Akame Ga KILL! ZERO

I

TAKAHIRO
KEI TORU

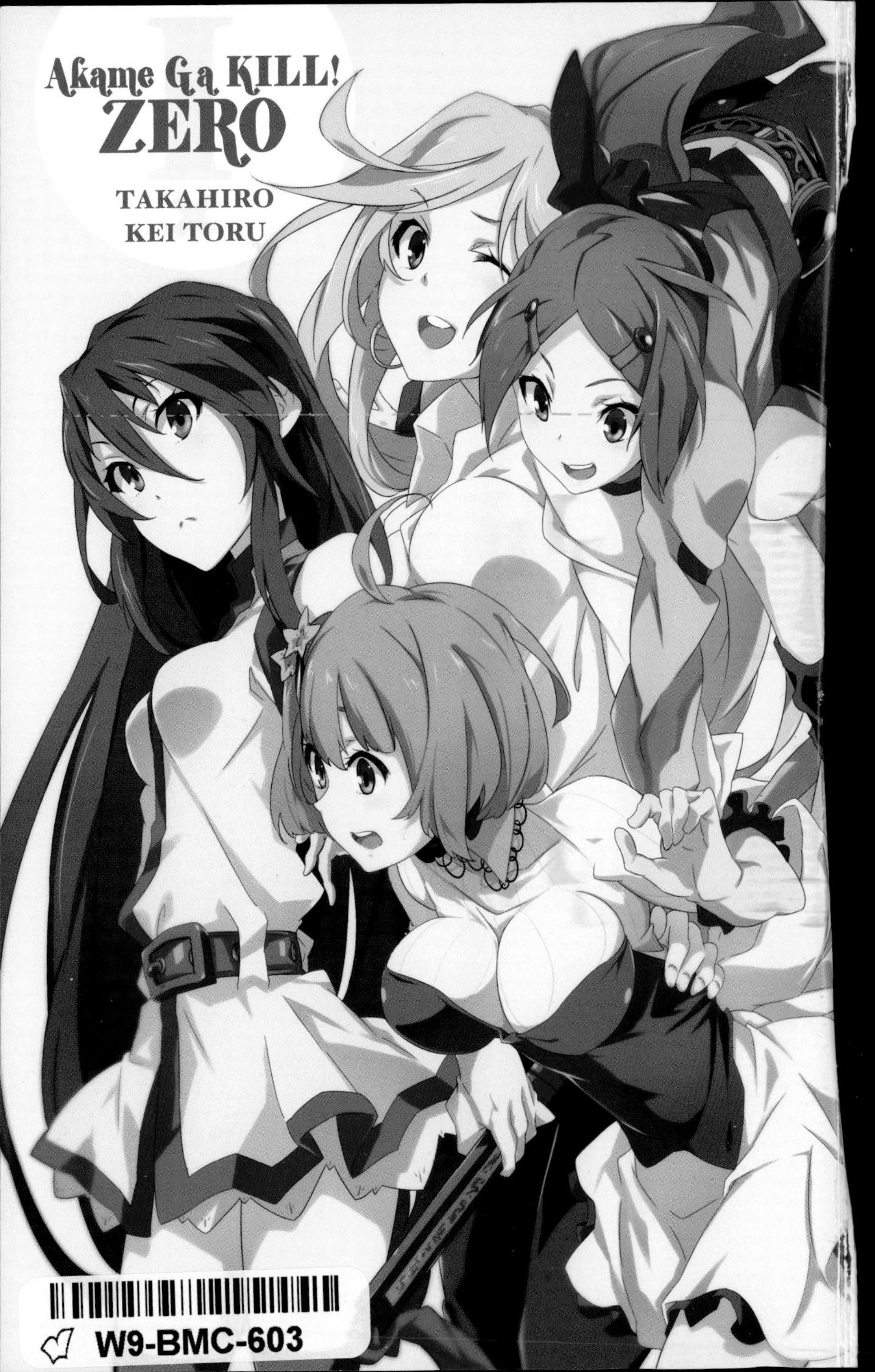

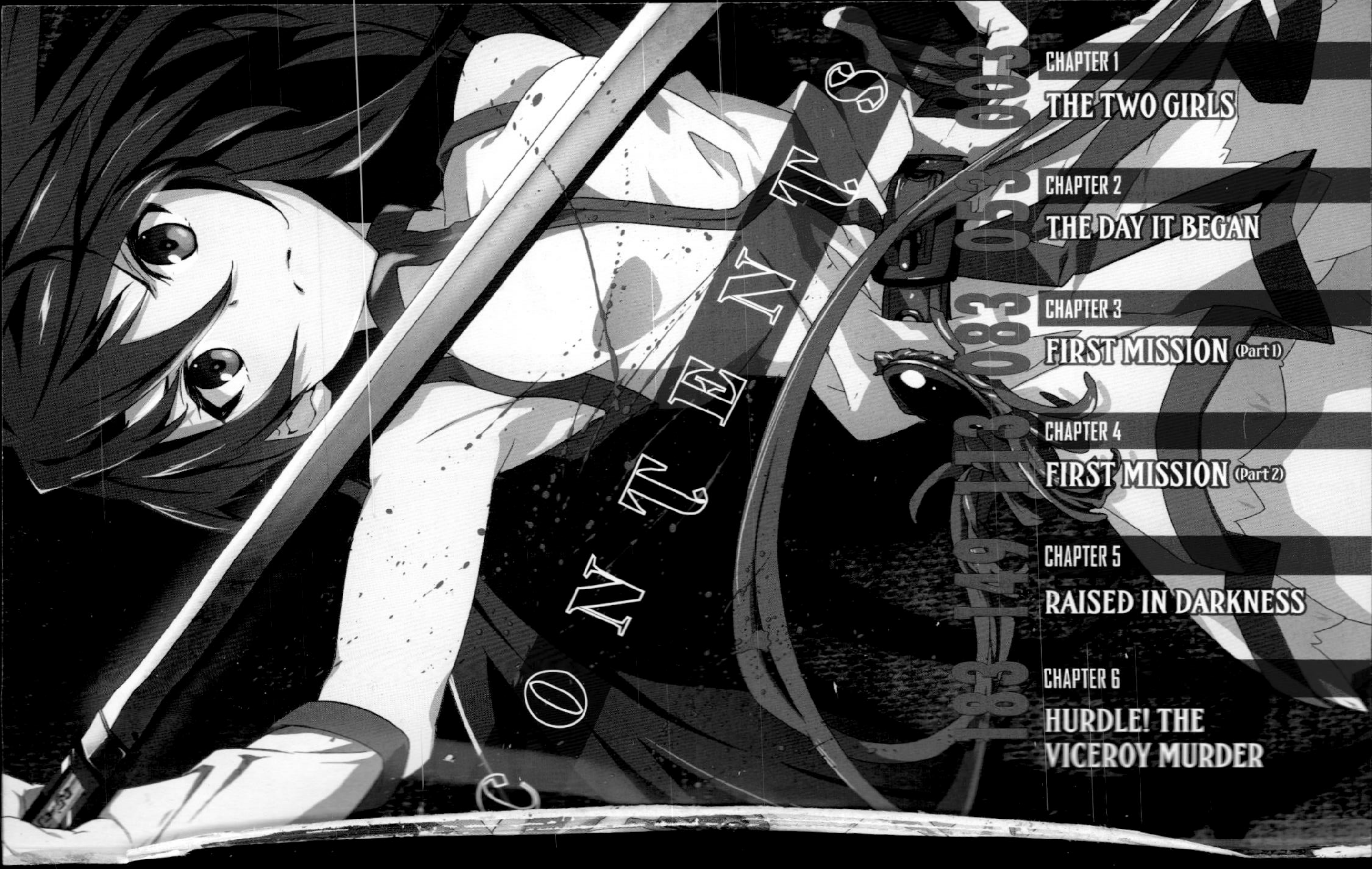

CONTENTS

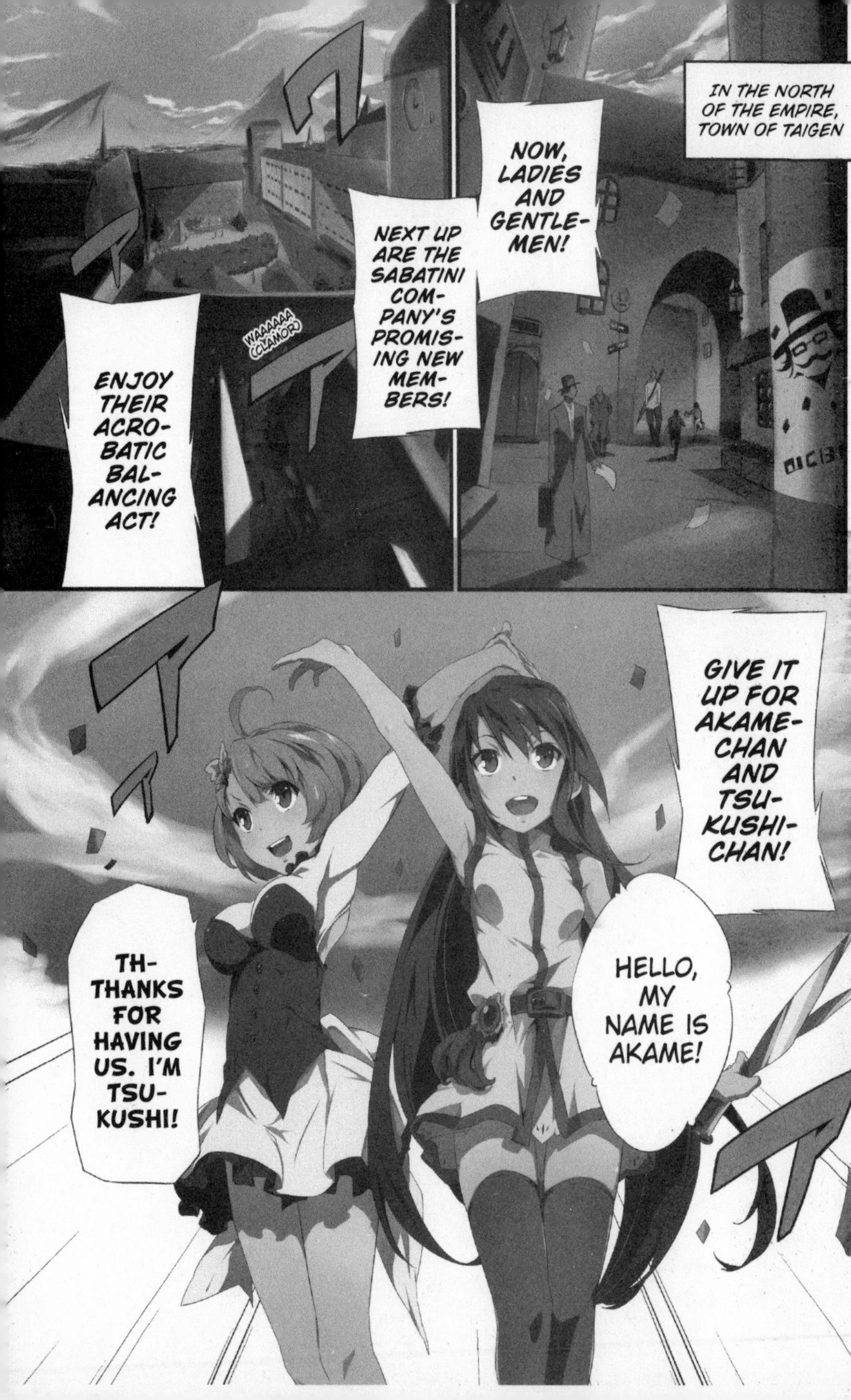
IN THE NORTH OF THE EMPIRE, TOWN OF TAIGEN
NOW, LADIES AND GENTLE-MEN!
NEXT UP ARE THE SABATINI COM-PANY'S PROMIS-ING NEW MEM-BERS!
WAAAAAA (CLAMOR)
ENJOY THEIR ACRO-BATIC BAL-ANCING ACT!
GIVE IT UP FOR AKAME-CHAN AND TSU-KUSHI-CHAN!
HELLO, MY NAME IS AKAME!
TH-THANKS FOR HAVING US. I'M TSU-KUSHI!

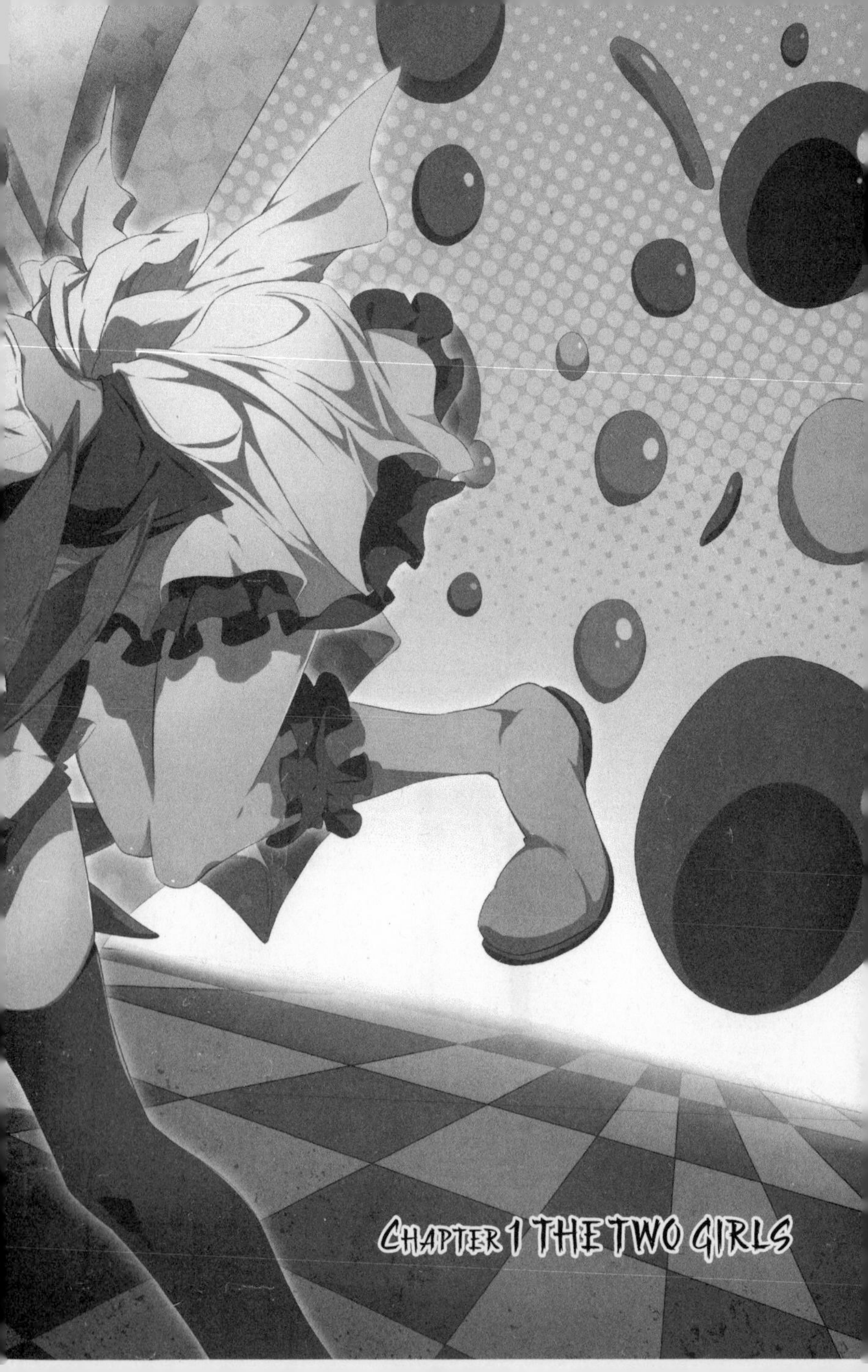

Chapter 1 The Two Girls

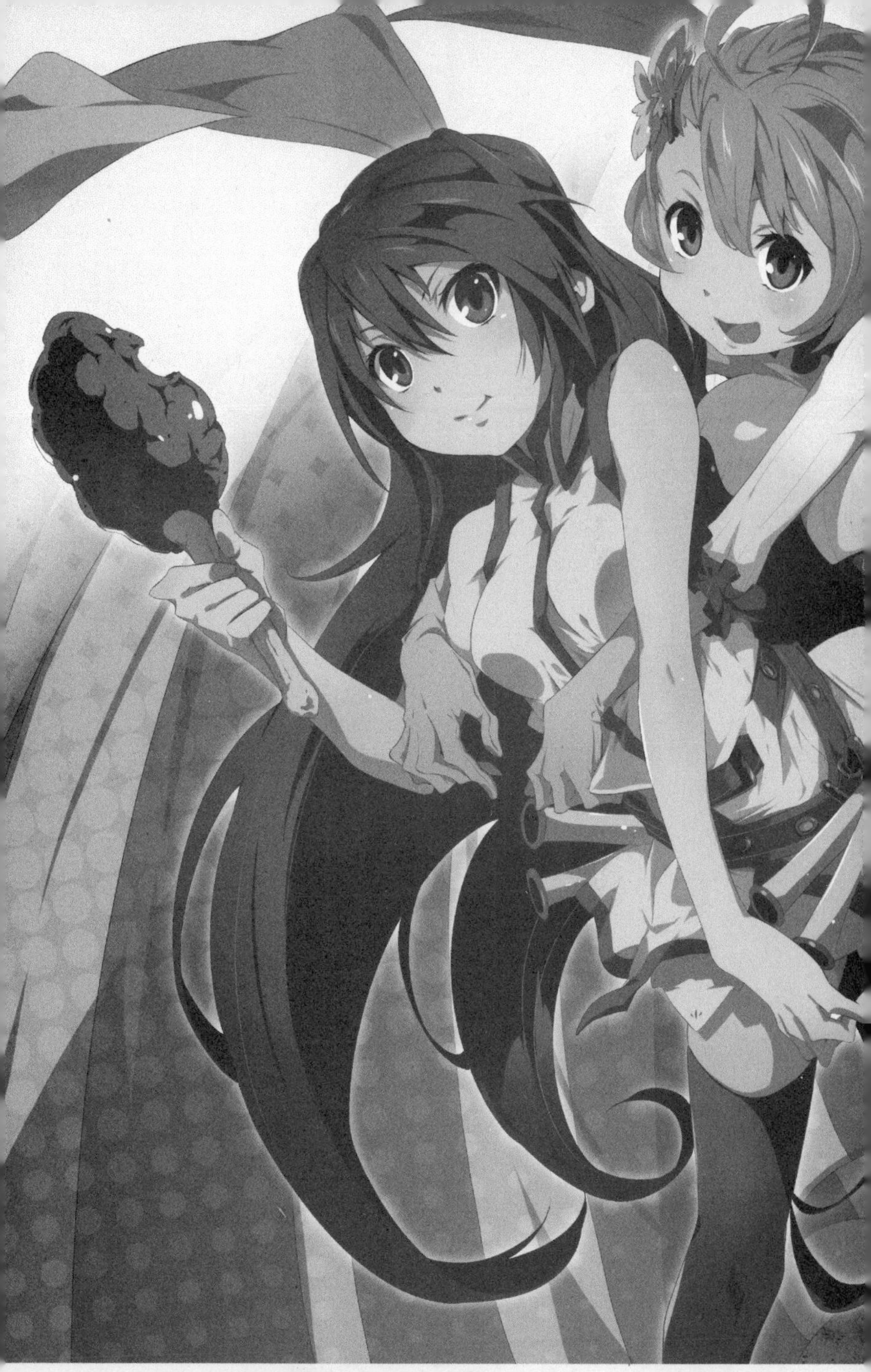

Akame ga KILL! ZERO

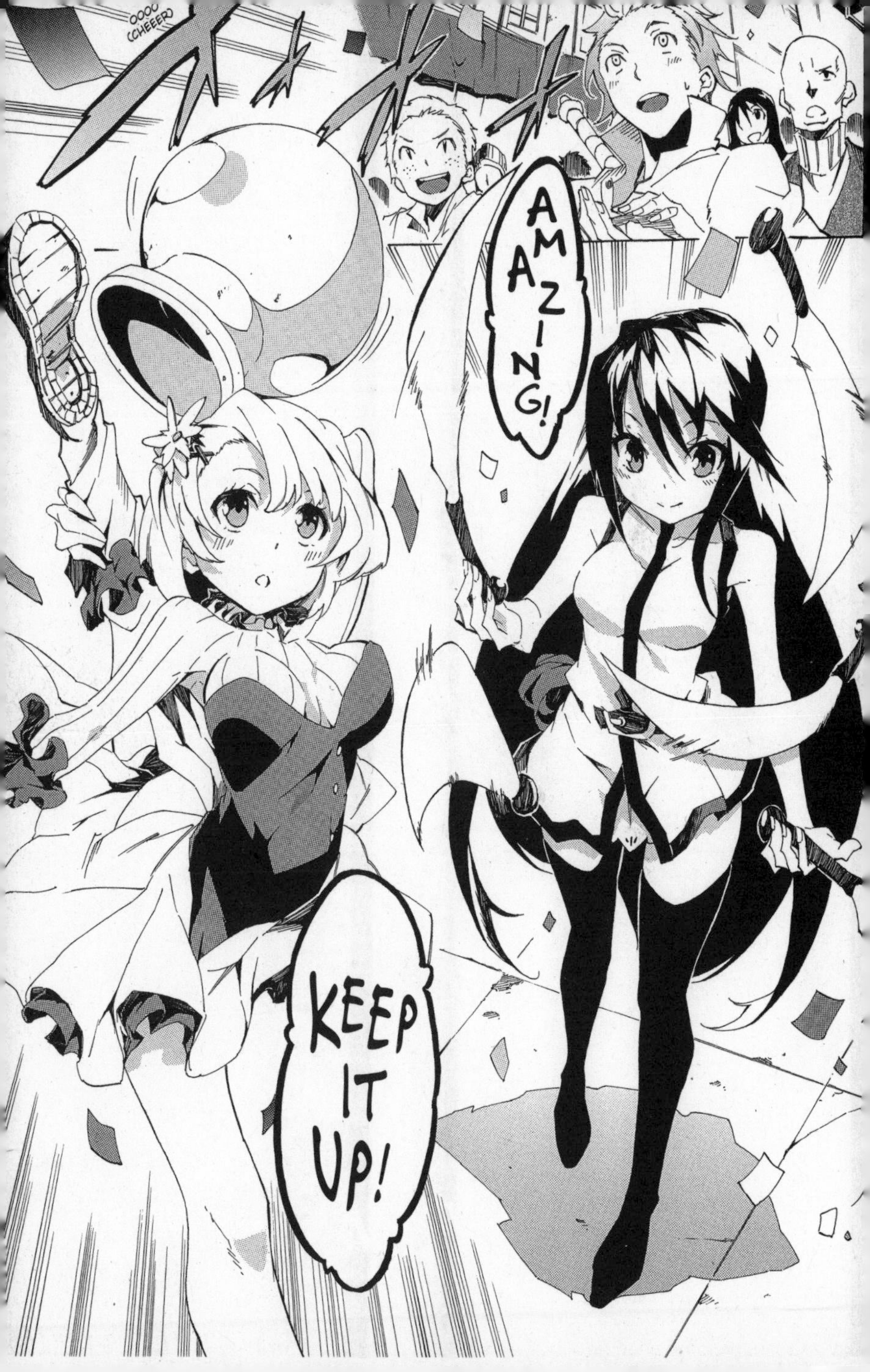
OOOO (CHEEER)
AMAZING!
KEEP IT UP!

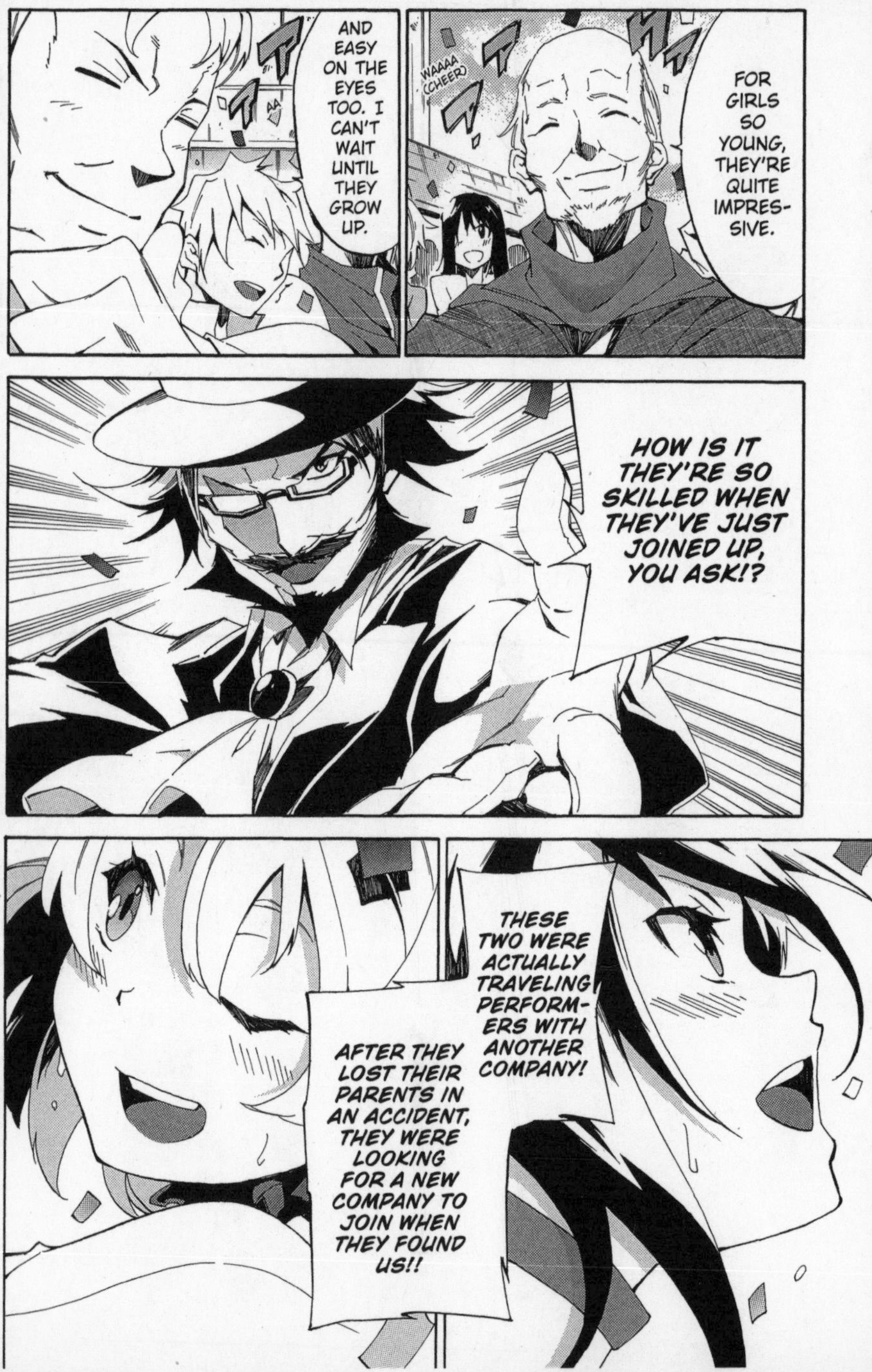
FOR GIRLS SO YOUNG, THEY'RE QUITE IMPRES- SIVE.
WAAAA (CHEER)
AND EASY ON THE EYES TOO. I CAN'T WAIT UNTIL THEY GROW UP.
AA
HOW IS IT THEY'RE SO SKILLED WHEN THEY'VE JUST JOINED UP, YOU ASK!?
THESE TWO WERE ACTUALLY TRAVELING PERFORM- ERS WITH ANOTHER COMPANY!
AFTER THEY LOST THEIR PARENTS IN AN ACCIDENT, THEY WERE LOOKING FOR A NEW COMPANY TO JOIN WHEN THEY FOUND US!!

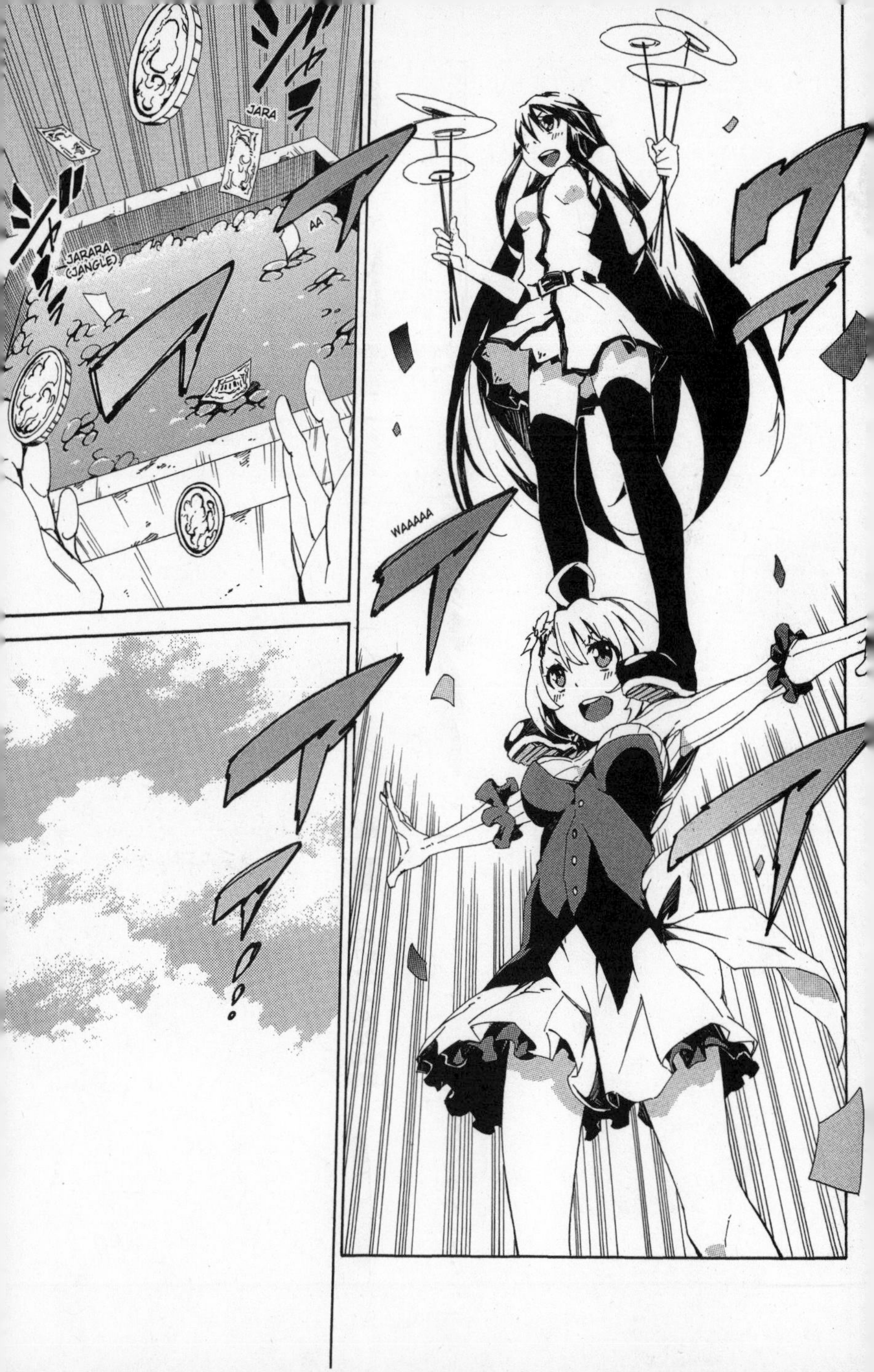

WAAAAA
JARA
AA
JARARA
(JANGLE)

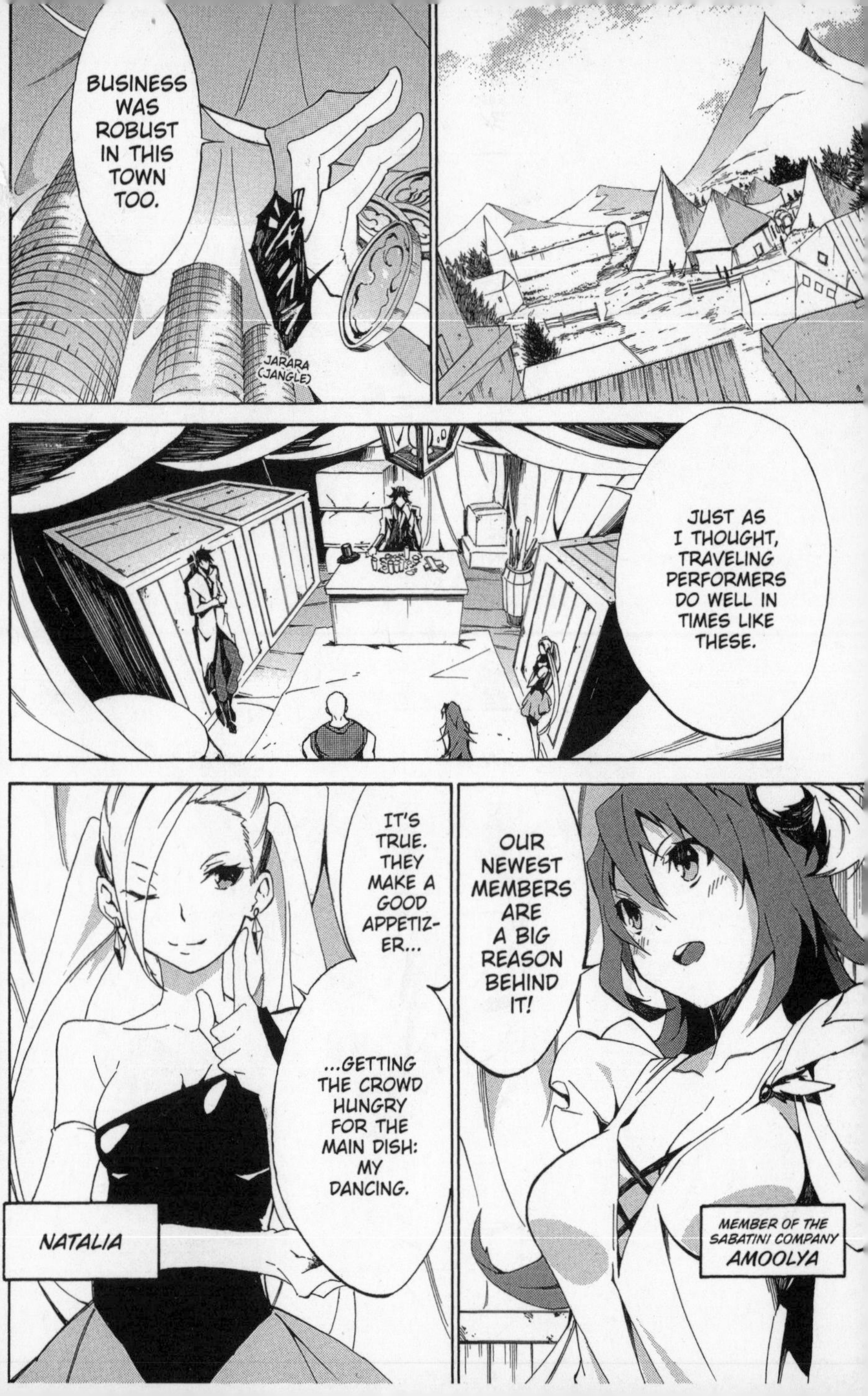
BUSINESS WAS ROBUST IN THIS TOWN TOO.
JARARA (JANGLE)
JUST AS I THOUGHT, TRAVELING PERFORMERS DO WELL IN TIMES LIKE THESE.
OUR NEWEST MEMBERS ARE A BIG REASON BEHIND IT!
IT'S TRUE. THEY MAKE A GOOD APPETIZER...
...GETTING THE CROWD HUNGRY FOR THE MAIN DISH: MY DANCING.
NATALIA
MEMBER OF THE SABATINI COMPANY
AMOOLYA

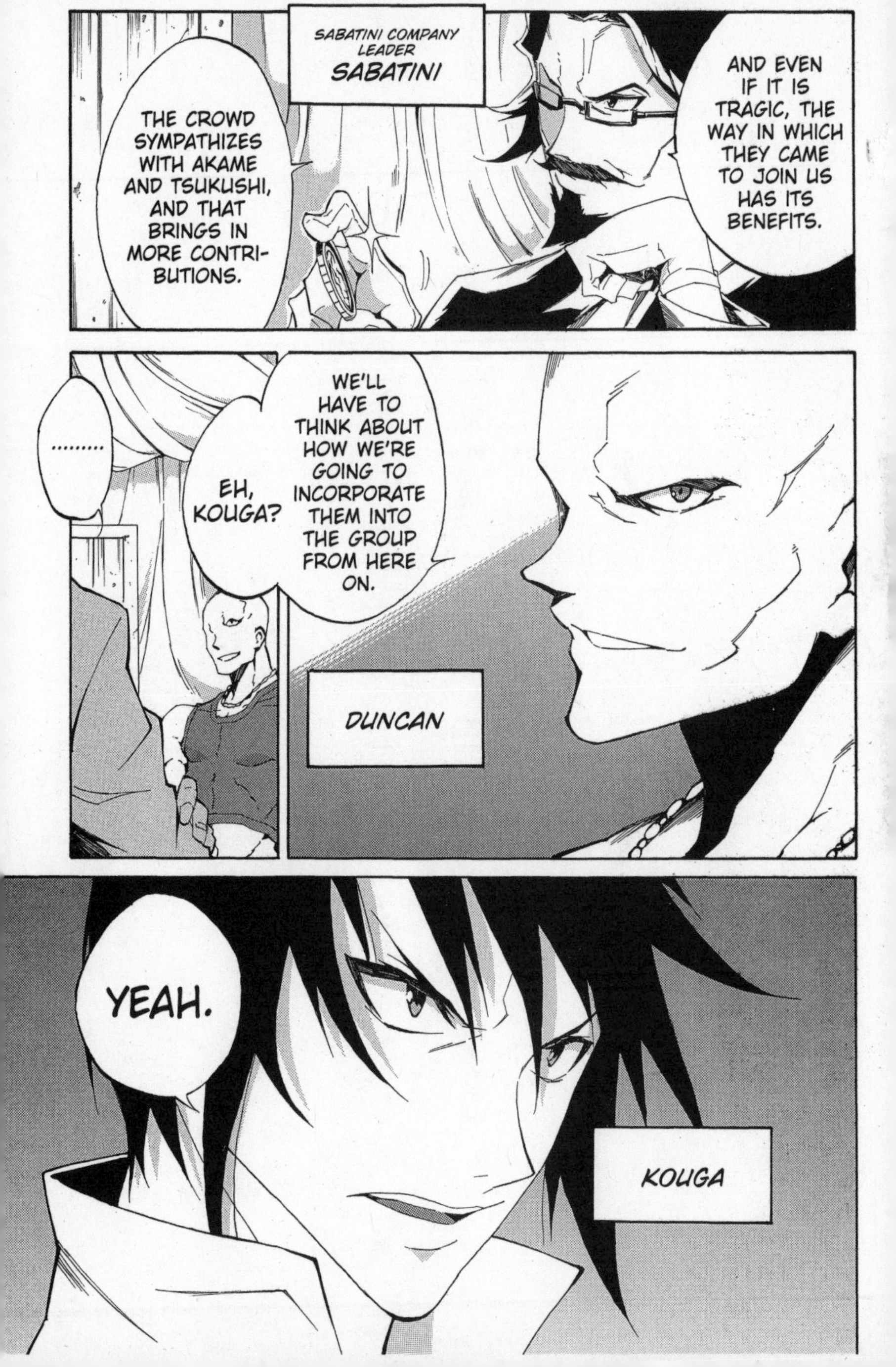
SABATINI COMPANY LEADER SABATINI
AND EVEN IF IT IS TRAGIC, THE WAY IN WHICH THEY CAME TO JOIN US HAS ITS BENEFITS.
THE CROWD SYMPATHIZES WITH AKAME AND TSUKUSHI, AND THAT BRINGS IN MORE CONTRI-BUTIONS.
WE'LL HAVE TO THINK ABOUT HOW WE'RE GOING TO INCORPORATE THEM INTO THE GROUP FROM HERE ON.
EH, KOUGA?
DUNCAN
....
YEAH.
KOUGA

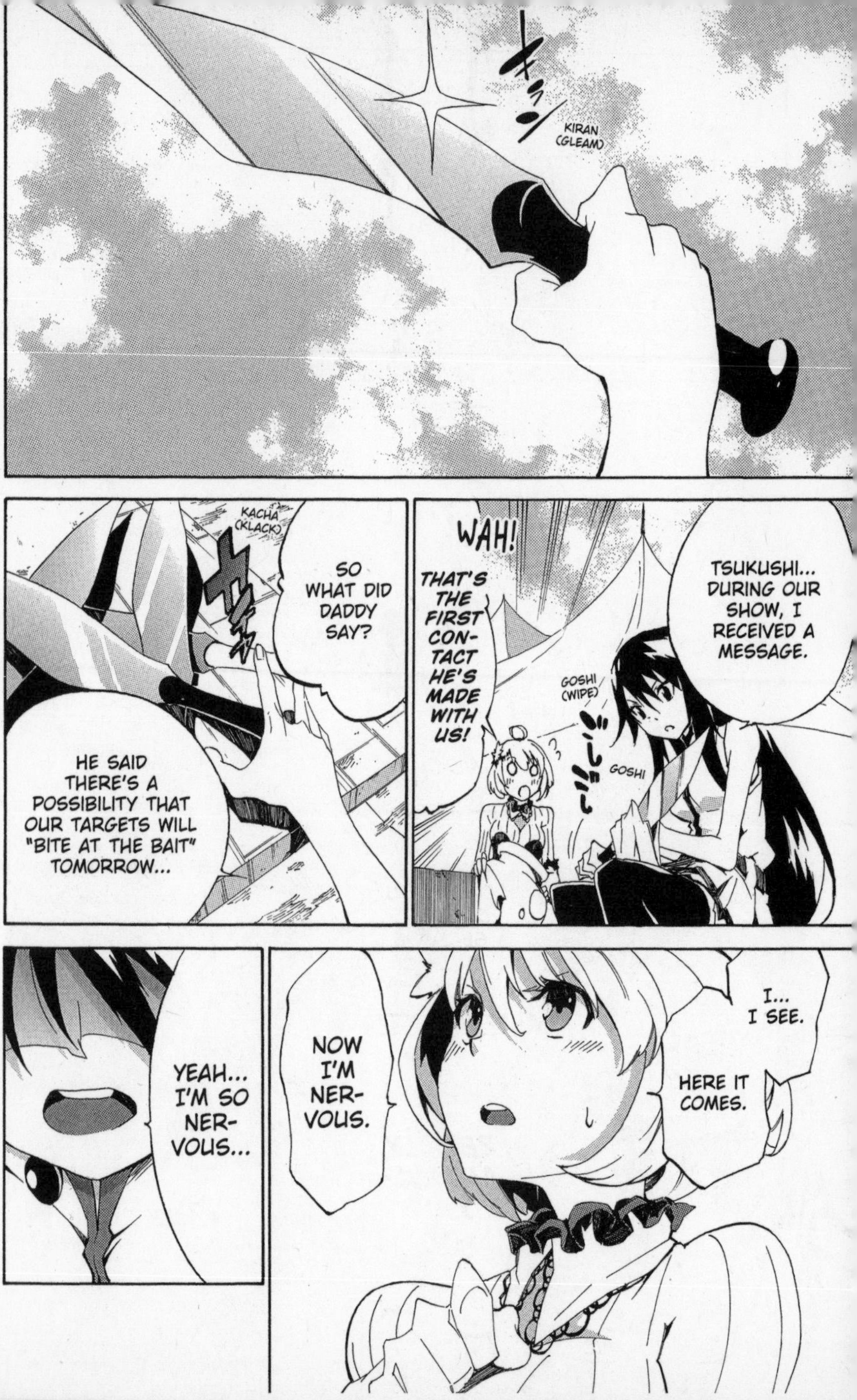
KIRAN (GLEAM)
TSUKUSHI... DURING OUR SHOW, I RECEIVED A MESSAGE.
GOSHI (WIPE)
GOSHI
WAH!
THAT'S THE FIRST CON-TACT HE'S MADE WITH US!
SO WHAT DID DADDY SAY?
KACHA (KLACK)
HE SAID THERE'S A POSSIBILITY THAT OUR TARGETS WILL "BITE AT THE BAIT" TOMORROW...
I... I SEE.
HERE IT COMES.
NOW I'M NER-VOUS.
YEAH... I'M SO NER-VOUS...

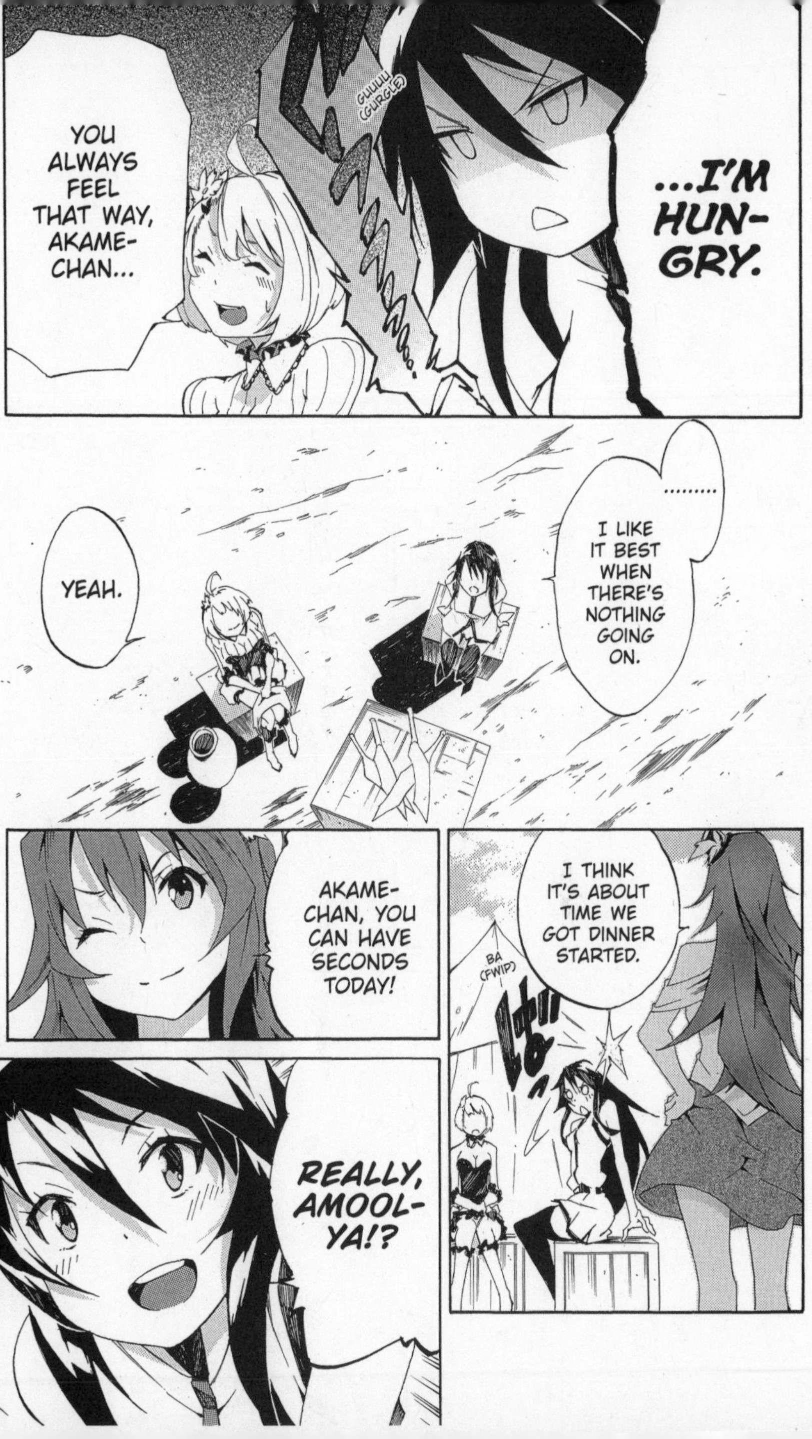
...I'M HUNGRY.
GUUUU (GURGLE)
YOU ALWAYS FEEL THAT WAY, AKAME-CHAN...
....
I LIKE IT BEST WHEN THERE'S NOTHING GOING ON.
YEAH.
I THINK IT'S ABOUT TIME WE GOT DINNER STARTED.
BA (FWIP)
AKAME-CHAN, YOU CAN HAVE SECONDS TODAY!
REALLY, AMOOLYA!?

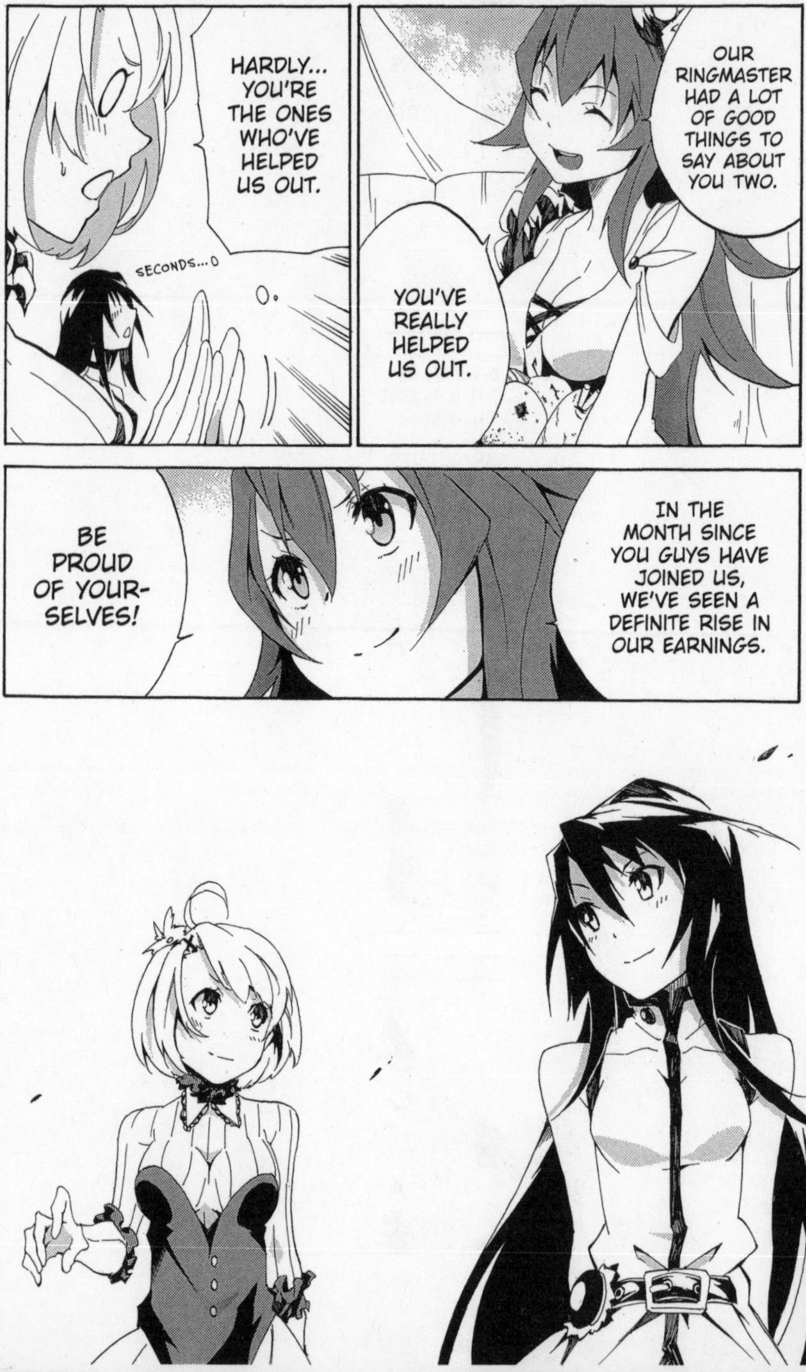
OUR RINGMASTER HAD A LOT OF GOOD THINGS TO SAY ABOUT YOU TWO.
YOU'VE REALLY HELPED US OUT.
HARDLY... YOU'RE THE ONES WHO'VE HELPED US OUT.
SECONDS...
IN THE MONTH SINCE YOU GUYS HAVE JOINED US, WE'VE SEEN A DEFINITE RISE IN OUR EARNINGS.
BE PROUD OF YOUR-SELVES!

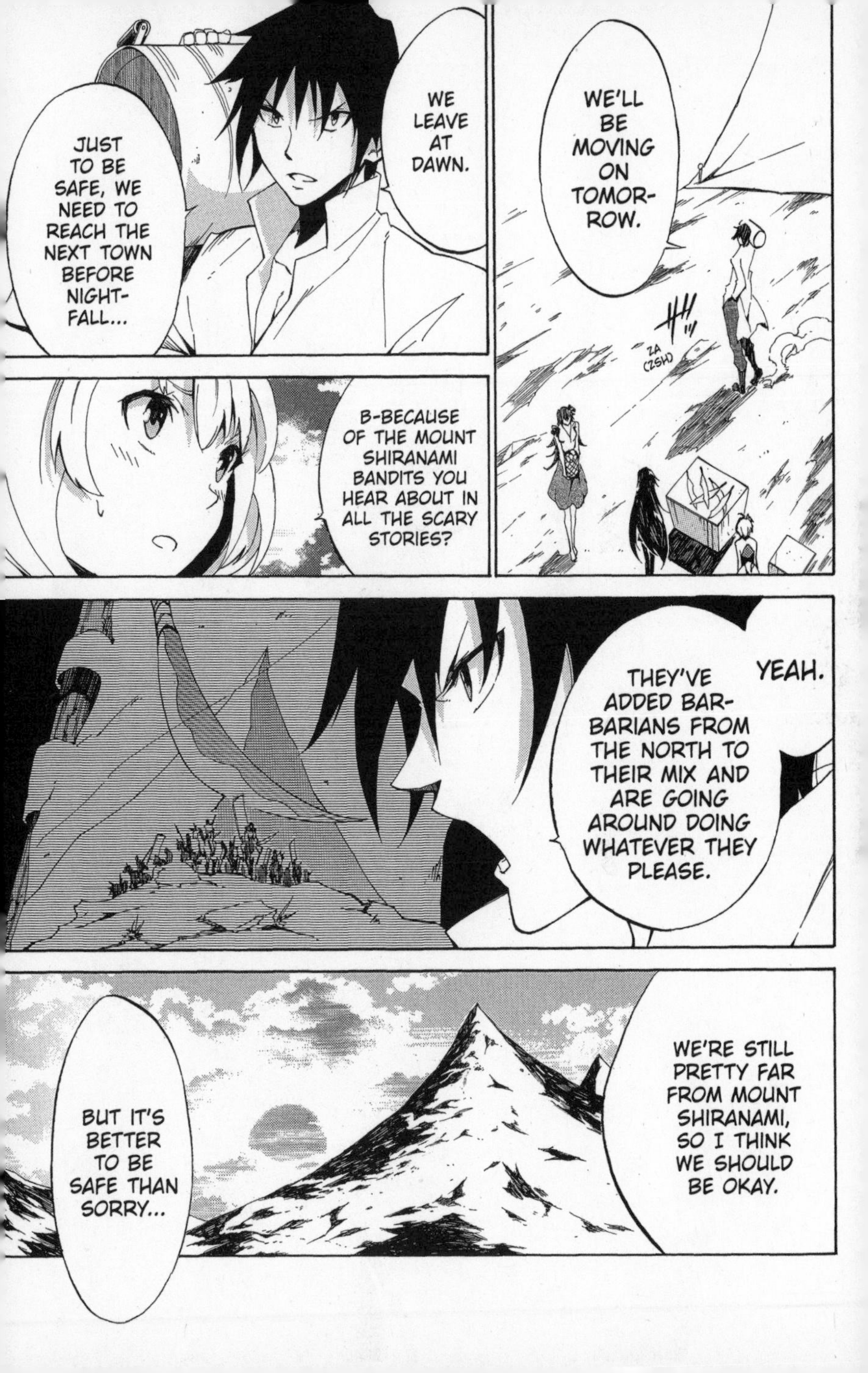
WE'LL BE MOVING ON TOMORROW.
ZA (ZSH)
WE LEAVE AT DAWN.
JUST TO BE SAFE, WE NEED TO REACH THE NEXT TOWN BEFORE NIGHTFALL...
B-BECAUSE OF THE MOUNT SHIRANAMI BANDITS YOU HEAR ABOUT IN ALL THE SCARY STORIES?
YEAH.
THEY'VE ADDED BARBARIANS FROM THE NORTH TO THEIR MIX AND ARE GOING AROUND DOING WHATEVER THEY PLEASE.
WE'RE STILL PRETTY FAR FROM MOUNT SHIRANAMI, SO I THINK WE SHOULD BE OKAY.
BUT IT'S BETTER TO BE SAFE THAN SORRY...

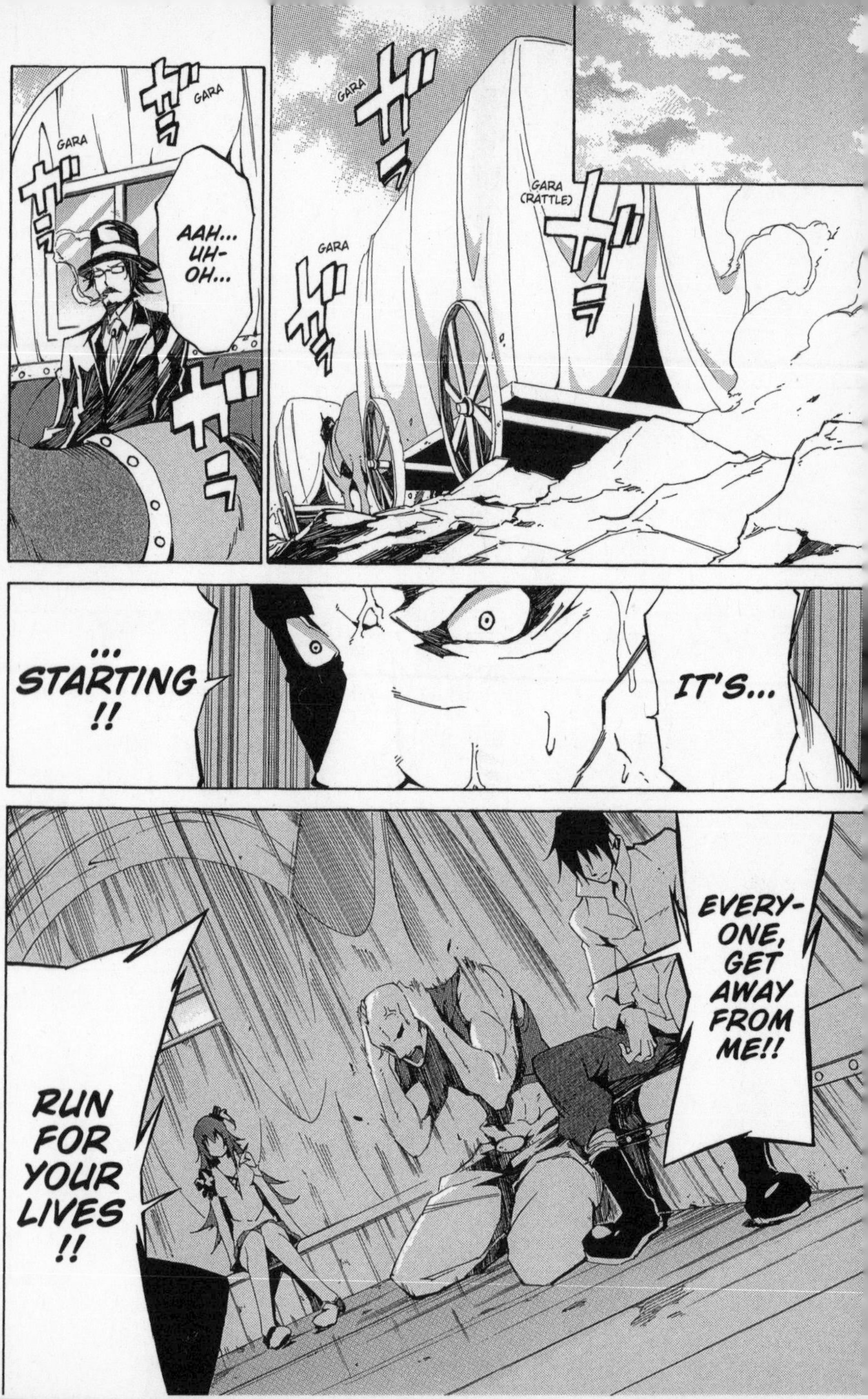

GARA
GARA (RATTLE)
GARA
GARA
GARA
AAH... UH-OH...
IT'S...
...STARTING!!
EVERYONE, GET AWAY FROM ME!!
RUN FOR YOUR LIVES!!

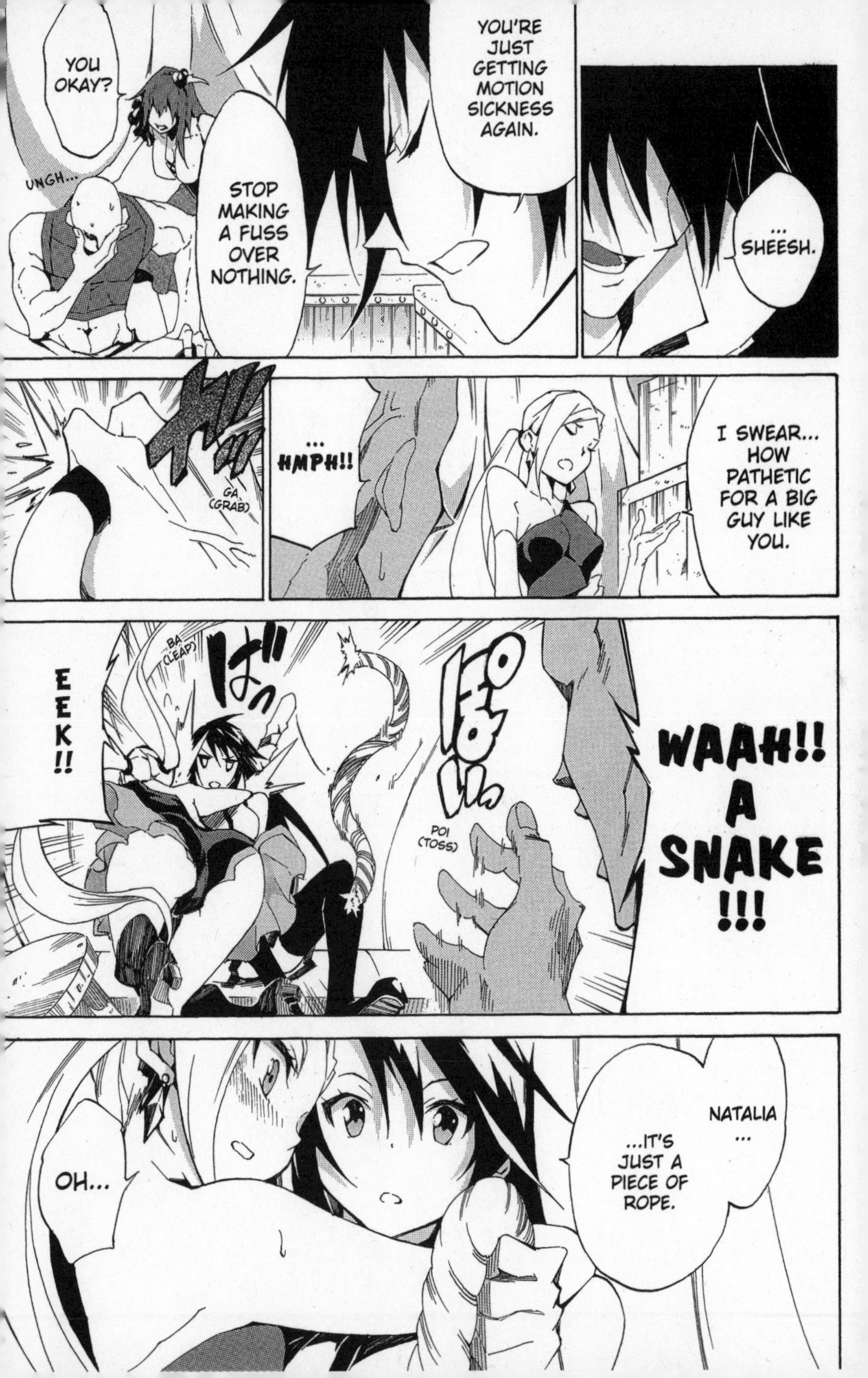
YOU'RE JUST GETTING MOTION SICKNESS AGAIN.
... SHEESH.
STOP MAKING A FUSS OVER NOTHING.
YOU OKAY?
UNGH...
I SWEAR... HOW PATHETIC FOR A BIG GUY LIKE YOU.
... HMPH!!
GA (GRAB)
WAAH!! A SNAKE !!!
POI (TOSS)
BA (LEAP)
EEK!!
NATALIA ...
...IT'S JUST A PIECE OF ROPE.
OH...

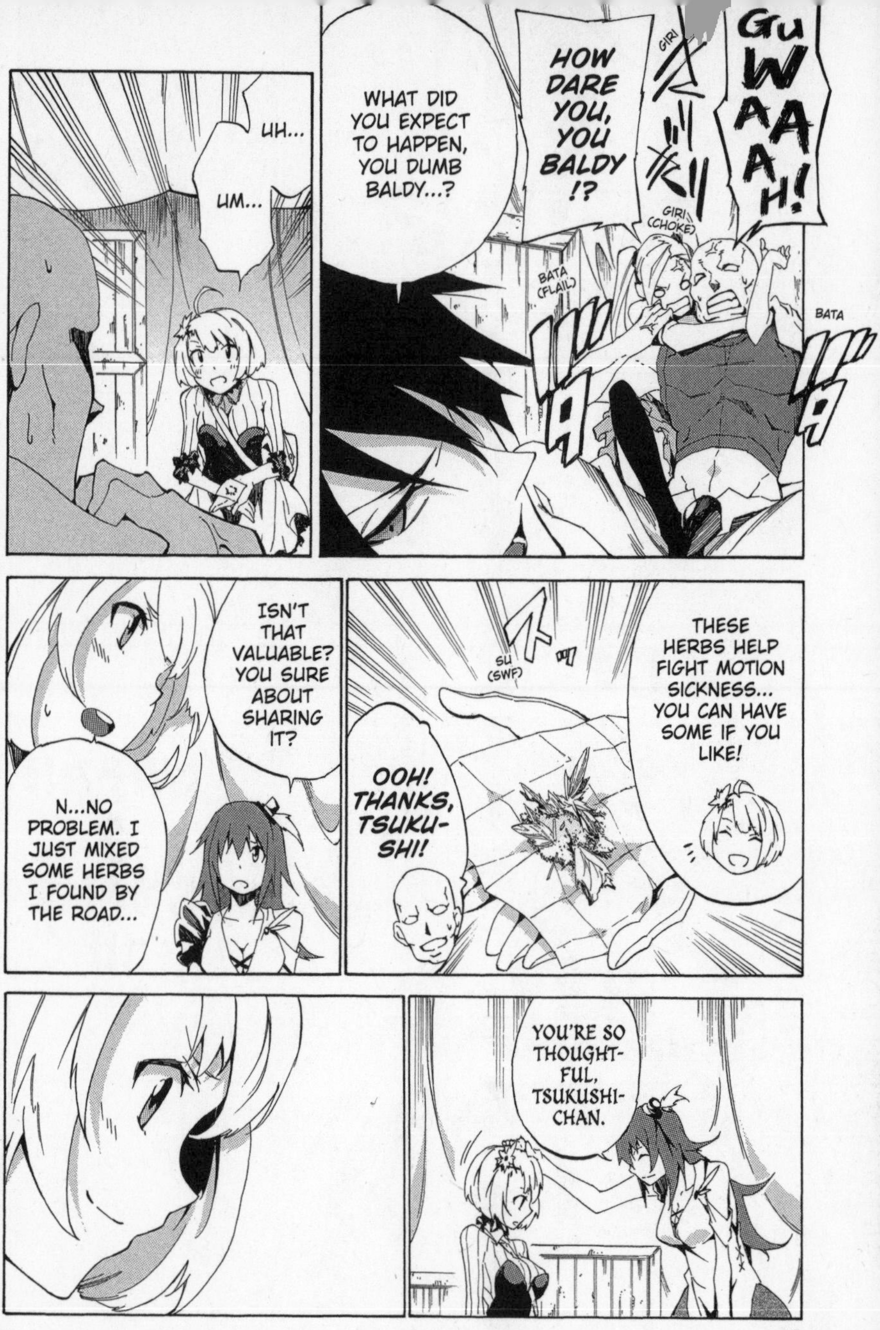
GUWAAAH!
HOW DARE YOU, YOU BALDY!?
GIRI
GIRI (CHOKE)
BATA (FLAIL)
BATA
WHAT DID YOU EXPECT TO HAPPEN, YOU DUMB BALDY...?
UH...
UM...
THESE HERBS HELP FIGHT MOTION SICKNESS... YOU CAN HAVE SOME IF YOU LIKE!
SU (SWF)
OOH! THANKS, TSUKUSHI!
ISN'T THAT VALUABLE? YOU SURE ABOUT SHARING IT?
N...NO PROBLEM. I JUST MIXED SOME HERBS I FOUND BY THE ROAD...
YOU'RE SO THOUGHTFUL, TSUKUSHI-CHAN.

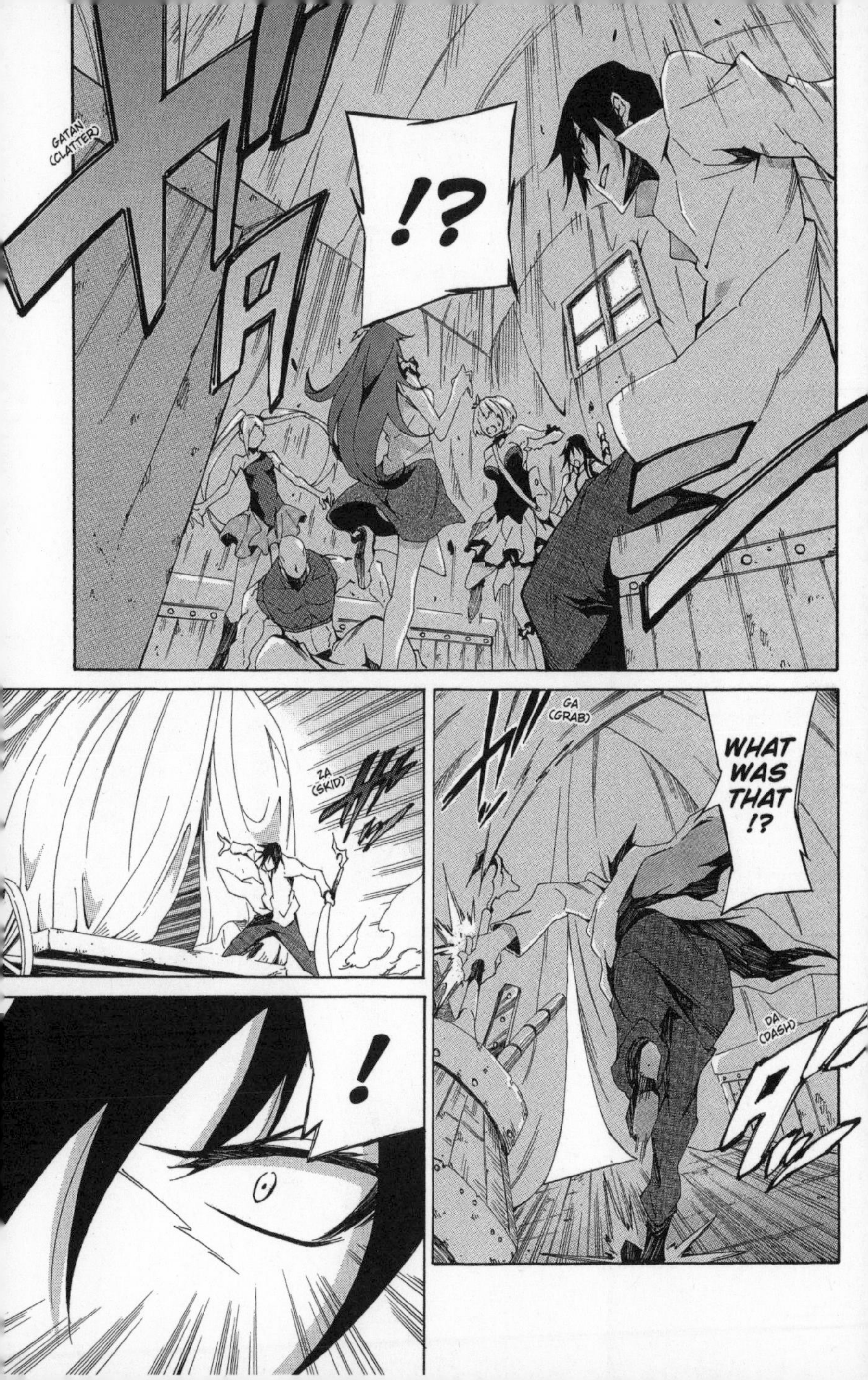
GATAN (CLATTER)
!?
GA (GRAB)
WHAT WAS THAT !?
ZA (SKID)
DA (DASH)
!

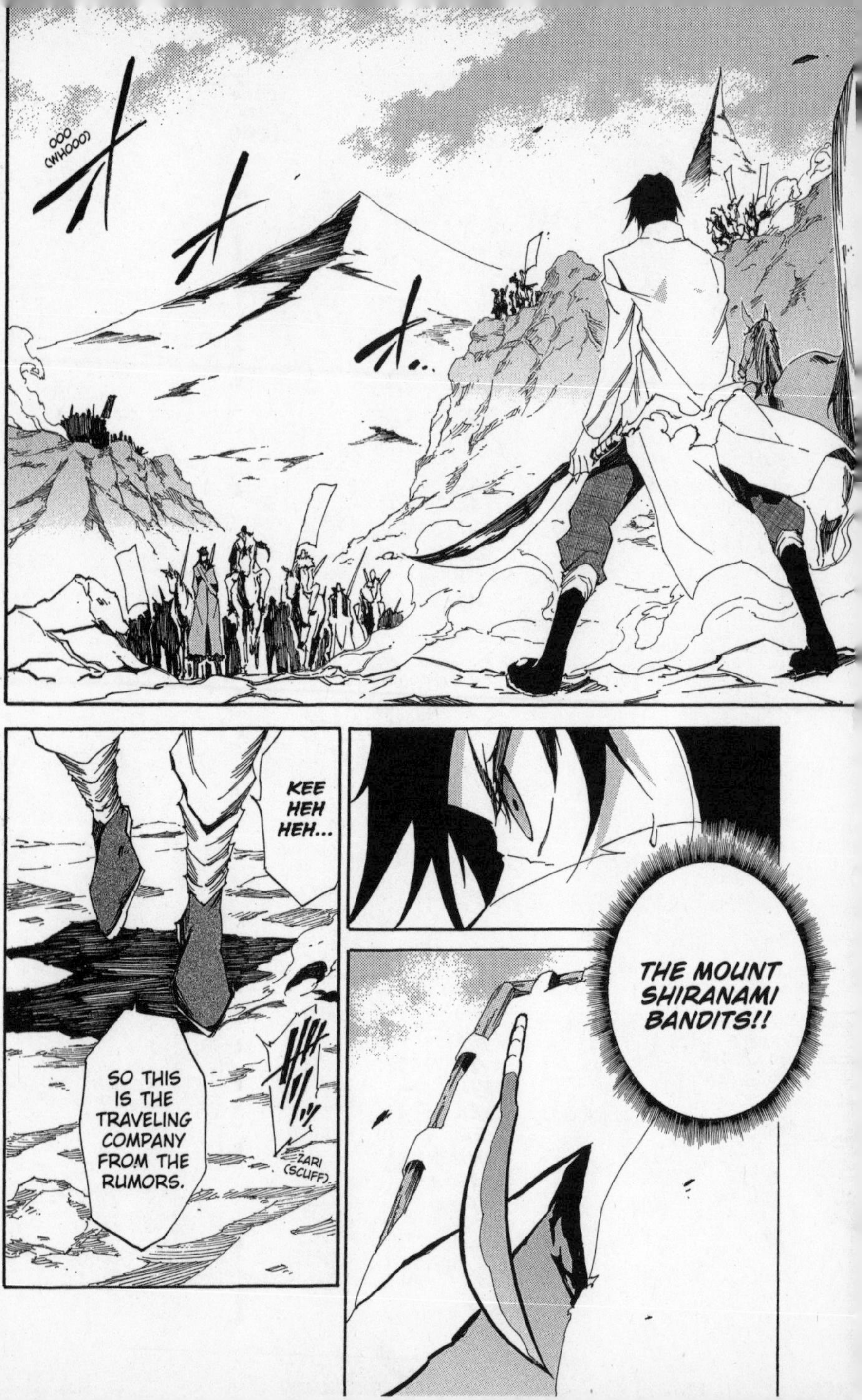
OOO
(WHOOO)
KEE
HEH
HEH...
THE MOUNT
SHIRANAMI
BANDITS!!
SO THIS
IS THE
TRAVELING
COMPANY
FROM THE
RUMORS.
ZARI
(SCUFF)

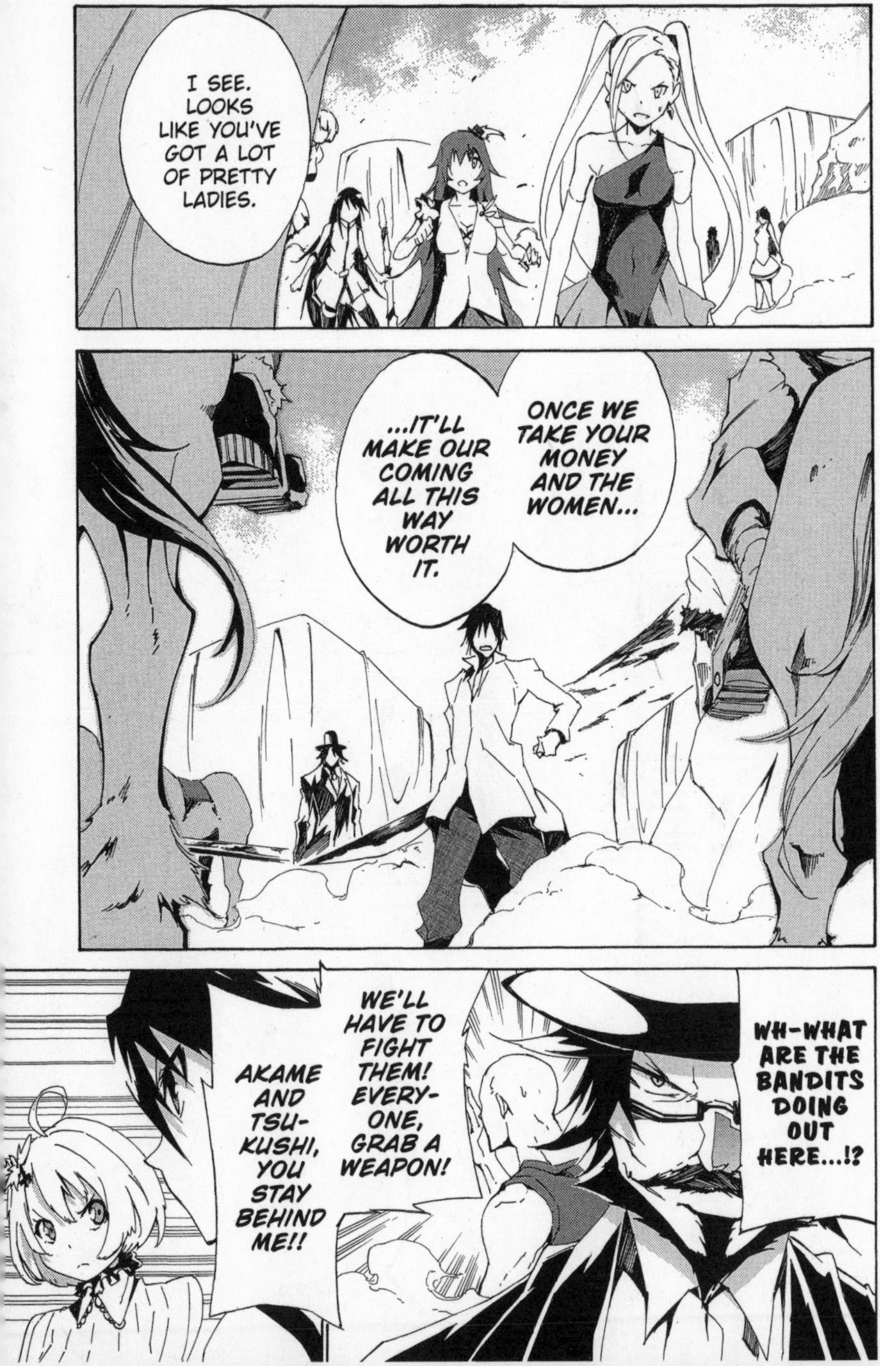
I SEE. LOOKS LIKE YOU'VE GOT A LOT OF PRETTY LADIES.
ONCE WE TAKE YOUR MONEY AND THE WOMEN...
...IT'LL MAKE OUR COMING ALL THIS WAY WORTH IT.
WH-WHAT ARE THE BANDITS DOING OUT HERE...!?
WE'LL HAVE TO FIGHT THEM! EVERYONE, GRAB A WEAPON!
AKAME AND TSUKUSHI, YOU STAY BEHIND ME!!

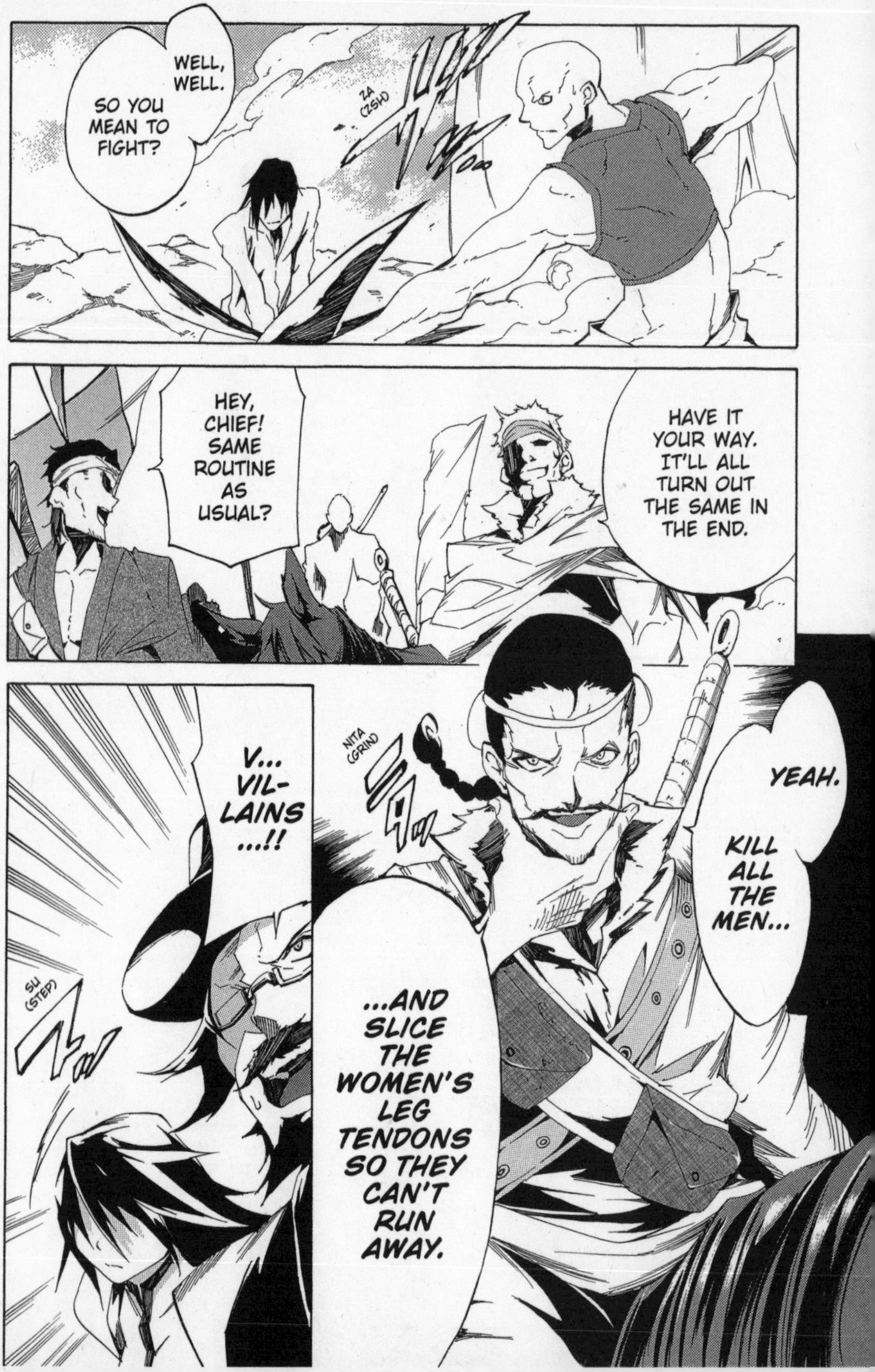
WELL, WELL.
SO YOU MEAN TO FIGHT?
ZA (ZSH)
HAVE IT YOUR WAY. IT'LL ALL TURN OUT THE SAME IN THE END.
HEY, CHIEF! SAME ROUTINE AS USUAL?
NITA (GRIN)
YEAH.
KILL ALL THE MEN...
...AND SLICE THE WOMEN'S LEG TENDONS SO THEY CAN'T RUN AWAY.
V... VIL-LAINS ...!!
SU (STEP)

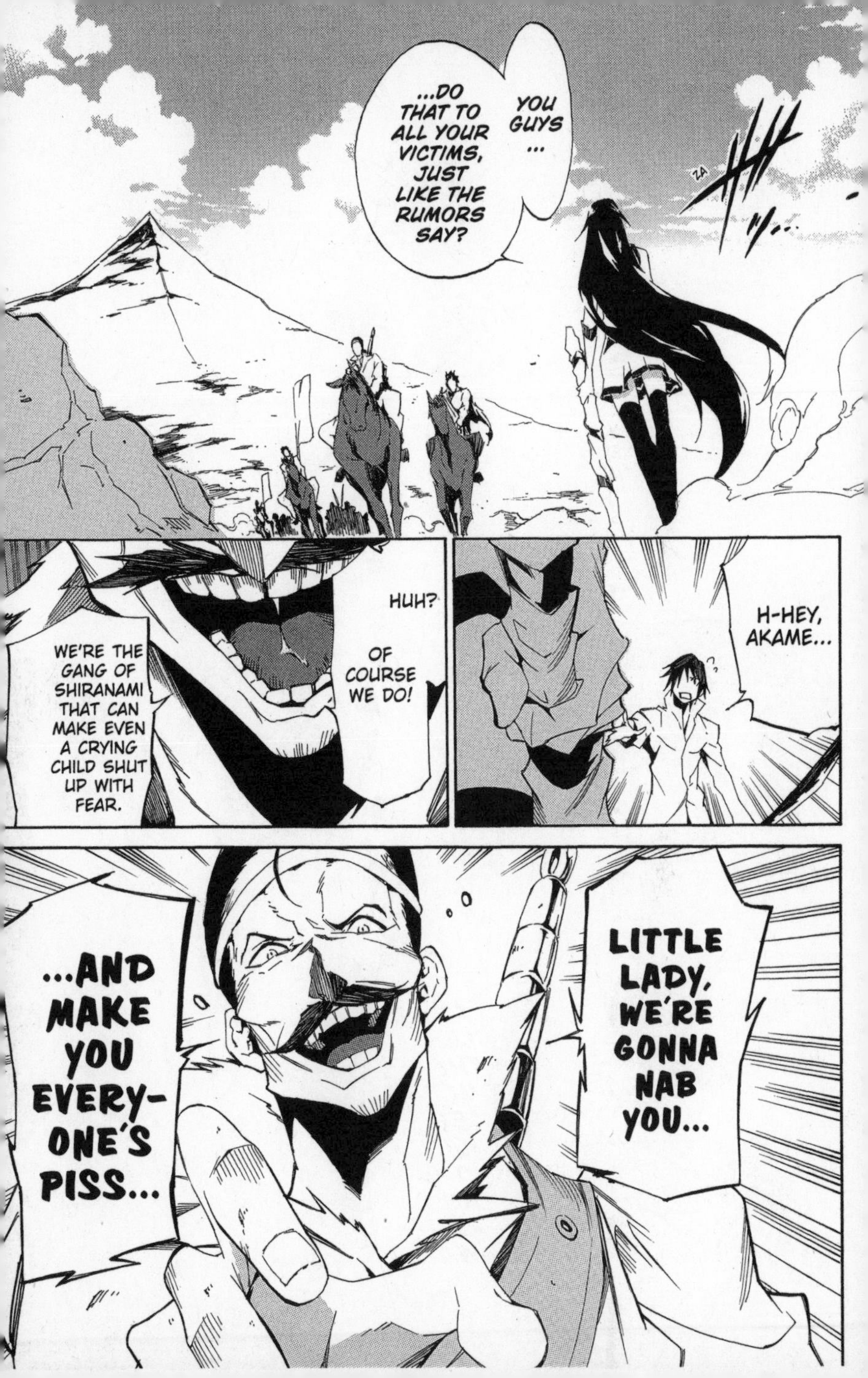
YOU GUYS ...
...DO THAT TO ALL YOUR VICTIMS, JUST LIKE THE RUMORS SAY?
ZA
H-HEY, AKAME...
HUH?
OF COURSE WE DO!
WE'RE THE GANG OF SHIRANAMI THAT CAN MAKE EVEN A CRYING CHILD SHUT UP WITH FEAR.
LITTLE LADY, WE'RE GONNA NAB YOU...
...AND MAKE YOU EVERYONE'S PISS...

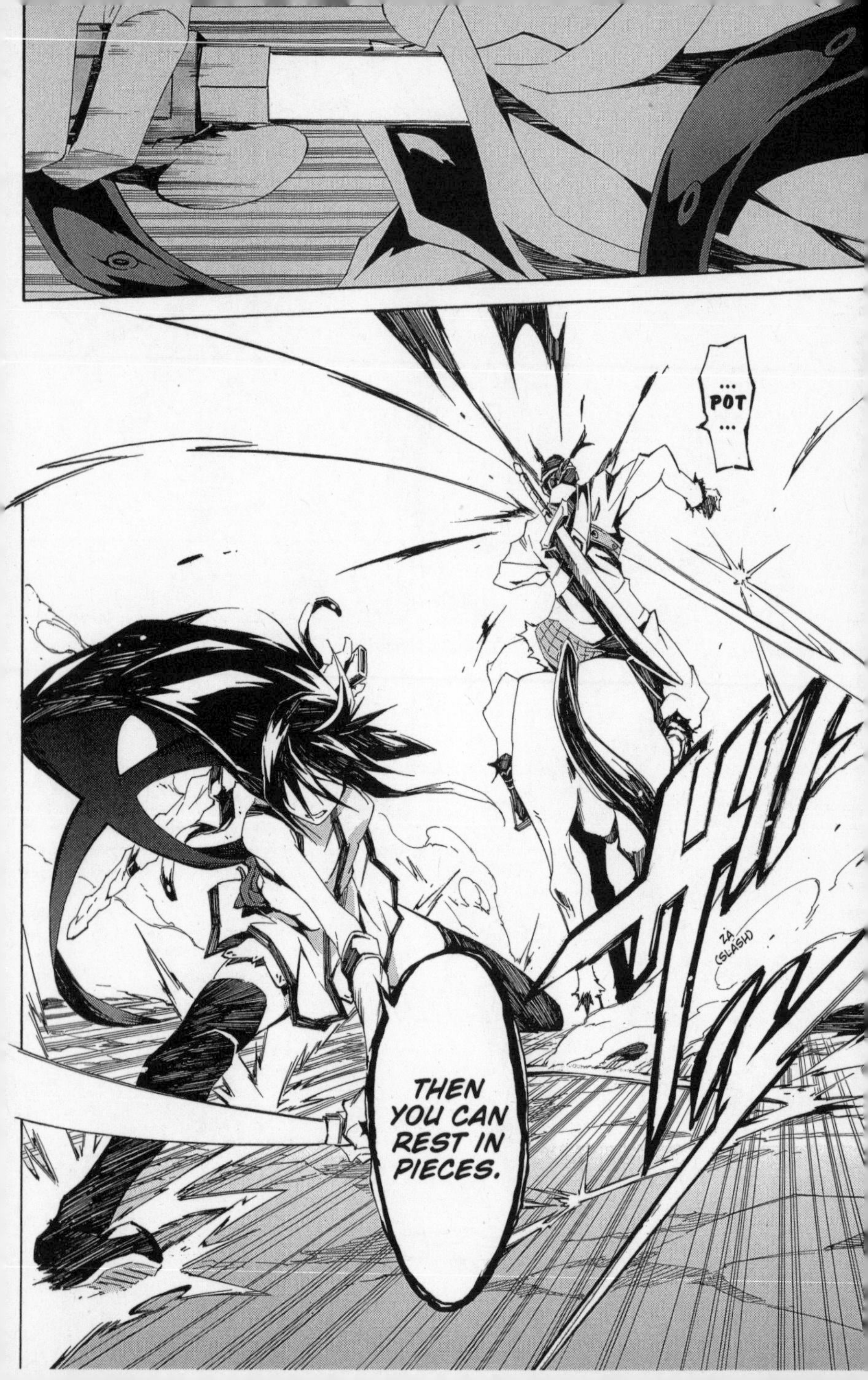
...POT...
ZA (SLASH)
THEN YOU CAN REST IN PIECES.

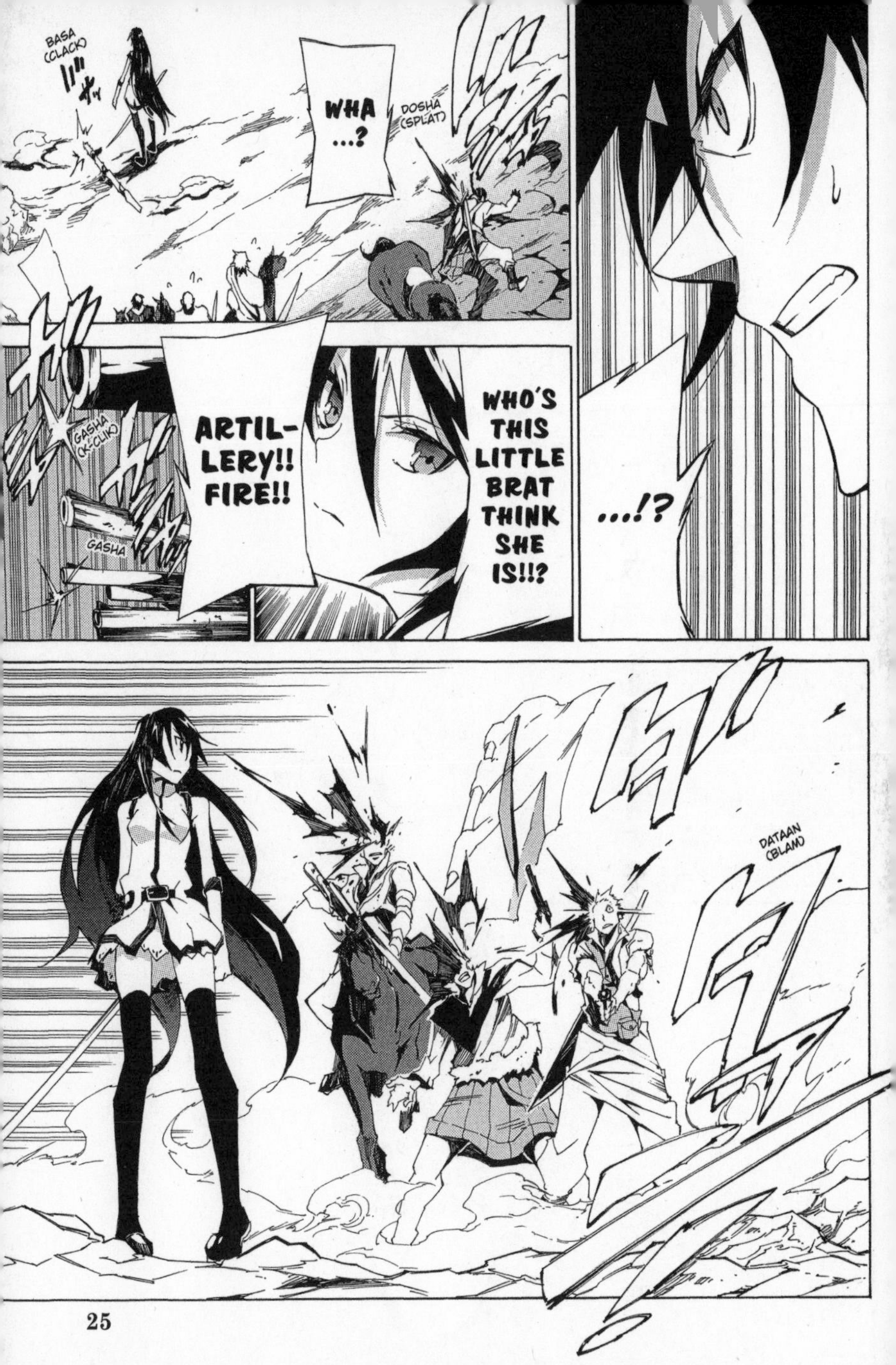

WHA ...?
DOSHA (SPLAT)
BASA (CLACK)
...!?
WHO'S THIS LITTLE BRAT THINK SHE IS!!?
ARTIL-LERY!! FIRE!!
GASHA (K-CLIK)
GASHA
DATAAN (BLAM)

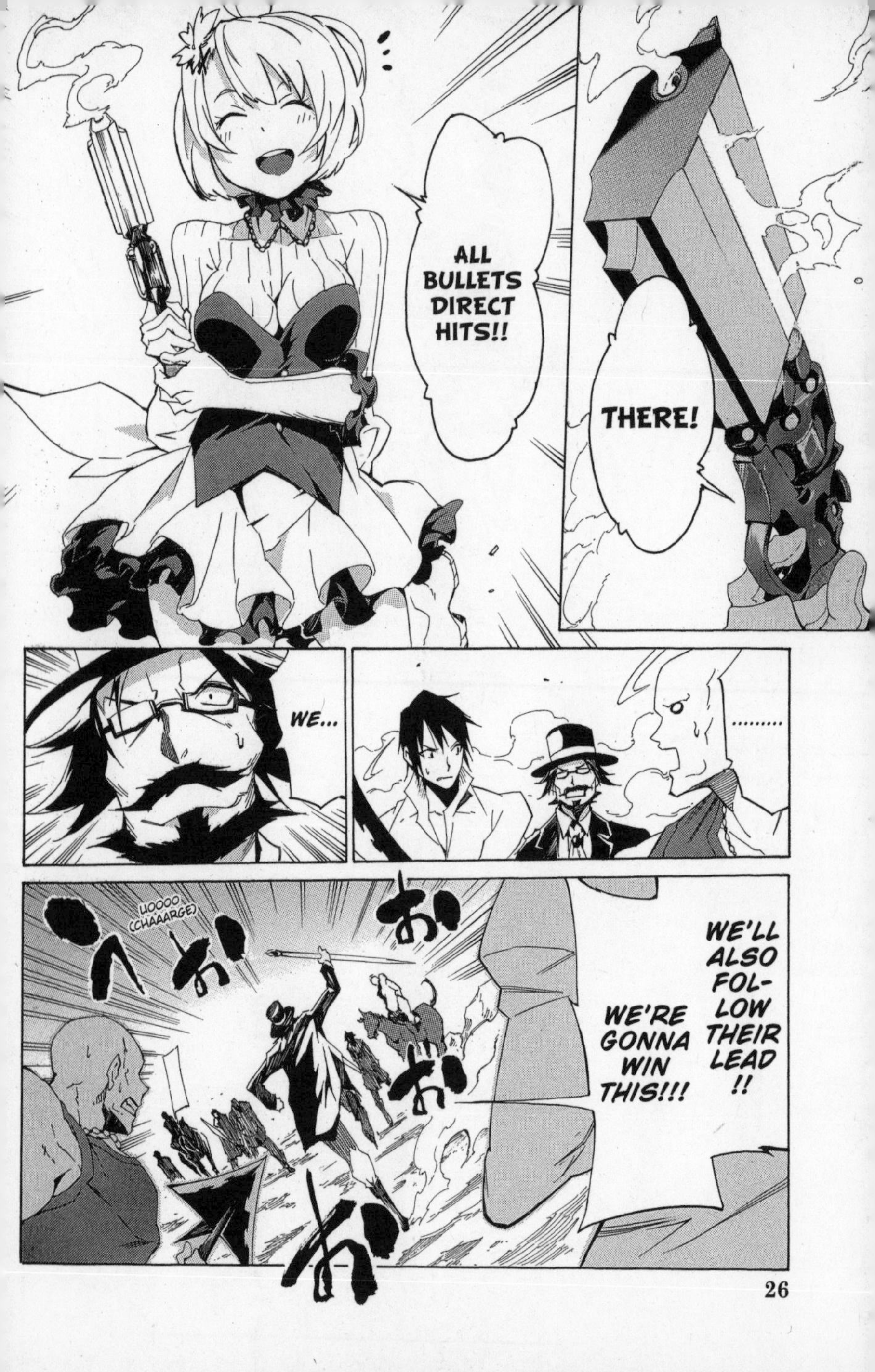
THERE!
ALL BULLETS DIRECT HITS!!
....
WE...
UOOOO (CHAAARGE)
WE'LL ALSO FOL-LOW THEIR LEAD!!
WE'RE GONNA WIN THIS!!!

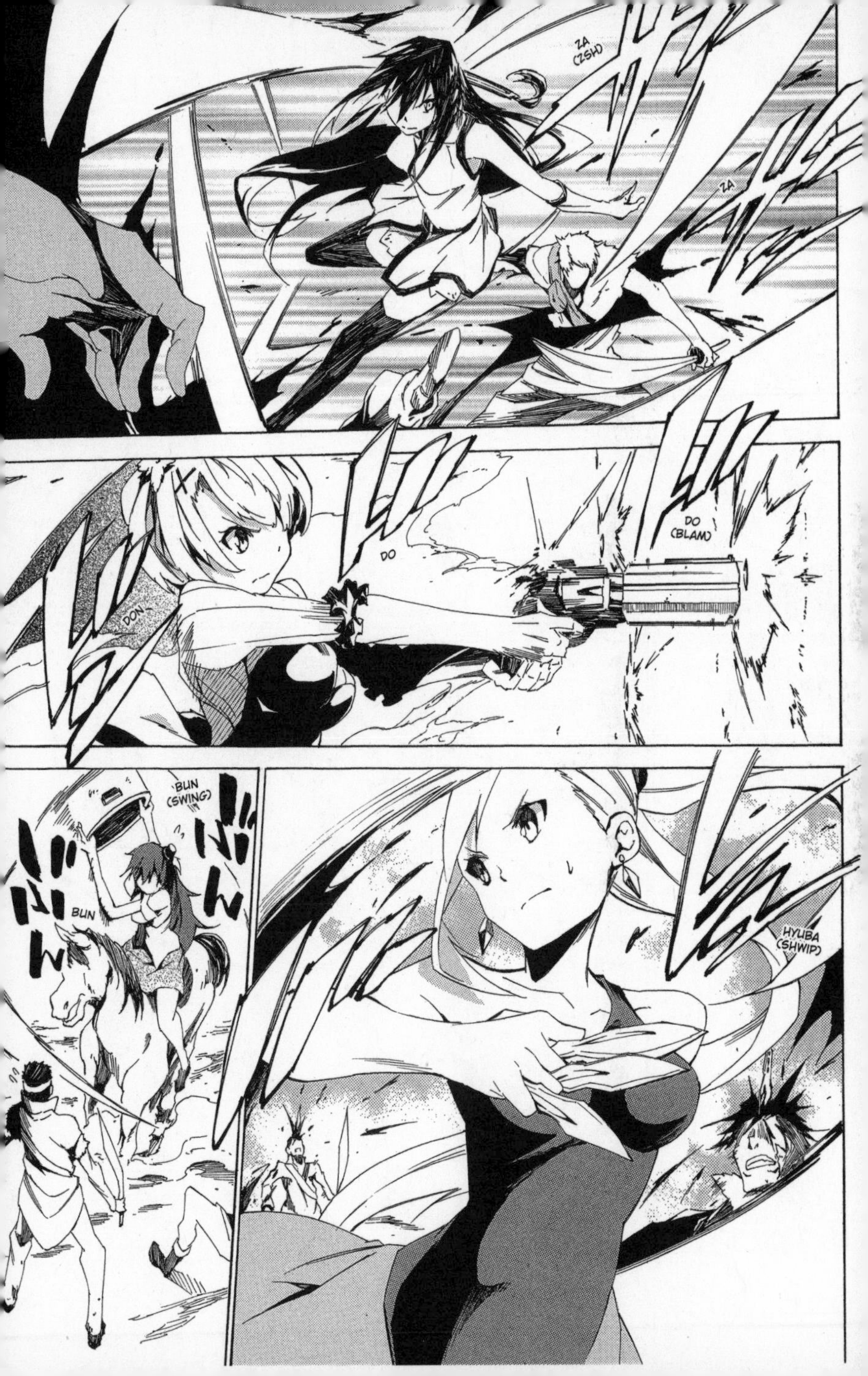
ZA
(ZSH)
ZA
DO
(BLAM)
DO
DON
HYUBA
(SHWIP)
BUN
(SWING)
BUN

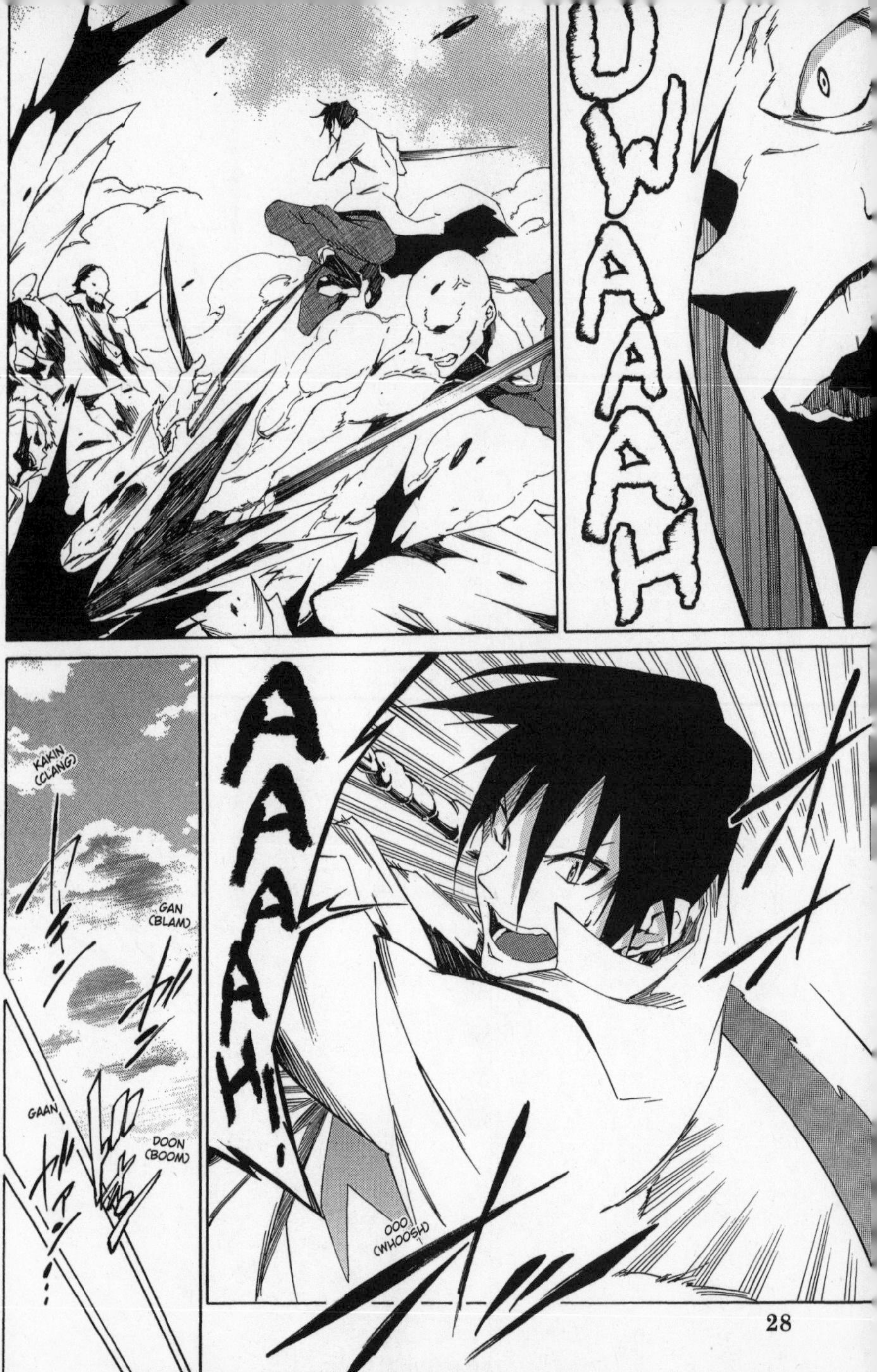
UWAAAAAH
AAAAAH!!
OOO (WHOOSH)
KAKIN (CLANG)
GAN (BLAM)
GAAN
DOON (BOOM)

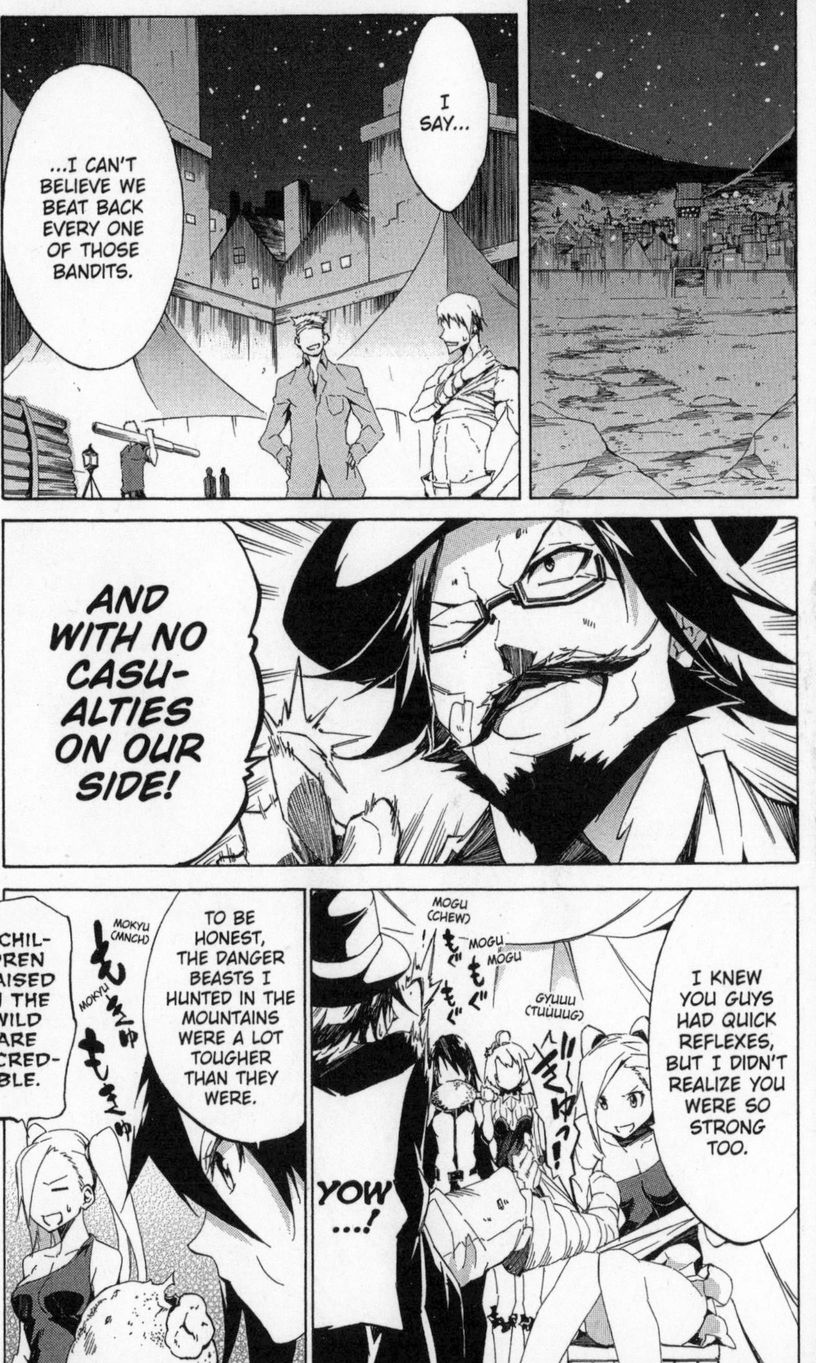
I SAY...
...I CAN'T BELIEVE WE BEAT BACK EVERY ONE OF THOSE BANDITS.
AND WITH NO CASU-ALTIES ON OUR SIDE!
I KNEW YOU GUYS HAD QUICK REFLEXES, BUT I DIDN'T REALIZE YOU WERE SO STRONG TOO.
GYUUU (TUUUUG)
MOGU (CHEW)
MOGU
MOGU
YOW ...!
TO BE HONEST, THE DANGER BEASTS I HUNTED IN THE MOUNTAINS WERE A LOT TOUGHER THAN THEY WERE.
MOKYU (MNCH)
MOKYU
...CHIL-DREN RAISED IN THE WILD ARE INCRED-IBLE.

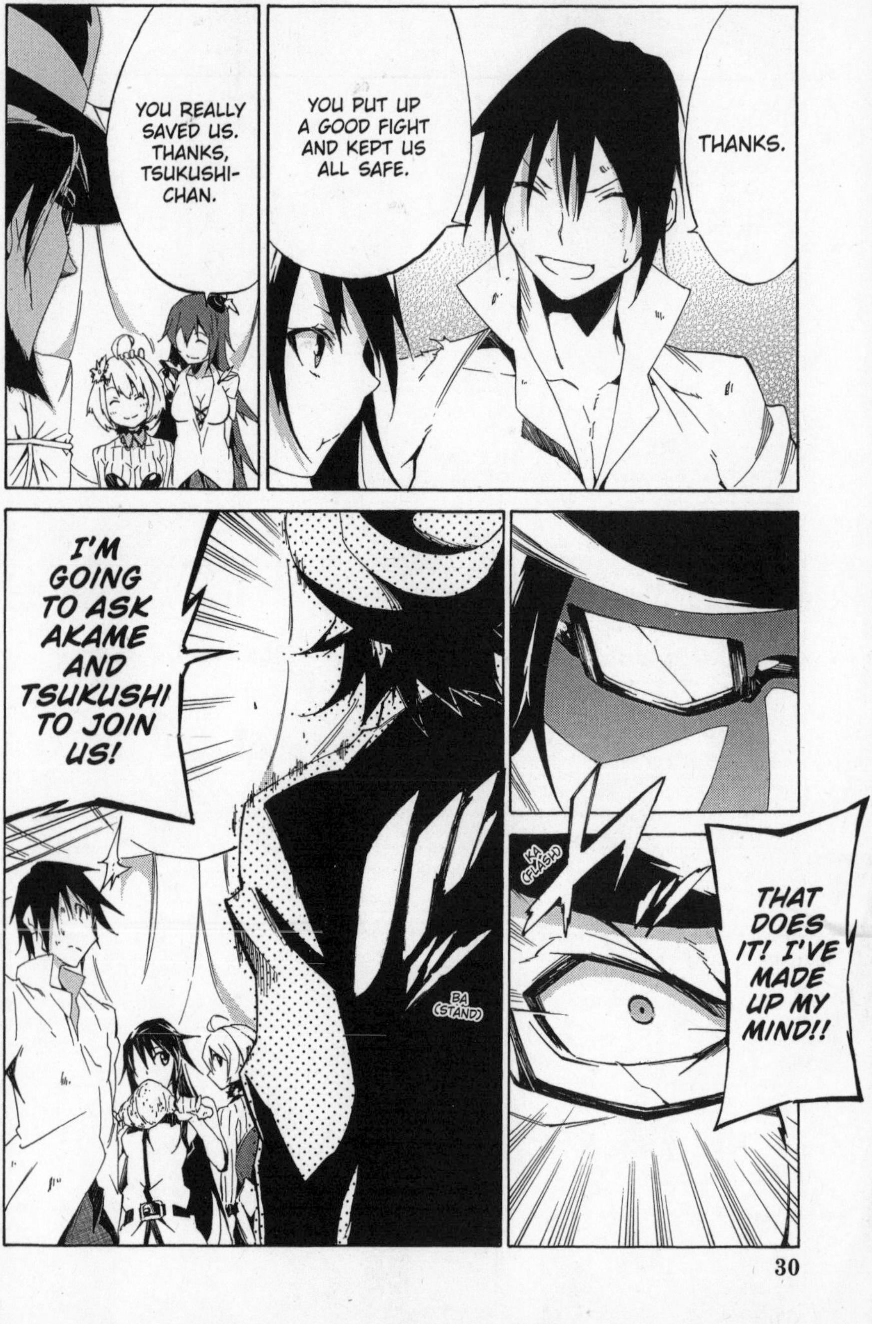
THANKS.
YOU PUT UP A GOOD FIGHT AND KEPT US ALL SAFE.
YOU REALLY SAVED US. THANKS, TSUKUSHI-CHAN.
KA (FLASH)
THAT DOES IT! I'VE MADE UP MY MIND!!
BA (STAND)
I'M GOING TO ASK AKAME AND TSUKUSHI TO JOIN US!

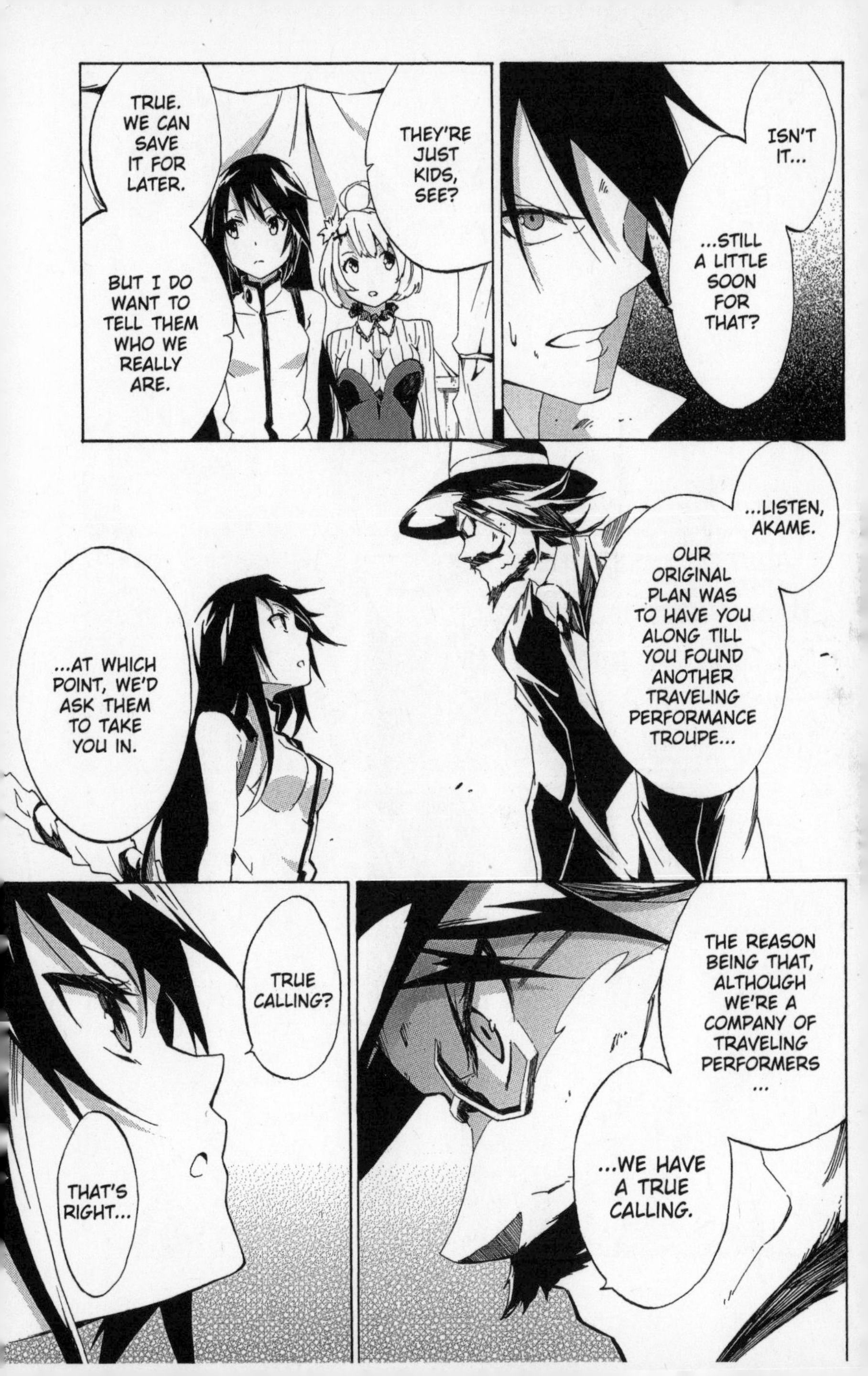

ISN'T IT...
...STILL A LITTLE SOON FOR THAT?
THEY'RE JUST KIDS, SEE?
TRUE. WE CAN SAVE IT FOR LATER.
BUT I DO WANT TO TELL THEM WHO WE REALLY ARE.
...LISTEN, AKAME.
OUR ORIGINAL PLAN WAS TO HAVE YOU ALONG TILL YOU FOUND ANOTHER TRAVELING PERFORMANCE TROUPE...
...AT WHICH POINT, WE'D ASK THEM TO TAKE YOU IN.
THE REASON BEING THAT, ALTHOUGH WE'RE A COMPANY OF TRAVELING PERFORMERS...
...WE HAVE A TRUE CALLING.
TRUE CALLING?
THAT'S RIGHT...

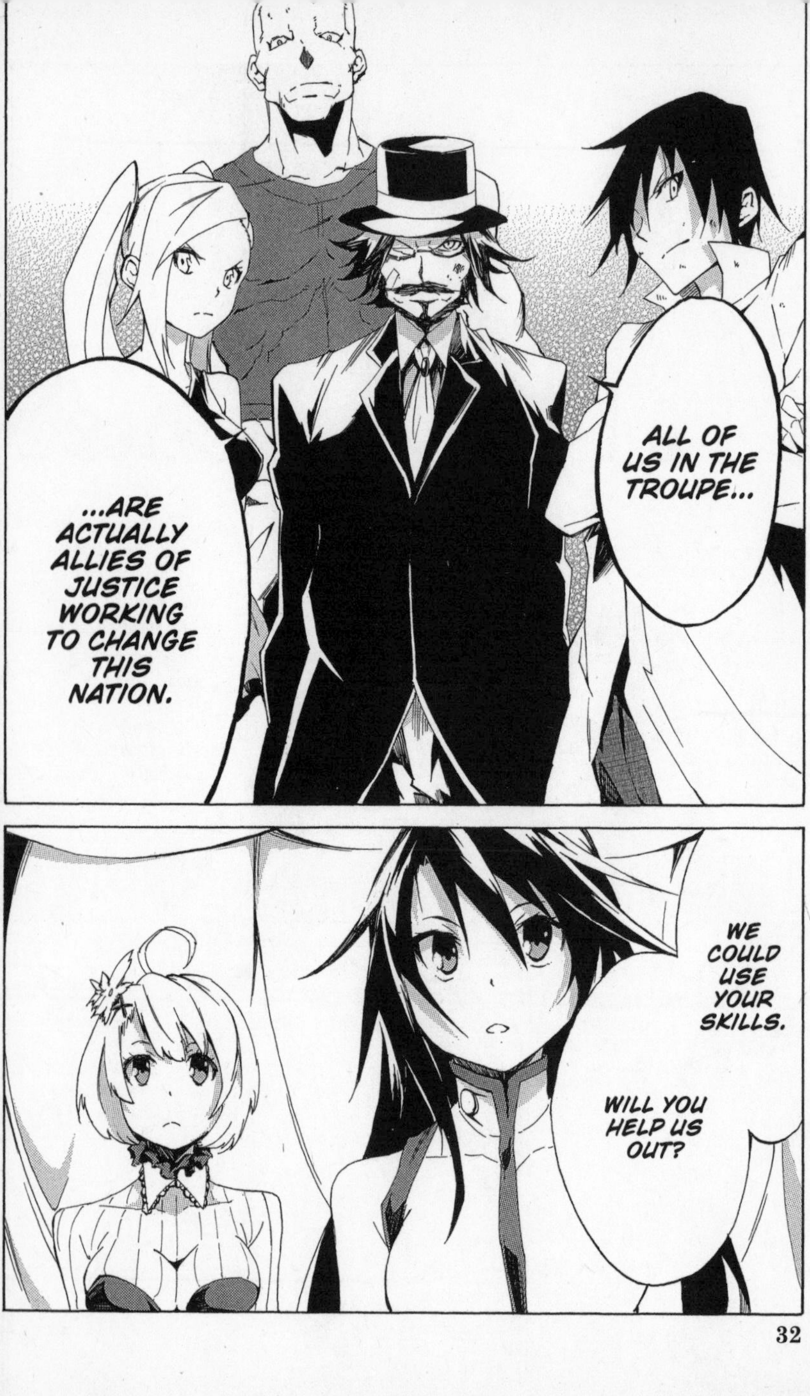
ALL OF US IN THE TROUPE...
...ARE ACTUALLY ALLIES OF JUSTICE WORKING TO CHANGE THIS NATION.
WE COULD USE YOUR SKILLS.
WILL YOU HELP US OUT?

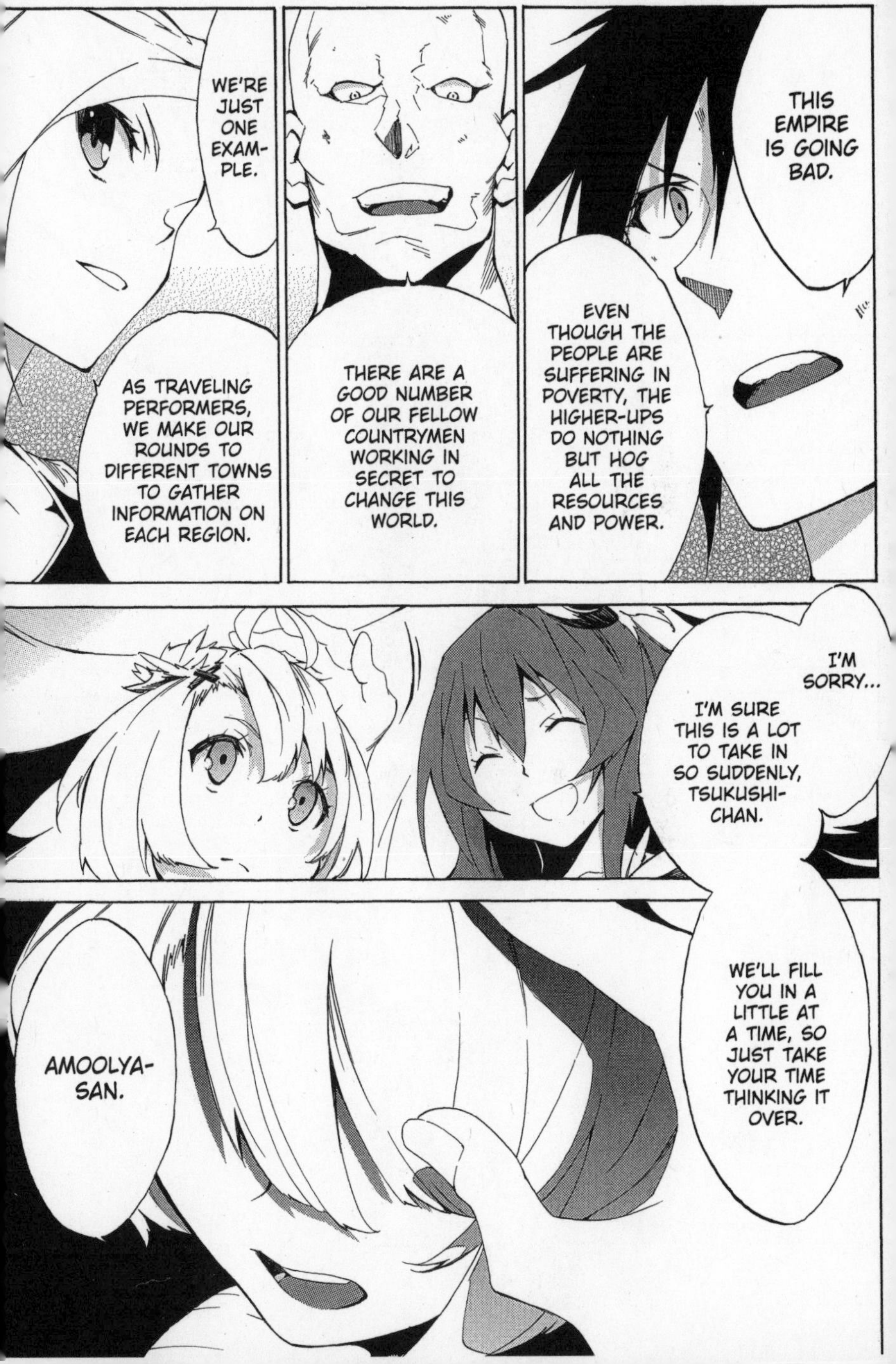
THIS EMPIRE IS GOING BAD.
EVEN THOUGH THE PEOPLE ARE SUFFERING IN POVERTY, THE HIGHER-UPS DO NOTHING BUT HOG ALL THE RESOURCES AND POWER.
THERE ARE A GOOD NUMBER OF OUR FELLOW COUNTRYMEN WORKING IN SECRET TO CHANGE THIS WORLD.
WE'RE JUST ONE EXAMPLE.
AS TRAVELING PERFORMERS, WE MAKE OUR ROUNDS TO DIFFERENT TOWNS TO GATHER INFORMATION ON EACH REGION.
I'M SORRY...
I'M SURE THIS IS A LOT TO TAKE IN SO SUDDENLY, TSUKUSHI-CHAN.
WE'LL FILL YOU IN A LITTLE AT A TIME, SO JUST TAKE YOUR TIME THINKING IT OVER.
AMOOLYA-SAN.

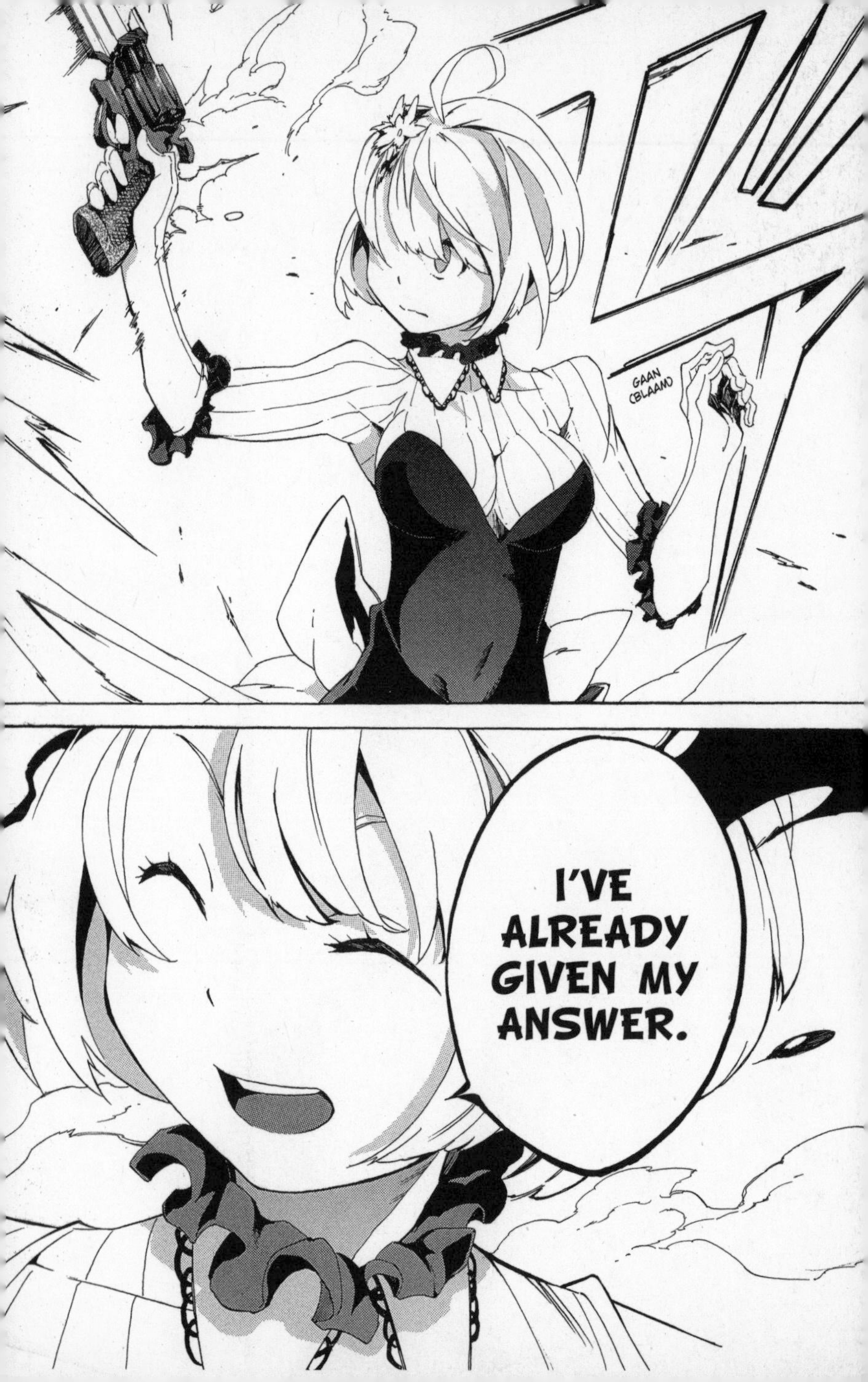
GAAN
(BLAAM)
I'VE ALREADY GIVEN MY ANSWER.

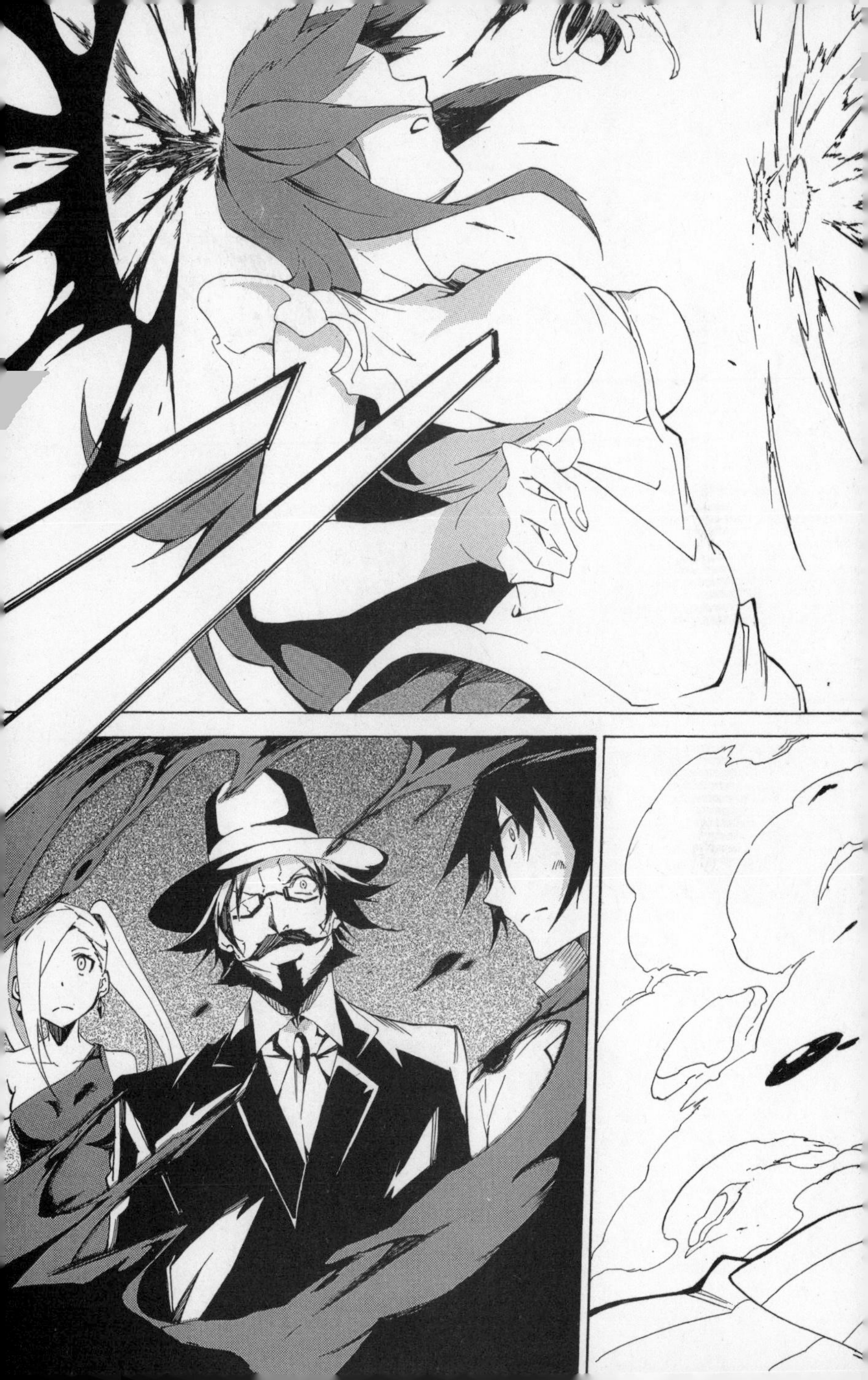

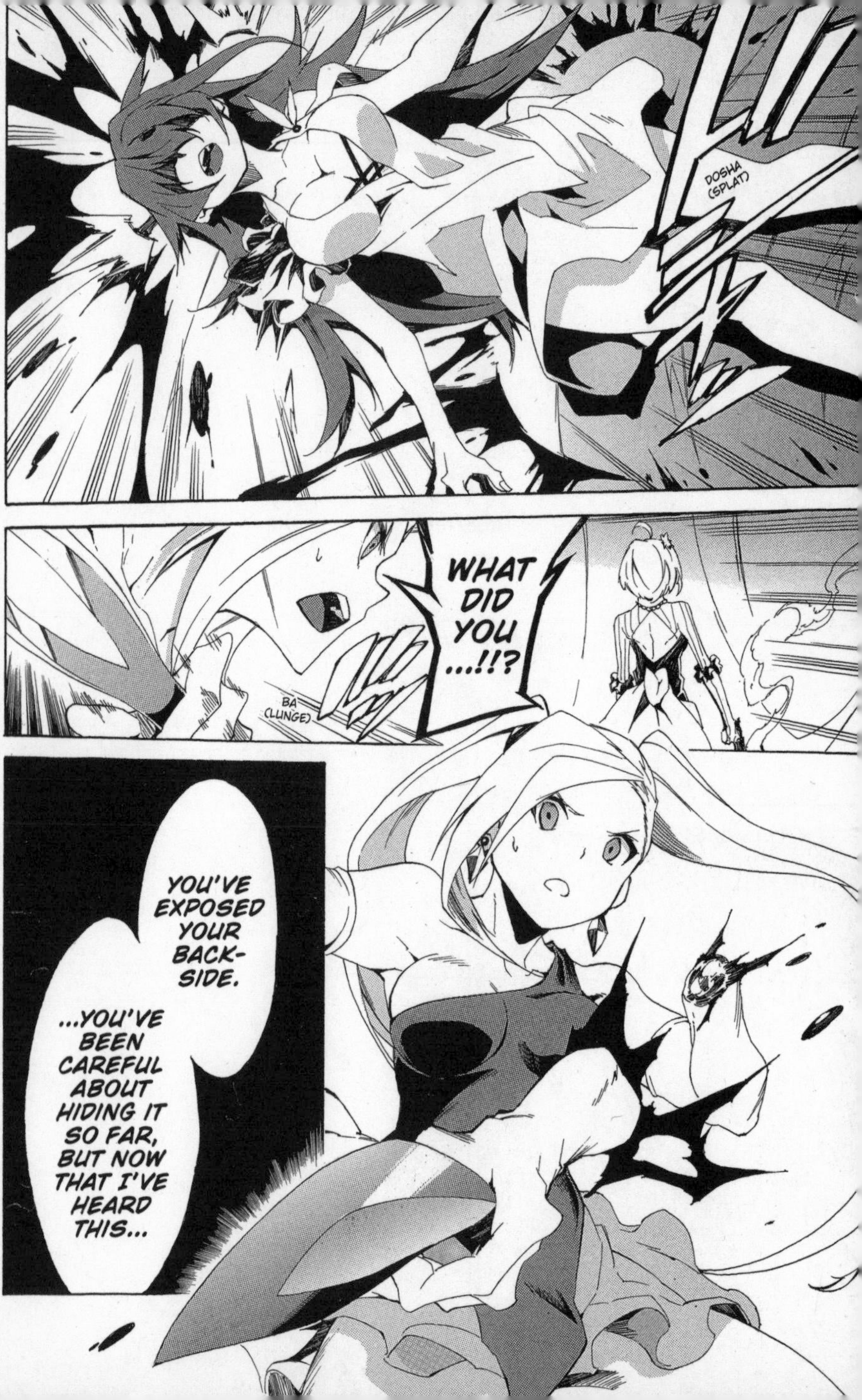
DOSHA (SPLAT)
WHAT DID YOU ...!!?
BA (LUNGE)
YOU'VE EXPOSED YOUR BACK-SIDE.
...YOU'VE BEEN CAREFUL ABOUT HIDING IT SO FAR, BUT NOW THAT I'VE HEARD THIS...

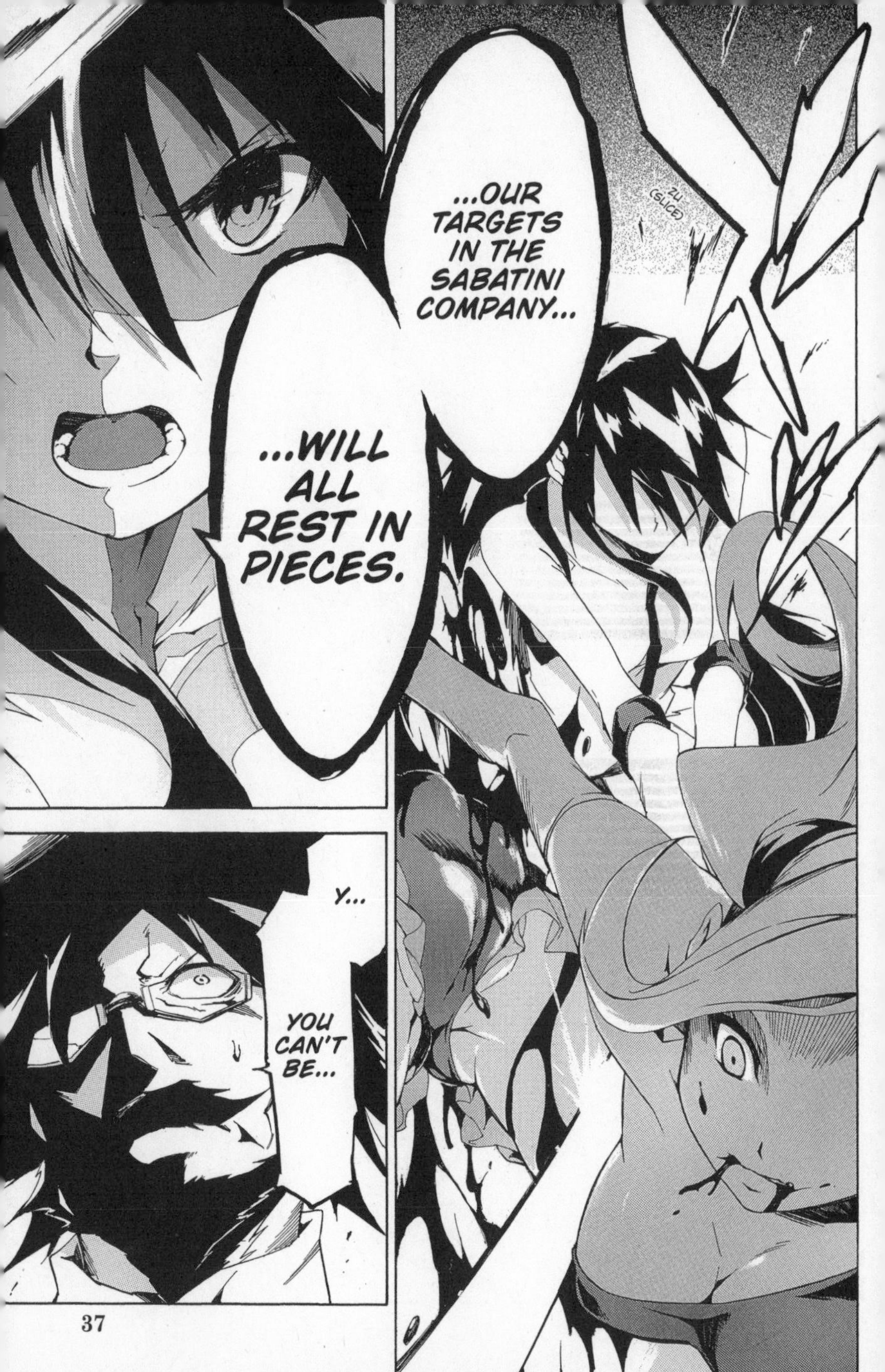
...OUR TARGETS IN THE SABATINI COMPANY...
...WILL ALL REST IN PIECES.
ZU (SLICE)
Y...
YOU CAN'T BE...

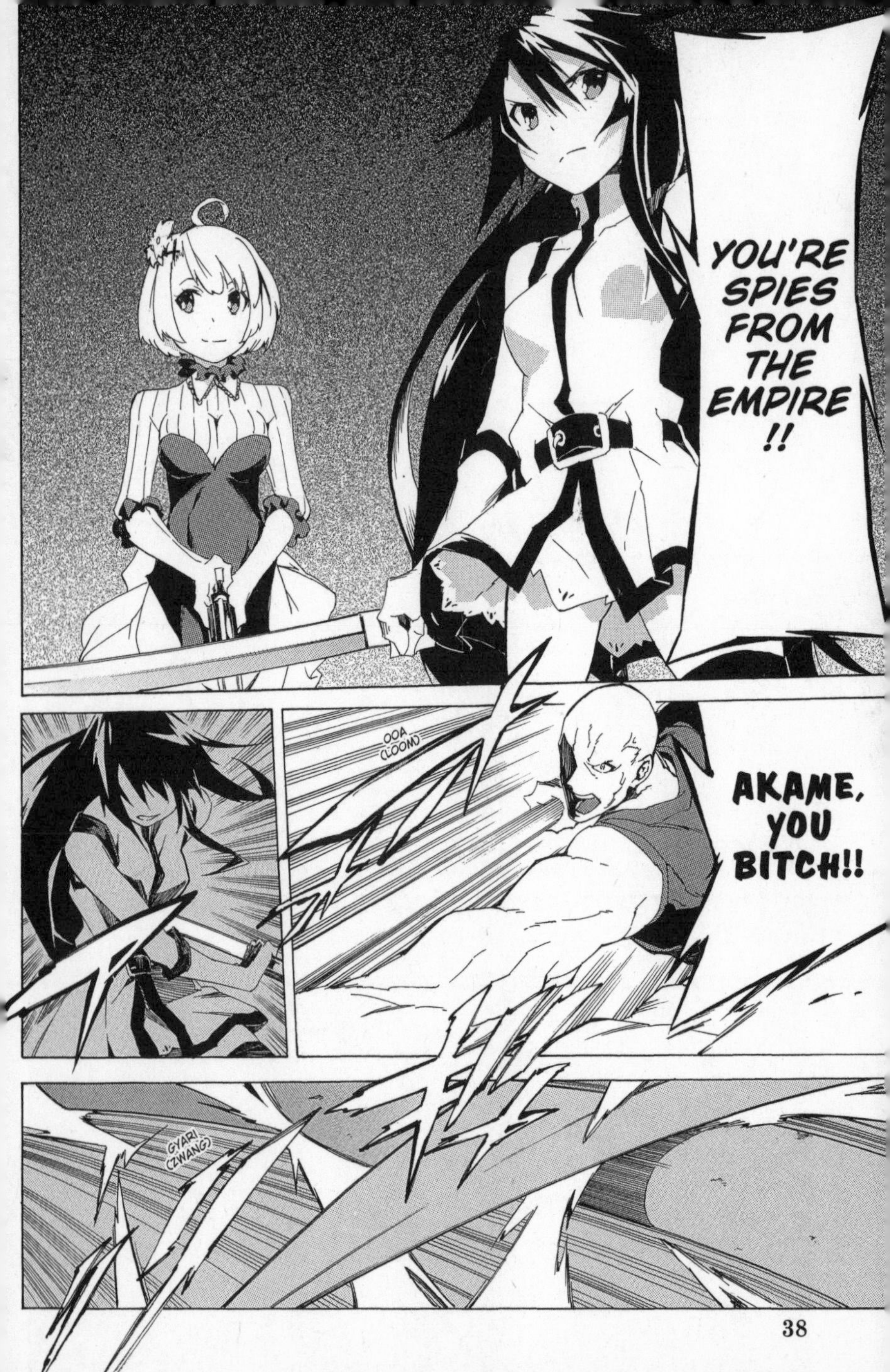

YOU'RE SPIES FROM THE EMPIRE !!
OOA (LOOM)
AKAME, YOU BITCH!!
GYARI (ZWANG)

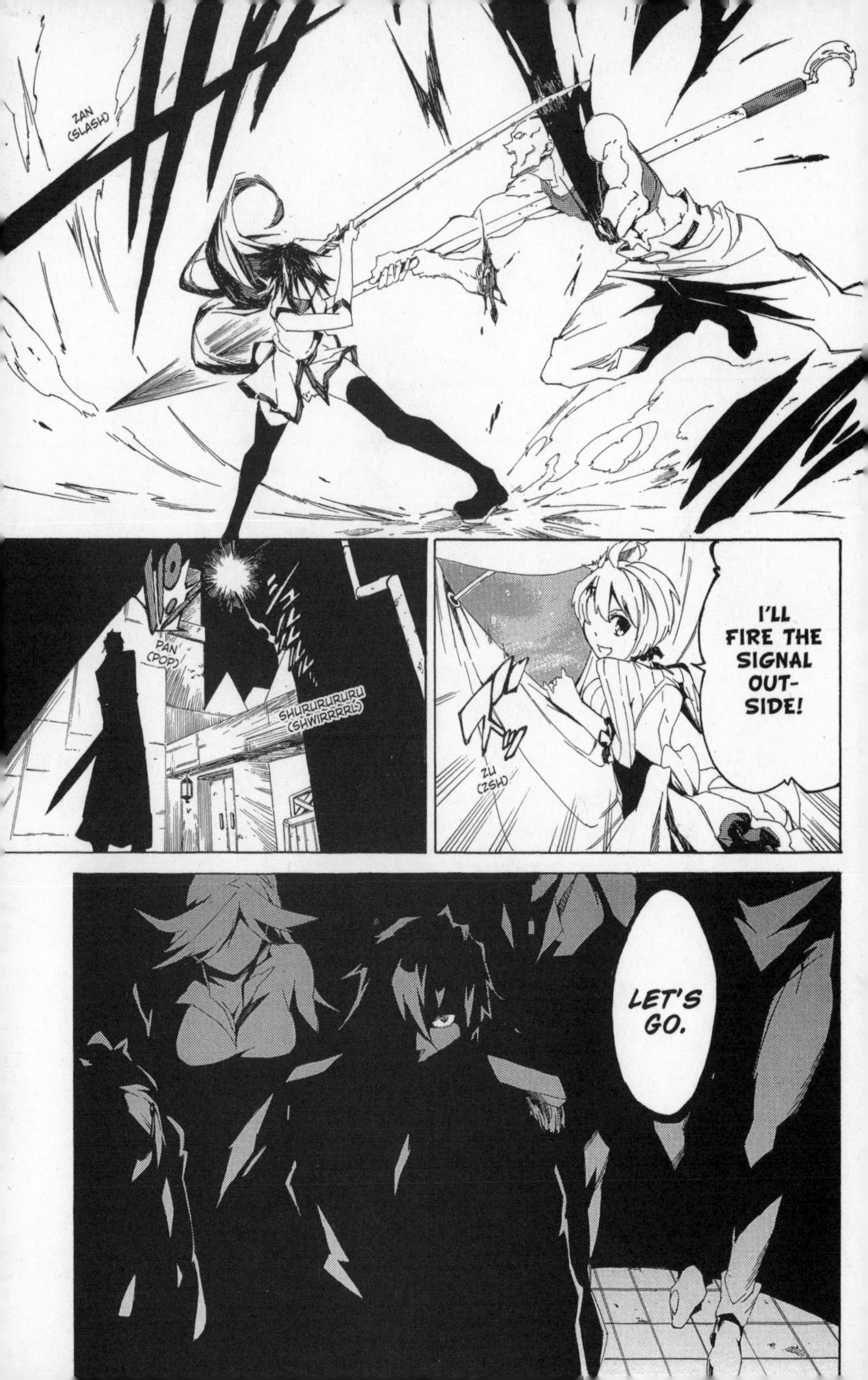
ZAN (SLASH)
I'LL FIRE THE SIGNAL OUT-SIDE!
ZU (ZSH)
PAN (POP)
SHURURURURU (SHWIRRRRR)
LET'S GO.

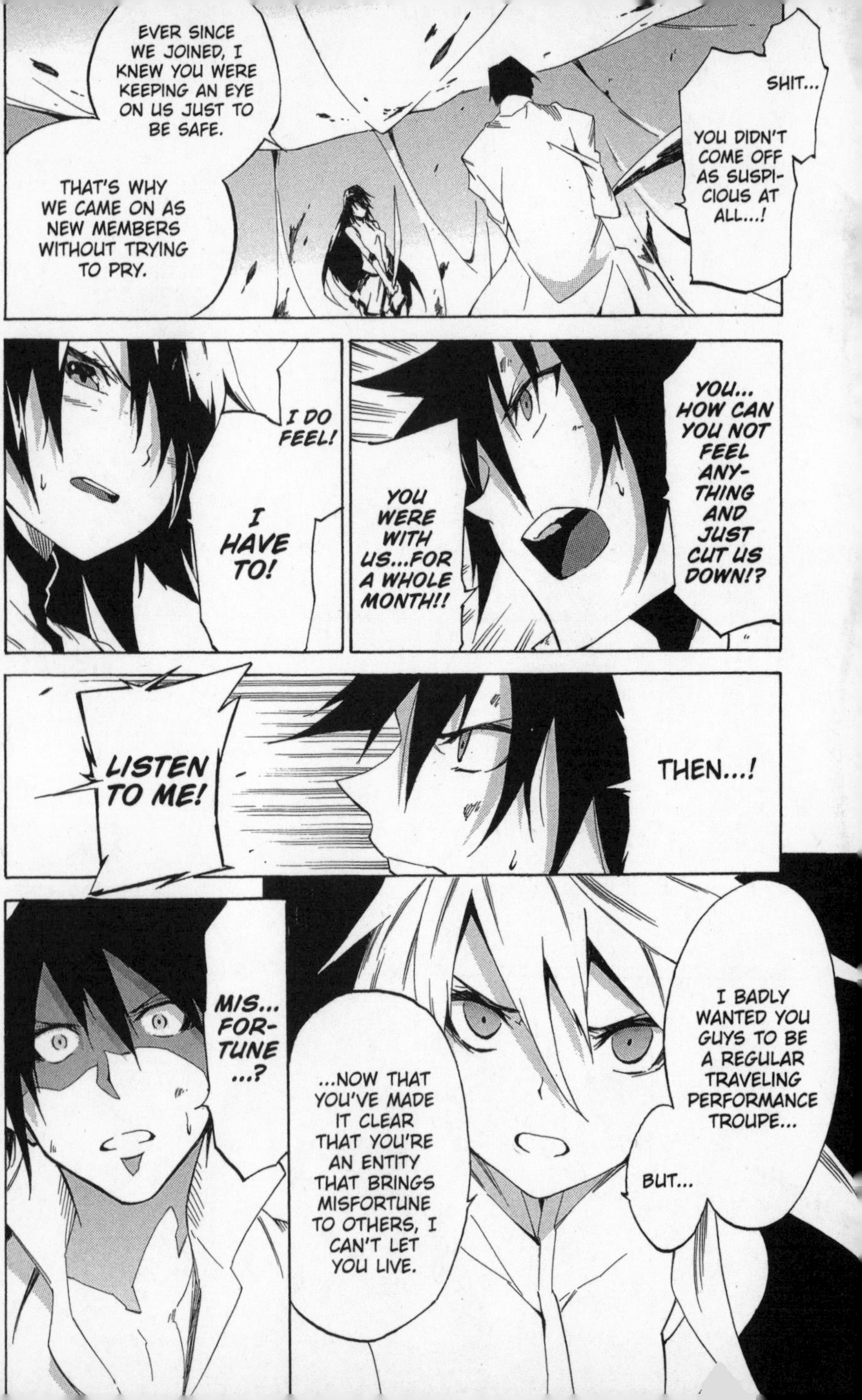

SHIT...
YOU DIDN'T COME OFF AS SUSPICIOUS AT ALL...!
EVER SINCE WE JOINED, I KNEW YOU WERE KEEPING AN EYE ON US JUST TO BE SAFE.
THAT'S WHY WE CAME ON AS NEW MEMBERS WITHOUT TRYING TO PRY.
YOU... HOW CAN YOU NOT FEEL ANYTHING AND JUST CUT US DOWN!?
YOU WERE WITH US...FOR A WHOLE MONTH!!
I DO FEEL!
I HAVE TO!
THEN...!
LISTEN TO ME!
I BADLY WANTED YOU GUYS TO BE A REGULAR TRAVELING PERFORMANCE TROUPE...
BUT...
...NOW THAT YOU'VE MADE IT CLEAR THAT YOU'RE AN ENTITY THAT BRINGS MISFORTUNE TO OTHERS, I CAN'T LET YOU LIVE.
MIS... FORTUNE ...?

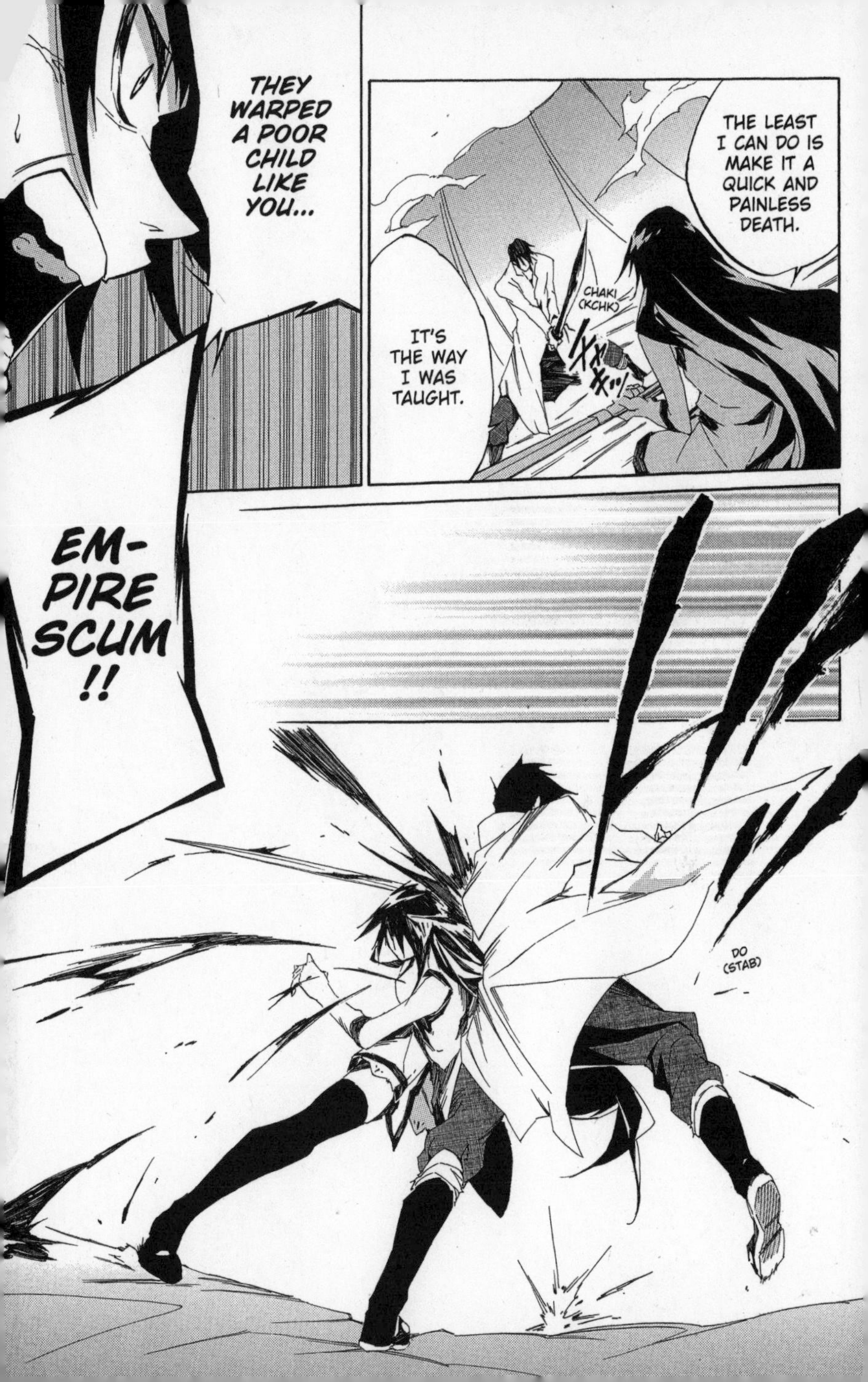THE LEAST I CAN DO IS MAKE IT A QUICK AND PAINLESS DEATH.
CHAKI (KCHK)
IT'S THE WAY I WAS TAUGHT.
THEY WARPED A POOR CHILD LIKE YOU...
DO (STAB)
EM-PIRE SCUM!!

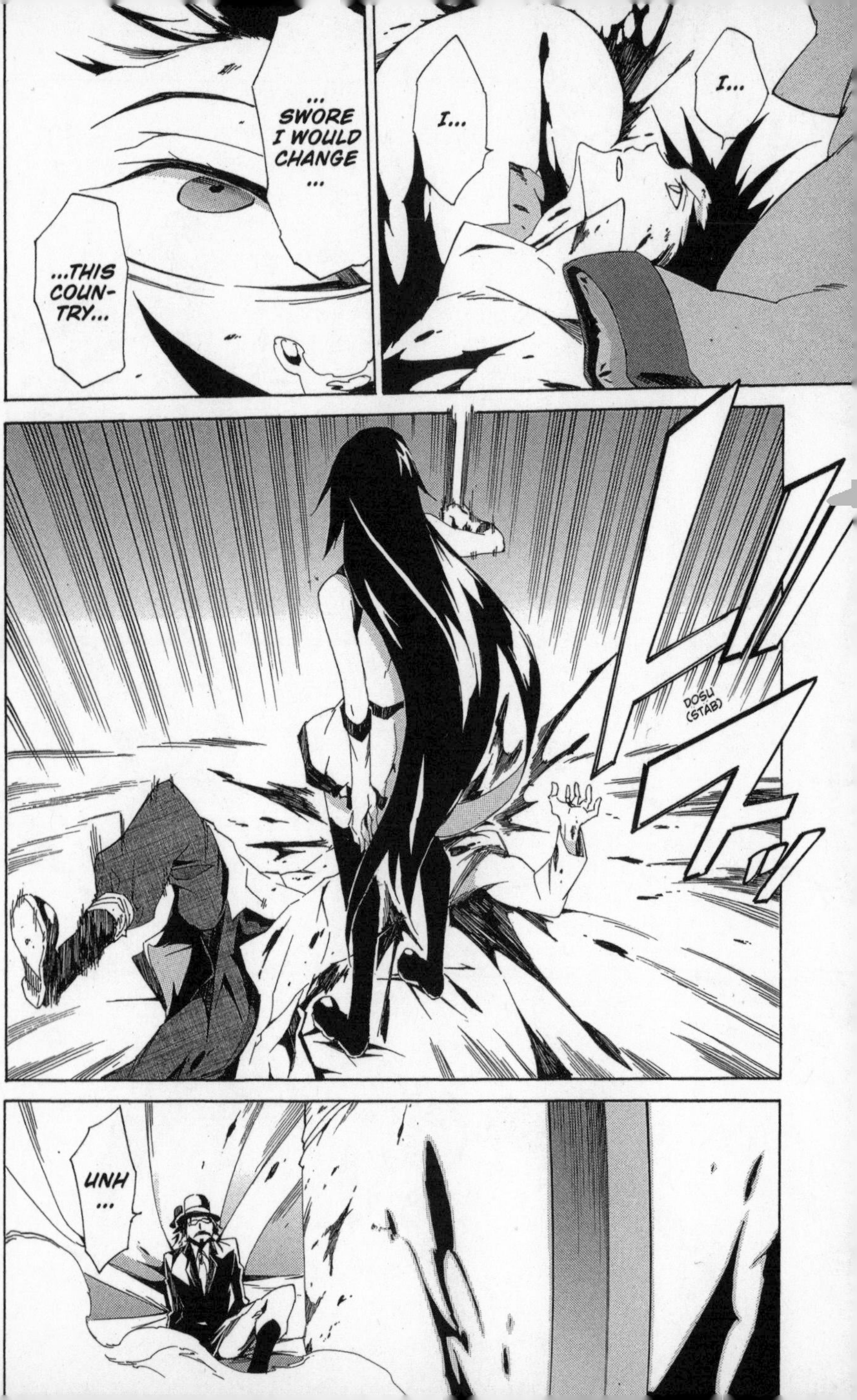
I...
I...
...SWORE I WOULD CHANGE...
...THIS COUNTRY...
DOSU (STAB)
UNH...

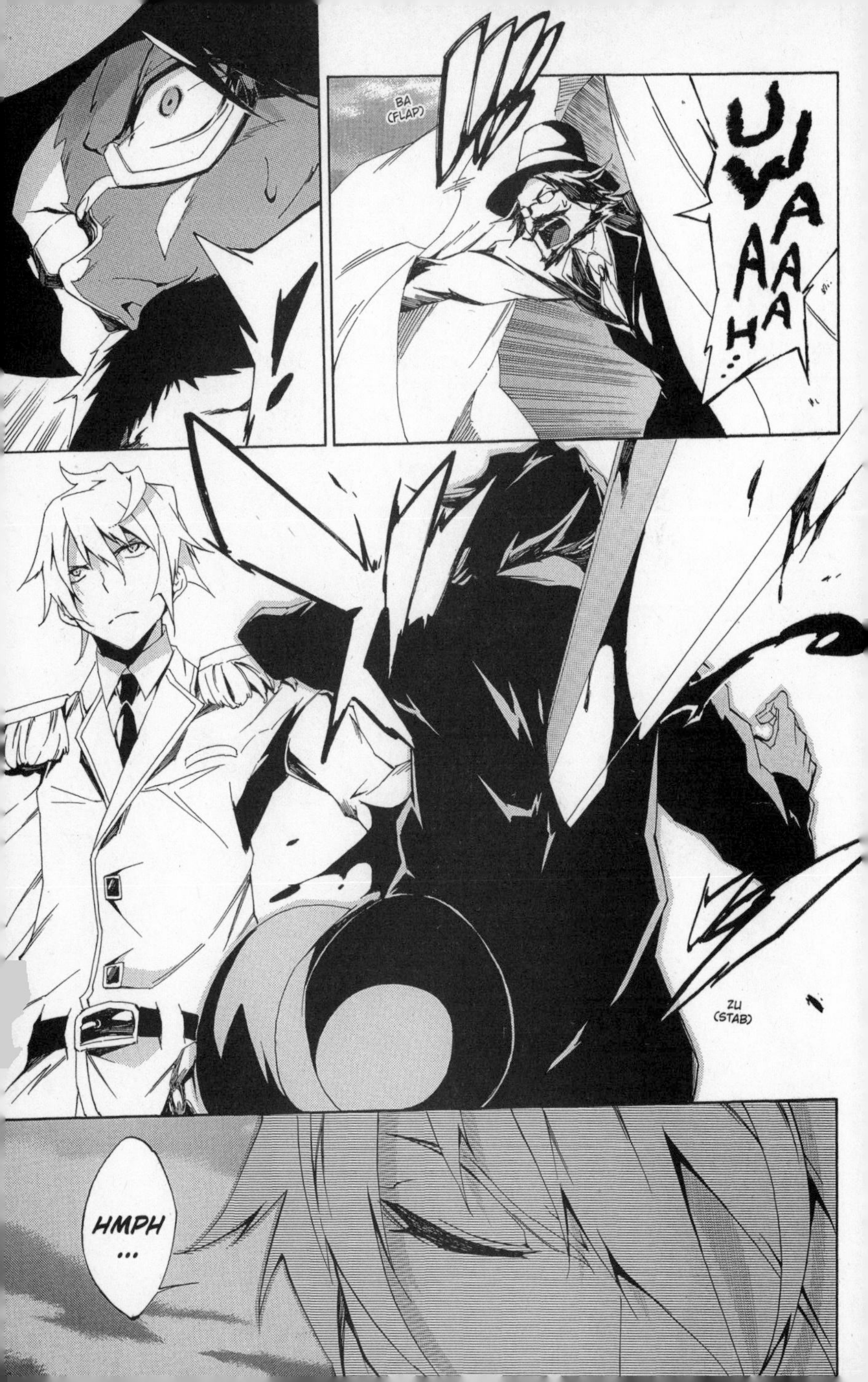
UWAAAAAH...
BA (FLAP)
ZU (STAB)
HMPH ...

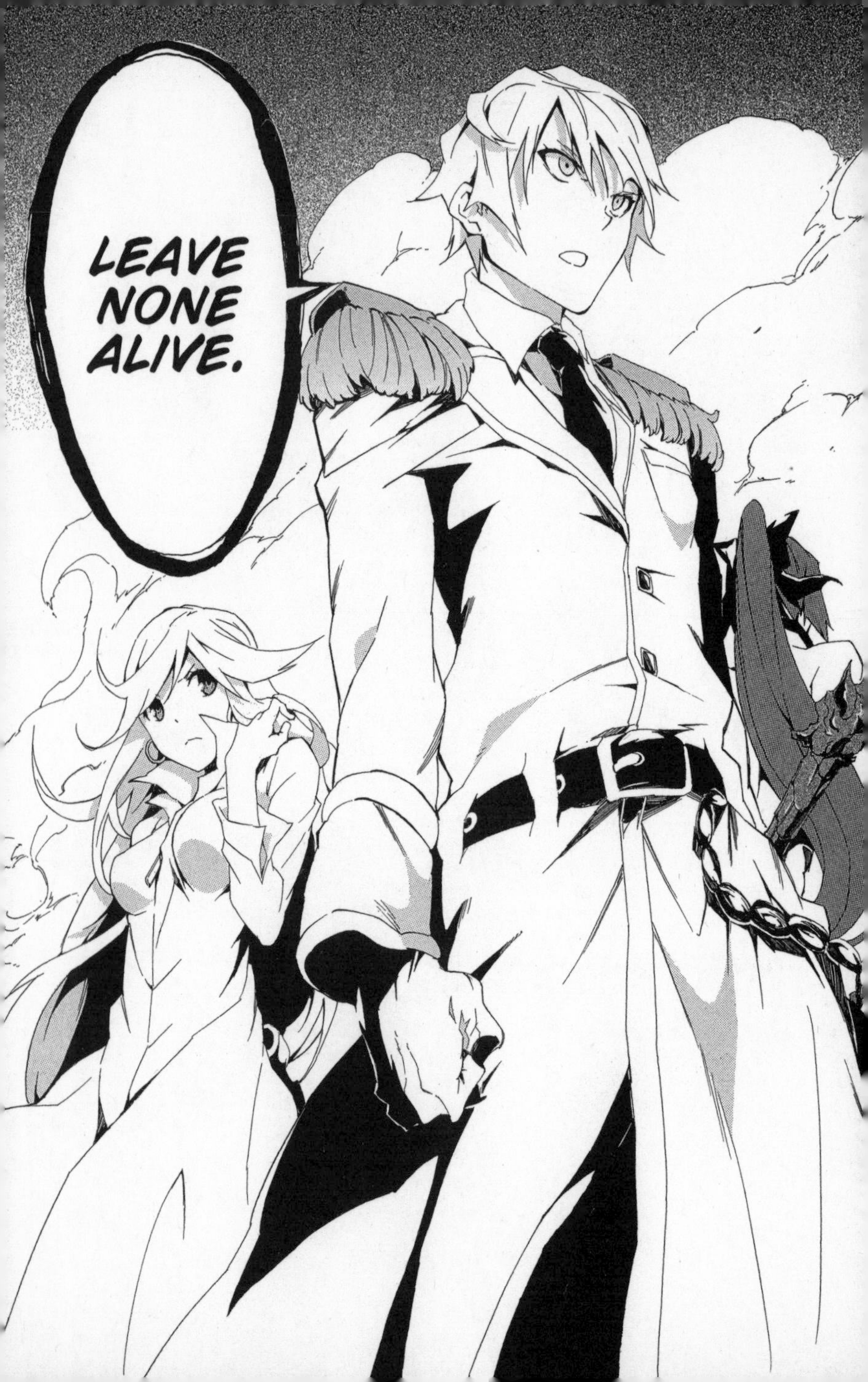
LEAVE NONE ALIVE.

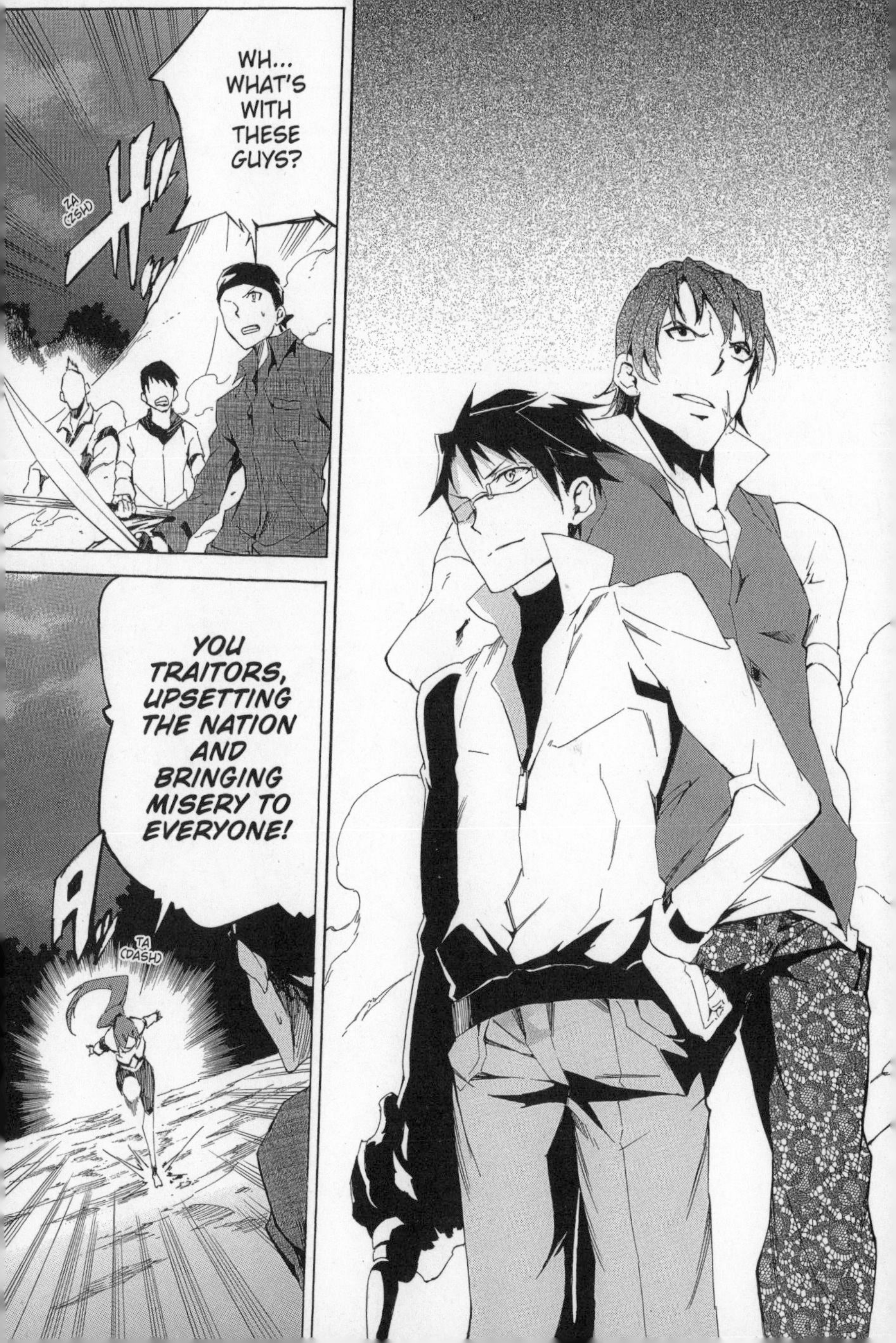
WH... WHAT'S WITH THESE GUYS?
ZA (ZISH)
YOU TRAITORS, UPSETTING THE NATION AND BRINGING MISERY TO EVERYONE!
TA (DASH)

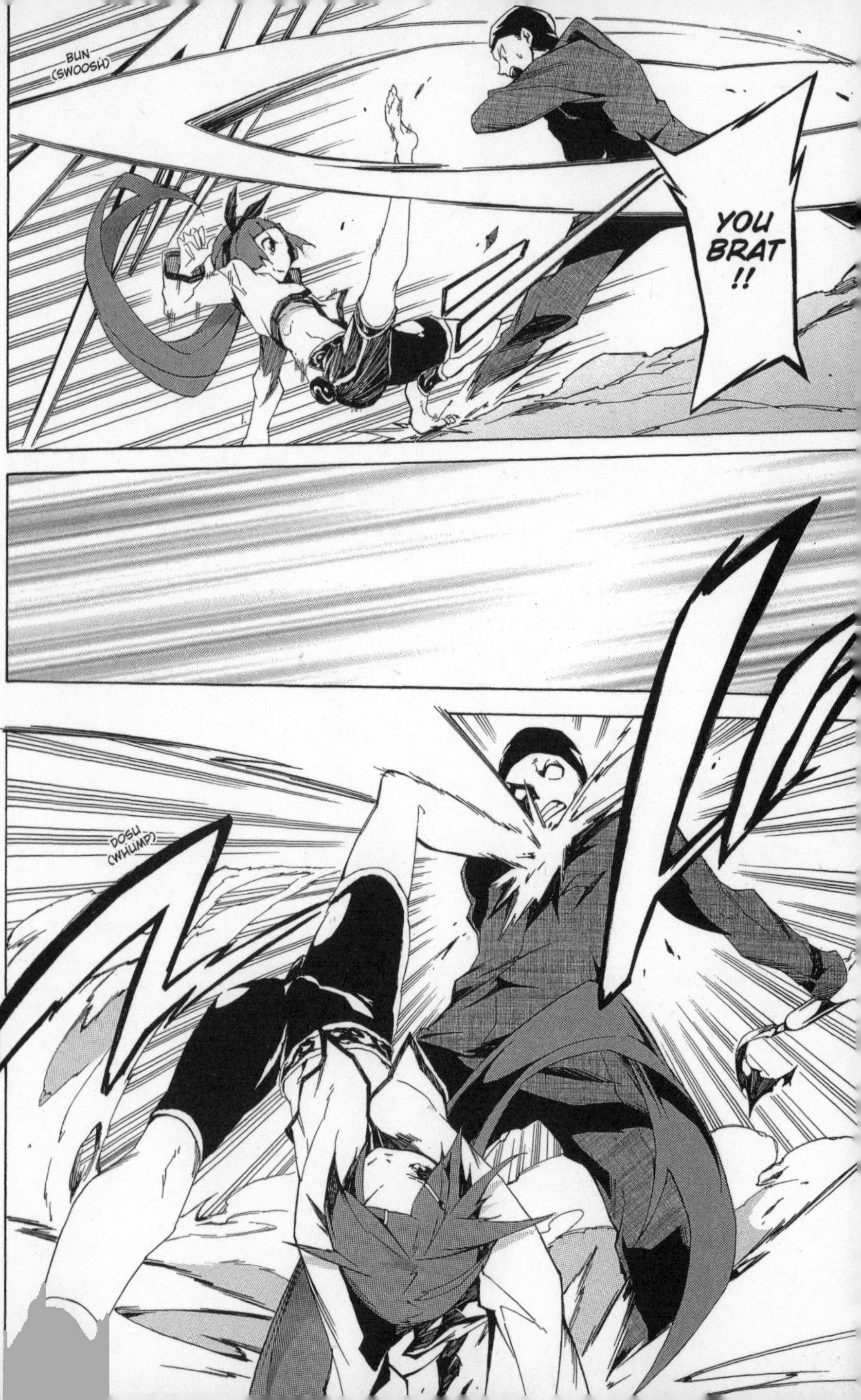
BUN (SWOOSH)
YOU BRAT !!
DOSU (WHUMP)

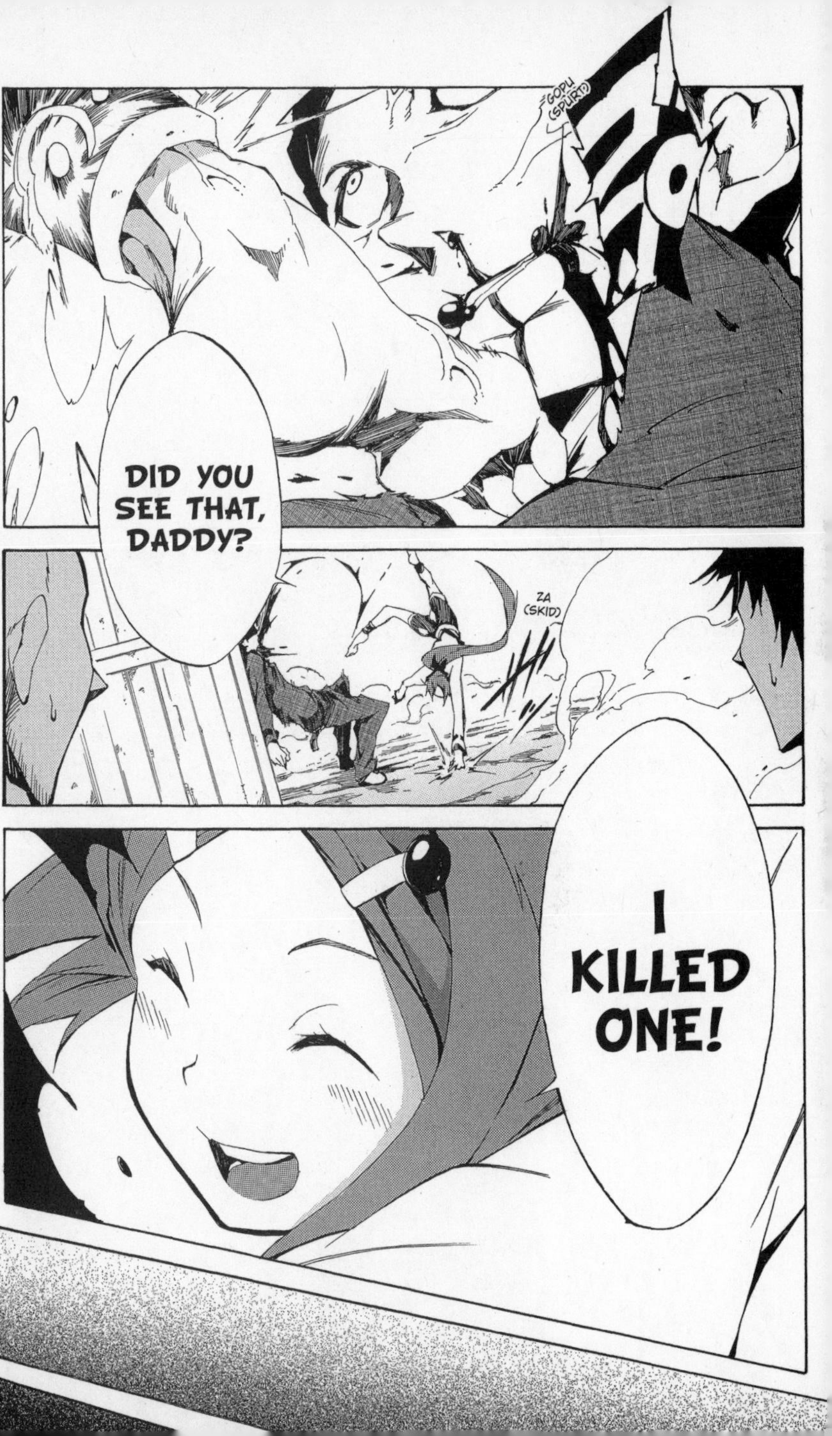GOPU (SPURT)
DID YOU SEE THAT, DADDY?
ZA (SKID)
I KILLED ONE!

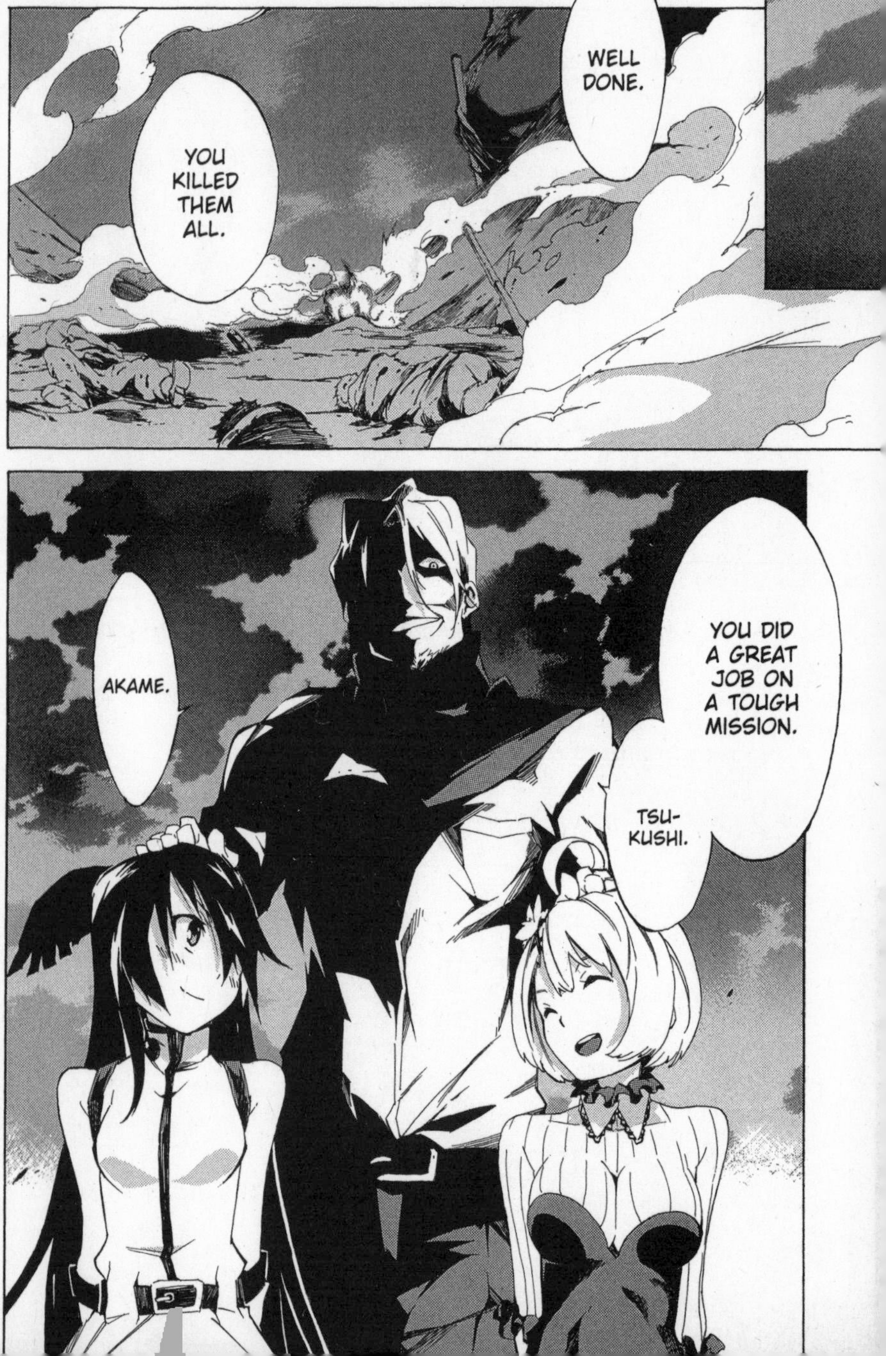
WELL DONE.
YOU KILLED THEM ALL.
YOU DID A GREAT JOB ON A TOUGH MISSION.
TSU-KUSHI.
AKAME.

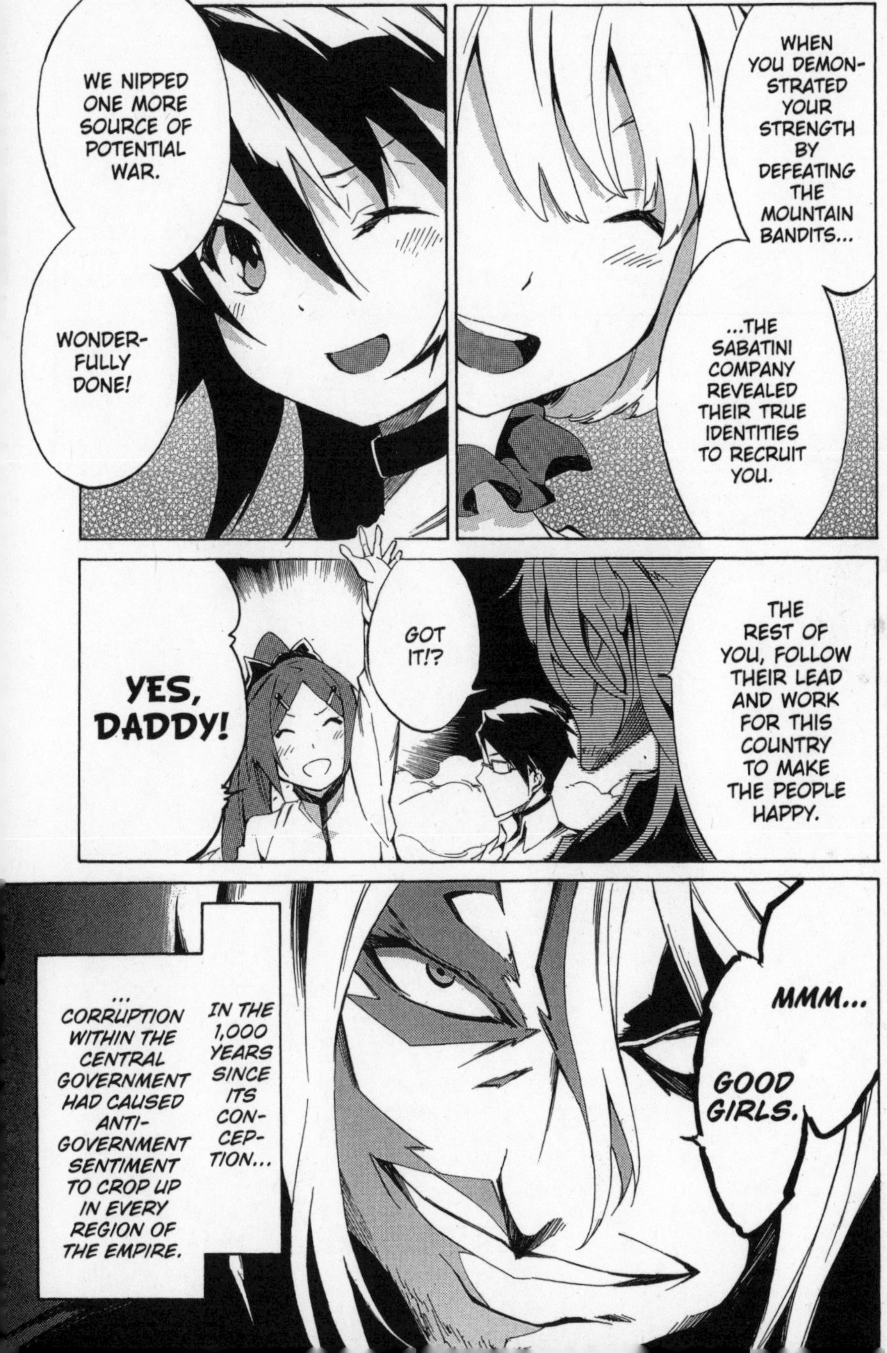

WHEN YOU DEMONSTRATED YOUR STRENGTH BY DEFEATING THE MOUNTAIN BANDITS...
...THE SABATINI COMPANY REVEALED THEIR TRUE IDENTITIES TO RECRUIT YOU.
WE NIPPED ONE MORE SOURCE OF POTENTIAL WAR.
WONDERFULLY DONE!
THE REST OF YOU, FOLLOW THEIR LEAD AND WORK FOR THIS COUNTRY TO MAKE THE PEOPLE HAPPY.
GOT IT!?
YES, DADDY!
MMM...
GOOD GIRLS.
IN THE 1,000 YEARS SINCE ITS CONCEPTION...
...CORRUPTION WITHIN THE CENTRAL GOVERNMENT HAD CAUSED ANTI-GOVERNMENT SENTIMENT TO CROP UP IN EVERY REGION OF THE EMPIRE.

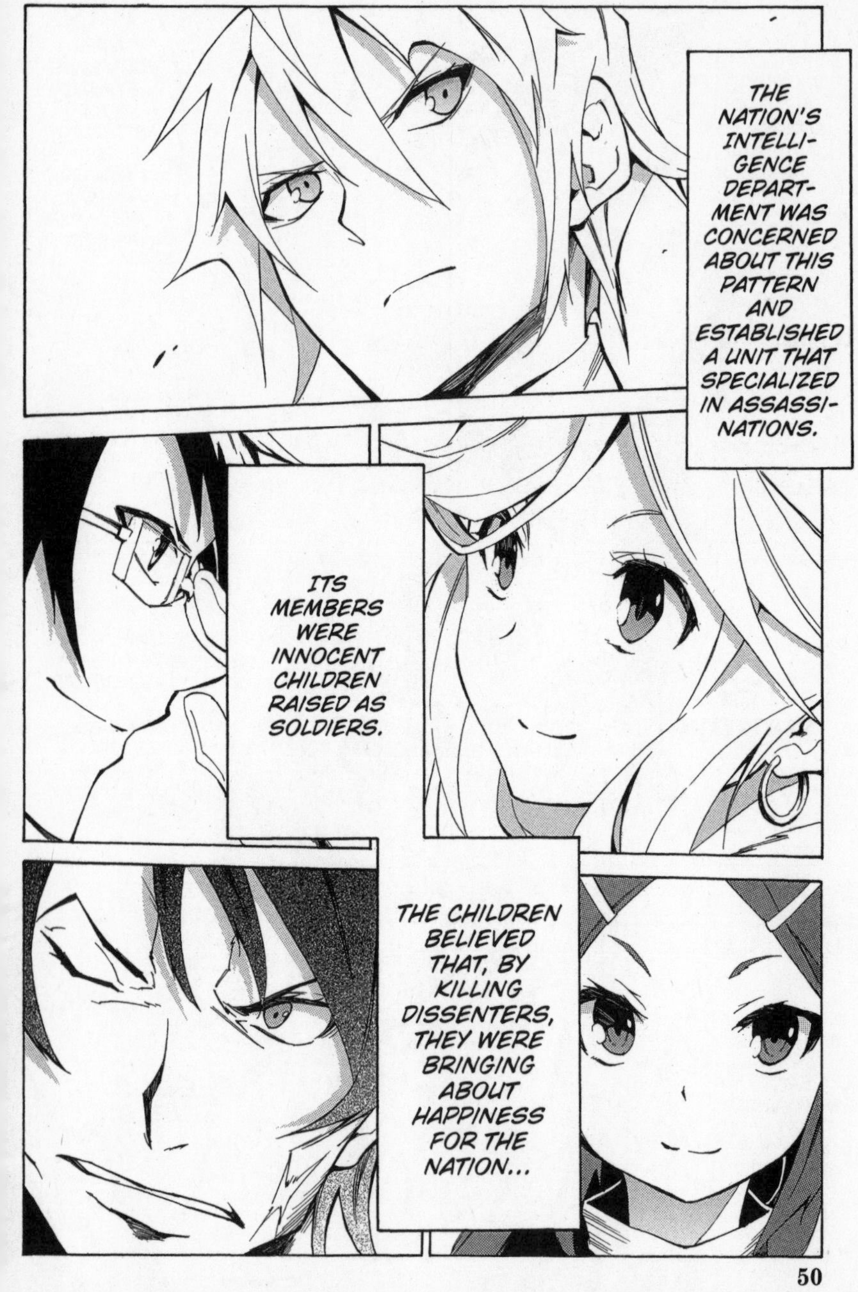
THE NATION'S INTELLIGENCE DEPARTMENT WAS CONCERNED ABOUT THIS PATTERN AND ESTABLISHED A UNIT THAT SPECIALIZED IN ASSASSINATIONS.
ITS MEMBERS WERE INNOCENT CHILDREN RAISED AS SOLDIERS.
THE CHILDREN BELIEVED THAT, BY KILLING DISSENTERS, THEY WERE BRINGING ABOUT HAPPINESS FOR THE NATION...

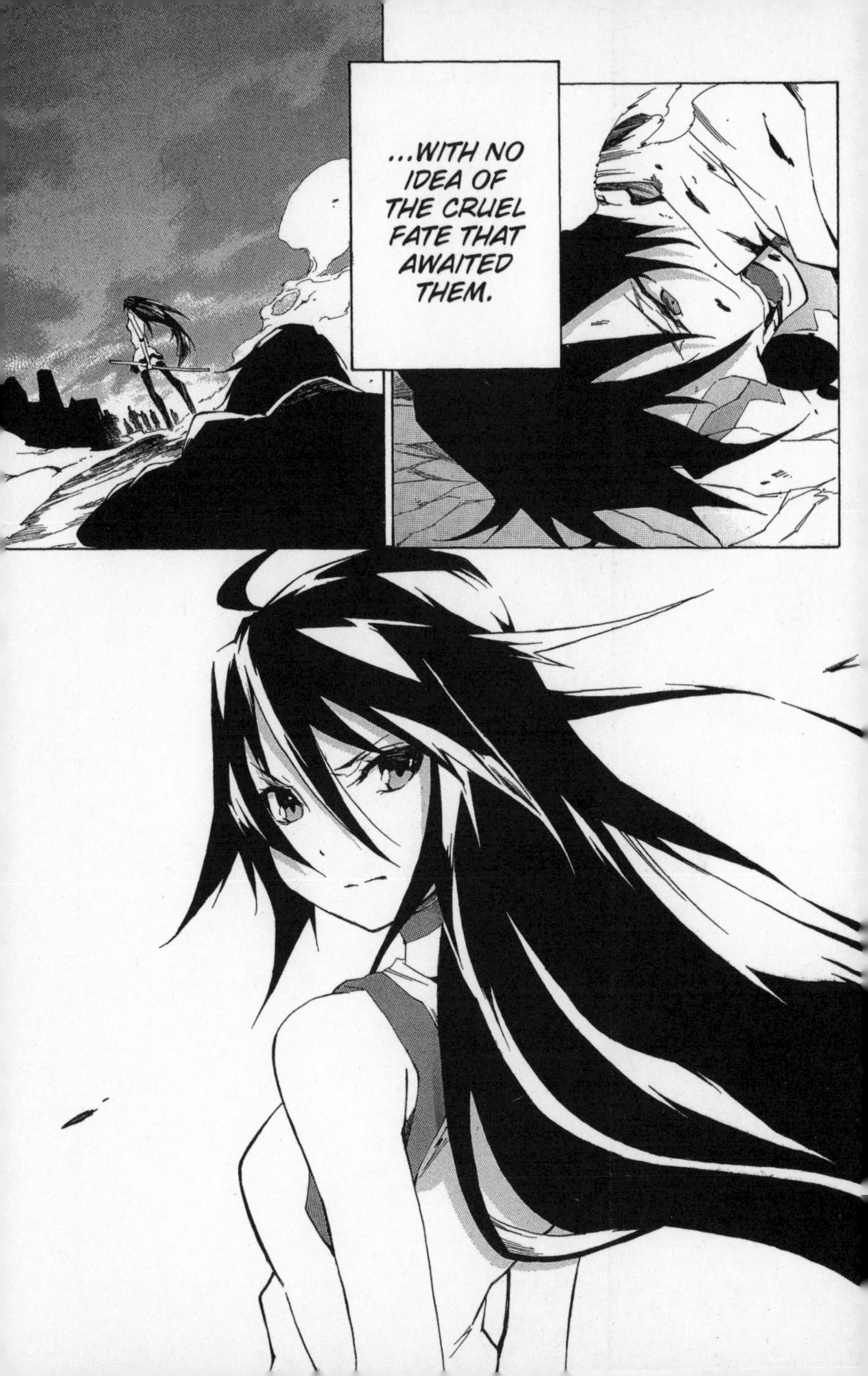
...WITH NO IDEA OF THE CRUEL FATE THAT AWAITED THEM.

Akame ga KILL! ZERO
Rough Sketches

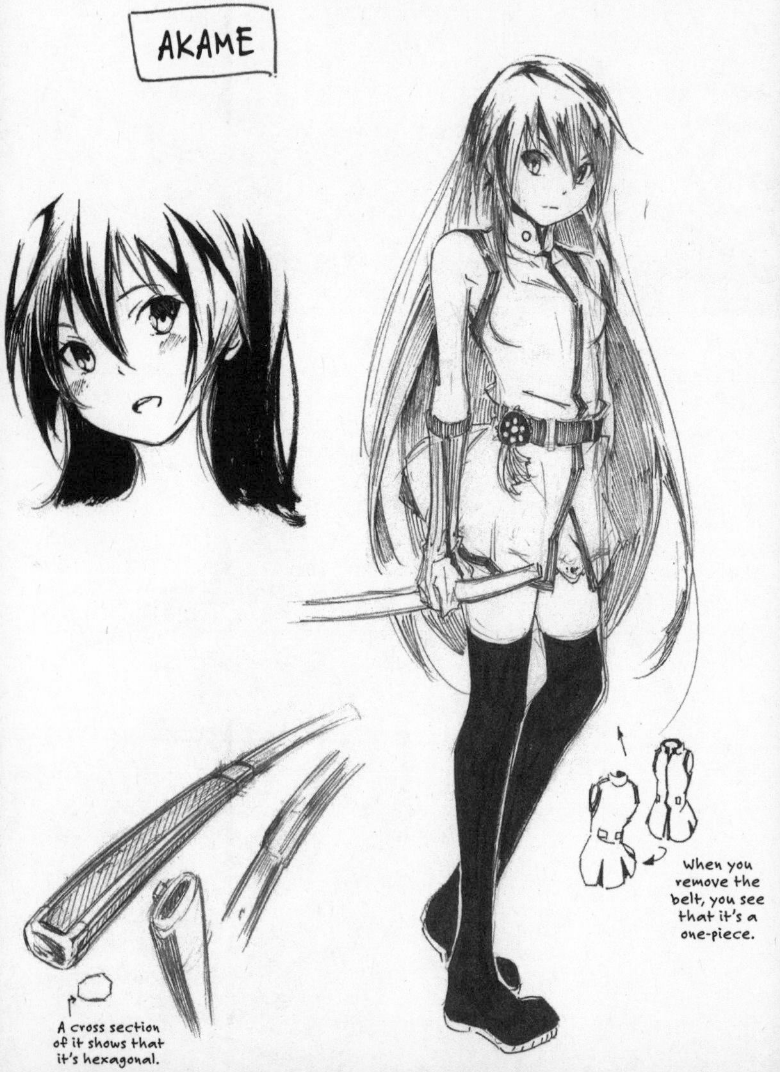
AKAME
When you remove the belt, you see that it's a one-piece.
A cross section of it shows that it's hexagonal.

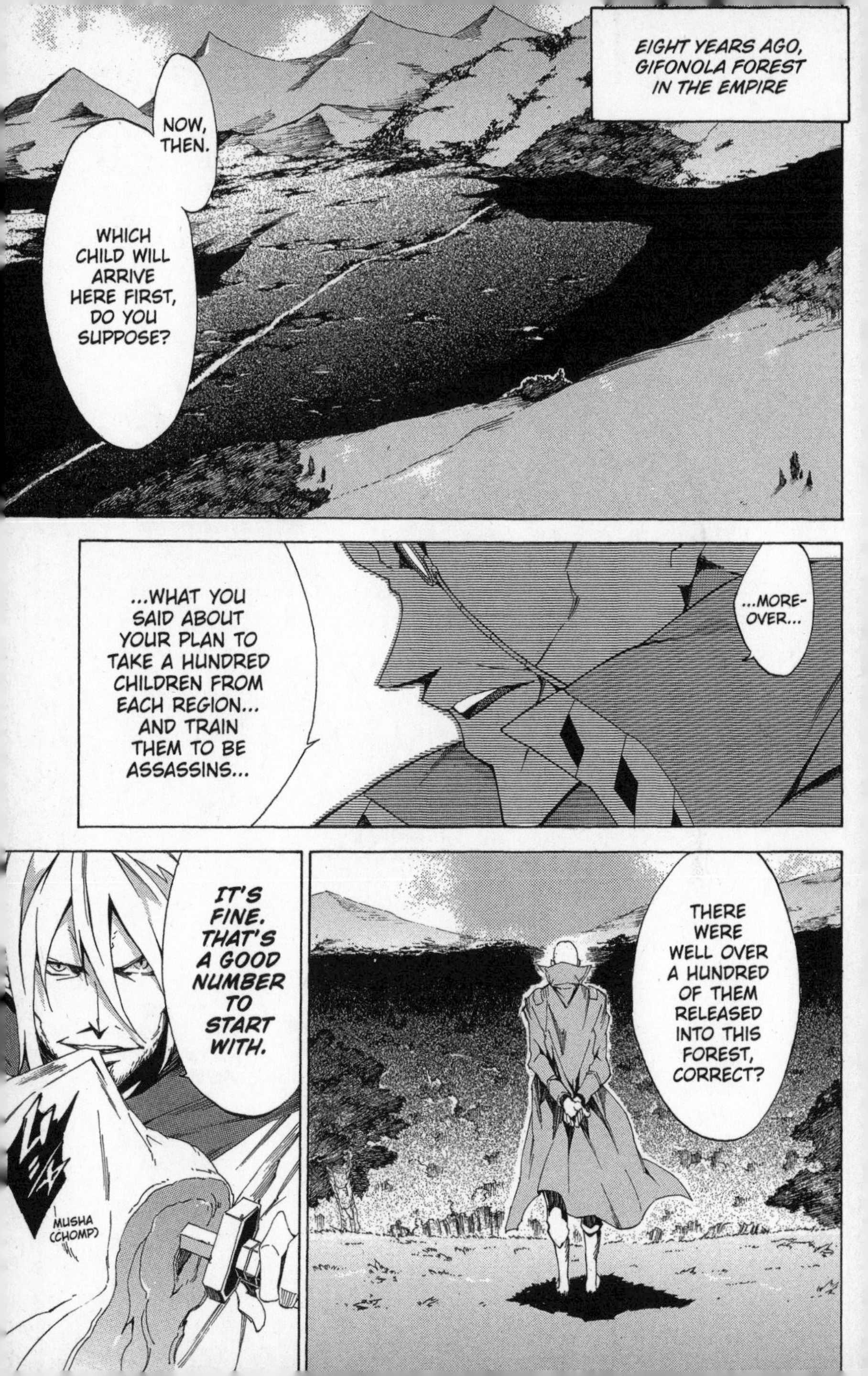
EIGHT YEARS AGO, GIFONOLA FOREST IN THE EMPIRE
NOW, THEN.
WHICH CHILD WILL ARRIVE HERE FIRST, DO YOU SUPPOSE?
...MORE-OVER...
...WHAT YOU SAID ABOUT YOUR PLAN TO TAKE A HUNDRED CHILDREN FROM EACH REGION... AND TRAIN THEM TO BE ASSASSINS...
THERE WERE WELL OVER A HUNDRED OF THEM RELEASED INTO THIS FOREST, CORRECT?
IT'S FINE. THAT'S A GOOD NUMBER TO START WITH.
MUSHA (CHOMP)

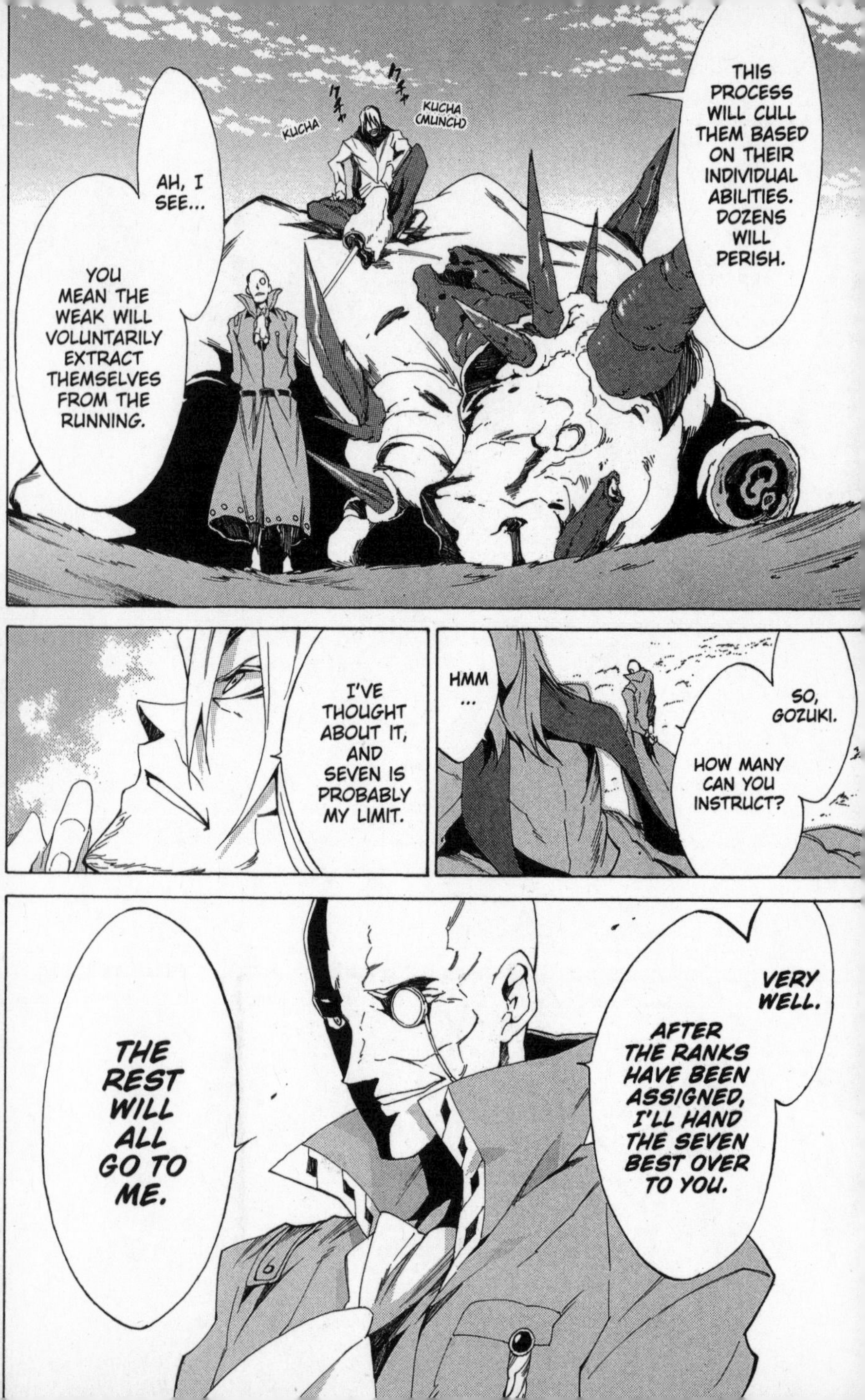
THIS PROCESS WILL CULL THEM BASED ON THEIR INDIVIDUAL ABILITIES. DOZENS WILL PERISH.
KUCHA (MUNCH)
KUCHA
AH, I SEE...
YOU MEAN THE WEAK WILL VOLUNTARILY EXTRACT THEMSELVES FROM THE RUNNING.
SO, GOZUKI.
HOW MANY CAN YOU INSTRUCT?
HMM ...
I'VE THOUGHT ABOUT IT, AND SEVEN IS PROBABLY MY LIMIT.
VERY WELL.
AFTER THE RANKS HAVE BEEN ASSIGNED, I'LL HAND THE SEVEN BEST OVER TO YOU.
THE REST WILL ALL GO TO ME.

Chapter 2
The Day It Began

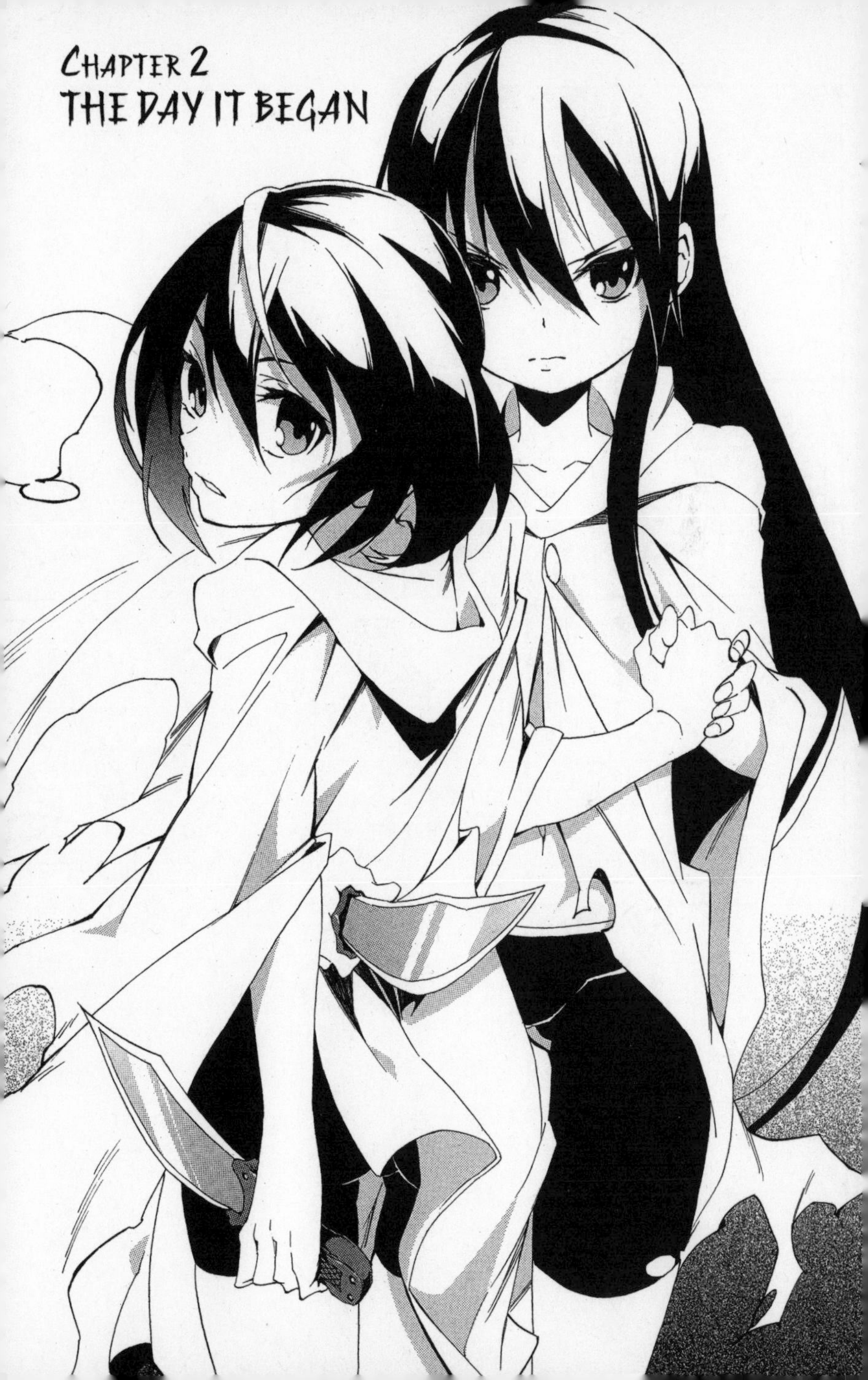

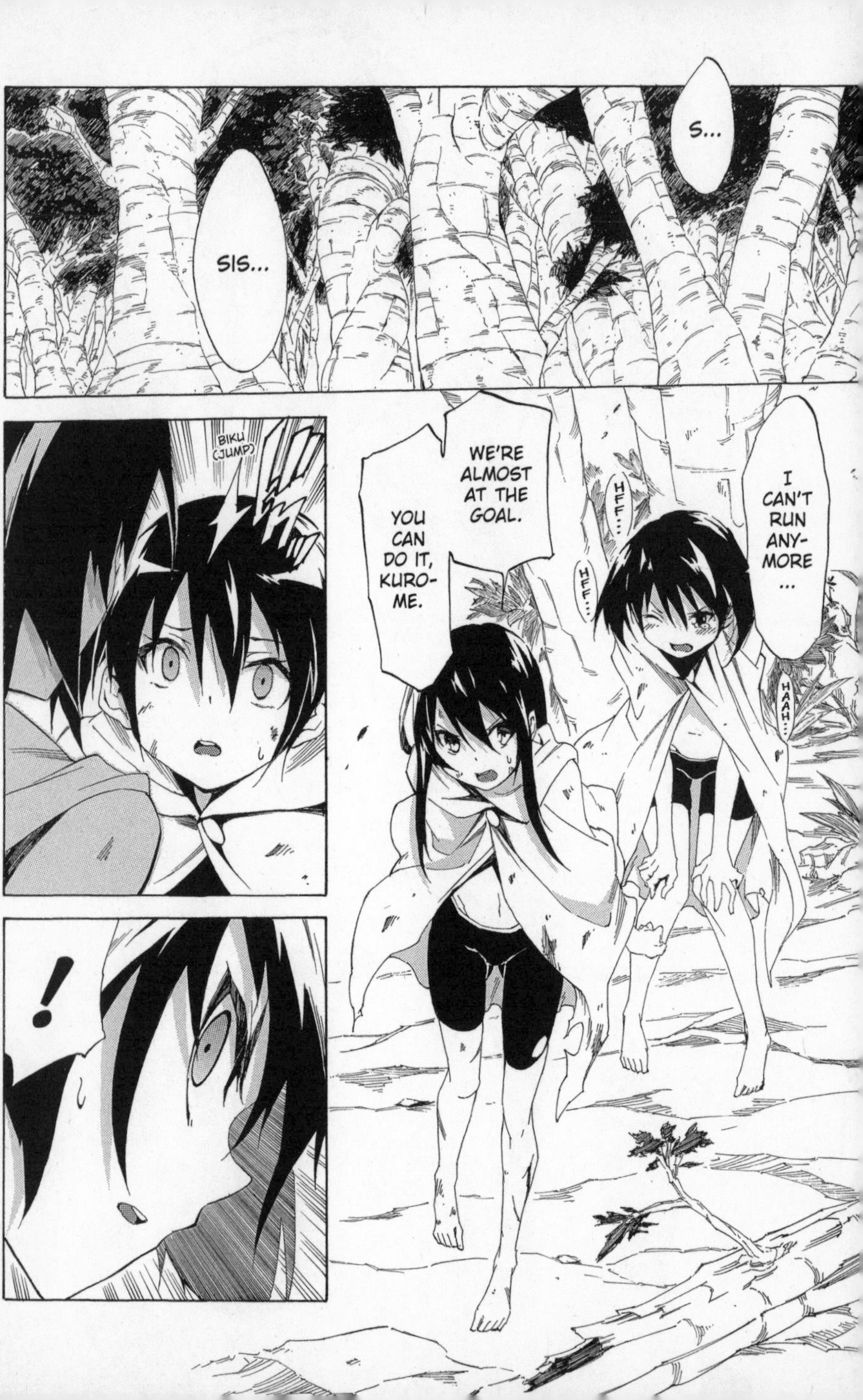
S...
SIS...
I CAN'T RUN ANYMORE...
HFF... HFF...
HAAH...
WE'RE ALMOST AT THE GOAL.
YOU CAN DO IT, KUROME.
BIKU (JUMP)
!

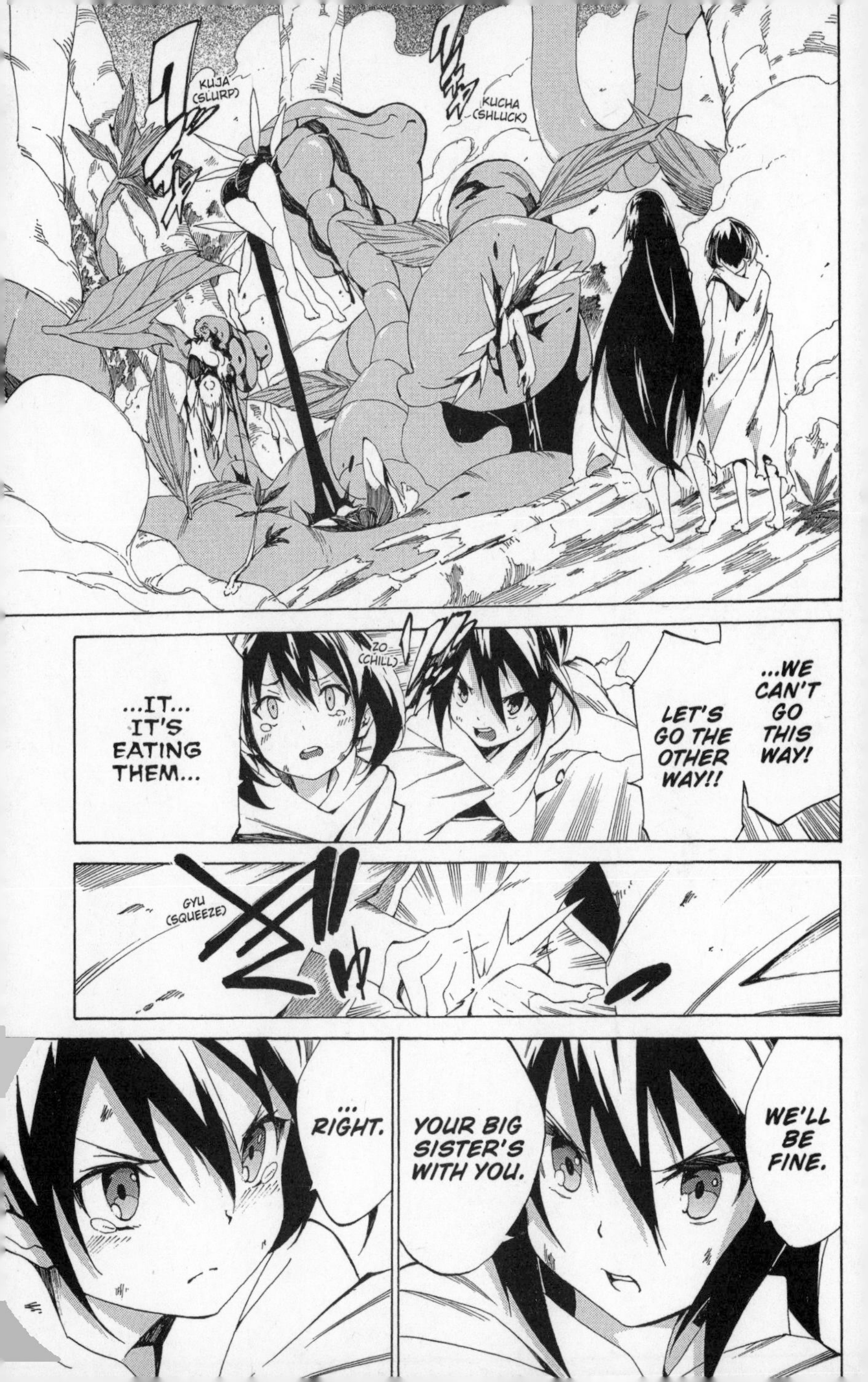
KUCHA (SHLUCK)
KUJA (SLURP)
ZO (CHILL)
...WE CAN'T GO THIS WAY!
LET'S GO THE OTHER WAY!!
...IT... IT'S EATING THEM...
GYU (SQUEEZE)
WE'LL BE FINE.
YOUR BIG SISTER'S WITH YOU.
... RIGHT.

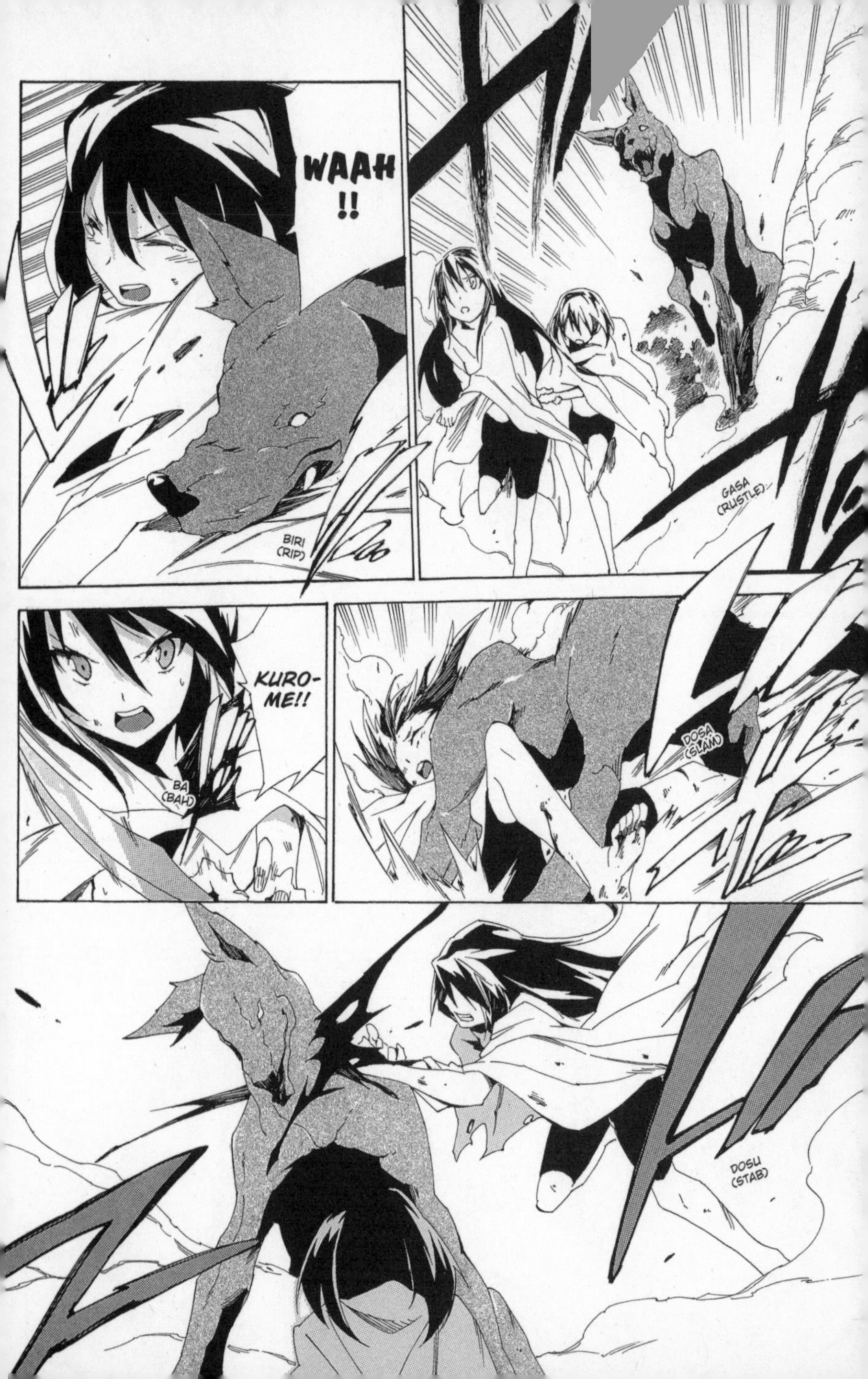
GASA (RUSTLE)
WAAH !!
BIRI (RIP)
DOSA (SLAM)
KURO-ME!!
BA (BAH)
DOSU (STAB)

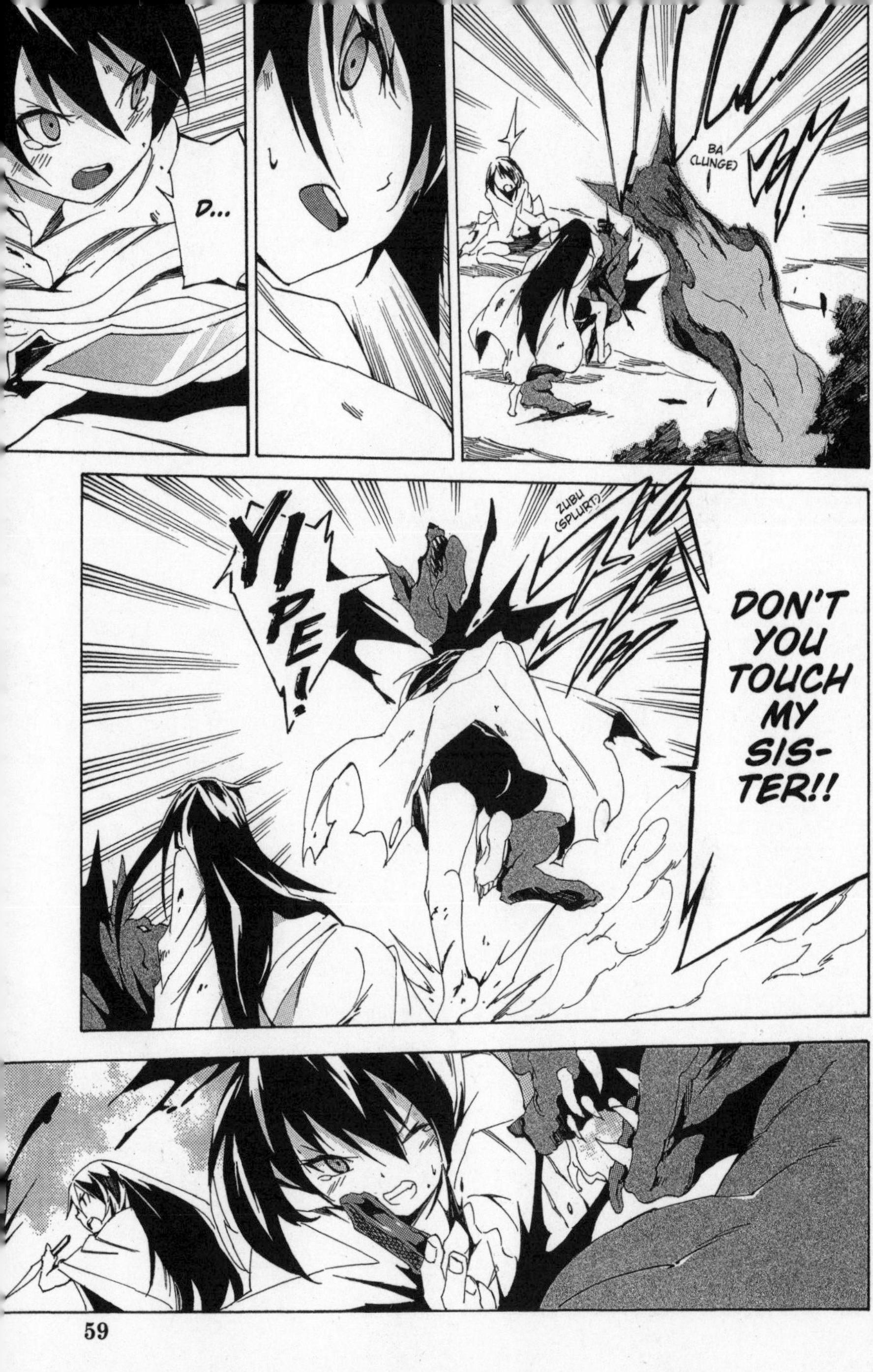
BA (LUNGE)
D...
ZUBU (SPLURT)
YIPE!!
DON'T YOU TOUCH MY SIS-TER!!

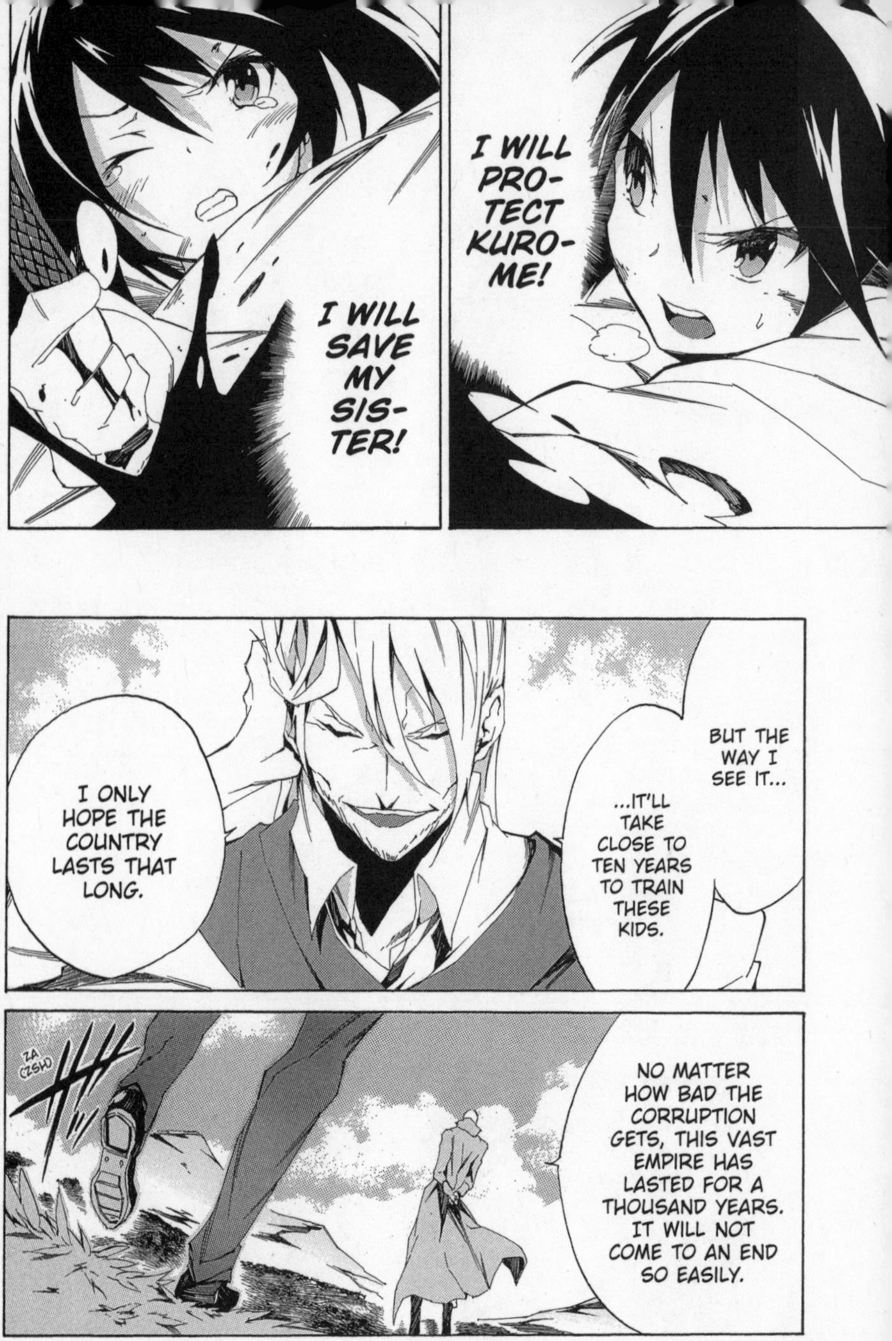
I WILL PROTECT KURO-ME!
I WILL SAVE MY SIS-TER!
BUT THE WAY I SEE IT...
...IT'LL TAKE CLOSE TO TEN YEARS TO TRAIN THESE KIDS.
I ONLY HOPE THE COUNTRY LASTS THAT LONG.
NO MATTER HOW BAD THE CORRUPTION GETS, THIS VAST EMPIRE HAS LASTED FOR A THOUSAND YEARS. IT WILL NOT COME TO AN END SO EASILY.

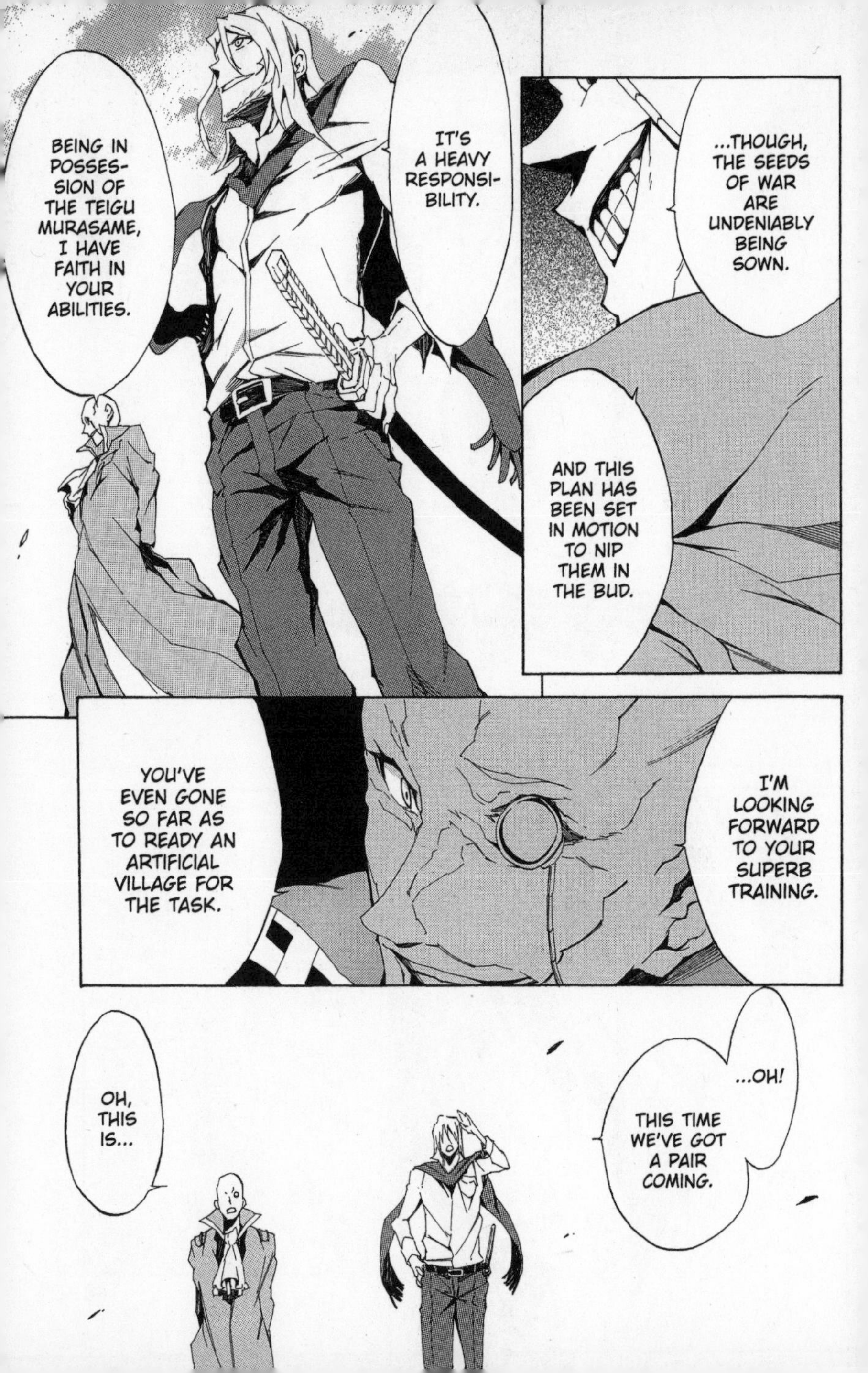
IT'S A HEAVY RESPONSIBILITY.
BEING IN POSSESSION OF THE TEIGU MURASAME, I HAVE FAITH IN YOUR ABILITIES.
...THOUGH, THE SEEDS OF WAR ARE UNDENIABLY BEING SOWN.
AND THIS PLAN HAS BEEN SET IN MOTION TO NIP THEM IN THE BUD.
I'M LOOKING FORWARD TO YOUR SUPERB TRAINING.
YOU'VE EVEN GONE SO FAR AS TO READY AN ARTIFICIAL VILLAGE FOR THE TASK.
...OH!
THIS TIME WE'VE GOT A PAIR COMING.
OH, THIS IS...

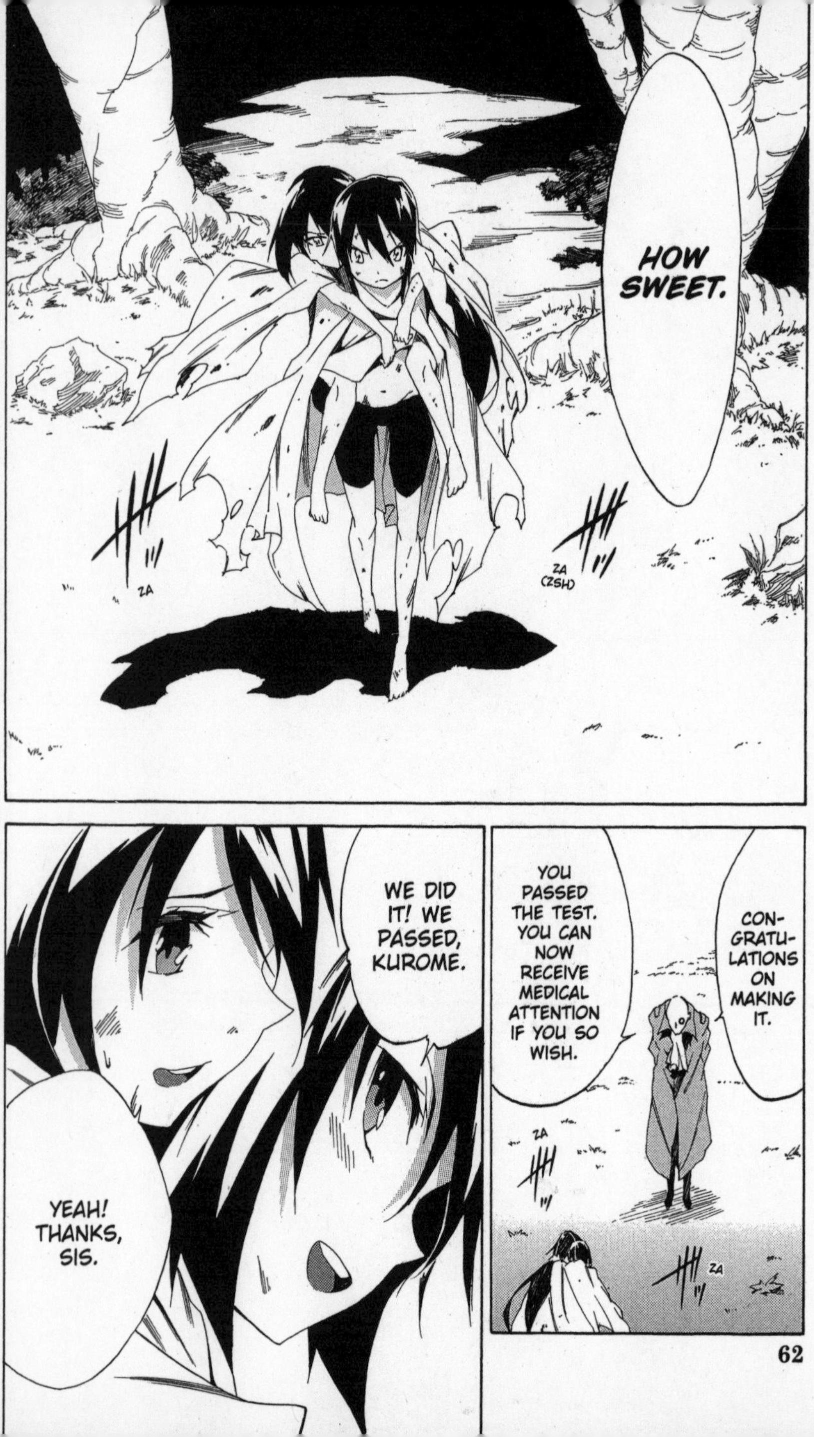
HOW SWEET.
ZA
ZA (ZSH)
CON-GRATU-LATIONS ON MAKING IT.
YOU PASSED THE TEST. YOU CAN NOW RECEIVE MEDICAL ATTENTION IF YOU SO WISH.
ZA
ZA
WE DID IT! WE PASSED, KUROME.
YEAH! THANKS, SIS.

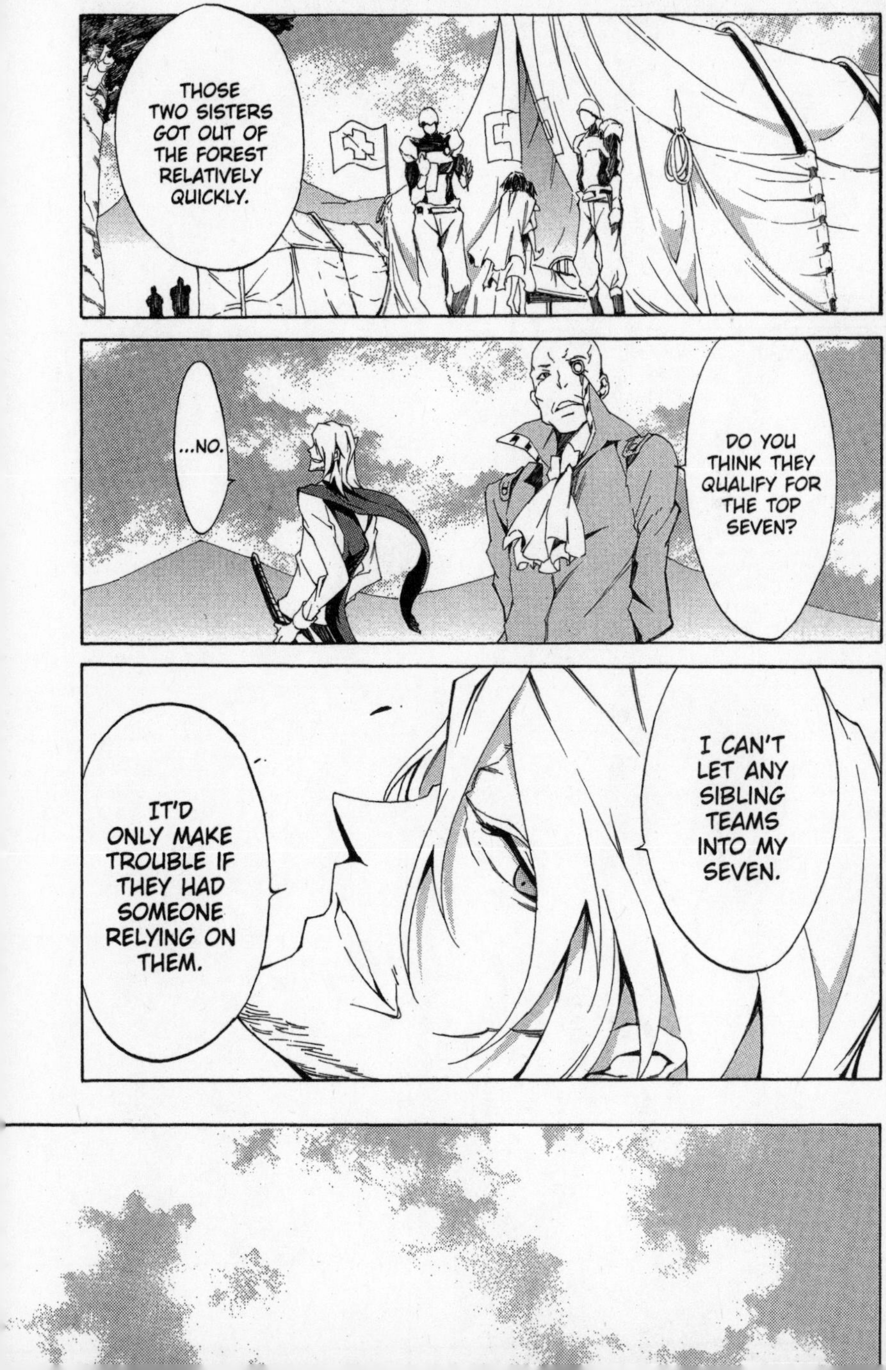
THOSE TWO SISTERS GOT OUT OF THE FOREST RELATIVELY QUICKLY.
DO YOU THINK THEY QUALIFY FOR THE TOP SEVEN?
...NO.
I CAN'T LET ANY SIBLING TEAMS INTO MY SEVEN.
IT'D ONLY MAKE TROUBLE IF THEY HAD SOMEONE RELYING ON THEM.

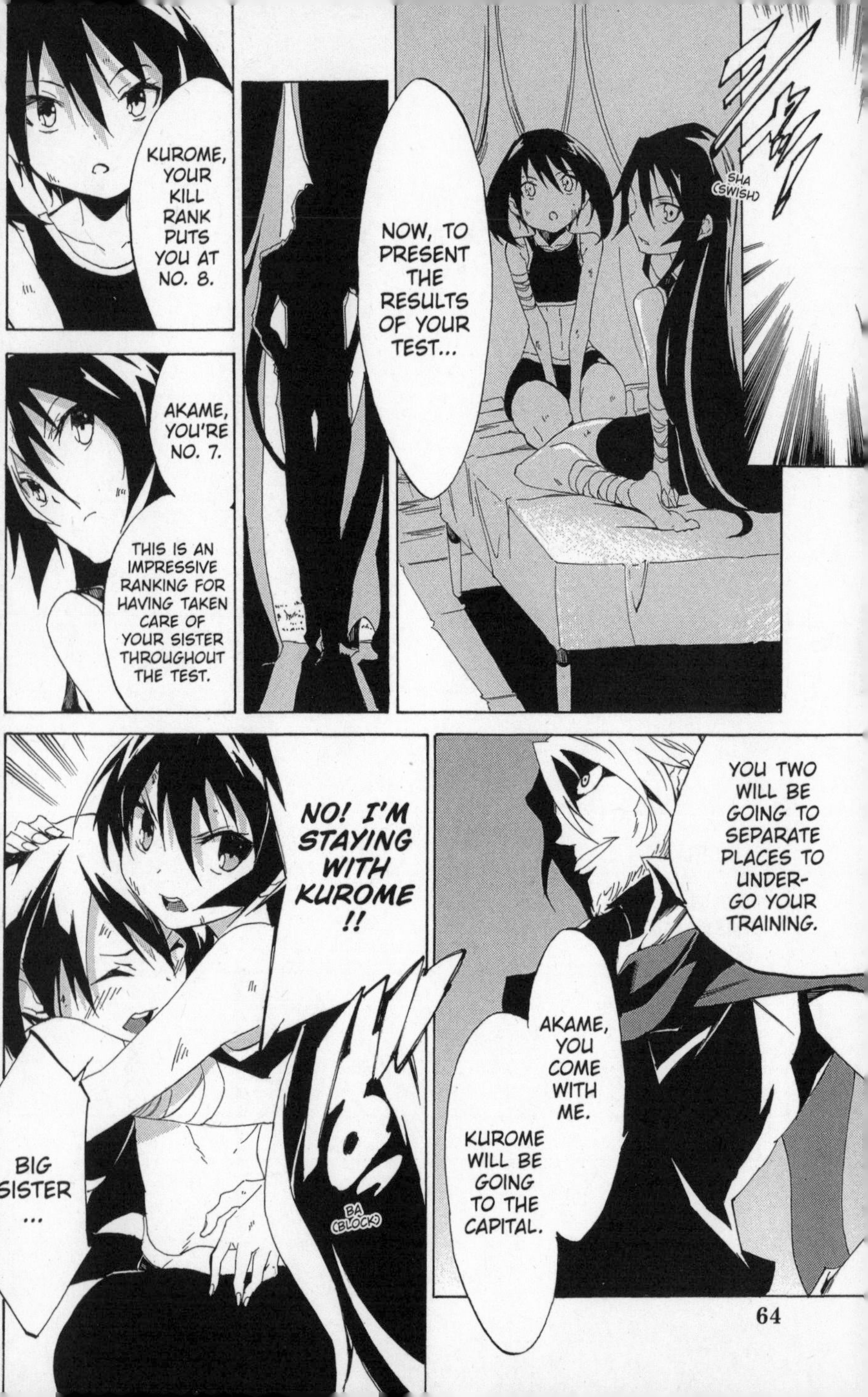
SHA (SWISH)
NOW, TO PRESENT THE RESULTS OF YOUR TEST...
KUROME, YOUR KILL RANK PUTS YOU AT NO. 8.
AKAME, YOU'RE NO. 7.
THIS IS AN IMPRESSIVE RANKING FOR HAVING TAKEN CARE OF YOUR SISTER THROUGHOUT THE TEST.
YOU TWO WILL BE GOING TO SEPARATE PLACES TO UNDER-GO YOUR TRAINING.
AKAME, YOU COME WITH ME.
KUROME WILL BE GOING TO THE CAPITAL.
NO! I'M STAYING WITH KUROME!!
BA (BLOCK)
BIG SISTER ...

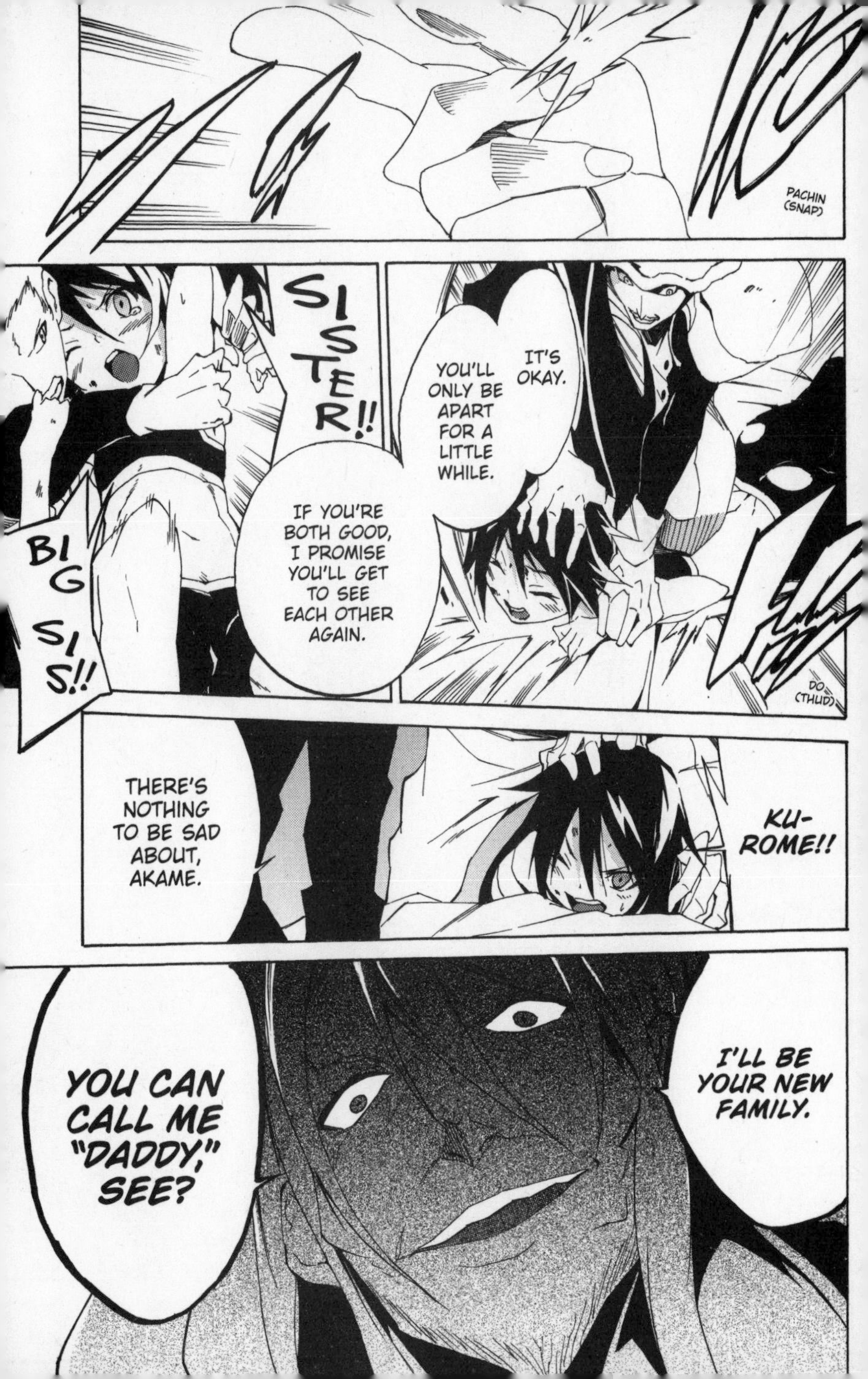
PACHIN (SNAP)
IT'S OKAY.
YOU'LL ONLY BE APART FOR A LITTLE WHILE.
IF YOU'RE BOTH GOOD, I PROMISE YOU'LL GET TO SEE EACH OTHER AGAIN.
DO (THUD)
SISTER!!
BIG SIS!!
KU-ROME!!
THERE'S NOTHING TO BE SAD ABOUT, AKAME.
I'LL BE YOUR NEW FAMILY.
YOU CAN CALL ME "DADDY," SEE?

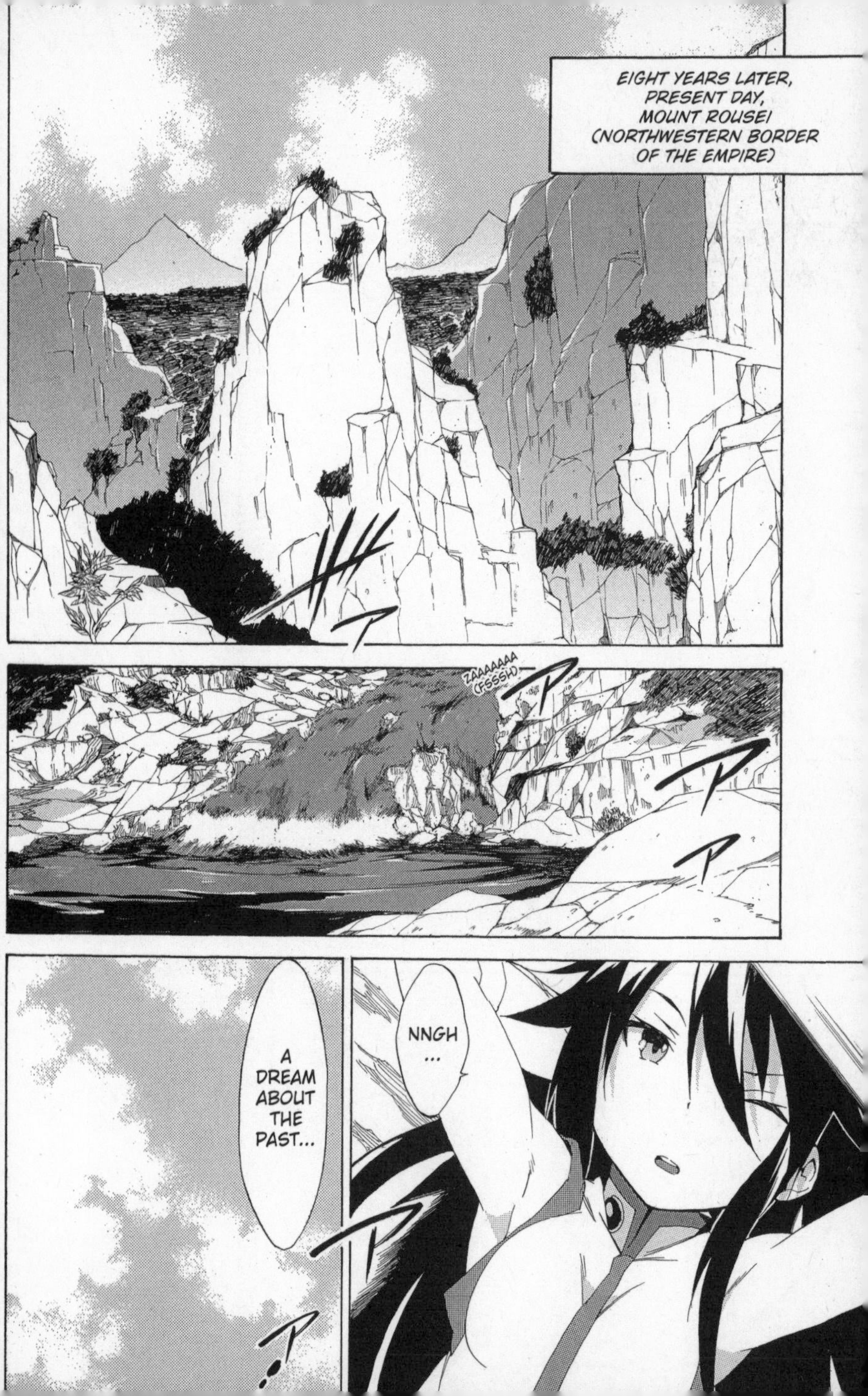
EIGHT YEARS LATER, PRESENT DAY, MOUNT ROUSEI (NORTHWESTERN BORDER OF THE EMPIRE)
ZAAAAAAA (FSSSH)
NNGH ...
A DREAM ABOUT THE PAST...

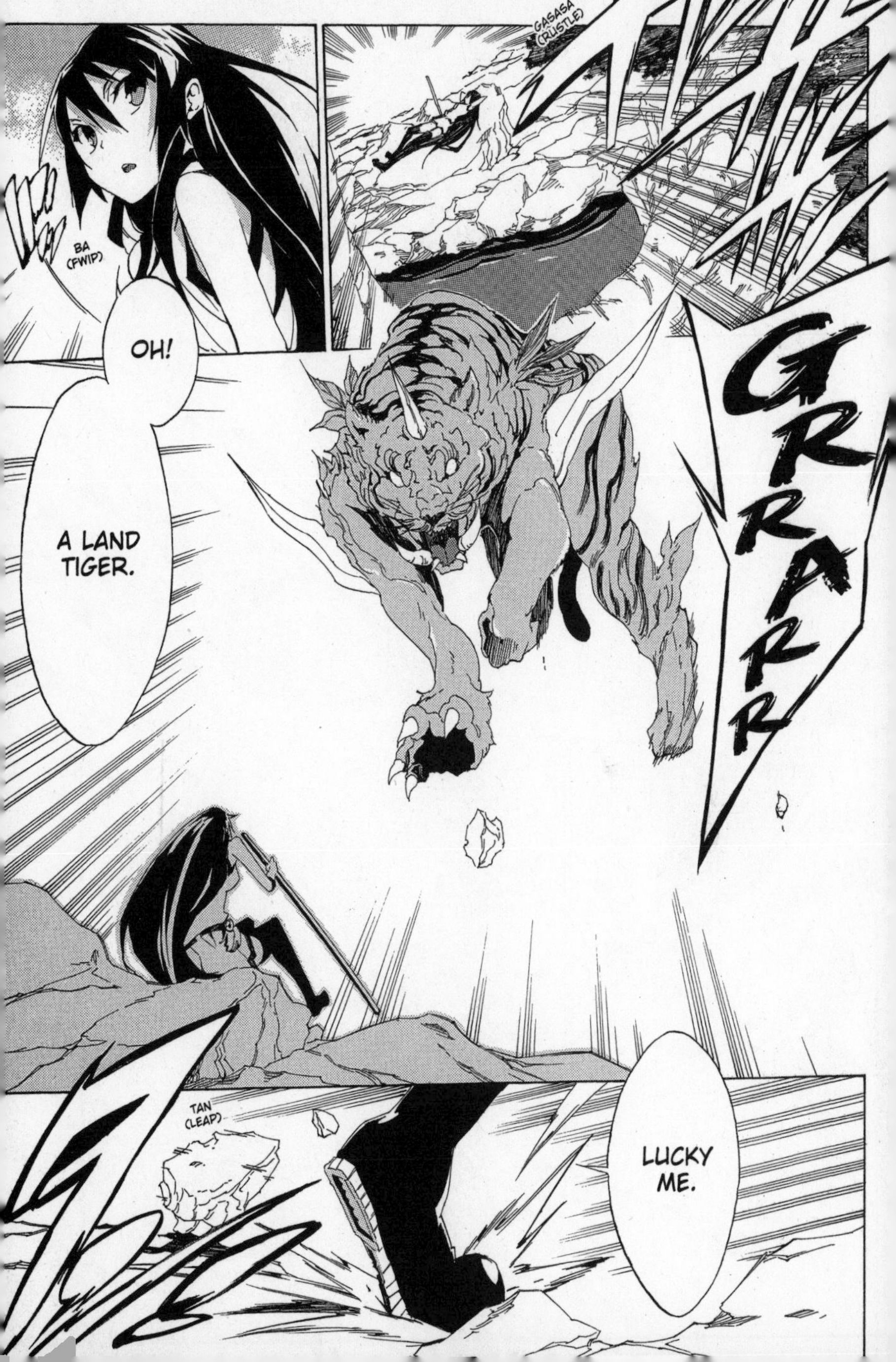
GASASA (RUSTLE)
BA (FWIP)
OH!
A LAND TIGER.
GRRARRR
TAN (LEAP)
LUCKY ME.

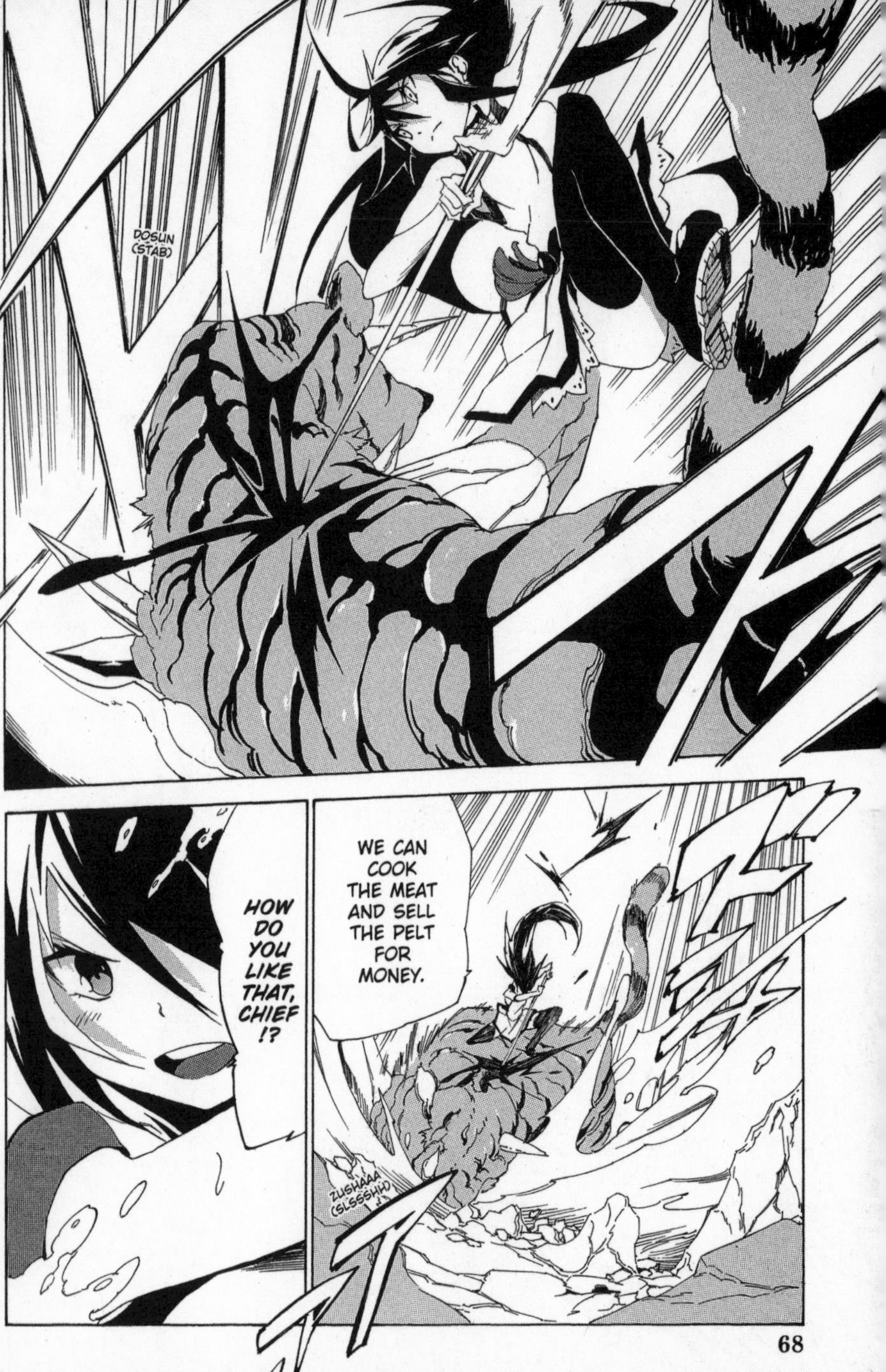
DOSUN (STAB)
WE CAN COOK THE MEAT AND SELL THE PELT FOR MONEY.
HOW DO YOU LIKE THAT, CHIEF!?
ZUSHAAA (SLSSSHH)

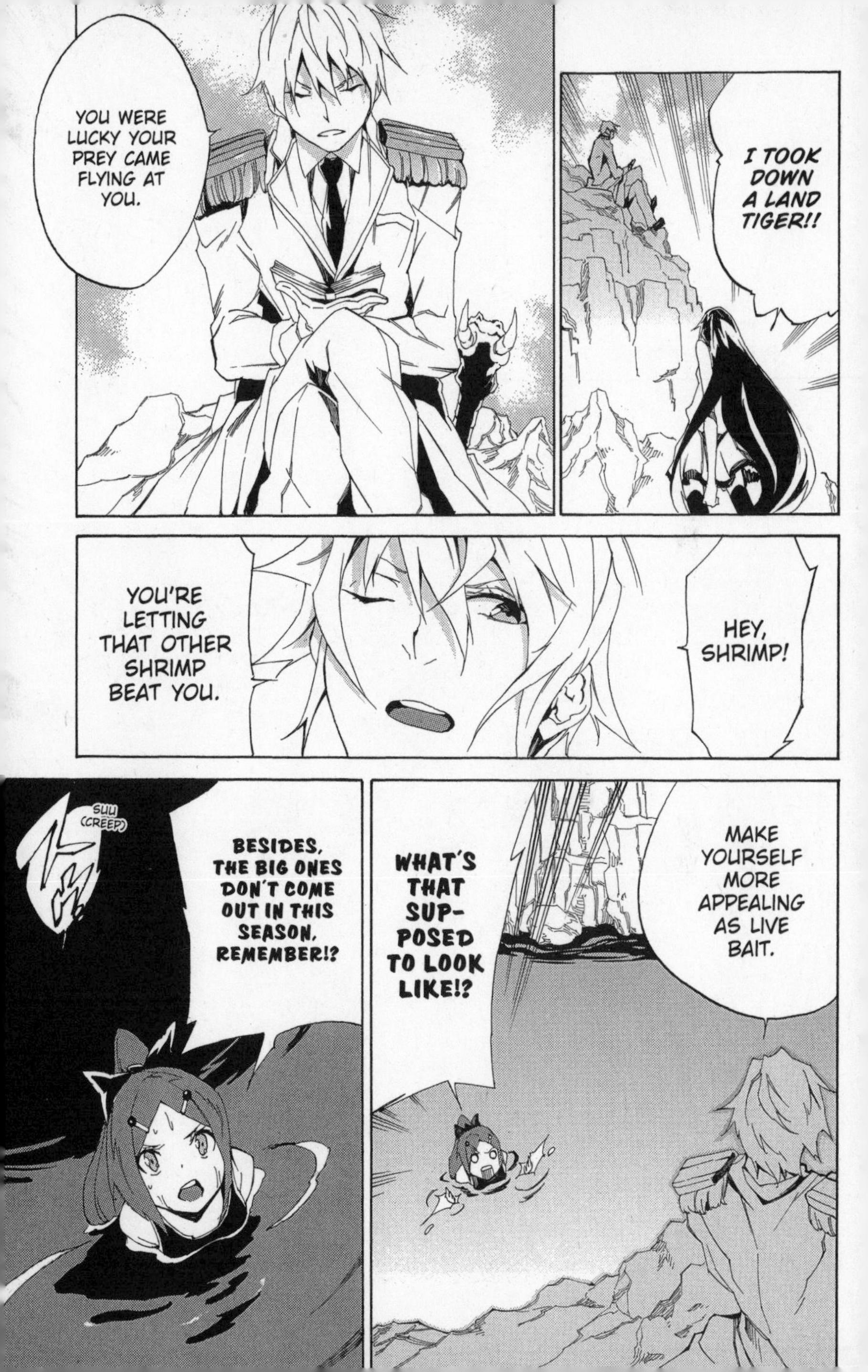
I TOOK DOWN A LAND TIGER!!
YOU WERE LUCKY YOUR PREY CAME FLYING AT YOU.
HEY, SHRIMP!
YOU'RE LETTING THAT OTHER SHRIMP BEAT YOU.
MAKE YOURSELF MORE APPEALING AS LIVE BAIT.
WHAT'S THAT SUP-POSED TO LOOK LIKE!?
BESIDES, THE BIG ONES DON'T COME OUT IN THIS SEASON, REMEMBER!?
SUU (CREEP)

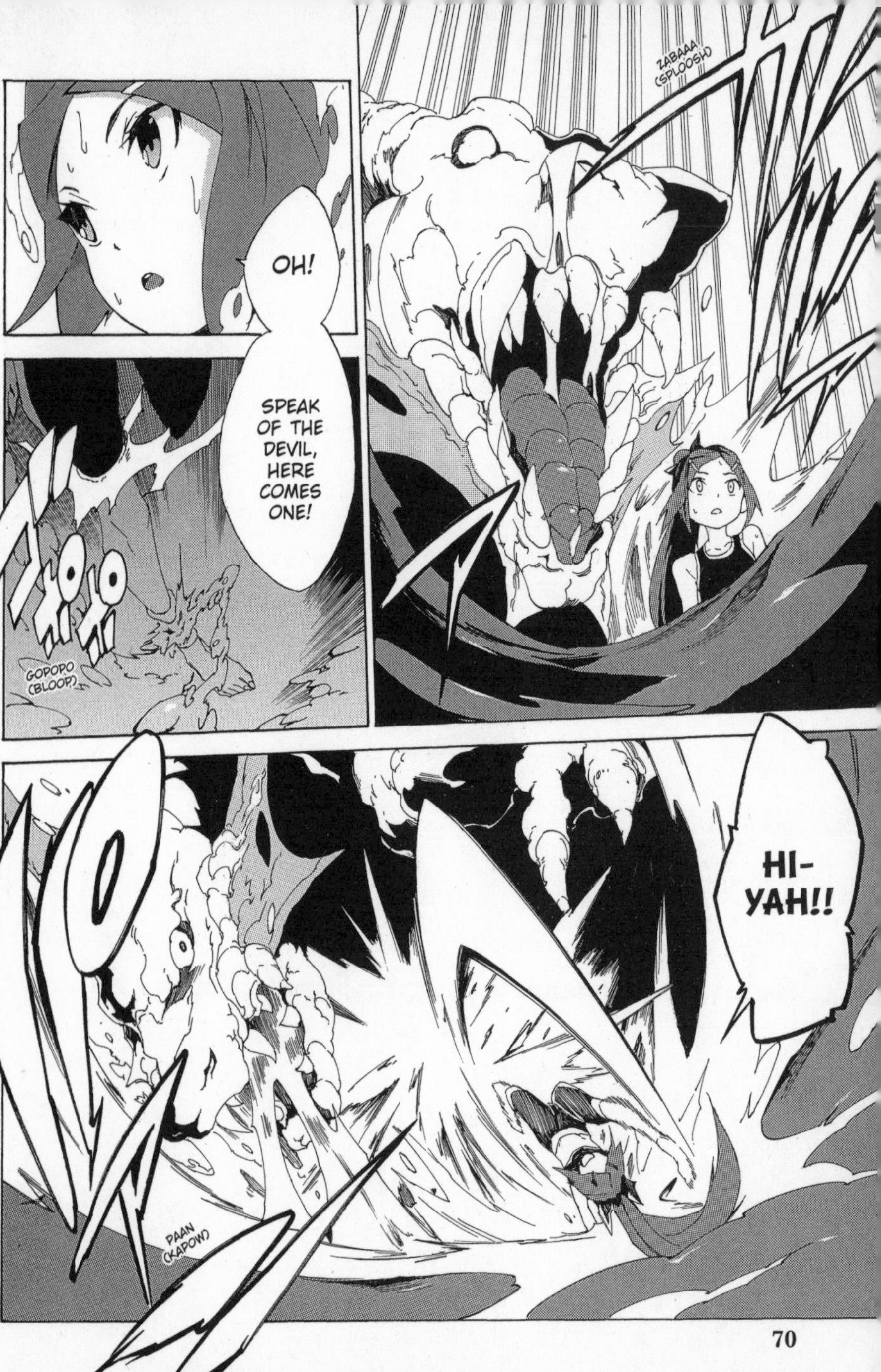
ZABAAA (SPLOOSH)
OH!
SPEAK OF THE DEVIL, HERE COMES ONE!
GOPOPO (BLOOP)
HI-YAH!!
PAAN (KAPOW)

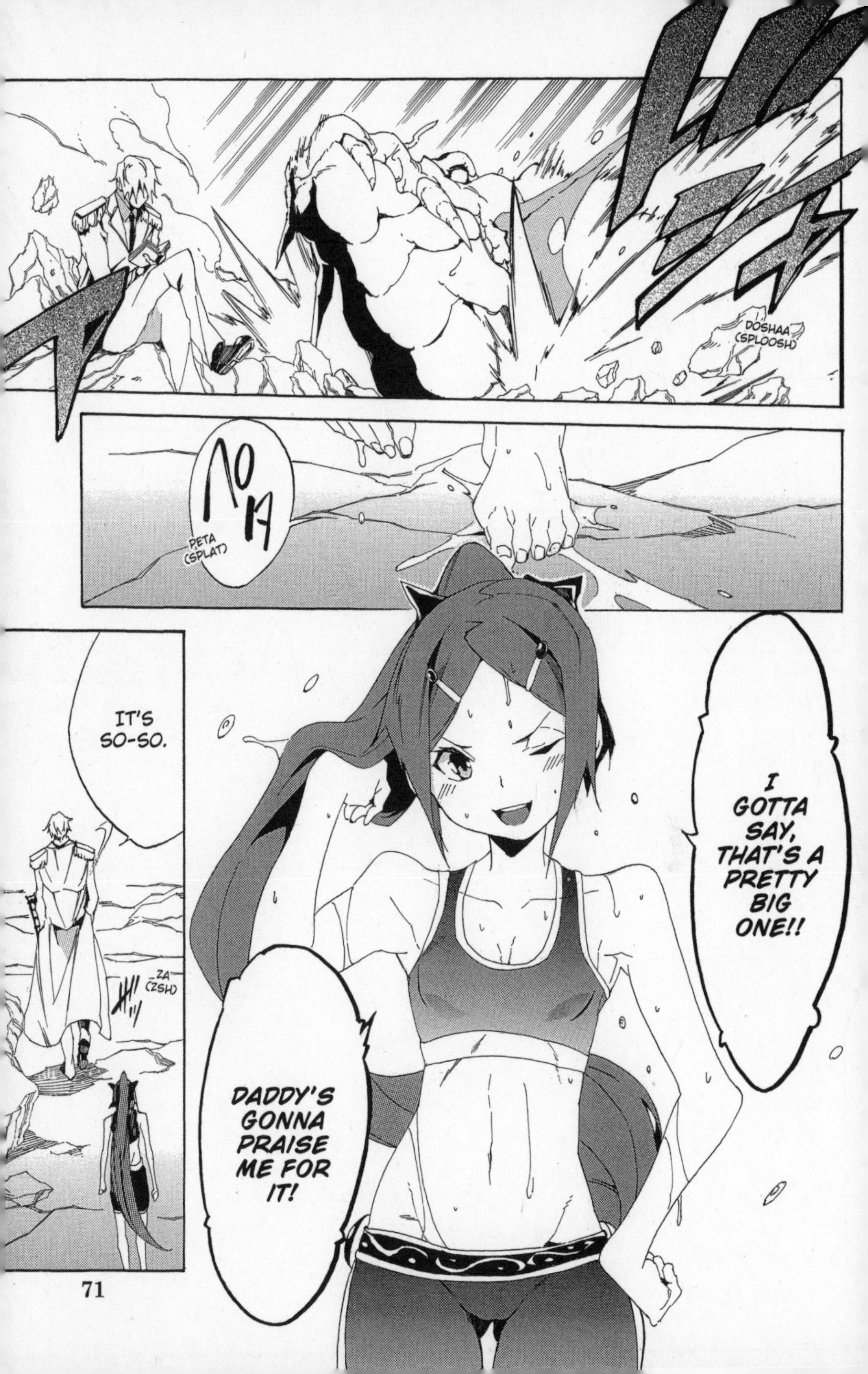
DOSHAA (SPLOOSH)
PETA (SPLAT)
I GOTTA SAY, THAT'S A PRETTY BIG ONE!!
DADDY'S GONNA PRAISE ME FOR IT!
IT'S SO-SO.
ZA (ZSH)

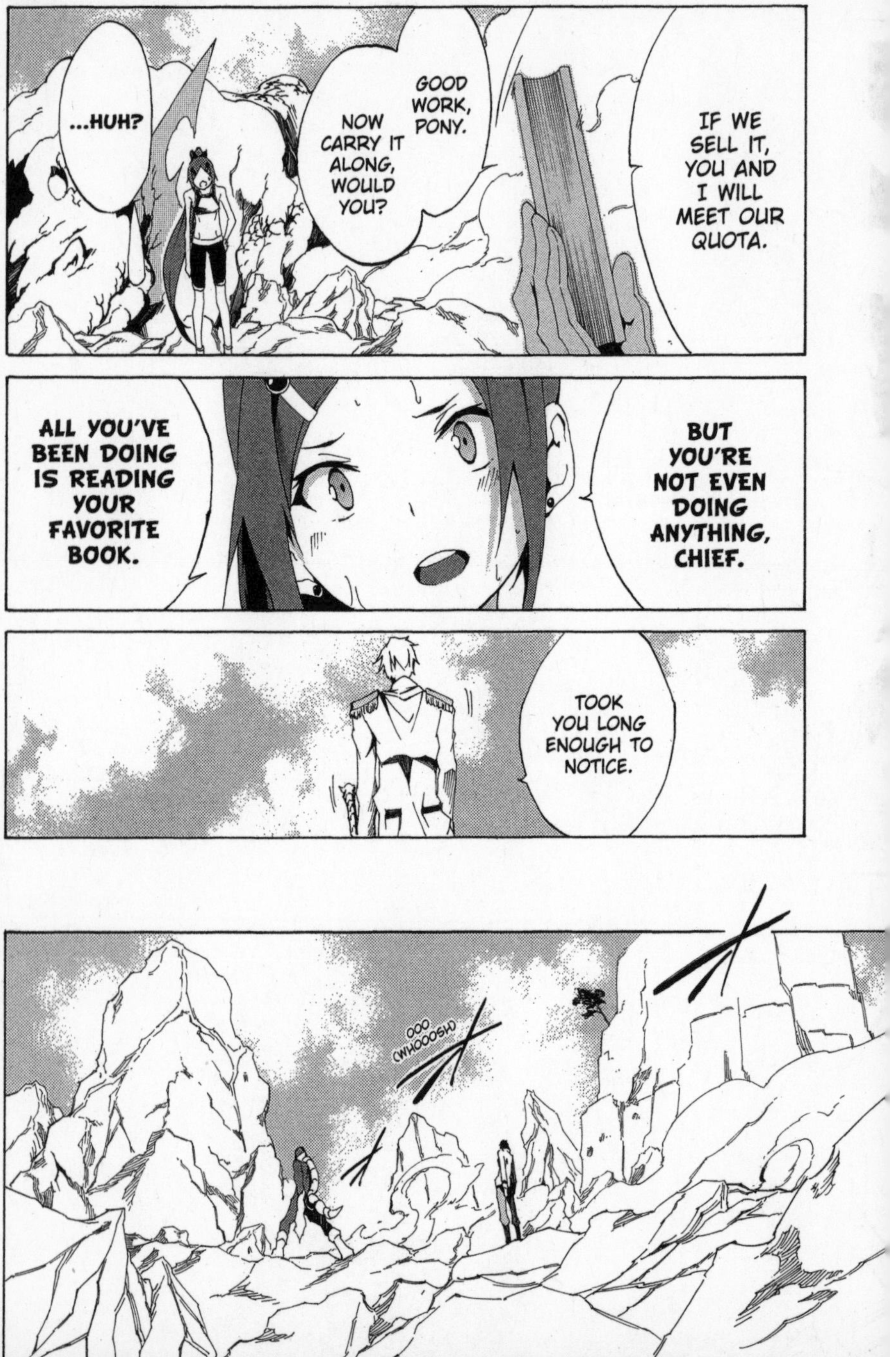
IF WE SELL IT, YOU AND I WILL MEET OUR QUOTA.
GOOD WORK, PONY.
NOW CARRY IT ALONG, WOULD YOU?
...HUH?
BUT YOU'RE NOT EVEN DOING ANYTHING, CHIEF.
ALL YOU'VE BEEN DOING IS READING YOUR FAVORITE BOOK.
TOOK YOU LONG ENOUGH TO NOTICE.
OOO (WHOOOSH)

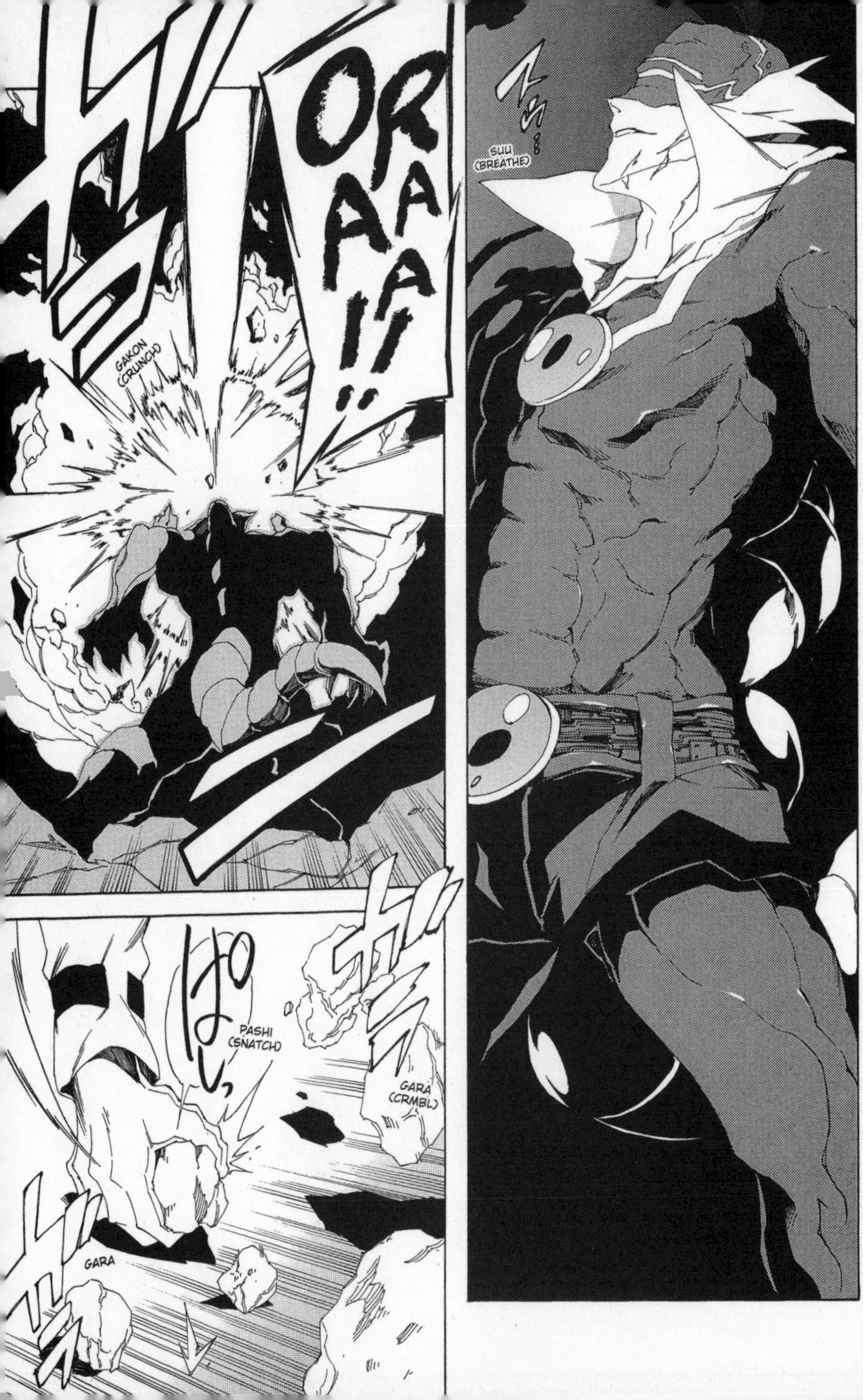
SUU
(BREATHE)
ORAAA!!
GAKON
(CRUNCH)
PASHI
(SNATCH)
GARA
(CRMBL)
GARA

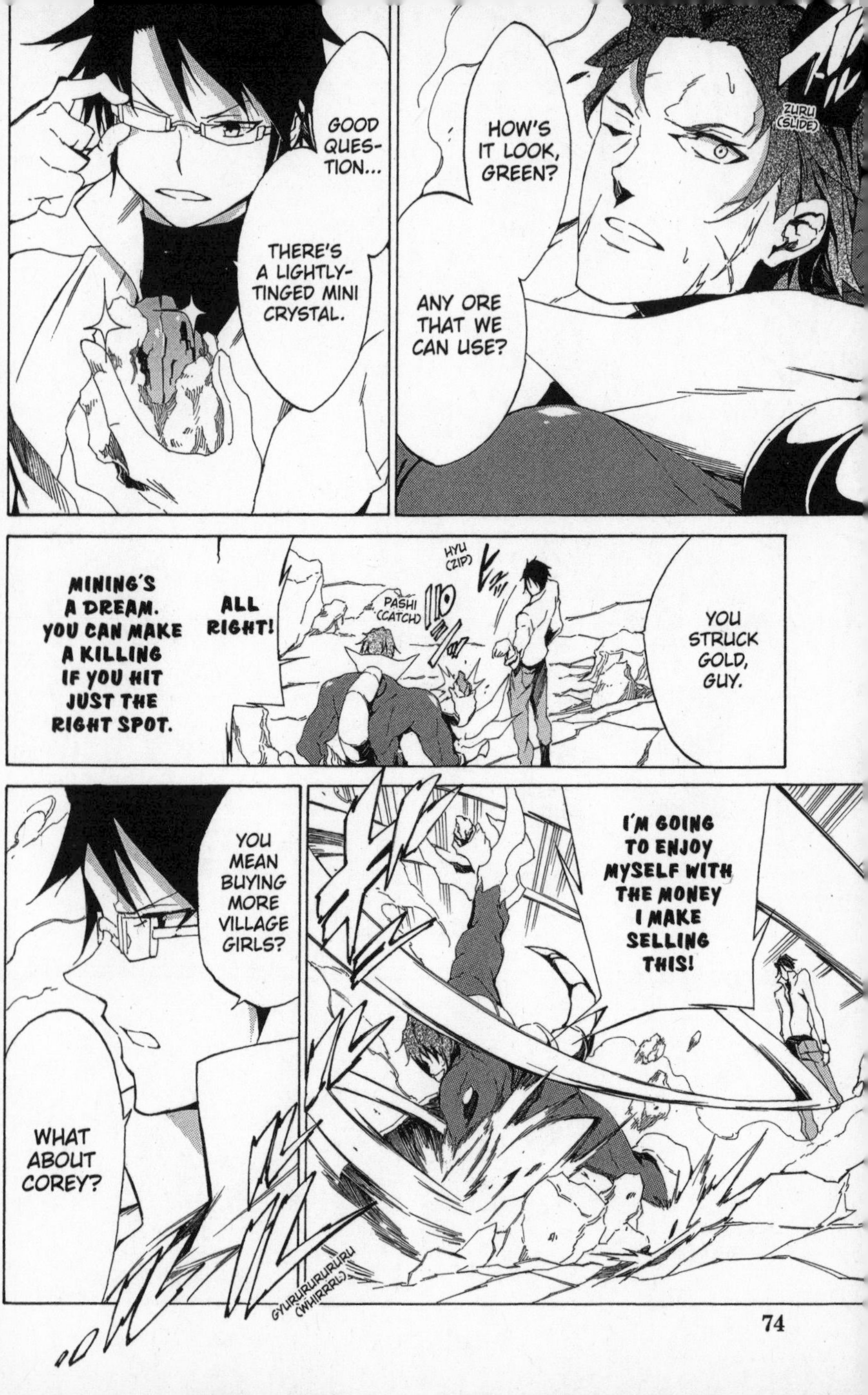
ZURU (SLIDE)
HOW'S IT LOOK, GREEN?
ANY ORE THAT WE CAN USE?
GOOD QUESTION...
THERE'S A LIGHTLY-TINGED MINI CRYSTAL.
YOU STRUCK GOLD, GUY.
HYU (ZIP)
PASHI (CATCH)
ALL RIGHT!
MINING'S A DREAM. YOU CAN MAKE A KILLING IF YOU HIT JUST THE RIGHT SPOT.
I'M GOING TO ENJOY MYSELF WITH THE MONEY I MAKE SELLING THIS!
GYURURURURURU (WHIRRRL)
YOU MEAN BUYING MORE VILLAGE GIRLS?
WHAT ABOUT COREY?

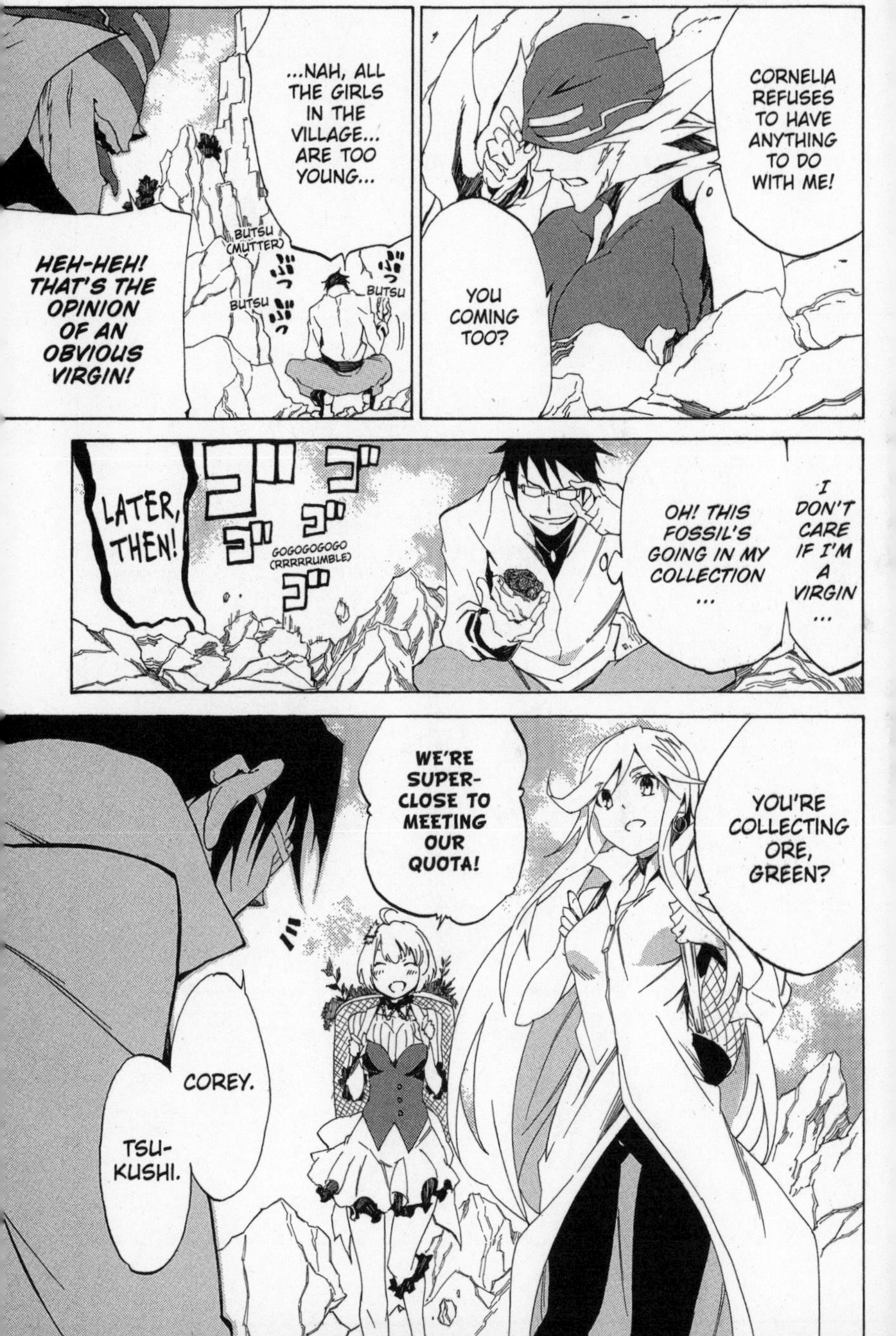
CORNELIA REFUSES TO HAVE ANYTHING TO DO WITH ME!
YOU COMING TOO?
...NAH, ALL THE GIRLS IN THE VILLAGE... ARE TOO YOUNG...
BUTSU (MUTTER)
BUTSU
BUTSU
HEH-HEH! THAT'S THE OPINION OF AN OBVIOUS VIRGIN!
I DON'T CARE IF I'M A VIRGIN...
OH! THIS FOSSIL'S GOING IN MY COLLECTION...
GOGOGOGOGO (RRRRRUMBLE)
LATER, THEN!
YOU'RE COLLECTING ORE, GREEN?
WE'RE SUPER-CLOSE TO MEETING OUR QUOTA!
COREY.
TSU-KUSHI.

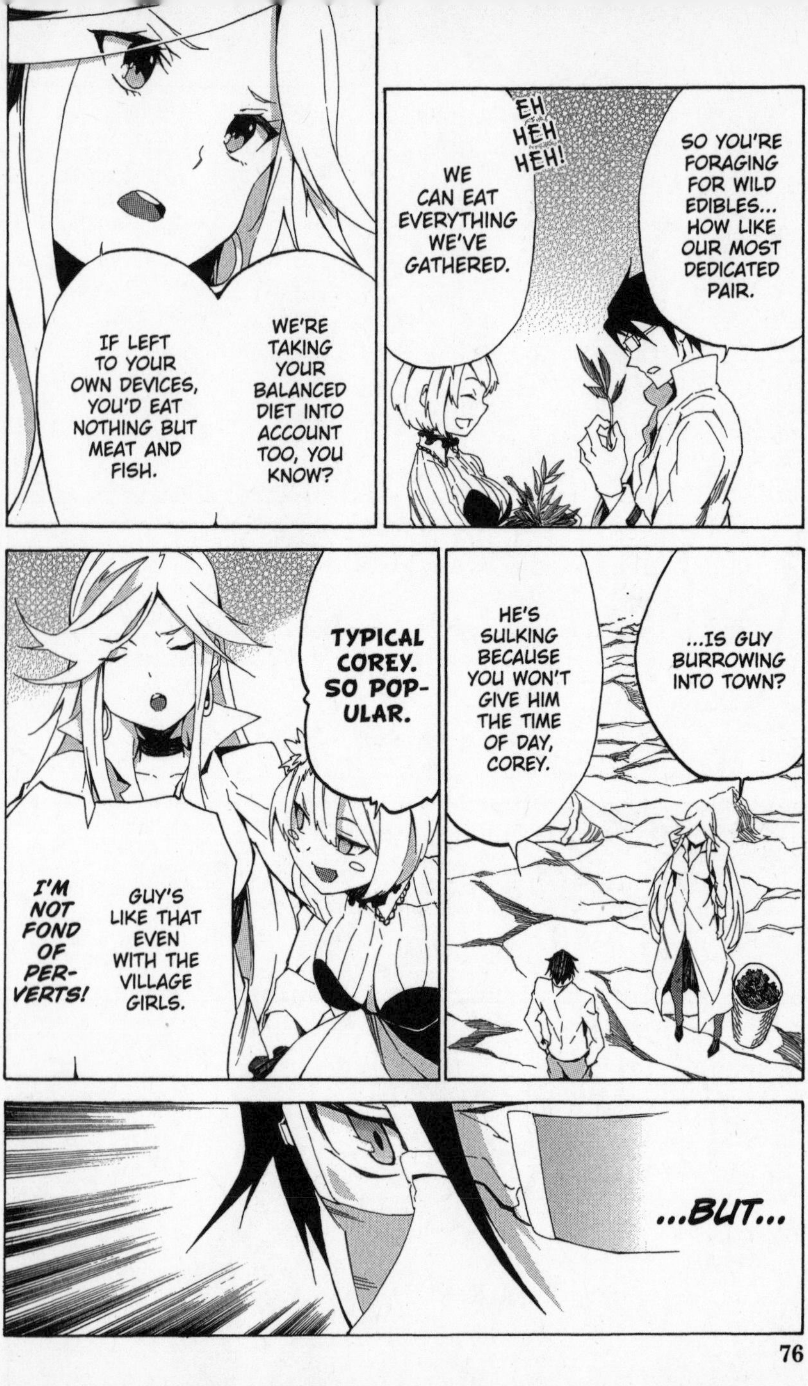
SO YOU'RE FORAGING FOR WILD EDIBLES... HOW LIKE OUR MOST DEDICATED PAIR.
EH HEH HEH!
WE CAN EAT EVERYTHING WE'VE GATHERED.
WE'RE TAKING YOUR BALANCED DIET INTO ACCOUNT TOO, YOU KNOW?
IF LEFT TO YOUR OWN DEVICES, YOU'D EAT NOTHING BUT MEAT AND FISH.
...IS GUY BURROWING INTO TOWN?
HE'S SULKING BECAUSE YOU WON'T GIVE HIM THE TIME OF DAY, COREY.
TYPICAL COREY. SO POP-ULAR.
GUY'S LIKE THAT EVEN WITH THE VILLAGE GIRLS.
I'M NOT FOND OF PER-VERTS!
...BUT...

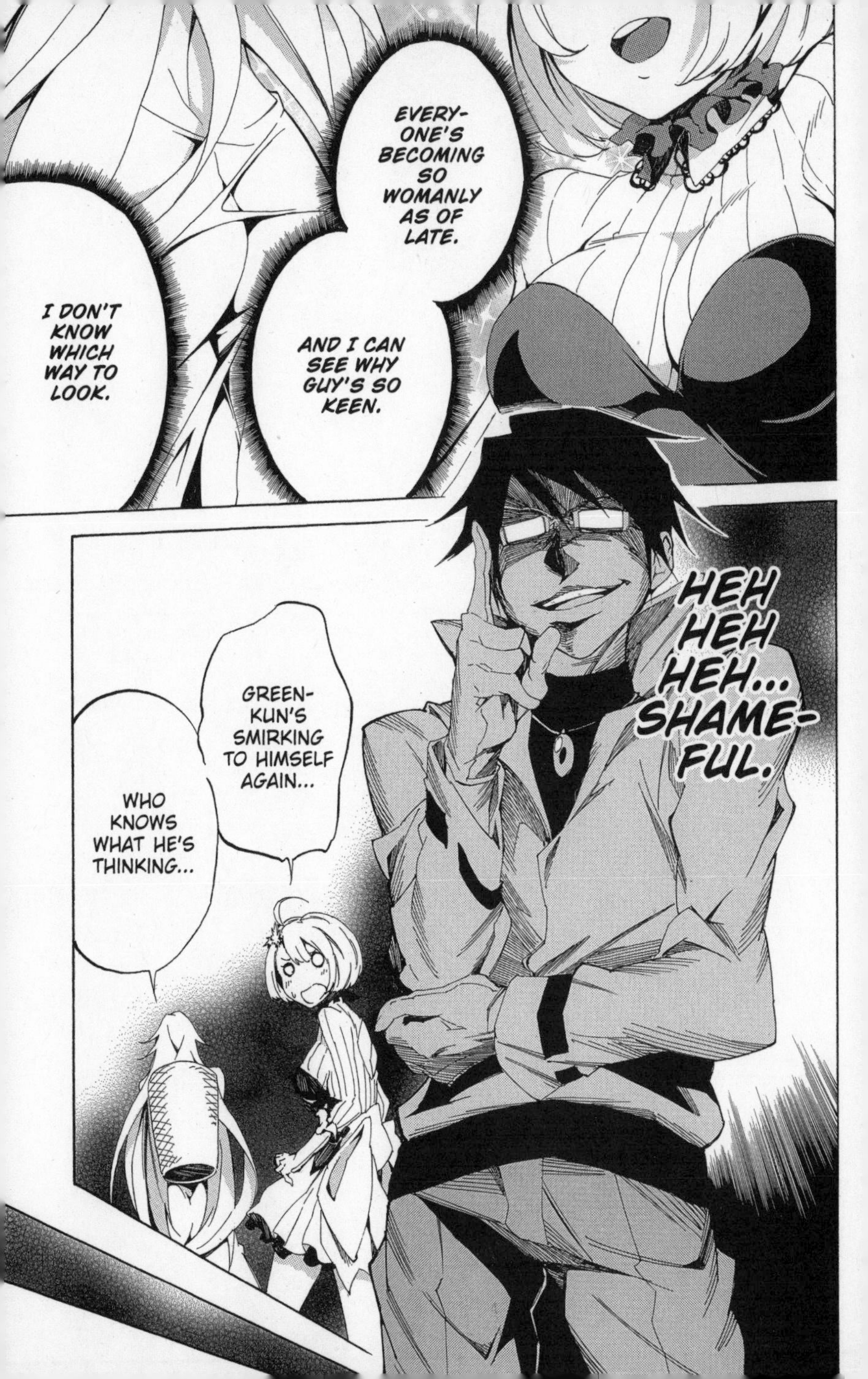
EVERY-ONE'S BECOMING SO WOMANLY AS OF LATE.
AND I CAN SEE WHY GUY'S SO KEEN.
I DON'T KNOW WHICH WAY TO LOOK.
HEH HEH HEH... SHAME-FUL.
GREEN-KUN'S SMIRKING TO HIMSELF AGAIN...
WHO KNOWS WHAT HE'S THINKING...

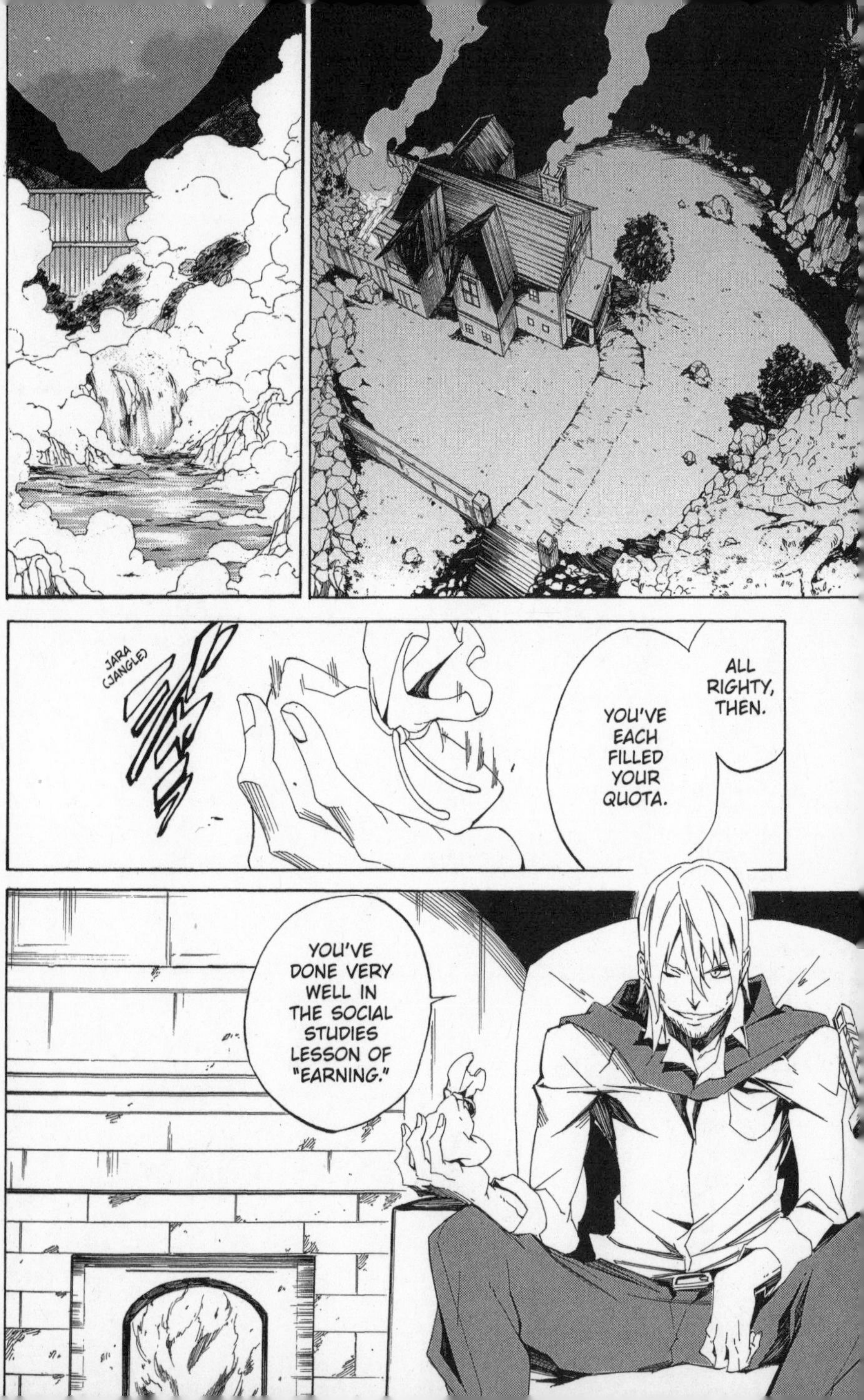
JARA (JANGLE)
ALL RIGHTY, THEN.
YOU'VE EACH FILLED YOUR QUOTA.
YOU'VE DONE VERY WELL IN THE SOCIAL STUDIES LESSON OF "EARNING."

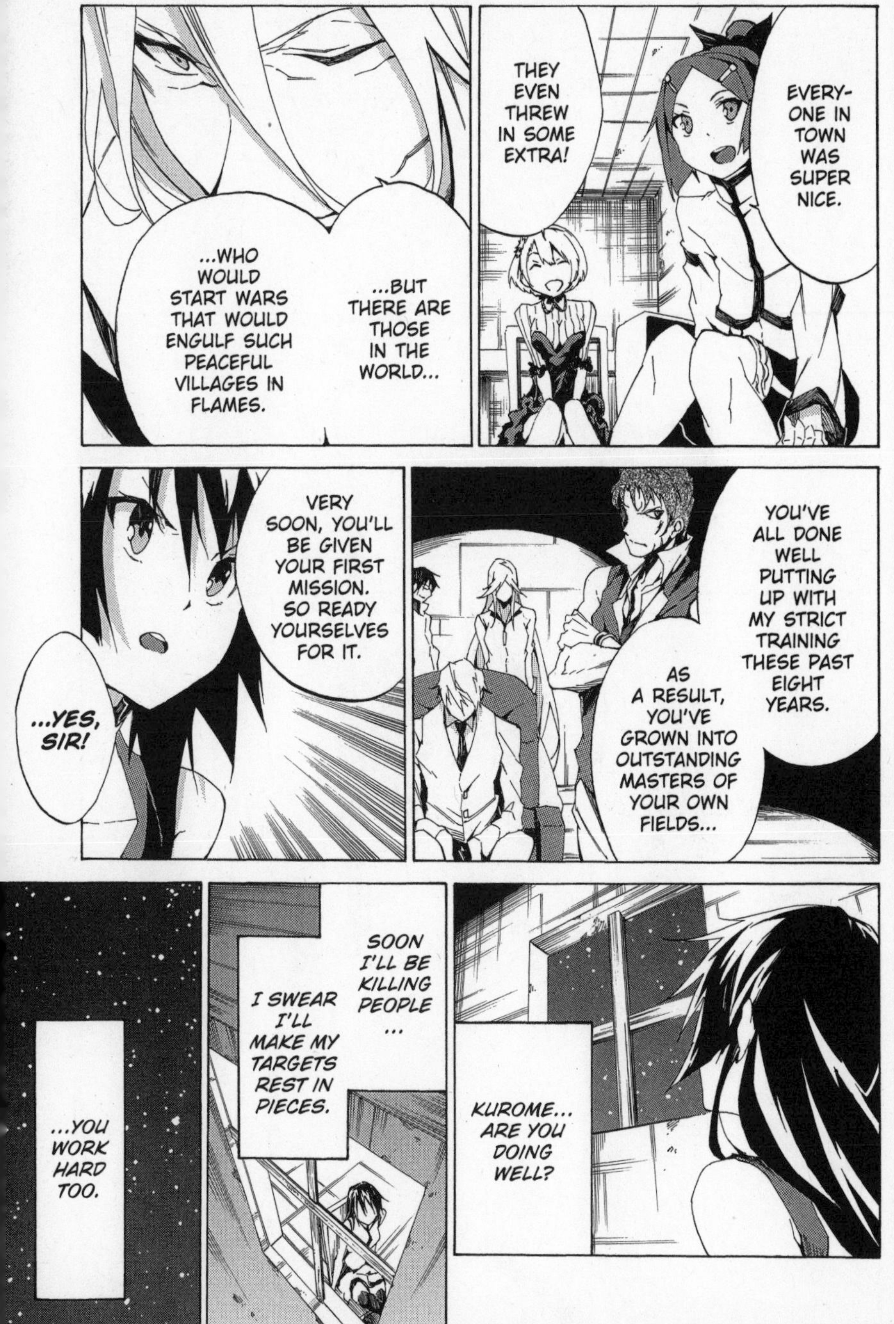
EVERY-ONE IN TOWN WAS SUPER NICE.
THEY EVEN THREW IN SOME EXTRA!
...BUT THERE ARE THOSE IN THE WORLD...
...WHO WOULD START WARS THAT WOULD ENGULF SUCH PEACEFUL VILLAGES IN FLAMES.
YOU'VE ALL DONE WELL PUTTING UP WITH MY STRICT TRAINING THESE PAST EIGHT YEARS.
AS A RESULT, YOU'VE GROWN INTO OUTSTANDING MASTERS OF YOUR OWN FIELDS...
VERY SOON, YOU'LL BE GIVEN YOUR FIRST MISSION. SO READY YOURSELVES FOR IT.
...YES, SIR!
KUROME... ARE YOU DOING WELL?
SOON I'LL BE KILLING PEOPLE...
I SWEAR I'LL MAKE MY TARGETS REST IN PIECES.
...YOU WORK HARD TOO.

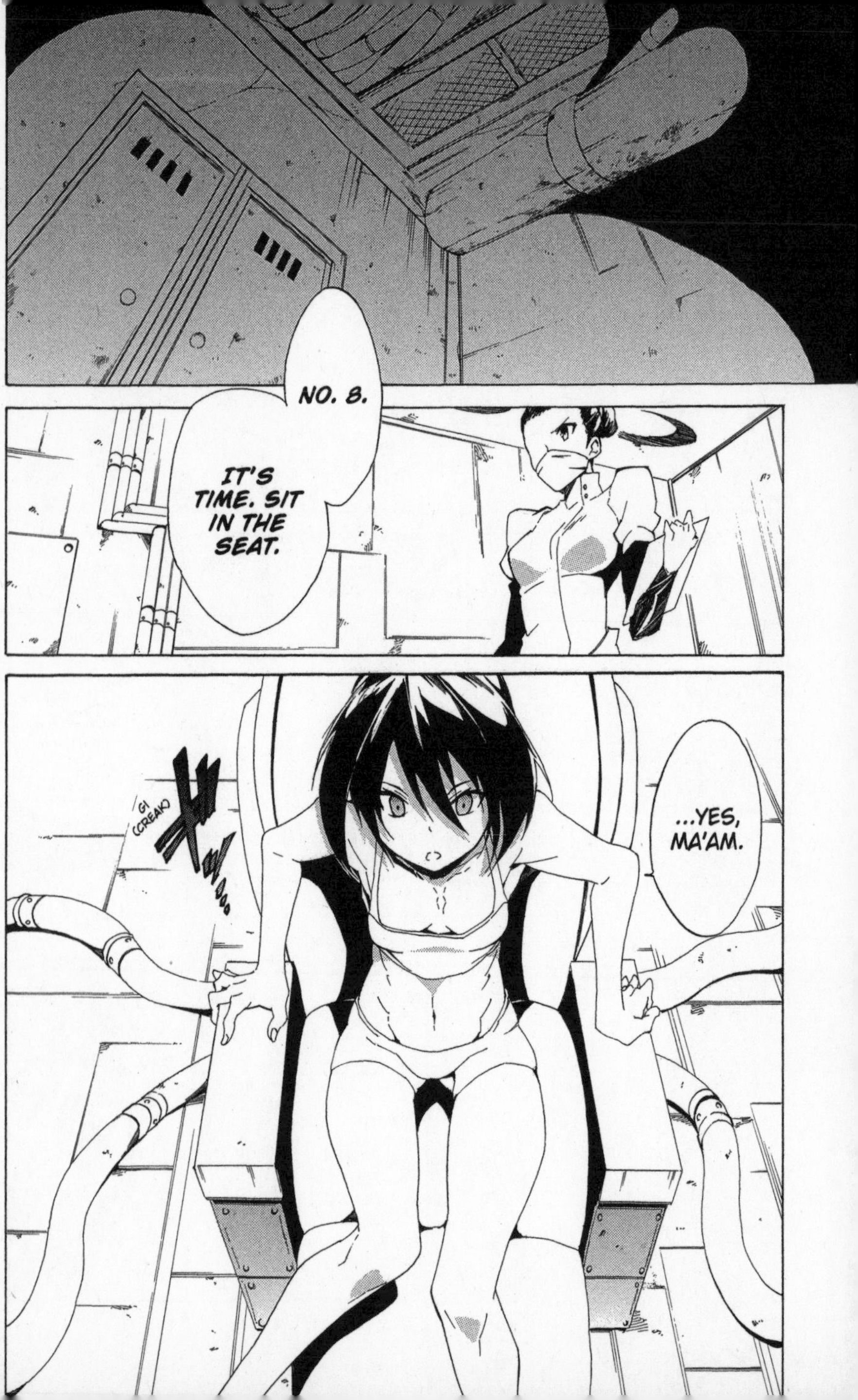
NO. 8.
IT'S TIME. SIT IN THE SEAT.
...YES, MA'AM.
GI (CREAK)

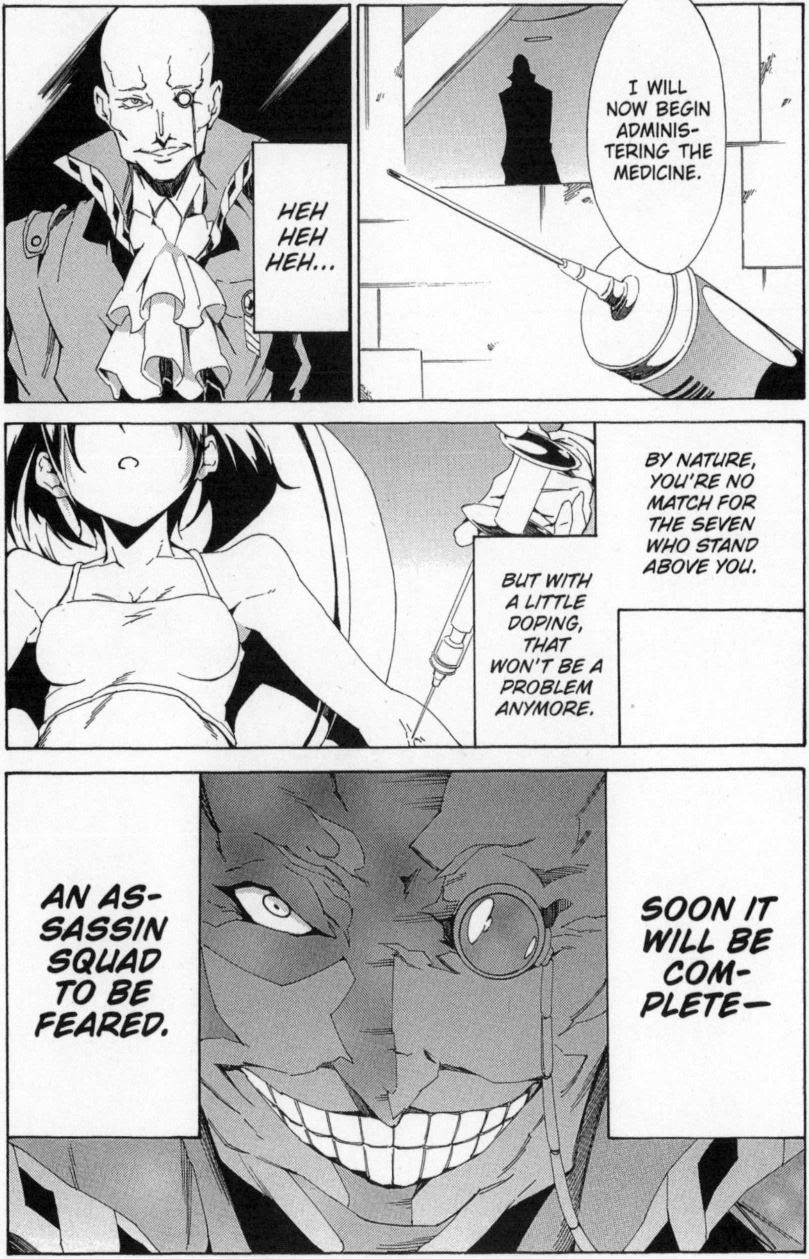
I WILL NOW BEGIN ADMINIS-TERING THE MEDICINE.
HEH HEH HEH...
BY NATURE, YOU'RE NO MATCH FOR THE SEVEN WHO STAND ABOVE YOU.
BUT WITH A LITTLE DOPING, THAT WON'T BE A PROBLEM ANYMORE.
SOON IT WILL BE COM-PLETE—
AN AS-SASSIN SQUAD TO BE FEARED.

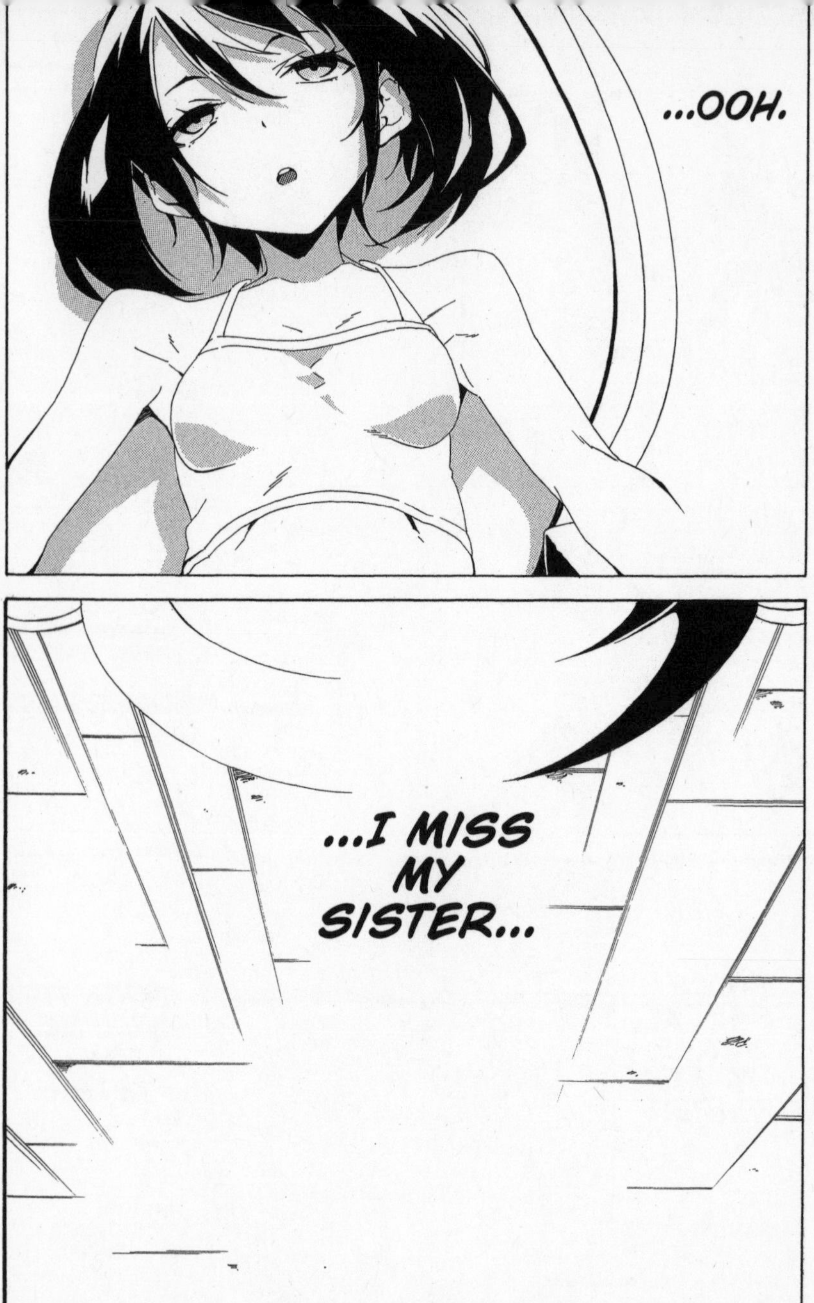
...OOH.
...I MISS MY SISTER...

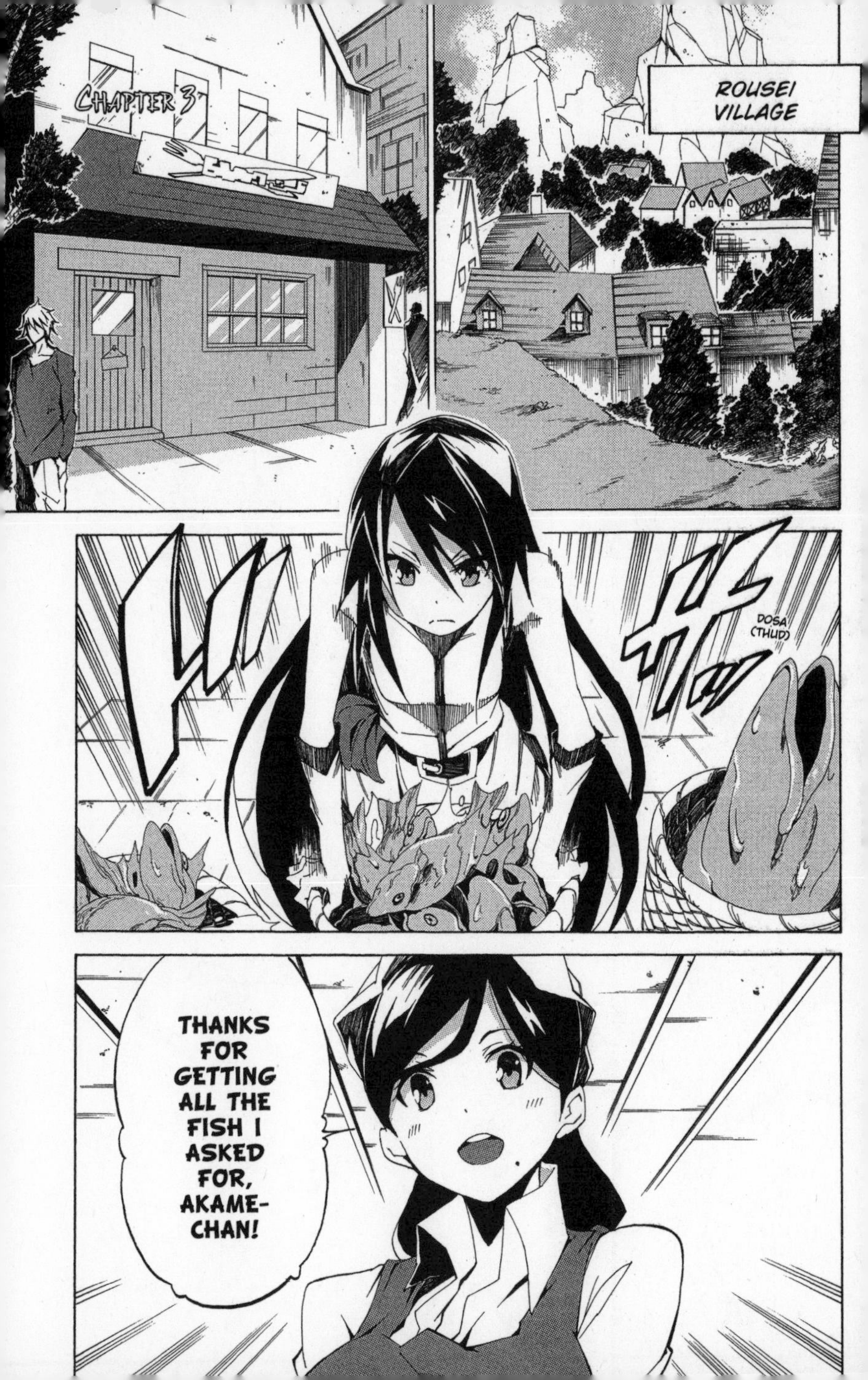

CHAPTER 3
ROUSEI VILLAGE
DOSA (THUD)
THANKS FOR GETTING ALL THE FISH I ASKED FOR, AKAME-CHAN!

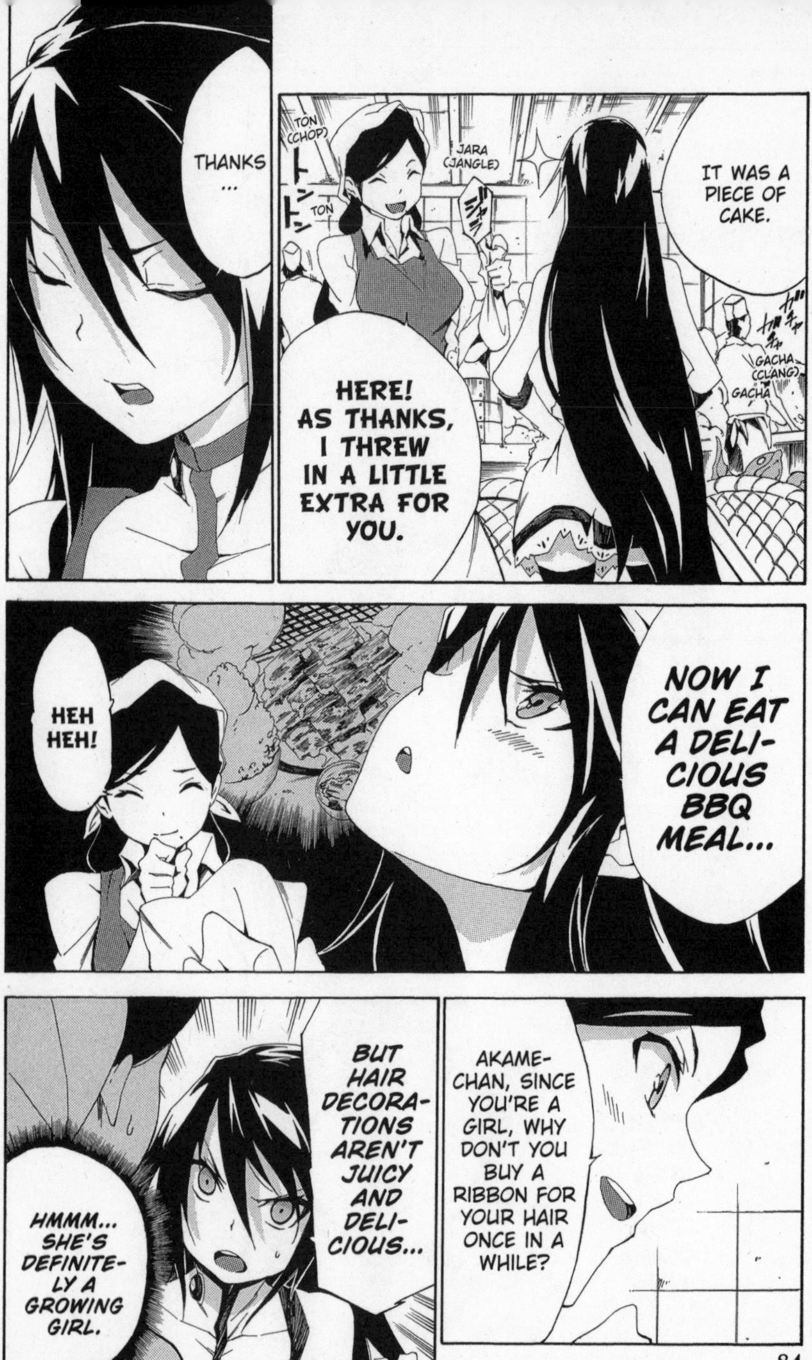
IT WAS A PIECE OF CAKE.
TON (CHOP)
TON
JARA (JANGLE)
GACHA (CLANG)
GACHA
HERE! AS THANKS, I THREW IN A LITTLE EXTRA FOR YOU.
THANKS ...
NOW I CAN EAT A DELI-CIOUS BBQ MEAL...
HEH HEH!
AKAME-CHAN, SINCE YOU'RE A GIRL, WHY DON'T YOU BUY A RIBBON FOR YOUR HAIR ONCE IN A WHILE?
BUT HAIR DECORA-TIONS AREN'T JUICY AND DELI-CIOUS...
HMMM... SHE'S DEFINITE-LY A GROWING GIRL.

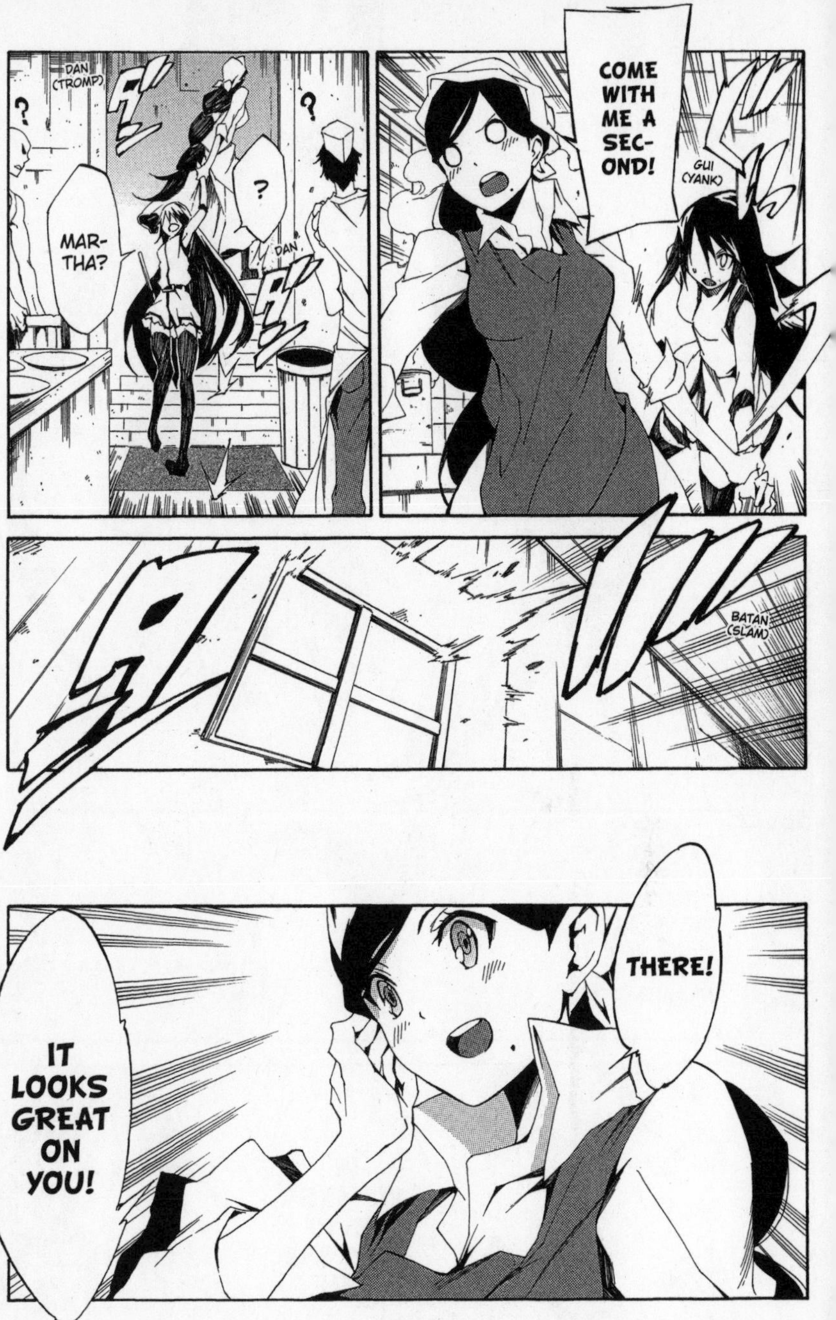
COME WITH ME A SEC-OND!
GUI (YANK)
DAN (TROMP)
?
?
?
MAR-THA?
DAN
BATAN (SLAM)
THERE!
IT LOOKS GREAT ON YOU!

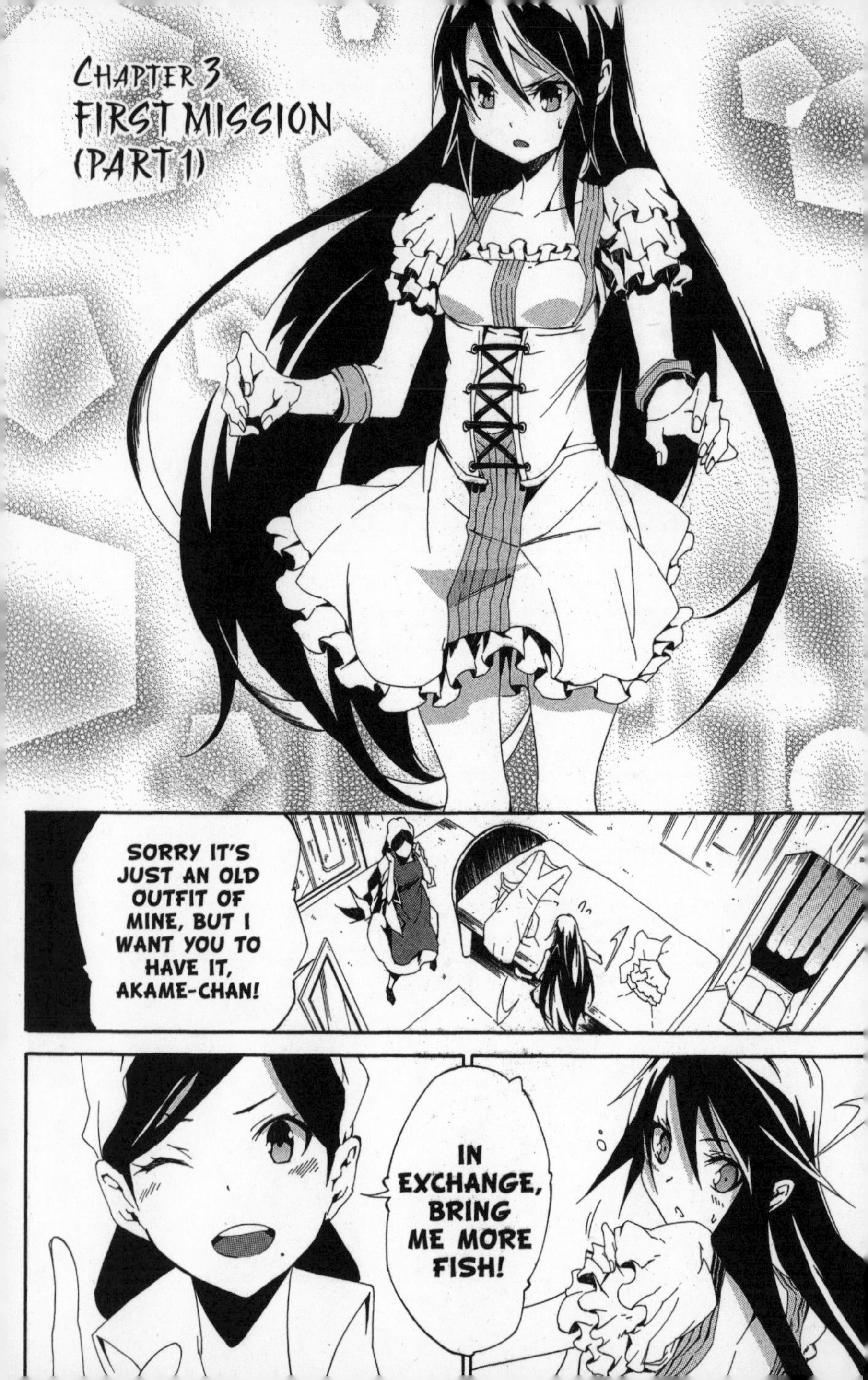
CHAPTER 3
FIRST MISSION
(PART 1)
SORRY IT'S JUST AN OLD OUTFIT OF MINE, BUT I WANT YOU TO HAVE IT, AKAME-CHAN!
IN EXCHANGE, BRING ME MORE FISH!

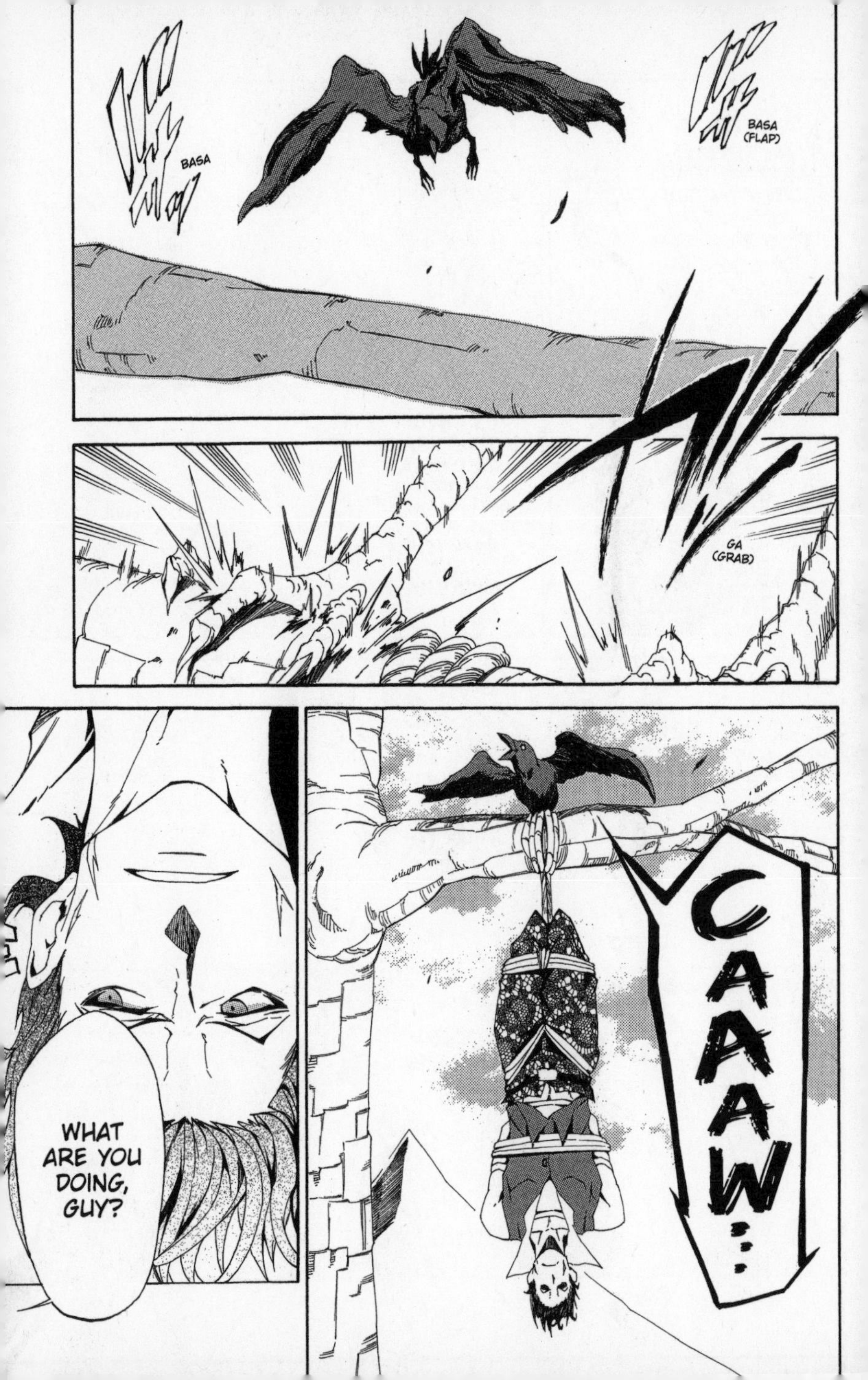
BASA (FLAP)
BASA
GA (GRAB)
CAAAW...
WHAT ARE YOU DOING, GUY?

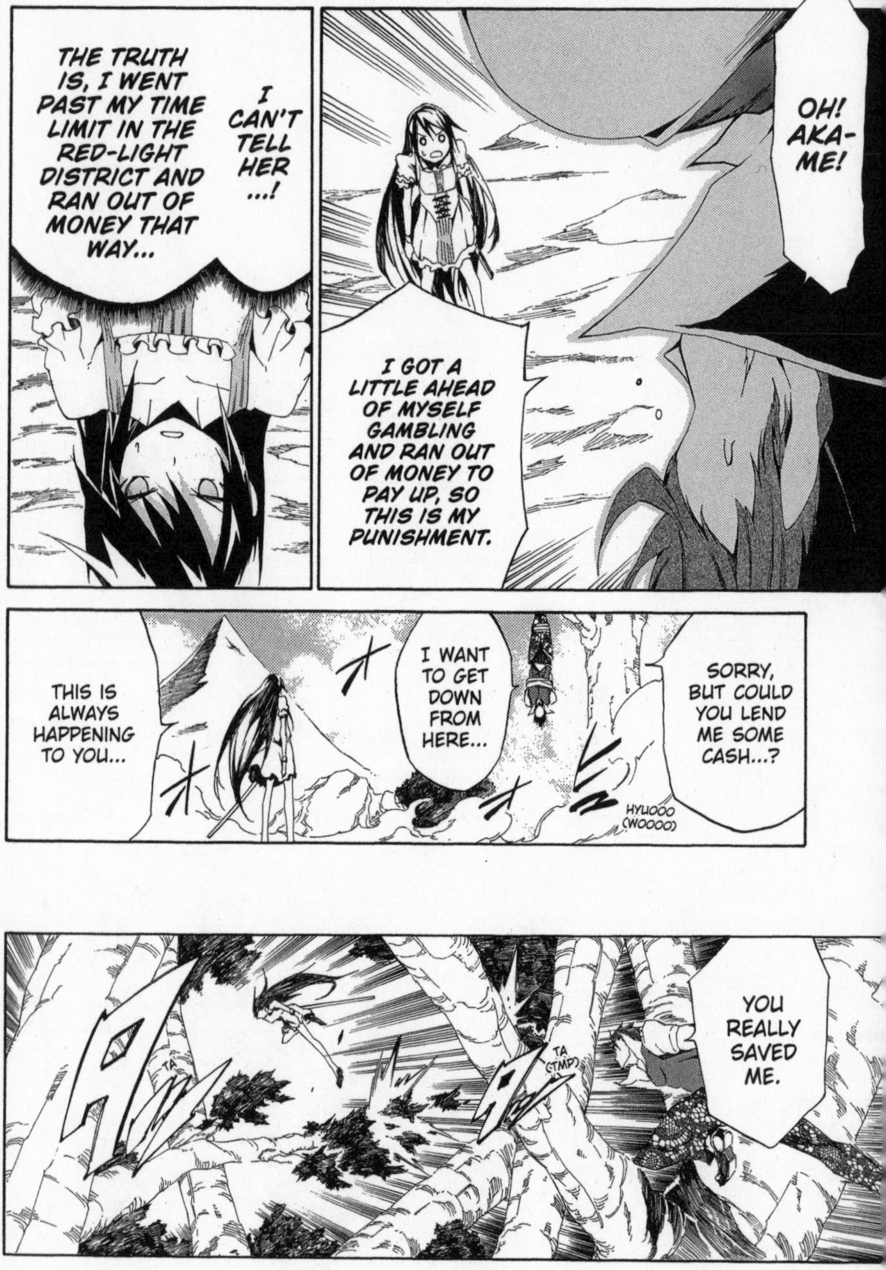
OH! AKA-ME!
I GOT A LITTLE AHEAD OF MYSELF GAMBLING AND RAN OUT OF MONEY TO PAY UP, SO THIS IS MY PUNISHMENT.
I CAN'T TELL HER ...!
THE TRUTH IS, I WENT PAST MY TIME LIMIT IN THE RED-LIGHT DISTRICT AND RAN OUT OF MONEY THAT WAY...
SORRY, BUT COULD YOU LEND ME SOME CASH...?
HYUOOO (WOOOO)
I WANT TO GET DOWN FROM HERE...
THIS IS ALWAYS HAPPENING TO YOU...
YOU REALLY SAVED ME.
TA (TMP)
TA

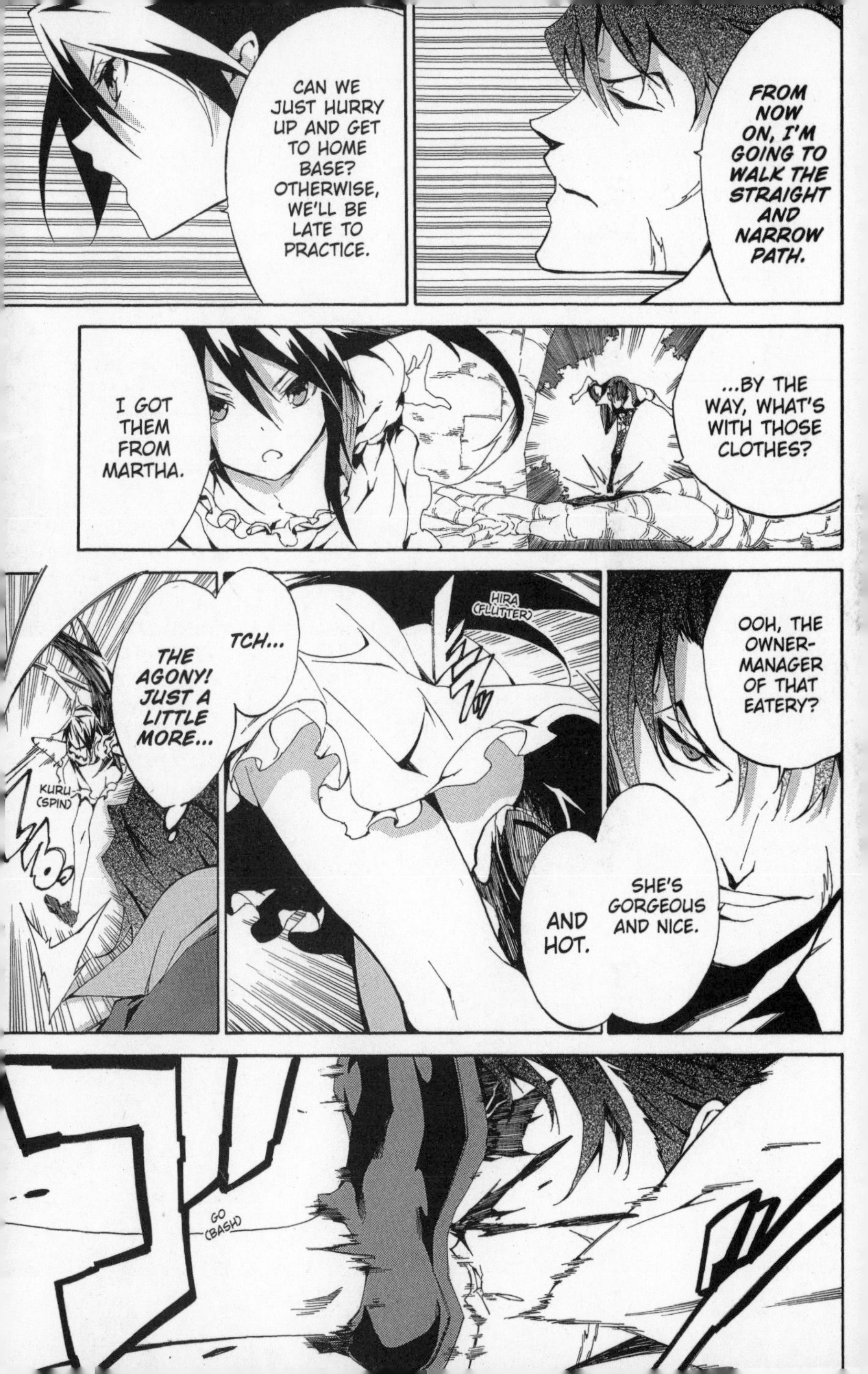
FROM NOW ON, I'M GOING TO WALK THE STRAIGHT AND NARROW PATH.
CAN WE JUST HURRY UP AND GET TO HOME BASE? OTHERWISE, WE'LL BE LATE TO PRACTICE.
...BY THE WAY, WHAT'S WITH THOSE CLOTHES?
I GOT THEM FROM MARTHA.
OOH, THE OWNER-MANAGER OF THAT EATERY?
SHE'S GORGEOUS AND NICE.
AND HOT.
HIRA (FLUTTER)
TCH...
THE AGONY! JUST A LITTLE MORE...
KURU (SPIN)
GO (BASH)

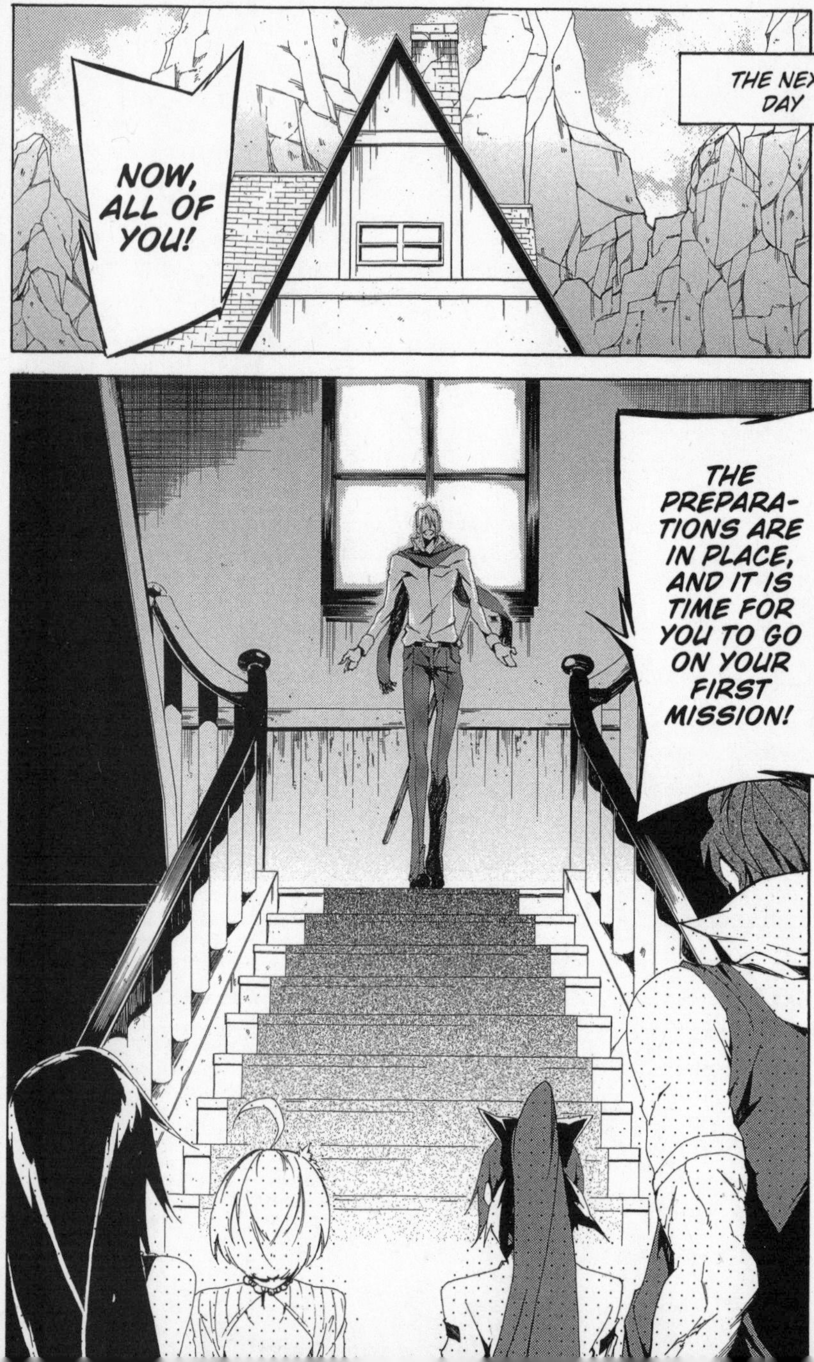
THE NEXT DAY
NOW, ALL OF YOU!
THE PREPARATIONS ARE IN PLACE, AND IT IS TIME FOR YOU TO GO ON YOUR FIRST MISSION!

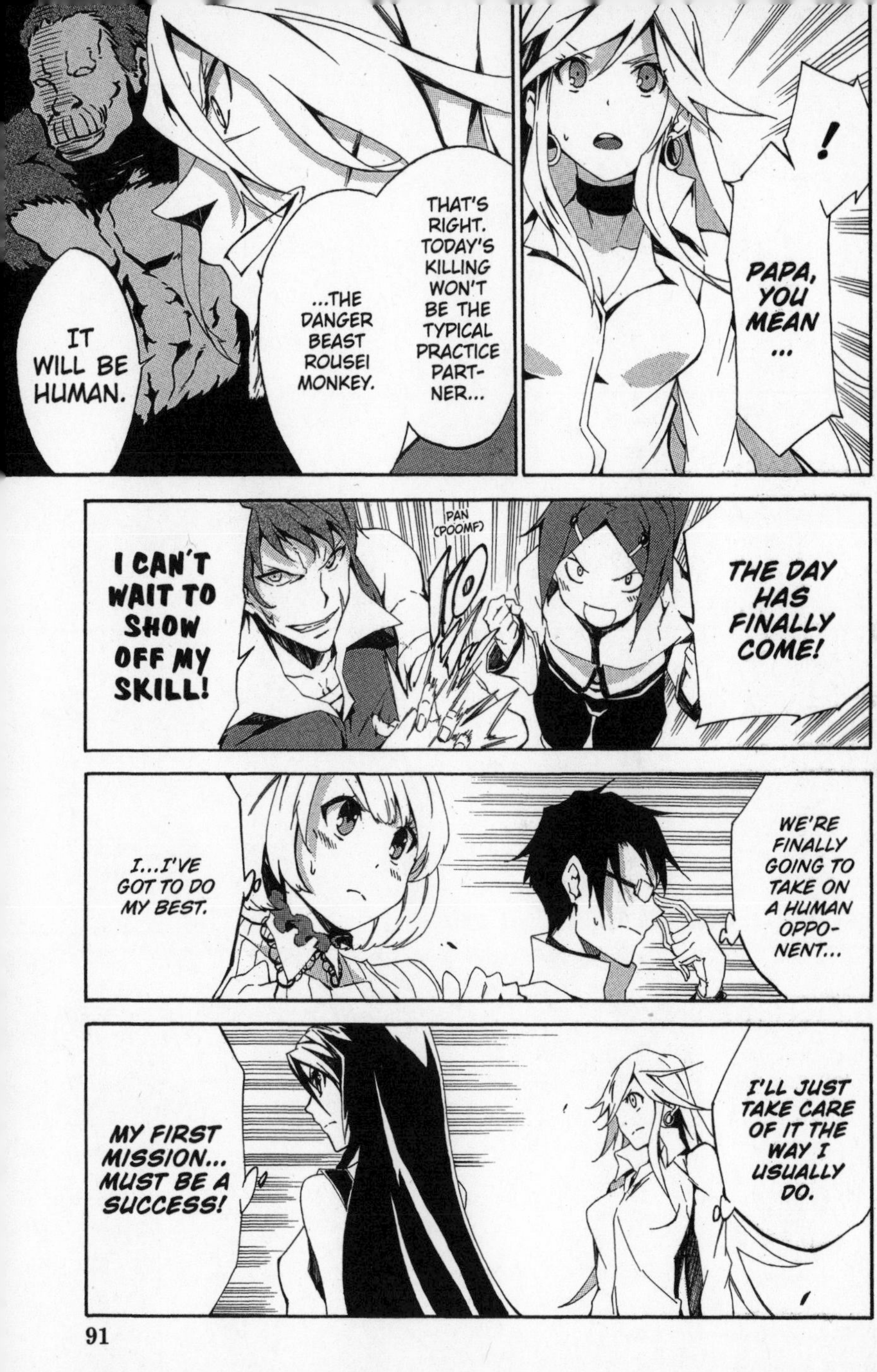
!
PAPA, YOU MEAN...
THAT'S RIGHT. TODAY'S KILLING WON'T BE THE TYPICAL PRACTICE PART-NER...
...THE DANGER BEAST ROUSEI MONKEY.
IT WILL BE HUMAN.
THE DAY HAS FINALLY COME!
PAN (POOMF)
I CAN'T WAIT TO SHOW OFF MY SKILL!
WE'RE FINALLY GOING TO TAKE ON A HUMAN OPPO-NENT...
I...I'VE GOT TO DO MY BEST.
I'LL JUST TAKE CARE OF IT THE WAY I USUALLY DO.
MY FIRST MISSION... MUST BE A SUCCESS!

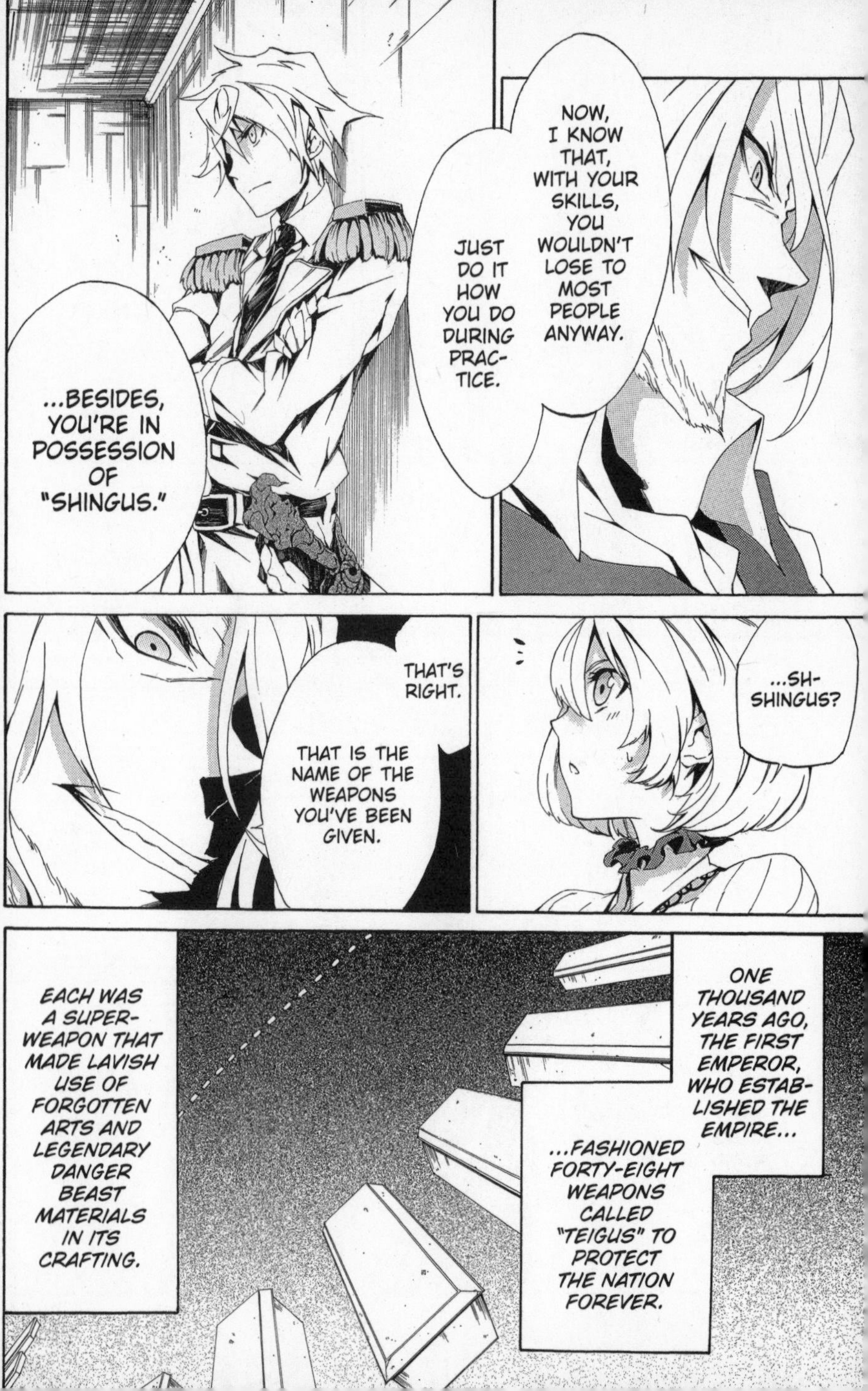
NOW, I KNOW THAT, WITH YOUR SKILLS, YOU WOULDN'T LOSE TO MOST PEOPLE ANYWAY.
JUST DO IT HOW YOU DO DURING PRAC-TICE.
...BESIDES, YOU'RE IN POSSESSION OF "SHINGUS."
...SH-SHINGUS?
THAT'S RIGHT.
THAT IS THE NAME OF THE WEAPONS YOU'VE BEEN GIVEN.
ONE THOUSAND YEARS AGO, THE FIRST EMPEROR, WHO ESTAB-LISHED THE EMPIRE...
...FASHIONED FORTY-EIGHT WEAPONS CALLED "TEIGUS" TO PROTECT THE NATION FOREVER.
EACH WAS A SUPER-WEAPON THAT MADE LAVISH USE OF FORGOTTEN ARTS AND LEGENDARY DANGER BEAST MATERIALS IN ITS CRAFTING.

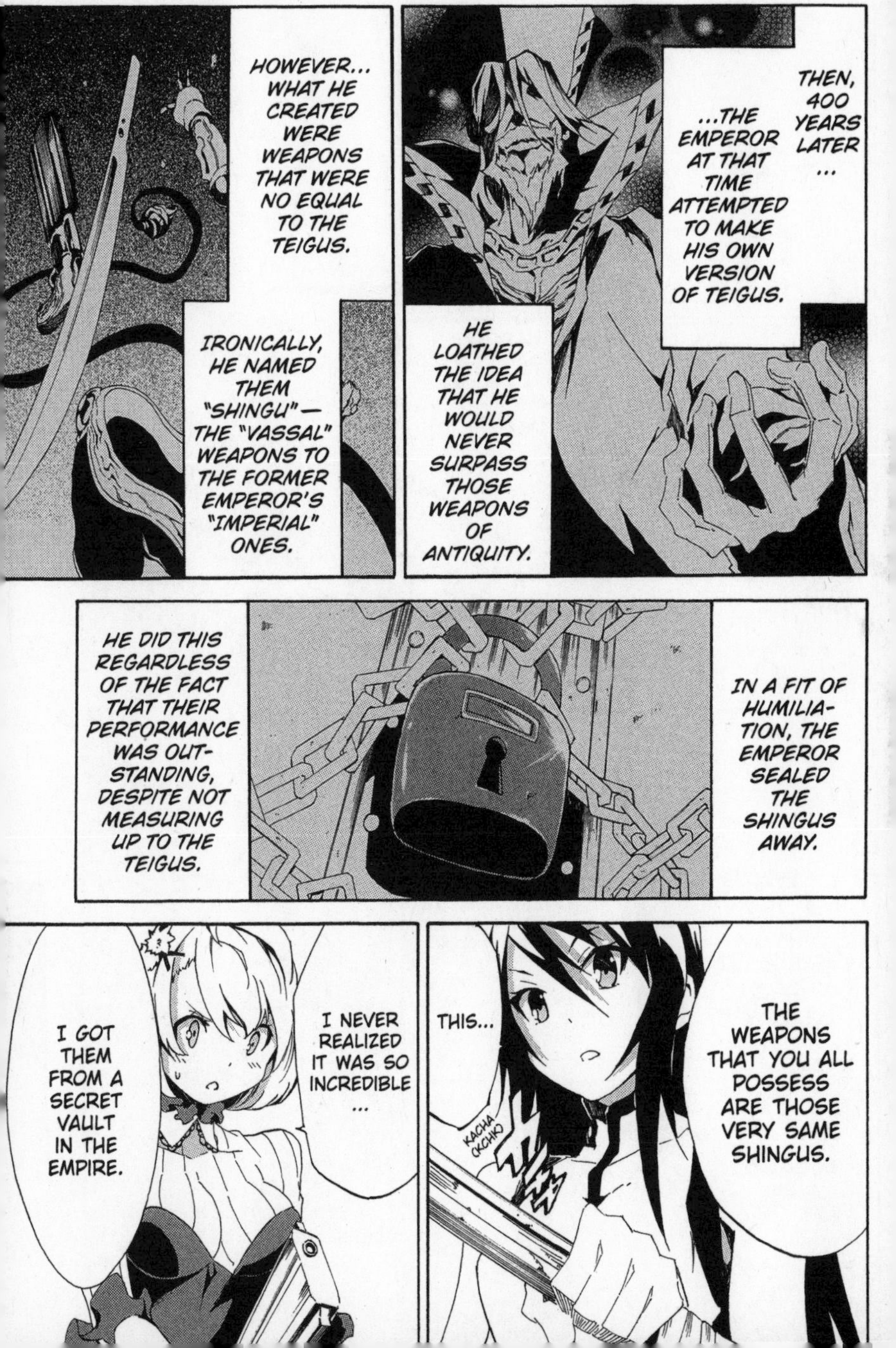
THEN, 400 YEARS LATER...
...THE EMPEROR AT THAT TIME ATTEMPTED TO MAKE HIS OWN VERSION OF TEIGUS.
HE LOATHED THE IDEA THAT HE WOULD NEVER SURPASS THOSE WEAPONS OF ANTIQUITY.
HOWEVER... WHAT HE CREATED WERE WEAPONS THAT WERE NO EQUAL TO THE TEIGUS.
IRONICALLY, HE NAMED THEM "SHINGU"—THE "VASSAL" WEAPONS TO THE FORMER EMPEROR'S "IMPERIAL" ONES.
IN A FIT OF HUMILIATION, THE EMPEROR SEALED THE SHINGUS AWAY.
HE DID THIS REGARDLESS OF THE FACT THAT THEIR PERFORMANCE WAS OUTSTANDING, DESPITE NOT MEASURING UP TO THE TEIGUS.
THE WEAPONS THAT YOU ALL POSSESS ARE THOSE VERY SAME SHINGUS.
KACHA CKCHK
THIS...
I NEVER REALIZED IT WAS SO INCREDIBLE...
I GOT THEM FROM A SECRET VAULT IN THE EMPIRE.

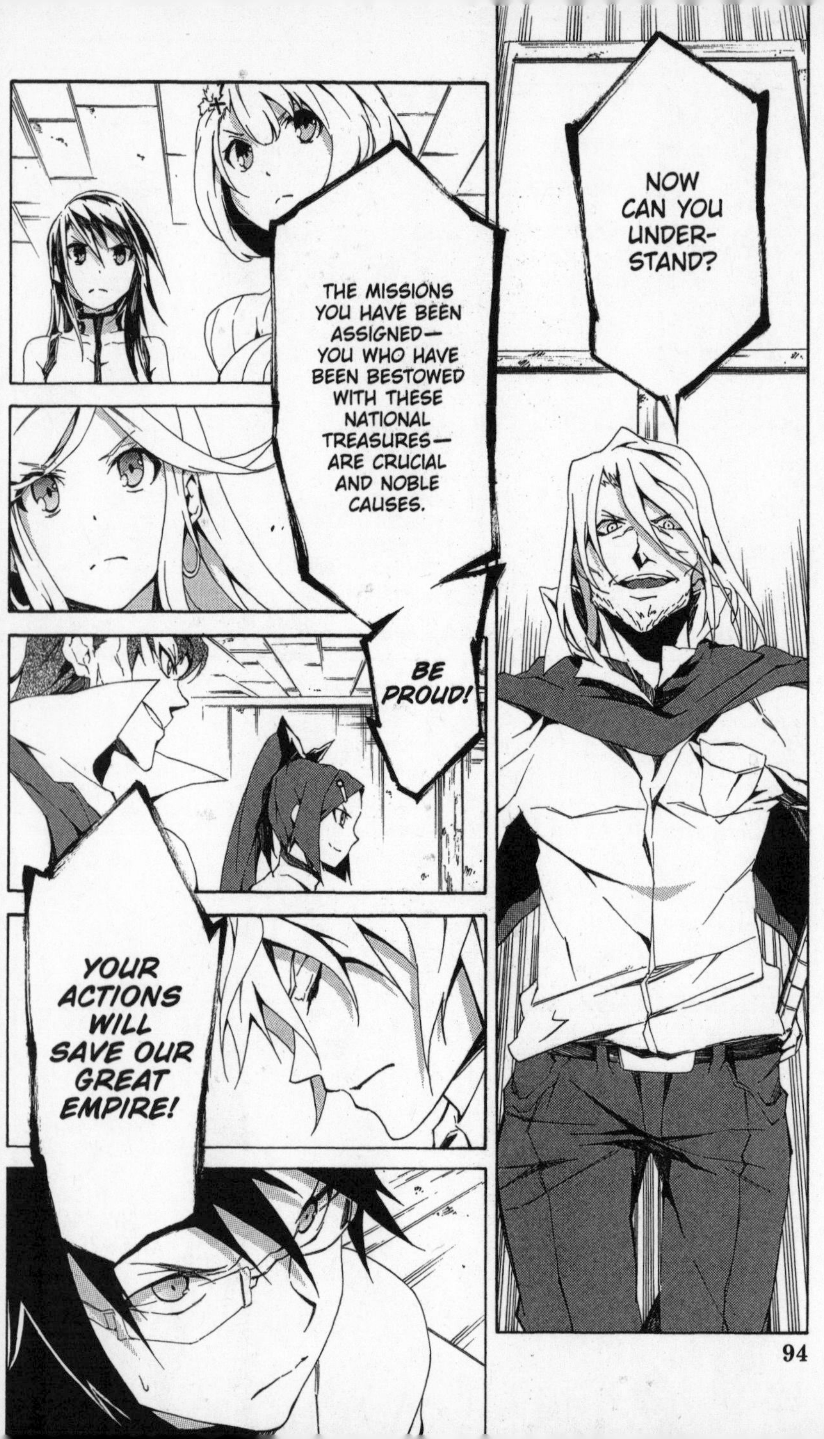
NOW CAN YOU UNDER-STAND?
THE MISSIONS YOU HAVE BEEN ASSIGNED— YOU WHO HAVE BEEN BESTOWED WITH THESE NATIONAL TREASURES— ARE CRUCIAL AND NOBLE CAUSES.
BE PROUD!
YOUR ACTIONS WILL SAVE OUR GREAT EMPIRE!

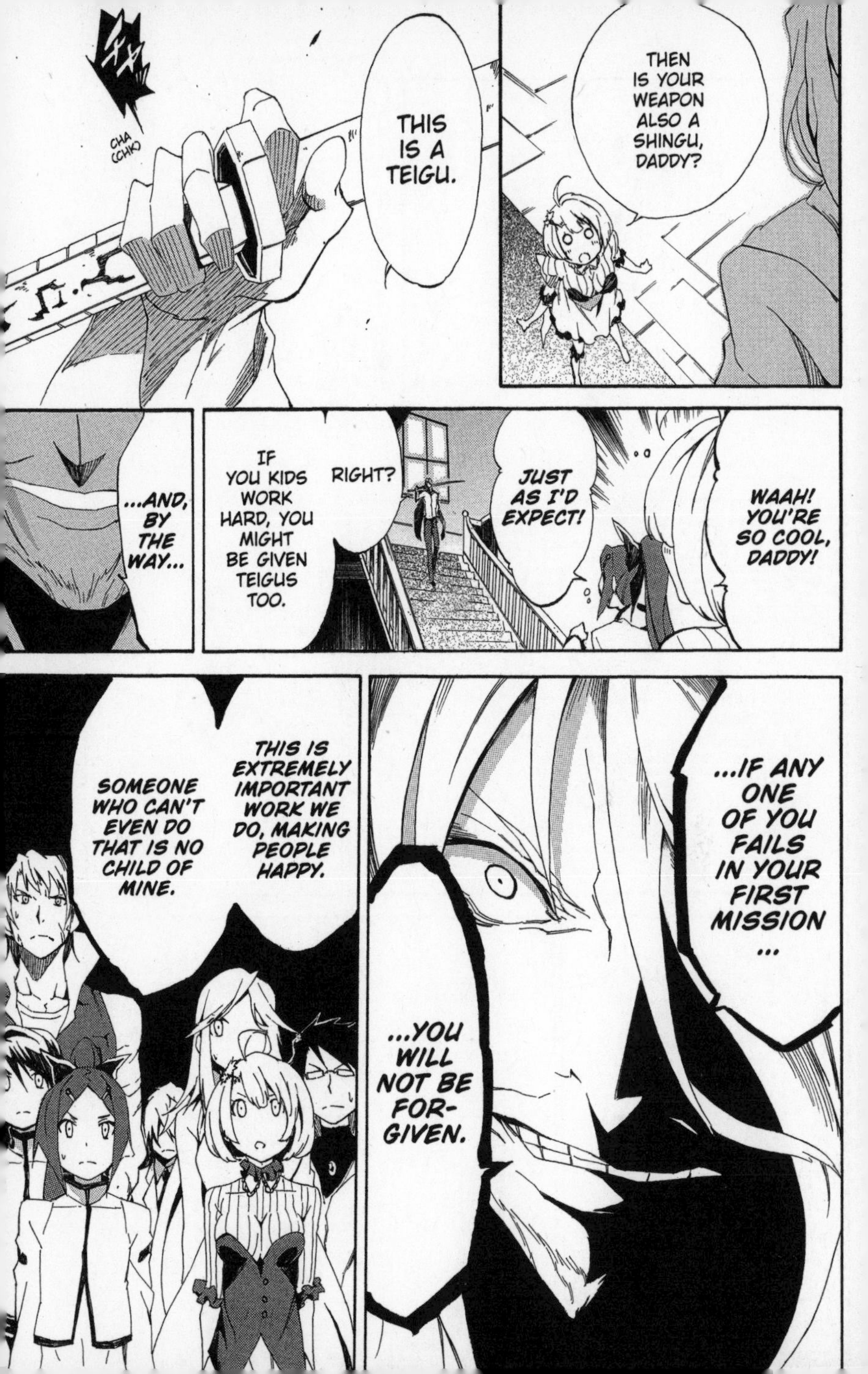
THEN IS YOUR WEAPON ALSO A SHINGU, DADDY?
THIS IS A TEIGU.
CHA (CHK)
WAAH! YOU'RE SO COOL, DADDY!
JUST AS I'D EXPECT!
RIGHT?
IF YOU KIDS WORK HARD, YOU MIGHT BE GIVEN TEIGUS TOO.
...AND, BY THE WAY...
...IF ANY ONE OF YOU FAILS IN YOUR FIRST MISSION ...
...YOU WILL NOT BE FOR-GIVEN.
THIS IS EXTREMELY IMPORTANT WORK WE DO, MAKING PEOPLE HAPPY.
SOMEONE WHO CAN'T EVEN DO THAT IS NO CHILD OF MINE.

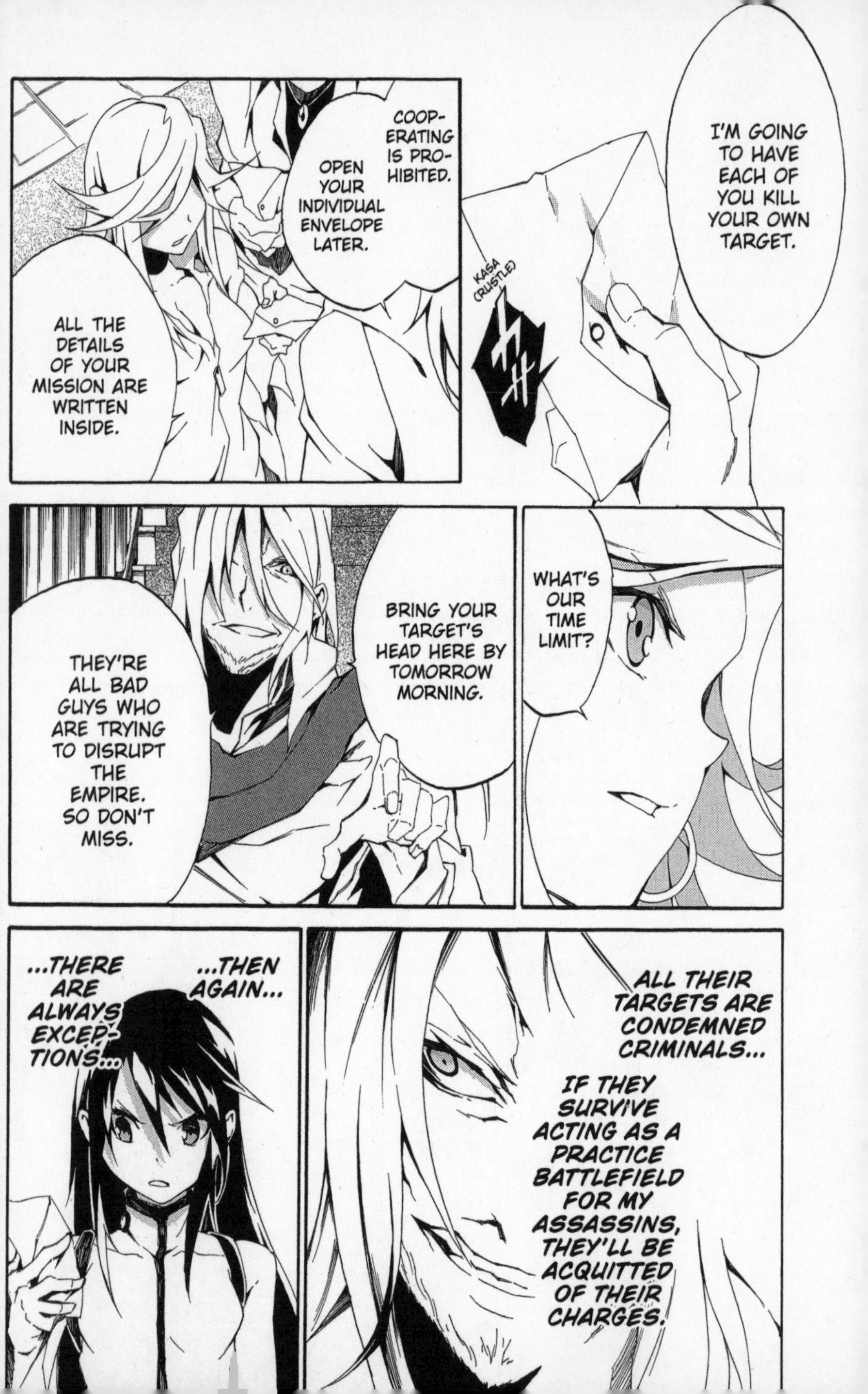
I'M GOING TO HAVE EACH OF YOU KILL YOUR OWN TARGET.
KASA (RUSTLE)
COOP-ERATING IS PRO-HIBITED.
OPEN YOUR INDIVIDUAL ENVELOPE LATER.
ALL THE DETAILS OF YOUR MISSION ARE WRITTEN INSIDE.
WHAT'S OUR TIME LIMIT?
BRING YOUR TARGET'S HEAD HERE BY TOMORROW MORNING.
THEY'RE ALL BAD GUYS WHO ARE TRYING TO DISRUPT THE EMPIRE. SO DON'T MISS.
ALL THEIR TARGETS ARE CONDEMNED CRIMINALS...
IF THEY SURVIVE ACTING AS A PRACTICE BATTLEFIELD FOR MY ASSASSINS, THEY'LL BE ACQUITTED OF THEIR CHARGES.
...THEN AGAIN...
...THERE ARE ALWAYS EXCEP-TIONS...

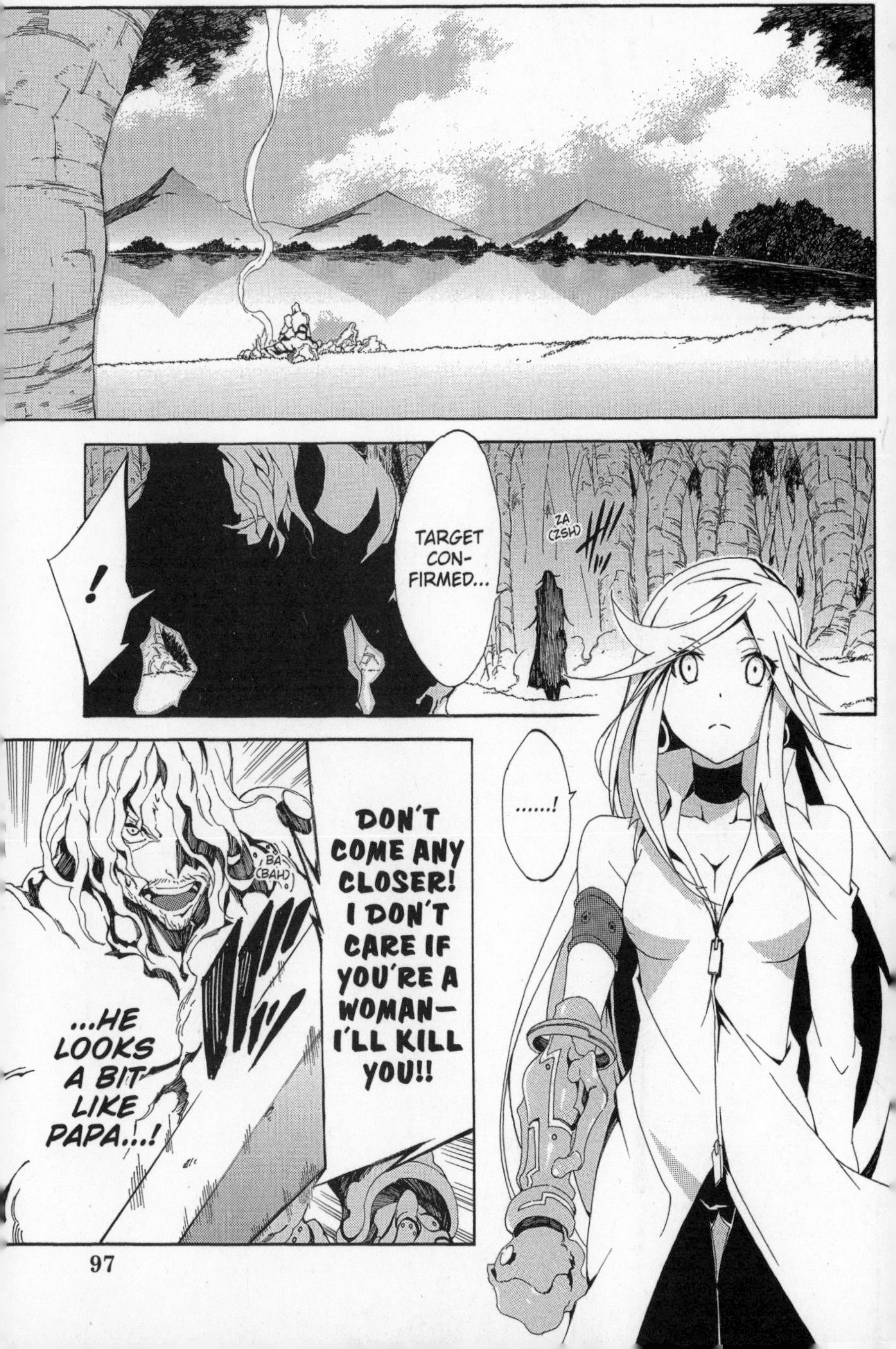

TARGET CON-FIRMED...
ZA (ZSH)
!
......!
DON'T COME ANY CLOSER! I DON'T CARE IF YOU'RE A WOMAN—I'LL KILL YOU!!
BA (BAH)
...HE LOOKS A BIT LIKE PAPA...!

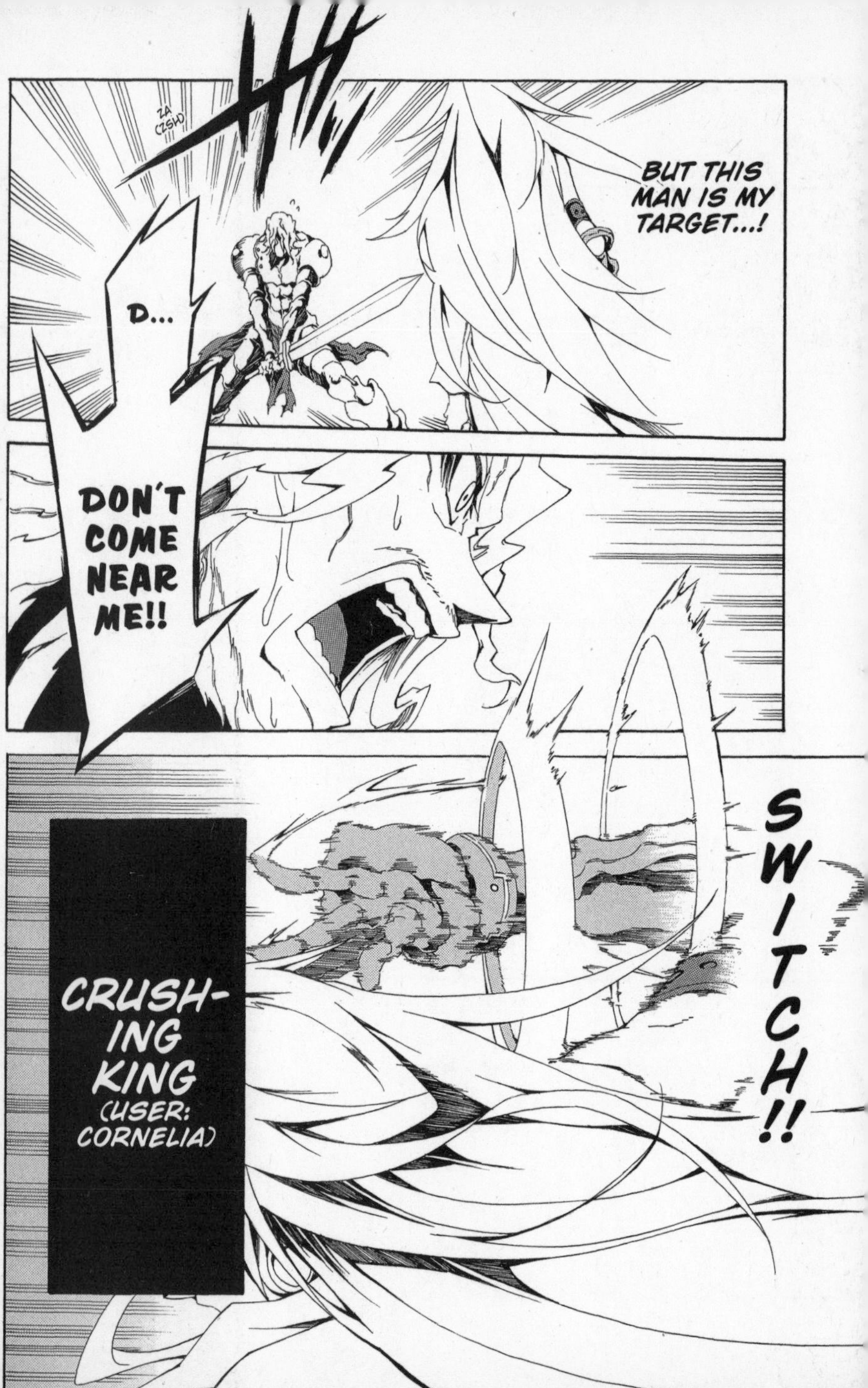
ZA (ZSH)
BUT THIS MAN IS MY TARGET...!
D...
DON'T COME NEAR ME!!
SWITCH!!
CRUSHING KING (USER: CORNELIA)

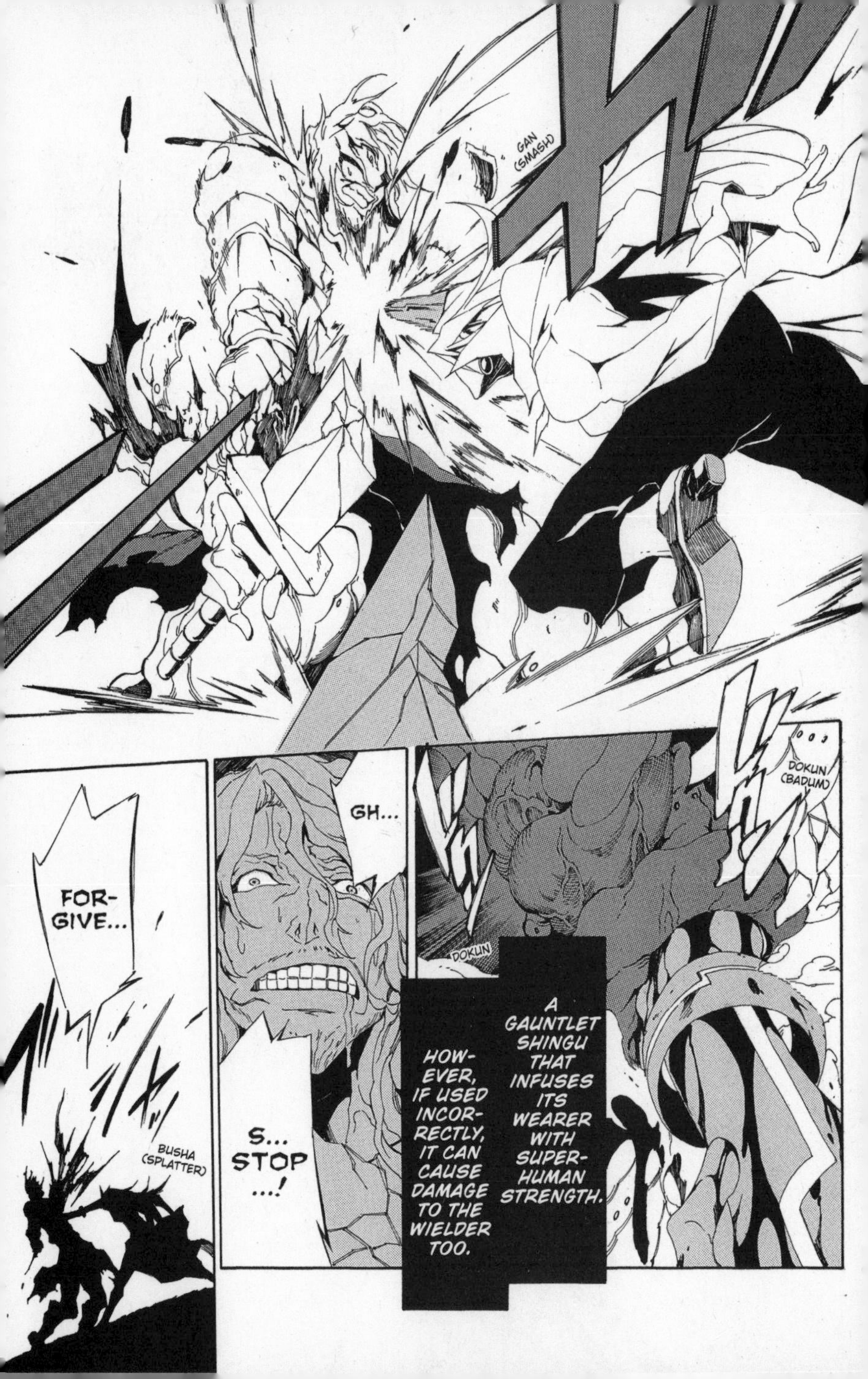
GAN (SMASH)
...
DOKUN (BADUM)
DOKUN
A GAUNTLET SHINGU THAT INFUSES ITS WEARER WITH SUPER-HUMAN STRENGTH.
HOW-EVER, IF USED INCOR-RECTLY, IT CAN CAUSE DAMAGE TO THE WIELDER TOO.
GH...
S... STOP ...!
FOR-GIVE...
BUSHA (SPLATTER)

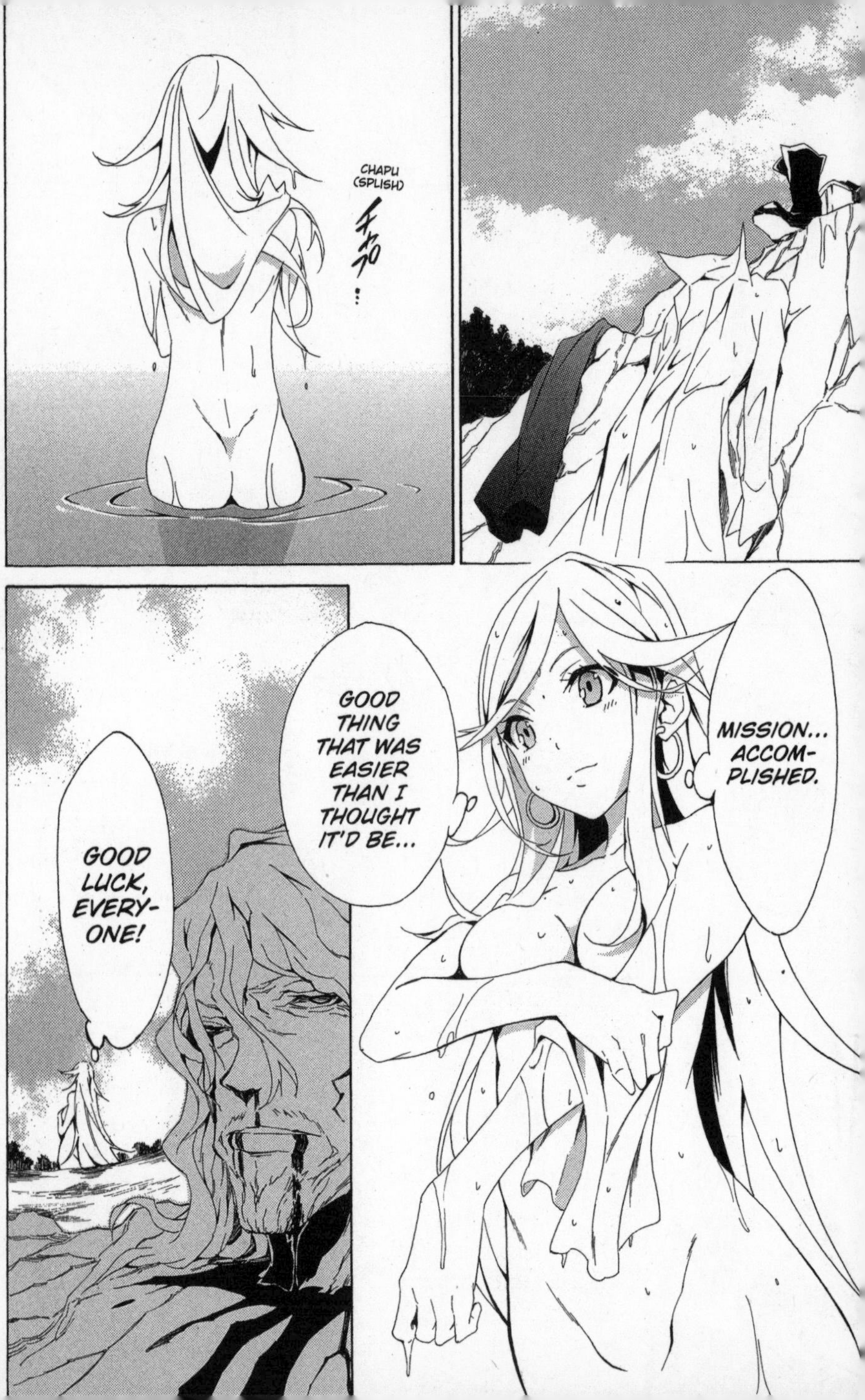
CHAPU (SPLISH)
チャプ…
MISSION... ACCOMPLISHED.
GOOD THING THAT WAS EASIER THAN I THOUGHT IT'D BE...
GOOD LUCK, EVERYONE!

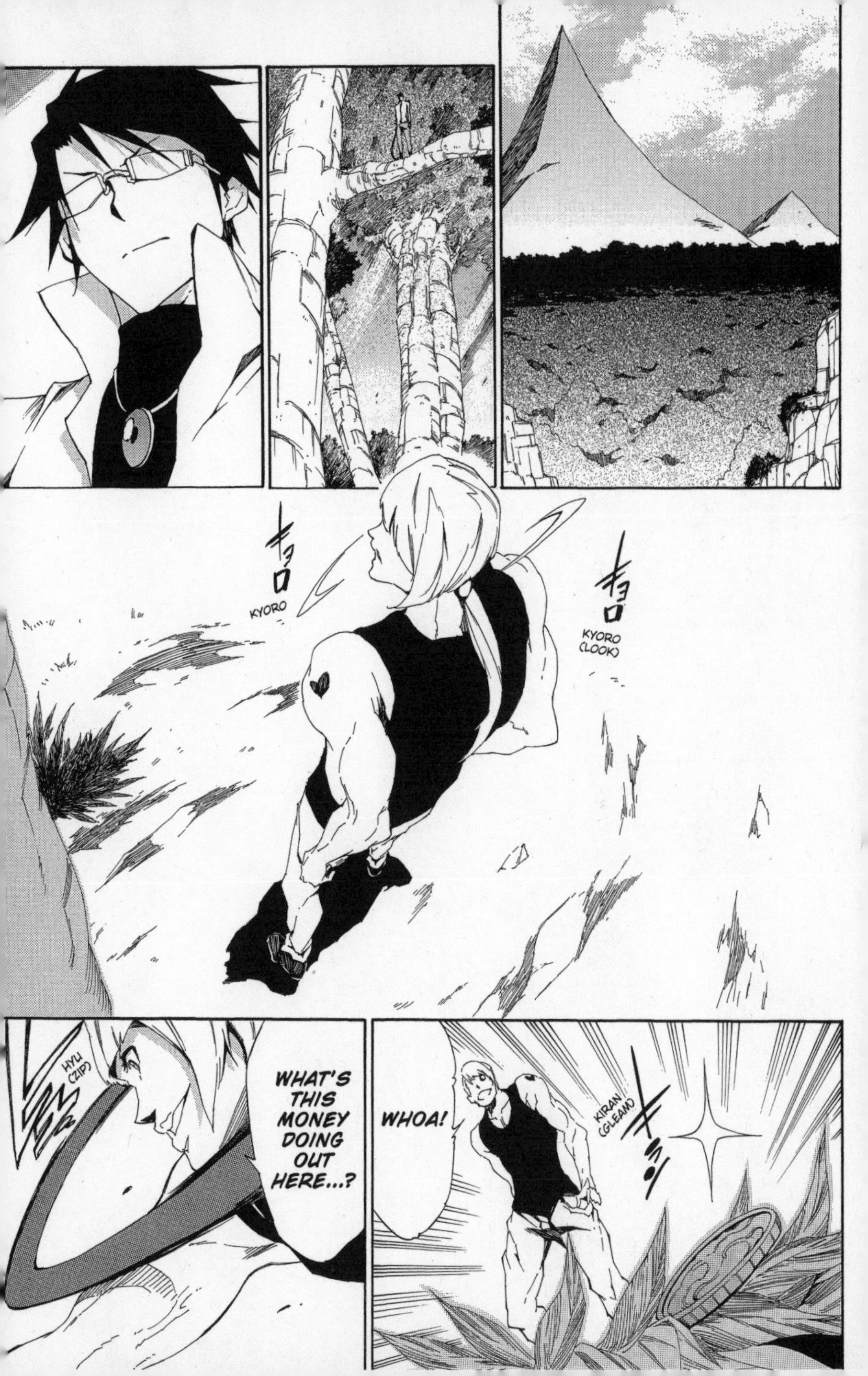
KYORO (LOOK)
KYORO
HYU (ZIP)
WHAT'S THIS MONEY DOING OUT HERE...?
WHOA!
KIRAN (GLEAM)

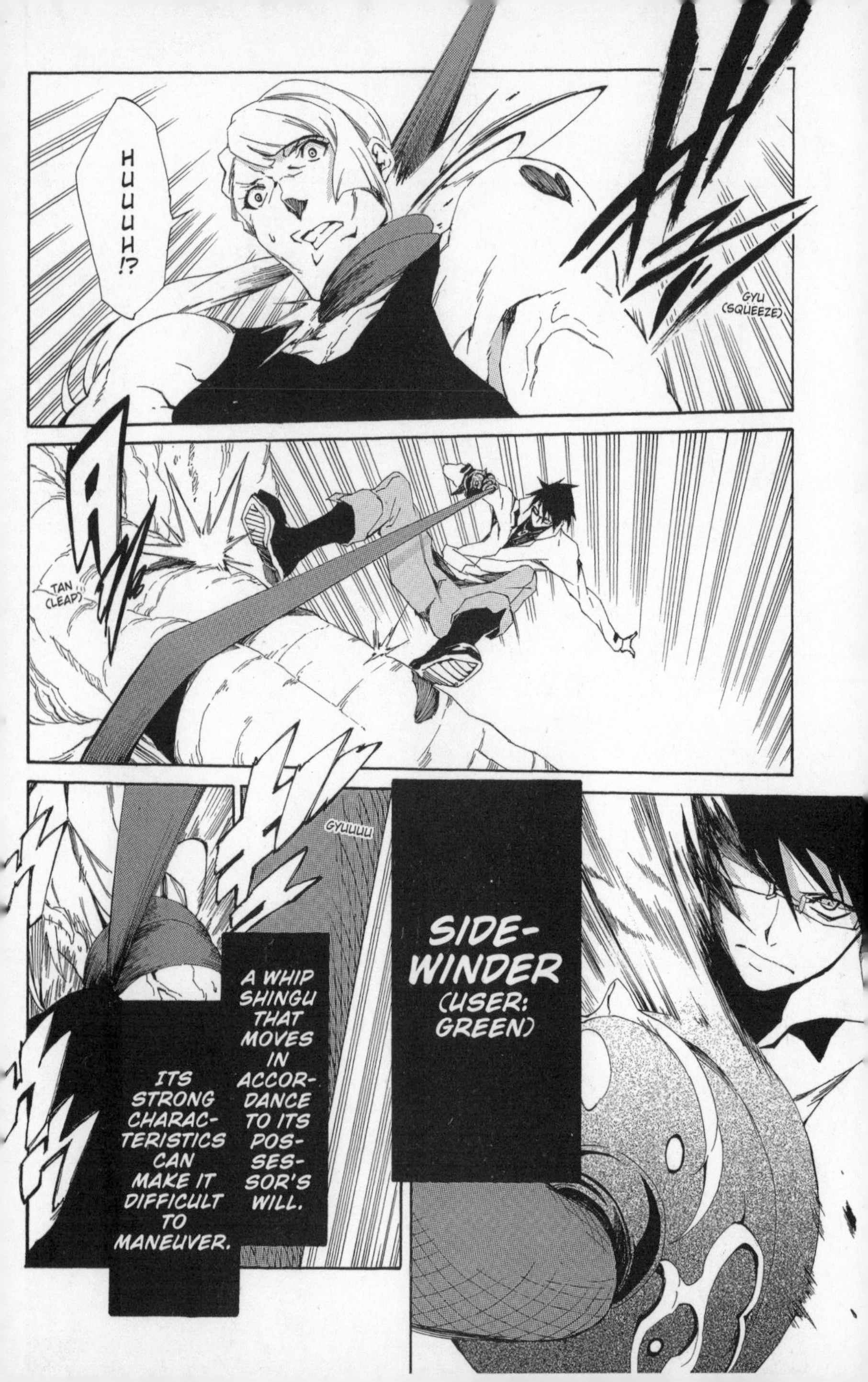
HUUUUH!?
GYU (SQUEEZE)
TAN (LEAP)
GYUUUU
SIDE-WINDER (USER: GREEN)
A WHIP SHINGU THAT MOVES IN ACCORDANCE TO ITS POSSESSOR'S WILL.
ITS STRONG CHARACTERISTICS CAN MAKE IT DIFFICULT TO MANEUVER.

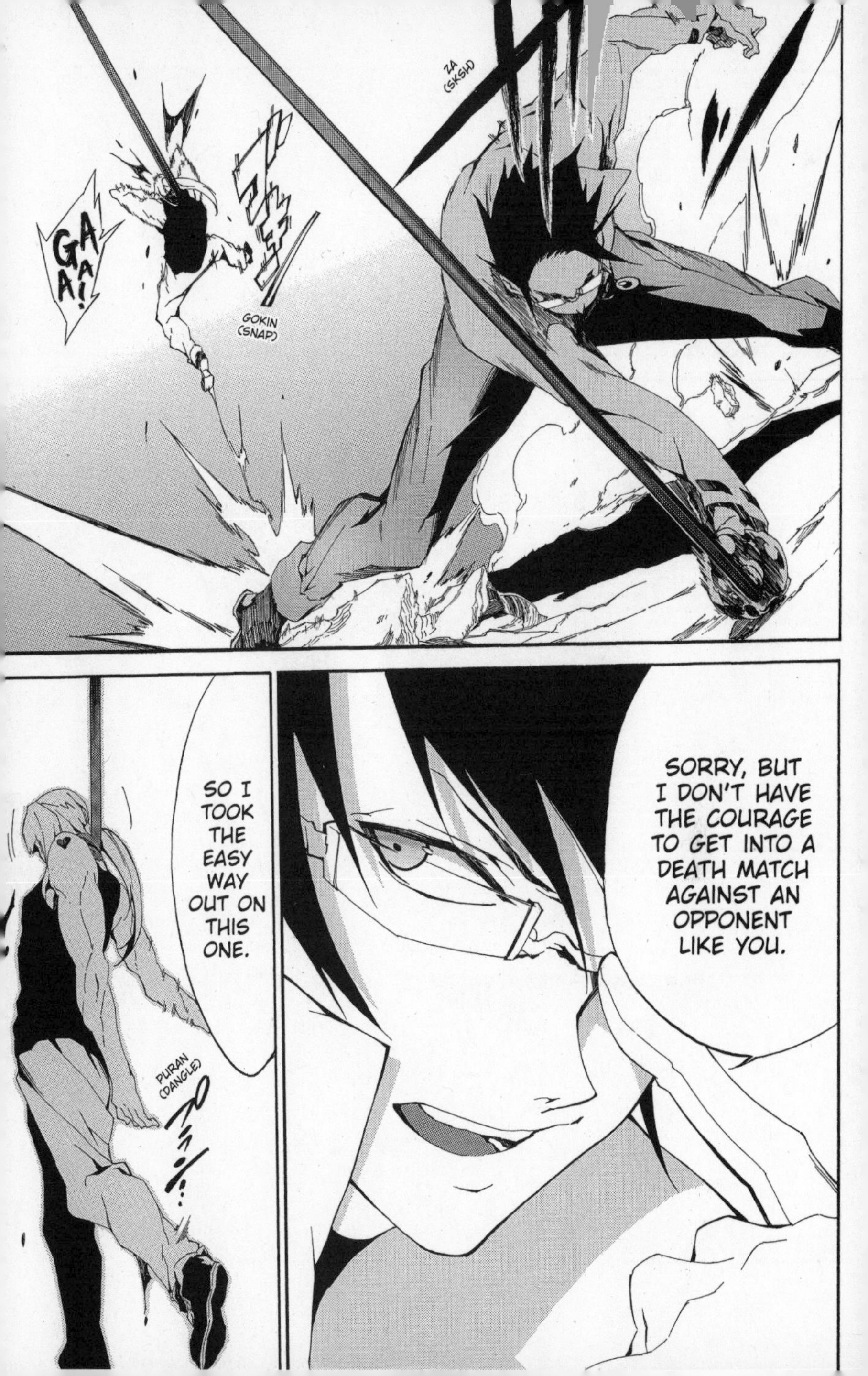
ZA (SKSH)
GOKIN (SNAP)
GAAA!
SORRY, BUT I DON'T HAVE THE COURAGE TO GET INTO A DEATH MATCH AGAINST AN OPPONENT LIKE YOU.
SO I TOOK THE EASY WAY OUT ON THIS ONE.
PURAN (DANGLE)

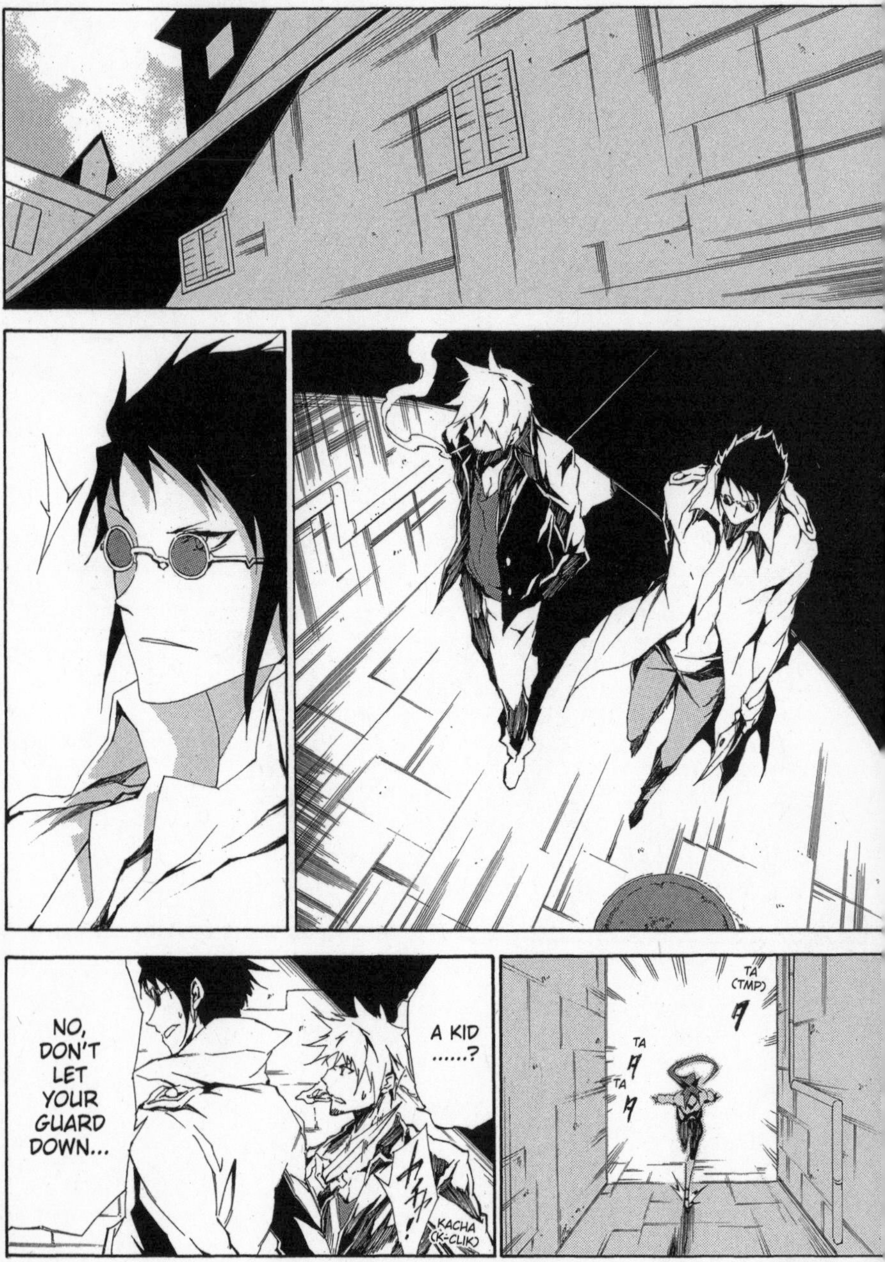
TA
(TMP)
TA
TA
A KID
......?
KACHA
(K-CLIK)
NO,
DON'T
LET
YOUR
GUARD
DOWN...

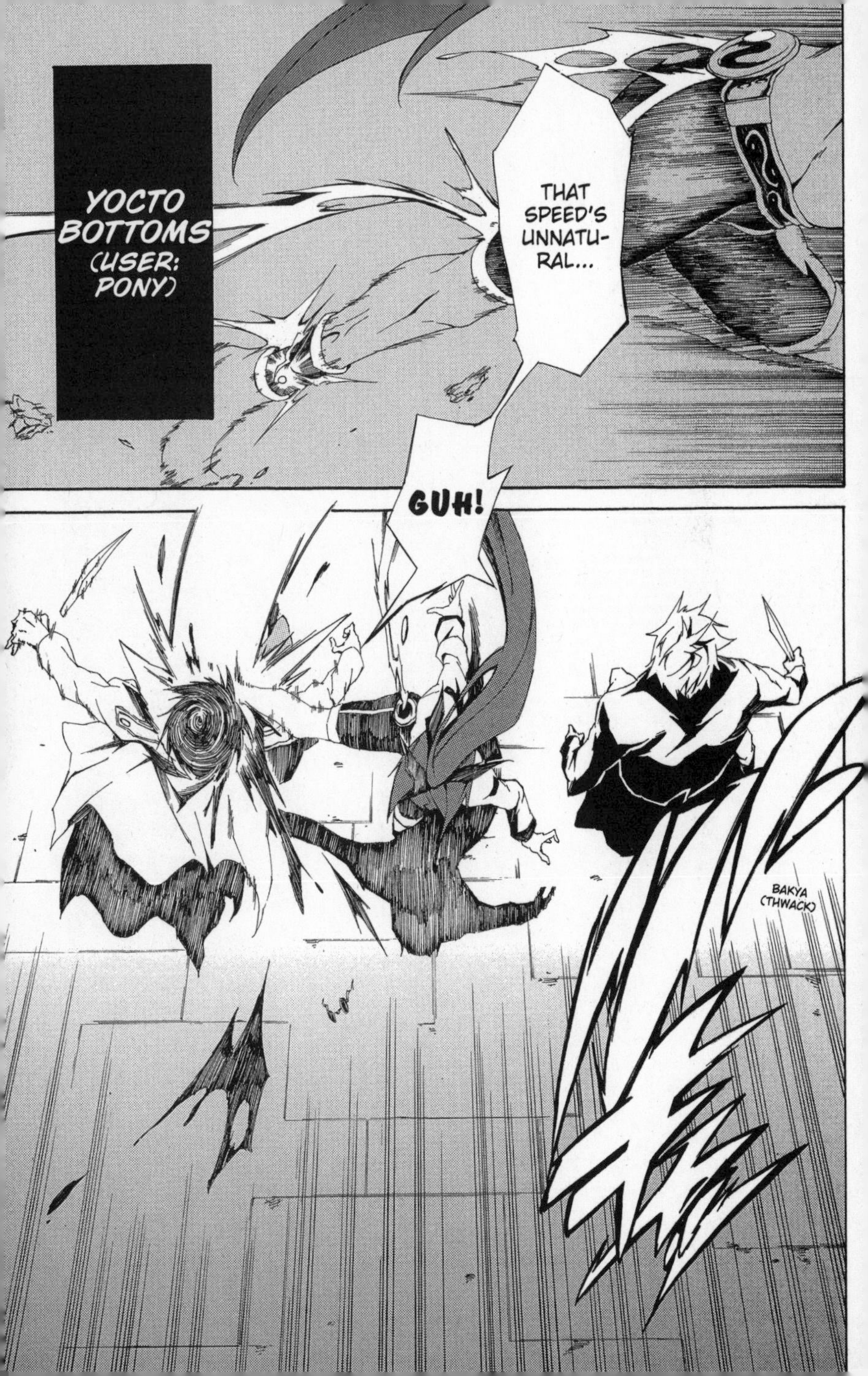
YOCTO BOTTOMS (USER: PONY)
THAT SPEED'S UNNATU-RAL...
GUH!
BAKYA (THWACK)

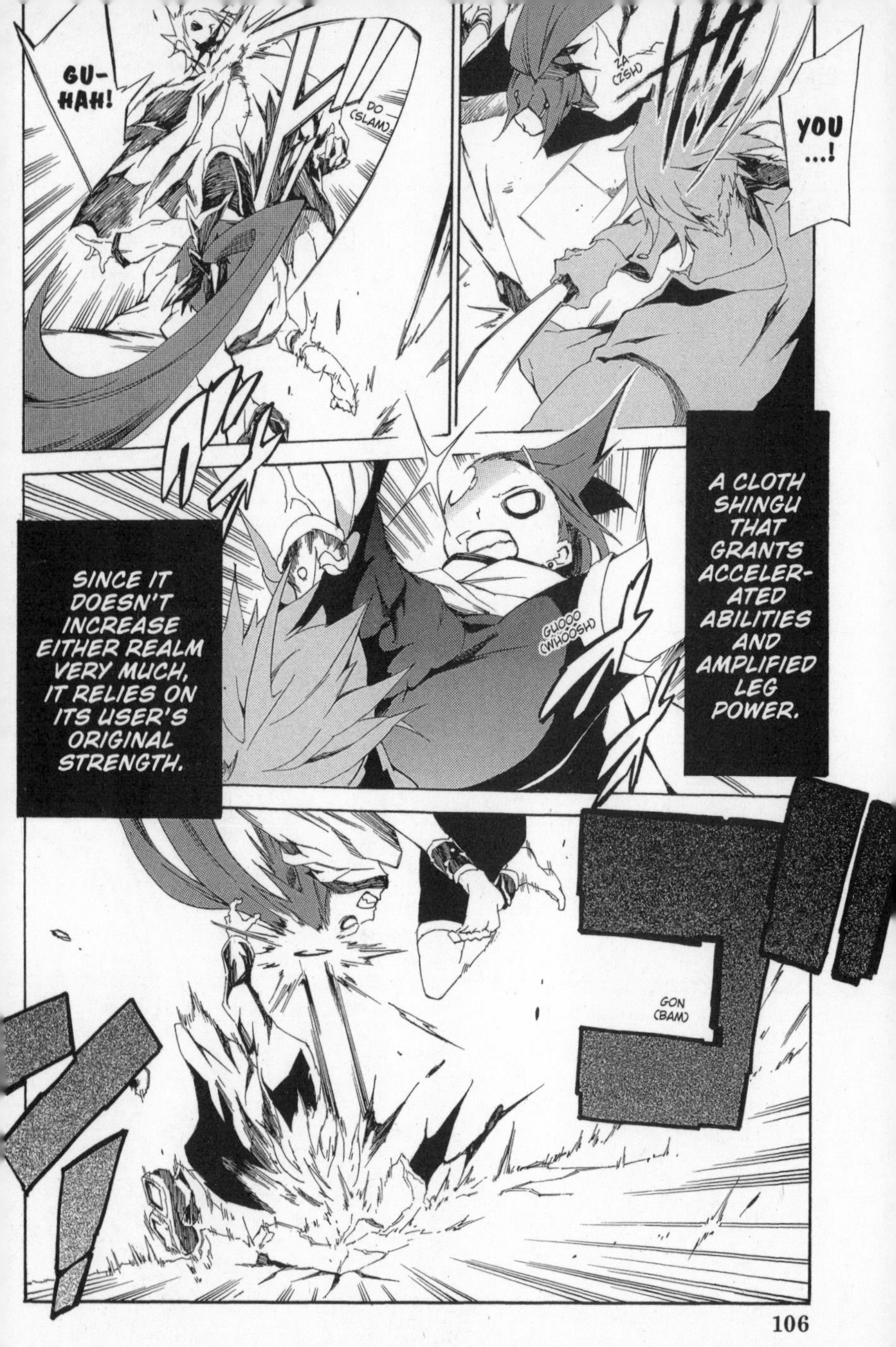

ZA (ZSH)
YOU ...!
GU-HAH!
DO (SLAM)
A CLOTH SHINGU THAT GRANTS ACCELERATED ABILITIES AND AMPLIFIED LEG POWER.
GUOOO (WHOOSH)
SINCE IT DOESN'T INCREASE EITHER REALM VERY MUCH, IT RELIES ON ITS USER'S ORIGINAL STRENGTH.
GON (BAM)

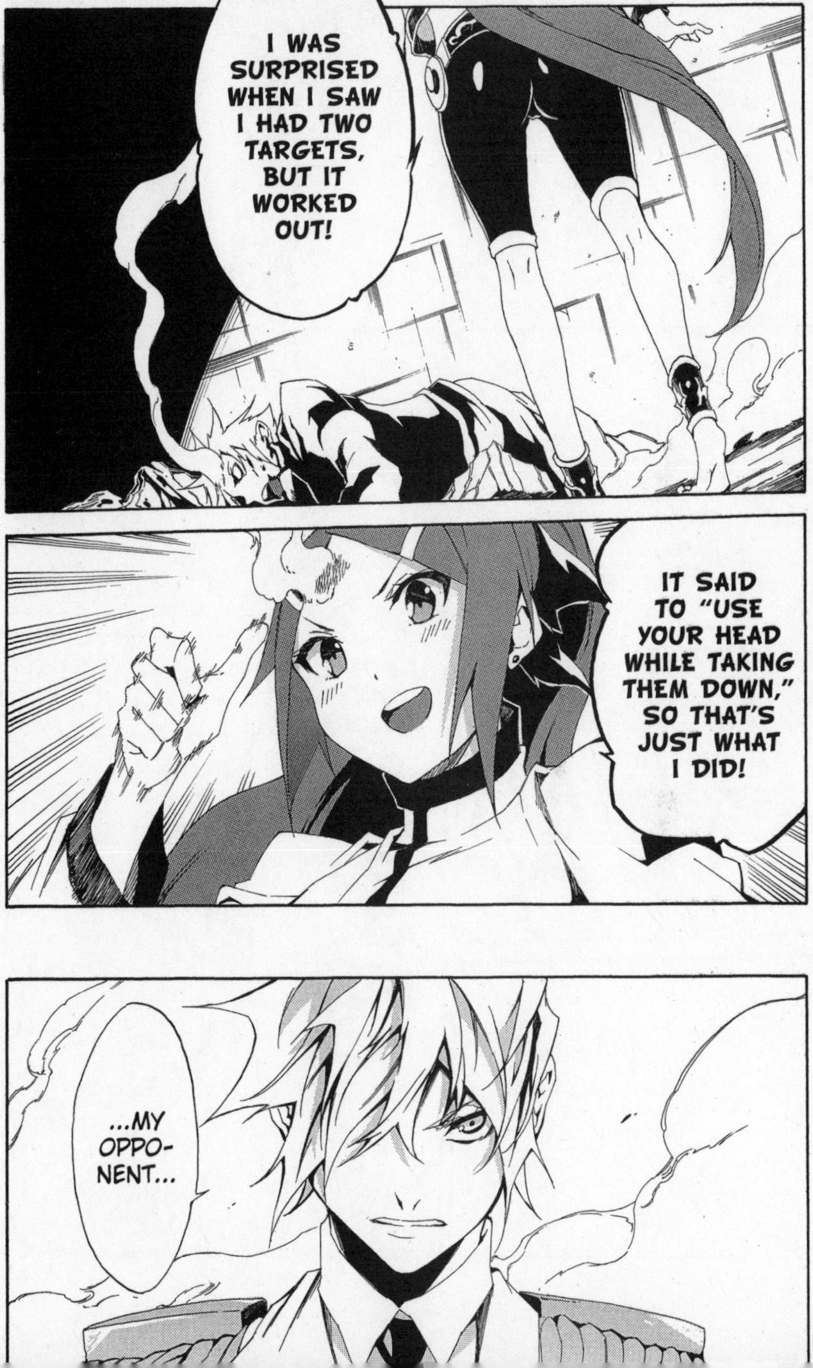
I WAS SURPRISED WHEN I SAW I HAD TWO TARGETS, BUT IT WORKED OUT!
IT SAID TO "USE YOUR HEAD WHILE TAKING THEM DOWN," SO THAT'S JUST WHAT I DID!
...MY OPPO-NENT...

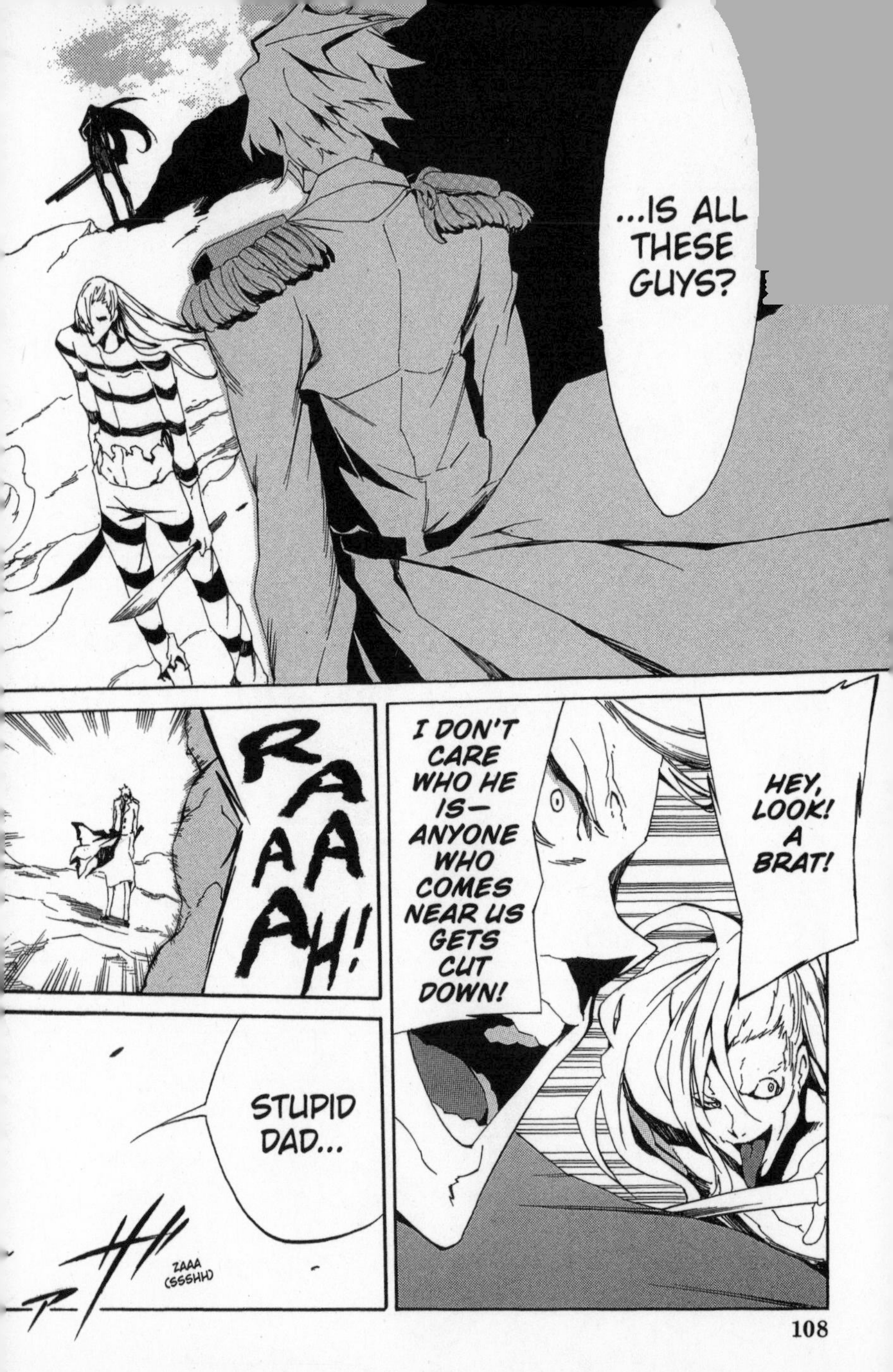
...IS ALL THESE GUYS?
HEY, LOOK! A BRAT!
I DON'T CARE WHO HE IS—ANYONE WHO COMES NEAR US GETS CUT DOWN!
RAAAAH!
STUPID DAD...
ZAAA (SSSHH)

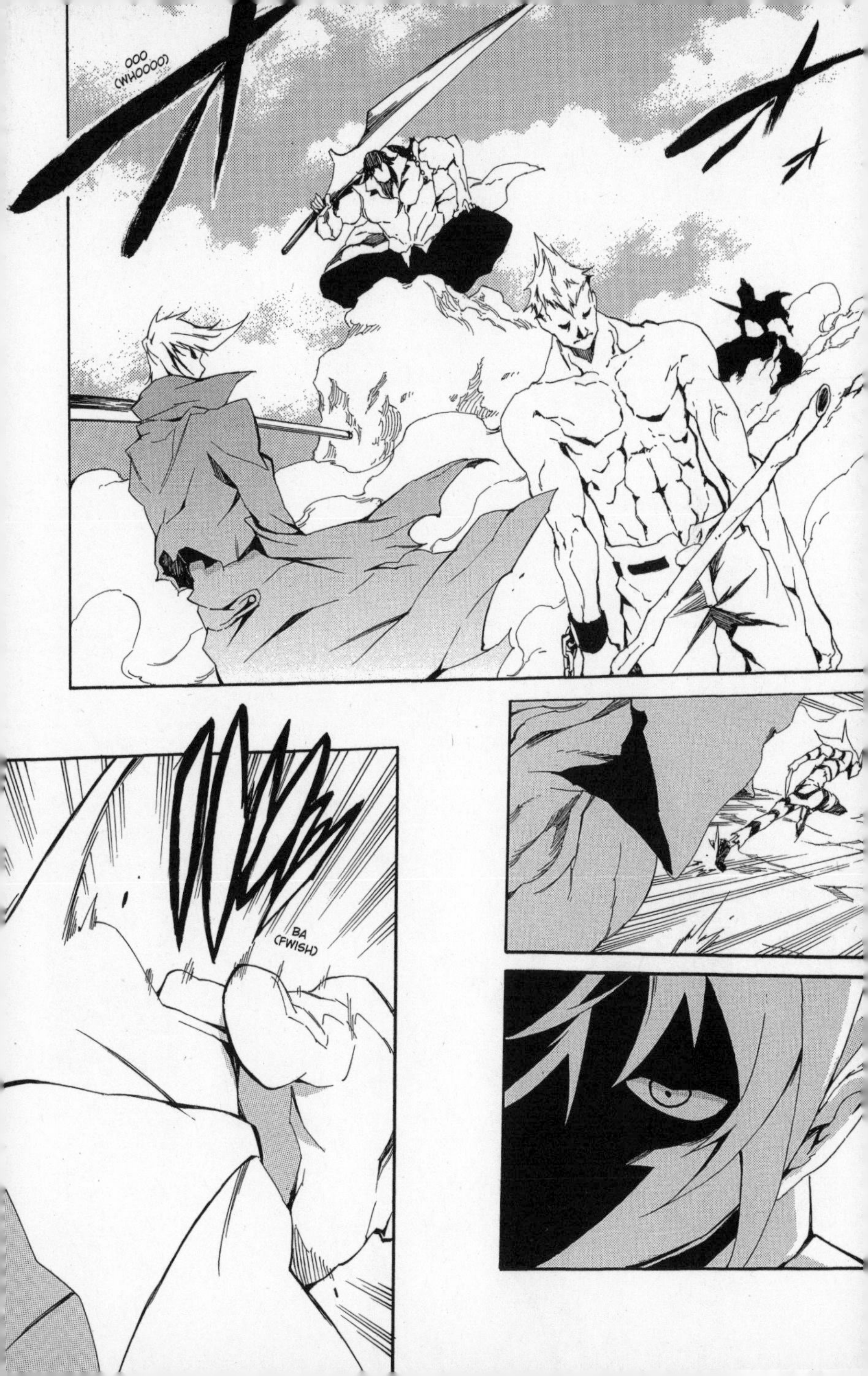
OOO
(WHOOOO)
BA
(FWISH)

IT'S GOING TO BE A PAIN BRINGING BACK ALL THESE HEADS.

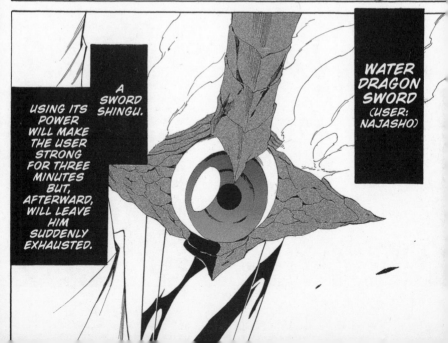

WATER DRAGON SWORD (USER: NAJASHO)

A SWORD SHINGU.

USING ITS POWER WILL MAKE THE USER STRONG FOR THREE MINUTES BUT, AFTERWARD, WILL LEAVE HIM SUDDENLY EXHAUSTED.

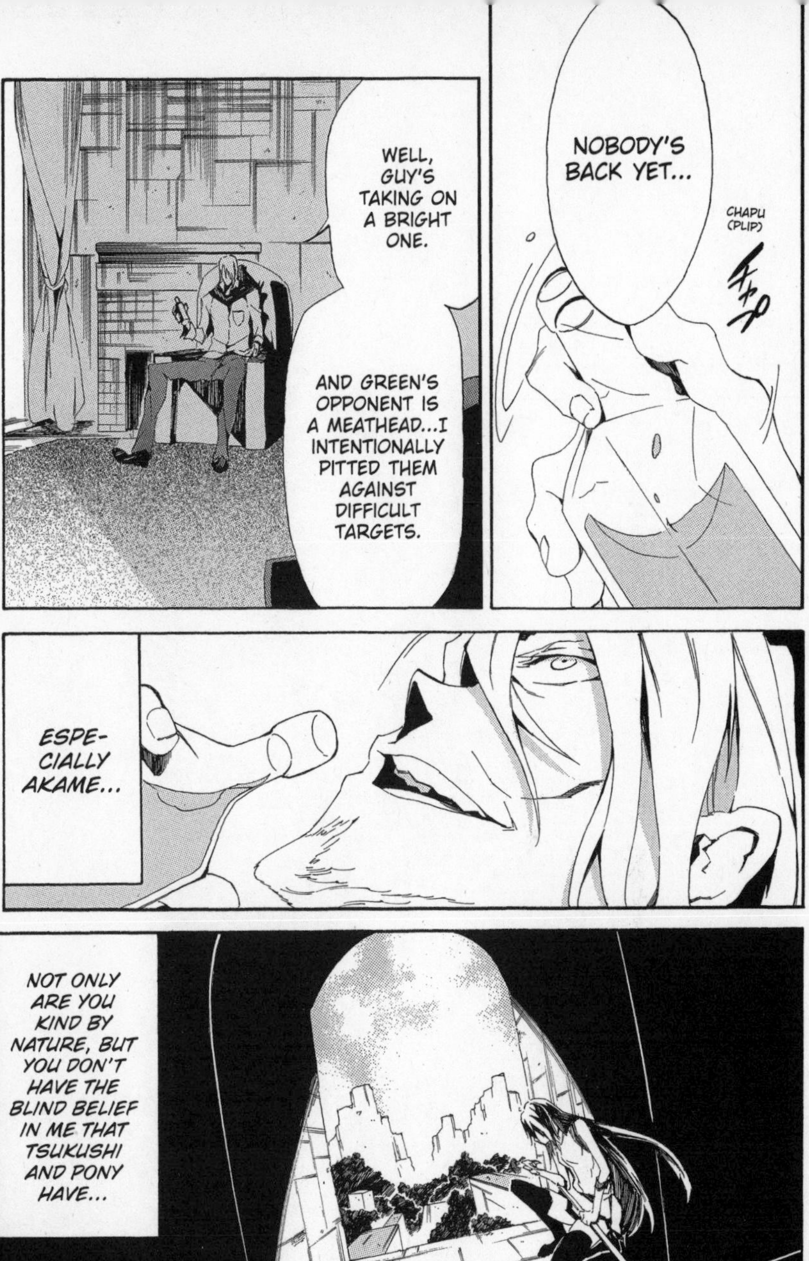
NOBODY'S BACK YET...
CHAPU (PLIP)
WELL, GUY'S TAKING ON A BRIGHT ONE.
AND GREEN'S OPPONENT IS A MEATHEAD...I INTENTIONALLY PITTED THEM AGAINST DIFFICULT TARGETS.
ESPE-CIALLY AKAME...
NOT ONLY ARE YOU KIND BY NATURE, BUT YOU DON'T HAVE THE BLIND BELIEF IN ME THAT TSUKUSHI AND PONY HAVE...

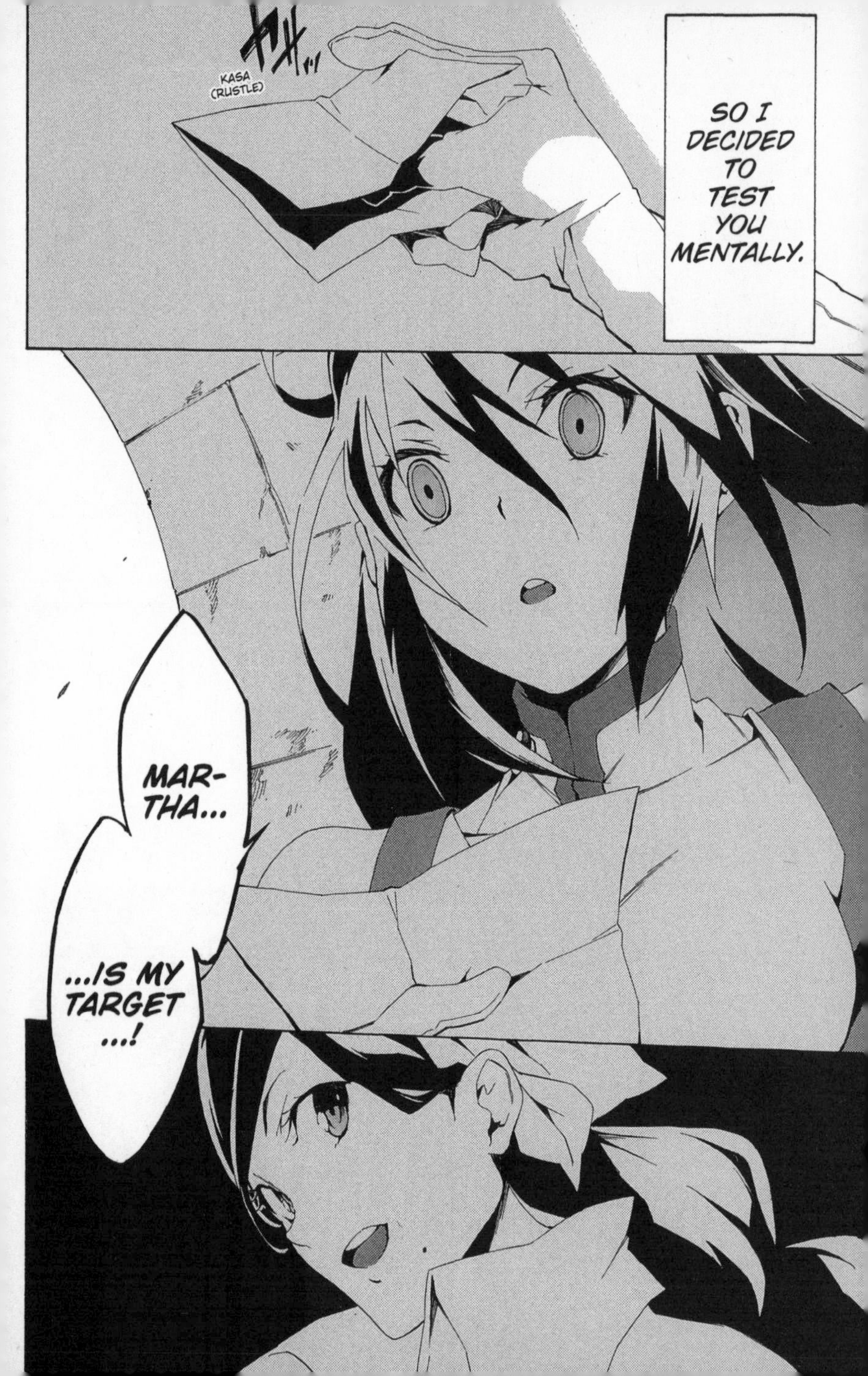
KASA (RUSTLE)
SO I DECIDED TO TEST YOU MENTALLY.
MARTHA...
...IS MY TARGET ...!

Chapter 4
First Mission (Part 2)

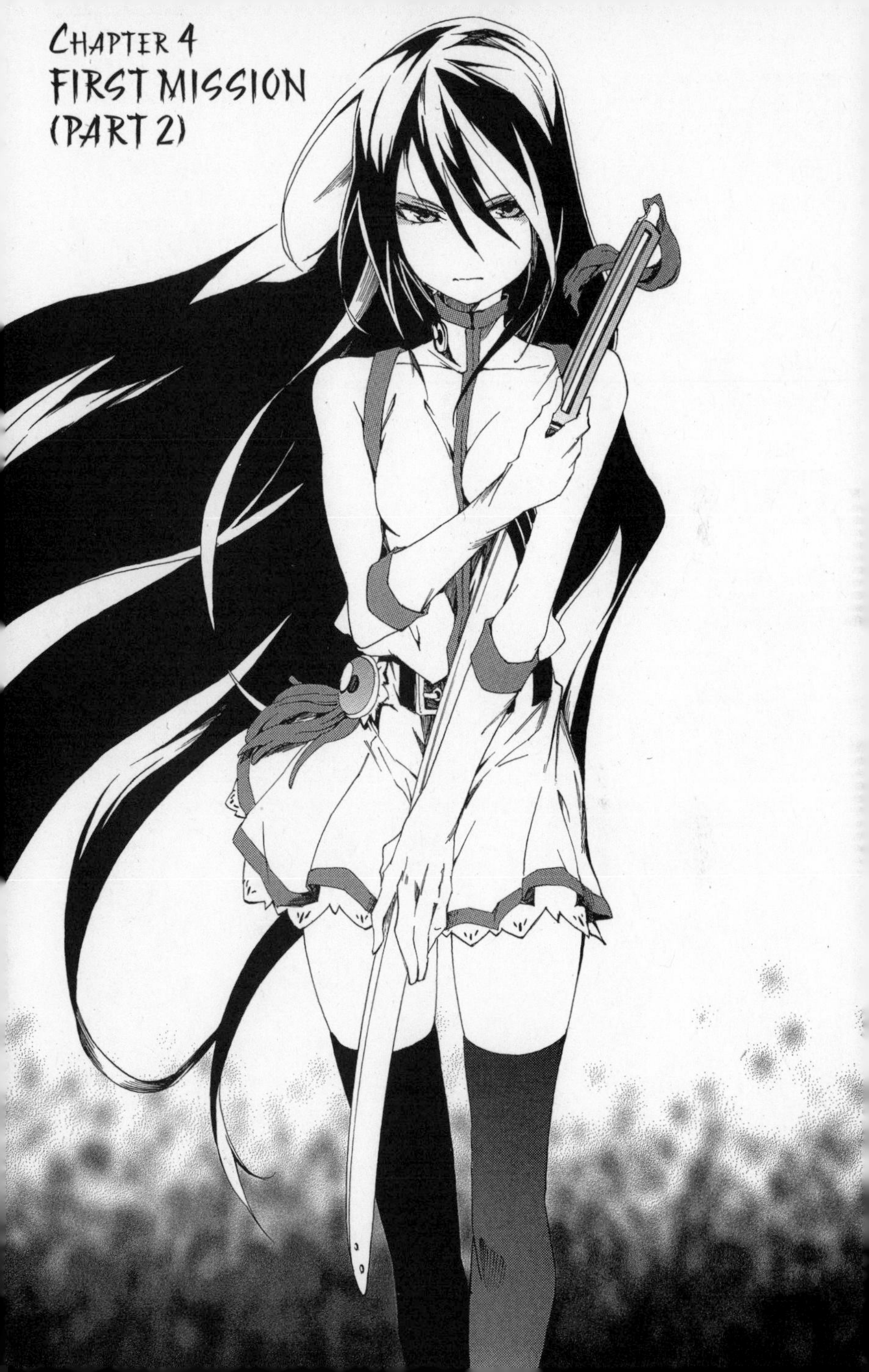

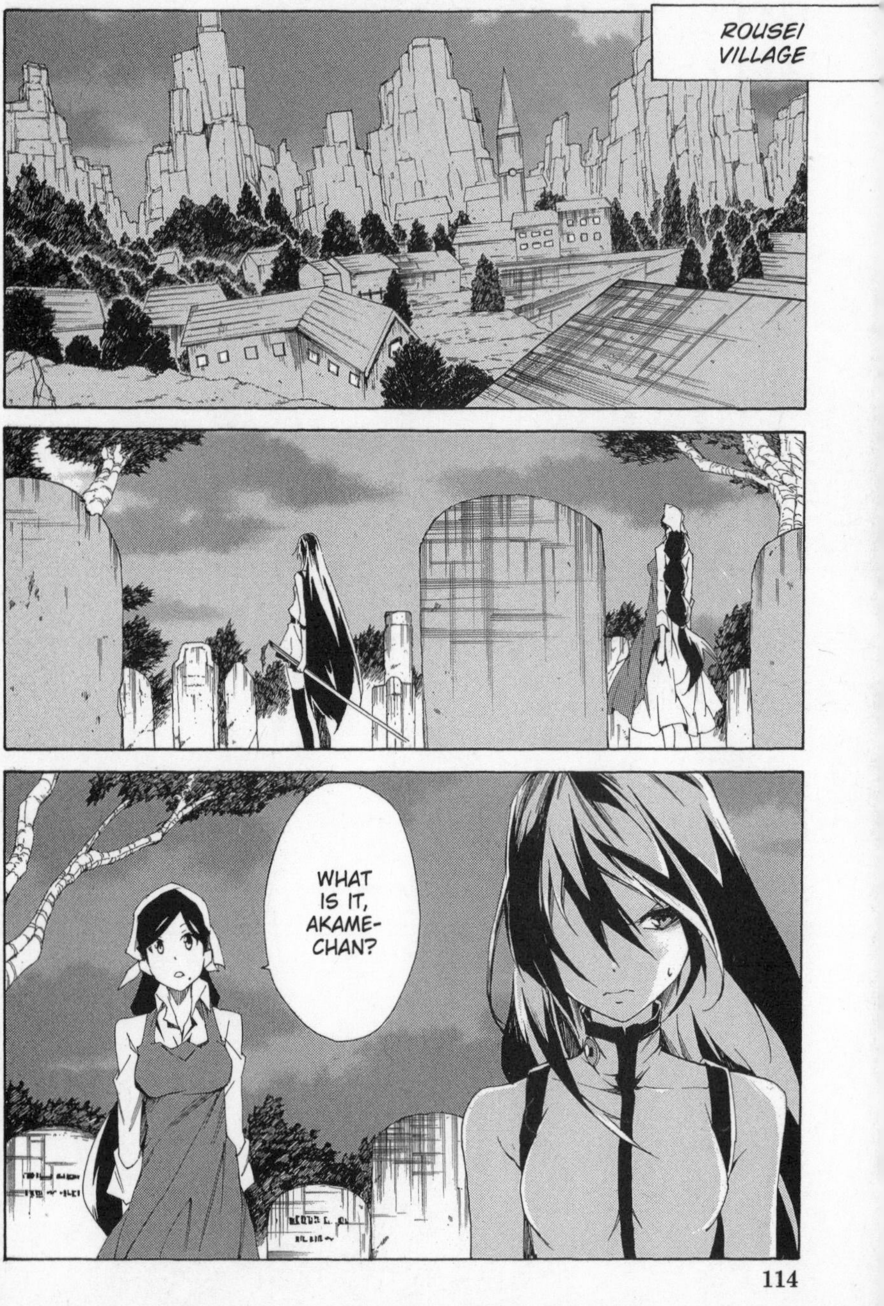
ROUSEI VILLAGE
WHAT IS IT, AKAME-CHAN?

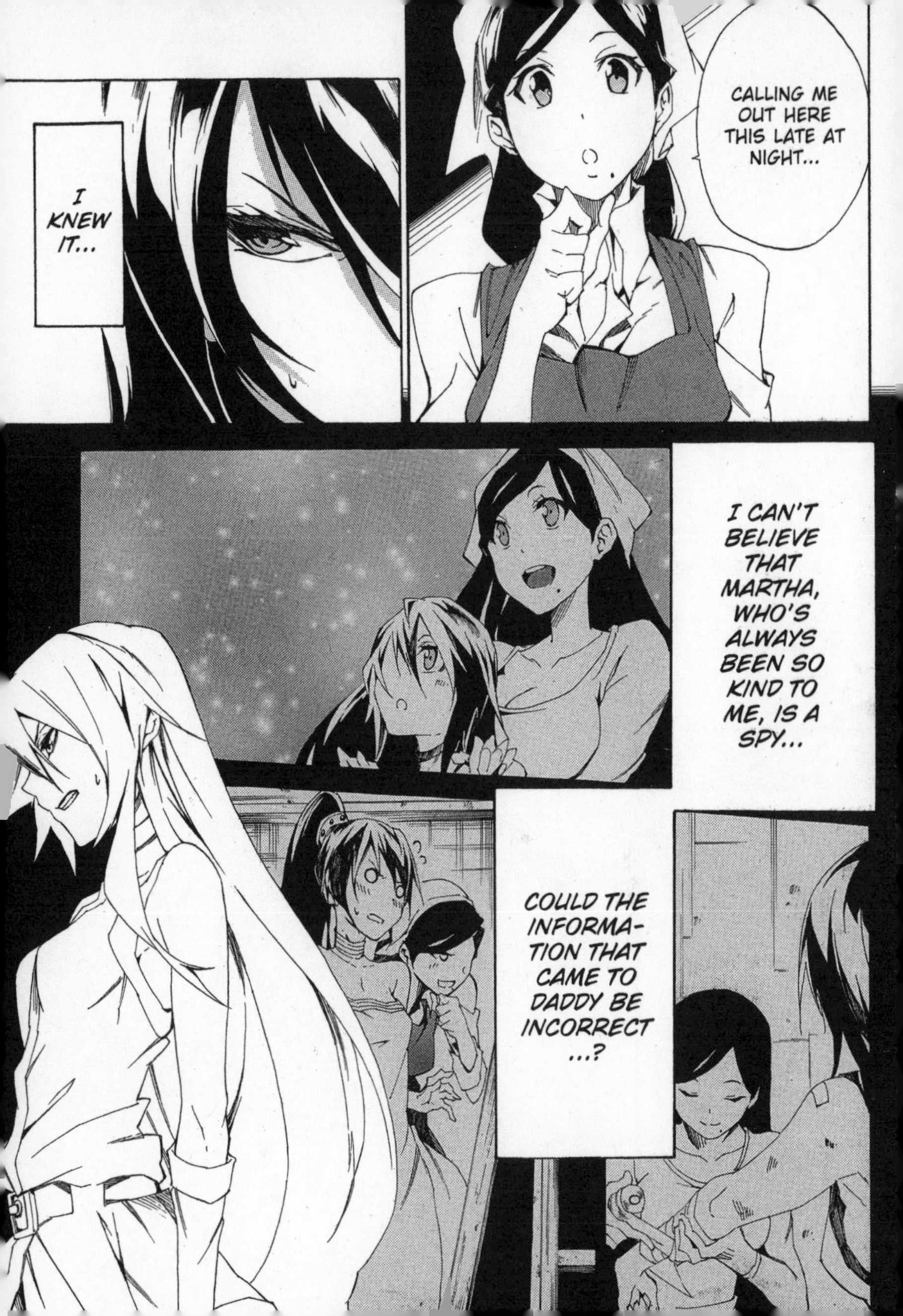
CALLING ME OUT HERE THIS LATE AT NIGHT...
I KNEW IT...
I CAN'T BELIEVE THAT MARTHA, WHO'S ALWAYS BEEN SO KIND TO ME, IS A SPY...
COULD THE INFORMATION THAT CAME TO DADDY BE INCORRECT ...?

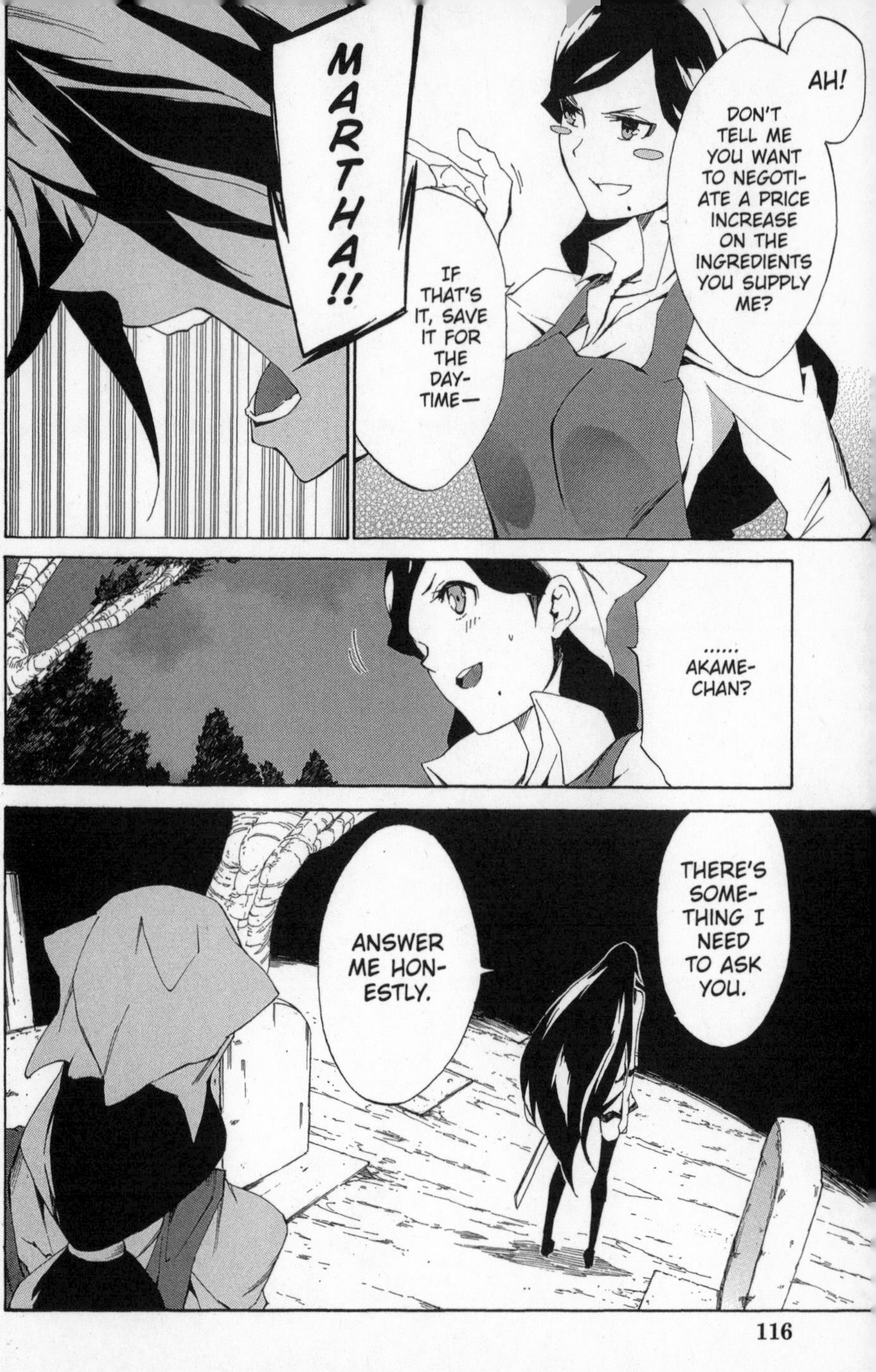
AH!
DON'T TELL ME YOU WANT TO NEGOTI-ATE A PRICE INCREASE ON THE INGREDIENTS YOU SUPPLY ME?
IF THAT'S IT, SAVE IT FOR THE DAY-TIME—
MARTHA!!
...... AKAME-CHAN?
THERE'S SOME-THING I NEED TO ASK YOU.
ANSWER ME HON-ESTLY.

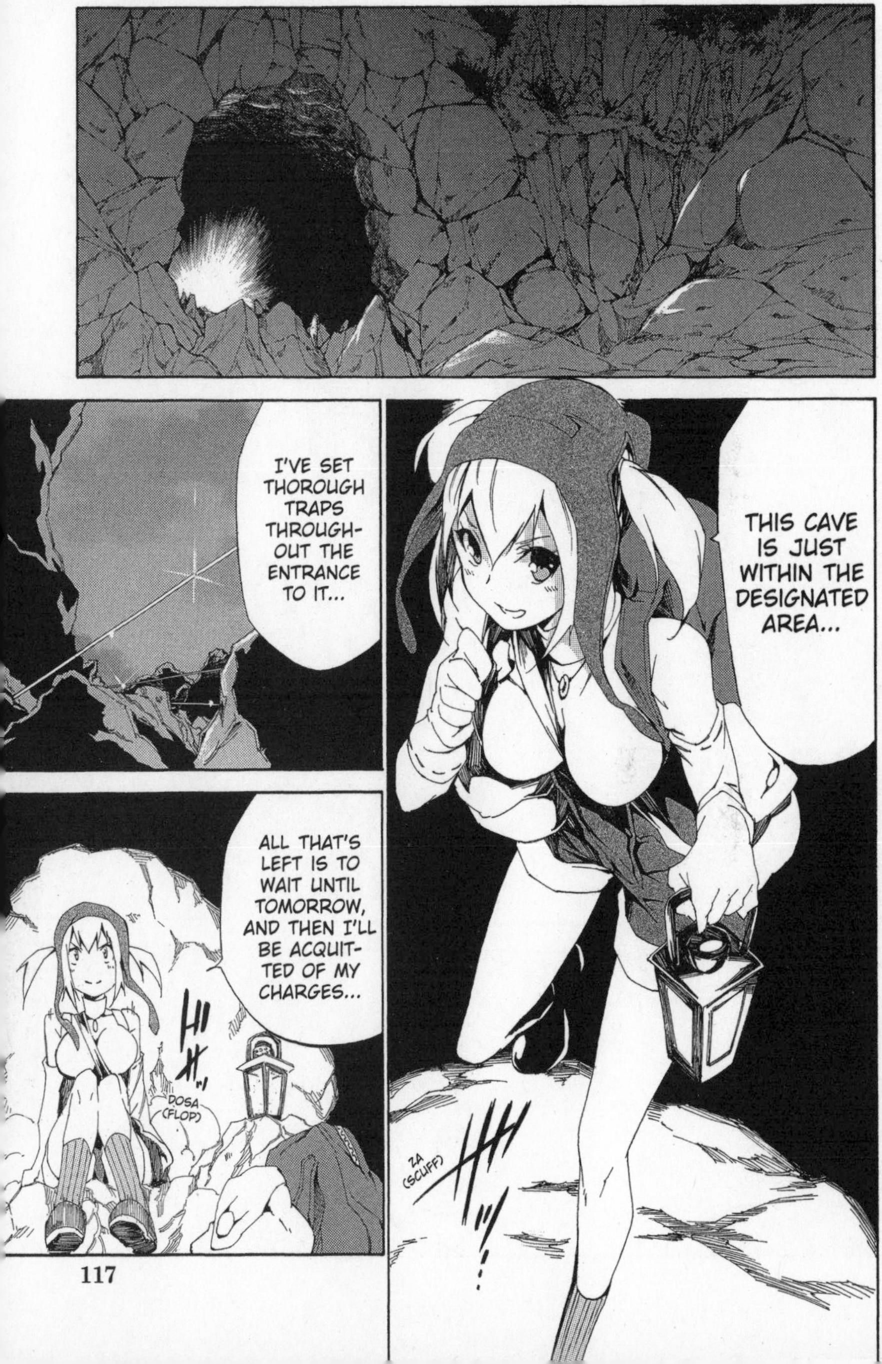
THIS CAVE IS JUST WITHIN THE DESIGNATED AREA...
ZA (SCUFF)
I'VE SET THOROUGH TRAPS THROUGHOUT THE ENTRANCE TO IT...
ALL THAT'S LEFT IS TO WAIT UNTIL TOMORROW, AND THEN I'LL BE ACQUITTED OF MY CHARGES...
DOSA (FLOP)

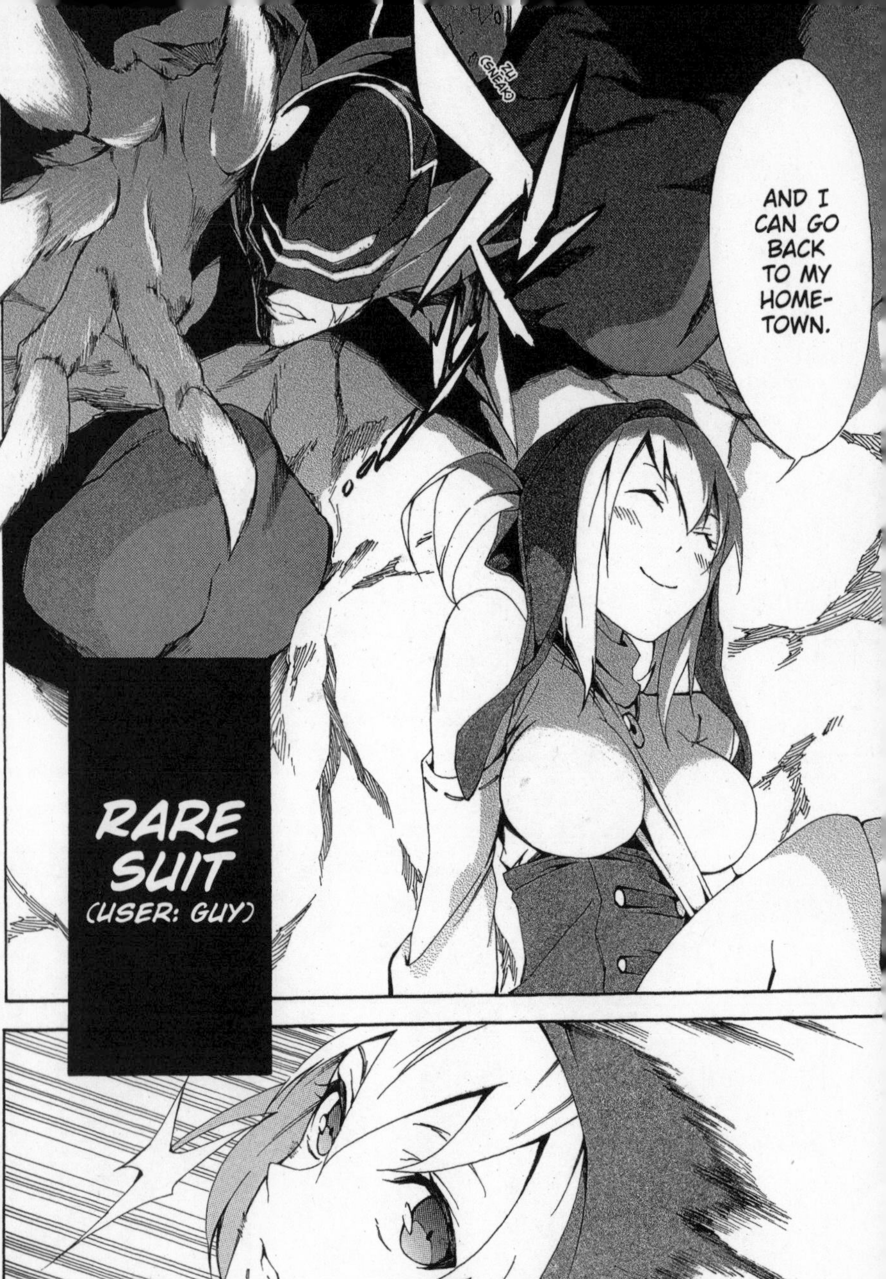
ZU
(SNEAK)
AND I CAN GO BACK TO MY HOME-TOWN.
RARE SUIT
(USER: GUY)

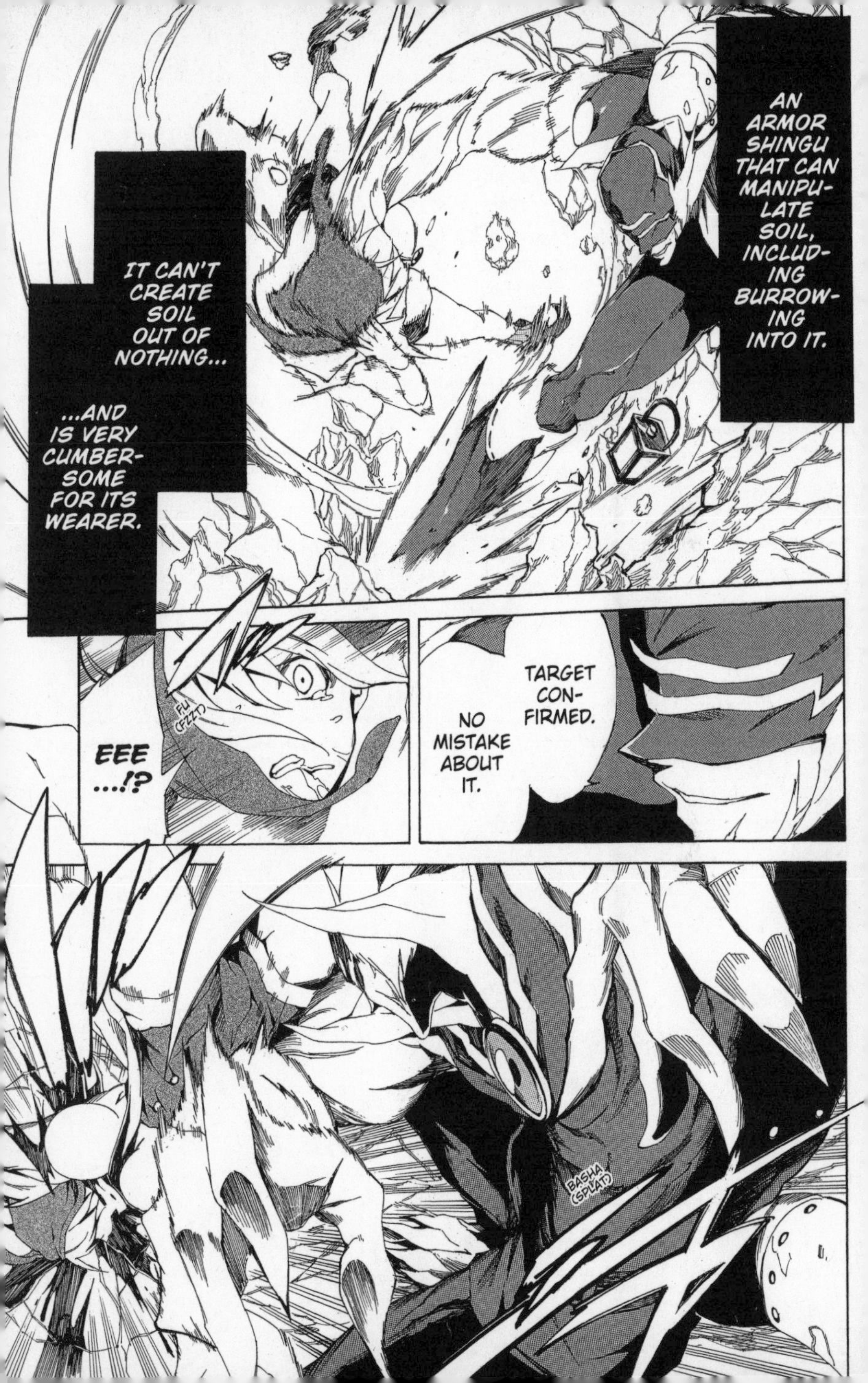
AN ARMOR SHINGU THAT CAN MANIPULATE SOIL, INCLUDING BURROWING INTO IT.
IT CAN'T CREATE SOIL OUT OF NOTHING...
...AND IS VERY CUMBERSOME FOR ITS WEARER.
TARGET CONFIRMED.
NO MISTAKE ABOUT IT.
FU (FZZZT)
EEE ...!?
BASHA (SPLAT)

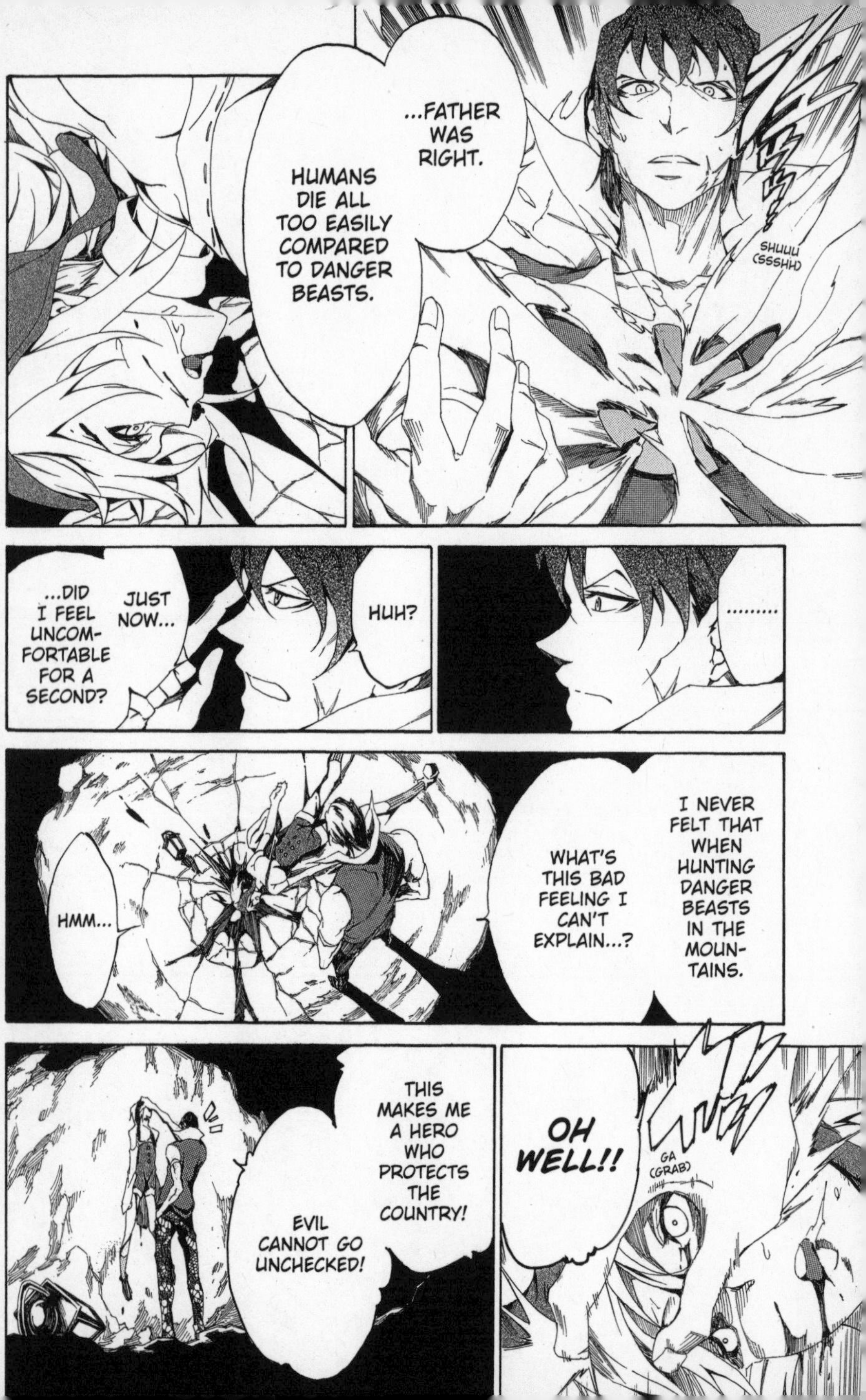
...FATHER WAS RIGHT.
HUMANS DIE ALL TOO EASILY COMPARED TO DANGER BEASTS.
SHUUU (SSSHH)
....
HUH?
JUST NOW...
...DID I FEEL UNCOM-FORTABLE FOR A SECOND?
I NEVER FELT THAT WHEN HUNTING DANGER BEASTS IN THE MOUN-TAINS.
WHAT'S THIS BAD FEELING I CAN'T EXPLAIN...?
HMM...
OH WELL!!
GA (GRAB)
THIS MAKES ME A HERO WHO PROTECTS THE COUNTRY!
EVIL CANNOT GO UNCHECKED!

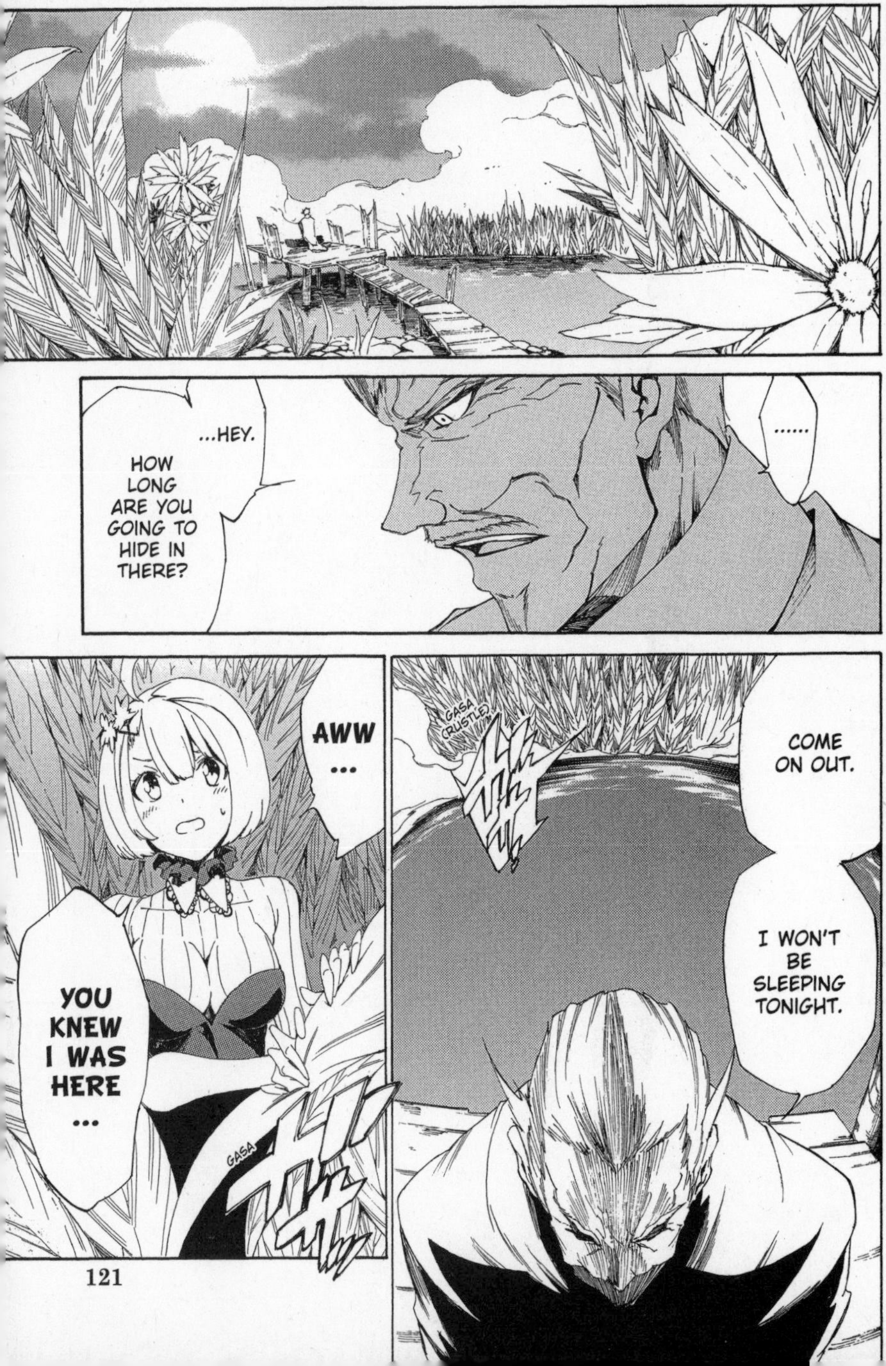
...
...HEY.
HOW LONG ARE YOU GOING TO HIDE IN THERE?
......
COME ON OUT.
GASA (RUSTLE)
AWW ...
I WON'T BE SLEEPING TONIGHT.
YOU KNEW I WAS HERE ...
GASA

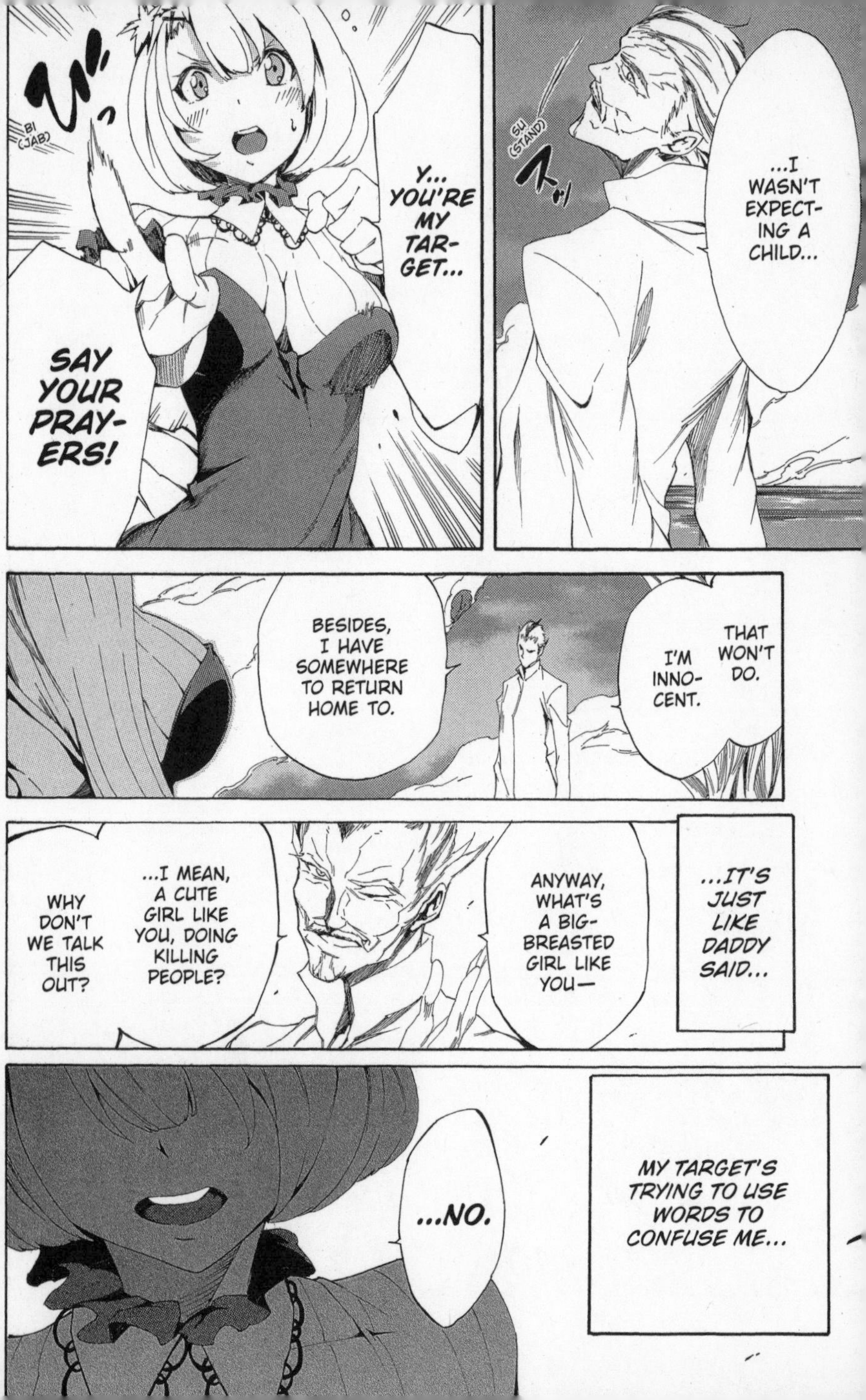
SU (STAND)
...I WASN'T EXPECTING A CHILD...
Y... YOU'RE MY TARGET...
BI (JAB)
SAY YOUR PRAYERS!
THAT WON'T DO.
I'M INNOCENT.
BESIDES, I HAVE SOMEWHERE TO RETURN HOME TO.
...IT'S JUST LIKE DADDY SAID...
ANYWAY, WHAT'S A BIG-BREASTED GIRL LIKE YOU—
...I MEAN, A CUTE GIRL LIKE YOU, DOING KILLING PEOPLE?
WHY DON'T WE TALK THIS OUT?
MY TARGET'S TRYING TO USE WORDS TO CONFUSE ME...
...NO.

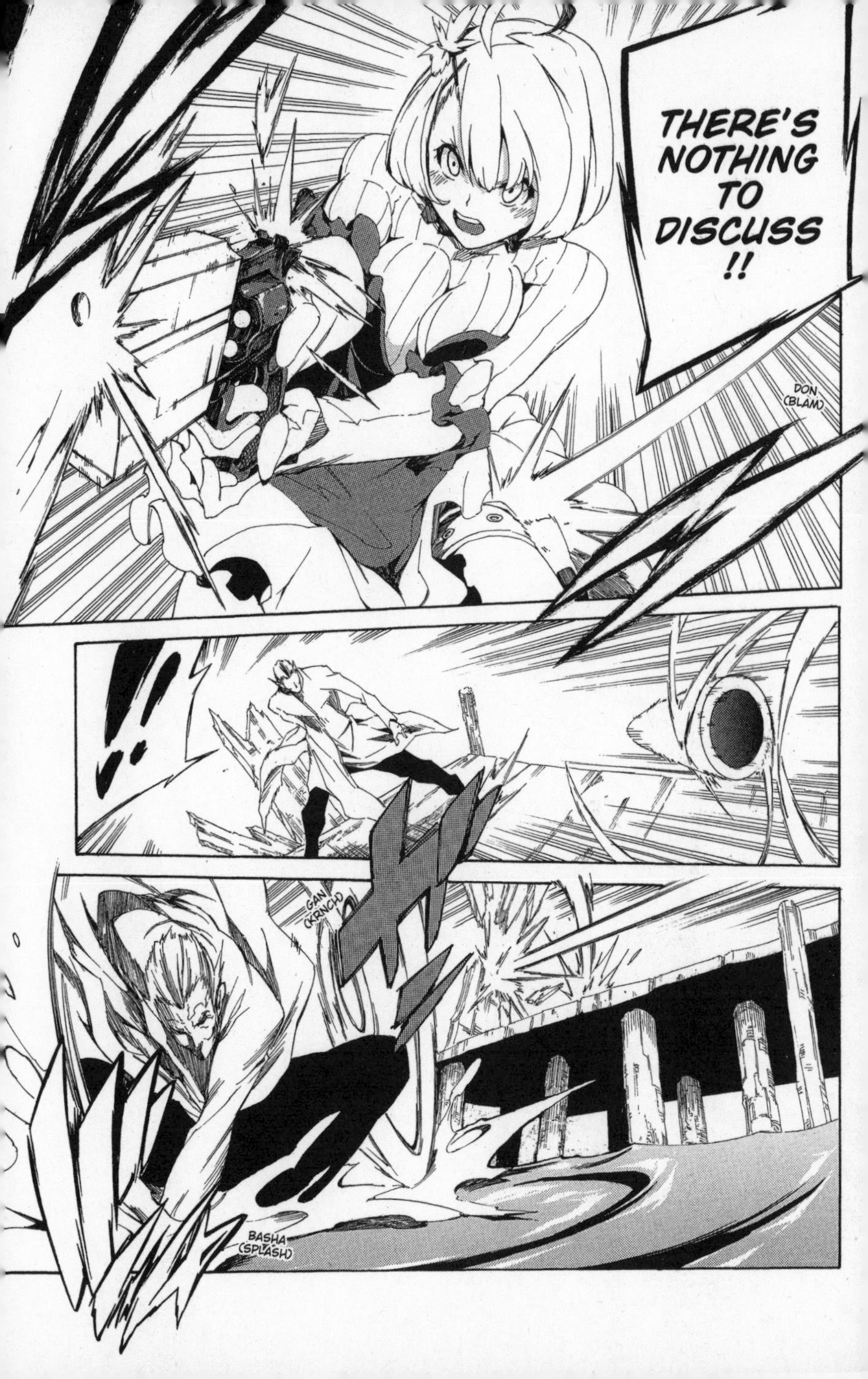
THERE'S NOTHING TO DISCUSS !!
DON (BLAM)
GAN (KRNCH)
BASHA (SPLASH)

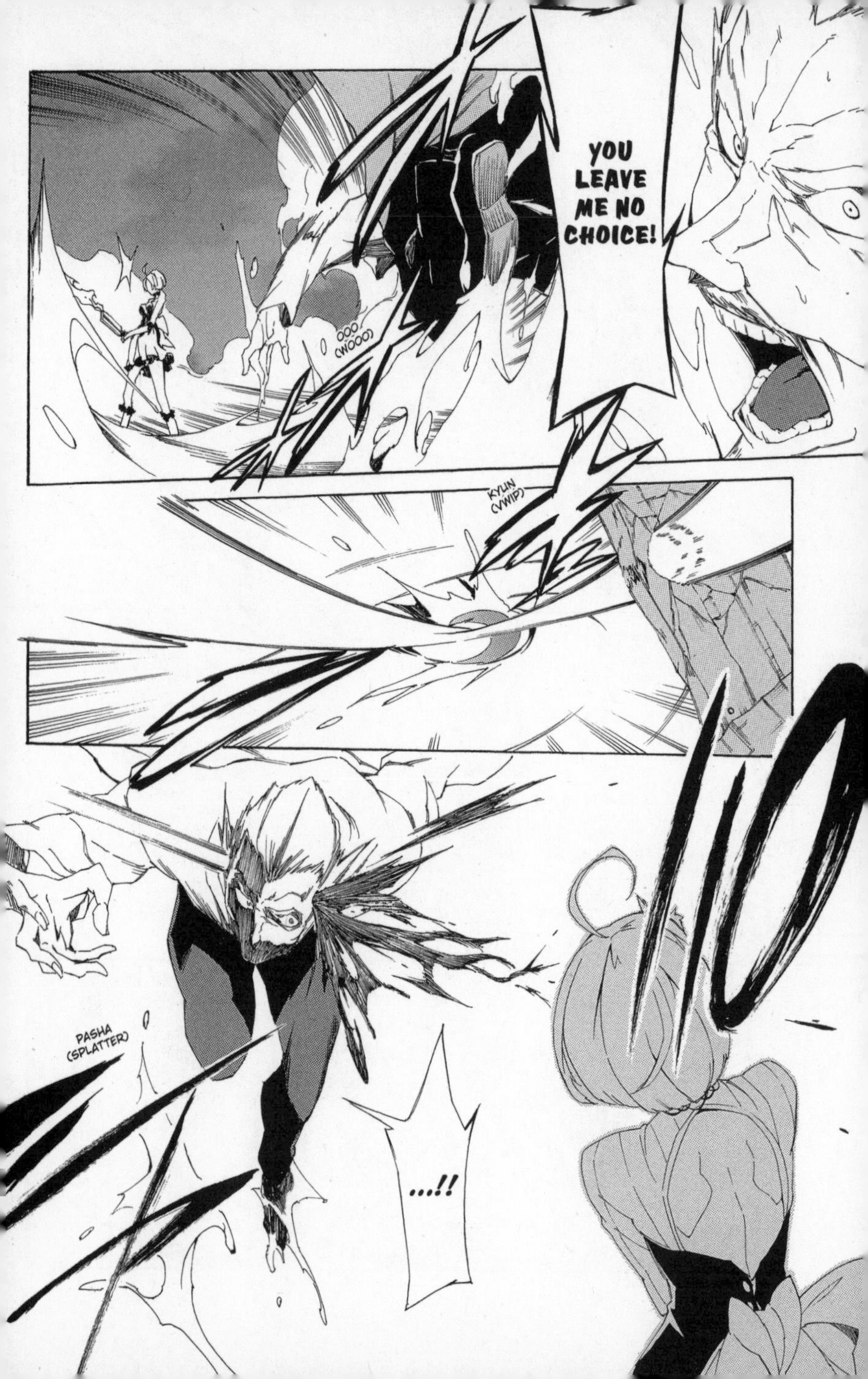
YOU LEAVE ME NO CHOICE!
OOO (WOOO)
KYUN (VWIP)
PASHA (SPLATTER)
...!!

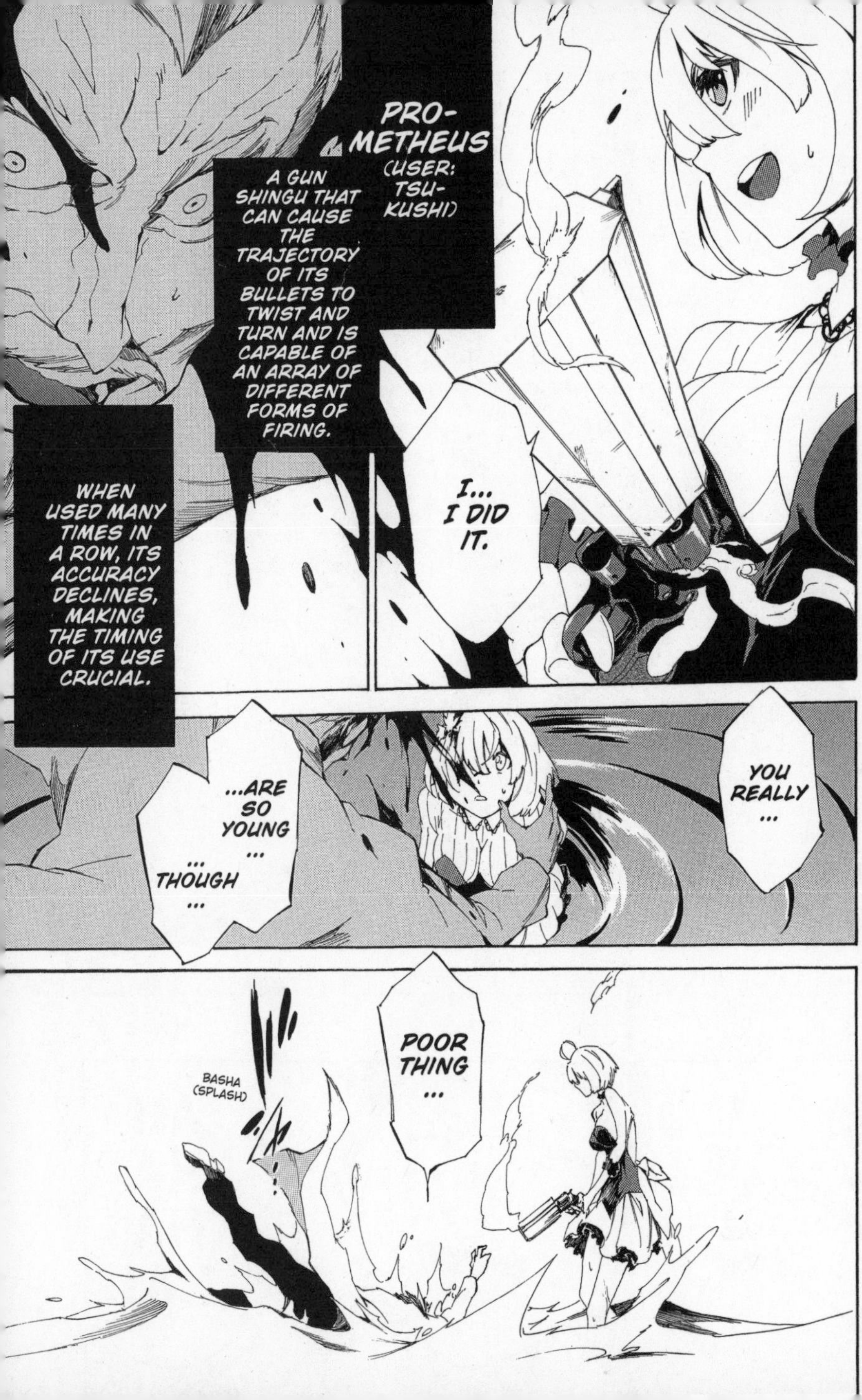
PRO-METHEUS (USER: TSU-KUSHI)
A GUN SHINGU THAT CAN CAUSE THE TRAJECTORY OF ITS BULLETS TO TWIST AND TURN AND IS CAPABLE OF AN ARRAY OF DIFFERENT FORMS OF FIRING.
WHEN USED MANY TIMES IN A ROW, ITS ACCURACY DECLINES, MAKING THE TIMING OF ITS USE CRUCIAL.
I... I DID IT.
YOU REALLY ...
...ARE SO YOUNG ... THOUGH ...
POOR THING ...
BASHA (SPLASH)

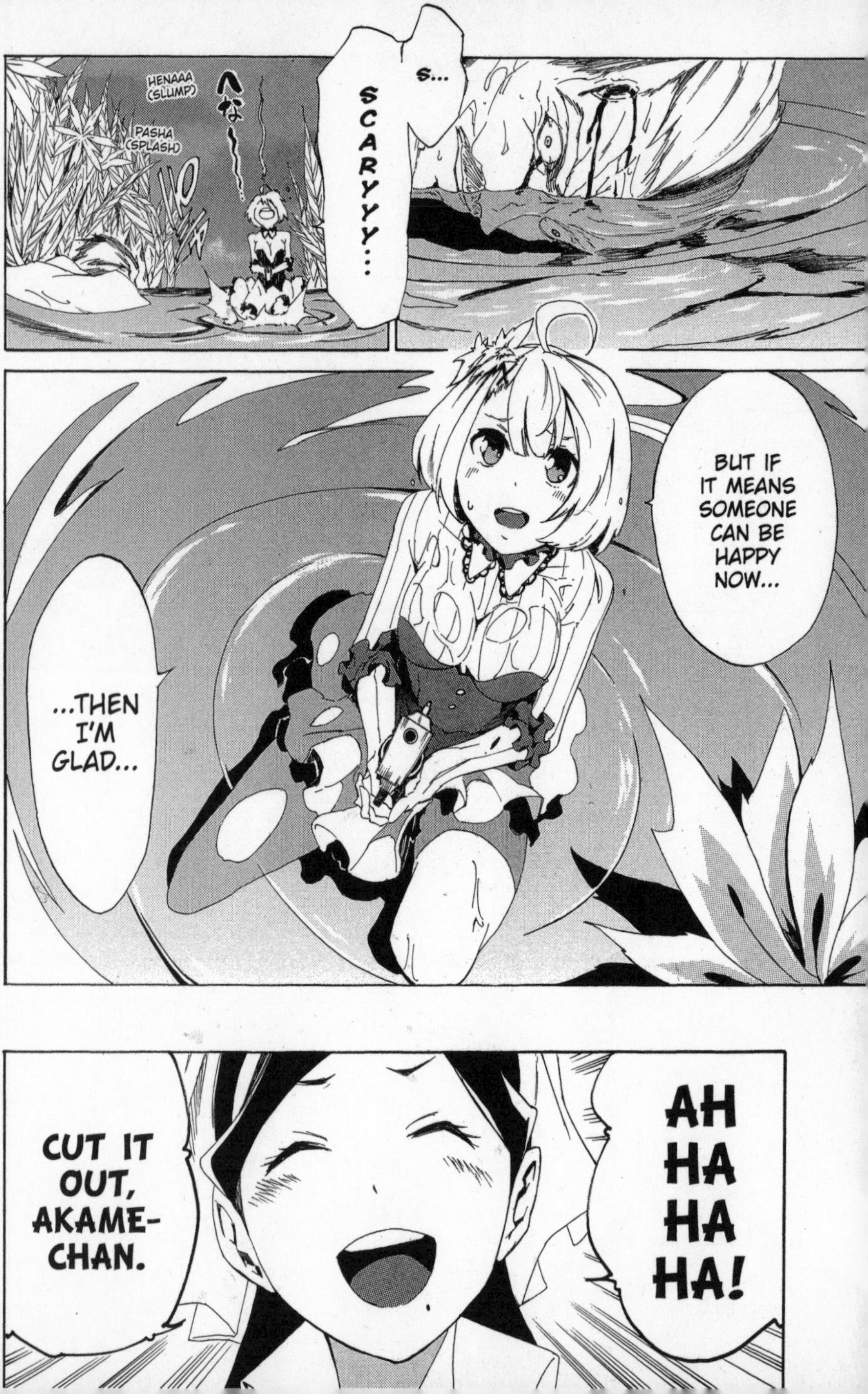
S...
SCARYYY...
へな～
HENAAA (SLUMP)
PASHA (SPLASH)
BUT IF IT MEANS SOMEONE CAN BE HAPPY NOW...
...THEN I'M GLAD...
AH HA HA HA HA!
CUT IT OUT, AKAME-CHAN.

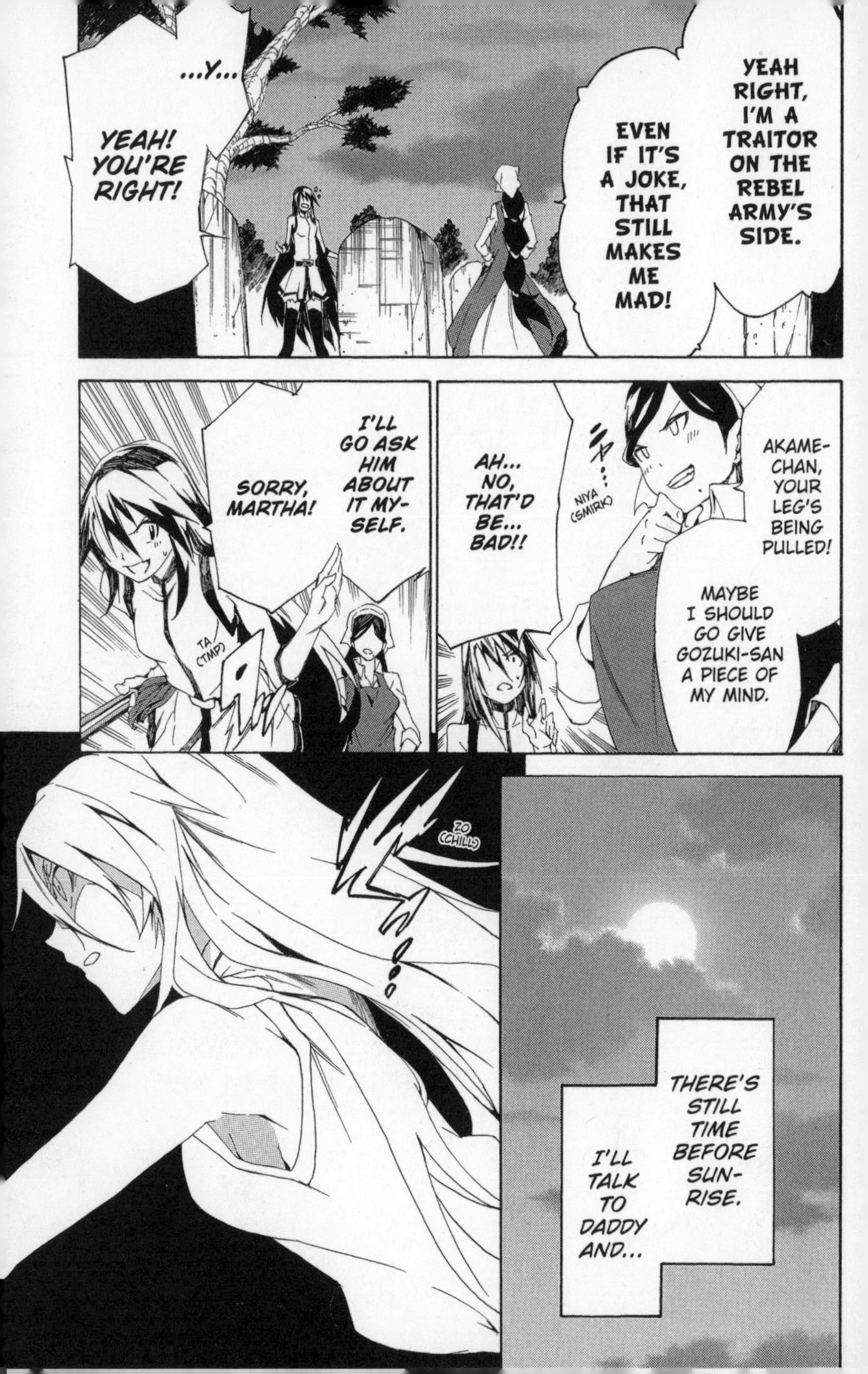
YEAH RIGHT, I'M A TRAITOR ON THE REBEL ARMY'S SIDE.
EVEN IF IT'S A JOKE, THAT STILL MAKES ME MAD!
...Y...
YEAH! YOU'RE RIGHT!
AKAME-CHAN, YOUR LEG'S BEING PULLED!
MAYBE I SHOULD GO GIVE GOZUKI-SAN A PIECE OF MY MIND.
NIYA (SMIRK)
AH... NO, THAT'D BE... BAD!!
I'LL GO ASK HIM ABOUT IT MY-SELF.
SORRY, MARTHA!
TA (TMP)
ZO (CHILL)
THERE'S STILL TIME BEFORE SUN-RISE.
I'LL TALK TO DADDY AND...

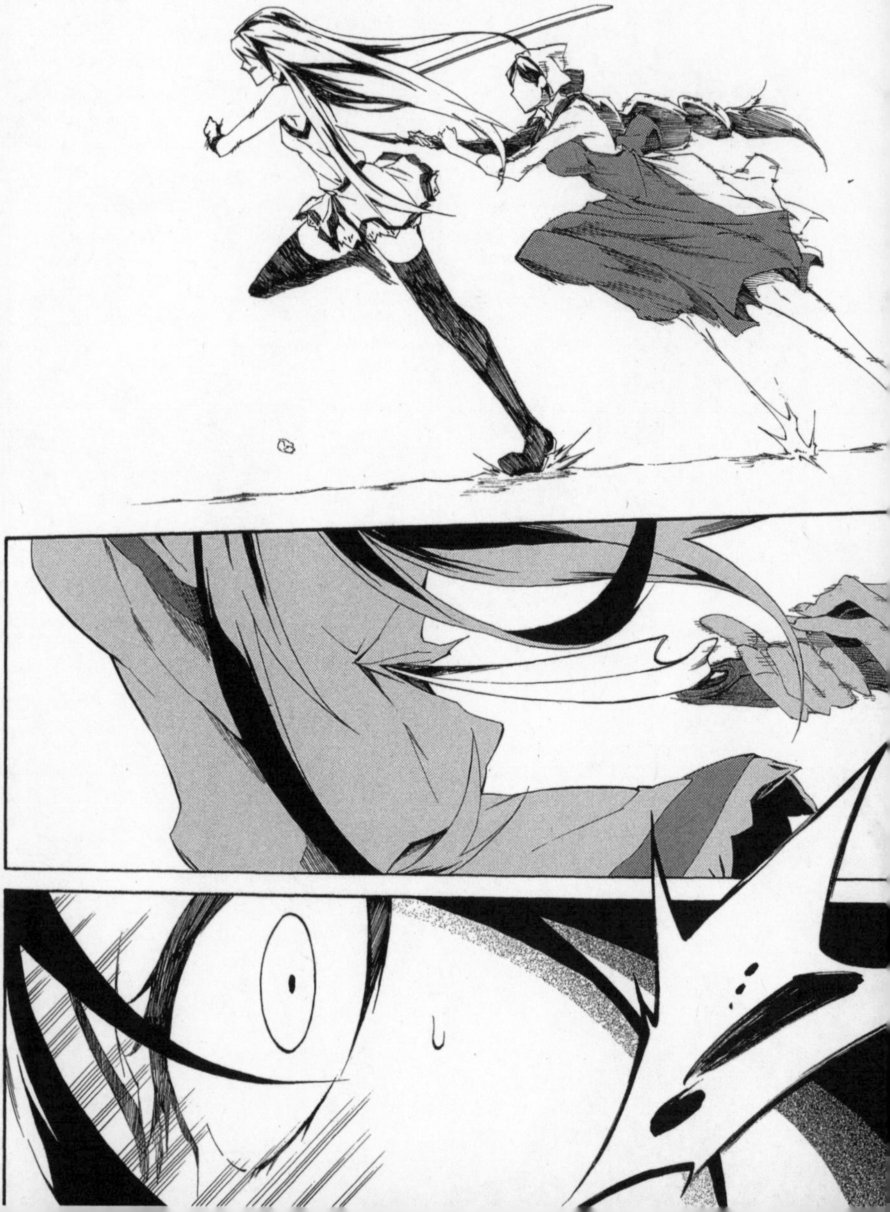

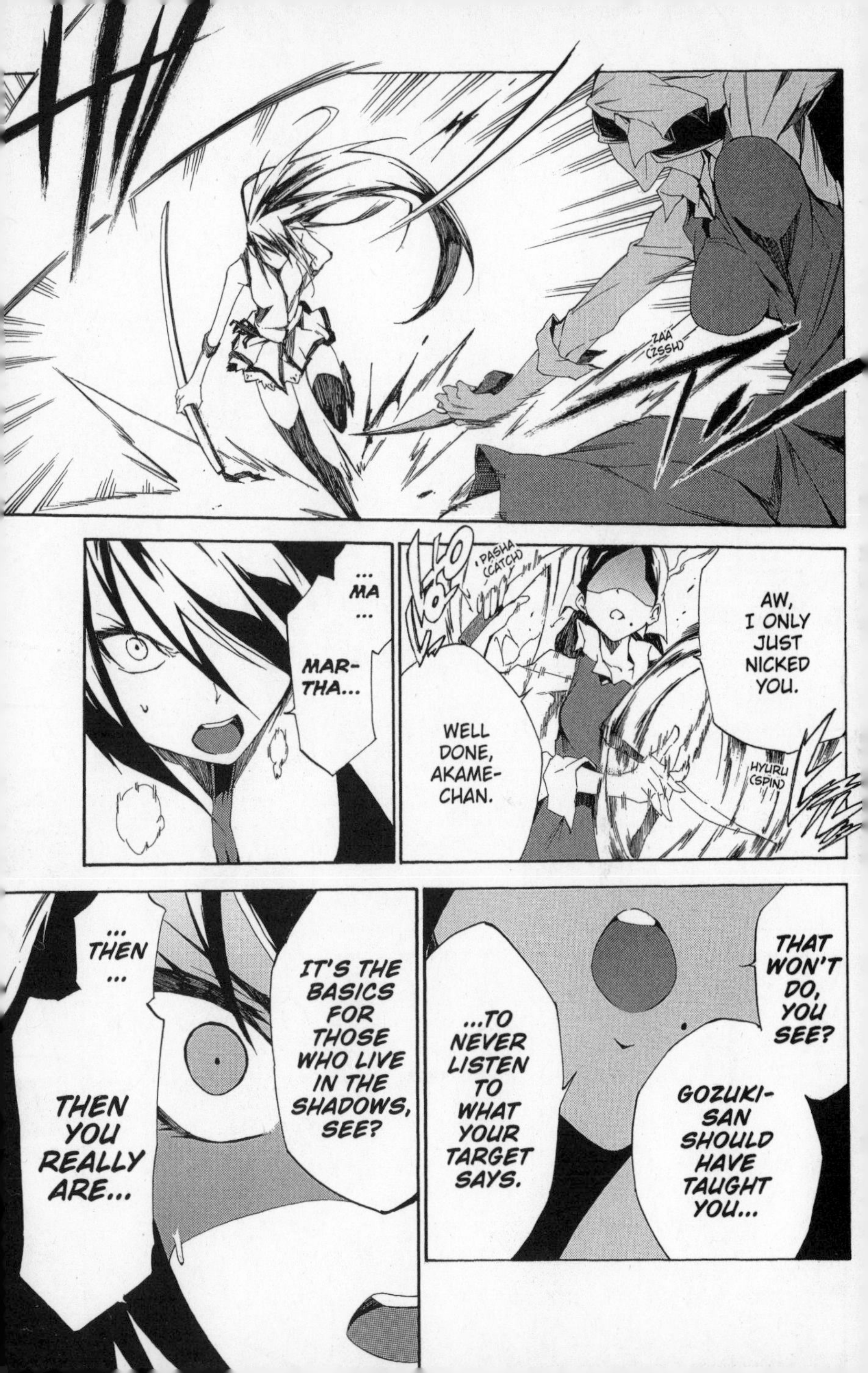
ZAA (ZSSH)
PASHA (CATCH)
AW, I ONLY JUST NICKED YOU.
WELL DONE, AKAME-CHAN.
HYURU (SPIN)
...MA...
MAR-THA...
THAT WON'T DO, YOU SEE?
GOZUKI-SAN SHOULD HAVE TAUGHT YOU...
...TO NEVER LISTEN TO WHAT YOUR TARGET SAYS.
IT'S THE BASICS FOR THOSE WHO LIVE IN THE SHADOWS, SEE?
...THEN...
THEN YOU REALLY ARE...

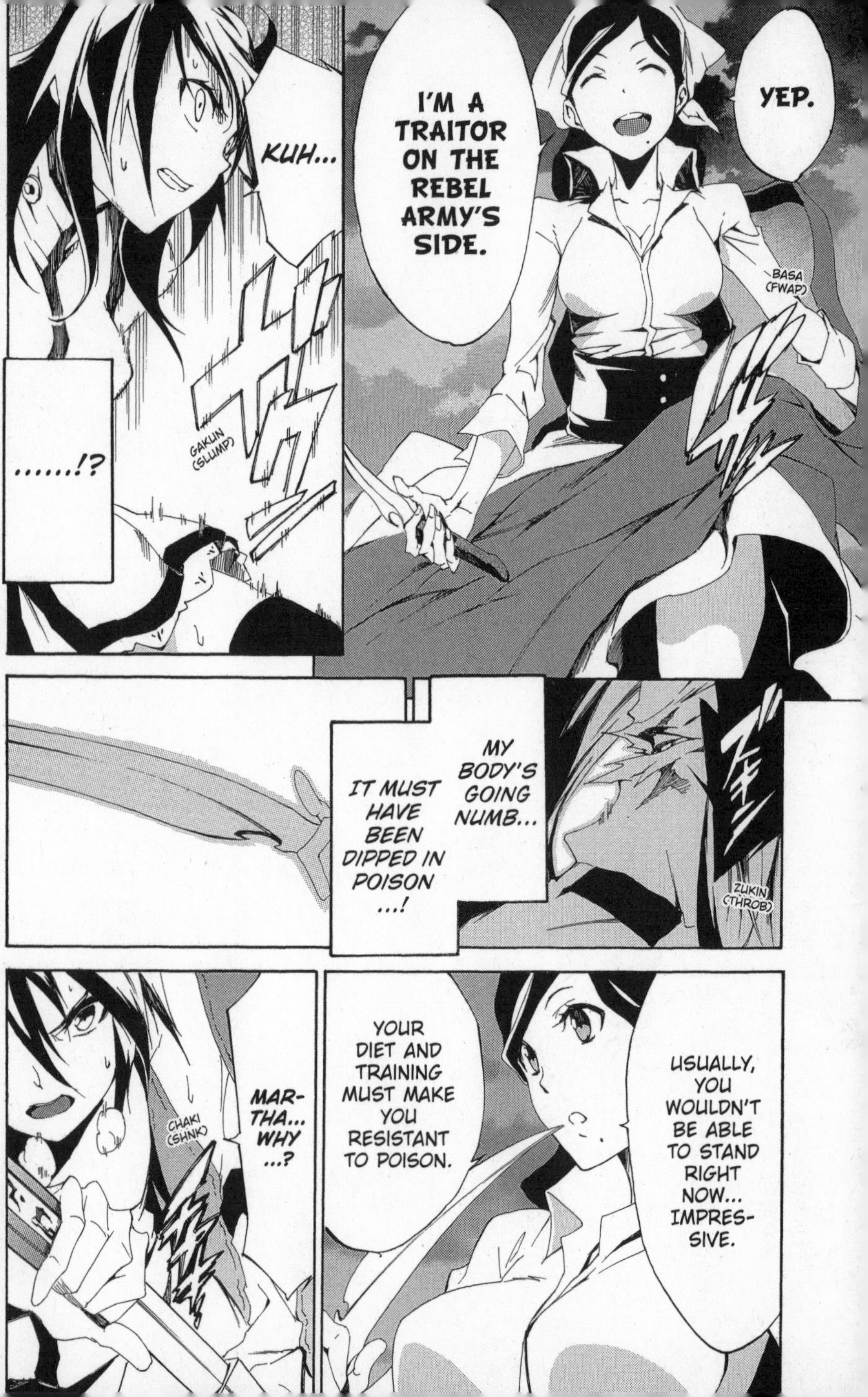
YEP.
I'M A TRAITOR ON THE REBEL ARMY'S SIDE.
BASA (FWAP)
KUH...
GAKUN (SLUMP)
......!?
ZUKIN (THROB)
MY BODY'S GOING NUMB...
IT MUST HAVE BEEN DIPPED IN POISON ...!
USUALLY, YOU WOULDN'T BE ABLE TO STAND RIGHT NOW... IMPRES- SIVE.
YOUR DIET AND TRAINING MUST MAKE YOU RESISTANT TO POISON.
MAR- THA... WHY ...?
CHAKI (SHNK)

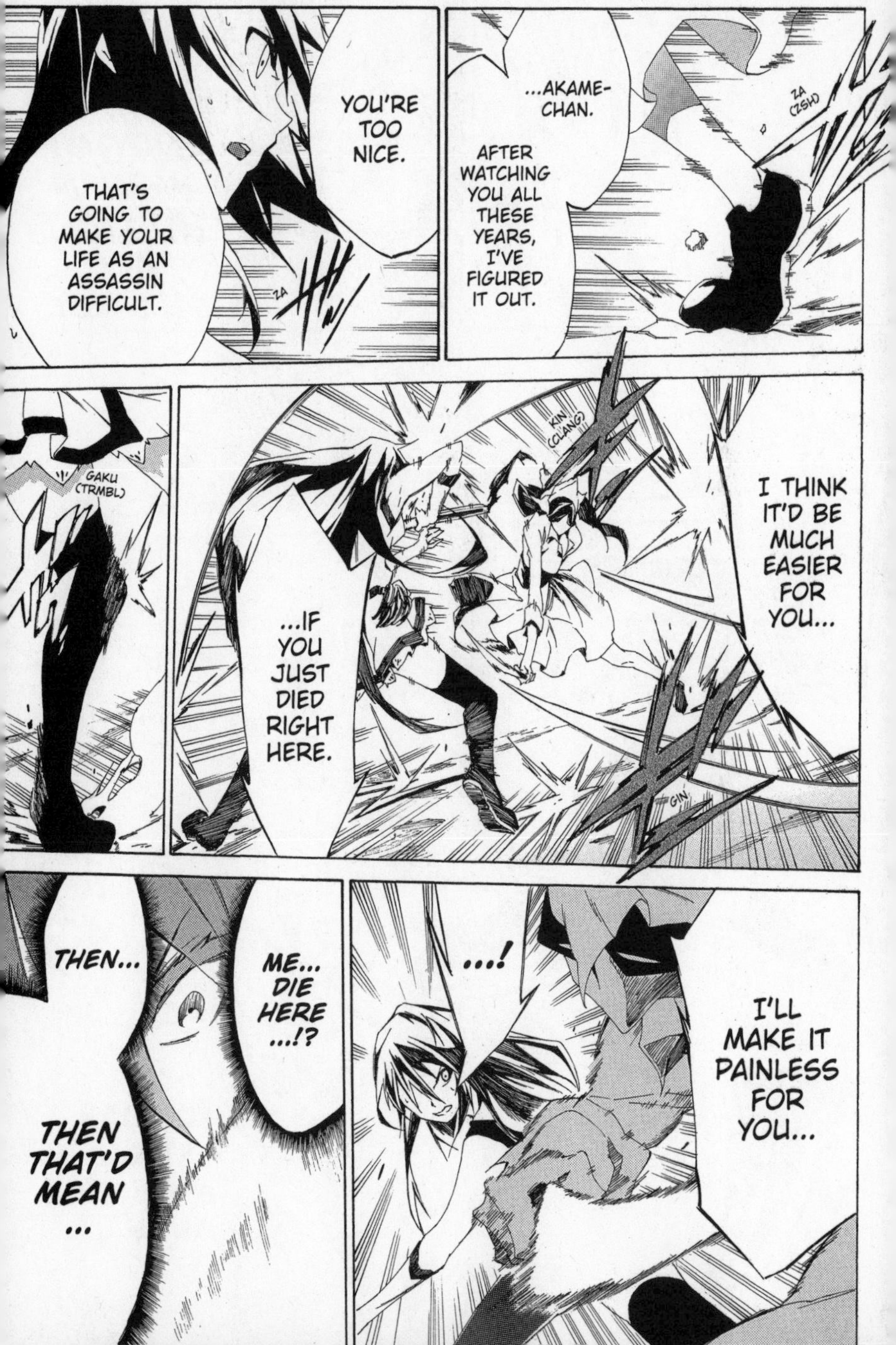
ZA (ZSH)
...AKAME-CHAN.
AFTER WATCHING YOU ALL THESE YEARS, I'VE FIGURED IT OUT.
YOU'RE TOO NICE.
THAT'S GOING TO MAKE YOUR LIFE AS AN ASSASSIN DIFFICULT.
ZA
I THINK IT'D BE MUCH EASIER FOR YOU...
KIN (CLANG)
...IF YOU JUST DIED RIGHT HERE.
GIN
GAKU (TRMBL)
I'LL MAKE IT PAINLESS FOR YOU...
...!
ME... DIE HERE ...!?
THEN...
THEN THAT'D MEAN ...

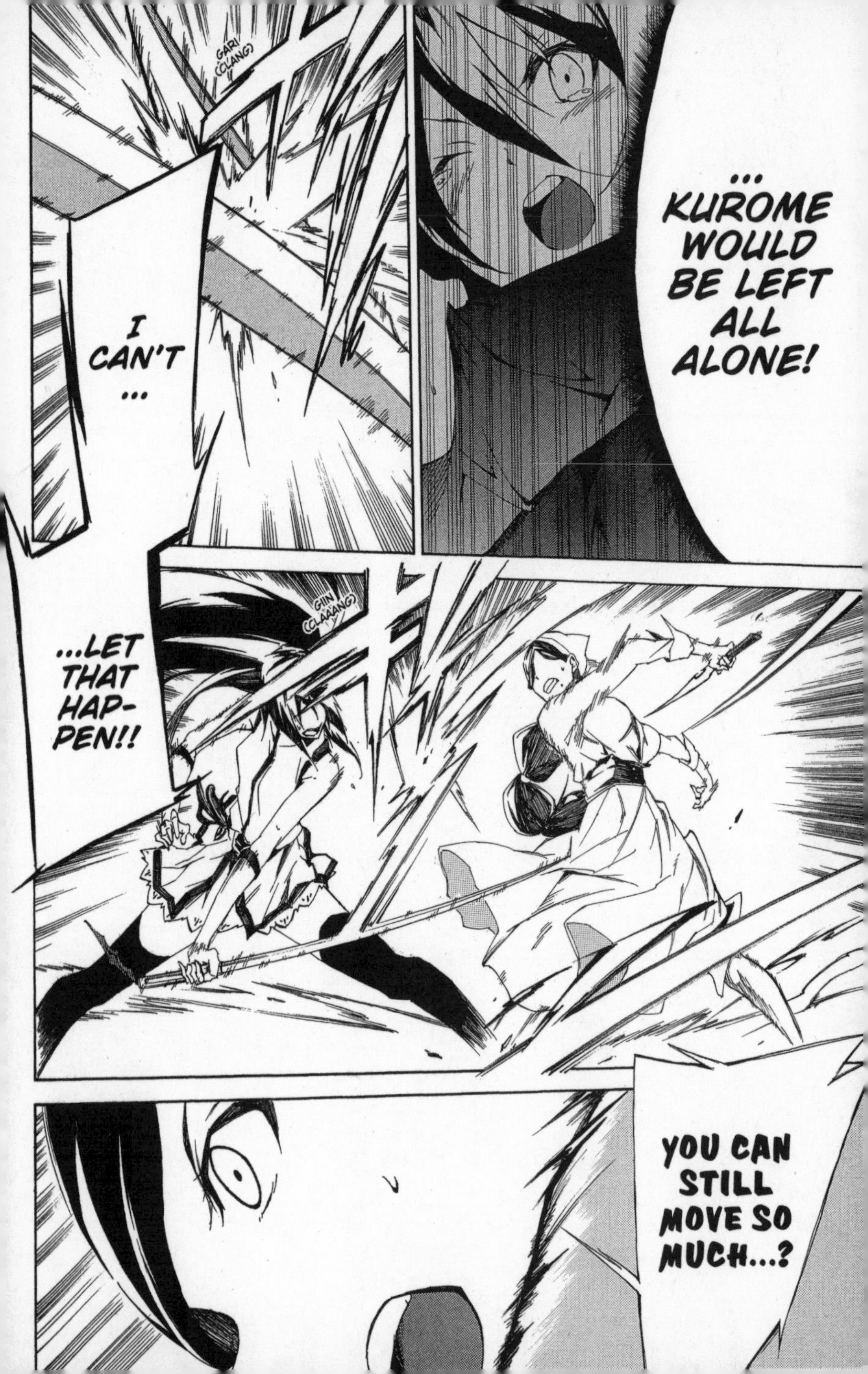
GARI (CLANG)
... KUROME WOULD BE LEFT ALL ALONE!
I CAN'T ...
GIN (CLAAANG)
...LET THAT HAP- PEN!!
YOU CAN STILL MOVE SO MUCH...?

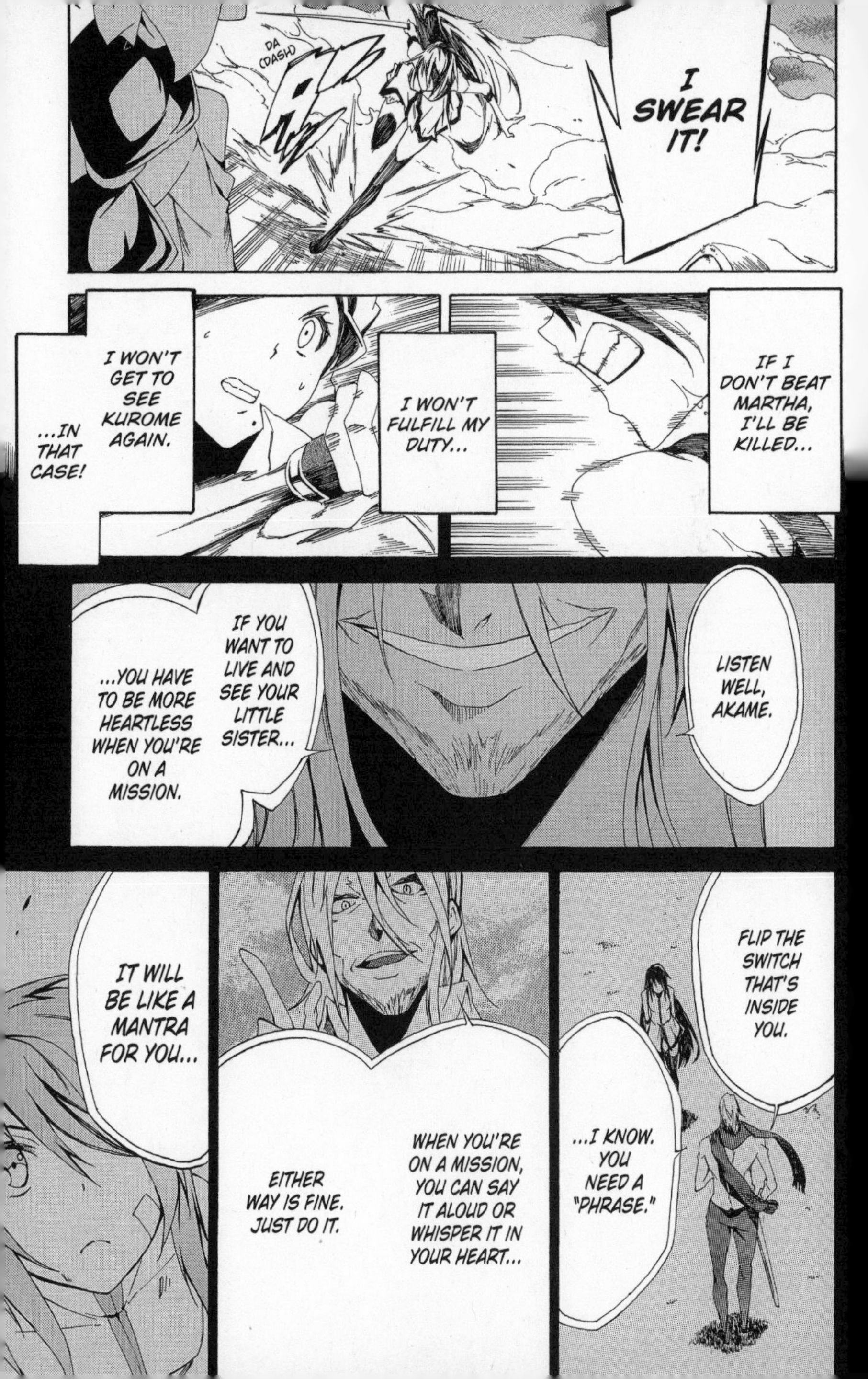
I SWEAR IT!
DA (DASH)
IF I DON'T BEAT MARTHA, I'LL BE KILLED...
I WON'T FULFILL MY DUTY...
I WON'T GET TO SEE KUROME AGAIN.
...IN THAT CASE!
LISTEN WELL, AKAME.
IF YOU WANT TO LIVE AND SEE YOUR LITTLE SISTER...
...YOU HAVE TO BE MORE HEARTLESS WHEN YOU'RE ON A MISSION.
FLIP THE SWITCH THAT'S INSIDE YOU.
...I KNOW. YOU NEED A "PHRASE."
WHEN YOU'RE ON A MISSION, YOU CAN SAY IT ALOUD OR WHISPER IT IN YOUR HEART...
EITHER WAY IS FINE. JUST DO IT.
IT WILL BE LIKE A MANTRA FOR YOU...

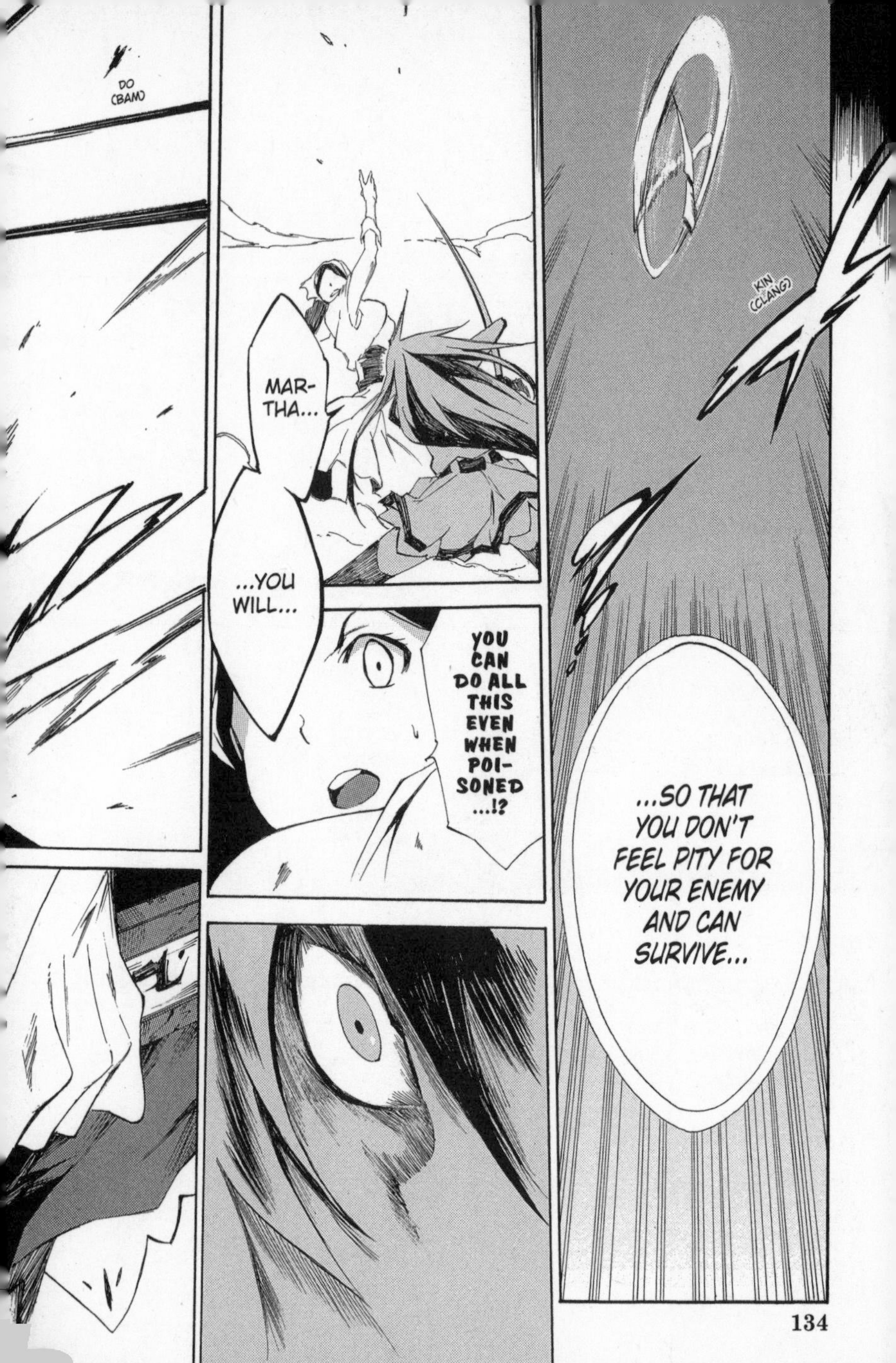
KIN (CLANG)
...SO THAT YOU DON'T FEEL PITY FOR YOUR ENEMY AND CAN SURVIVE...
MAR-THA...
...YOU WILL...
DO (BAM)
YOU CAN DO ALL THIS EVEN WHEN POI-SONED ...!?

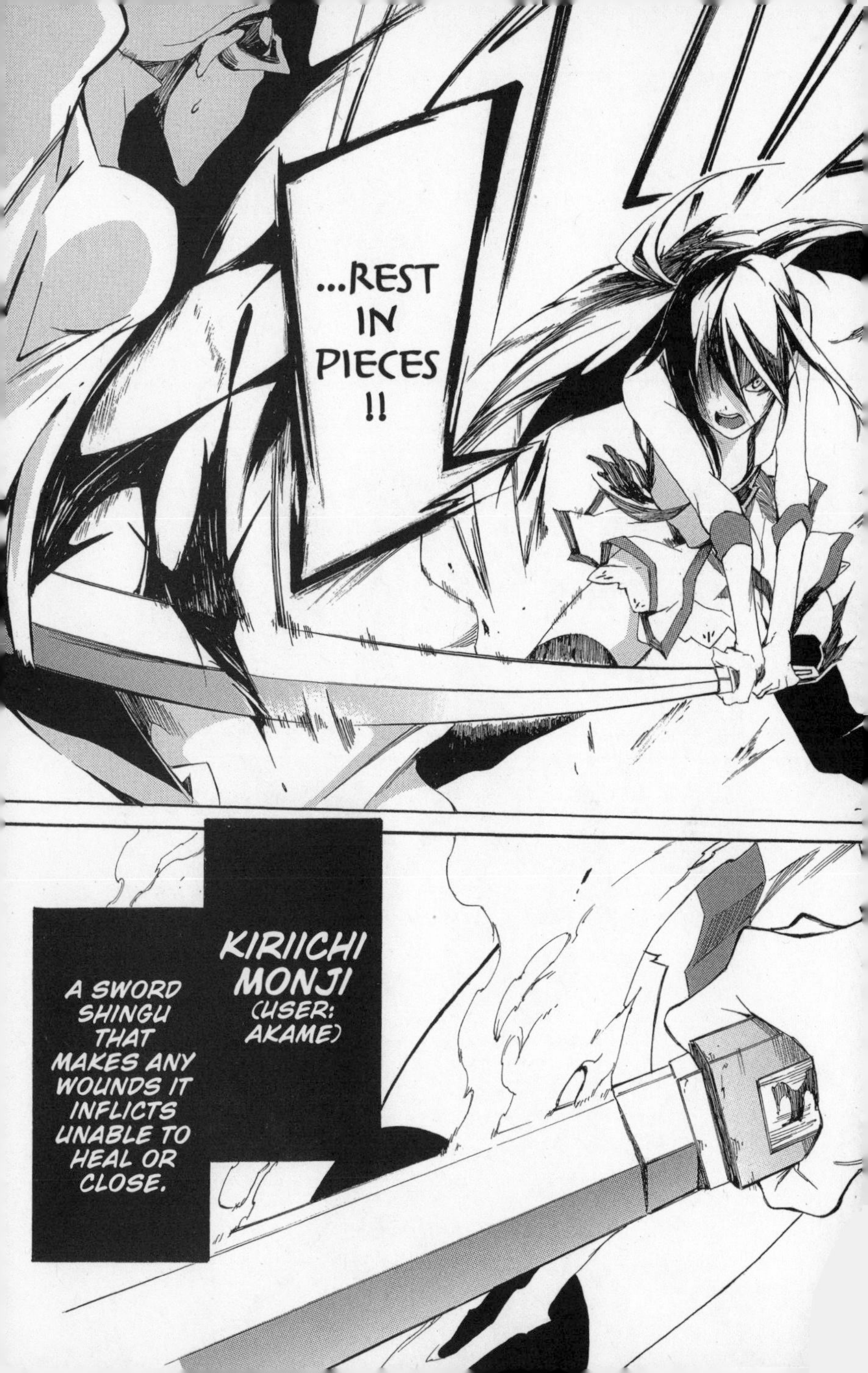
...REST IN PIECES !!
KIRIICHI MONJI (USER: AKAME)
A SWORD SHINGU THAT MAKES ANY WOUNDS IT INFLICTS UNABLE TO HEAL OR CLOSE.

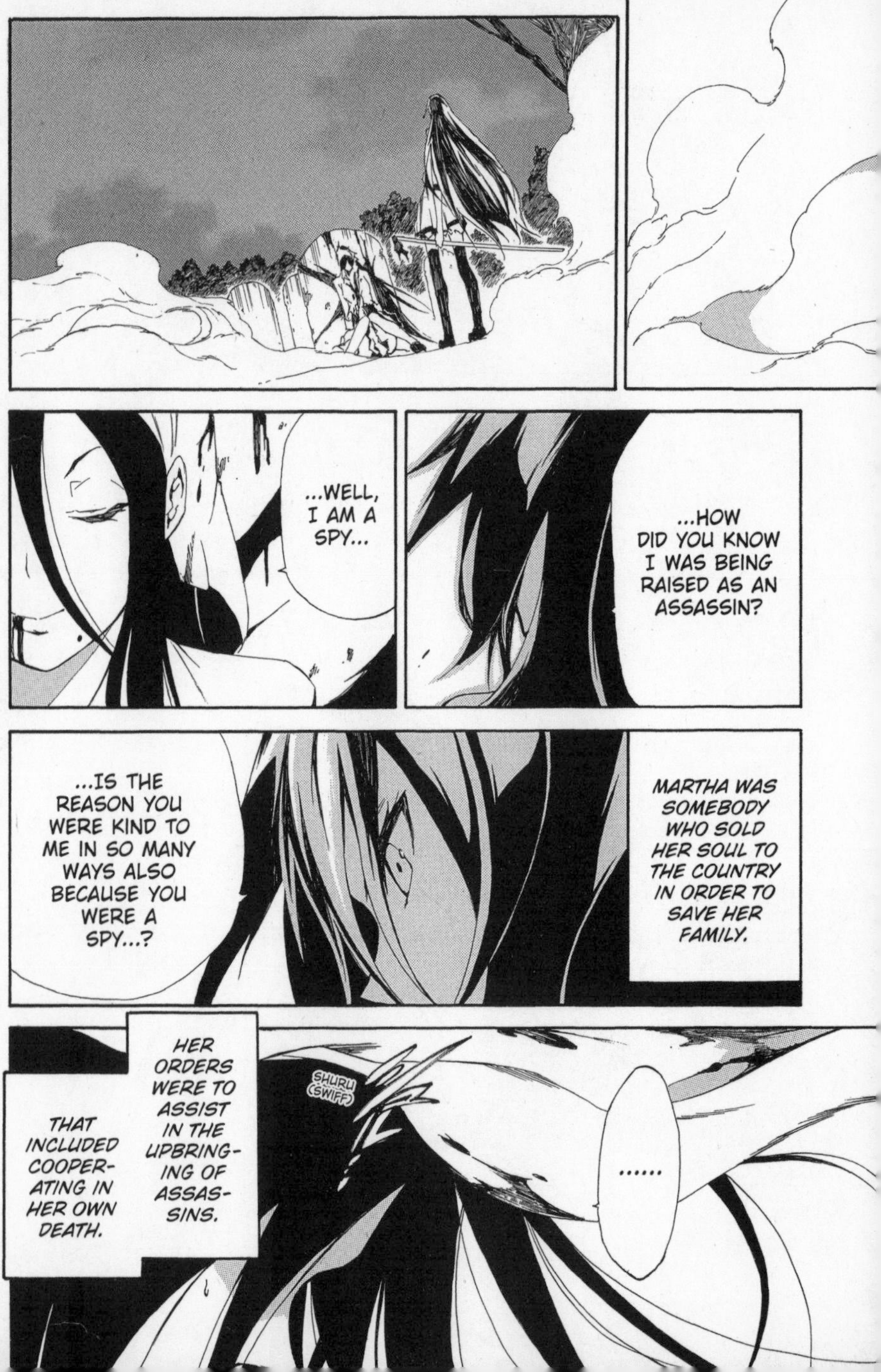

...WELL, I AM A SPY...
...HOW DID YOU KNOW I WAS BEING RAISED AS AN ASSASSIN?
MARTHA WAS SOMEBODY WHO SOLD HER SOUL TO THE COUNTRY IN ORDER TO SAVE HER FAMILY.
...IS THE REASON YOU WERE KIND TO ME IN SO MANY WAYS ALSO BECAUSE YOU WERE A SPY...?
......
SHURU (SWIFF)
HER ORDERS WERE TO ASSIST IN THE UPBRINGING OF ASSASSINS.
THAT INCLUDED COOPERATING IN HER OWN DEATH.

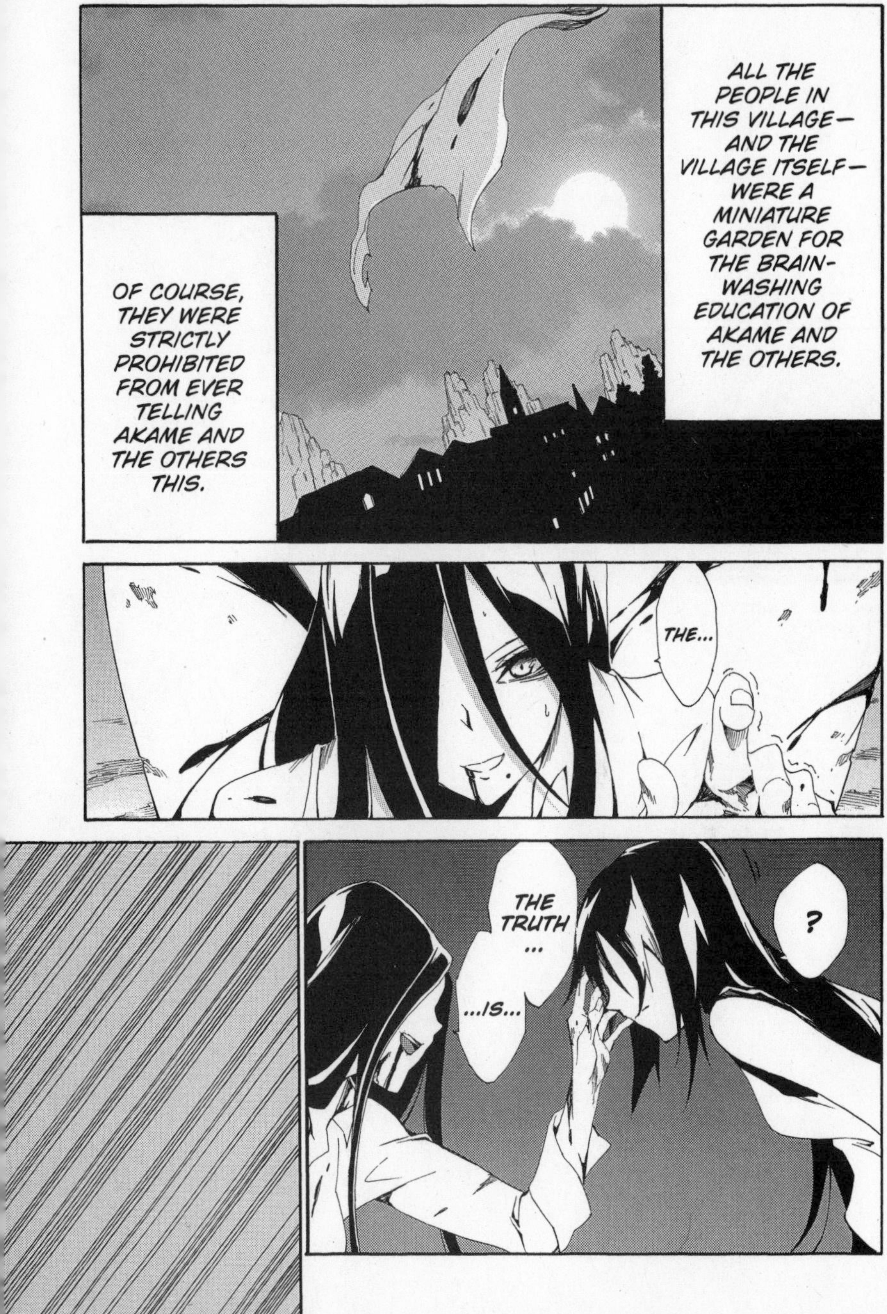
ALL THE PEOPLE IN THIS VILLAGE—AND THE VILLAGE ITSELF—WERE A MINIATURE GARDEN FOR THE BRAIN-WASHING EDUCATION OF AKAME AND THE OTHERS.
OF COURSE, THEY WERE STRICTLY PROHIBITED FROM EVER TELLING AKAME AND THE OTHERS THIS.
THE...
?
THE TRUTH...
...IS...

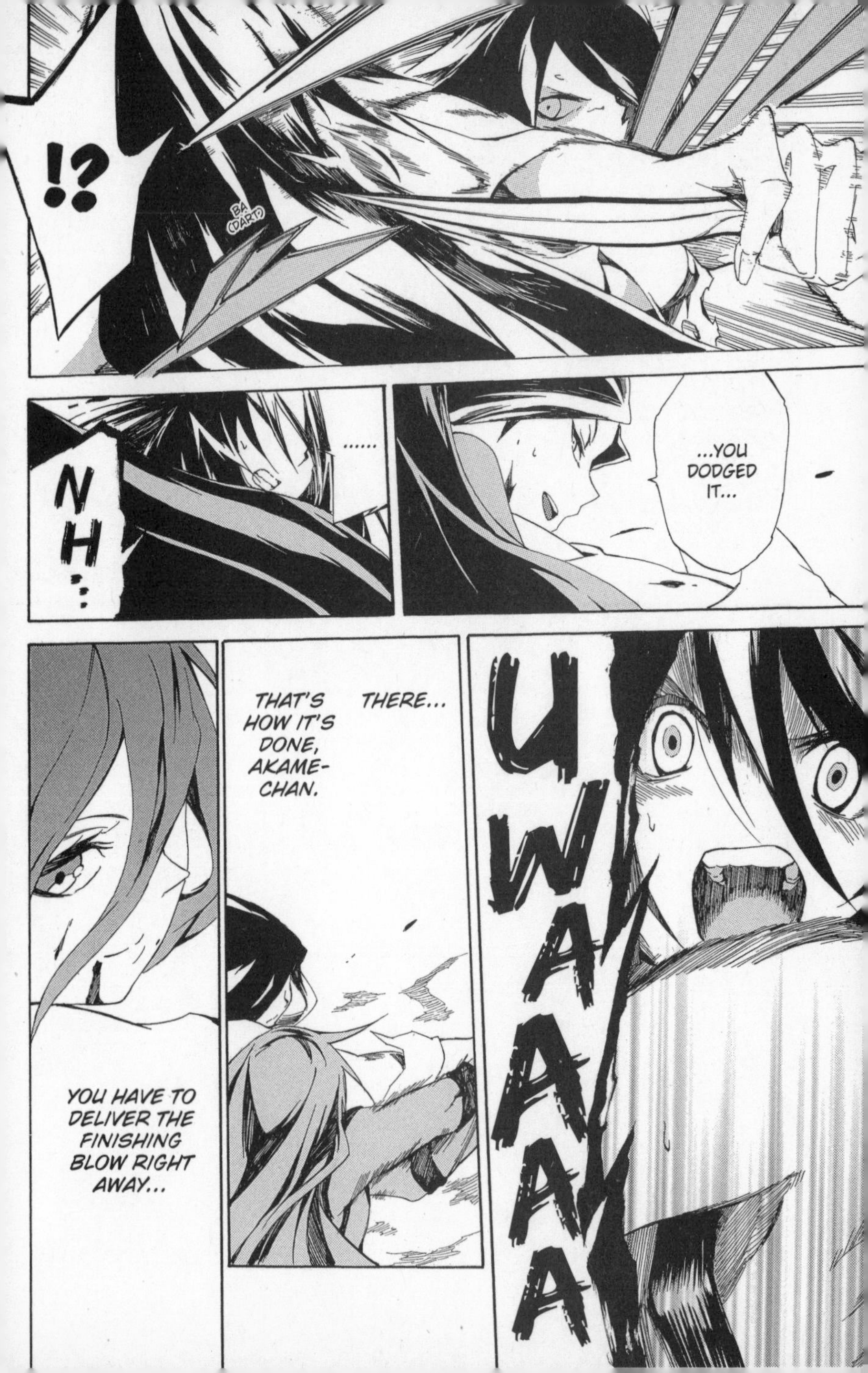
!?
BA (DART)
...YOU DODGED IT...
......
NH..
UWAAAAAA
THERE...
THAT'S HOW IT'S DONE, AKAME-CHAN.
YOU HAVE TO DELIVER THE FINISHING BLOW RIGHT AWAY...

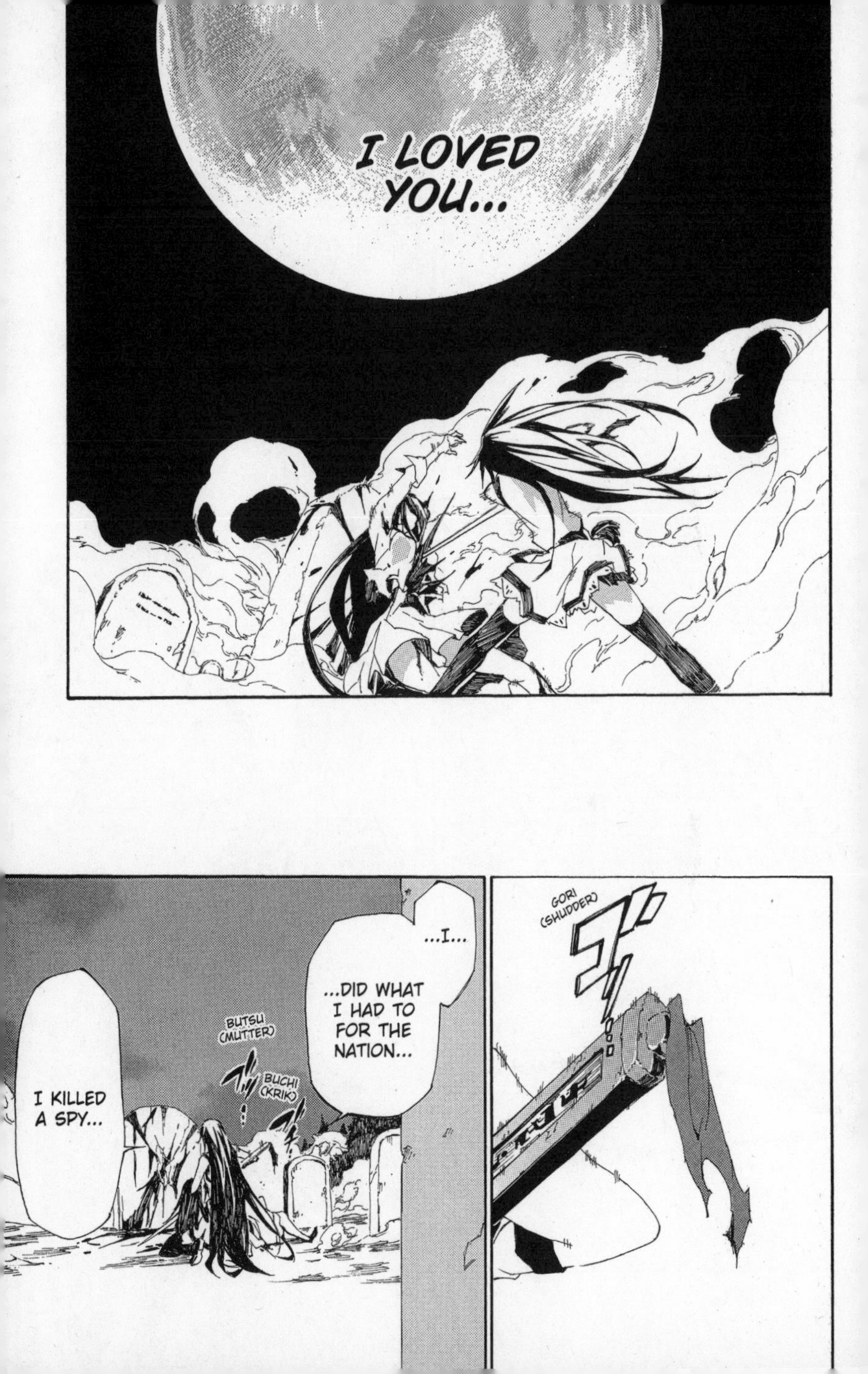
I LOVED YOU...
GORI (SHUDDER)
...I...
...DID WHAT I HAD TO FOR THE NATION...
BUTSU (MUTTER)
BUCHI (KRIK)
I KILLED A SPY...

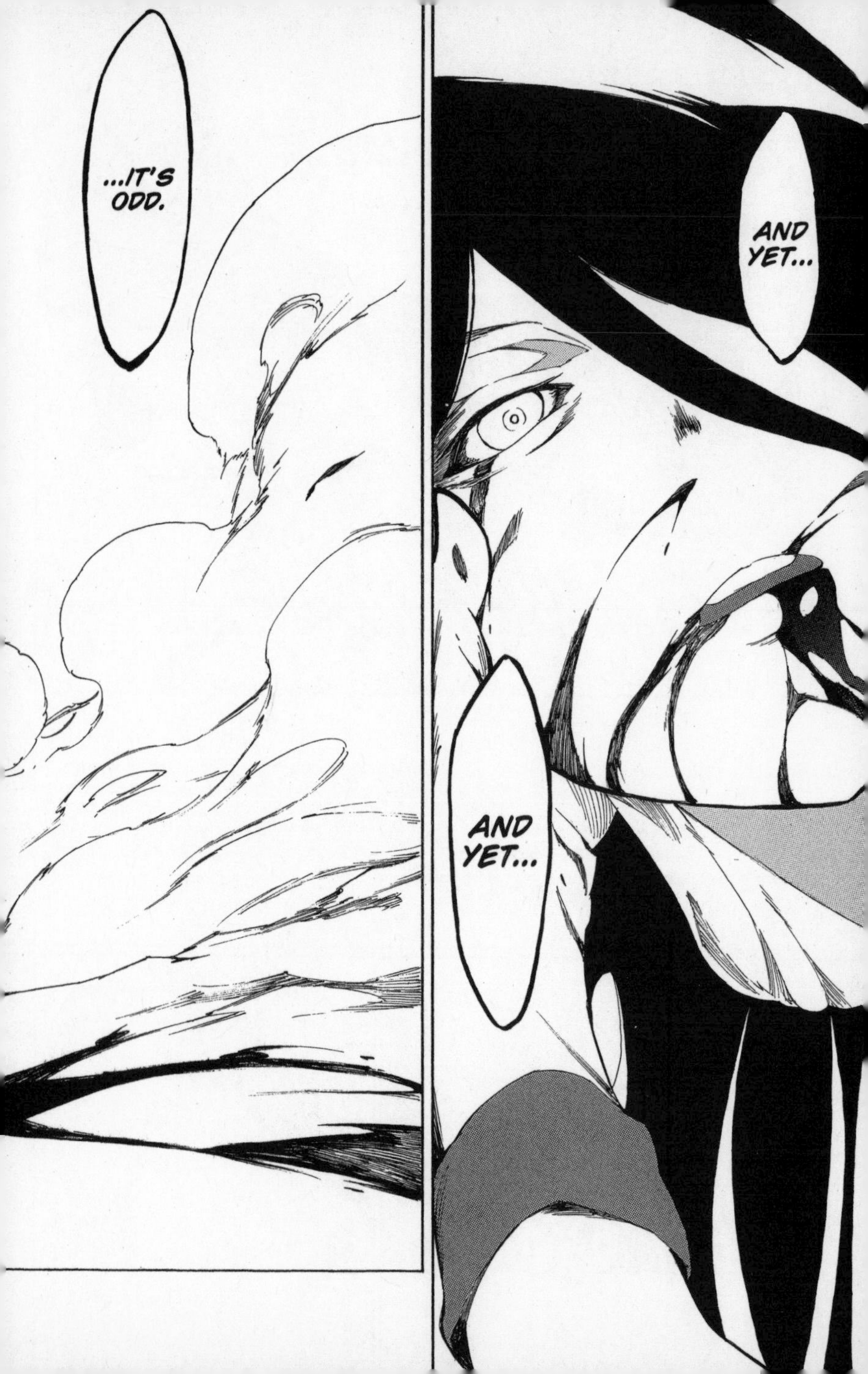
AND YET...
AND YET...
...IT'S ODD.

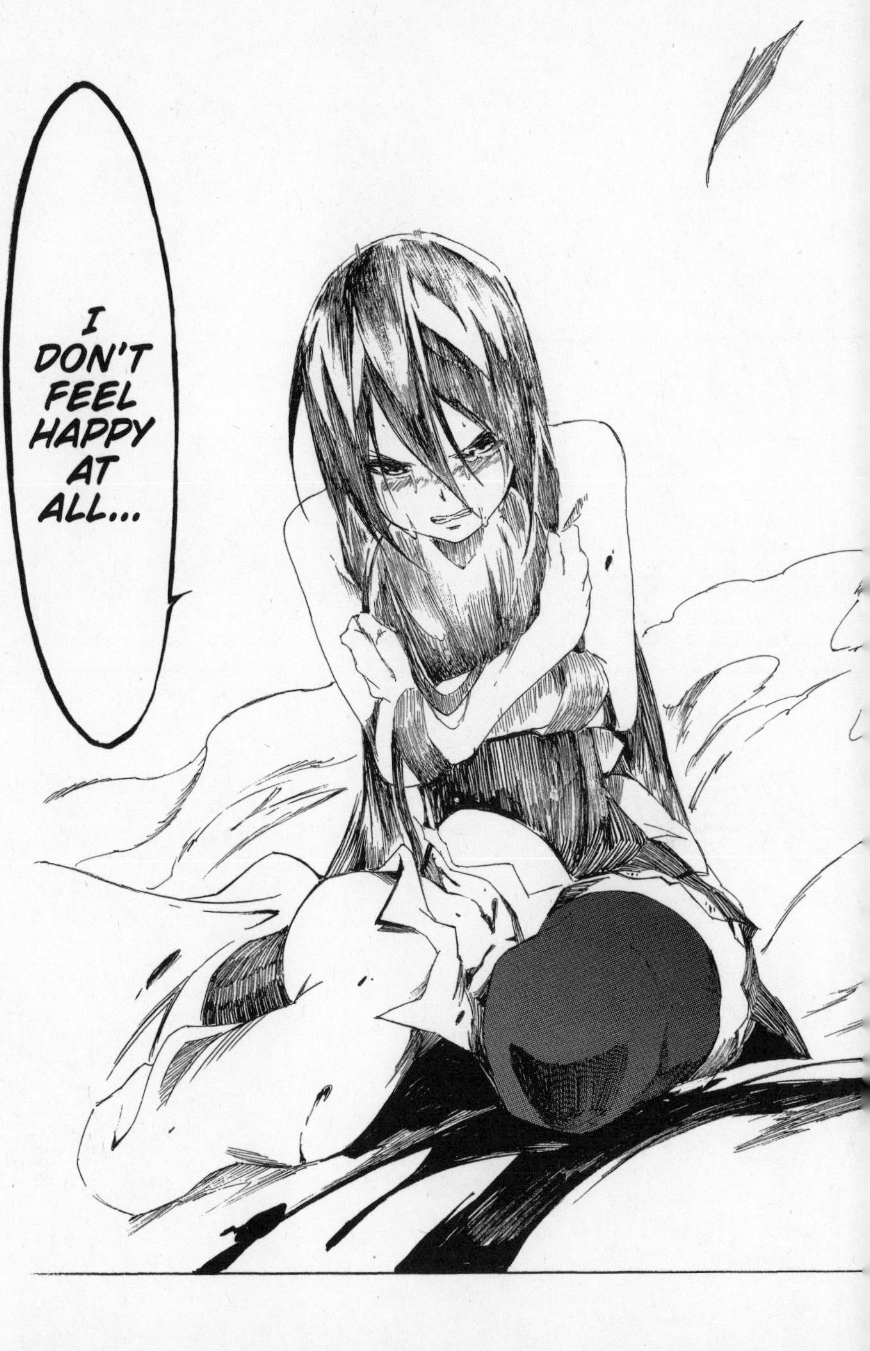
I DON'T FEEL HAPPY AT ALL...

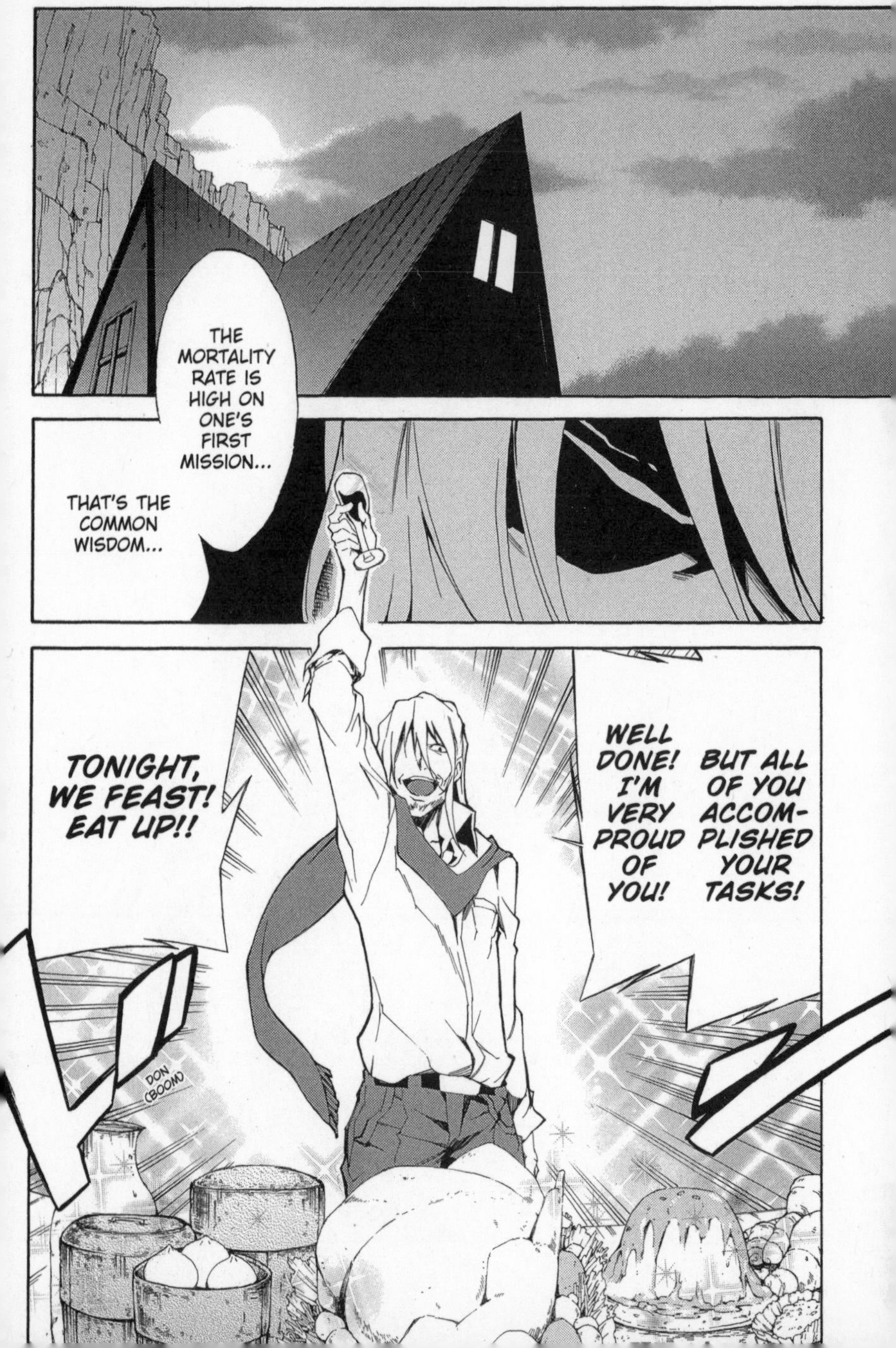
THE MORTALITY RATE IS HIGH ON ONE'S FIRST MISSION...
THAT'S THE COMMON WISDOM...
BUT ALL OF YOU ACCOMPLISHED YOUR TASKS!
WELL DONE! I'M VERY PROUD OF YOU!
TONIGHT, WE FEAST! EAT UP!!
DON (BOOM)

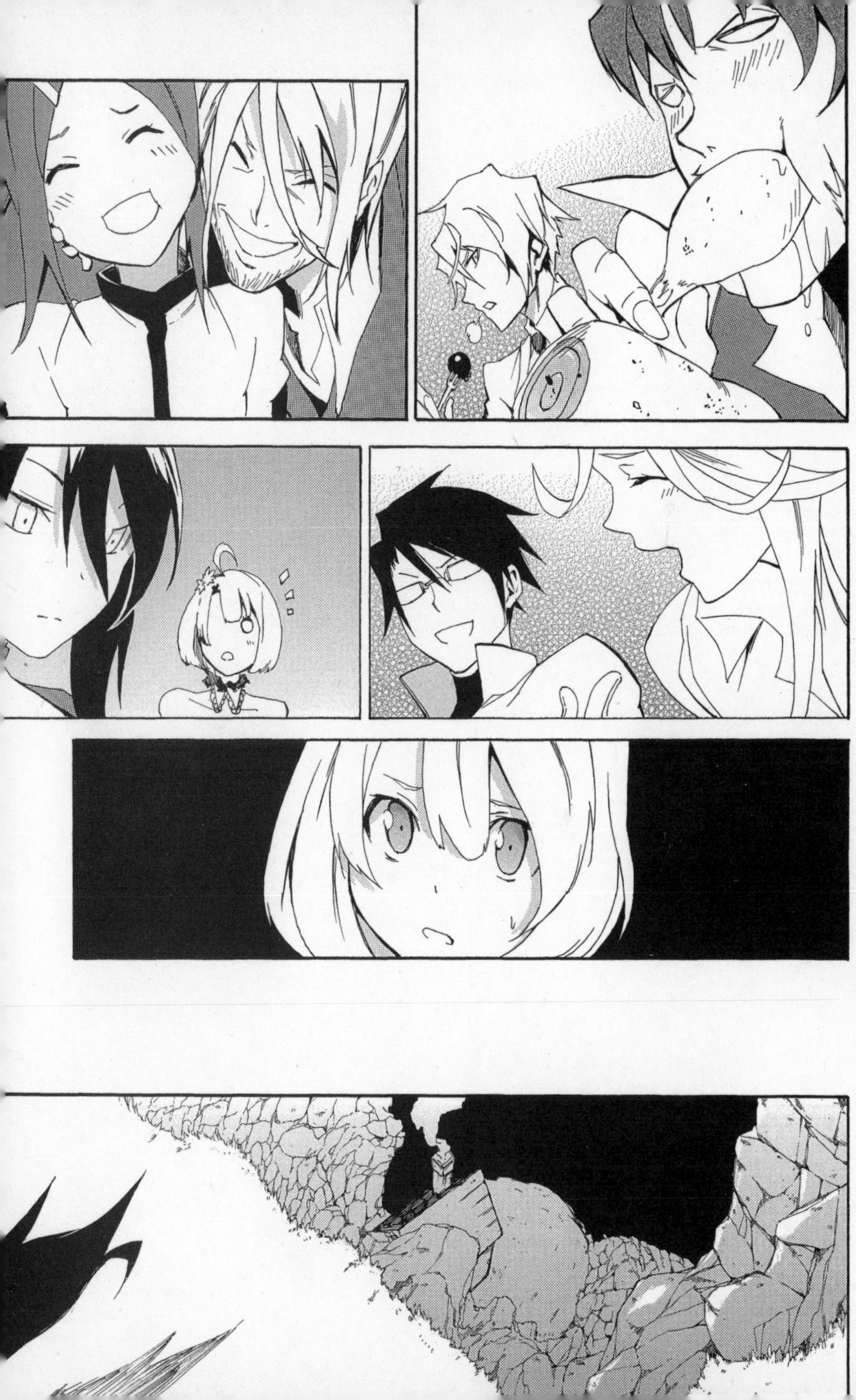

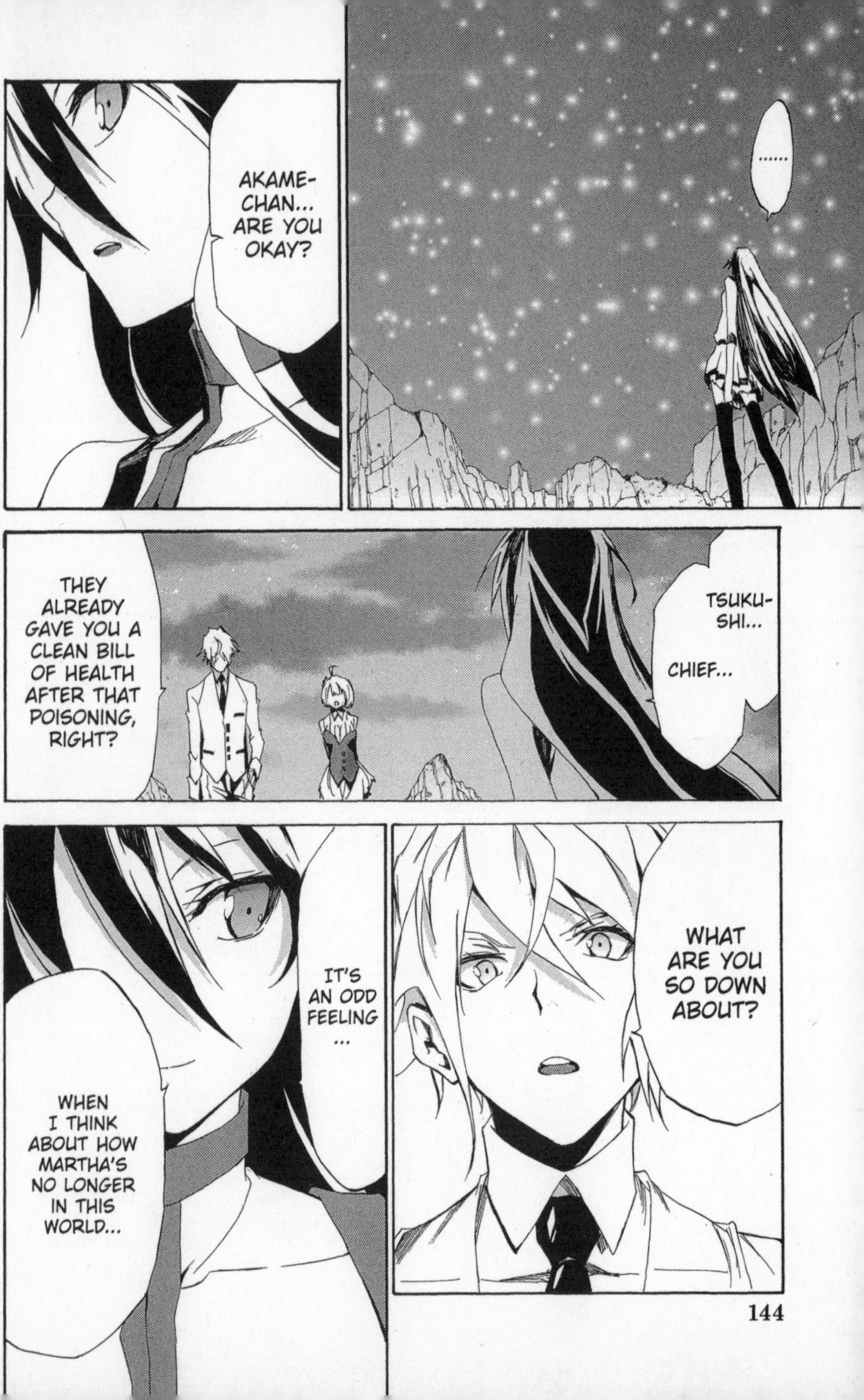
......
AKAME-CHAN... ARE YOU OKAY?
TSUKU-SHI...
CHIEF...
THEY ALREADY GAVE YOU A CLEAN BILL OF HEALTH AFTER THAT POISONING, RIGHT?
WHAT ARE YOU SO DOWN ABOUT?
IT'S AN ODD FEELING...
WHEN I THINK ABOUT HOW MARTHA'S NO LONGER IN THIS WORLD...

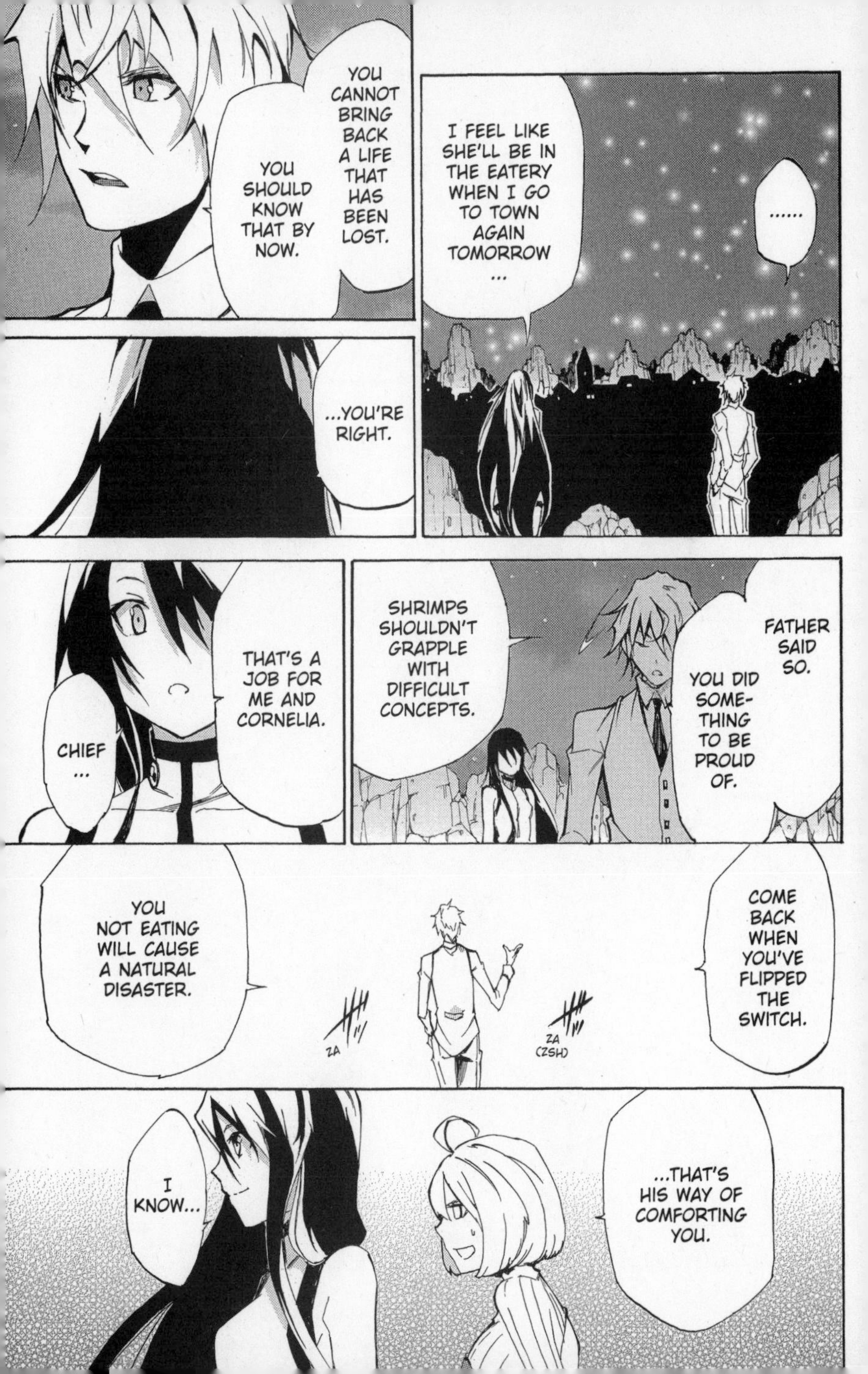
......
I FEEL LIKE SHE'LL BE IN THE EATERY WHEN I GO TO TOWN AGAIN TOMORROW ...
YOU CANNOT BRING BACK A LIFE THAT HAS BEEN LOST.
YOU SHOULD KNOW THAT BY NOW.
...YOU'RE RIGHT.
FATHER SAID SO.
YOU DID SOME-THING TO BE PROUD OF.
SHRIMPS SHOULDN'T GRAPPLE WITH DIFFICULT CONCEPTS.
THAT'S A JOB FOR ME AND CORNELIA.
CHIEF ...
COME BACK WHEN YOU'VE FLIPPED THE SWITCH.
ZA (ZSH)
ZA
YOU NOT EATING WILL CAUSE A NATURAL DISASTER.
...THAT'S HIS WAY OF COMFORTING YOU.
I KNOW...

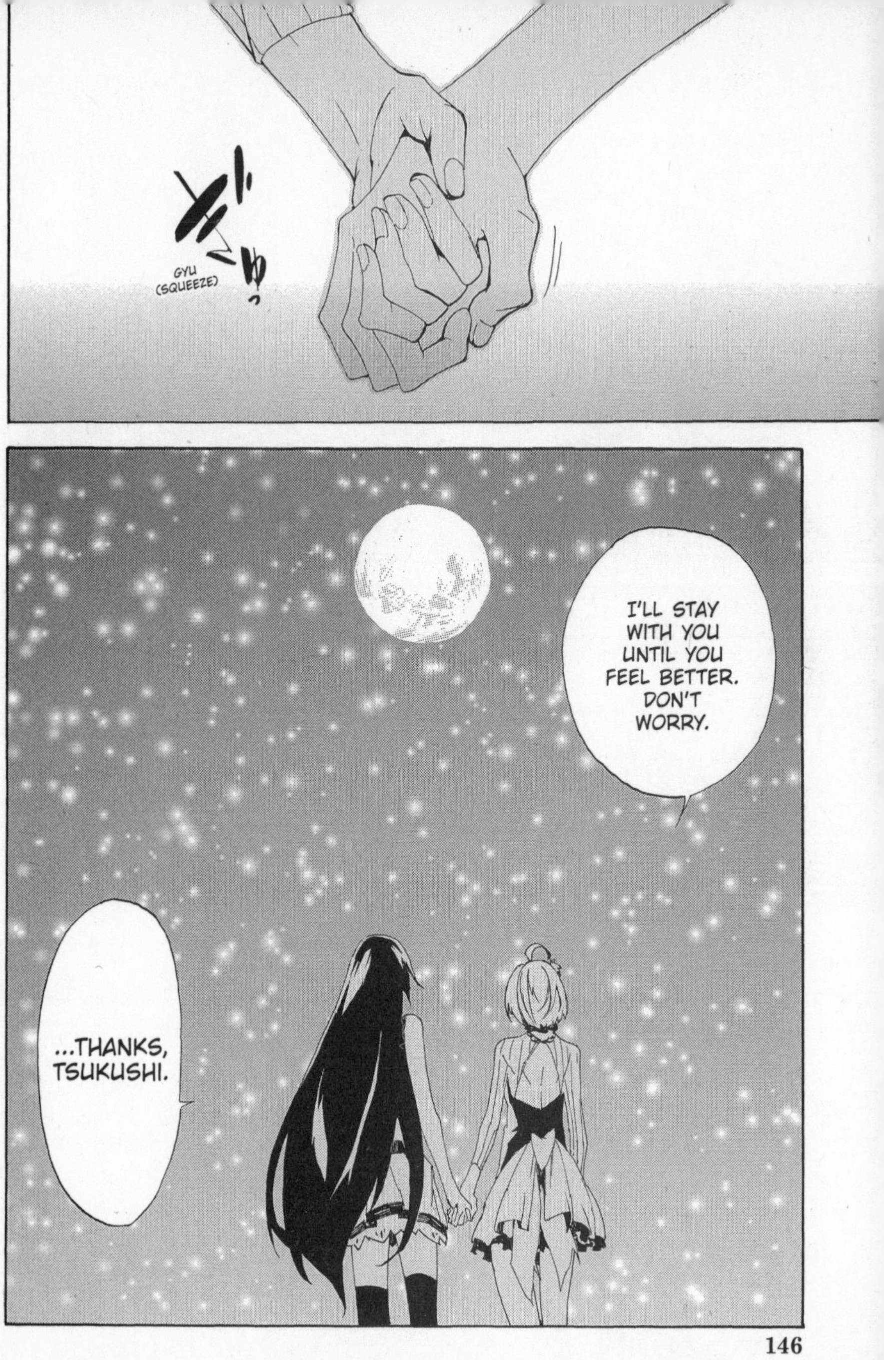
GYU (SQUEEZE)
I'LL STAY WITH YOU UNTIL YOU FEEL BETTER. DON'T WORRY.
...THANKS, TSUKUSHI.

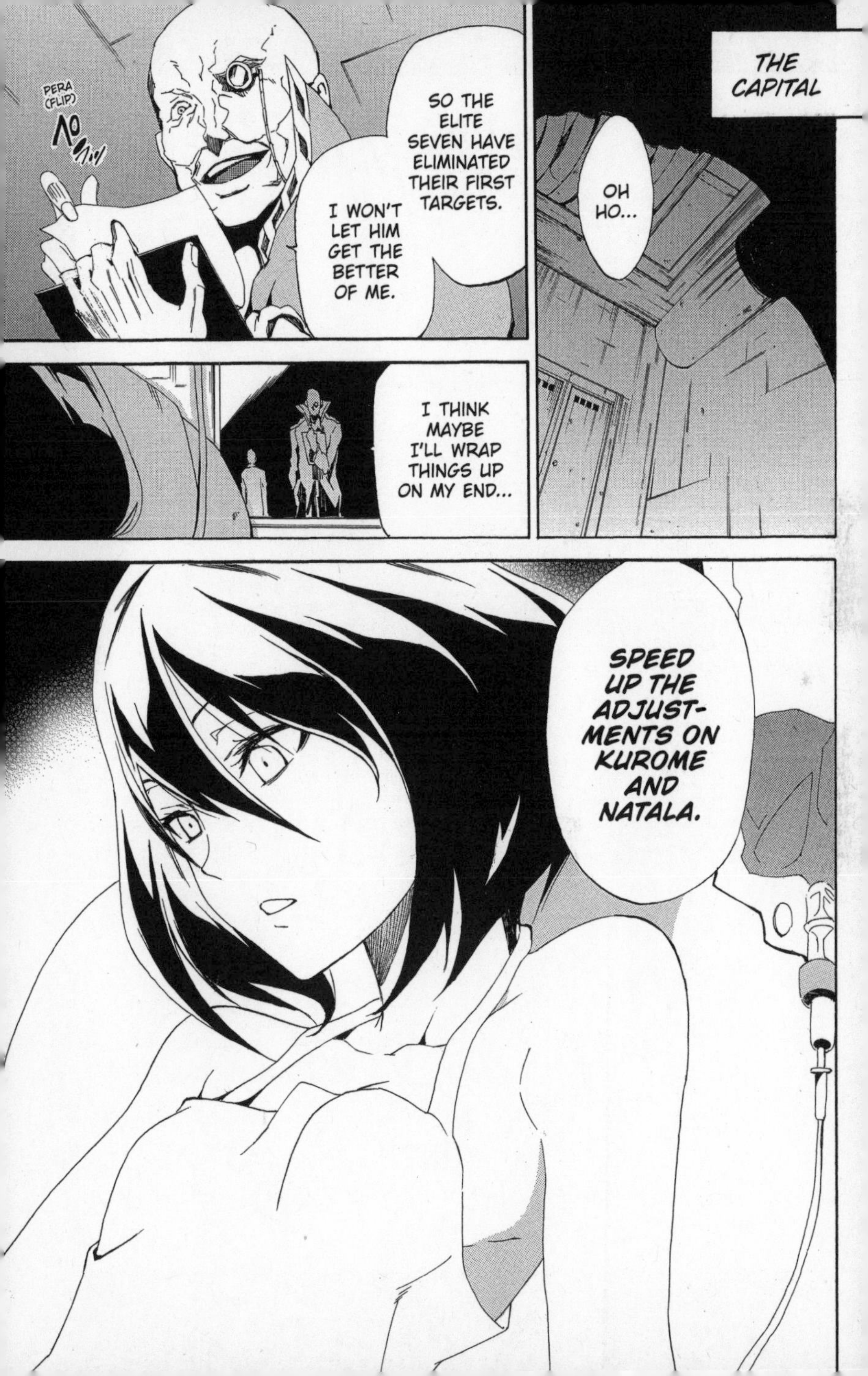
THE CAPITAL
OH HO...
SO THE ELITE SEVEN HAVE ELIMINATED THEIR FIRST TARGETS.
I WON'T LET HIM GET THE BETTER OF ME.
PERA (FLIP)
I THINK MAYBE I'LL WRAP THINGS UP ON MY END...
SPEED UP THE ADJUST-MENTS ON KUROME AND NATALA.

Akame ga KILL! ZERO
Rough Sketches

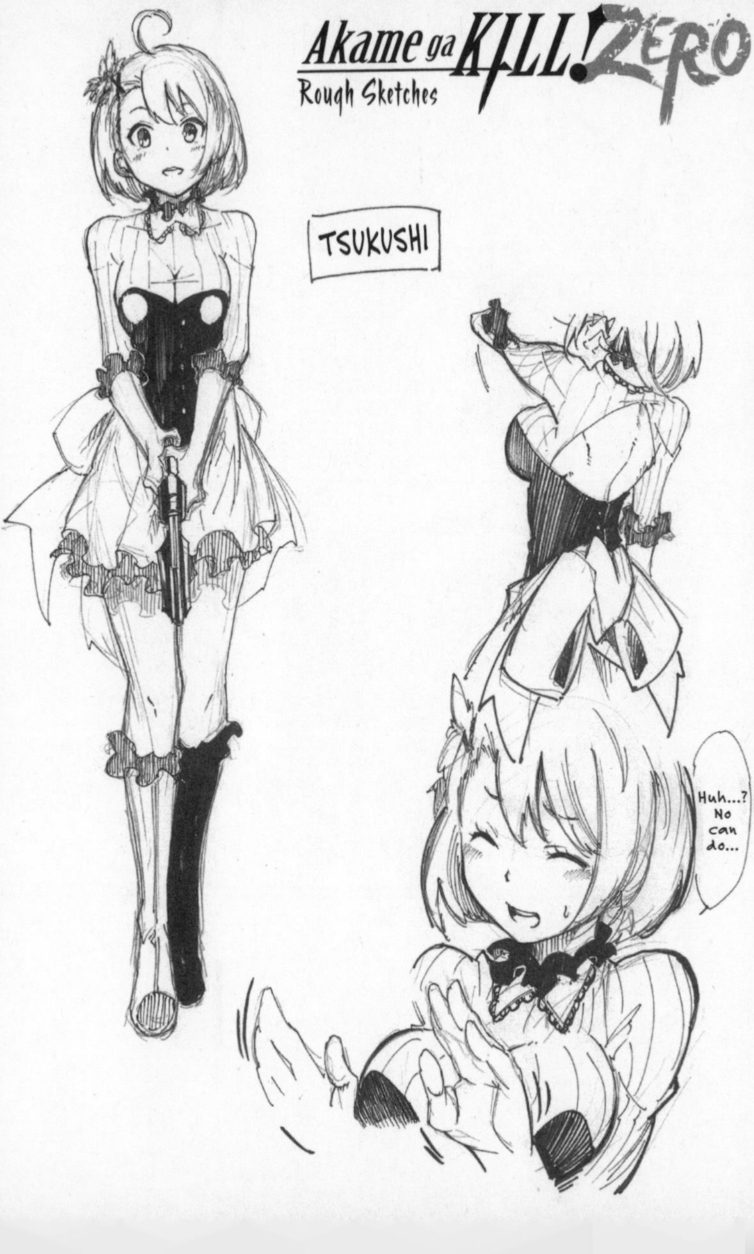
TSUKUSHI
Huh...? No can do...

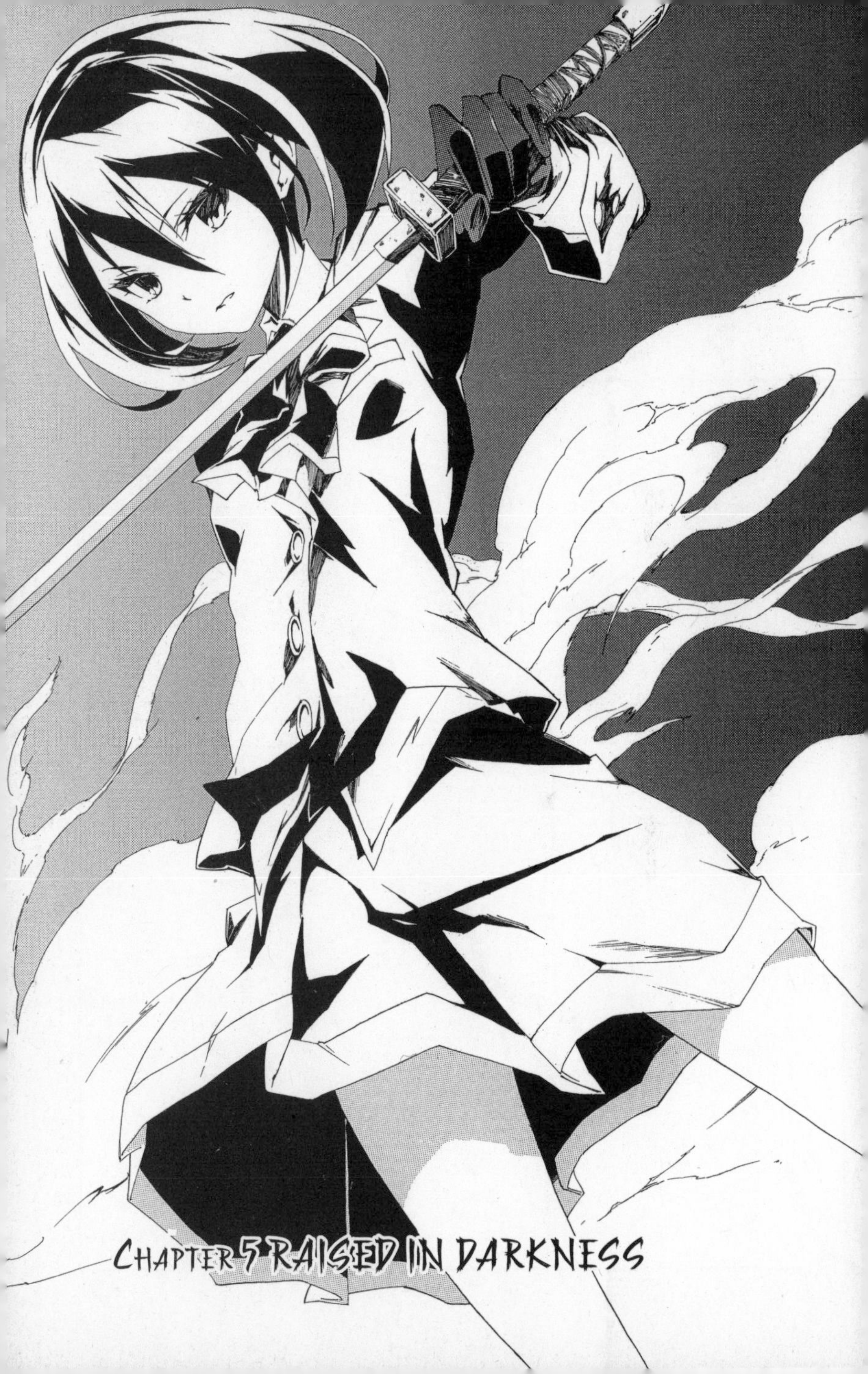
Chapter 5 Raised in Darkness

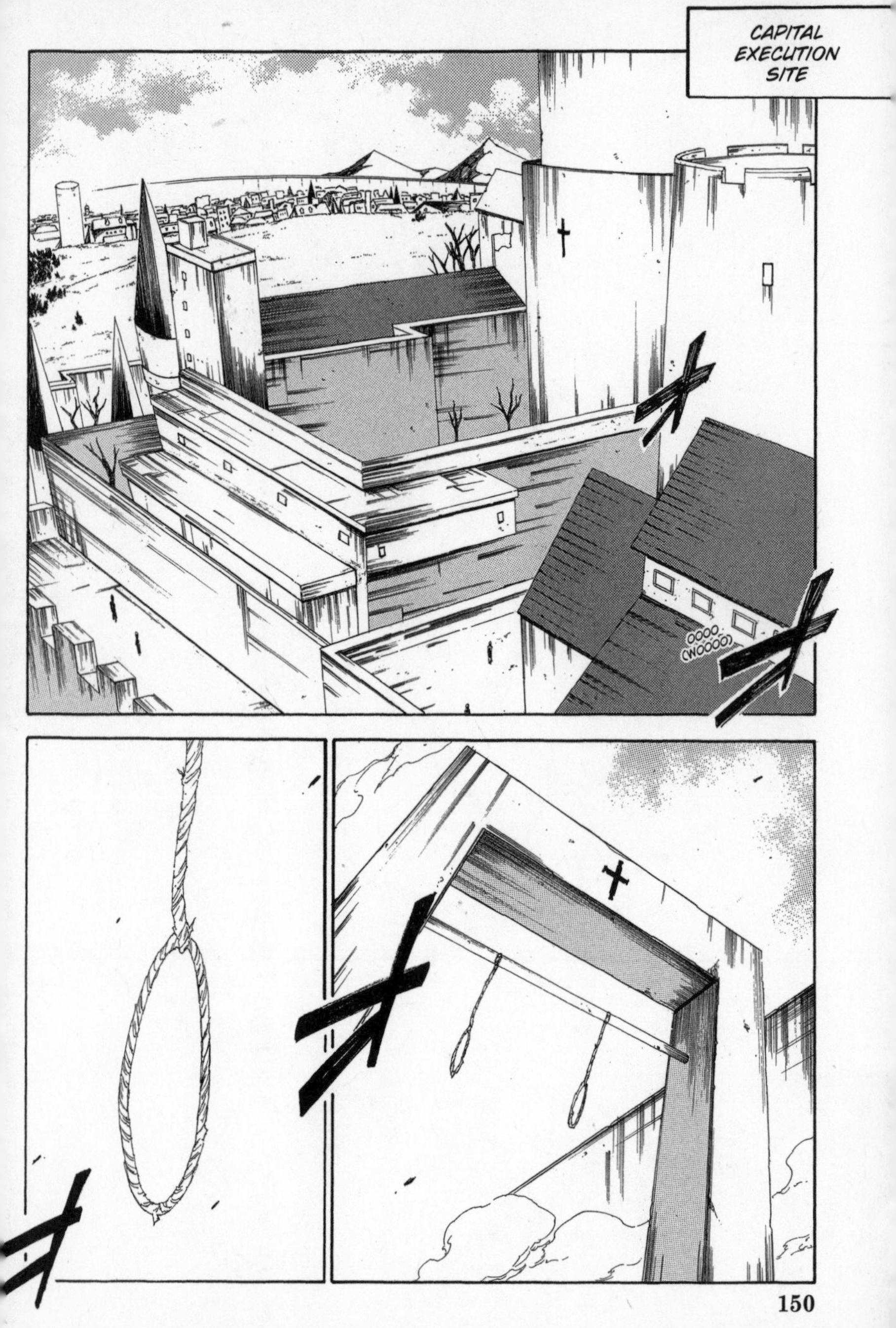
CAPITAL EXECUTION SITE
OOOO (WOOOO)

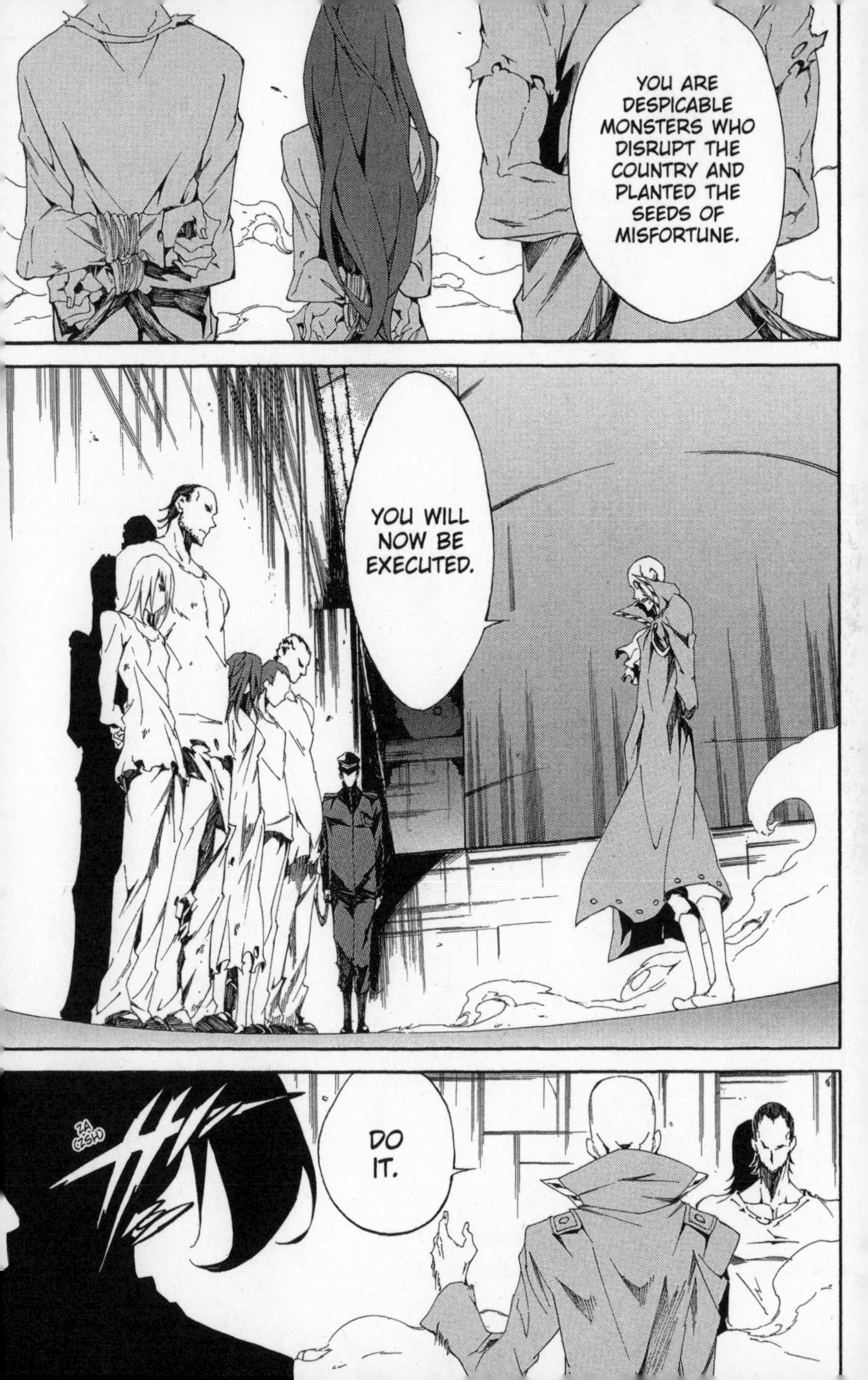
YOU ARE DESPICABLE MONSTERS WHO DISRUPT THE COUNTRY AND PLANTED THE SEEDS OF MISFORTUNE.
YOU WILL NOW BE EXECUTED.
DO IT.
ZA (ZSH)

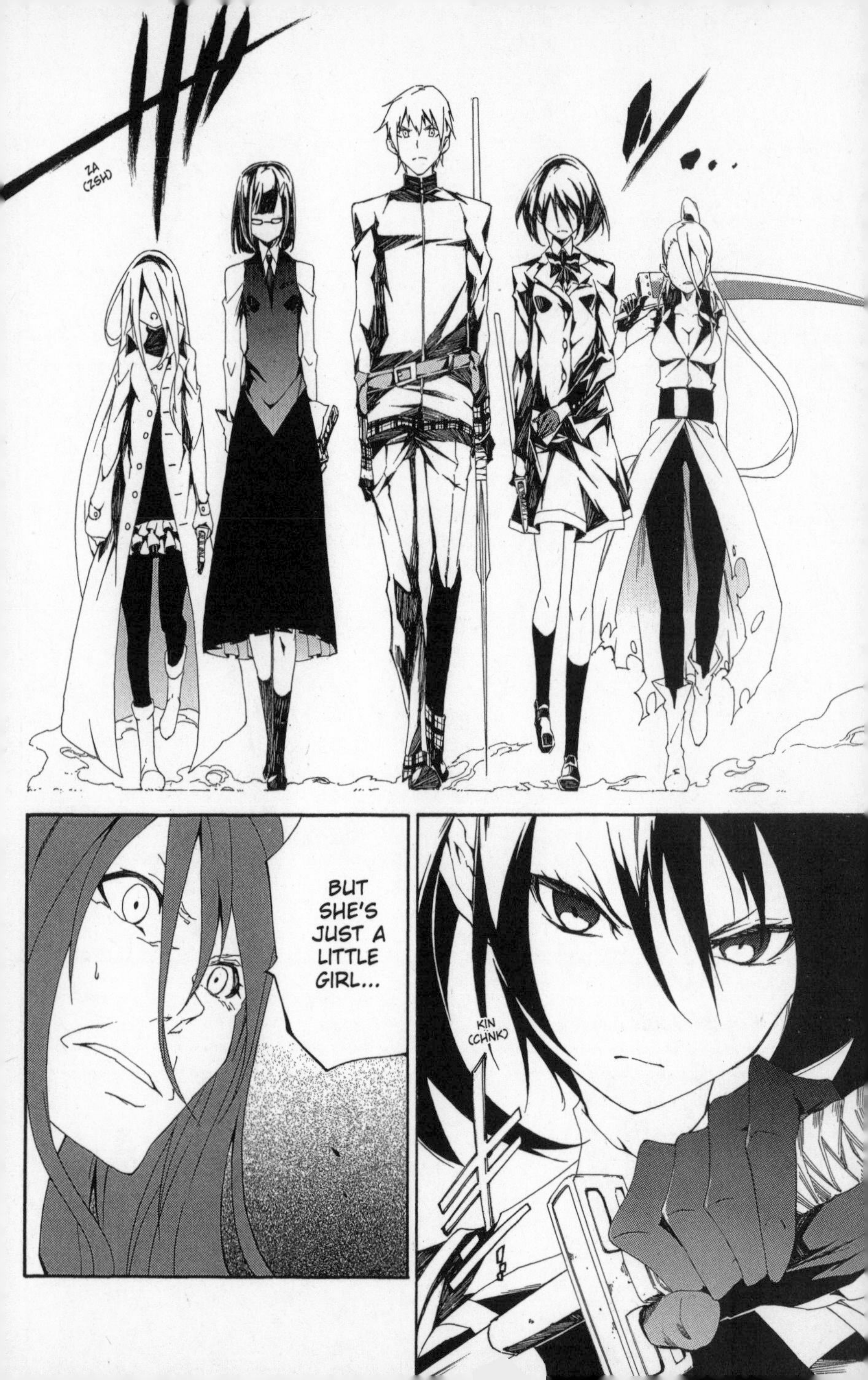
ZA (ZSH)
BUT SHE'S JUST A LITTLE GIRL...
KIN (CHNK)

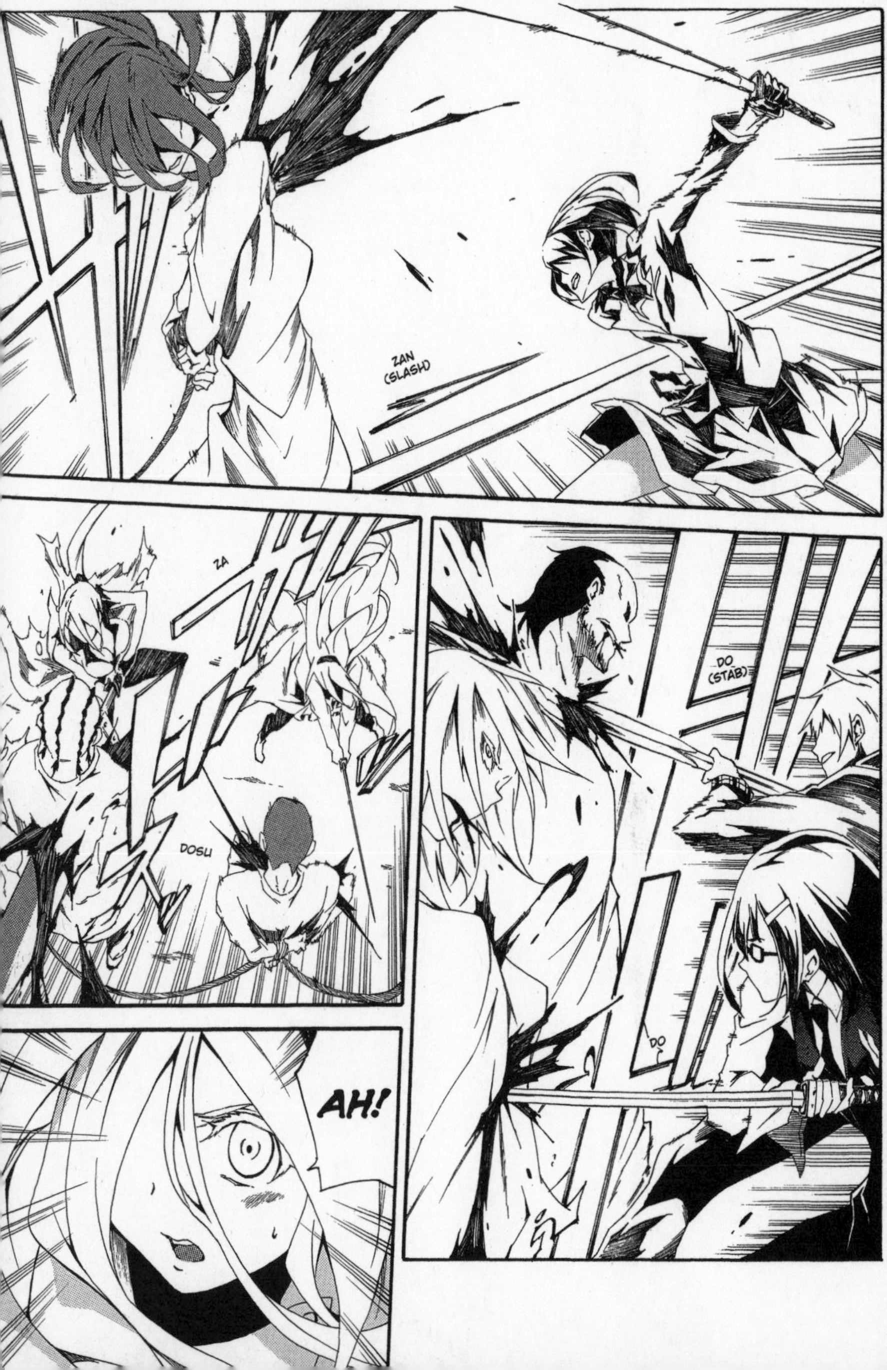
ZAN
(SLASH)
DO
(STAB)
ZA
DOSU
DO
AH!

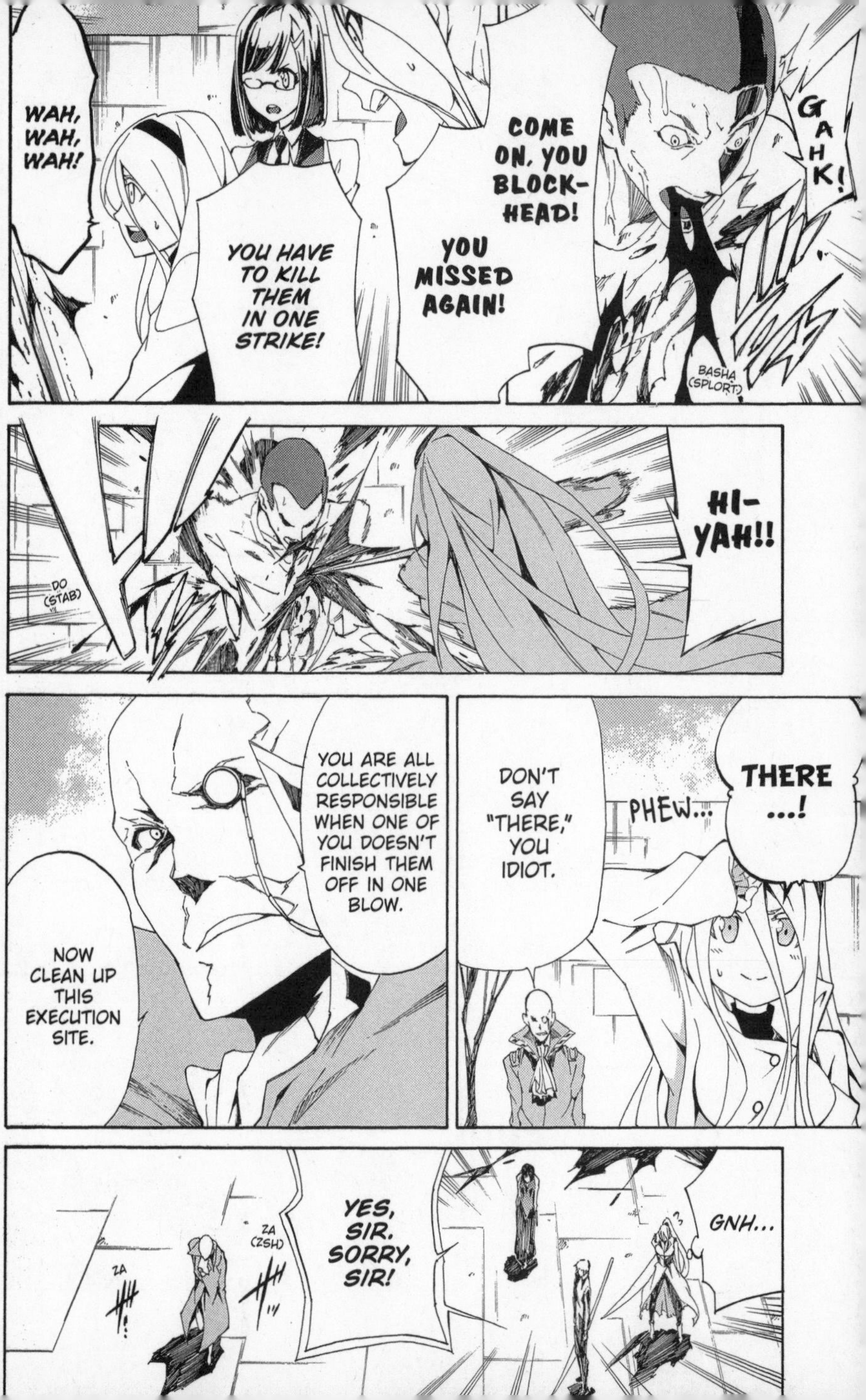
GAHK!
BASHA (SPLORT)
COME ON, YOU BLOCKHEAD!
YOU MISSED AGAIN!
YOU HAVE TO KILL THEM IN ONE STRIKE!
WAH, WAH, WAH!
HI-YAH!!
DO (STAB)
THERE ...!
PHEW...
DON'T SAY "THERE," YOU IDIOT.
YOU ARE ALL COLLECTIVELY RESPONSIBLE WHEN ONE OF YOU DOESN'T FINISH THEM OFF IN ONE BLOW.
NOW CLEAN UP THIS EXECUTION SITE.
GNH...
YES, SIR. SORRY, SIR!
ZA (ZSH)
ZA

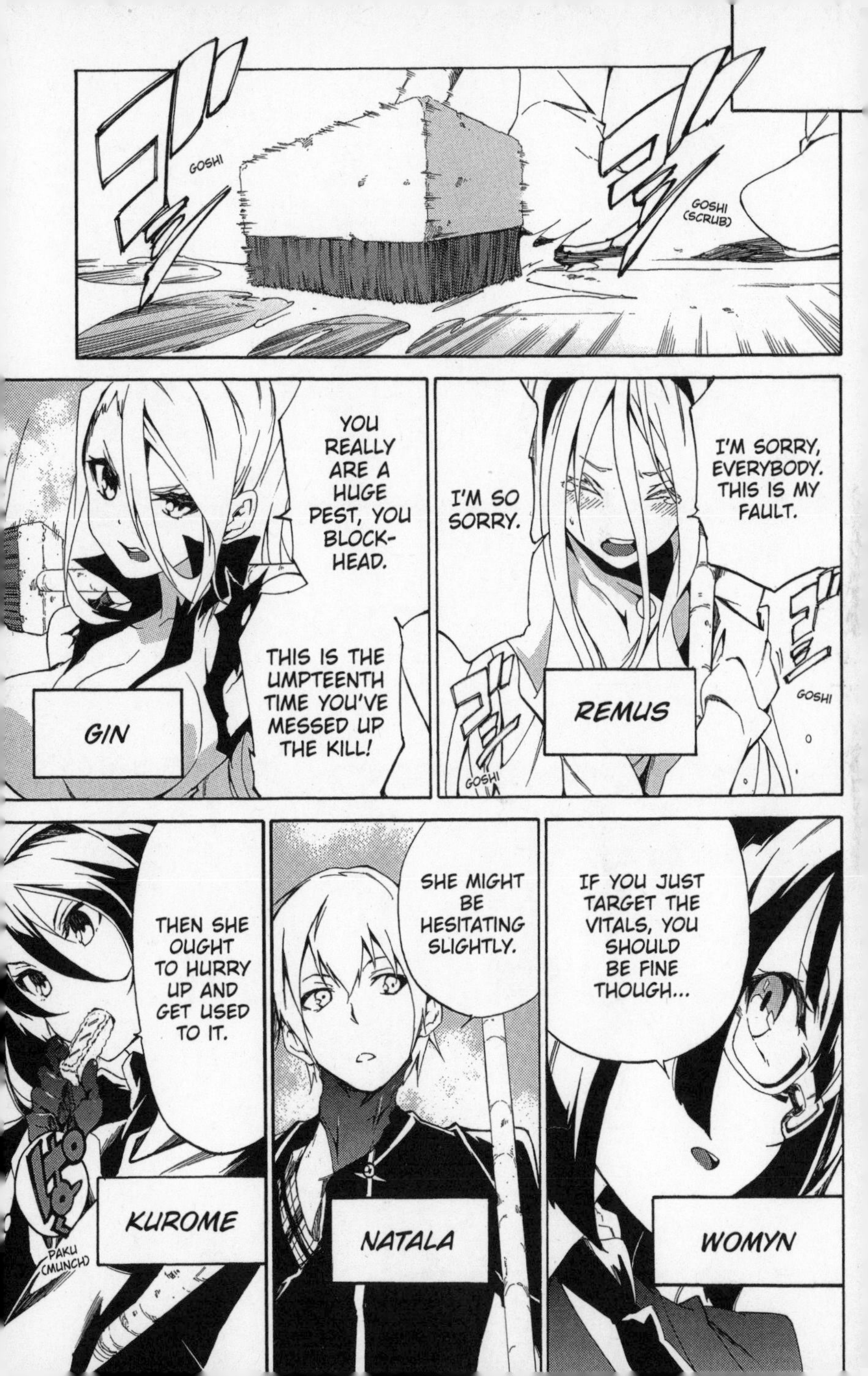
GOSHI (SCRUB)
GOSHI
I'M SORRY, EVERYBODY. THIS IS MY FAULT.
I'M SO SORRY.
REMUS
GOSHI
GOSHI
YOU REALLY ARE A HUGE PEST, YOU BLOCK-HEAD.
THIS IS THE UMPTEENTH TIME YOU'VE MESSED UP THE KILL!
GIN
IF YOU JUST TARGET THE VITALS, YOU SHOULD BE FINE THOUGH...
WOMYN
SHE MIGHT BE HESITATING SLIGHTLY.
NATALA
THEN SHE OUGHT TO HURRY UP AND GET USED TO IT.
KUROME
PAKU (MUNCH)

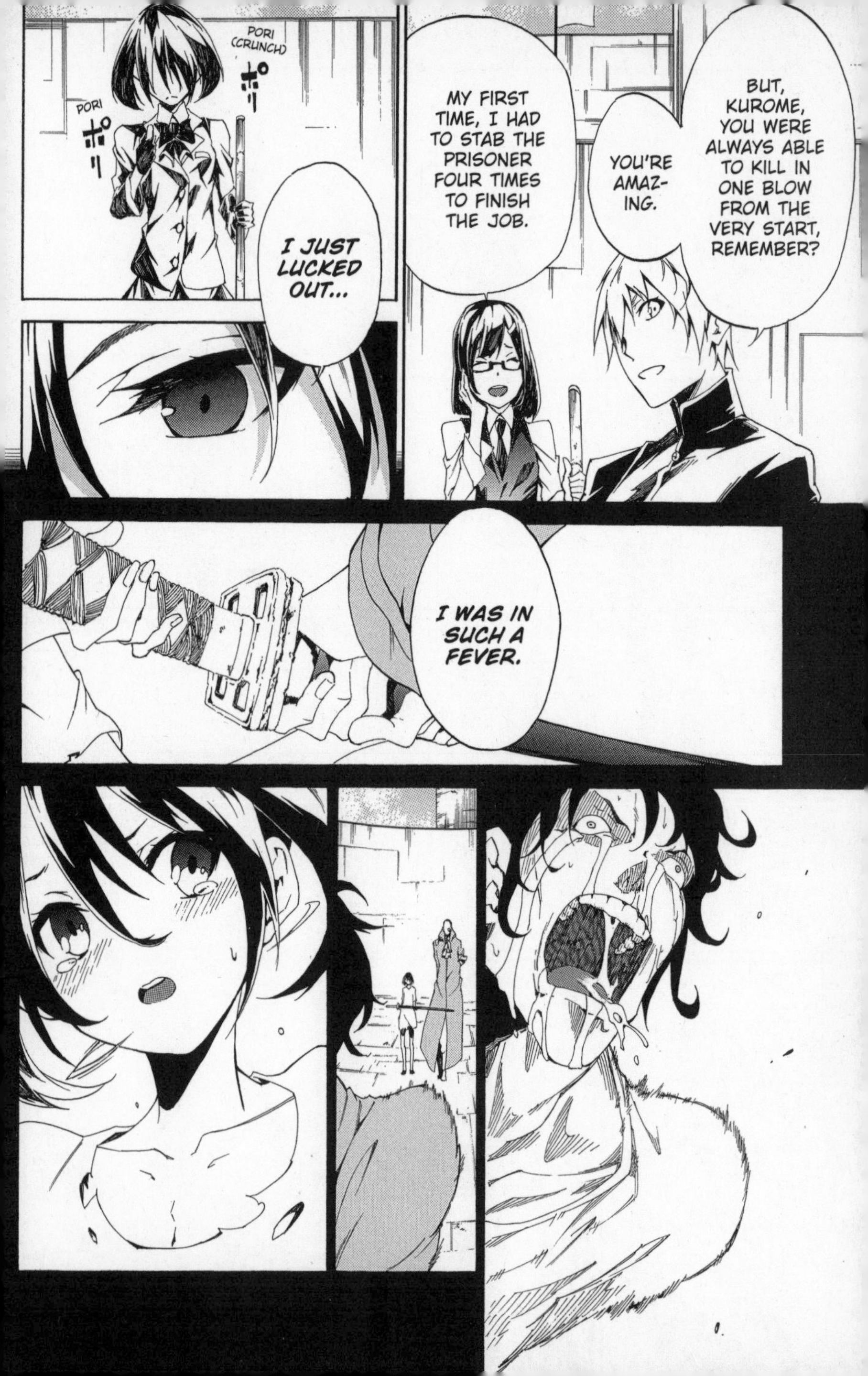
BUT, KUROME, YOU WERE ALWAYS ABLE TO KILL IN ONE BLOW FROM THE VERY START, REMEMBER?
YOU'RE AMAZ-ING.
MY FIRST TIME, I HAD TO STAB THE PRISONER FOUR TIMES TO FINISH THE JOB.
PORI (CRUNCH)
ポリ
PORI
ポリ
I JUST LUCKED OUT...
I WAS IN SUCH A FEVER.

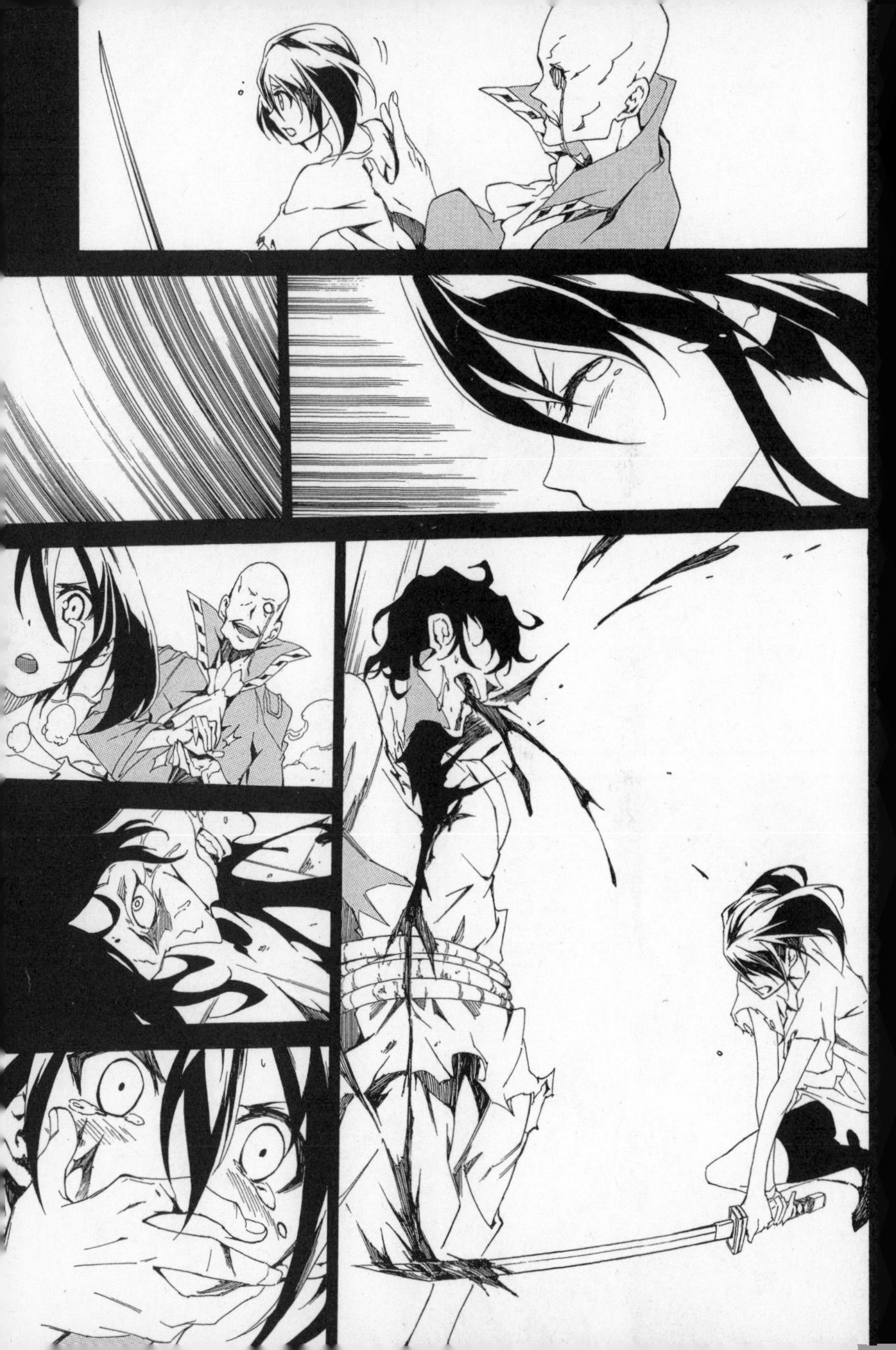

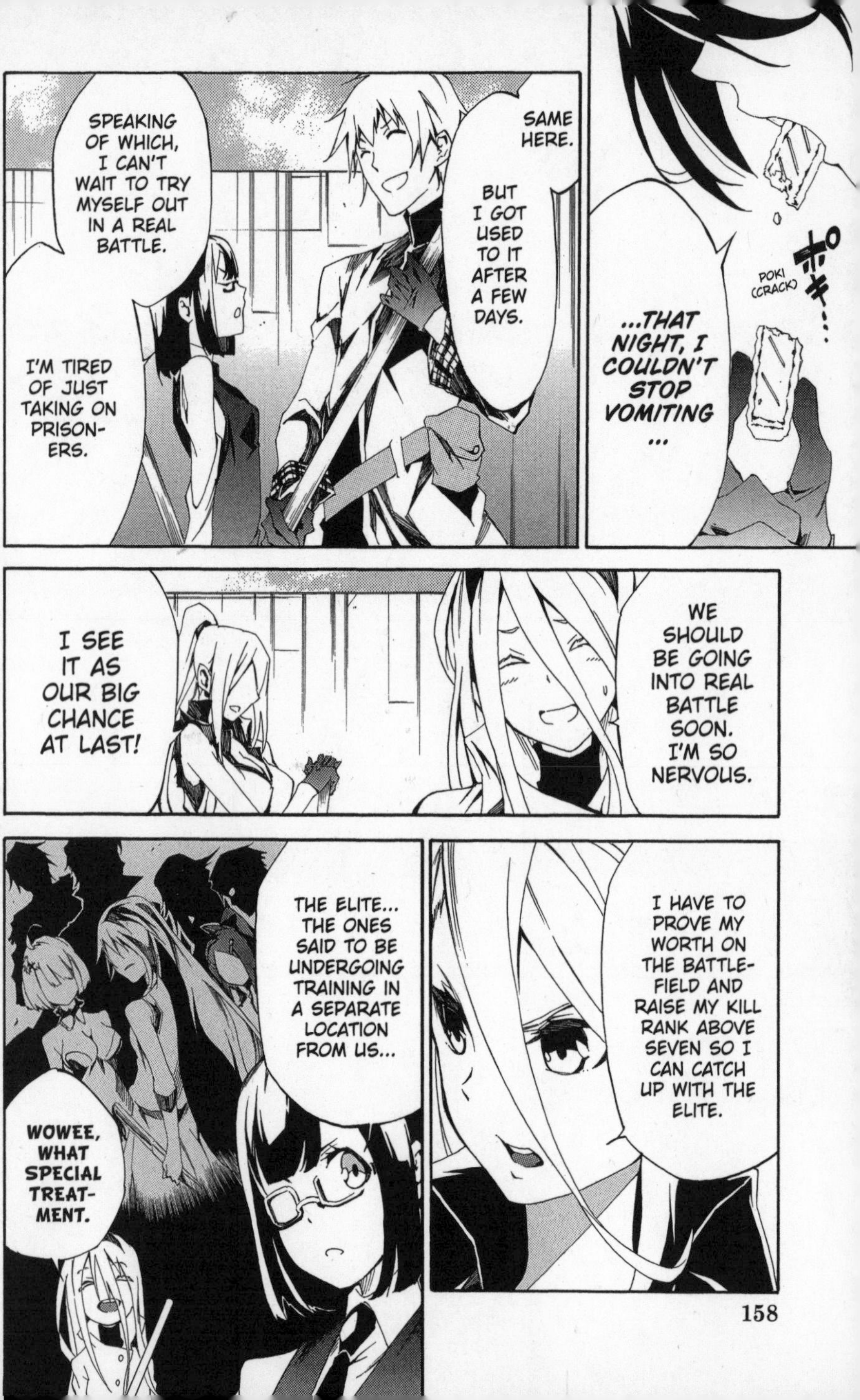
...THAT NIGHT, I COULDN'T STOP VOMITING ...
POKI (CRACK)
SAME HERE.
BUT I GOT USED TO IT AFTER A FEW DAYS.
SPEAKING OF WHICH, I CAN'T WAIT TO TRY MYSELF OUT IN A REAL BATTLE.
I'M TIRED OF JUST TAKING ON PRISON-ERS.
WE SHOULD BE GOING INTO REAL BATTLE SOON. I'M SO NERVOUS.
I SEE IT AS OUR BIG CHANCE AT LAST!
I HAVE TO PROVE MY WORTH ON THE BATTLE-FIELD AND RAISE MY KILL RANK ABOVE SEVEN SO I CAN CATCH UP WITH THE ELITE.
THE ELITE... THE ONES SAID TO BE UNDERGOING TRAINING IN A SEPARATE LOCATION FROM US...
WOWEE, WHAT SPECIAL TREAT-MENT.

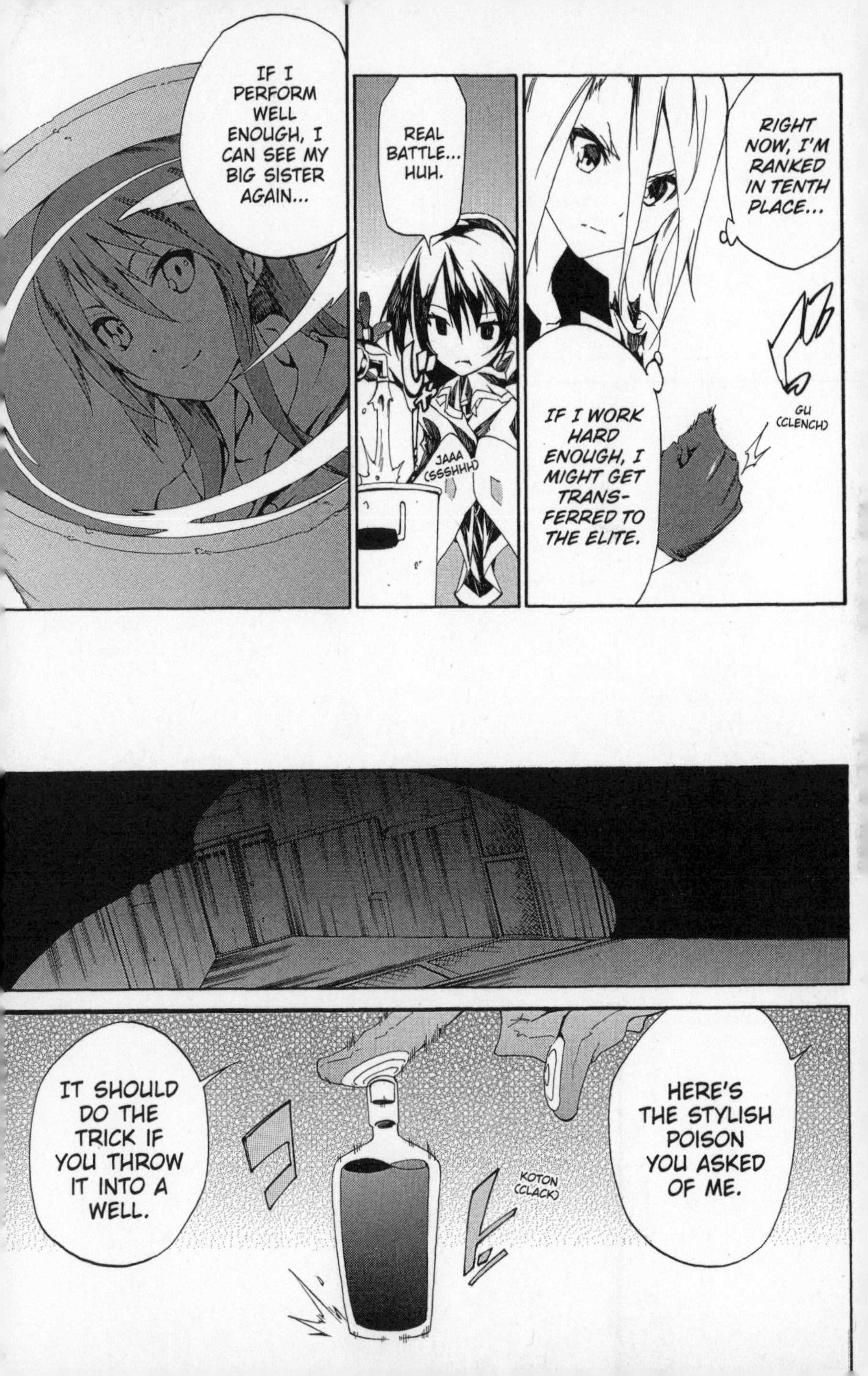
RIGHT NOW, I'M RANKED IN TENTH PLACE...
IF I WORK HARD ENOUGH, I MIGHT GET TRANS-FERRED TO THE ELITE.
GU (CLENCH)
REAL BATTLE... HUH.
JAAA (SSSHHH)
IF I PERFORM WELL ENOUGH, I CAN SEE MY BIG SISTER AGAIN...
HERE'S THE STYLISH POISON YOU ASKED OF ME.
KOTON (CLACK)
IT SHOULD DO THE TRICK IF YOU THROW IT INTO A WELL.

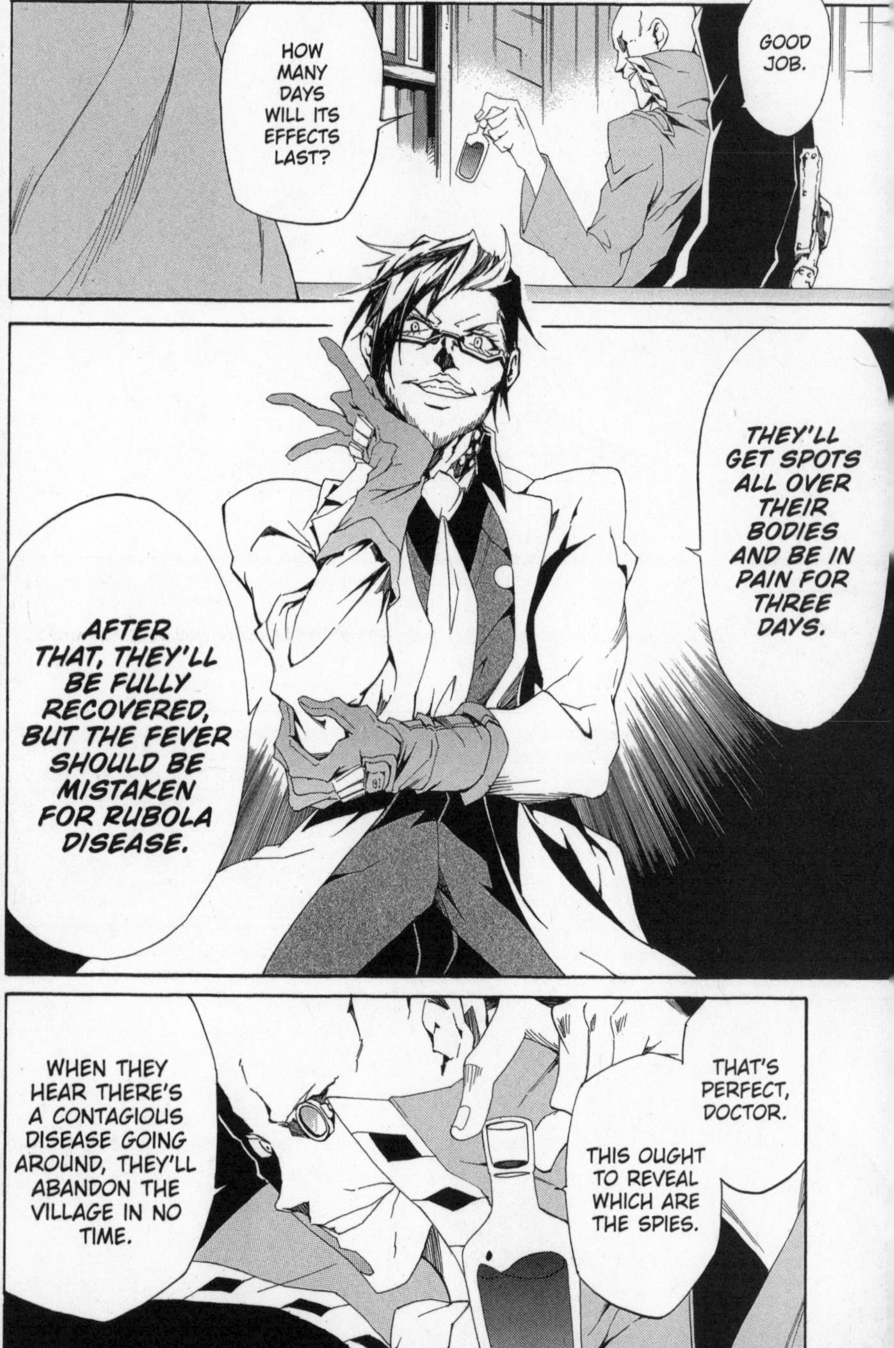
GOOD JOB.
HOW MANY DAYS WILL ITS EFFECTS LAST?
THEY'LL GET SPOTS ALL OVER THEIR BODIES AND BE IN PAIN FOR THREE DAYS.
AFTER THAT, THEY'LL BE FULLY RECOVERED, BUT THE FEVER SHOULD BE MISTAKEN FOR RUBOLA DISEASE.
THAT'S PERFECT, DOCTOR.
THIS OUGHT TO REVEAL WHICH ARE THE SPIES.
WHEN THEY HEAR THERE'S A CONTAGIOUS DISEASE GOING AROUND, THEY'LL ABANDON THE VILLAGE IN NO TIME.

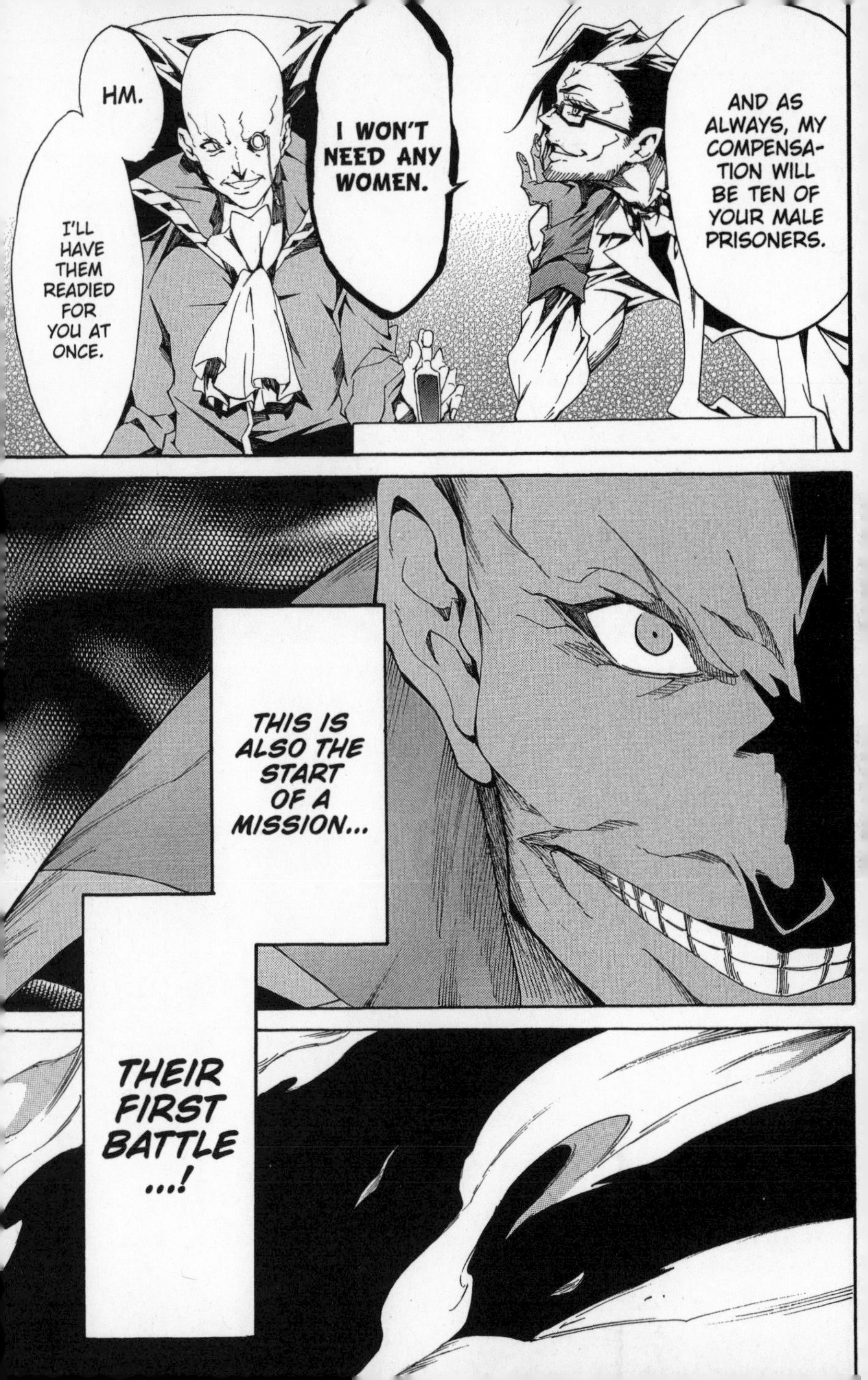
AND AS ALWAYS, MY COMPENSATION WILL BE TEN OF YOUR MALE PRISONERS.
I WON'T NEED ANY WOMEN.
HM.
I'LL HAVE THEM READIED FOR YOU AT ONCE.
THIS IS ALSO THE START OF A MISSION...
THEIR FIRST BATTLE ...!

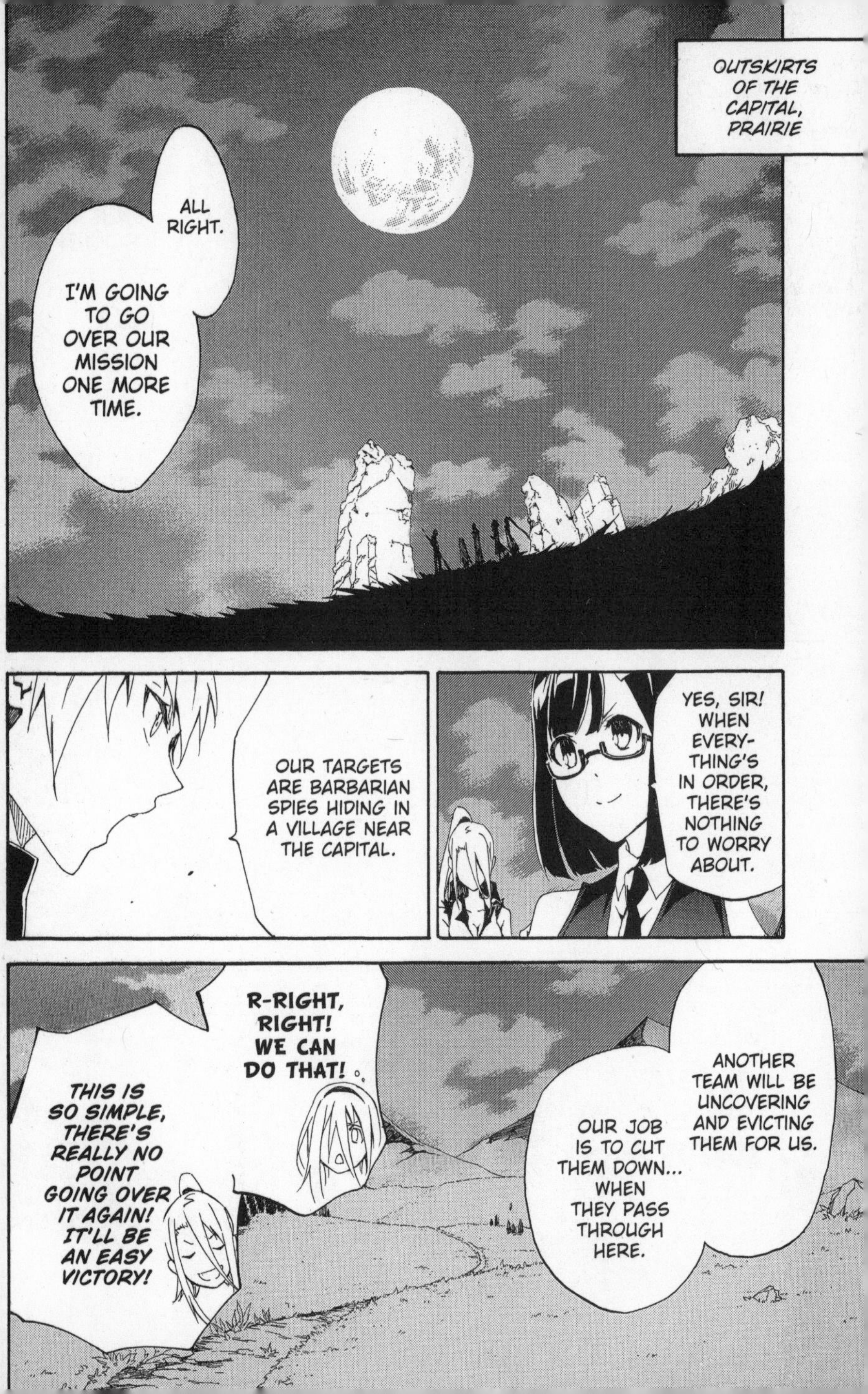
OUTSKIRTS OF THE CAPITAL, PRAIRIE
ALL RIGHT.
I'M GOING TO GO OVER OUR MISSION ONE MORE TIME.
YES, SIR! WHEN EVERY-THING'S IN ORDER, THERE'S NOTHING TO WORRY ABOUT.
OUR TARGETS ARE BARBARIAN SPIES HIDING IN A VILLAGE NEAR THE CAPITAL.
ANOTHER TEAM WILL BE UNCOVERING AND EVICTING THEM FOR US.
OUR JOB IS TO CUT THEM DOWN... WHEN THEY PASS THROUGH HERE.
R-RIGHT, RIGHT! WE CAN DO THAT!
THIS IS SO SIMPLE, THERE'S REALLY NO POINT GOING OVER IT AGAIN! IT'LL BE AN EASY VICTORY!

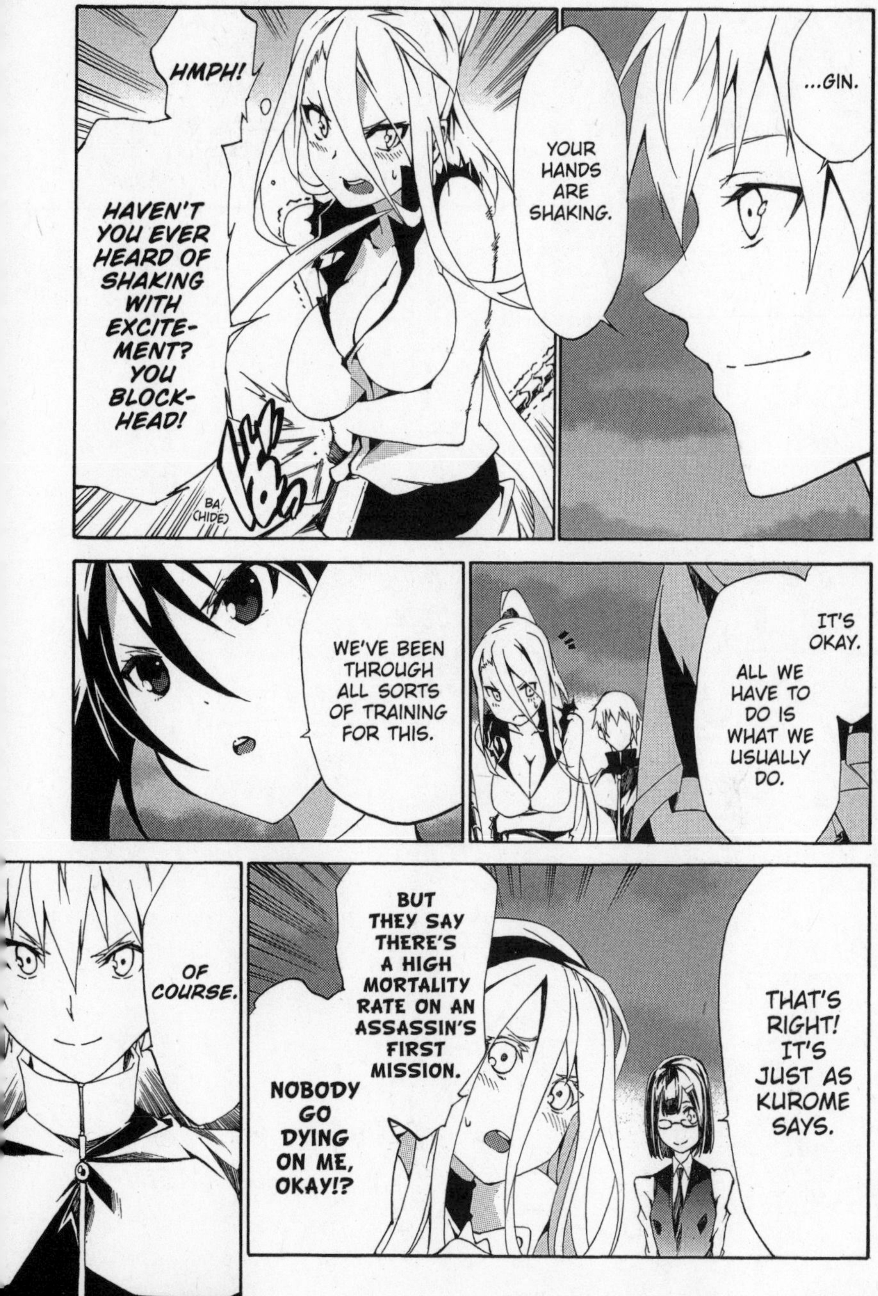
...GIN.
YOUR HANDS ARE SHAKING.
HMPH!
HAVEN'T YOU EVER HEARD OF SHAKING WITH EXCITE-MENT? YOU BLOCK-HEAD!
BA (HIDE)
IT'S OKAY.
ALL WE HAVE TO DO IS WHAT WE USUALLY DO.
WE'VE BEEN THROUGH ALL SORTS OF TRAINING FOR THIS.
THAT'S RIGHT! IT'S JUST AS KUROME SAYS.
BUT THEY SAY THERE'S A HIGH MORTALITY RATE ON AN ASSASSIN'S FIRST MISSION.
NOBODY GO DYING ON ME, OKAY!?
OF COURSE.

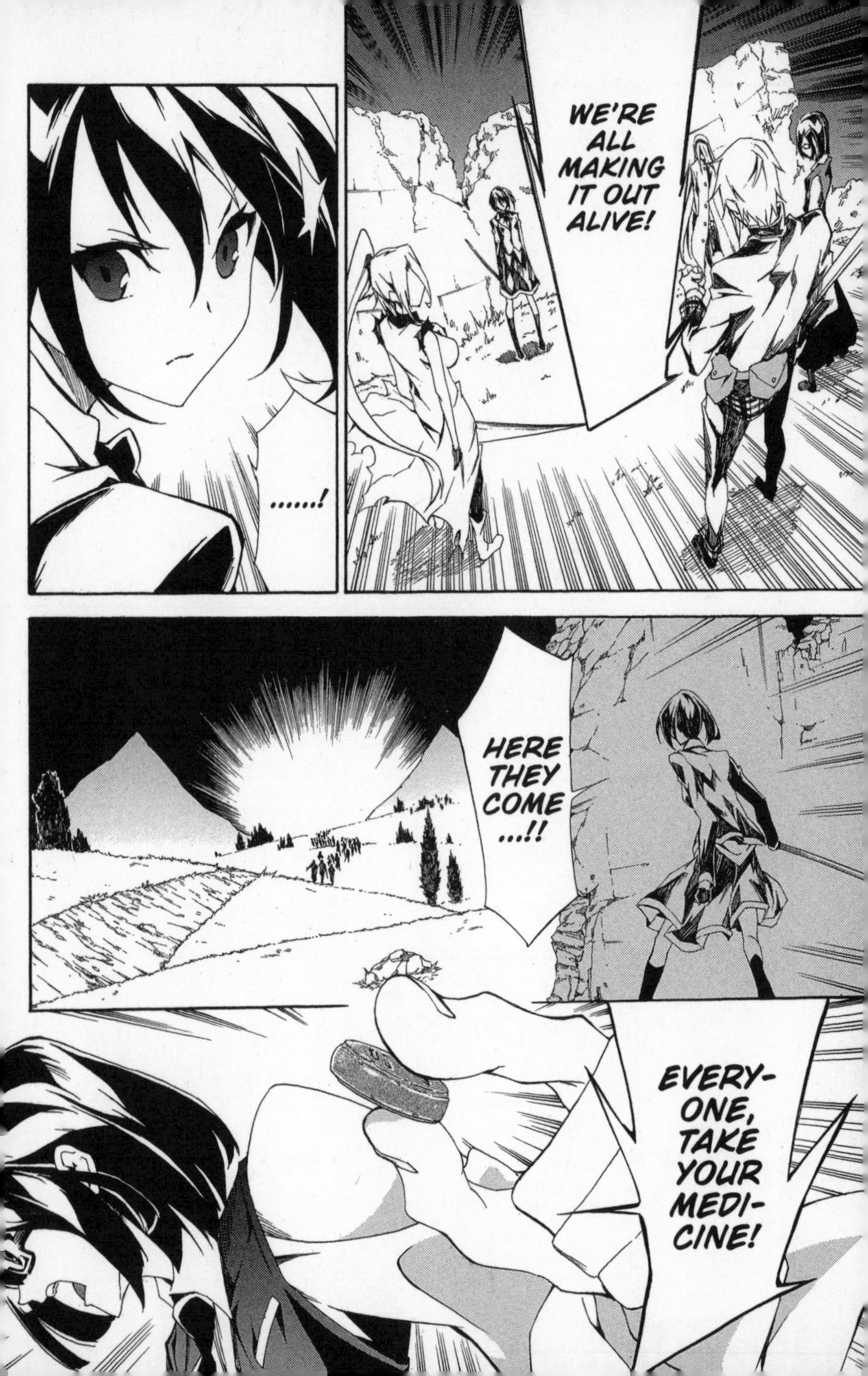
WE'RE ALL MAKING IT OUT ALIVE!
......!
HERE THEY COME ...!!
EVERY-ONE, TAKE YOUR MEDI-CINE!

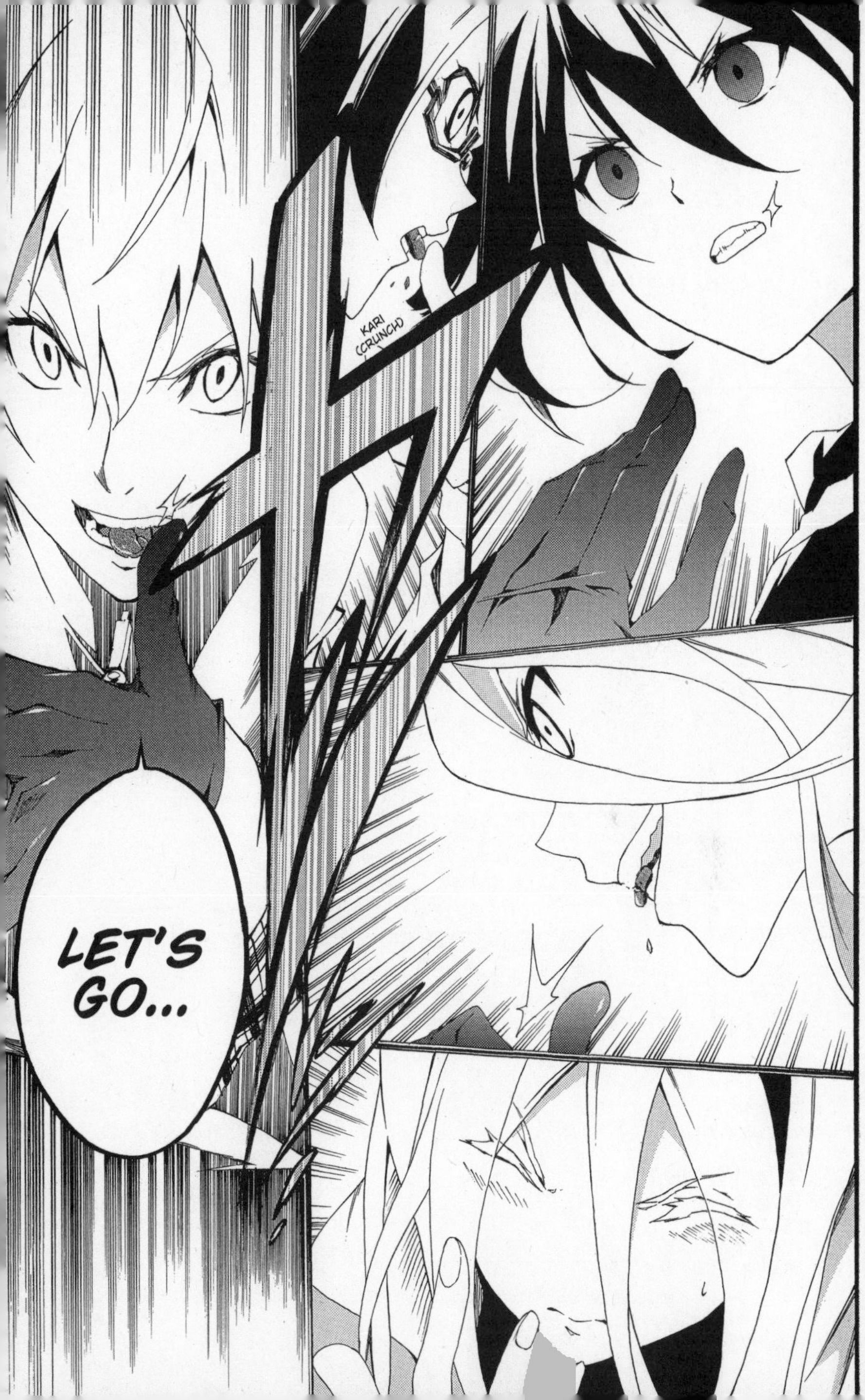
KARI (CRUNCH)
LET'S GO...

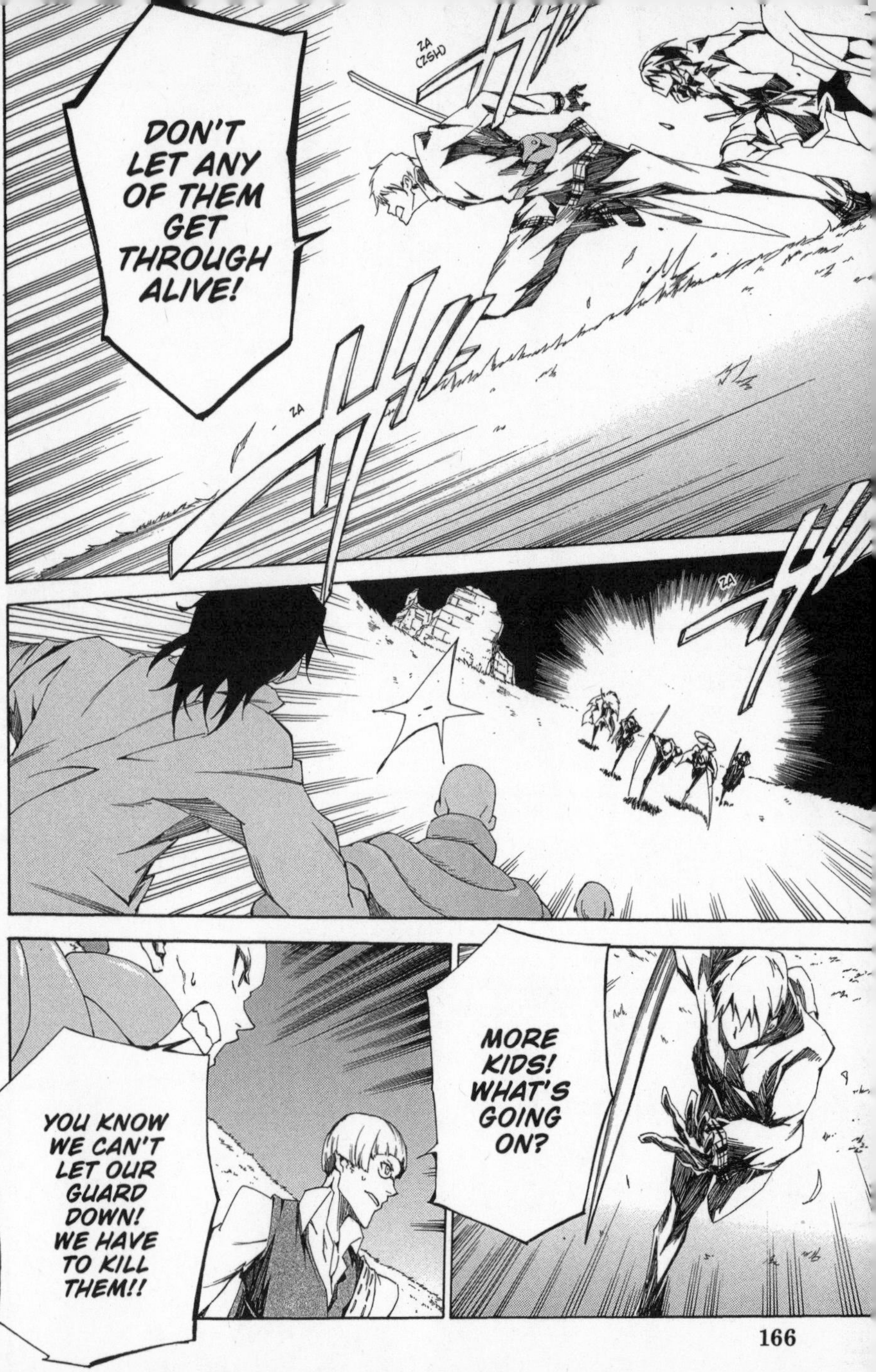
ZA (ZSH)
DON'T LET ANY OF THEM GET THROUGH ALIVE!
ZA
ZA
MORE KIDS! WHAT'S GOING ON?
YOU KNOW WE CAN'T LET OUR GUARD DOWN! WE HAVE TO KILL THEM!!

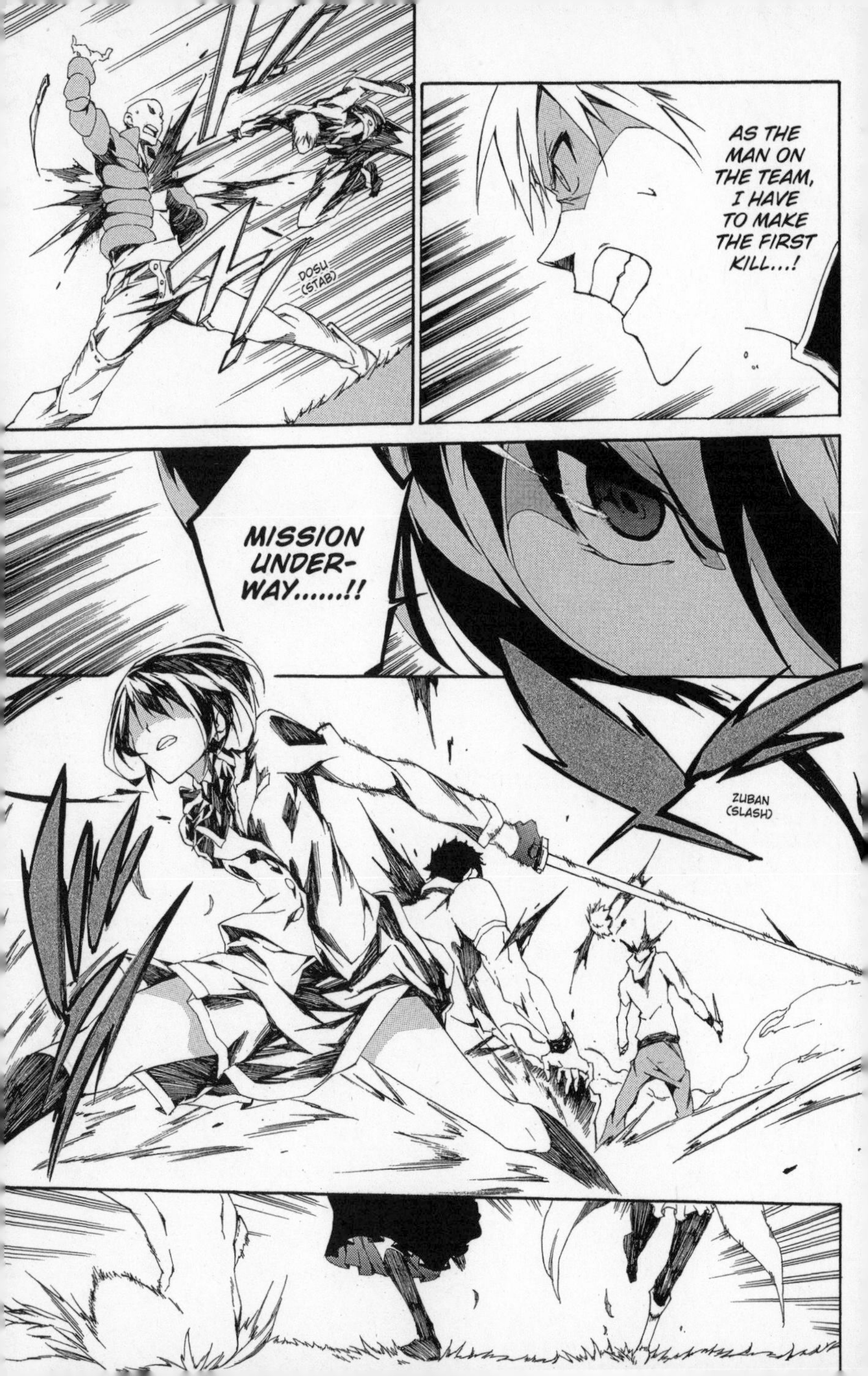
AS THE MAN ON THE TEAM, I HAVE TO MAKE THE FIRST KILL...!
DOSU (STAB)
MISSION UNDER-WAY......!!
ZUBAN (SLASH)

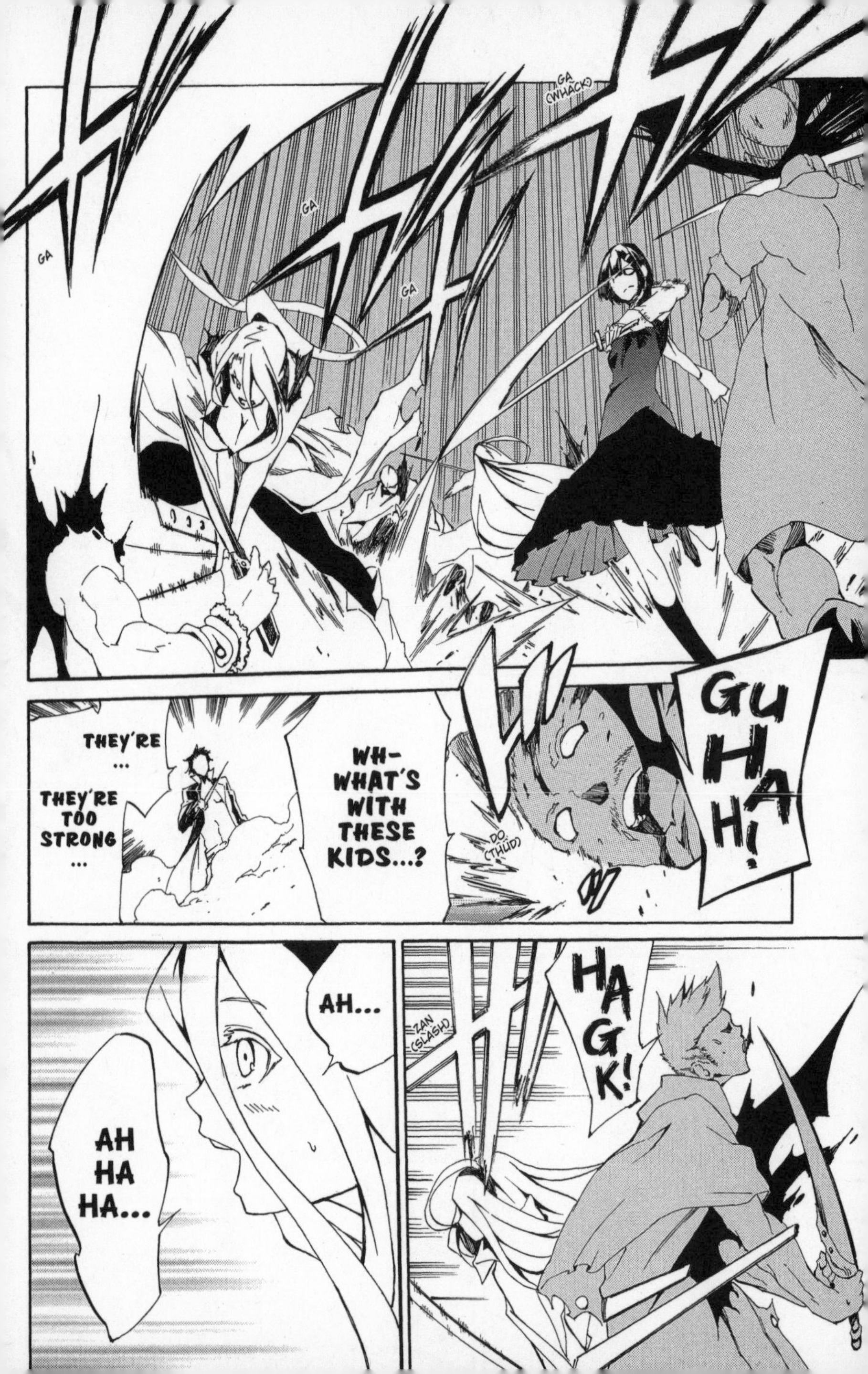
GA (WHACK)
GA
GA
GA
GUHAH!
DO (THUD)
WH-WHAT'S WITH THESE KIDS...?
THEY'RE ... THEY'RE TOO STRONG ...
HAGK!
ZAN (SLASH)
AH...
AH HA HA...

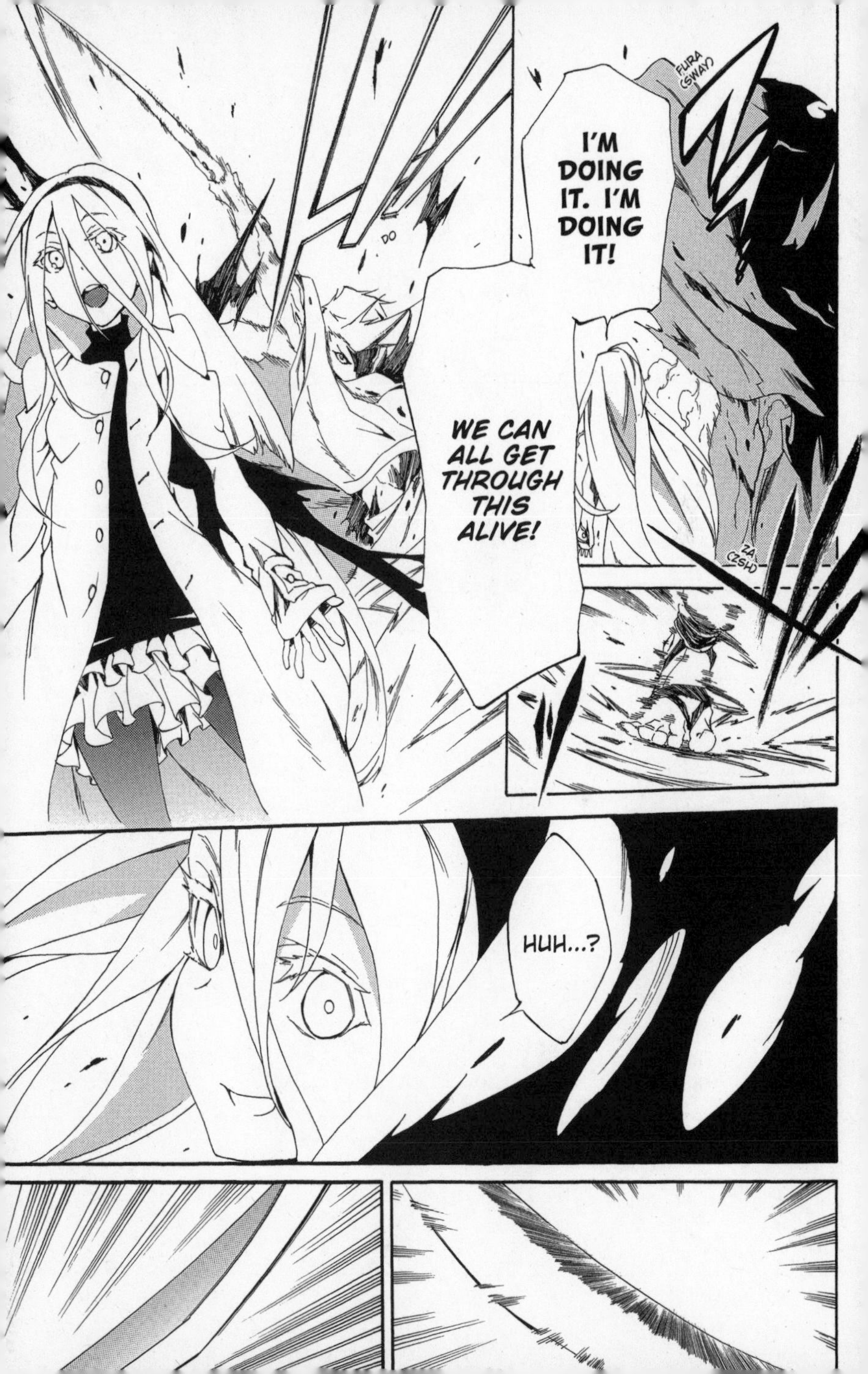
FURA (SWAY)
DO
I'M DOING IT. I'M DOING IT!
WE CAN ALL GET THROUGH THIS ALIVE!
ZA (ZSH)
HUH...?

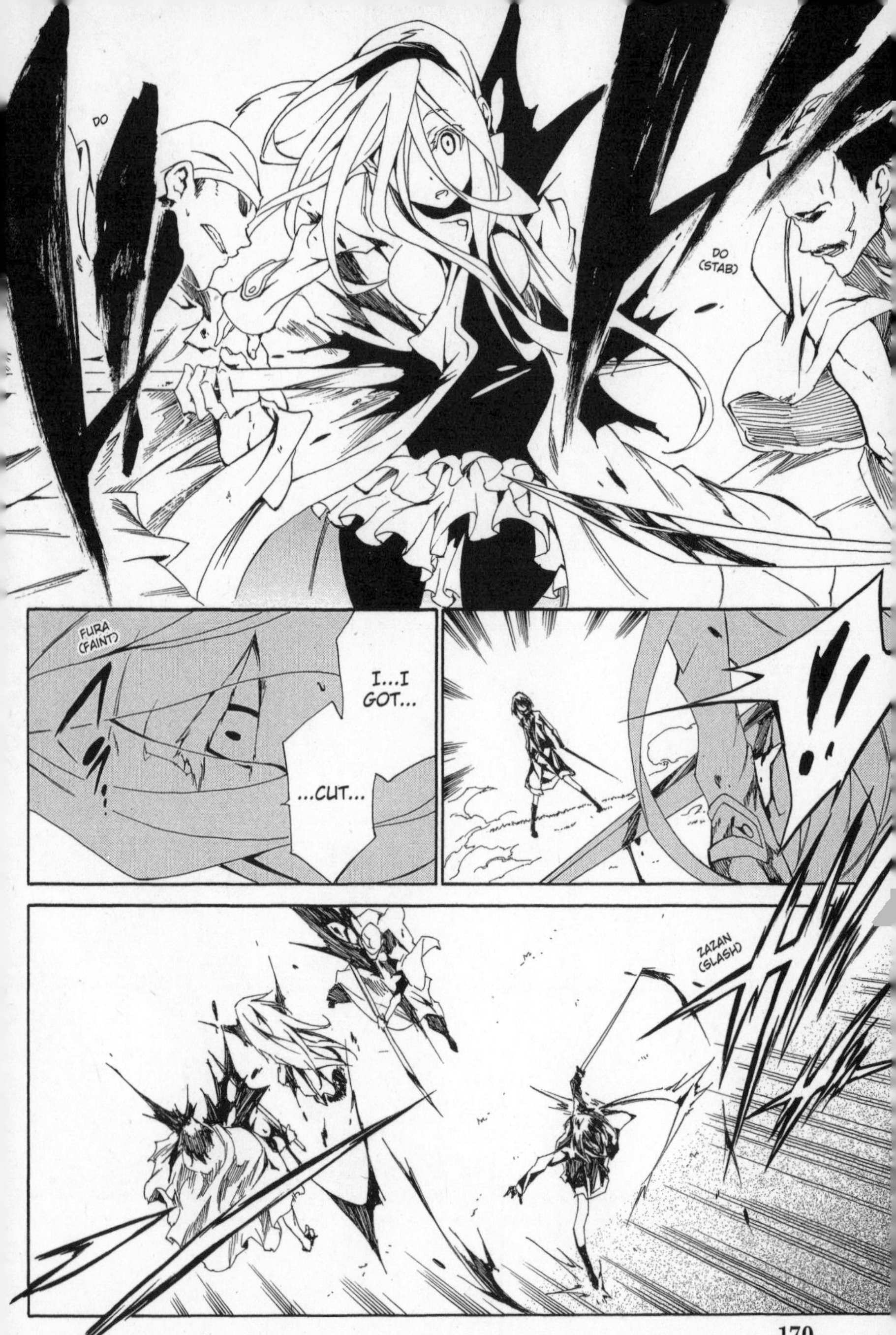
DO (STAB)
DO
FURA (FAINT)
I...I GOT...
...CUT...
ZAZAN (SLASH)

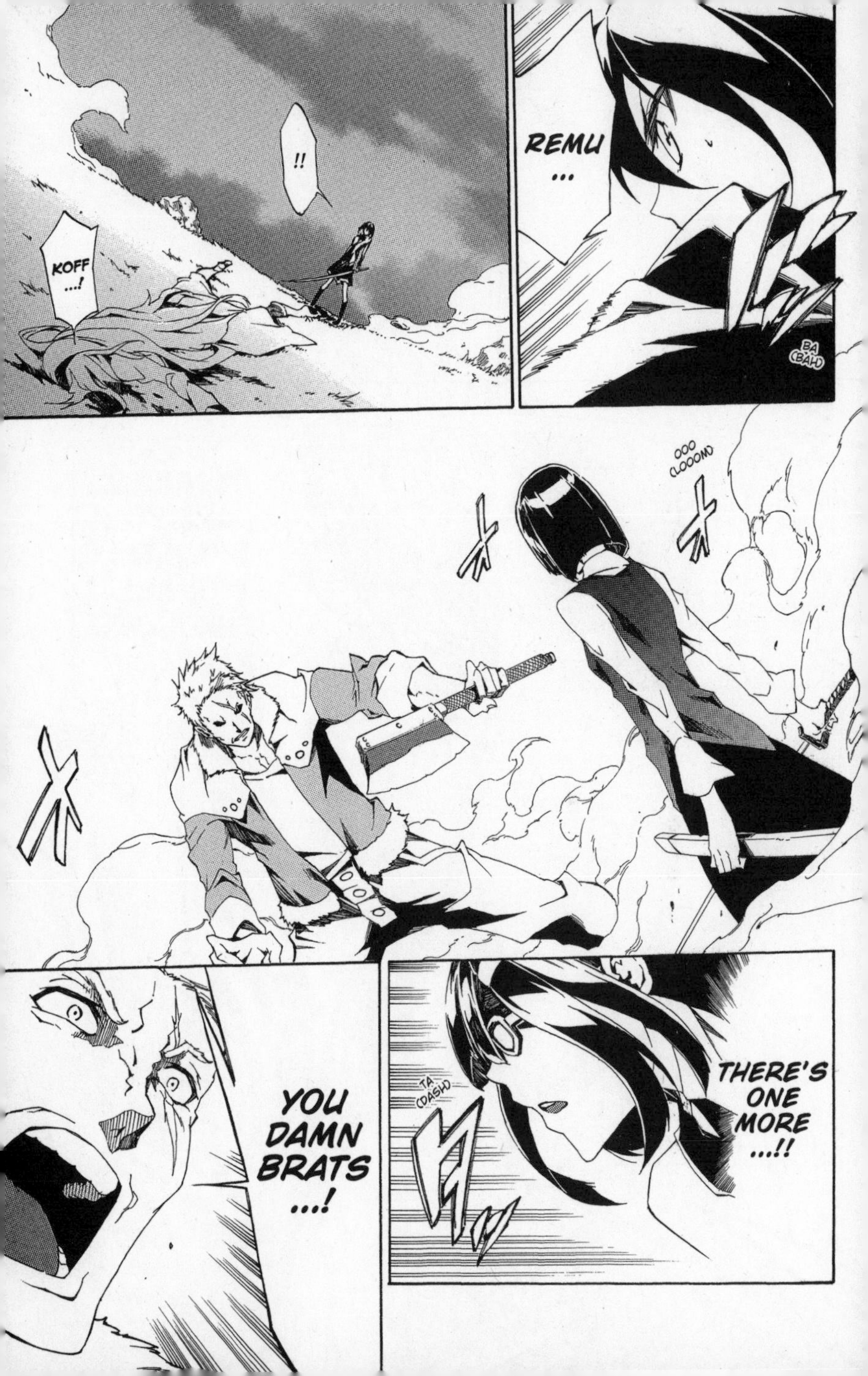
REMU
...
BA (BAH)
!!
KOFF ...!
OOO (LOOOM)
THERE'S ONE MORE ...!!
TA (DASH)
YOU DAMN BRATS ...!

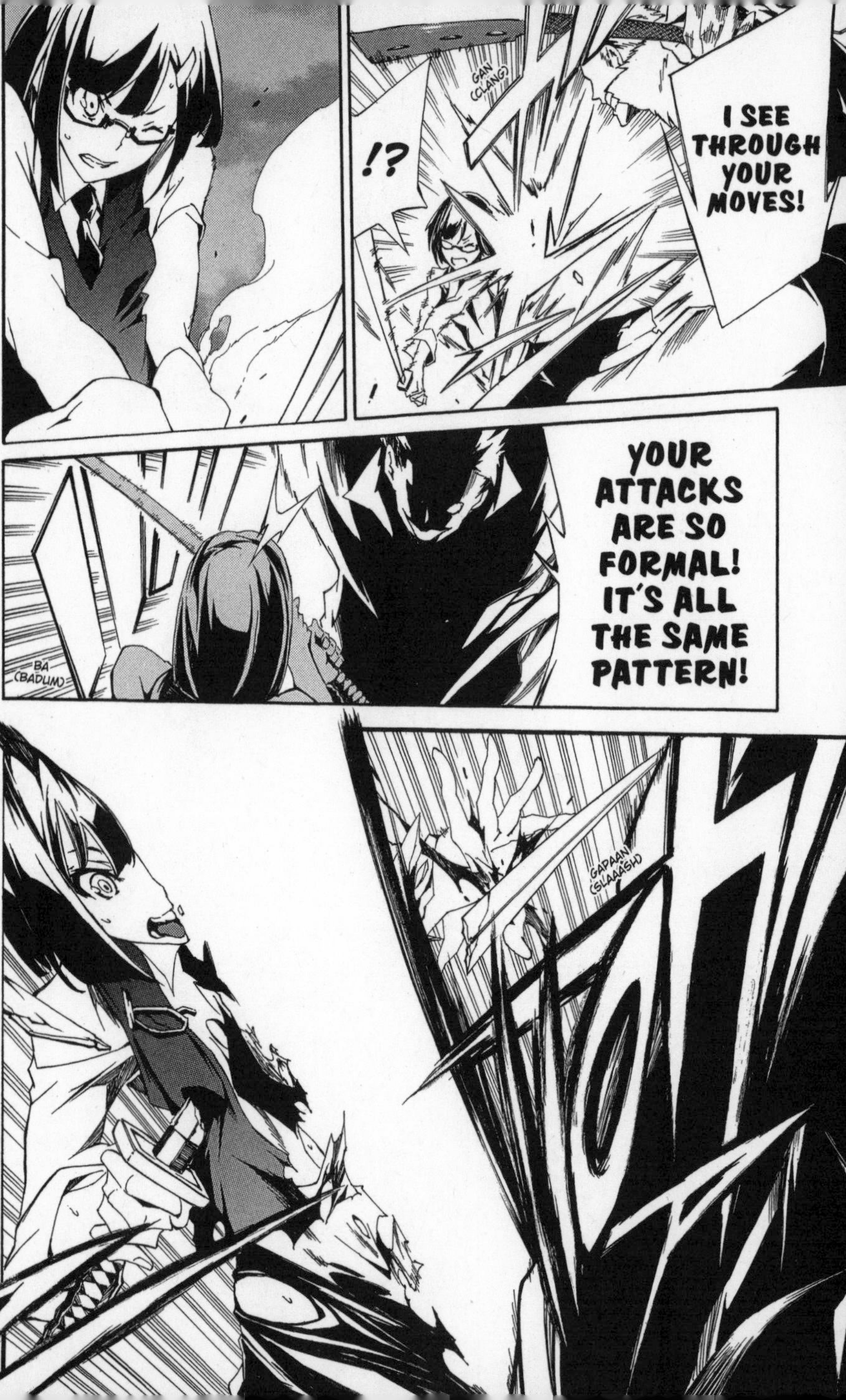

I SEE THROUGH YOUR MOVES!
GAN (CLANG)
!?
YOUR ATTACKS ARE SO FORMAL! IT'S ALL THE SAME PATTERN!
BA (BADUM)
GAPAAN (SLAAASH)

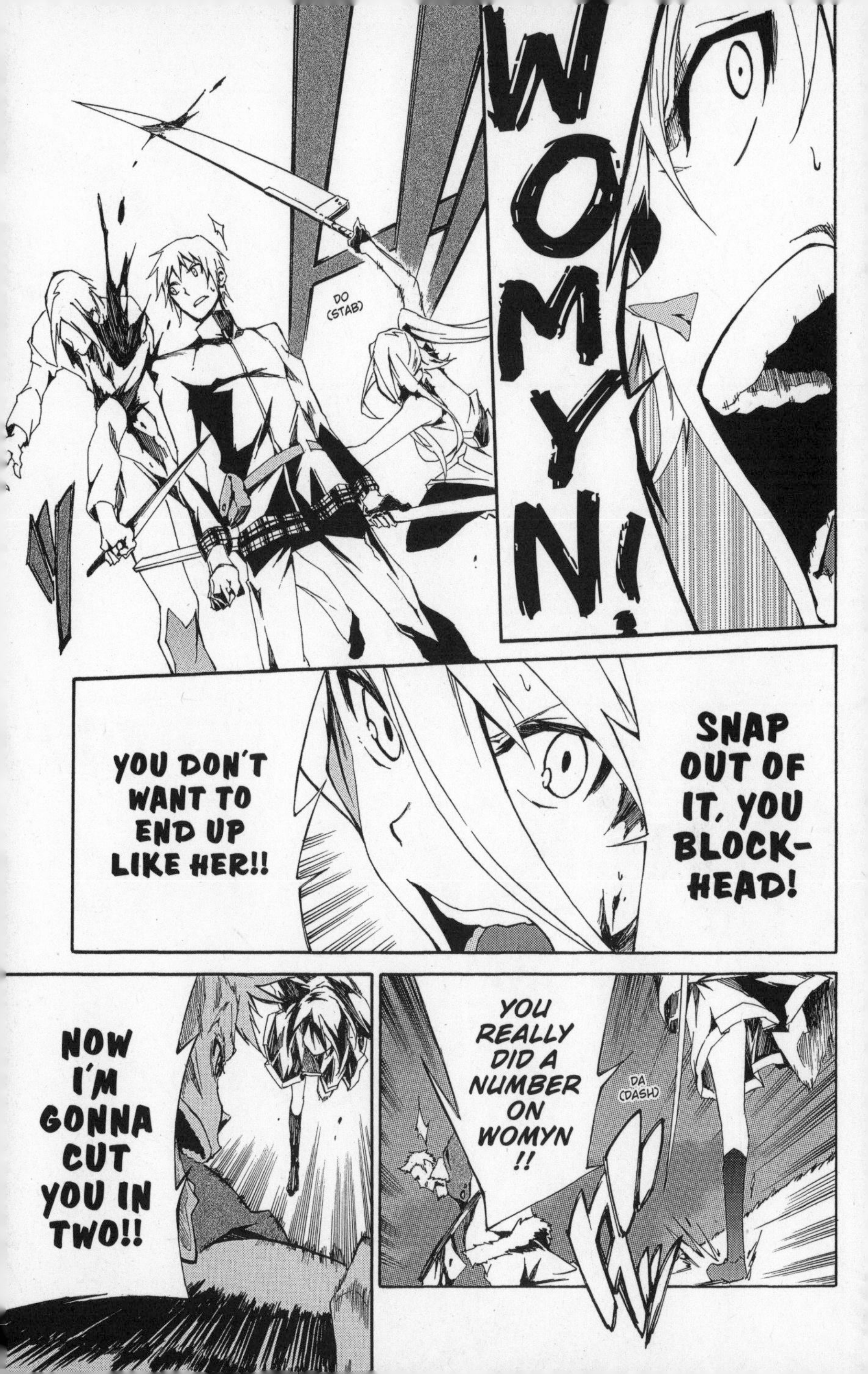
WOMYN!
DO (STAB)
SNAP OUT OF IT, YOU BLOCK-HEAD!
YOU DON'T WANT TO END UP LIKE HER!!
YOU REALLY DID A NUMBER ON WOMYN!!
DA (DASH)
NOW I'M GONNA CUT YOU IN TWO!!

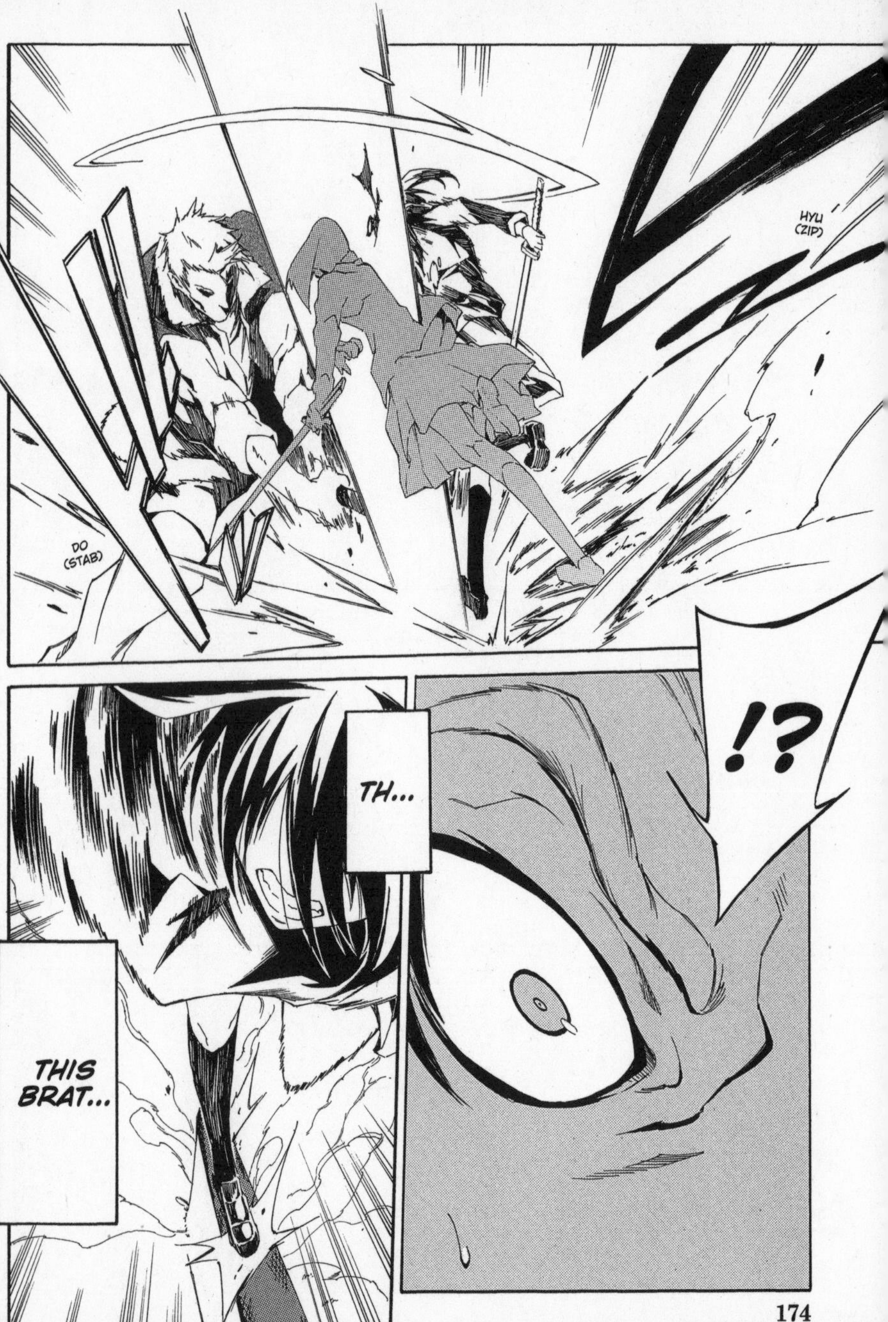
HYU
(ZIP)
DO
(STAB)
!?
TH...
THIS
BRAT...

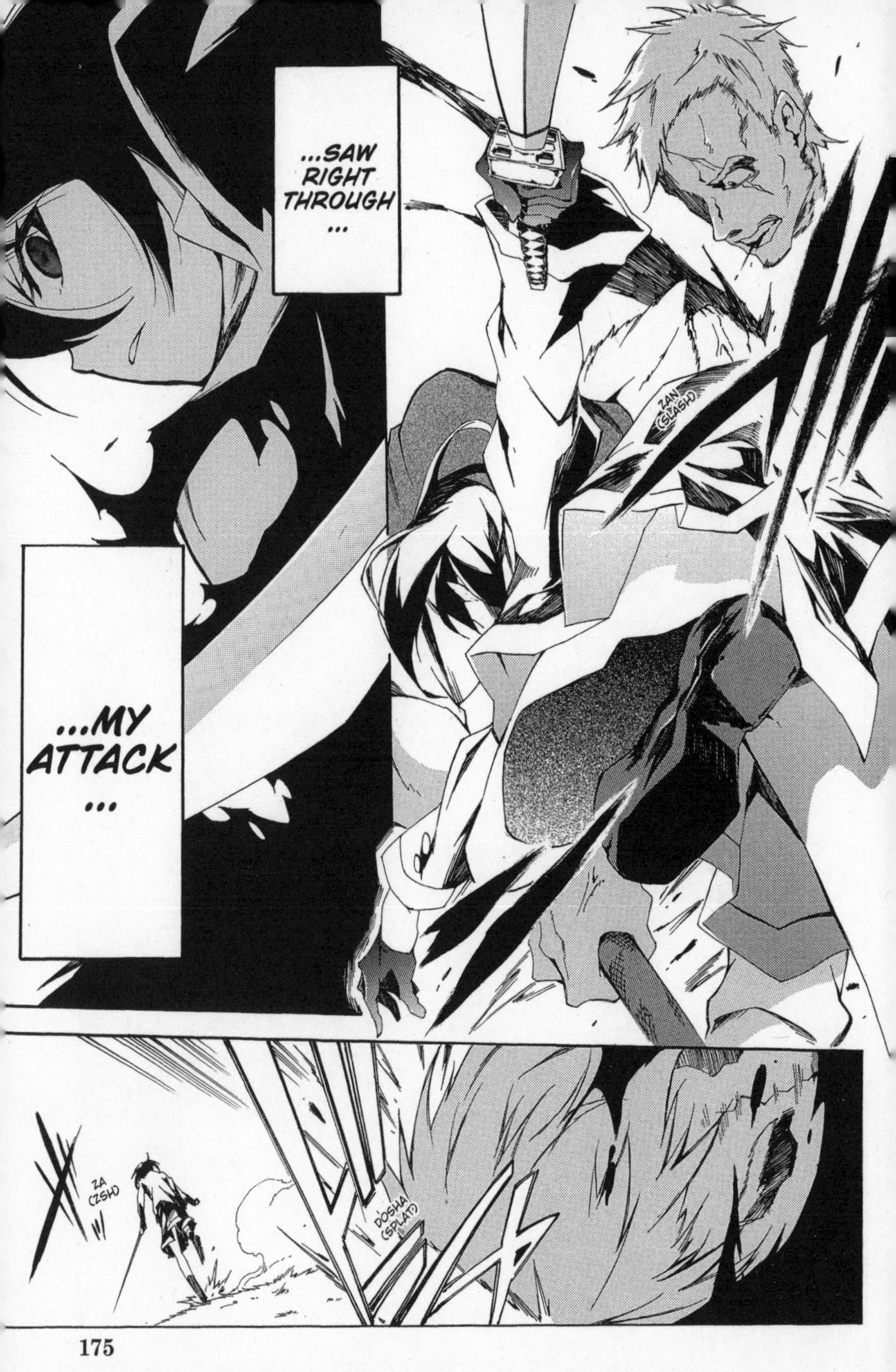
...SAW RIGHT THROUGH ...
ZAN (SLASH)
...MY ATTACK ...
DOSHA (SPLAT)
ZA (ZSH)

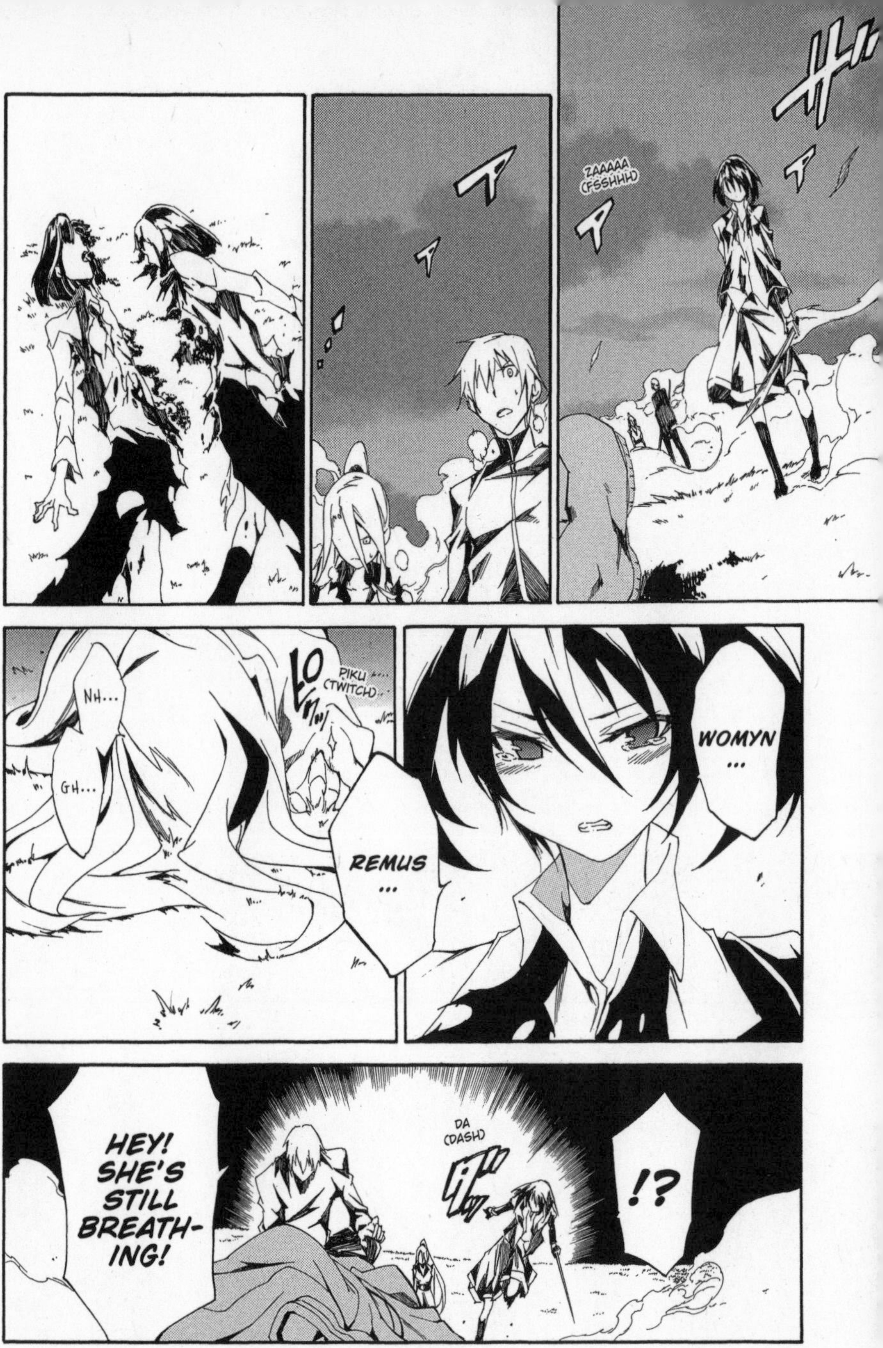
ZAAAAA (FSSHHH)
PIKU (TWITCH)
WOMYN ...
REMUS ...
NH...
GH...
!?
DA (DASH)
HEY! SHE'S STILL BREATH-ING!

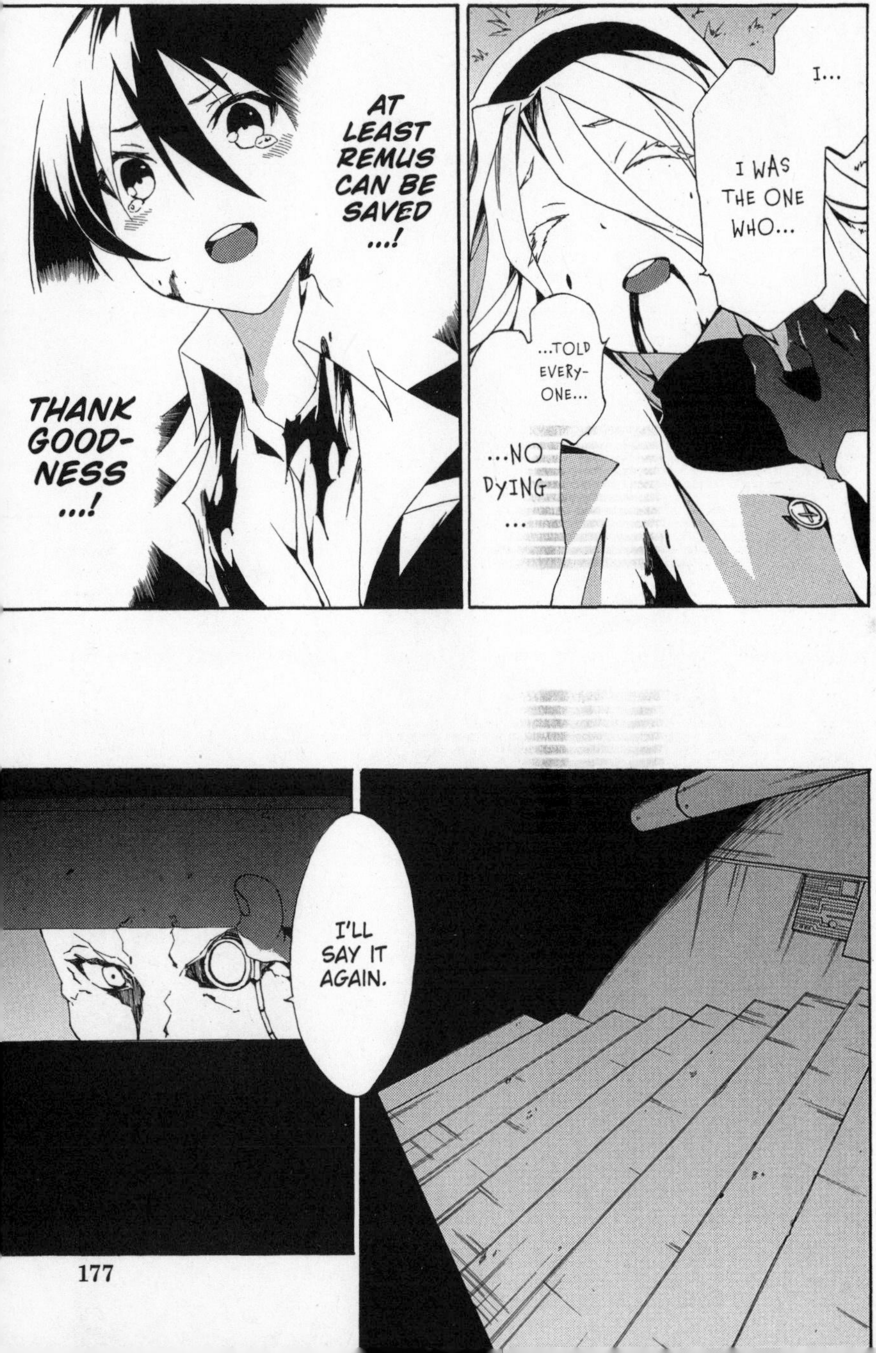
I...
I WAS THE ONE WHO...
...TOLD EVERY-ONE...
...NO DYING ...
AT LEAST REMUS CAN BE SAVED ...!
THANK GOOD-NESS ...!
I'LL SAY IT AGAIN.

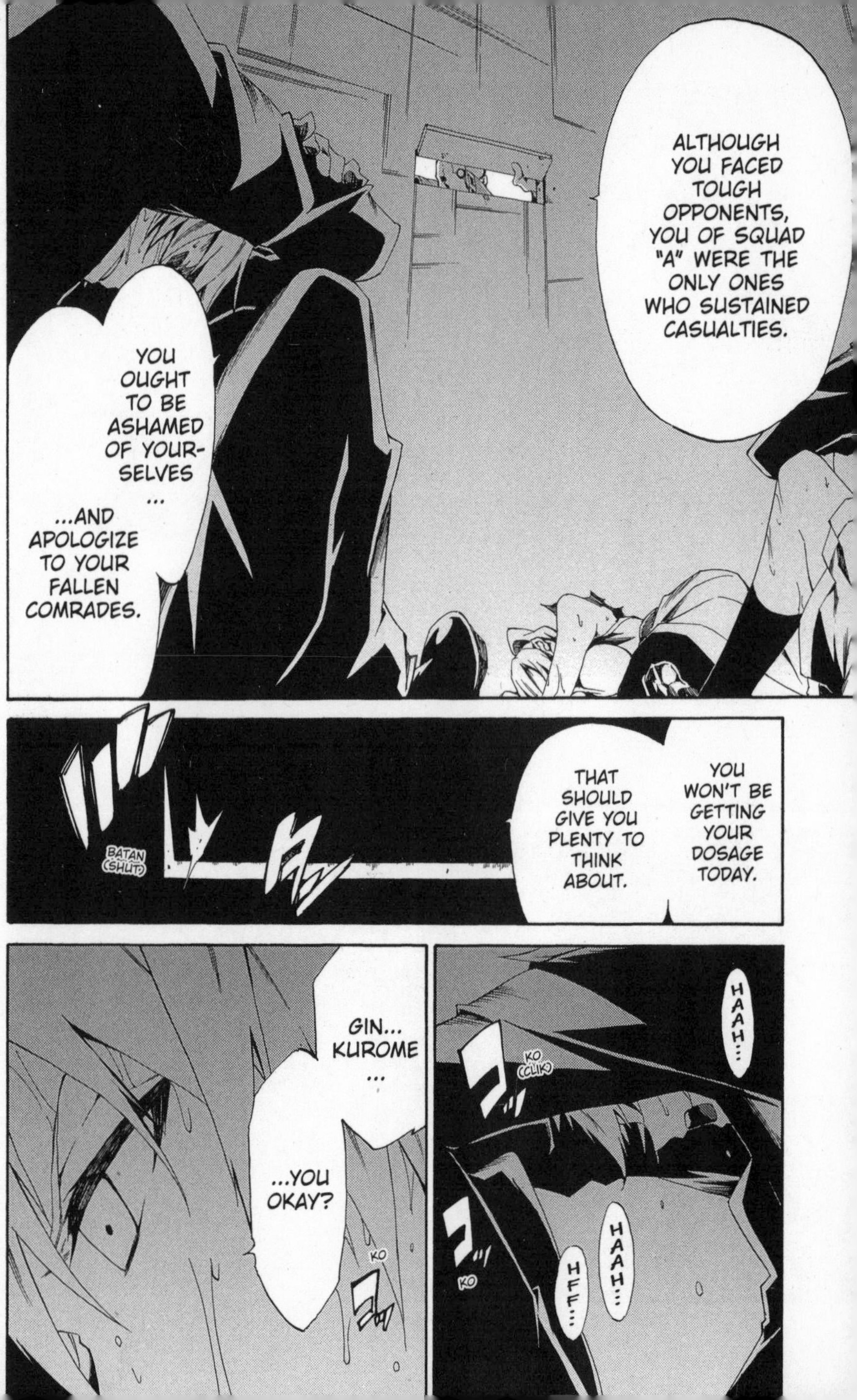
ALTHOUGH YOU FACED TOUGH OPPONENTS, YOU OF SQUAD "A" WERE THE ONLY ONES WHO SUSTAINED CASUALTIES.
YOU OUGHT TO BE ASHAMED OF YOUR-SELVES ...
...AND APOLOGIZE TO YOUR FALLEN COMRADES.
YOU WON'T BE GETTING YOUR DOSAGE TODAY.
THAT SHOULD GIVE YOU PLENTY TO THINK ABOUT.
BATAN (SHUT)
HAAAH...
KO (CLIK)
HAAAH...
HFF...
KO
GIN... KUROME ...
...YOU OKAY?
KO

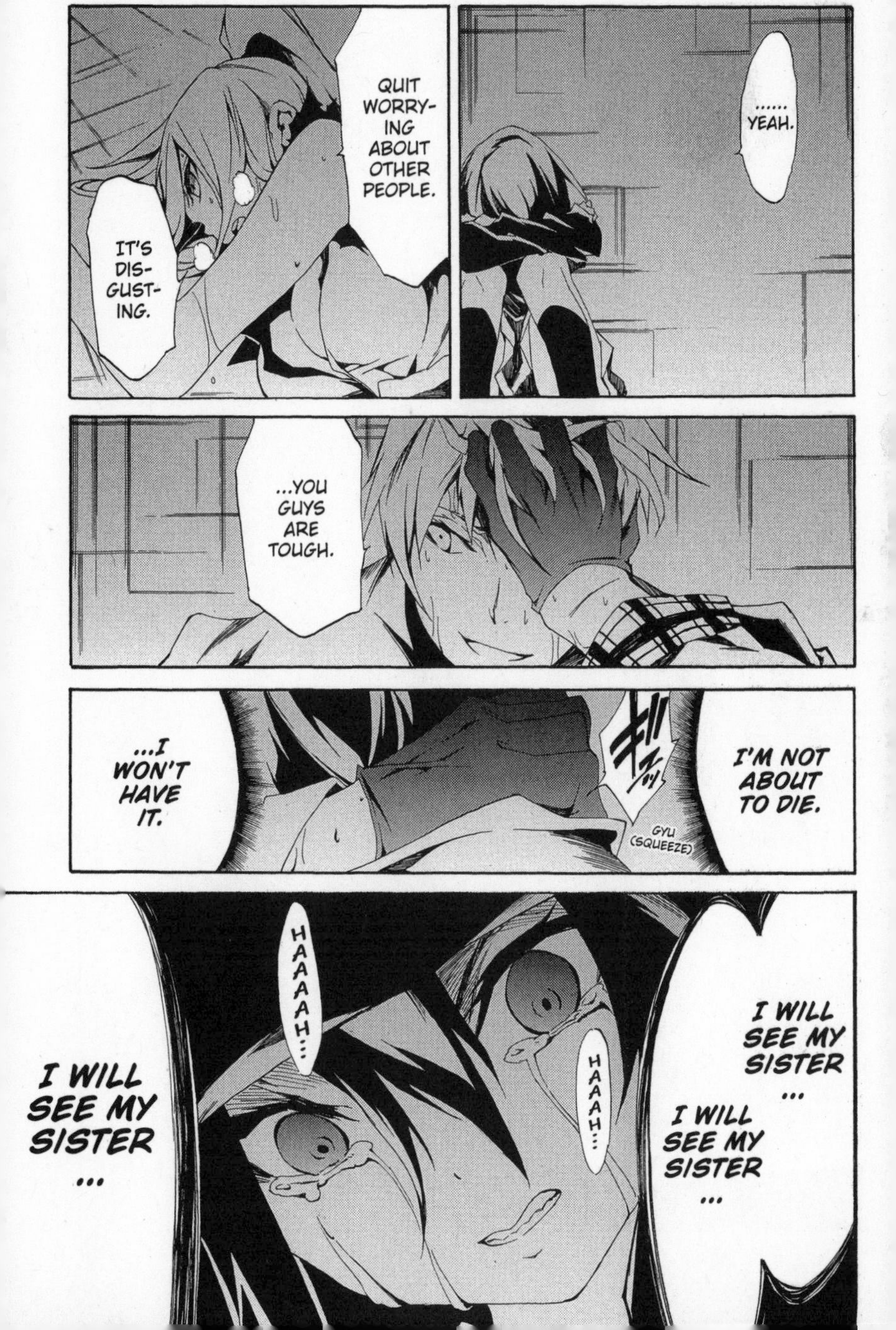
QUIT WORRYING ABOUT OTHER PEOPLE.
IT'S DISGUSTING.
......YEAH.
...YOU GUYS ARE TOUGH.
I'M NOT ABOUT TO DIE.
GYU (SQUEEZE)
...I WON'T HAVE IT.
I WILL SEE MY SISTER...
I WILL SEE MY SISTER...
HAAAAH...
HAAAH...
I WILL SEE MY SISTER...

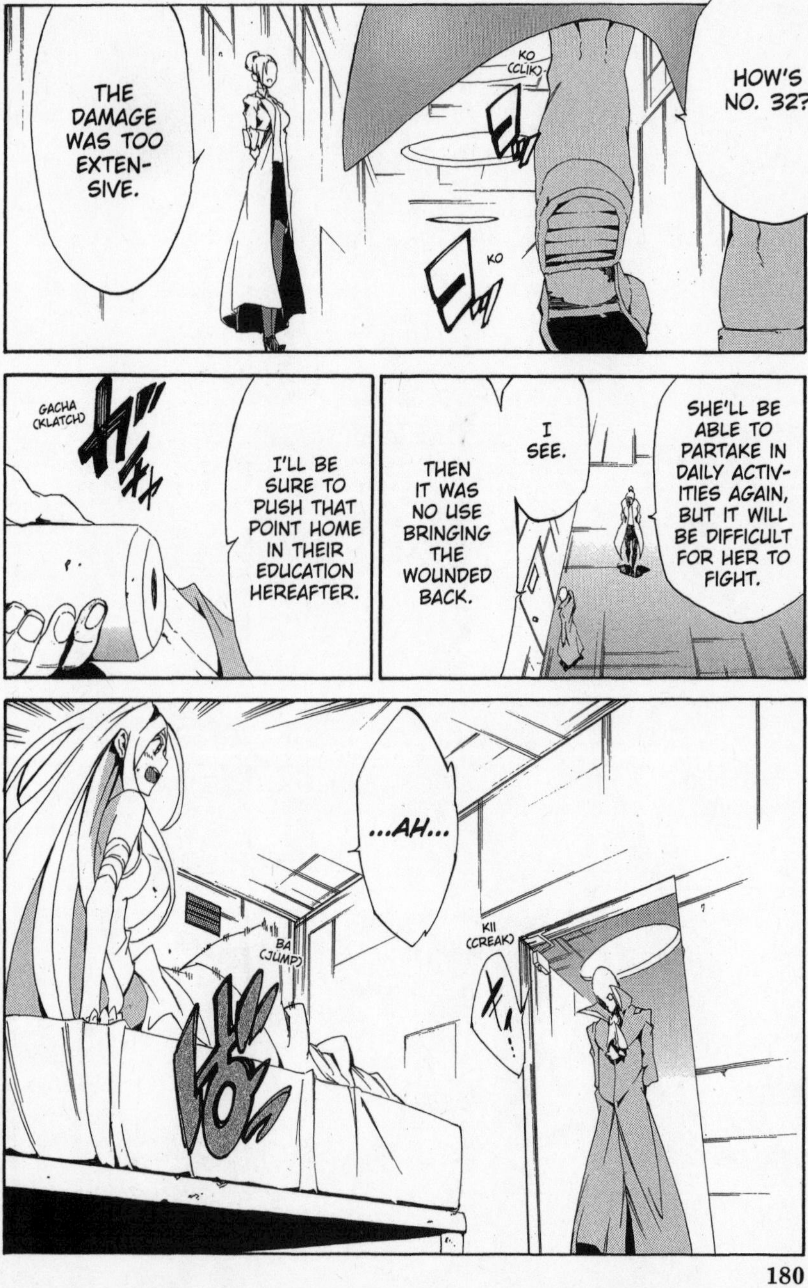
HOW'S NO. 32?
KO (CLIK)
KO
THE DAMAGE WAS TOO EXTEN-SIVE.
SHE'LL BE ABLE TO PARTAKE IN DAILY ACTIV-ITIES AGAIN, BUT IT WILL BE DIFFICULT FOR HER TO FIGHT.
I SEE.
THEN IT WAS NO USE BRINGING THE WOUNDED BACK.
GACHA (KLATCH)
I'LL BE SURE TO PUSH THAT POINT HOME IN THEIR EDUCATION HEREAFTER.
KII (CREAK)
...AH...
BA (JUMP)

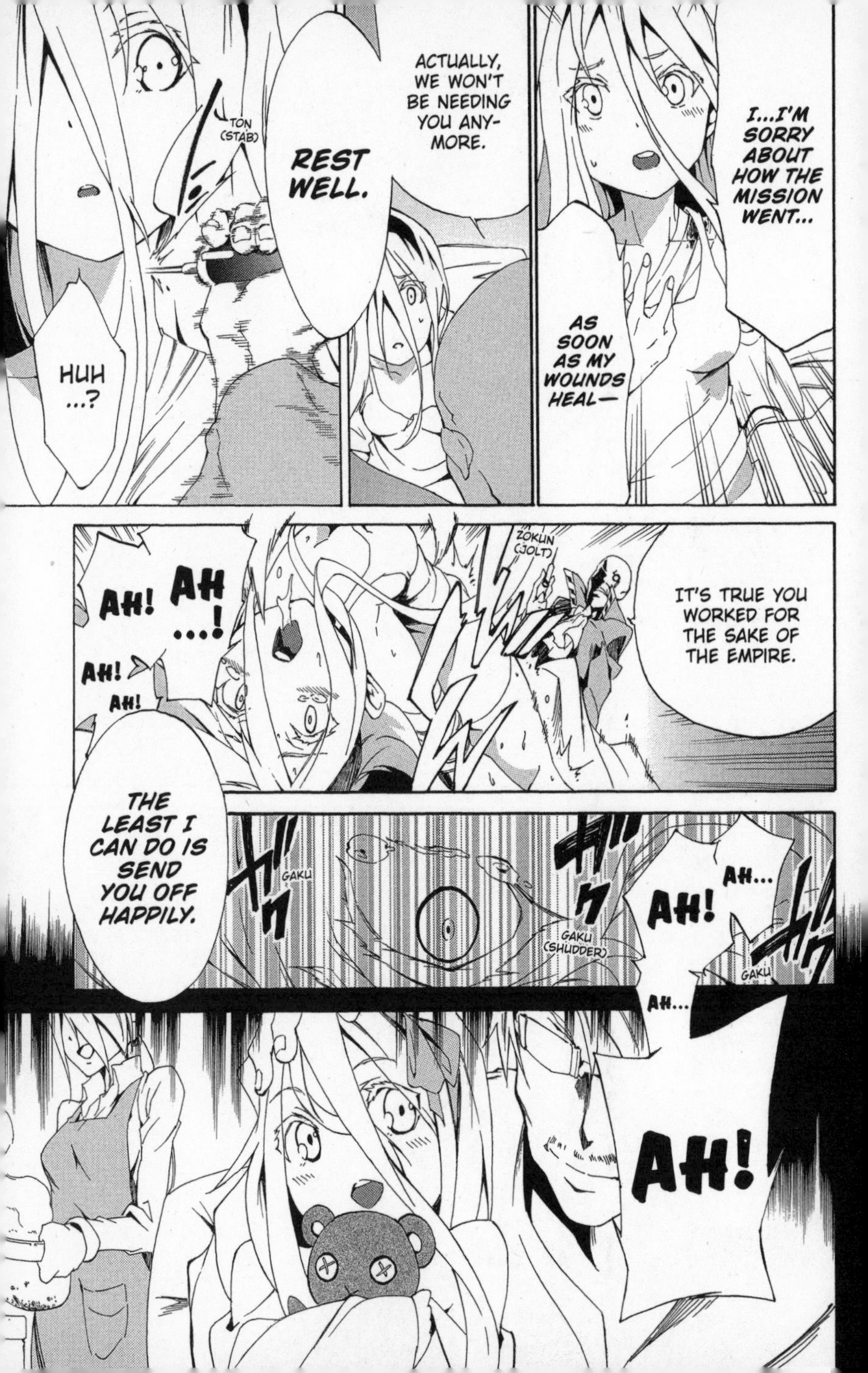
I...I'M SORRY ABOUT HOW THE MISSION WENT...
AS SOON AS MY WOUNDS HEAL—
ACTUALLY, WE WON'T BE NEEDING YOU ANY-MORE.
REST WELL.
TON (STAB)
HUH ...?
IT'S TRUE YOU WORKED FOR THE SAKE OF THE EMPIRE.
ZOKUN (JOLT)
AH ...!
AH!
AH!
AH!
THE LEAST I CAN DO IS SEND YOU OFF HAPPILY.
GAKU
AH...
AH!
GAKU
GAKU (SHUDDER)
GAKU
AH...
AH!

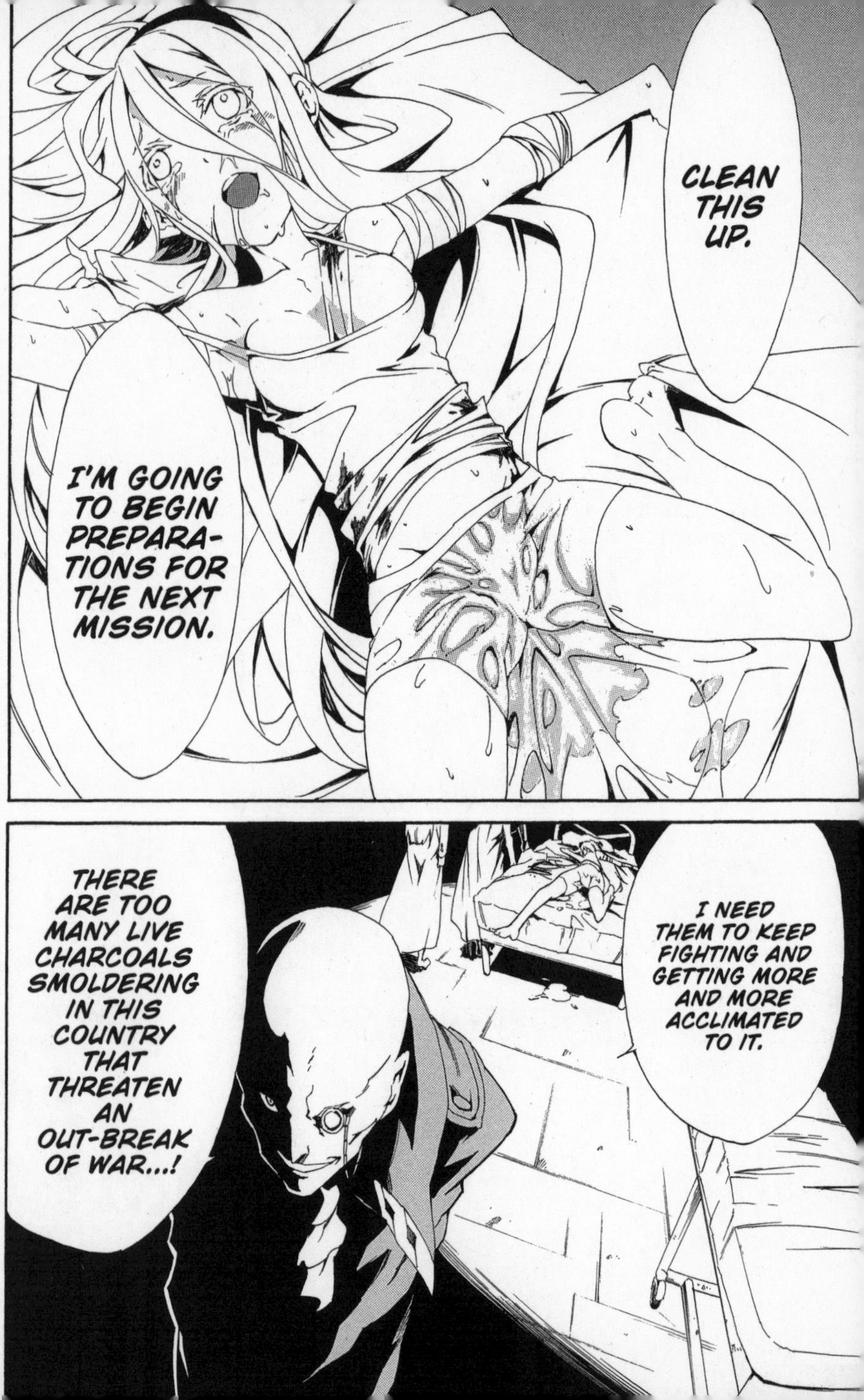
CLEAN THIS UP.
I'M GOING TO BEGIN PREPARA-TIONS FOR THE NEXT MISSION.
I NEED THEM TO KEEP FIGHTING AND GETTING MORE AND MORE ACCLIMATED TO IT.
THERE ARE TOO MANY LIVE CHARCOALS SMOLDERING IN THIS COUNTRY THAT THREATEN AN OUT-BREAK OF WAR...!

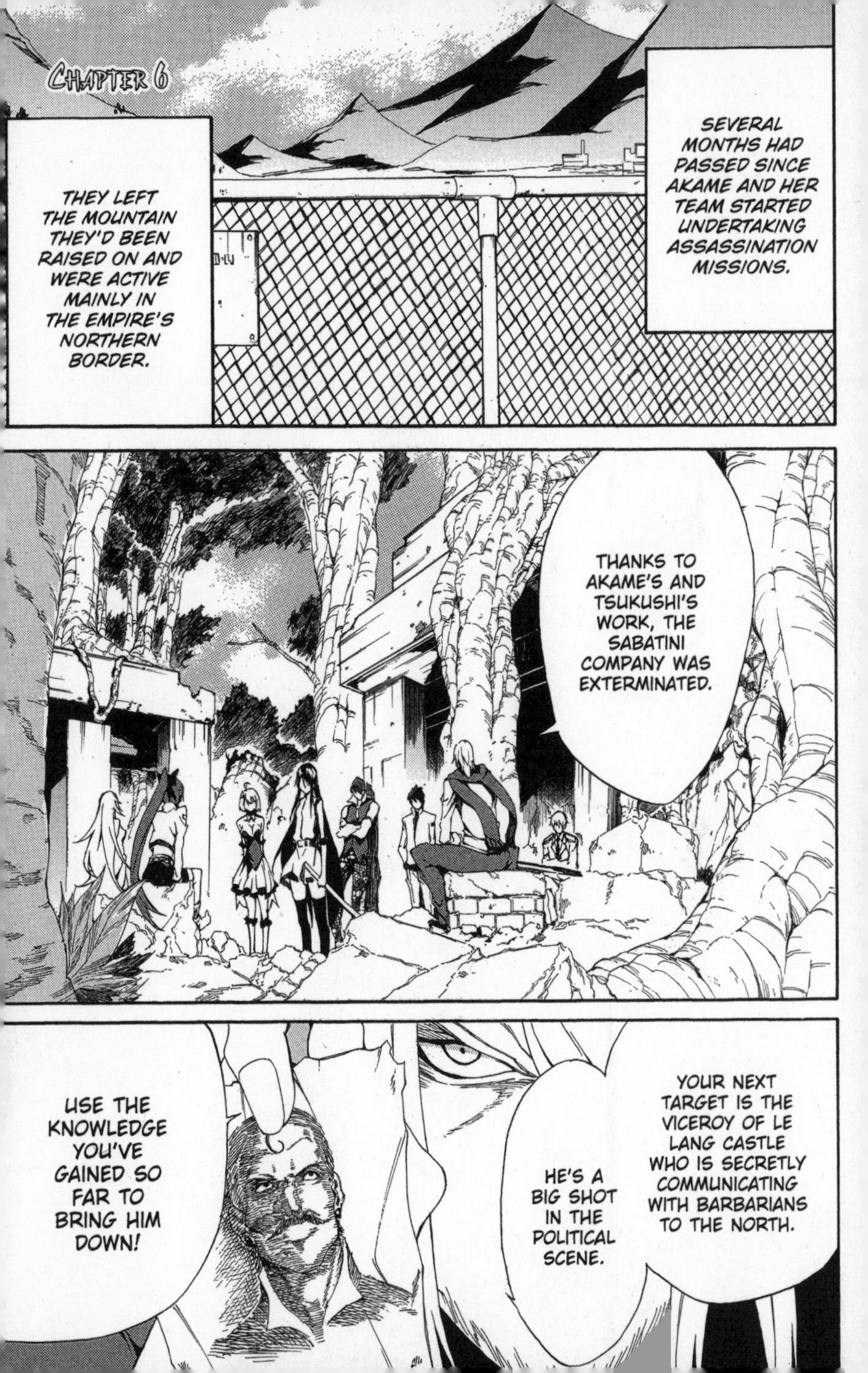
CHAPTER 6
SEVERAL MONTHS HAD PASSED SINCE AKAME AND HER TEAM STARTED UNDERTAKING ASSASSINATION MISSIONS.
THEY LEFT THE MOUNTAIN THEY'D BEEN RAISED ON AND WERE ACTIVE MAINLY IN THE EMPIRE'S NORTHERN BORDER.
THANKS TO AKAME'S AND TSUKUSHI'S WORK, THE SABATINI COMPANY WAS EXTERMINATED.
YOUR NEXT TARGET IS THE VICEROY OF LE LANG CASTLE WHO IS SECRETLY COMMUNICATING WITH BARBARIANS TO THE NORTH.
HE'S A BIG SHOT IN THE POLITICAL SCENE.
USE THE KNOWLEDGE YOU'VE GAINED SO FAR TO BRING HIM DOWN!

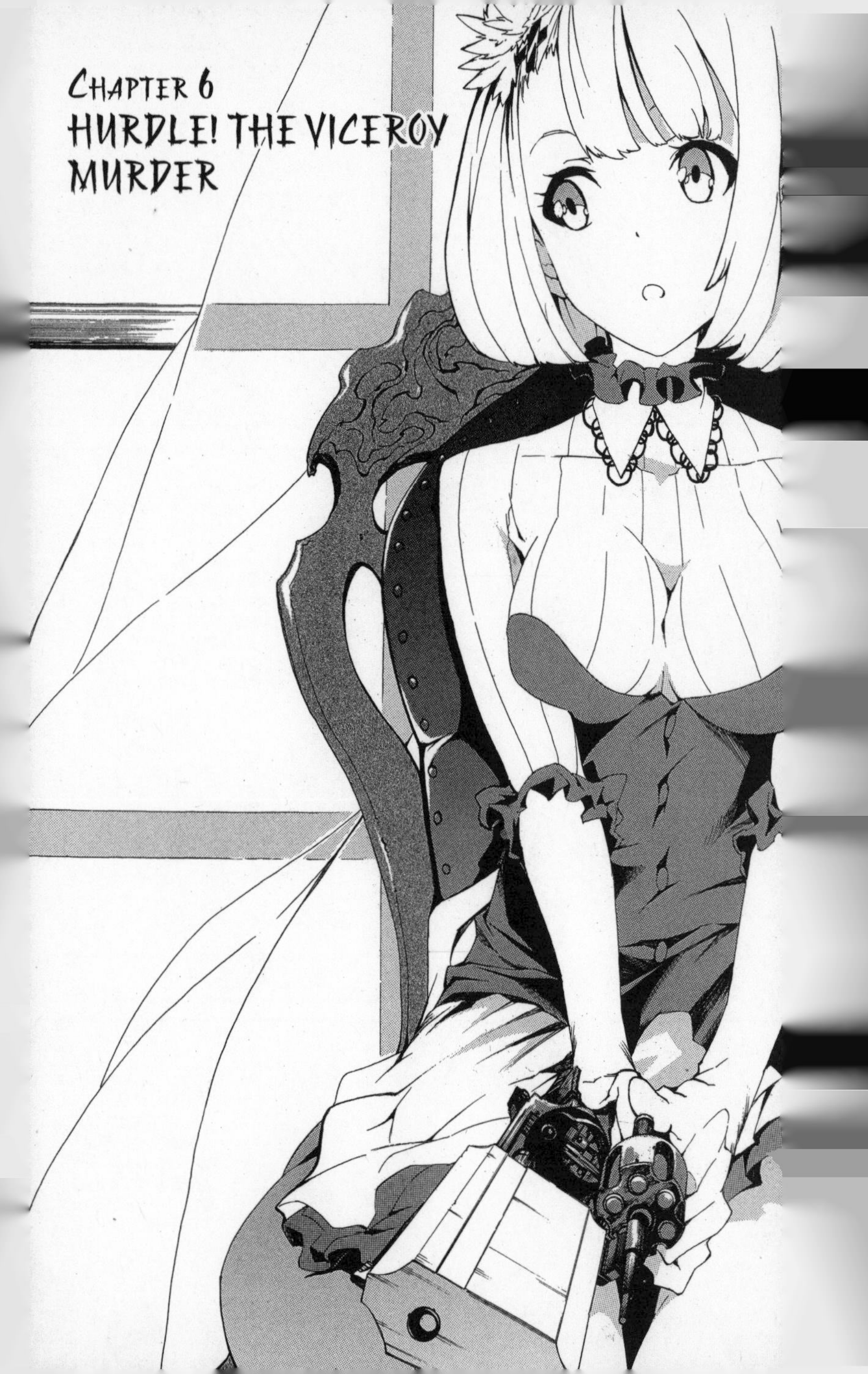
CHAPTER 6
HURDLE! THE VICEROY MURDER

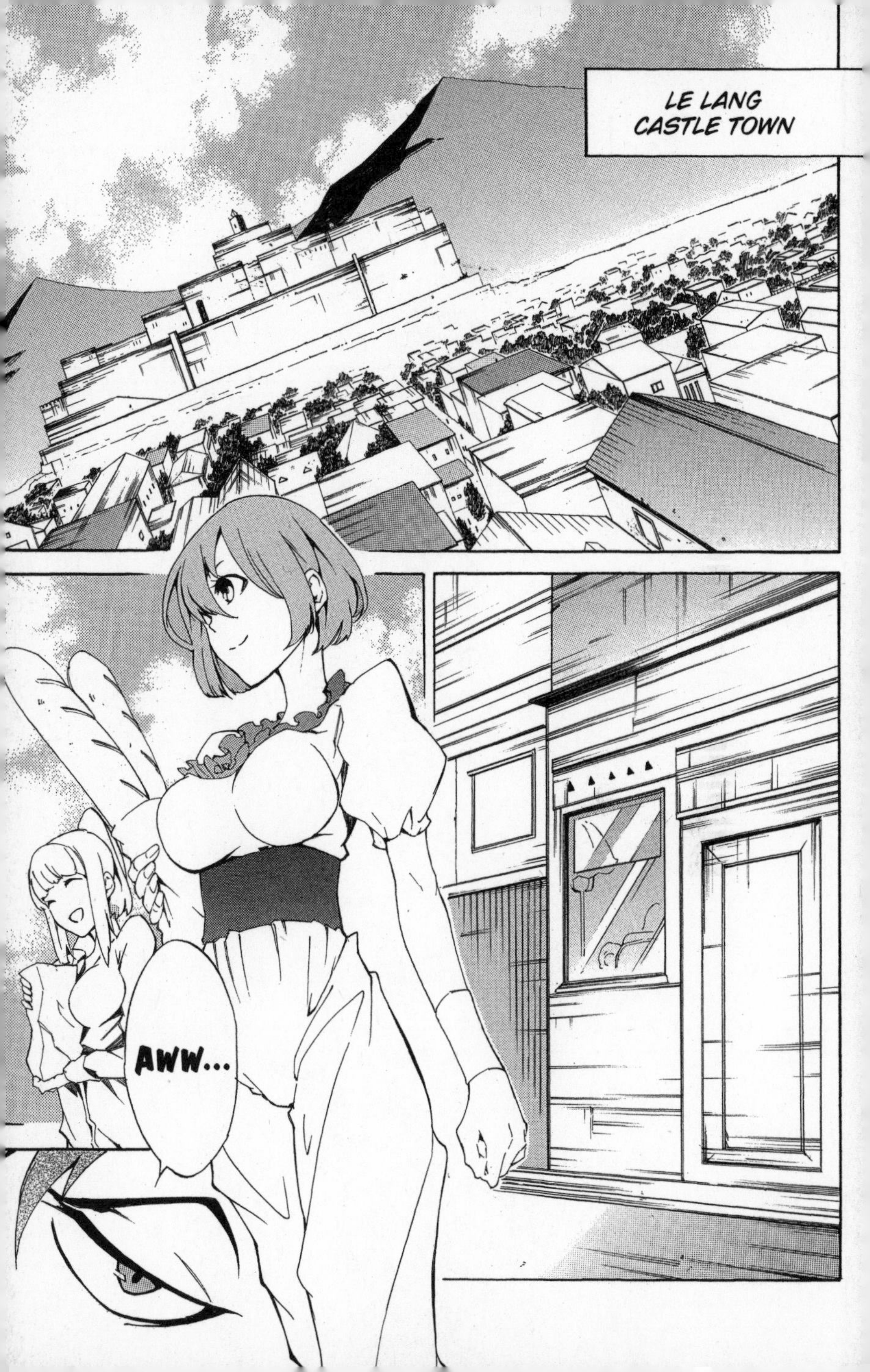
LE LANG CASTLE TOWN
AWW...

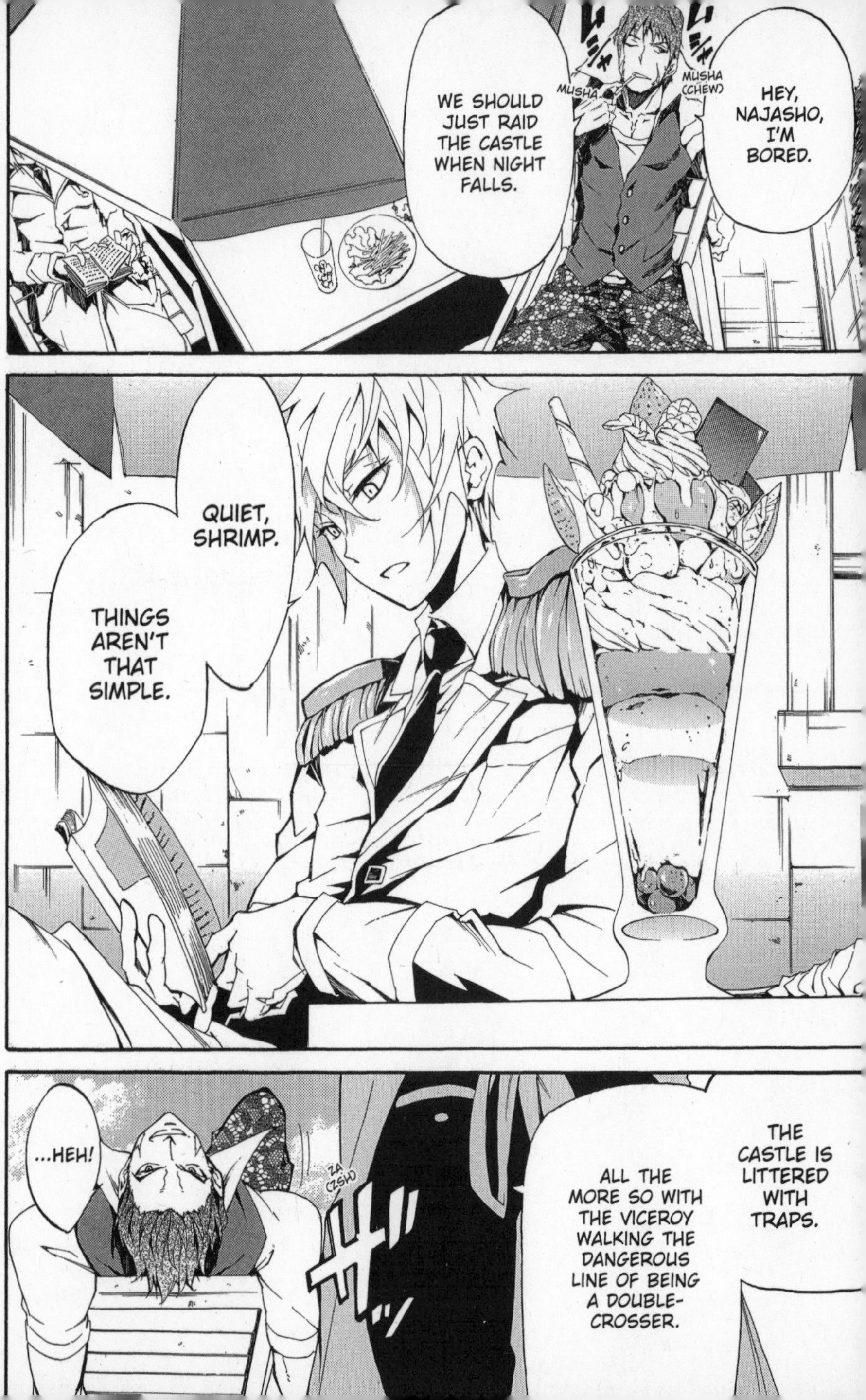
HEY, NAJASHO, I'M BORED.
MUSHA (CHEW)
MUSHA
WE SHOULD JUST RAID THE CASTLE WHEN NIGHT FALLS.
QUIET, SHRIMP.
THINGS AREN'T THAT SIMPLE.
THE CASTLE IS LITTERED WITH TRAPS.
ALL THE MORE SO WITH THE VICEROY WALKING THE DANGEROUS LINE OF BEING A DOUBLE-CROSSER.
ZA (ZSH)
...HEH!

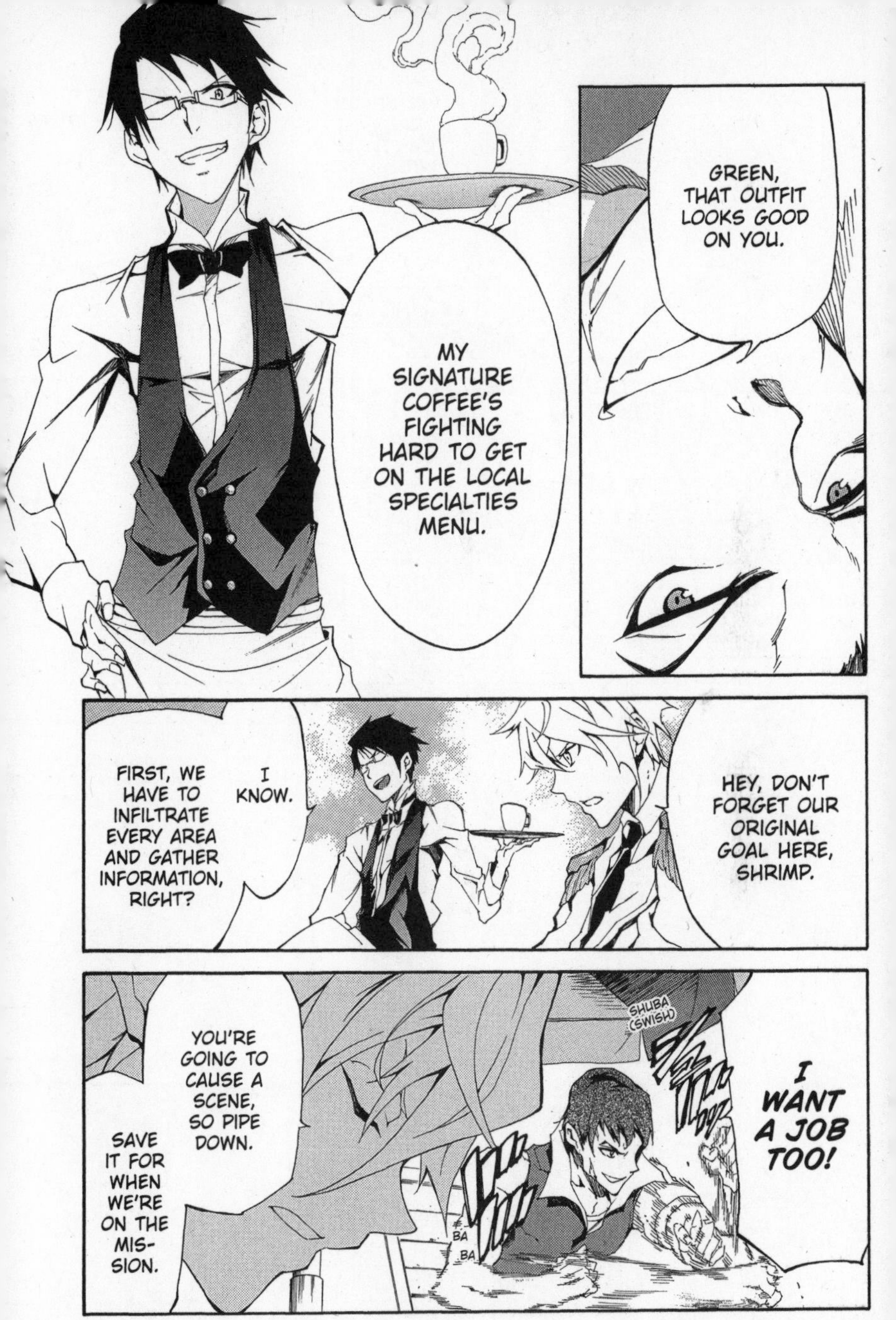
GREEN, THAT OUTFIT LOOKS GOOD ON YOU.
MY SIGNATURE COFFEE'S FIGHTING HARD TO GET ON THE LOCAL SPECIALTIES MENU.
HEY, DON'T FORGET OUR ORIGINAL GOAL HERE, SHRIMP.
I KNOW.
FIRST, WE HAVE TO INFILTRATE EVERY AREA AND GATHER INFORMATION, RIGHT?
SHUBA (SWISH)
I WANT A JOB TOO!
BA BA
YOU'RE GOING TO CAUSE A SCENE, SO PIPE DOWN.
SAVE IT FOR WHEN WE'RE ON THE MIS-SION.

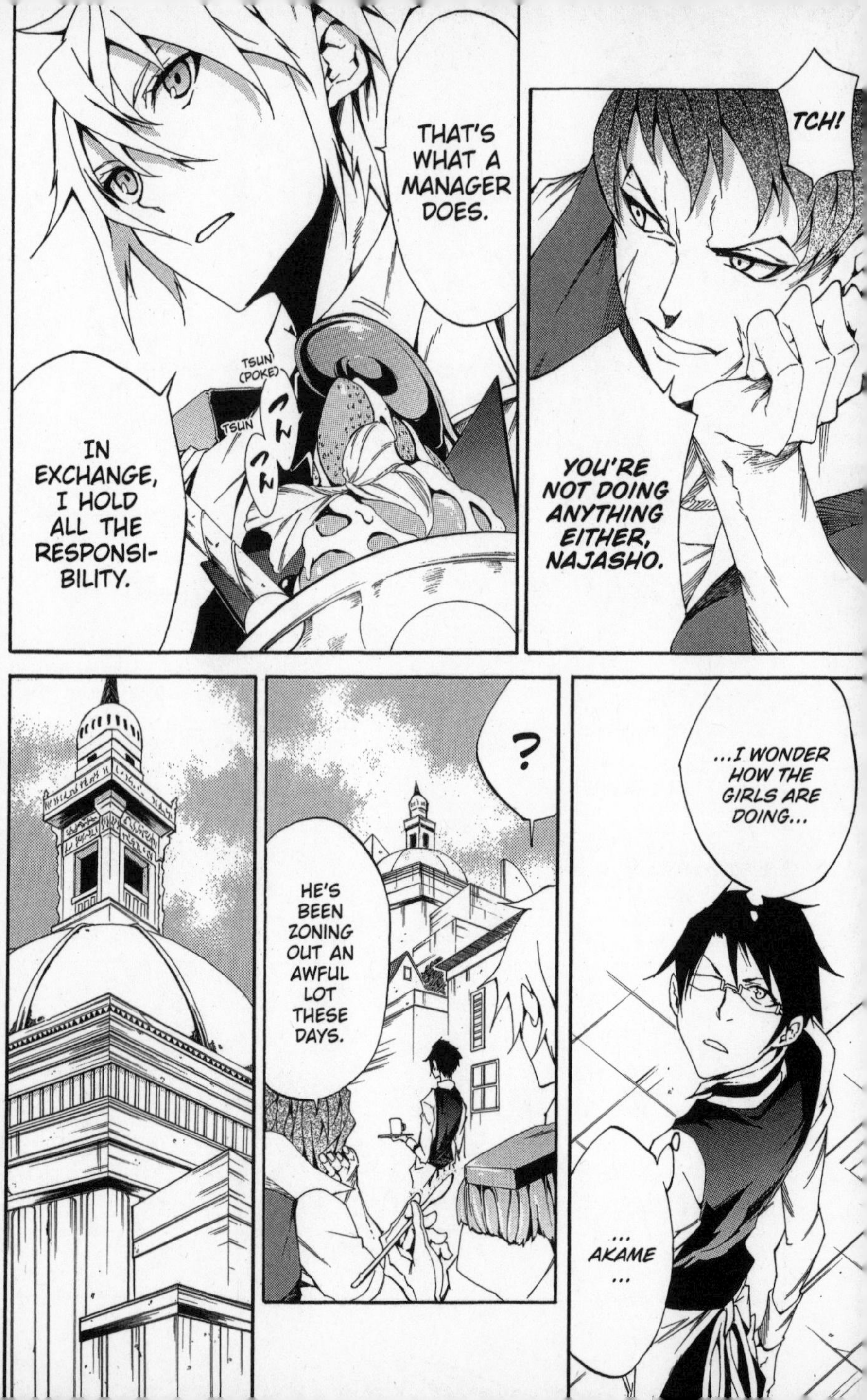

TCH!
YOU'RE NOT DOING ANYTHING EITHER, NAJASHO.
THAT'S WHAT A MANAGER DOES.
TSUN (POKE)
TSUN
IN EXCHANGE, I HOLD ALL THE RESPONSI-BILITY.
...I WONDER HOW THE GIRLS ARE DOING...
... AKAME ...
?
HE'S BEEN ZONING OUT AN AWFUL LOT THESE DAYS.

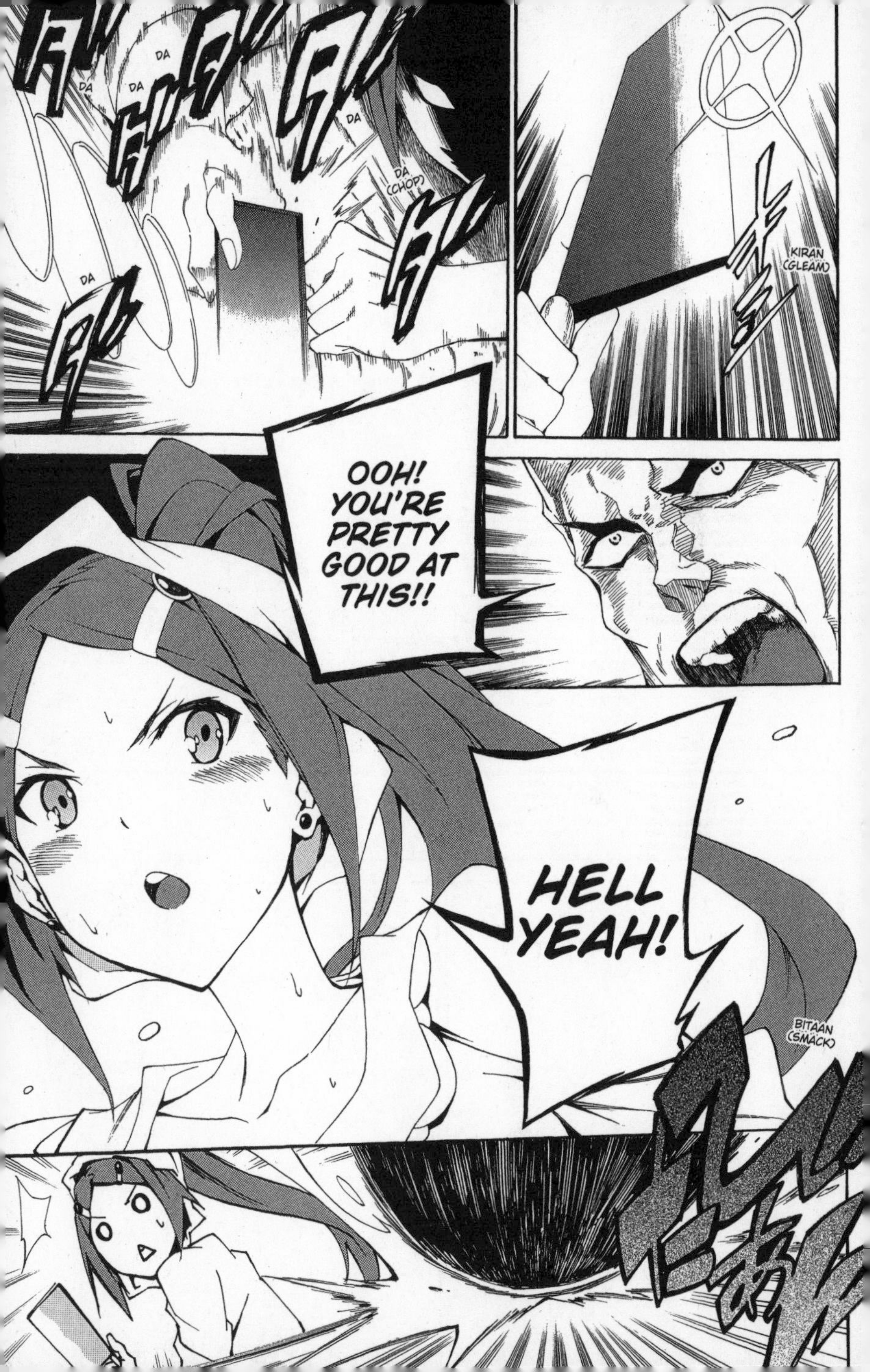
KIRAN (GLEAM)
DA
DA
DA
DA
DA (CHOP)
DA
OOH! YOU'RE PRETTY GOOD AT THIS!!
HELL YEAH!
BITAAN (SMACK)

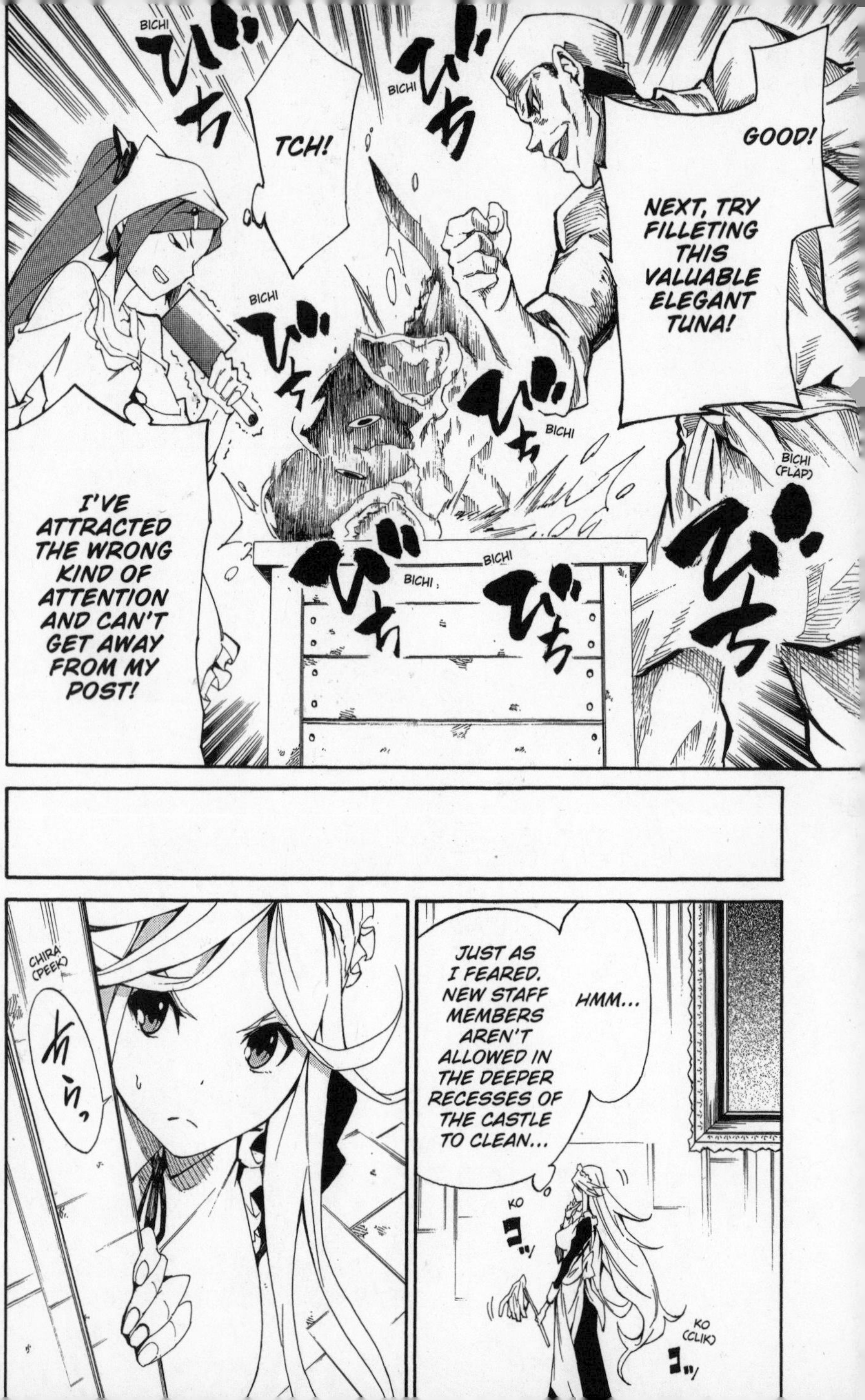
GOOD!
NEXT, TRY FILLETING THIS VALUABLE ELEGANT TUNA!
BICHI
TCH!
BICHI
BICHI
BICHI
BICHI (FLAP)
BICHI
BICHI
I'VE ATTRACTED THE WRONG KIND OF ATTENTION AND CAN'T GET AWAY FROM MY POST!
HMM...
JUST AS I FEARED. NEW STAFF MEMBERS AREN'T ALLOWED IN THE DEEPER RECESSES OF THE CASTLE TO CLEAN...
KO
KO (CLIK)
CHIRA (PEEK)

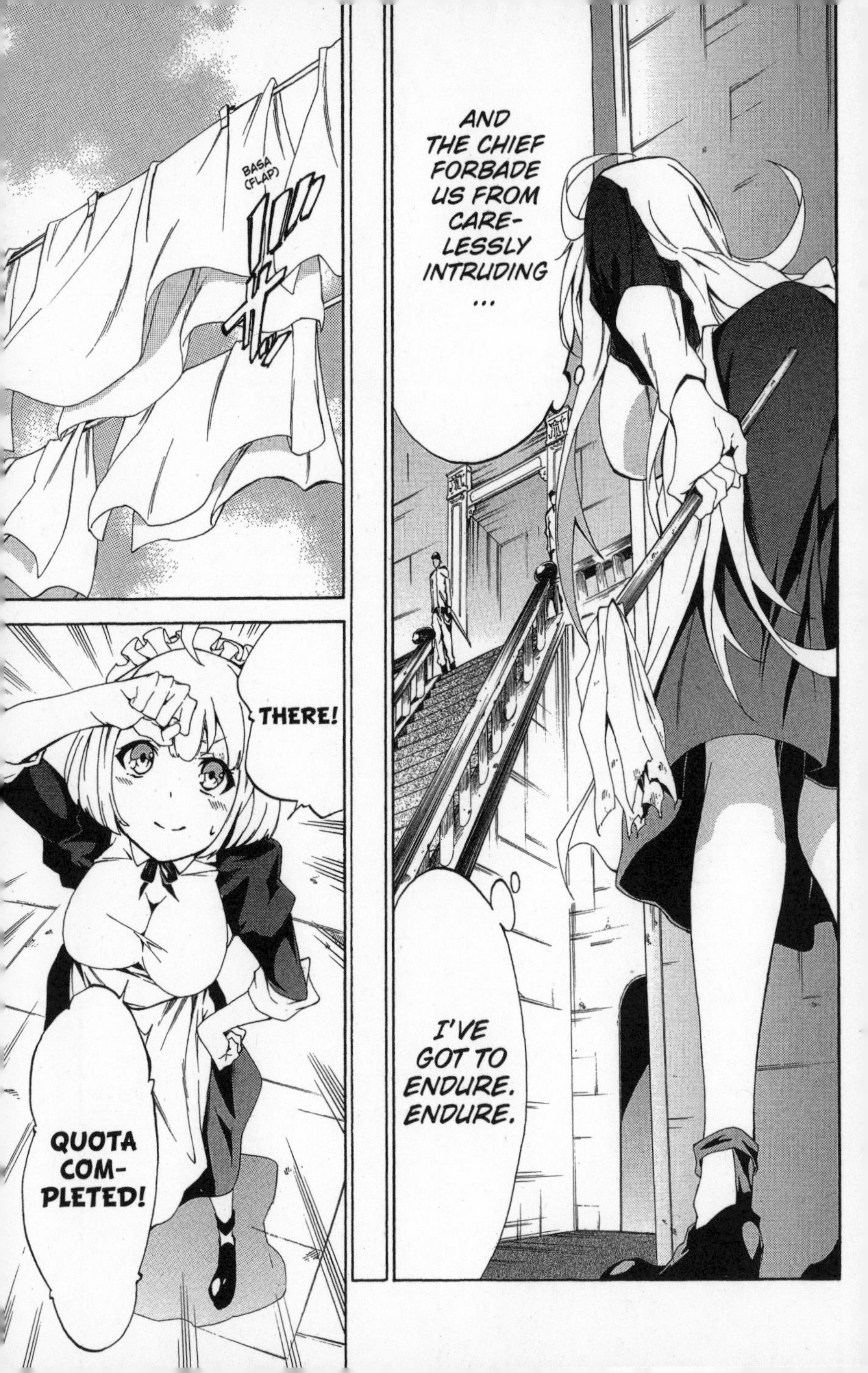
AND THE CHIEF FORBADE US FROM CARE-LESSLY INTRUDING ...
I'VE GOT TO ENDURE. ENDURE.
BASA (FLAP)
THERE!
QUOTA COM-PLETED!

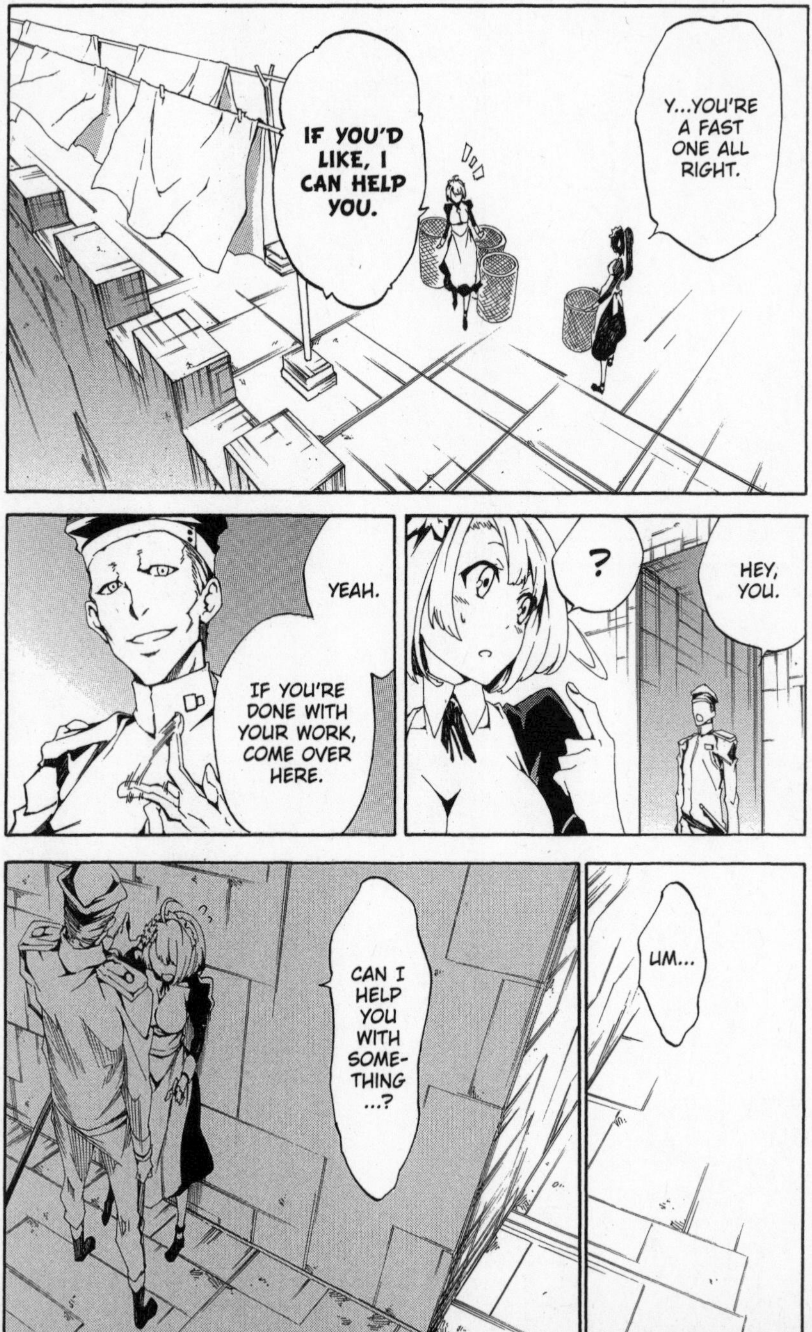
Y...YOU'RE A FAST ONE ALL RIGHT.
IF YOU'D LIKE, I CAN HELP YOU.
HEY, YOU.
?
YEAH.
IF YOU'RE DONE WITH YOUR WORK, COME OVER HERE.
UM...
CAN I HELP YOU WITH SOME-THING...?

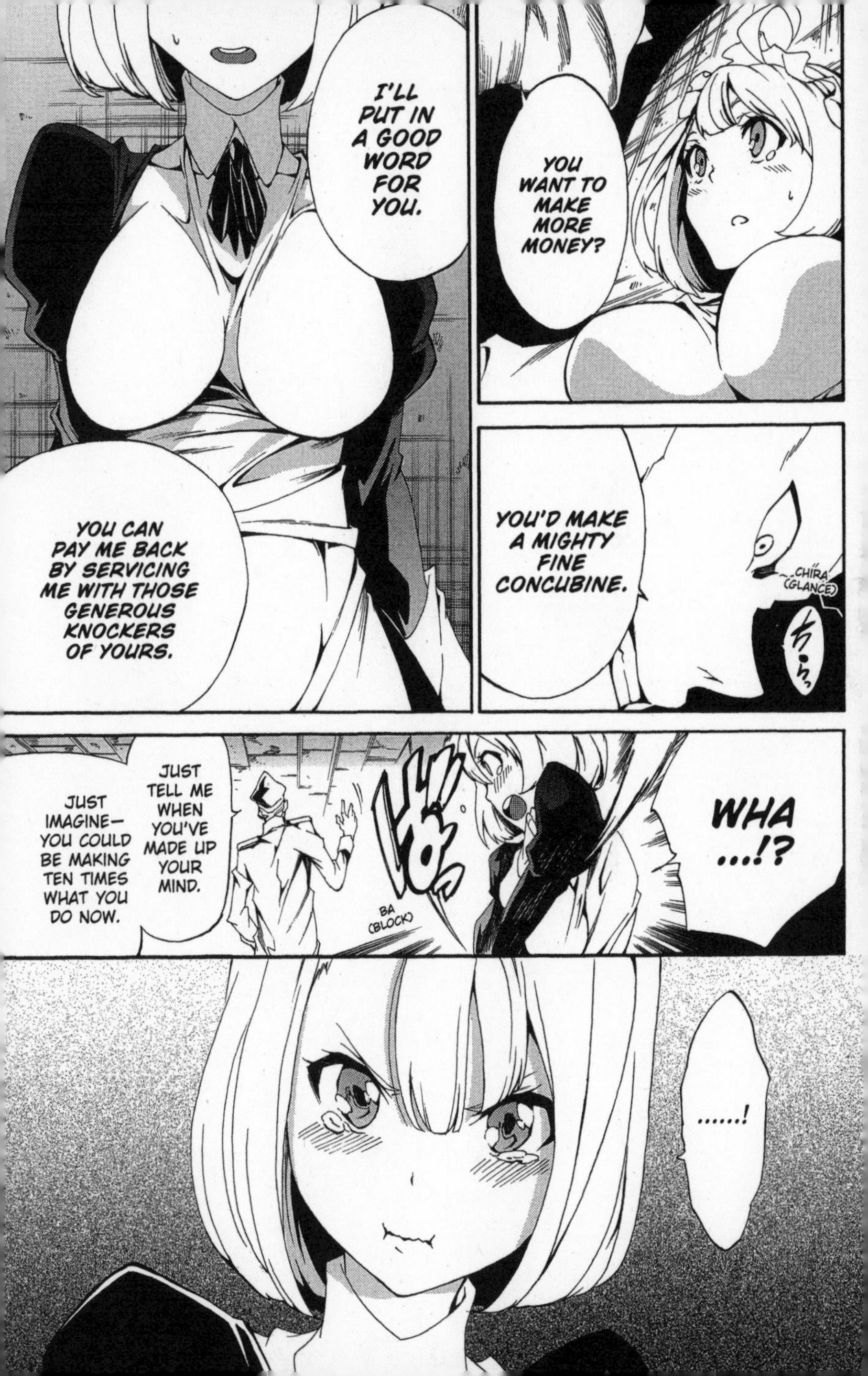
YOU WANT TO MAKE MORE MONEY?
I'LL PUT IN A GOOD WORD FOR YOU.
YOU'D MAKE A MIGHTY FINE CONCUBINE.
CHIRA (GLANCE)
YOU CAN PAY ME BACK BY SERVICING ME WITH THOSE GENEROUS KNOCKERS OF YOURS.
WHA ...!?
BA (BLOCK)
JUST TELL ME WHEN YOU'VE MADE UP YOUR MIND.
JUST IMAGINE—YOU COULD BE MAKING TEN TIMES WHAT YOU DO NOW.
......!

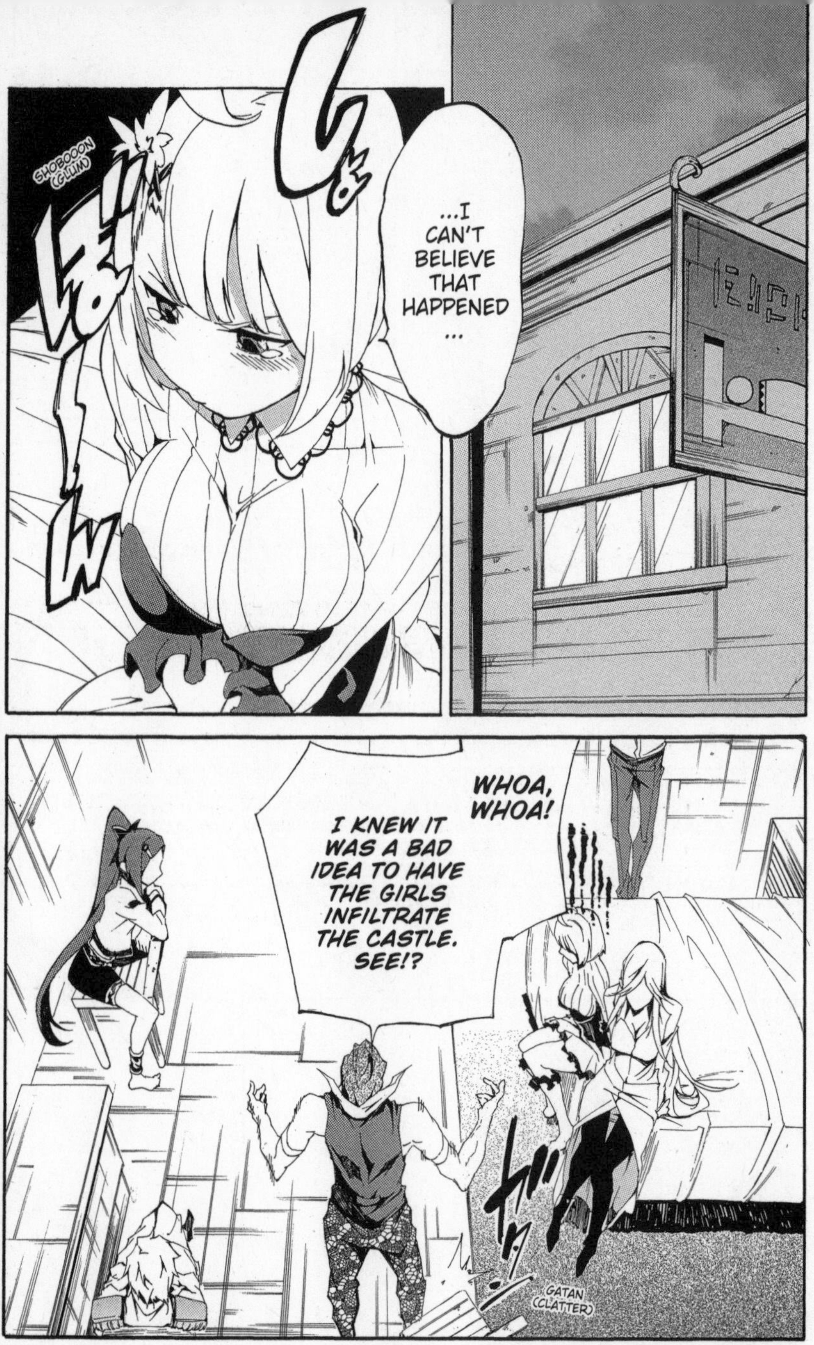
SHOBOOON (GLUM)
...I CAN'T BELIEVE THAT HAPPENED ...
WHOA, WHOA!
I KNEW IT WAS A BAD IDEA TO HAVE THE GIRLS INFILTRATE THE CASTLE. SEE!?
GATAN (CLATTER)

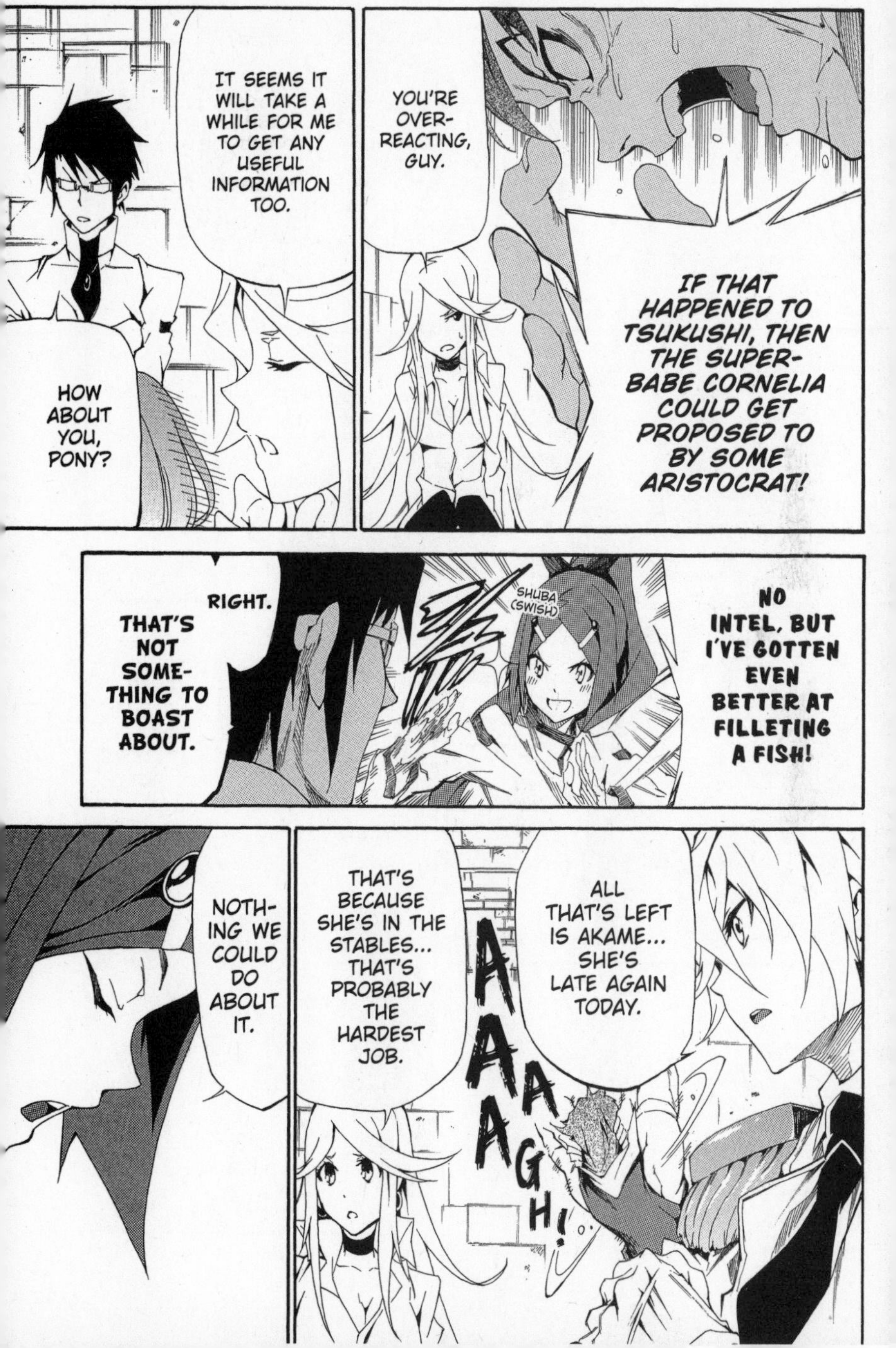
IF THAT HAPPENED TO TSUKUSHI, THEN THE SUPER-BABE CORNELIA COULD GET PROPOSED TO BY SOME ARISTOCRAT!
YOU'RE OVER-REACTING, GUY.
IT SEEMS IT WILL TAKE A WHILE FOR ME TO GET ANY USEFUL INFORMATION TOO.
HOW ABOUT YOU, PONY?
NO INTEL, BUT I'VE GOTTEN EVEN BETTER AT FILLETING A FISH!
SHUBA (SWISH)
RIGHT.
THAT'S NOT SOME-THING TO BOAST ABOUT.
ALL THAT'S LEFT IS AKAME... SHE'S LATE AGAIN TODAY.
AAAAGH!
THAT'S BECAUSE SHE'S IN THE STABLES... THAT'S PROBABLY THE HARDEST JOB.
NOTH-ING WE COULD DO ABOUT IT.

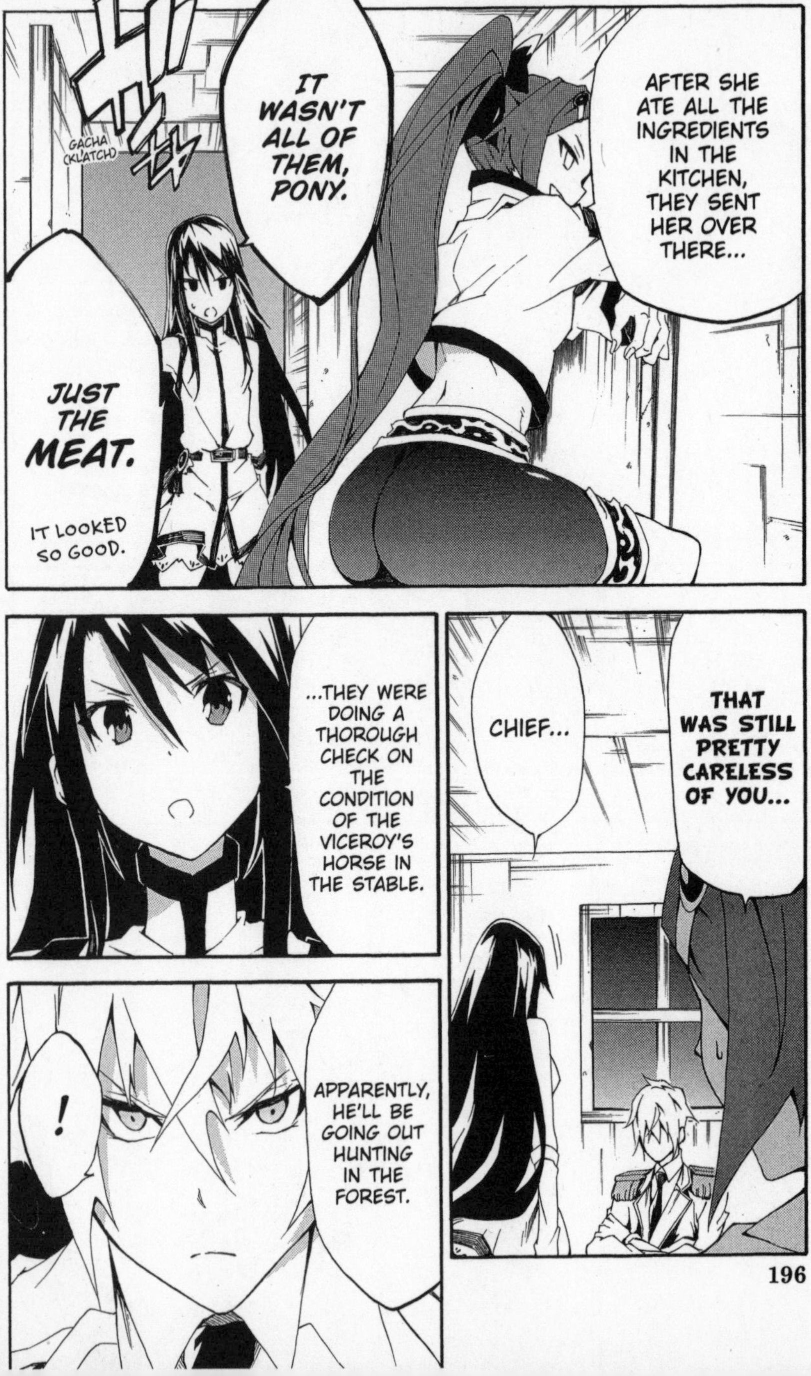
AFTER SHE ATE ALL THE INGREDIENTS IN THE KITCHEN, THEY SENT HER OVER THERE...
IT WASN'T ALL OF THEM, PONY.
GACHA (KLATCH)
JUST THE MEAT.
IT LOOKED SO GOOD.
THAT WAS STILL PRETTY CARELESS OF YOU...
CHIEF...
...THEY WERE DOING A THOROUGH CHECK ON THE CONDITION OF THE VICEROY'S HORSE IN THE STABLE.
APPARENTLY, HE'LL BE GOING OUT HUNTING IN THE FOREST.
!

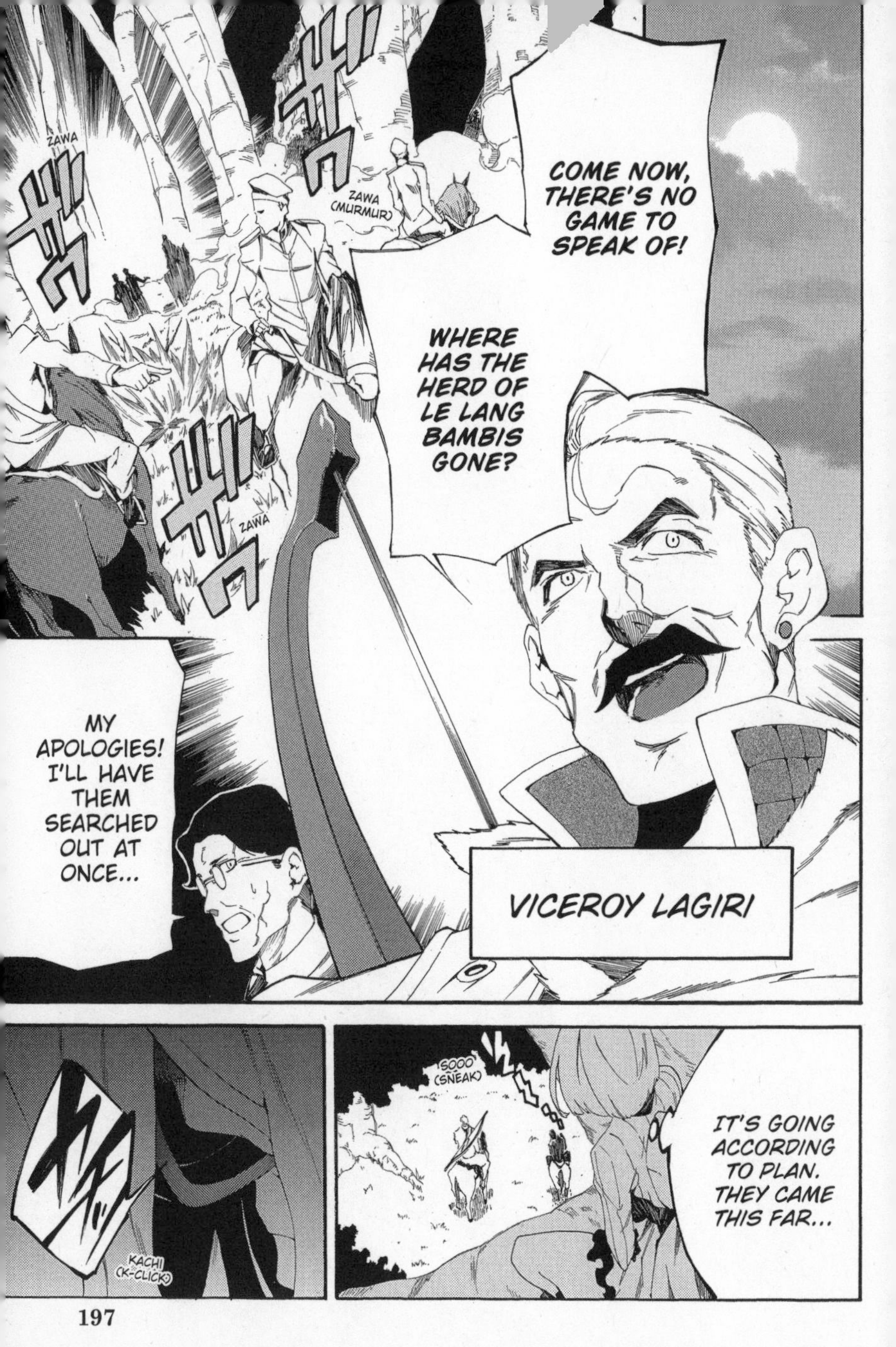
ZAWA
ZAWA (MURMUR)
ZAWA
COME NOW, THERE'S NO GAME TO SPEAK OF!
WHERE HAS THE HERD OF LE LANG BAMBIS GONE?
VICEROY LAGIRI
MY APOLOGIES! I'LL HAVE THEM SEARCHED OUT AT ONCE...
SOOO (SNEAK)
IT'S GOING ACCORDING TO PLAN. THEY CAME THIS FAR...
KACHI (K-CLICK)

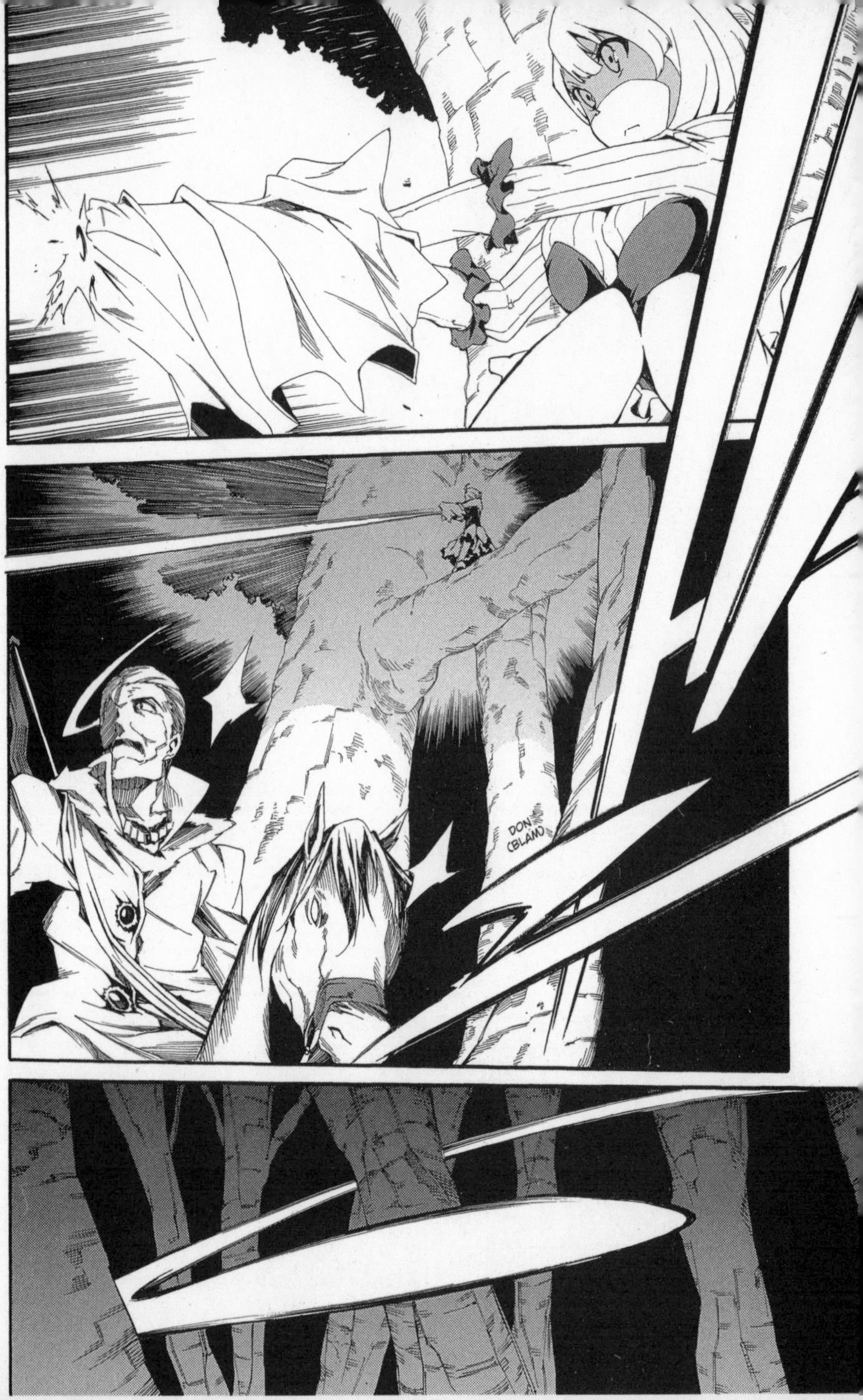
DON
(BLAM)

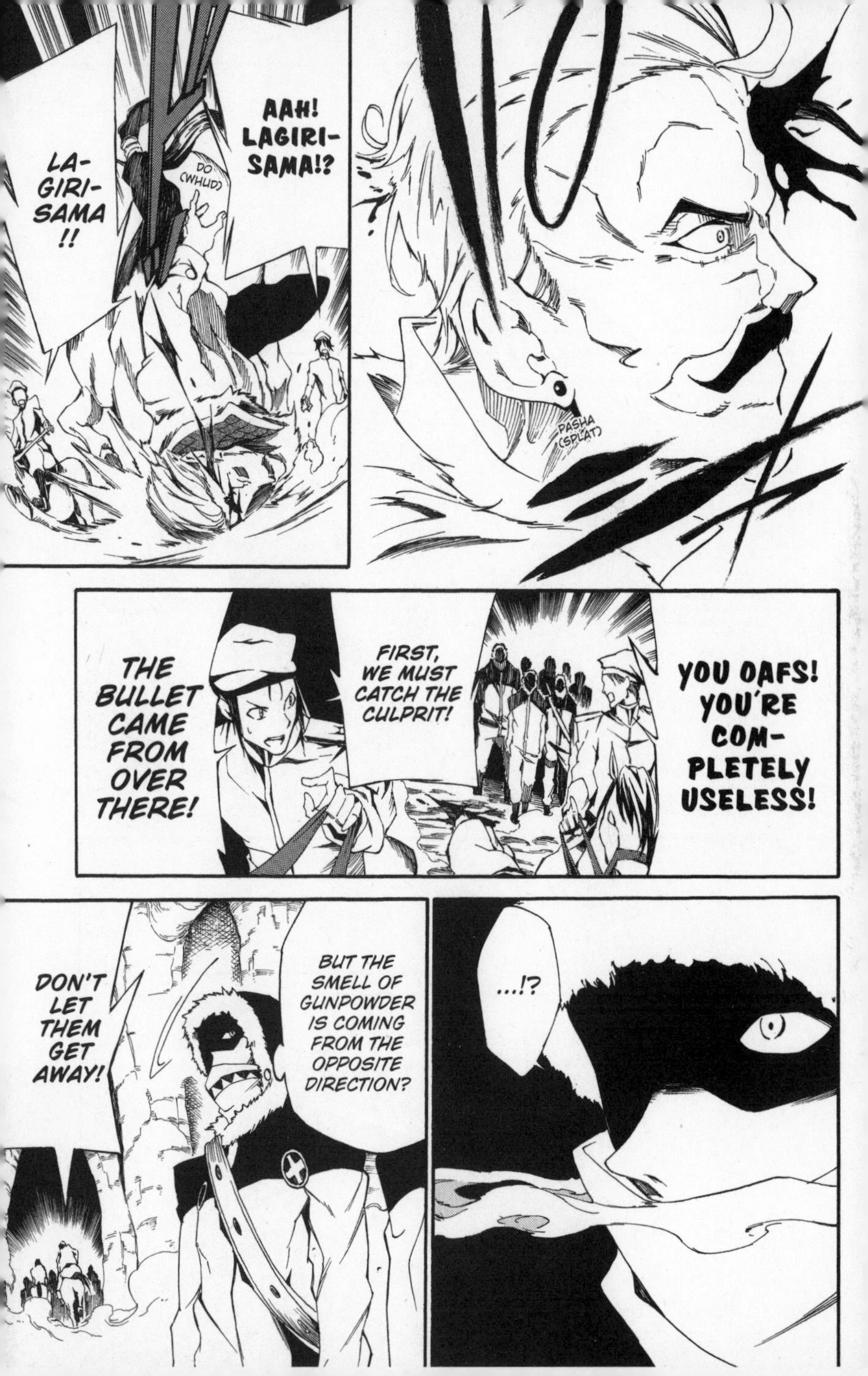
PASHA (SPLAT)
AAH! LAGIRI-SAMA!?
DO (WHUD)
LA-GIRI-SAMA!!
YOU OAFS! YOU'RE COM-PLETELY USELESS!
FIRST, WE MUST CATCH THE CULPRIT!
THE BULLET CAME FROM OVER THERE!
...!?
BUT THE SMELL OF GUNPOWDER IS COMING FROM THE OPPOSITE DIRECTION?
DON'T LET THEM GET AWAY!

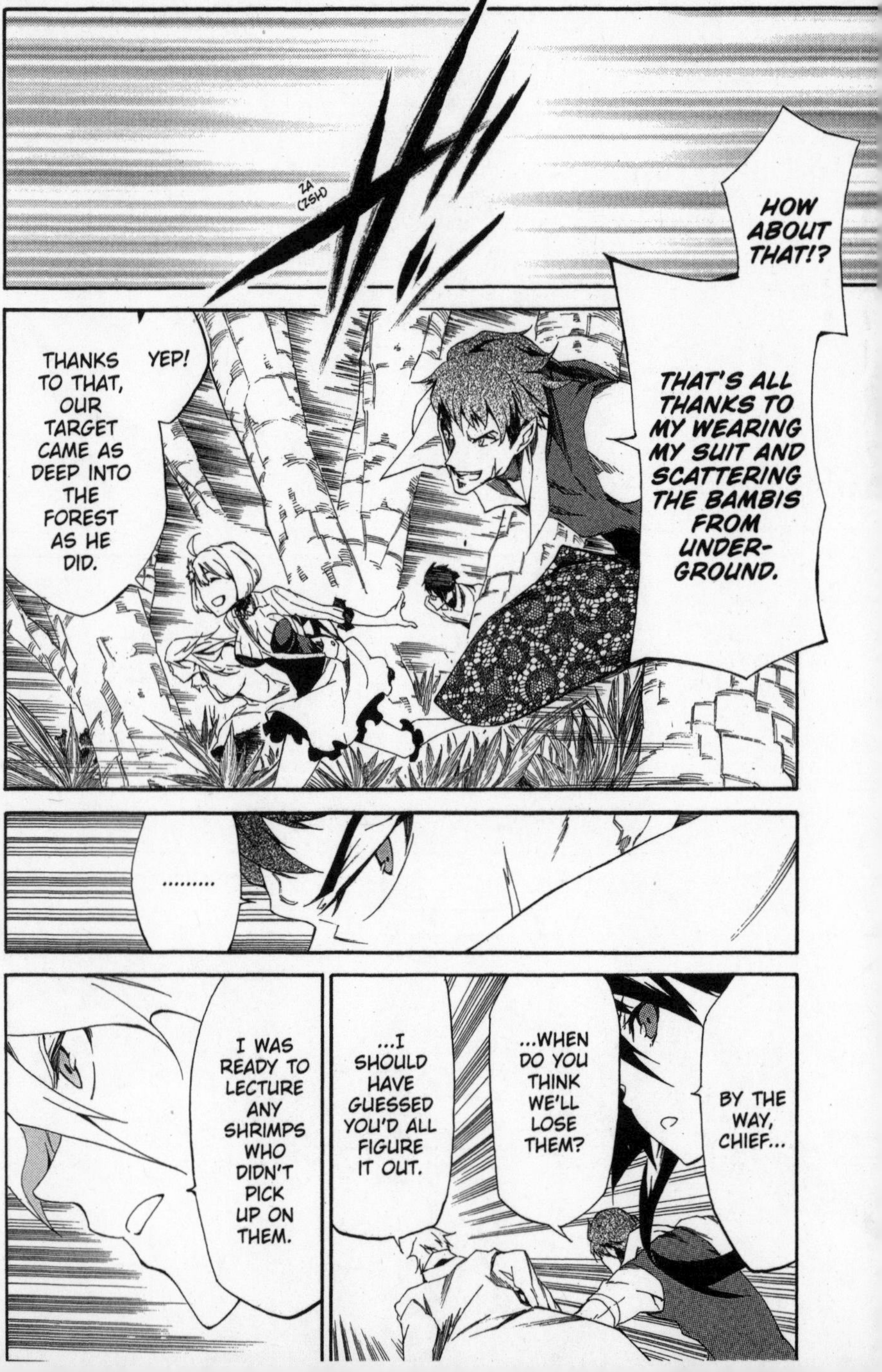
ZA (ZSH)
HOW ABOUT THAT!?
THAT'S ALL THANKS TO MY WEARING MY SUIT AND SCATTERING THE BAMBIS FROM UNDER-GROUND.
YEP!
THANKS TO THAT, OUR TARGET CAME AS DEEP INTO THE FOREST AS HE DID.
....
BY THE WAY, CHIEF...
...WHEN DO YOU THINK WE'LL LOSE THEM?
...I SHOULD HAVE GUESSED YOU'D ALL FIGURE IT OUT.
I WAS READY TO LECTURE ANY SHRIMPS WHO DIDN'T PICK UP ON THEM.

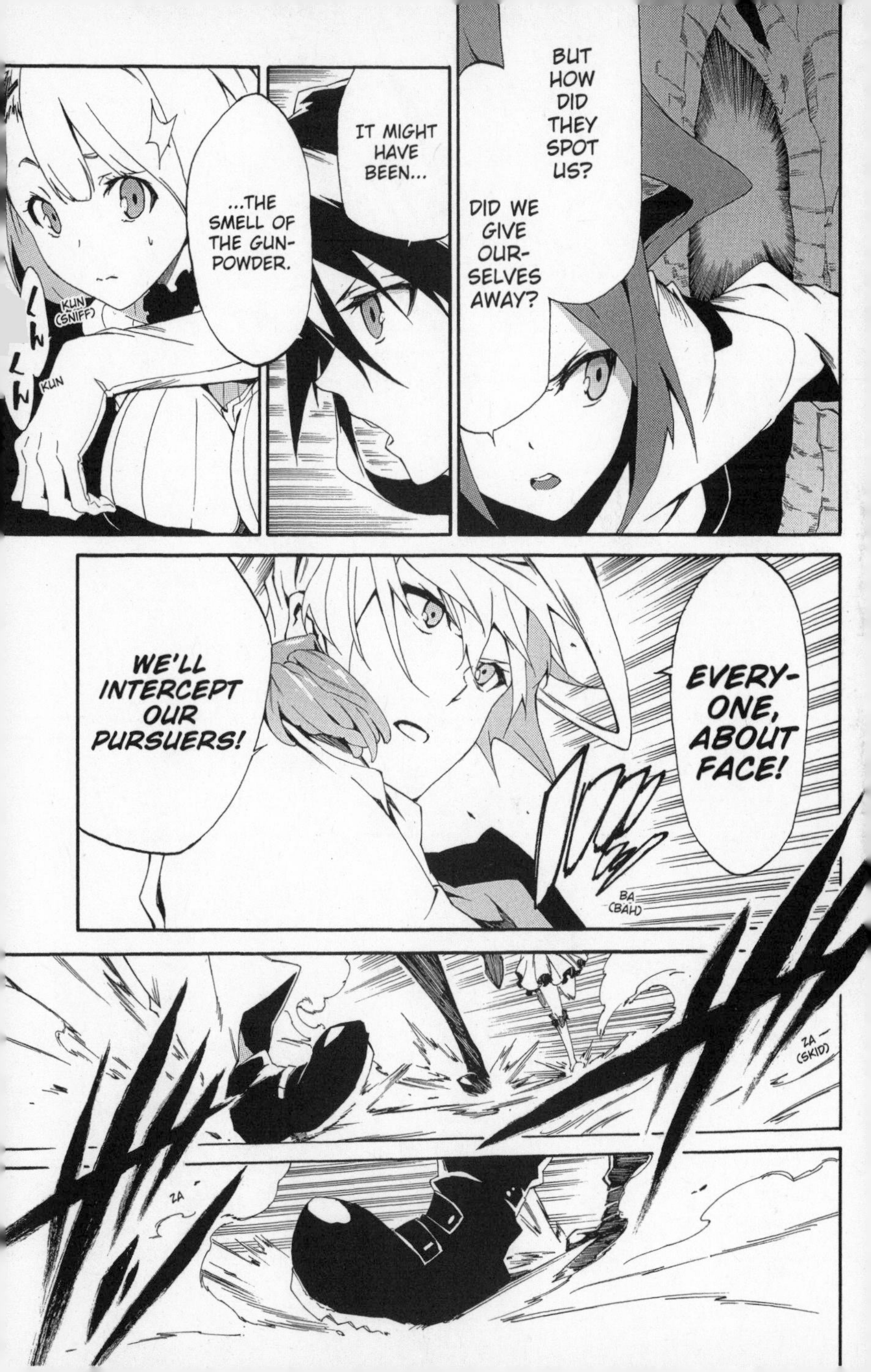
BUT HOW DID THEY SPOT US?
DID WE GIVE OUR-SELVES AWAY?
IT MIGHT HAVE BEEN...
...THE SMELL OF THE GUN-POWDER.
KUN (SNIFF)
KUN
EVERY-ONE, ABOUT FACE!
WE'LL INTERCEPT OUR PURSUERS!
BA (BAH)
ZA (SKID)
ZA

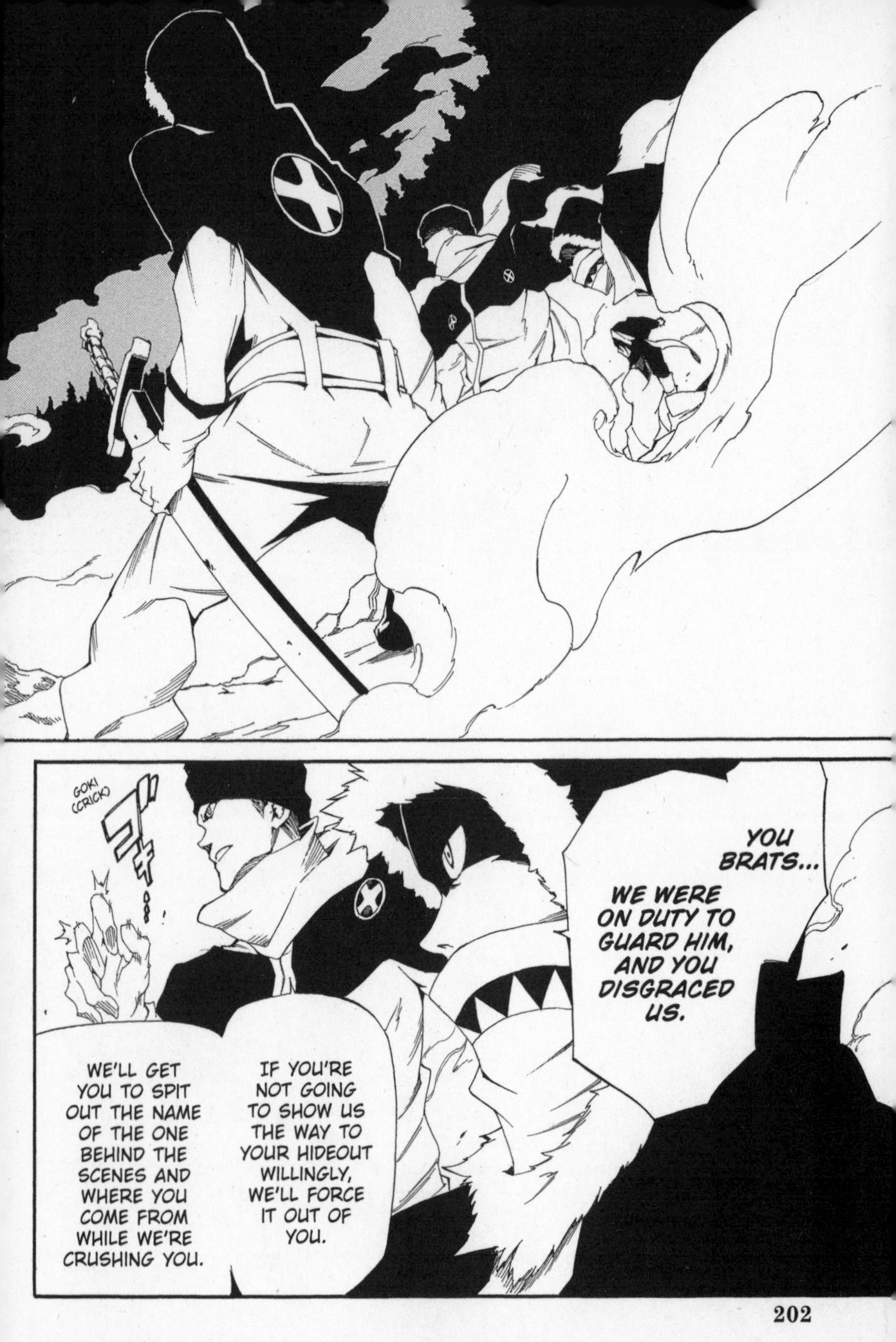
YOU BRATS...
WE WERE ON DUTY TO GUARD HIM, AND YOU DISGRACED US.
GOKI (CRICK)
IF YOU'RE NOT GOING TO SHOW US THE WAY TO YOUR HIDEOUT WILLINGLY, WE'LL FORCE IT OUT OF YOU.
WE'LL GET YOU TO SPIT OUT THE NAME OF THE ONE BEHIND THE SCENES AND WHERE YOU COME FROM WHILE WE'RE CRUSHING YOU.

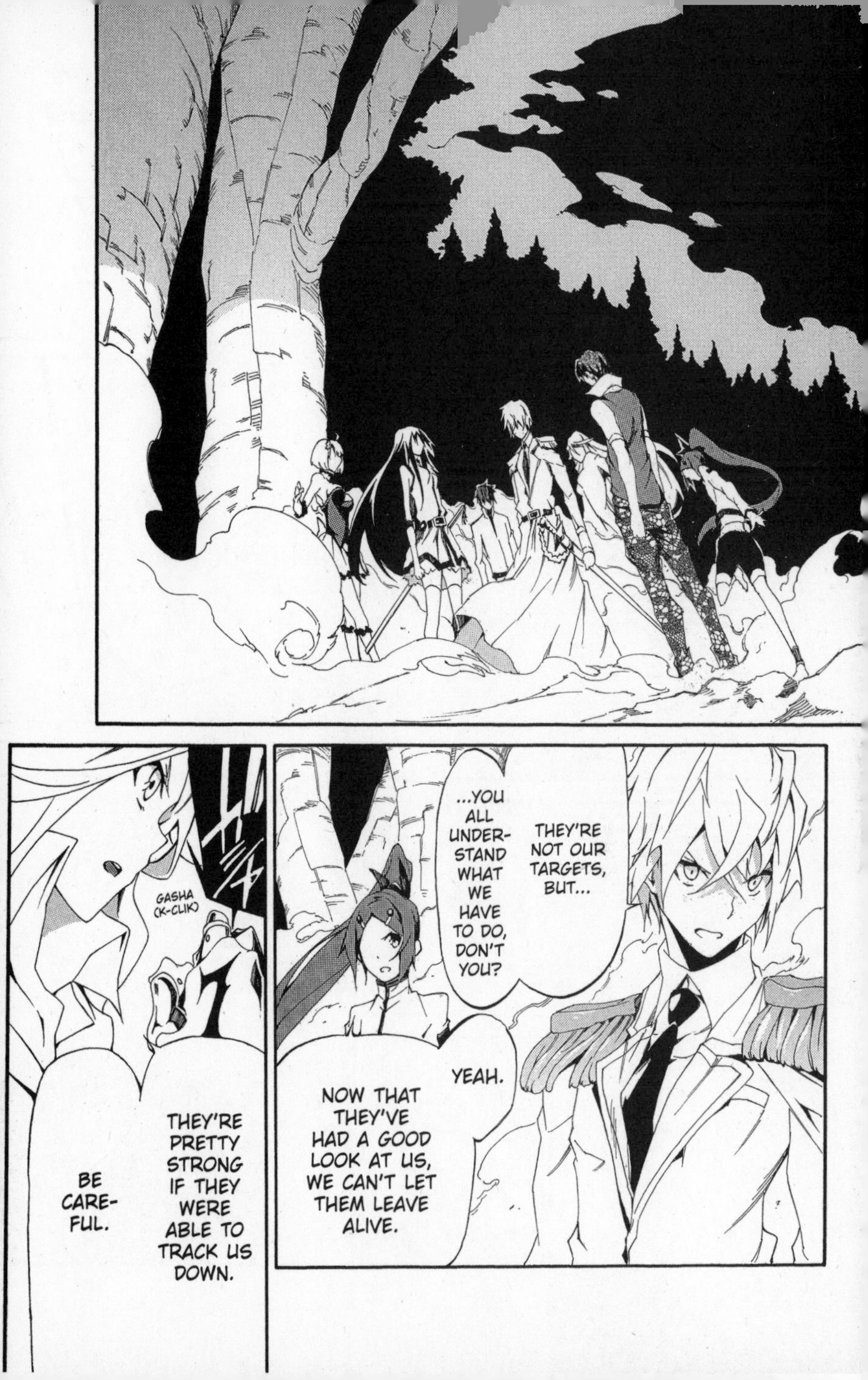
THEY'RE NOT OUR TARGETS, BUT...
...YOU ALL UNDERSTAND WHAT WE HAVE TO DO, DON'T YOU?
YEAH.
NOW THAT THEY'VE HAD A GOOD LOOK AT US, WE CAN'T LET THEM LEAVE ALIVE.
GASHA (K-CLIK)
THEY'RE PRETTY STRONG IF THEY WERE ABLE TO TRACK US DOWN.
BE CARE-FUL.

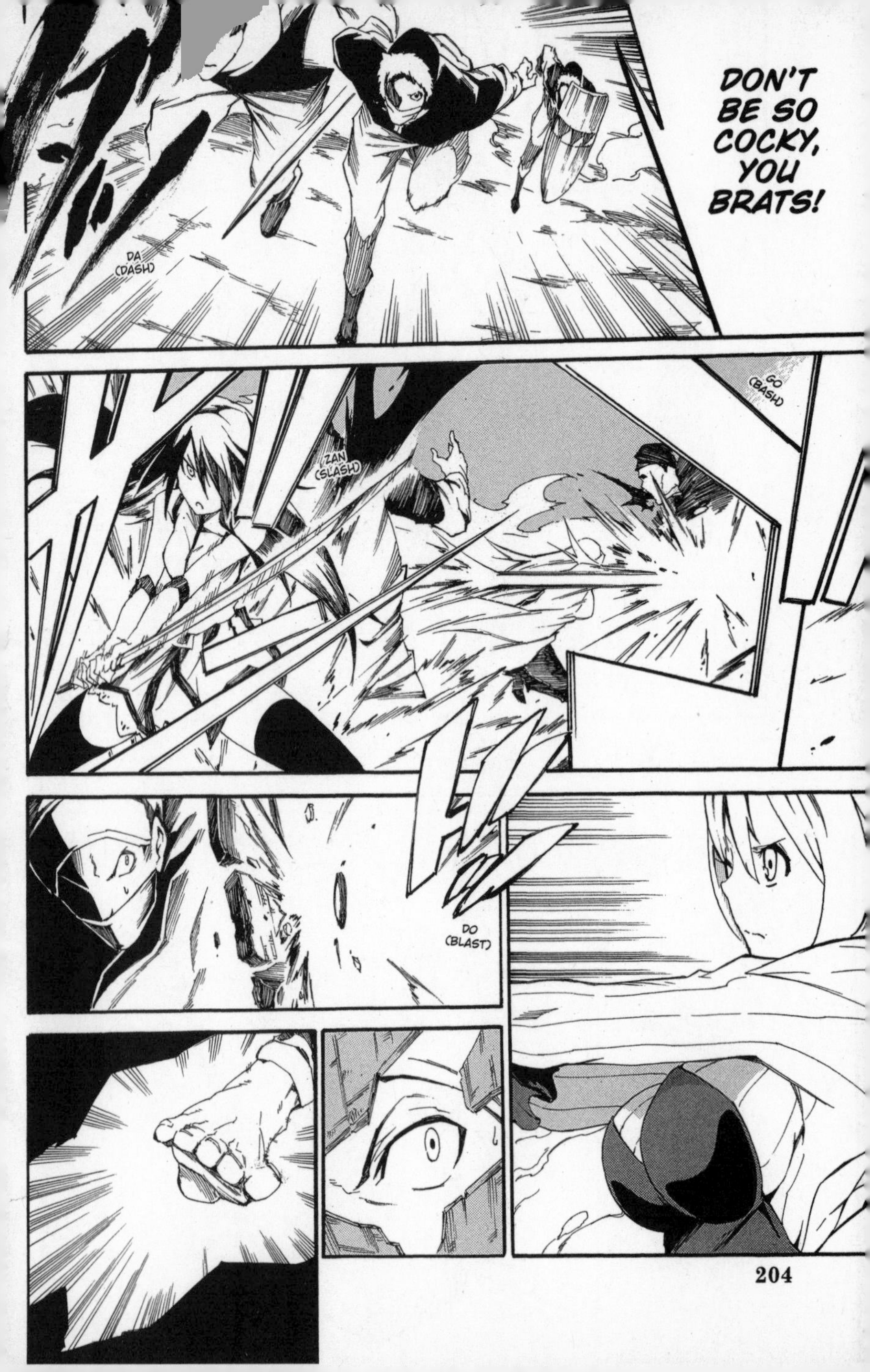
DON'T BE SO COCKY, YOU BRATS!
DA
(DASH)
GO
(BASH)
ZAN
(SLASH)
DO
(BLAST)

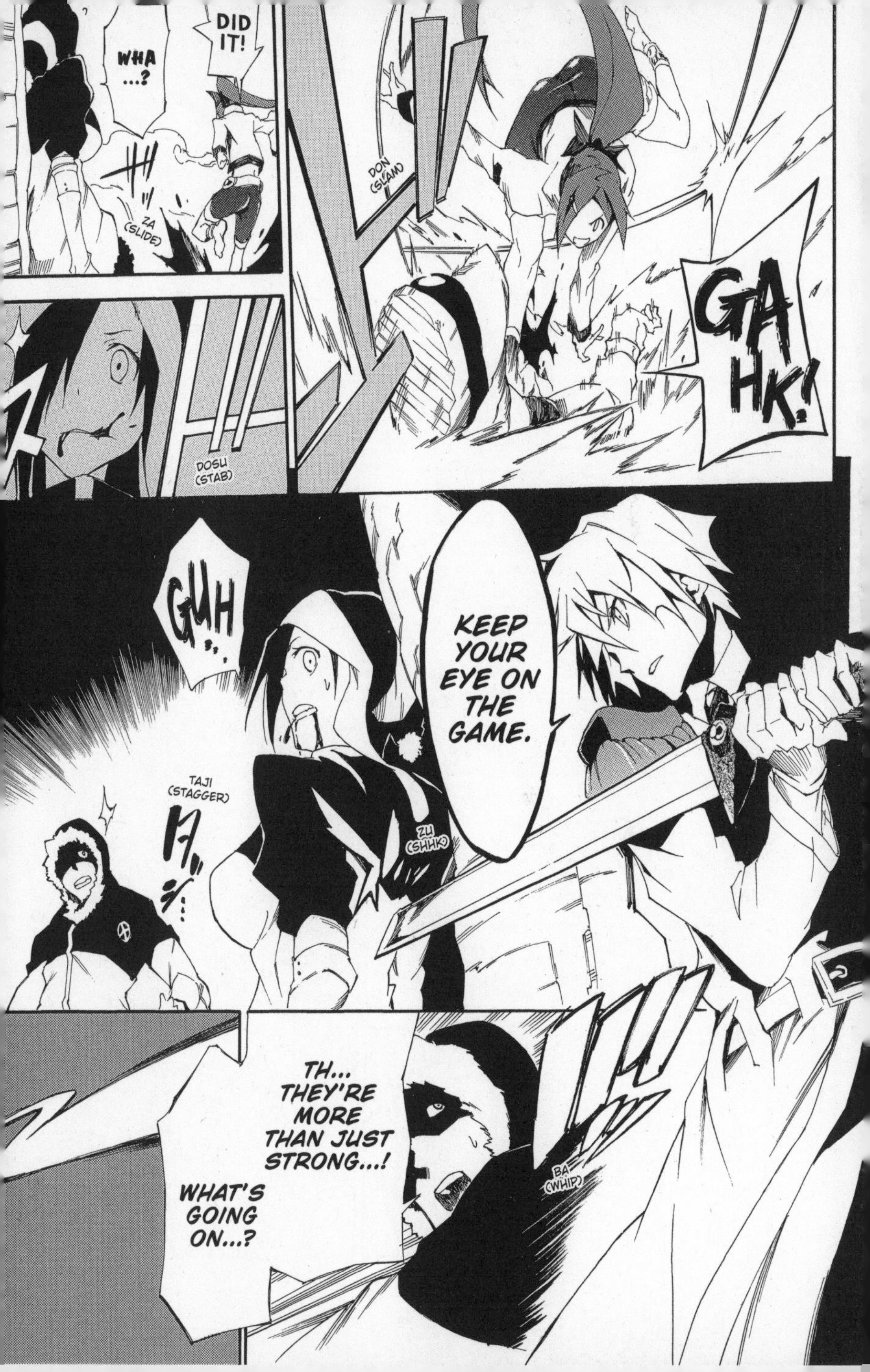
DON (SLAM)
DID IT!
WHA ...?
ZA (SLIDE)
GAHK!
DOSU (STAB)
KEEP YOUR EYE ON THE GAME.
GUH...
ZU (SHHK)
TAJI (STAGGER)
TH... THEY'RE MORE THAN JUST STRONG...!
WHAT'S GOING ON...?
BA (WHIP)

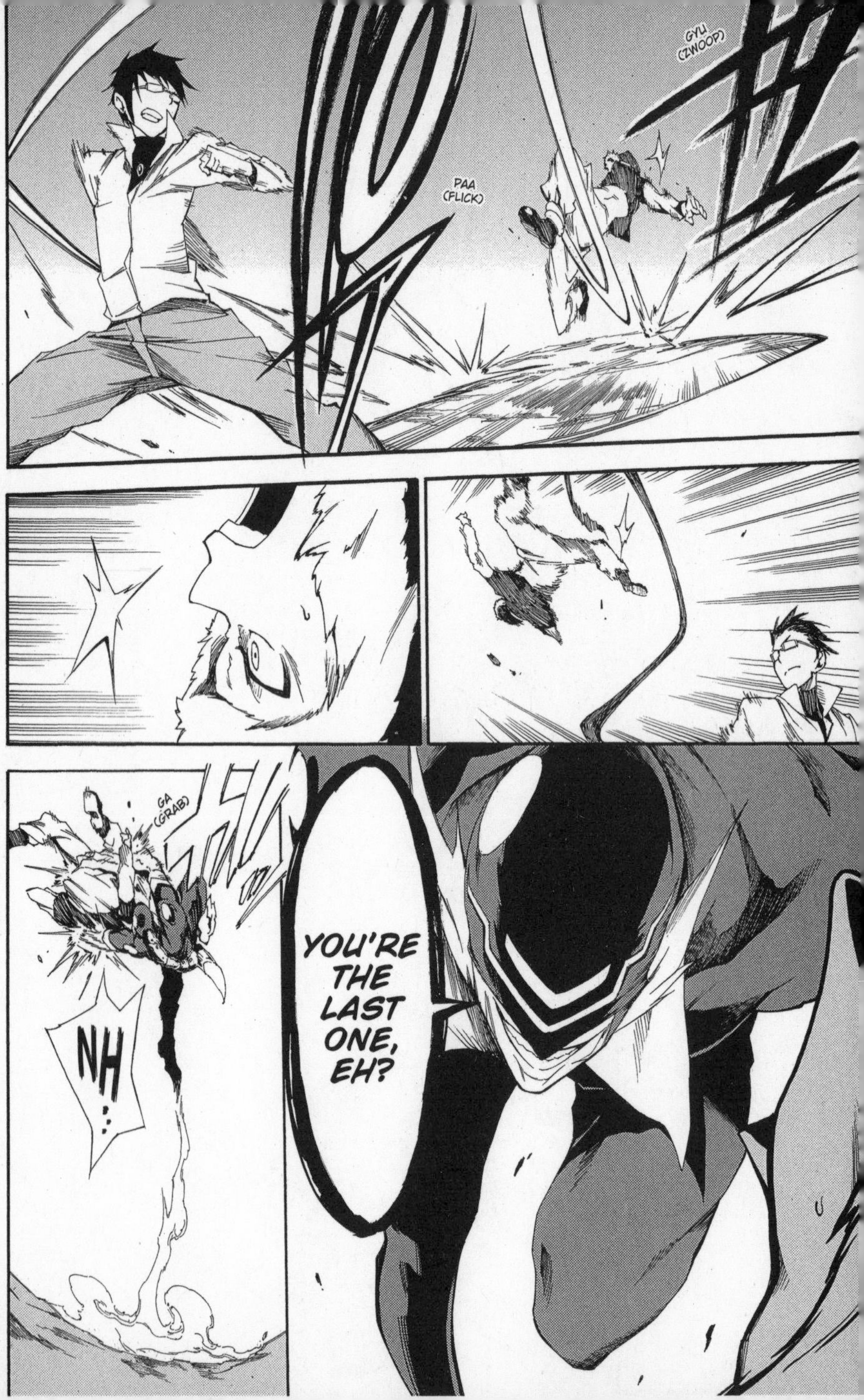
GYU
(ZWOOP)
PAA
(FLICK)
YOU'RE THE LAST ONE, EH?
GA
(GRAB)
NH...

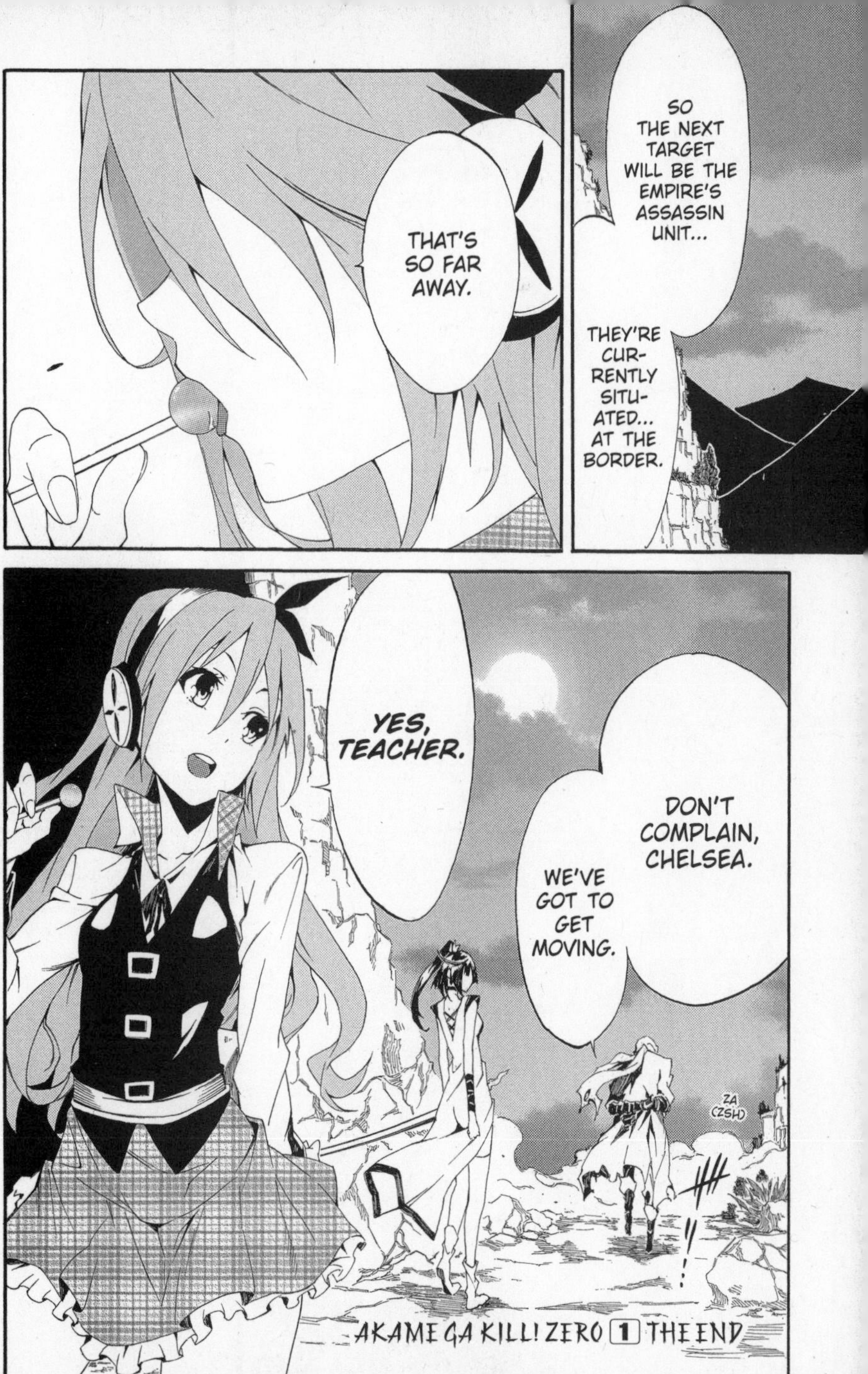
SO THE NEXT TARGET WILL BE THE EMPIRE'S ASSASSIN UNIT...
THEY'RE CUR-RENTLY SITU-ATED... AT THE BORDER.
THAT'S SO FAR AWAY.
DON'T COMPLAIN, CHELSEA.
WE'VE GOT TO GET MOVING.
ZA (ZSH)
YES, TEACHER.
AKAME GA KILL! ZERO 1 THE END

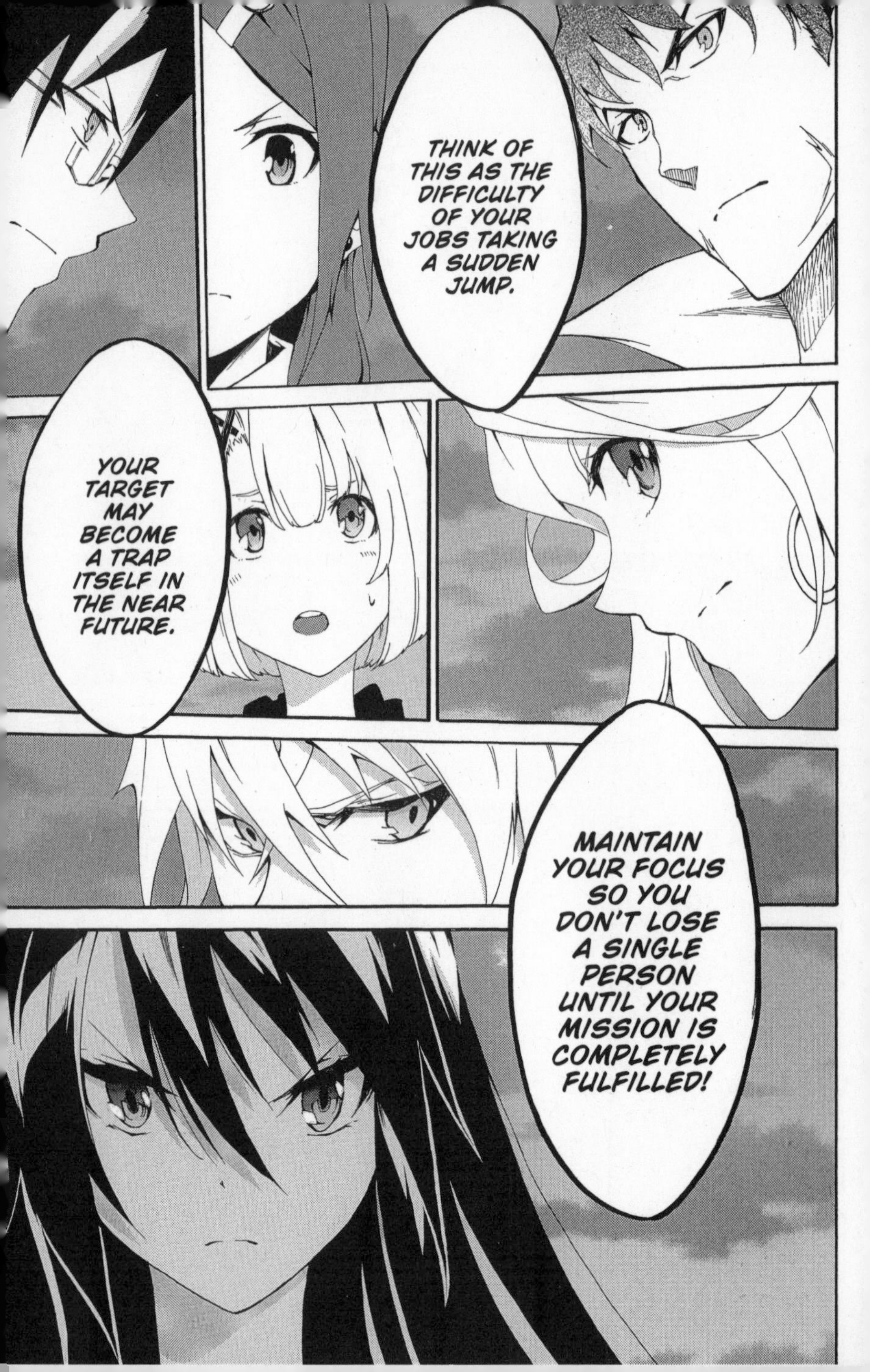
THINK OF THIS AS THE DIFFICULTY OF YOUR JOBS TAKING A SUDDEN JUMP.
YOUR TARGET MAY BECOME A TRAP ITSELF IN THE NEAR FUTURE.
MAINTAIN YOUR FOCUS SO YOU DON'T LOSE A SINGLE PERSON UNTIL YOUR MISSION IS COMPLETELY FULFILLED!

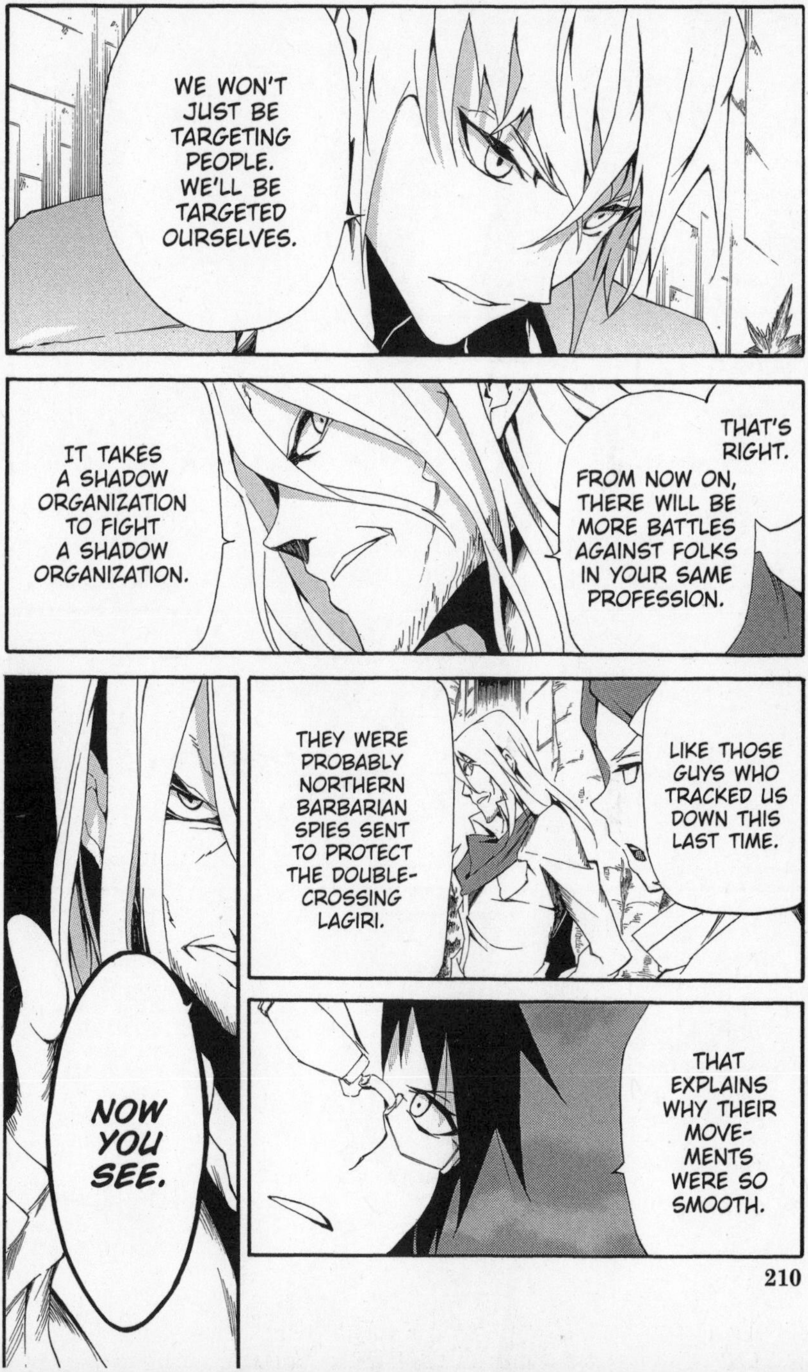
WE WON'T JUST BE TARGETING PEOPLE. WE'LL BE TARGETED OURSELVES.
THAT'S RIGHT.
FROM NOW ON, THERE WILL BE MORE BATTLES AGAINST FOLKS IN YOUR SAME PROFESSION.
IT TAKES A SHADOW ORGANIZATION TO FIGHT A SHADOW ORGANIZATION.
LIKE THOSE GUYS WHO TRACKED US DOWN THIS LAST TIME.
THEY WERE PROBABLY NORTHERN BARBARIAN SPIES SENT TO PROTECT THE DOUBLE-CROSSING LAGIRI.
THAT EXPLAINS WHY THEIR MOVE-MENTS WERE SO SMOOTH.
NOW YOU SEE.

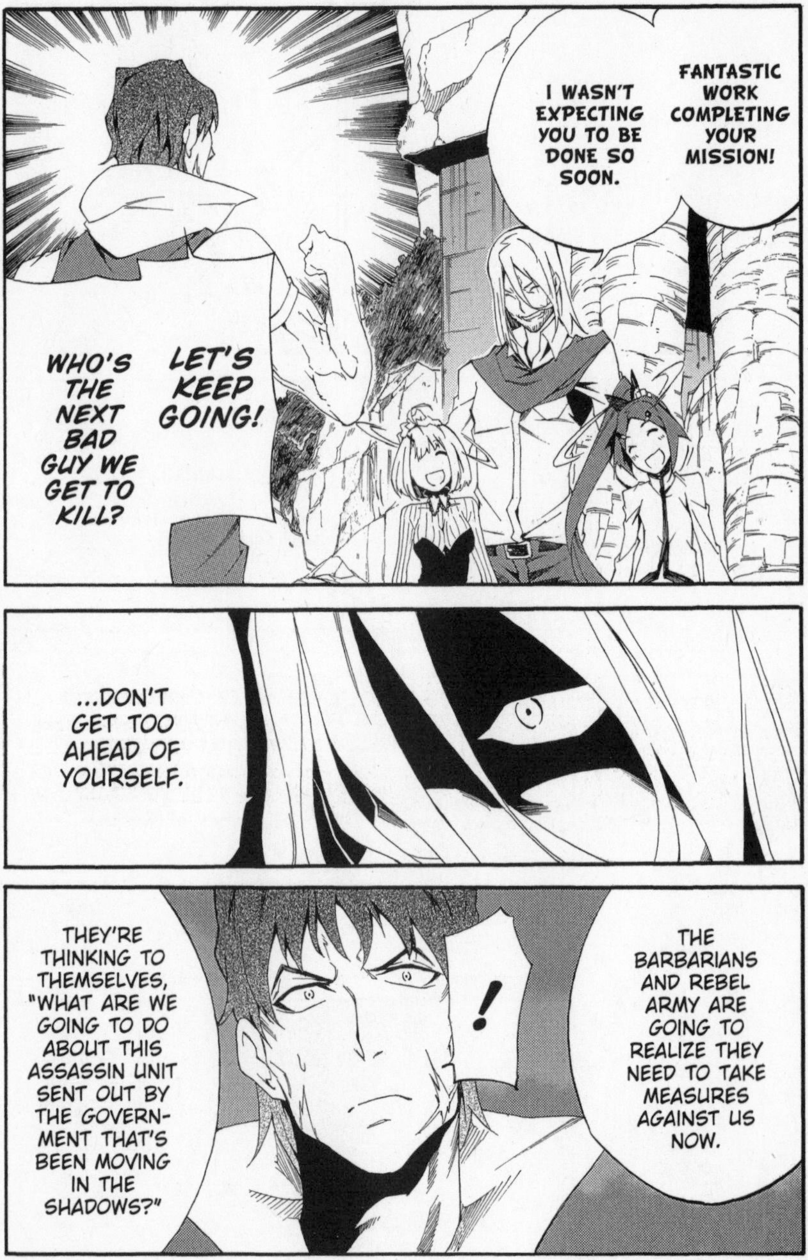
FANTASTIC WORK COMPLETING YOUR MISSION!
I WASN'T EXPECTING YOU TO BE DONE SO SOON.
LET'S KEEP GOING!
WHO'S THE NEXT BAD GUY WE GET TO KILL?
...DON'T GET TOO AHEAD OF YOURSELF.
!
THE BARBARIANS AND REBEL ARMY ARE GOING TO REALIZE THEY NEED TO TAKE MEASURES AGAINST US NOW.
THEY'RE THINKING TO THEMSELVES, "WHAT ARE WE GOING TO DO ABOUT THIS ASSASSIN UNIT SENT OUT BY THE GOVERN-MENT THAT'S BEEN MOVING IN THE SHADOWS?"

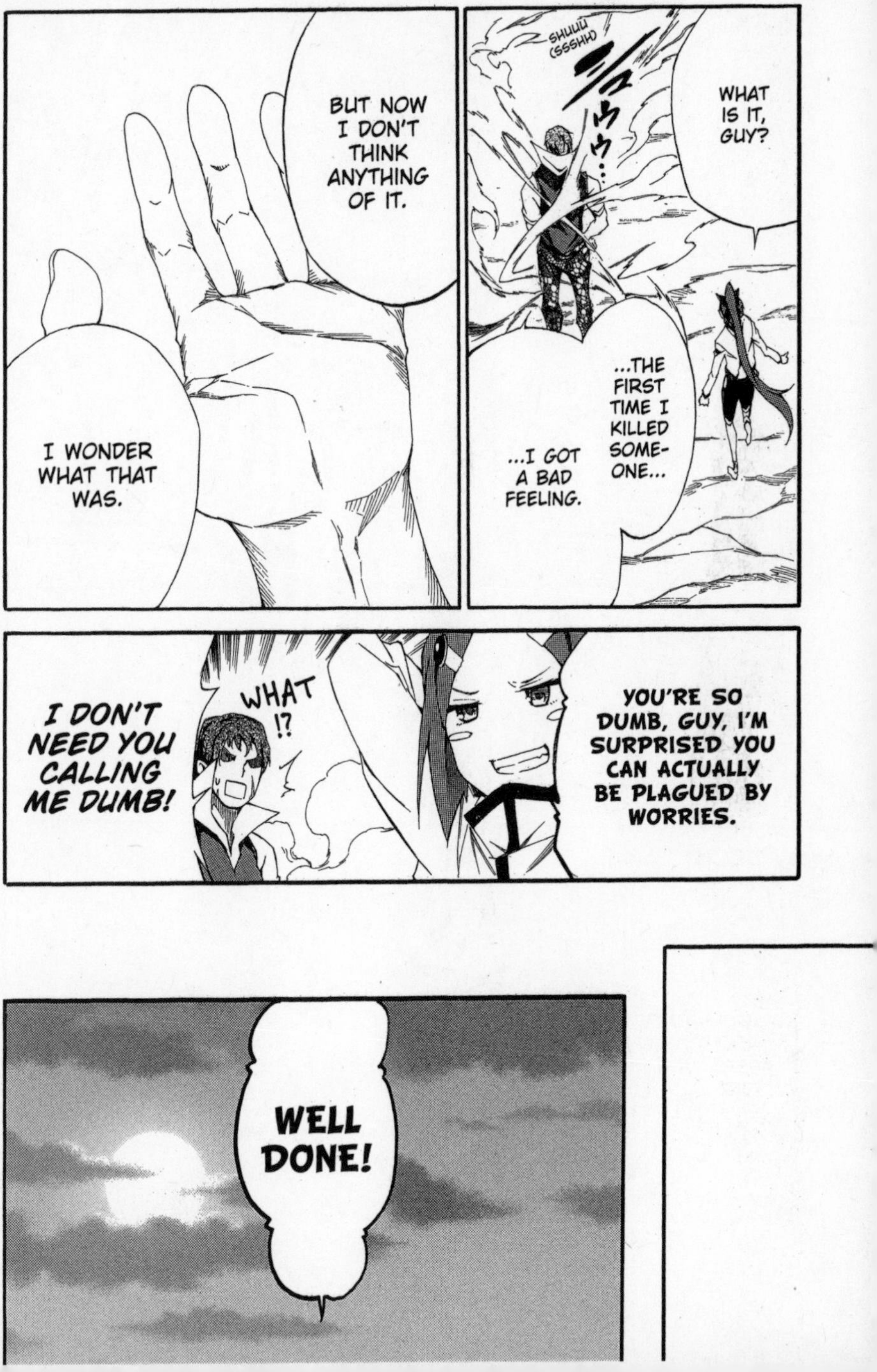
SHUUU (SSSHH)
WHAT IS IT, GUY?
...THE FIRST TIME I KILLED SOME-ONE...
...I GOT A BAD FEELING.
BUT NOW I DON'T THINK ANYTHING OF IT.
I WONDER WHAT THAT WAS.
YOU'RE SO DUMB, GUY, I'M SURPRISED YOU CAN ACTUALLY BE PLAGUED BY WORRIES.
WHAT!?
I DON'T NEED YOU CALLING ME DUMB!
WELL DONE!

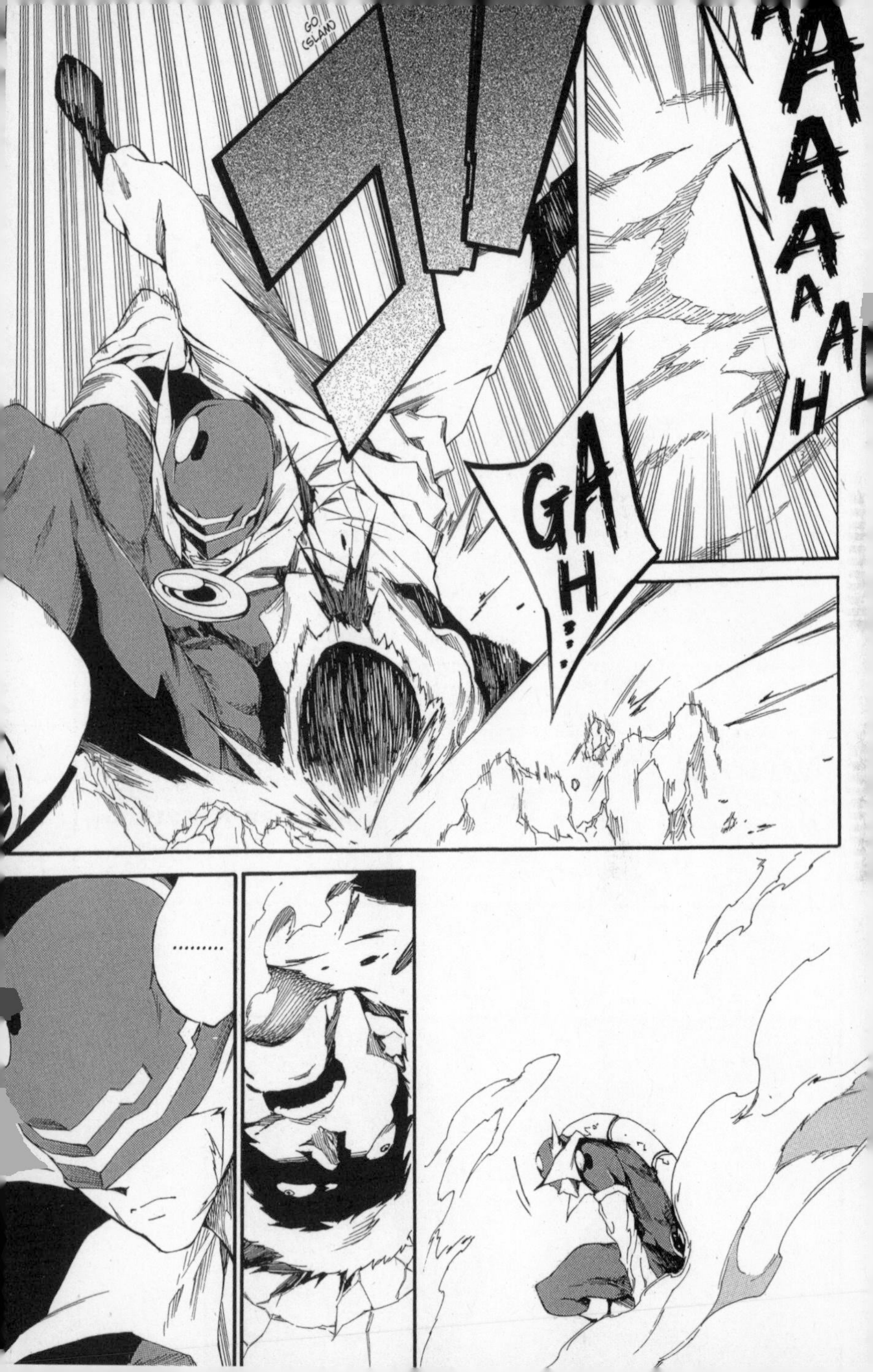
GO (SLAM)
AAAAAAAH
GAH...!!
....

Akame ga KILL! ZERO
Rough Sketches

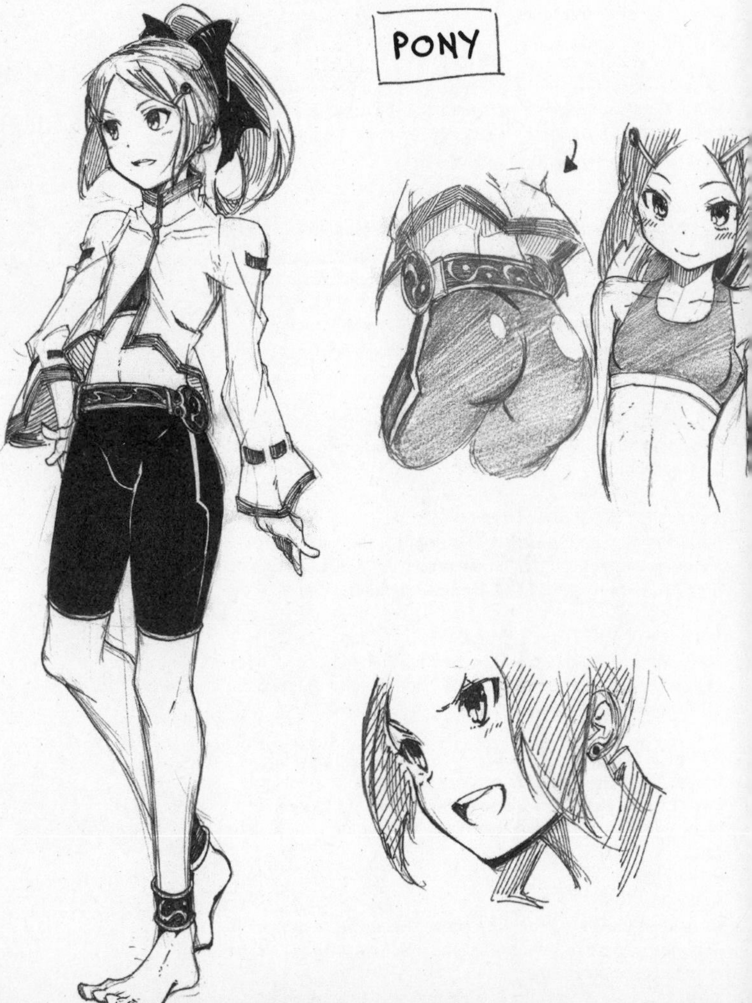
PONY

TAKAHIRO's
PostScript

Hello, this is Takahiro from Minato Soft.
I'd like to use this bonus page as an opportunity to introduce
Akame and her fun team.

◆**Akame & Kurome**
When asked, "Who is the person you love most in the whole, wide
world?" neither would hesitate to say the other's name. They're
both working hard on their missions in the hopes of seeing each
other again someday.

◆**Tsukushi - 4' 11" / Blood Type AB**
Akame's best friend and the healer of the team. She has a bubble-
brain personality but carries out her killings thoroughly.

◆**Green - 5' 5" / Blood Type A**
He's seeking a position that will keep him safe from dying, making
him a bit of the comedic relief. He's prone to being sullen.

◆**Pony - 5' 1" / Blood Type O**
She sleeps a lot, eats a lot, plays a lot, and kills a lot on her
missions. She's a peppy young girl with absolute faith in Gozuki.
A little stupid.

◆**Cornelia - 5' 6" / Blood Type O**
A hard worker and the big-sister type who will say things with
absolute conviction. Her teammates trust her, and she has a
high level of femininity and excels at domestic chores.

◆**Najasho - 5' 4" / Blood Type B**
The chief of Akame's team. He's as hard on himself as he is
on others. He'll call his teammates "shrimps," but it's in an
affectionate(ish) way.

◆**Guy - 5' 11" / Blood Type O**
He has a simple and clear personality and is single-minded. He
awoke to his sexuality ahead of the others, and when he gets
money, he goes to buy women in the village. He's reliable in a
fight.

◆**Gozuki**
An assassin working for the Empire who possesses the Teigu
Murasame. He has a daughter named Mezu, but that will be
touched upon next time.

That's all for now.

AKAME GA KILL! ZERO VOLUME 1

THANK YOU FOR BUYING THIS BOOK!

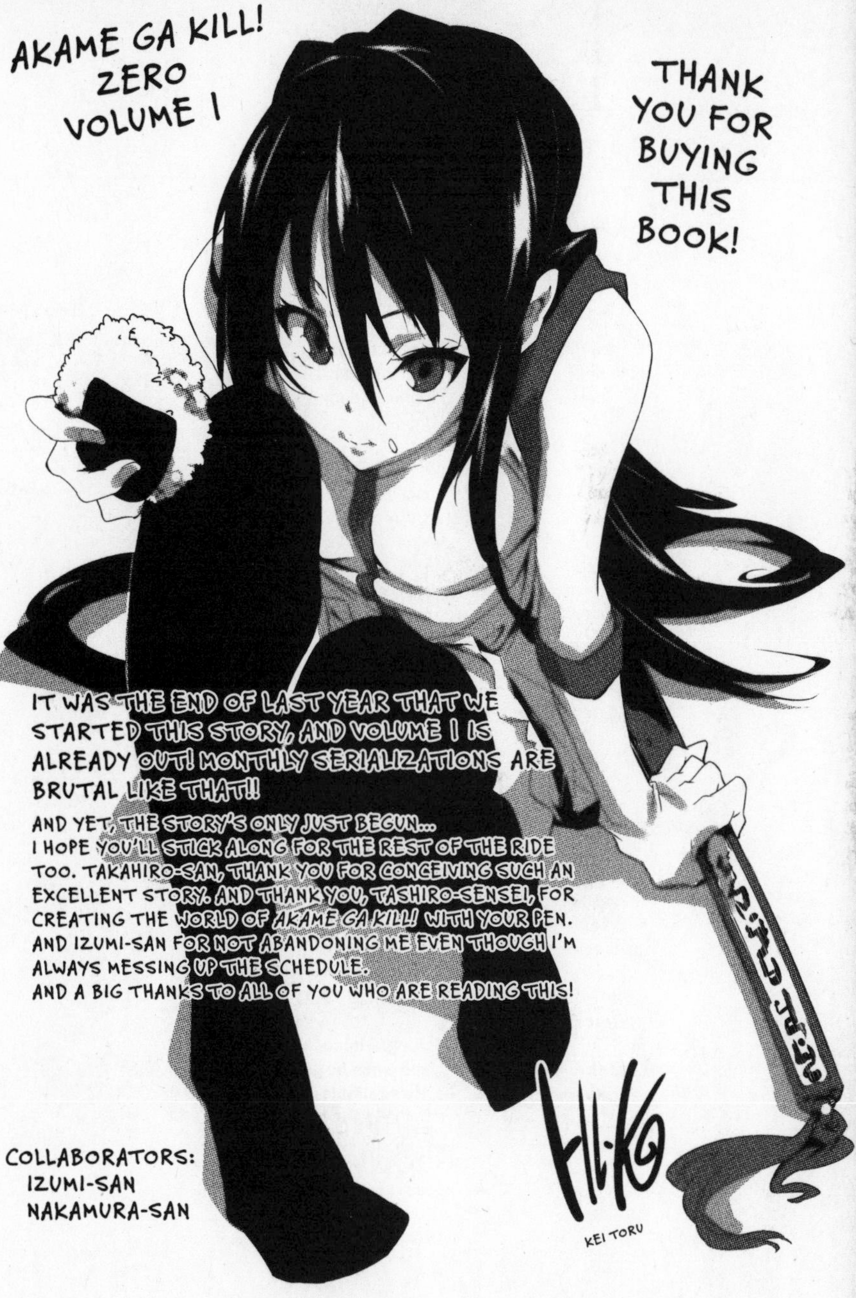

IT WAS THE END OF LAST YEAR THAT WE STARTED THIS STORY, AND VOLUME 1 IS ALREADY OUT! MONTHLY SERIALIZATIONS ARE BRUTAL LIKE THAT!!

AND YET, THE STORY'S ONLY JUST BEGUN...
I HOPE YOU'LL STICK ALONG FOR THE REST OF THE RIDE TOO. TAKAHIRO-SAN, THANK YOU FOR CONCEIVING SUCH AN EXCELLENT STORY. AND THANK YOU, TASHIRO-SENSEI, FOR CREATING THE WORLD OF *AKAME GA KILL!* WITH YOUR PEN.
AND IZUMI-SAN FOR NOT ABANDONING ME EVEN THOUGH I'M ALWAYS MESSING UP THE SCHEDULE.
AND A BIG THANKS TO ALL OF YOU WHO ARE READING THIS!

KEI TORU

COLLABORATORS:
IZUMI-SAN
NAKAMURA-SAN

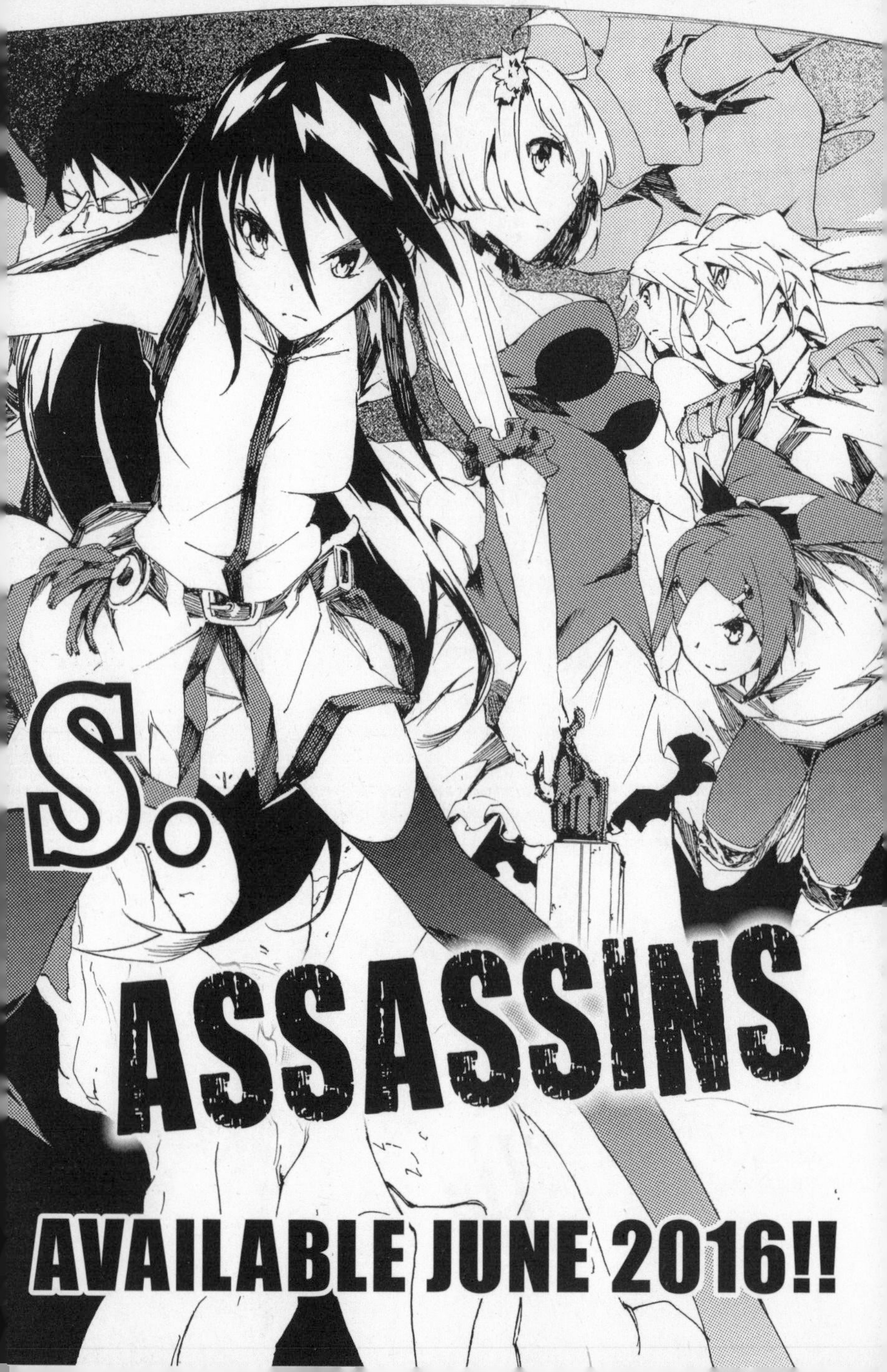

S.
ASSASSINS
AVAILABLE JUNE 2016!!

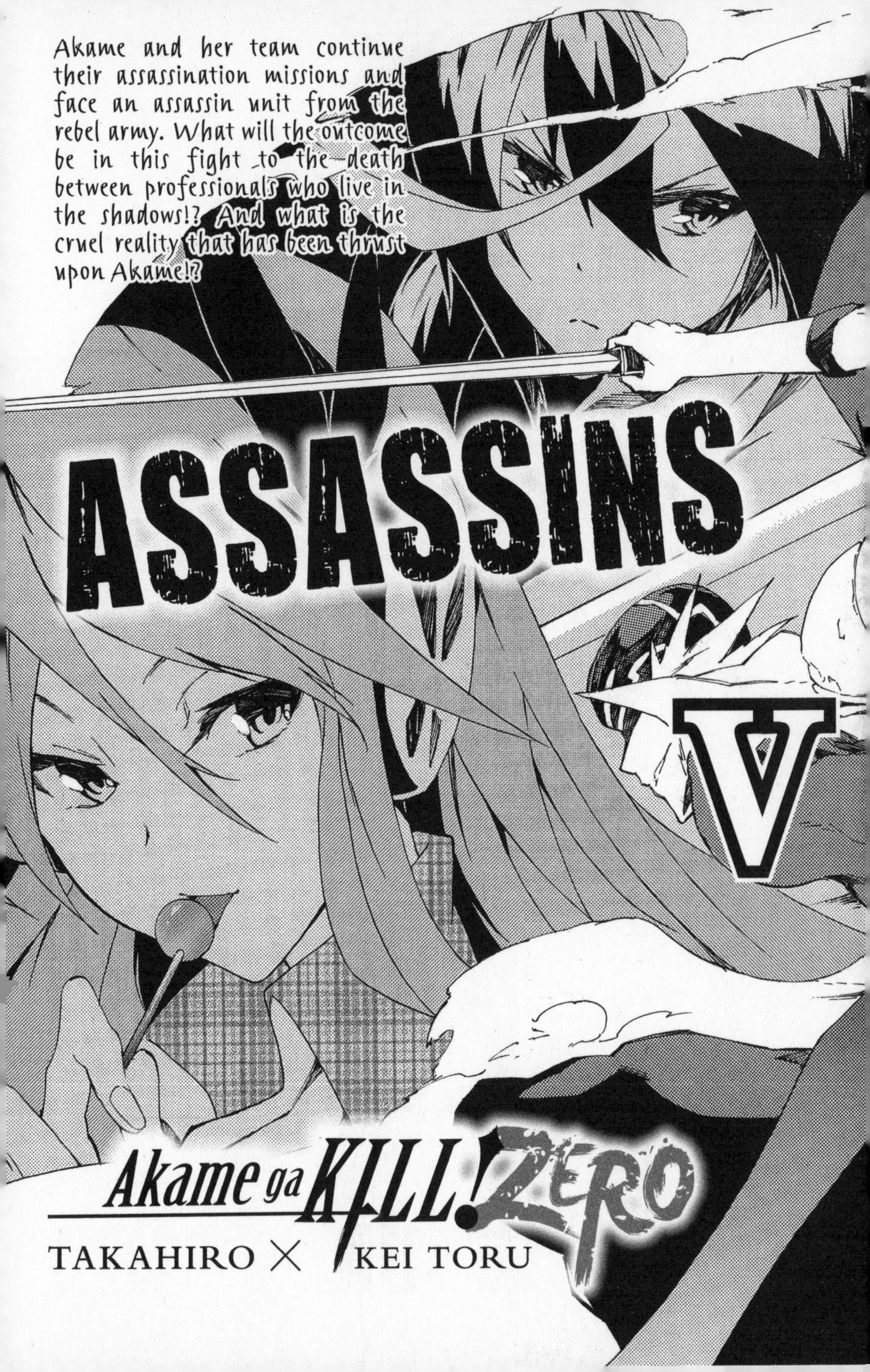
Akame and her team continue their assassination missions and face an assassin unit from the rebel army. What will the outcome be in this fight to the death between professionals who live in the shadows!? And what is the cruel reality that has been thrust upon Akame!?
ASSASSINS
V
Akame ga KILL! ZERO
TAKAHIRO × KEI TORU

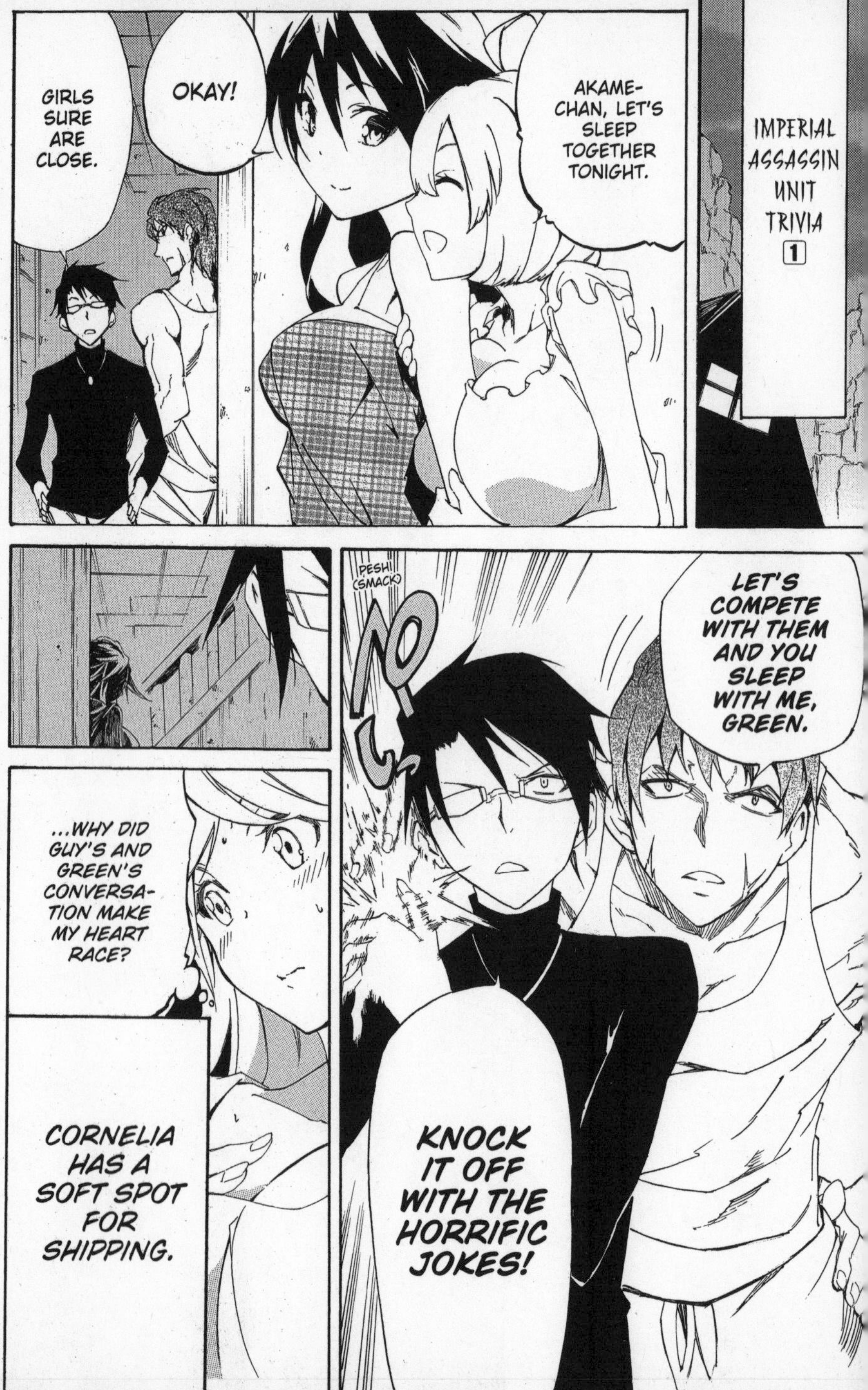
IMPERIAL ASSASSIN UNIT TRIVIA 1
AKAME-CHAN, LET'S SLEEP TOGETHER TONIGHT.
OKAY!
GIRLS SURE ARE CLOSE.
LET'S COMPETE WITH THEM AND YOU SLEEP WITH ME, GREEN.
PESHI (SMACK)
KNOCK IT OFF WITH THE HORRIFIC JOKES!
...WHY DID GUY'S AND GREEN'S CONVERSATION MAKE MY HEART RACE?
CORNELIA HAS A SOFT SPOT FOR SHIPPING.

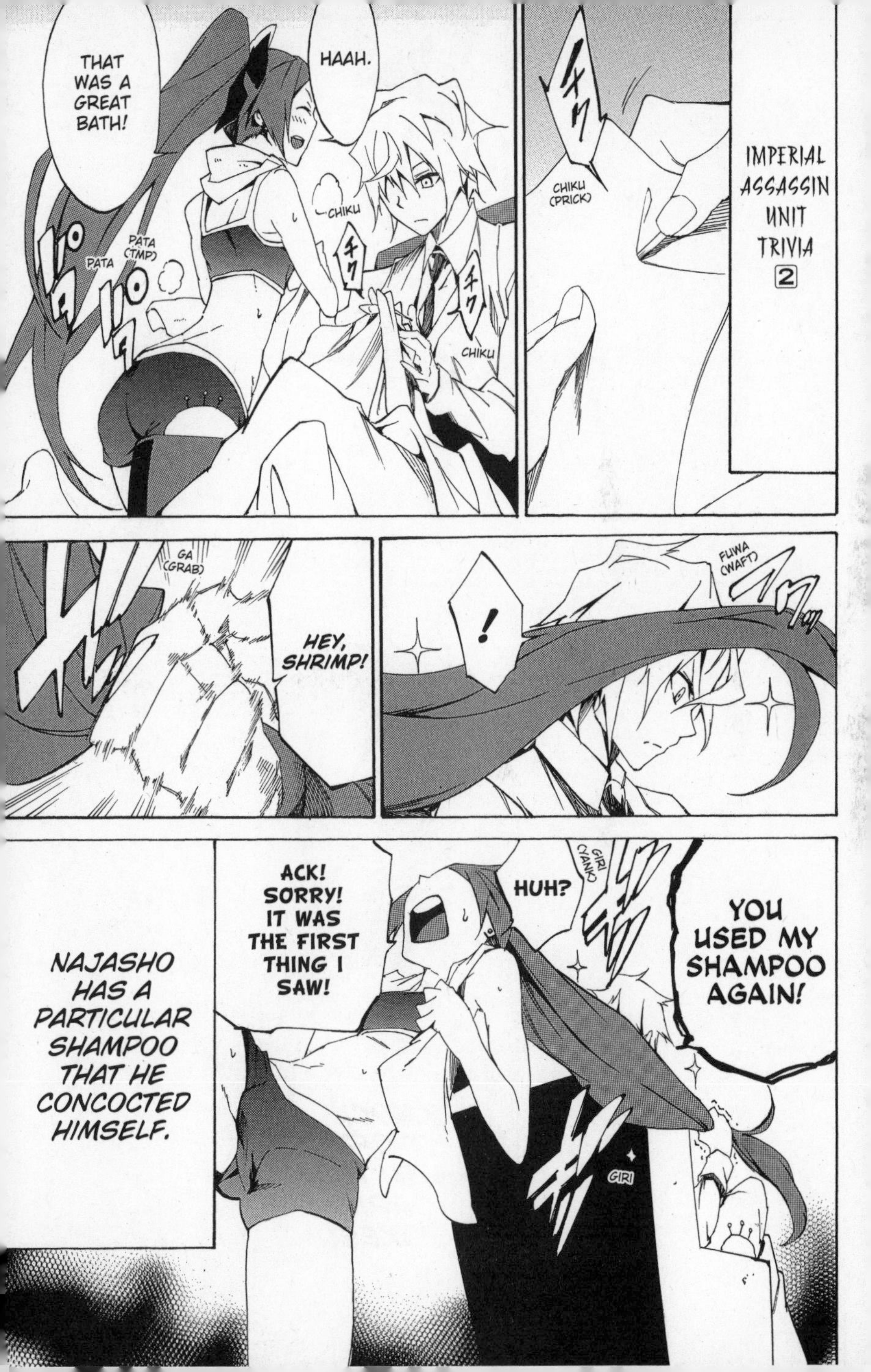
IMPERIAL ASSASSIN UNIT TRIVIA 2
CHIKU (PRICK)
HAAH.
THAT WAS A GREAT BATH!
CHIKU
CHIKU
PATA (TMP)
PATA
FUWA (WAFT)
!
HEY, SHRIMP!
GA (GRAB)
YOU USED MY SHAMPOO AGAIN!
GIRI (YANK)
HUH?
ACK! SORRY! IT WAS THE FIRST THING I SAW!
GIRI
NAJASHO HAS A PARTICULAR SHAMPOO THAT HE CONCOCTED HIMSELF.

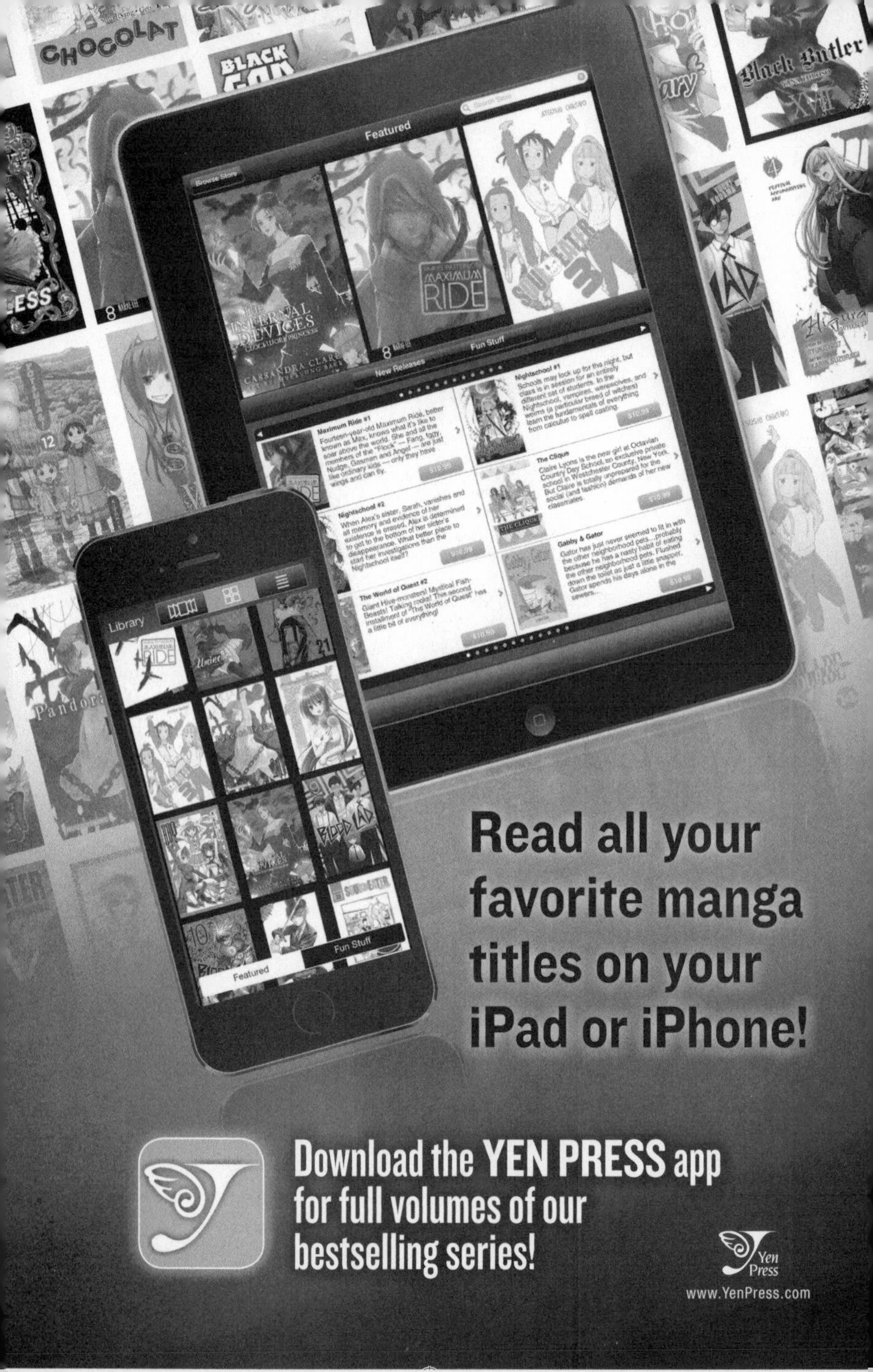
Read all your favorite manga titles on your iPad or iPhone!
Download the YEN PRESS app for full volumes of our bestselling series!
Yen Press
www.YenPress.com

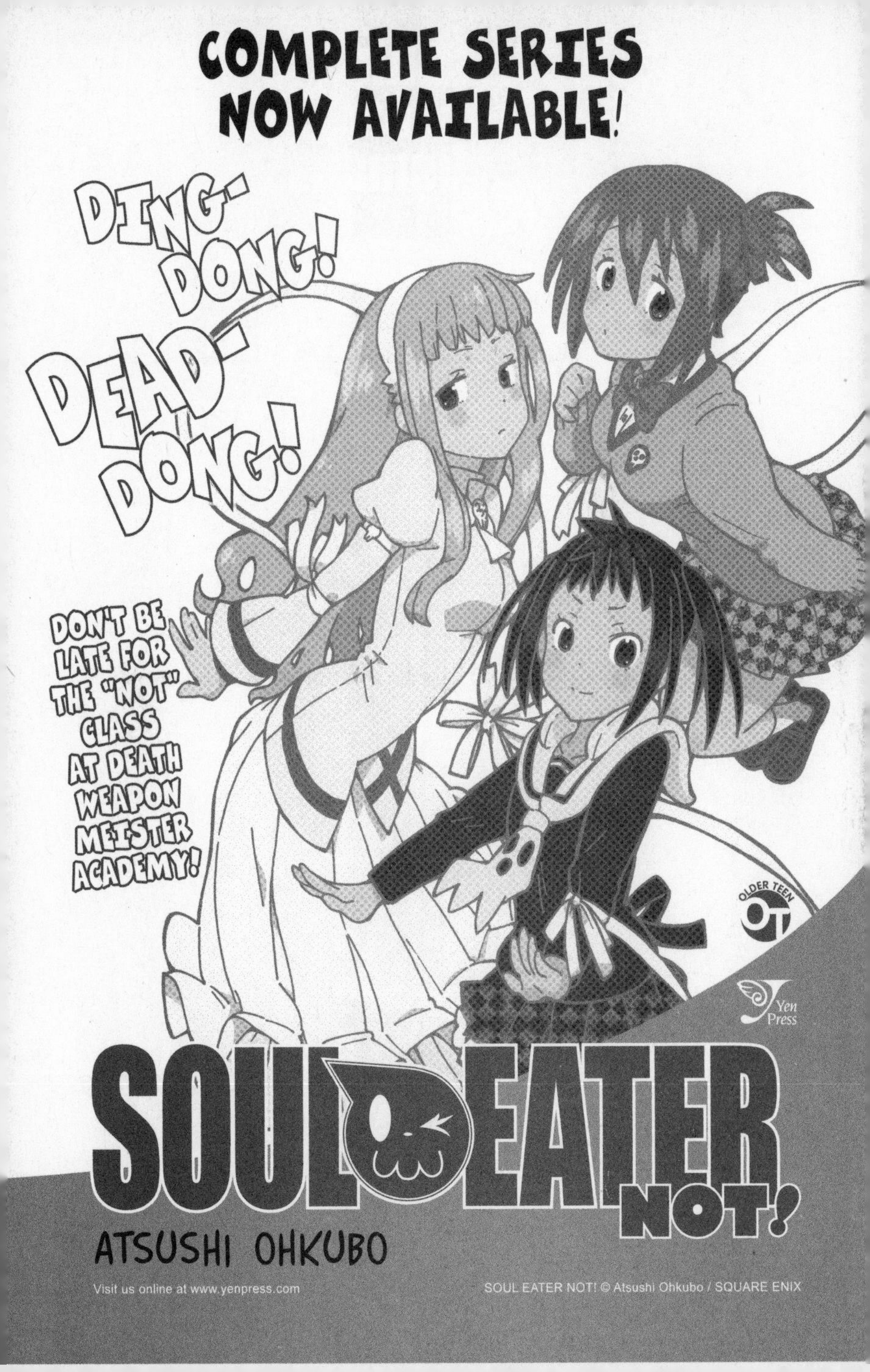
COMPLETE SERIES NOW AVAILABLE!
DING-DONG!
DEAD-DONG!
DON'T BE LATE FOR THE "NOT" CLASS AT DEATH WEAPON MEISTER ACADEMY!
OLDER TEEN OT
Yen Press
SOUL EATER NOT!
ATSUSHI OHKUBO
Visit us online at www.yenpress.com
SOUL EATER NOT! © Atsushi Ohkubo / SQUARE ENIX

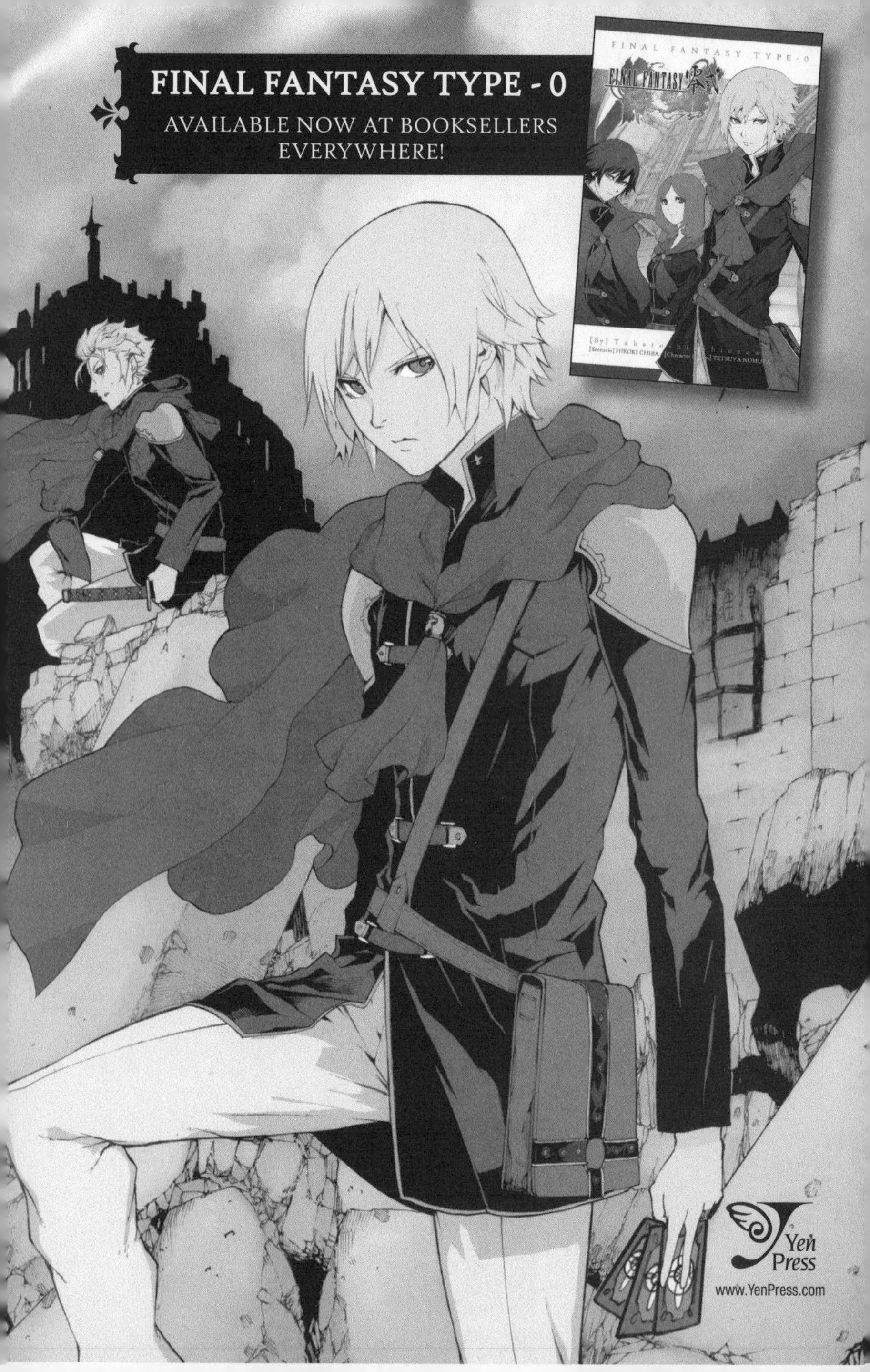
FINAL FANTASY TYPE - 0
AVAILABLE NOW AT BOOKSELLERS EVERYWHERE!
FINAL FANTASY TYPE-0
Yen Press
www.YenPress.com

FINAL FANTASY 零式 TYPE-0™

Art: TAKATOSHI SHIOZAWA
Character Design: TETSUYA NOMURA
Scenario: HIROKI CHIBA

The cadets of Akademeia's Class Zero are legends, with strength and magic unrivaled, and crimson capes symbolizing the great Vermilion Bird of the Dominion. But will their elite training be enough to keep them alive when a war breaks out and the Class Zero cadets find themselves at the front and center of a bloody political battlefield?!

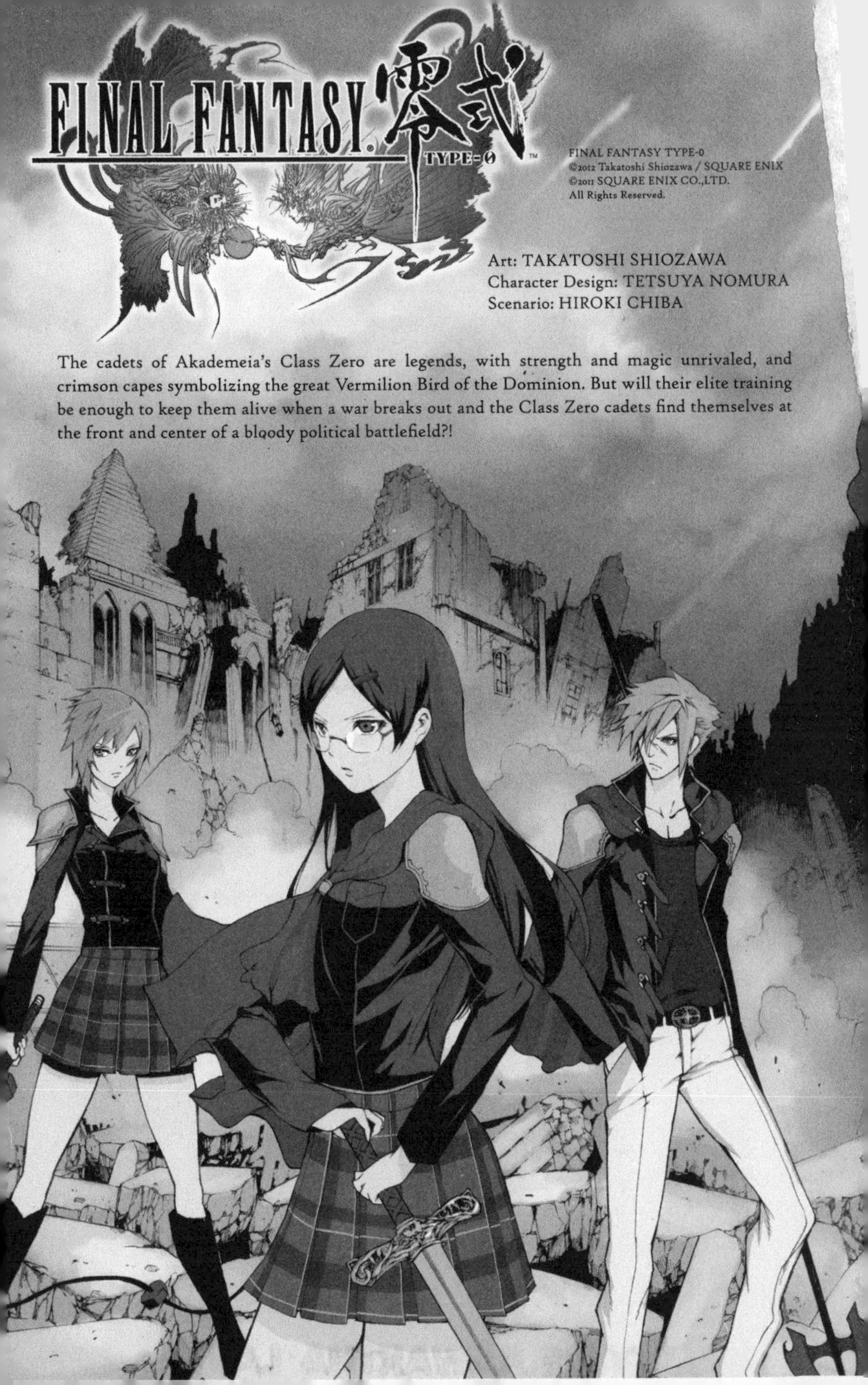

AKAME GA KILL! ZERO ☐1

TAKAHIRO
KEI TORU

Translation: Christine Dashiell • Lettering: Abigail Blackman

AKAME GA KILL! ZERO Vol. 1
© 2014 Takahiro, Kei Toru / SQUARE ENIX CO., LTD. First published in Japan in 2014 by SQUARE ENIX CO., LTD. English translation rights arranged with SQUARE ENIX CO., LTD. and Yen Press, LLC through Tuttle-Mori Agency, Inc., Tokyo.

English translation © 2016 by SQUARE ENIX CO., LTD.

Yen Press
1290 Avenue of the Americas
New York, NY 10104

Visit us at yenpress.com
facebook.com/yenpress
twitter.com/yenpress
yenpress.tumblr.com
instagram.com/yenpress

First Yen Press Edition: March 2016

Yen Press is an imprint of Yen Press, LLC.
The Yen Press name and logo are trademarks of Yen Press, LLC.

The publisher is not responsible for websites (or their content) that are not owned by the publisher.

Library of Congress Control Number: 2015956843

ISBN: 978-0-316-31468-8 (paperback)

10 9 8 7 6 5 4 3

BVG

Printed in the United States of America